At the breaking point, my body inhaled involuntarily. I closed my sightless eyes. Wrapped my arms around Lou, buried my nose in her neck. At least Morgane wouldn't have us. At least I wouldn't know life without her. Small victories. Important ones.

But the water never came. Instead, impossibly crisp air flooded my mouth, and with it, the sweetest relief. Though I still couldn't see—though the cold remained debilitating—I could *breathe*. I could *think*. Coherency returned in a disorienting wave. I took another deep breath. Then another, and another. This—this was impossible. I was *breathing underwater*. Like Jonah's fish. Like the melusines. Like—

Like magic.

Also by Shelby Mahurin
Serpent & Dove
Gods & Monsters

BLOOD & HONEY

SHELBY MAHURIN

HARPER TEEN

An Imprint of HarperCollinsPublishers

For Beau, James, and Rose *who I love unconditionally*

PART I

Il n'y a pas plus sourd que celui qui ne veut pas entendre.

There are none so deaf as those that will not hear.

—French proverb

TOMORROW

Lou

Dark clouds gathered overhead.

Though I couldn't see the sky through the thick canopy of La Fôret des Yeux—or feel the bitter winds rising outside our camp—I knew a storm was brewing. The trees swayed in the gray twilight, and the animals had gone to ground. Several days ago, we'd burrowed into our own sort of hole: a peculiar basin in the forest floor, where the trees had grown roots like fingers, thrusting in and out of the cold earth. I affectionately called it the Hollow. Though snow dusted everything outside it, the flakes melted on contact with the protective magic Madame Labelle had cast.

Adjusting the baking stone over the fire, I poked hopefully at the misshapen lump atop it. It couldn't be called *bread*, exactly, as I'd cobbled the concoction together from nothing but ground bark and water, but I refused to eat another meal of pine nuts and milk thistle root. I simply refused. A girl needed *something* with *taste* now and again—and I didn't mean the wild onions Coco had found this morning. My breath still smelled like a dragon's.

"I'm not eating that," Beau said flatly, eyeing the pine bread as if it'd soon sprout legs and attack him. His black hair—usually styled with immaculate detail—stuck out in disheveled waves, and dirt streaked his tawny cheek. Though his velvet suit would've been the height of fashion in Cesarine, it too was now sullied with grime.

I grinned at him. "Fine. Starve."

"Is it . . ." Ansel edged closer, wrinkling his nose surreptitiously. Eyes bright from hunger and hair tangled from the wind, he hadn't fared in the wilderness much better than Beau. But Ansel—with his olive skin and willowy build, his curling lashes and his genuine smile—would always be beautiful. He couldn't help it. "Do you think it's—"

"Edible?" Beau supplied, arching a dark brow. "No."

"I wasn't going to say that!" Pink colored Ansel's cheeks, and he shot me an apologetic look. "I was going to say, er—good. Do you think it's good?"

"Also no." Beau turned away to rummage in his pack. Triumphant, he straightened a moment later with a handful of onions, popping one into his mouth. "*This* will be my dinner tonight, thank you."

When I opened my mouth with a scathing reply, Reid's arm came across my shoulders, heavy and warm and comforting. He brushed a kiss against my temple. "I'm sure the bread is delicious."

"That's right." I leaned into him, preening at the compliment.

"It *will* be delicious. And we won't smell like ass—er, *onion*—for the rest of the night." I smiled sweetly at Beau, who paused with his hand halfway to his mouth, scowling between me and his onion. "Those are going to seep out of your pores for the next day, at least."

Chuckling, Reid bent low to kiss my shoulder, and his voice—slow and deep—rumbled against my skin. "You know, there's a stream up the way."

Instinctively, I extended my neck, and he placed another kiss on my throat, right beneath my jaw. My pulse spiked against his mouth. Though Beau curled his lip in disgust at our public display, I ignored him, reveling in Reid's nearness. We hadn't been properly alone since I'd woken after Modraniht. "Maybe we should go there," I said a bit breathlessly. As usual, Reid pulled away too soon. "We could pack up our bread and . . . picnic."

Madame Labelle's head jerked toward us from across camp, where she and Coco argued within the roots of an ancient fir. They clutched a piece of parchment between them, their shoulders tense and their faces drawn. Ink and blood dotted Coco's fingers. Already, she'd sent two notes to La Voisin at the blood camp, pleading for sanctuary. Her aunt hadn't responded to either. I doubted a third note would change that. "Absolutely not," Madame Labelle said. "You cannot leave camp. I've forbidden it. Besides, a storm is brewing."

Forbidden it. The words rankled. No one had *forbidden* me from doing anything since I was three.

"Might I remind you," she continued, her nose in the air and her tone insufferable, "that the forest is still crawling with huntsmen, and though we have not seen them, the witches cannot be far behind. That's not to mention the king's guard. Word has spread about Florin's death on Modraniht"—Reid and I stiffened in each other's arms—"and bounties have risen. Even peasants know your faces. You cannot leave this camp until we've formed some sort of offensive strategy."

I didn't miss the subtle emphasis she placed on *you*, or the way she glanced between Reid and me. *We* were the ones forbidden from leaving camp. *We* were the ones with our faces plastered all over Saint-Loire—and by now, probably every other village in the kingdom too. Coco and Ansel had pinched a couple of the wanted posters after their foray into Saint-Loire for supplies— one depicting Reid's handsome face, his hair colored red with common madder, and one depicting mine.

The artist had given me a wart on my chin.

Scowling at the memory, I flipped the loaf of pine bread, revealing a burnt, blackened crust on the underside. We all stared at it a moment.

"You're right, Reid. So delicious." Beau grinned wide. Behind him, Coco squeezed blood from her palm onto the note. The drops sizzled and smoked where they fell, burning the parchment away into nothing. Transporting it to wherever La Voisin and the Dames Rouges currently camped. Beau waved the rest of his onions directly beneath my nose, reclaiming my attention. "Are you sure you wouldn't like one?"

I knocked them out of his hand. "Piss off."

With a squeeze of my shoulders, Reid swept the burnt loaf from the stone and cut a slice with expert precision. "You don't have to eat it," I said sullenly.

His lips quirked in a grin. "*Bon appétit.*"

We watched, transfixed, as he stuffed the bread into his mouth—and choked.

Beau roared with laughter.

Eyes watering, Reid hastened to swallow as Ansel pounded on his back. "It's good," he assured me, still coughing and trying to chew. "Really. It tastes like—like—"

"Char?" Beau bent double at my expression, laughing riotously, and Reid glowered, still choking but lifting a foot to kick his ass. Literally. Losing his balance, Beau toppled forward into the moss and lichen of the forest floor, a boot print clearly visible against the seat of his velvet pants.

He spat mud from his mouth as Reid finally swallowed the bread. "Prick."

Before he could take another bite, I knocked the bread back into the fire. "Your chivalry is noted, husband mine, and shall be thusly rewarded."

He pulled me into a hug, his smile genuine now. And shamefully relieved. "I would've eaten it."

"I should've let you."

"And now all of you will go hungry," Beau said.

Ignoring my stomach's traitorous growl, I pulled out the bottle of wine I'd hidden amidst the contents of Reid's rucksack. I hadn't been able to pack for the journey myself, what with

Morgane snatching me from the steps of Cathédral Saint-Cécile d'Cesarine. Fortunately, I'd just *happened* to wander a bit too far from camp yesterday, securing a handful of useful items from a peddler on the road. The wine had been essential. As had new clothes. Though Coco and Reid had cobbled together an ensemble for me to wear instead of my bloody ceremonial dress, their clothing hung from my slim frame—a frame made slimmer, no, waiflike from my time at the Chateau. So far, I'd managed to keep the fruits of my little excursion hidden—both within Reid's rucksack and beneath Madame Labelle's borrowed cloak—but the bandage had to come off eventually.

There was no time like the present.

Reid's eyes sharpened on the bottle of wine, and his smile vanished. "What is that?"

"A gift, of course. Don't you know what day it is?" Determined to save the evening, I pressed the bottle into Ansel's unsuspecting hands. His fingers closed around its neck, and he smiled, blushing anew. My heart swelled. "*Bon anniversaire, mon petit chou!*"

"It isn't my birthday until next month," he said sheepishly, but he clutched the bottle to his chest anyway. The fire cast flickering light on his quiet joy. "No one's ever—" He cleared his throat and swallowed hard. "I've never received a present before."

The happiness in my chest punctured slightly.

As a child, my own birthdays had been revered as holy days. Witches from all over the kingdom had journeyed to Chateau le Blanc to celebrate, and together, we'd danced beneath the light of the moon until our feet had ached. Magic had coated the temple with its sharp scent, and my mother had showered me with extravagant gifts—a tiara of diamonds and pearls one year, a bouquet of eternal ghost orchids the next. She'd once parted the tides of L'Eau Mélancolique for me to walk the seafloor, and melusines had pressed their beautiful, eerie faces against the walls of water to watch us, tossing their luminous hair and flashing their silver tails.

Even then, I'd known my sisters celebrated less my life and more my death, but I'd later wondered—in my weaker moments—if the same had been true for my mother. "We are star-crossed, you and I," she'd murmured on my fifth birthday, pressing a kiss to my forehead. Though I couldn't remember the details clearly—only the shadows in my bedroom, the cold night air on my skin, the eucalyptus oil in my hair—I thought a tear had trickled down her cheek. In those weaker moments, I'd known Morgane hadn't celebrated my birthdays at all.

She'd mourned them.

"I believe the proper response is thank you." Coco sidled up to examine the bottle of wine, tossing her black curls over a shoulder. Ansel's color deepened. With a smirk, she trailed a suggestive finger down the curve of the glass, pressing her own curves into his lanky frame. "What vintage is it?"

Beau rolled his eyes at her obvious performance, stooping to retrieve his onions. She watched him from the corner of her dark eyes. The two hadn't spoken a civil word in days. It'd been entertaining at first, watching Coco chop at the prince's bloated head quip by quip, but she'd recently brought Ansel into the carnage. I'd have to talk to her about it soon. My eyes flicked to Ansel, who still smiled from ear to ear as he gazed at the wine.

Tomorrow. I'd talk to her tomorrow.

Placing her fingers over Ansel's, Coco lifted the bottle to study the crumbling label. The firelight illuminated the myriad scars on her brown skin. "*Boisaîné,*" she read slowly, struggling to discern the letters. She rubbed a bit of dirt away with the hem of her cloak. "Elderwood." She glanced at me. "I've never heard of such a place. It looks *ancient*, though. Must've cost a fortune."

"Much less than you'd think, actually." Grinning again at Reid's suspicious expression, I swiped the bottle from her with a wink. A towering summer oak adorned its label, and beside it, a monstrous man with antlers and hooves wore a crown of branches. Luminescent yellow paint colored his eyes, which had pupils like a cat's.

"He looks scary," Ansel commented, leaning over my shoulder to peer closer at the label.

"He's the Woodwose." Nostalgia hit me in an unexpected wave. "The wild man of the forest, the king of all flora and fauna. Morgane used to tell me stories about him when I was little."

The effect of my mother's name was instantaneous. Beau stopped scowling abruptly. Ansel stopped blushing, and Coco stopped smirking. Reid scanned the shadows around us and slid a hand to the Balisarda in his bandolier. Even the flames of the fire guttered, as if Morgane herself had blown a cold breath through the trees to extinguish them.

I fixed my smile in place.

We hadn't heard a word from Morgane since Modraniht. Days had passed, but we hadn't seen a single witch. To be fair, we hadn't seen much of anything beyond this cage of roots. I couldn't truly complain about the Hollow, however. Indeed—despite the lack of privacy and Madame Labelle's autocratic rule—I'd been almost relieved when we hadn't heard back from La Voisin. We'd been granted a reprieve. And we had everything we needed here, anyway. Madame Labelle's magic kept the danger away—warming us, cloaking us from spying eyes—and Coco had found the mountain-fed stream nearby. Its current kept the water from freezing, and certainly Ansel would catch a fish one of these days.

In this moment, it felt as if we lived in a pocket of time and space separate from the rest of the world. Morgane and her Dames Blanches, Jean Luc and his Chasseurs, even King Auguste—they ceased to exist in this place. No one could touch us. It was . . . strangely peaceful.

Like the calm before a storm.

Madame Labelle echoed my unspoken fear. "You know we cannot hide forever," she said, repeating the same tired argument. Coco and I shared an aggrieved look as she joined us, confiscating the wine. If I had to hear *one more* dire warning, I would upend the bottle and drown her in it. "Your mother will find you. We alone cannot keep you from her. However, if we were to gather allies, rally others to our cause, perhaps we could—"

"The blood witches' silence couldn't be louder." I grabbed the bottle back from her, wrestling with the cork. "They won't risk Morgane's wrath by *rallying to our cause*. Whatever the hell our *cause* even is."

"Don't be obtuse. If Josephine refuses to help us, there are other powerful players we can—"

"I need more time," I interrupted loudly, hardly listening,

gesturing to my throat. Though Reid's magic had closed the wound, saving my life, a thick crust remained. It still hurt like a bitch. But that wasn't the reason I wanted to linger here. "You're barely healed yourself, Helene. We'll strategize tomorrow."

"Tomorrow." Her eyes narrowed at the empty promise. I'd said the same for days now. This time, however, even I could hear the words landed different—true. Madame Labelle would no longer accept otherwise. As if to affirm my thoughts, she said, "Tomorrow we *will* talk, whether or not La Voisin answers our call. Agreed?"

I plunged my knife into the bottle's cork, twisting sharply. Everyone flinched. Grinning anew, I dipped my chin in the briefest of nods. "Who's thirsty?" I flicked the cork at Reid's nose, and he swatted it away in exasperation. "Ansel?"

His eyes widened. "Oh, I don't—"

"Perhaps we should procure a nipple." Beau snatched the bottle from under Ansel's nose and took a hearty swig. "It might be more palatable to him that way."

I choked on a laugh. "Stop it, Beau—"

"You're right. He'd have no idea what to do with a breast."

"Have you ever had a drink before, Ansel?" Coco asked curiously.

Face darkening, Ansel jerked the wine from Beau and drank deeply. Instead of spluttering, he seemed to unhinge his jaw and inhale half the bottle. When he'd finished, he merely wiped his mouth with the back of his hand and shoved the bottle toward Coco. His cheeks were still pink. "It goes down smooth."

I didn't know which was funnier—Coco and Beau's gobsmacked expressions or Ansel's smug one. I clapped my hands together in delight. "Oh, well done, Ansel. When you told me you liked wine, I didn't realize you could drink like a fish."

He shrugged and looked away. "I lived in Saint-Cécile for years. I learned to like it." His eyes flicked back to the bottle in Coco's hand. "That one tastes a lot better than anything in the sanctuary, though. Where did you get it?"

"Yes," Reid said, his voice not nearly as amused as the situation warranted. "Where *did* you get it? Clearly Coco and Ansel didn't purchase it with our supplies."

They both had the decency to look apologetic.

"Ah." I batted my lashes as Beau offered the bottle to Madame Labelle, who shook her head curtly. She waited for my answer with pursed lips. "Ask me no questions, *mon amour*, and I shall tell you no lies."

When he clenched his jaw, clearly battling his temper, I braced myself for the inquisition. Though Reid no longer wore his blue uniform, he just couldn't seem to help himself. The law was the law. It didn't matter on which side of it he stood. Bless him. "Tell me you didn't steal it," he said. "Tell me you found it in a hole somewhere."

"All right. I didn't steal it. I found it in a hole somewhere."

He folded his arms across his chest, leveling me with a stern gaze. "Lou."

"What?" I asked innocently. In a helpful gesture, Coco offered me the bottle, and I took a long pull of my own, admiring his biceps—his square jaw, his full mouth, his copper hair—with unabashed appreciation. I reached up to pat his cheek. "You didn't ask for the truth."

He trapped my hand against his face. "I am now."

I stared at him, the impulse to lie rising like a tide in my throat. But—no. I frowned at myself, examining the base instinct with a pause. He mistook my silence for refusal, shifting closer to coax me into answering. "Did you steal it, Lou? The truth, please."

"Well, that was *dripping* with condescension. Shall we try again?"

With an exasperated sigh, he turned his head to kiss my fingers. "You're impossible."

"I'm impractical, improbable, but never impossible." I rose to my toes and pressed my lips to his. Shaking his head, chuckling despite himself, he bent low to fold me in his arms and deepen the kiss. Delicious heat washed through me, and it took considerable self-restraint not to tackle him to the ground and have my wicked way with him.

"My God," Beau said, voice thick with disgust. "It looks like he's eating her face."

But Madame Labelle wasn't listening. Her eyes—so familiar and blue—shone with anger. "Answer the question, Louise." I stiffened at her sharp tone. To my surprise, Reid did too. He turned to look at her slowly. "Did you leave camp?"

For Reid's sake, I kept my own voice pleasant.

"I didn't steal anything. At least"—I shrugged, forcing myself to maintain an easy smile—"I didn't steal the *wine*. I bought it from a peddler on the road this morning with a few of Reid's *couronnes*."

"You stole from my son?"

Reid held out a calming hand. "Easy. She didn't steal anything from—"

"He's my *husband*." My jaw ached from smiling so hard, and I lifted my left hand for emphasis. Her own mother-of-pearl stone still gleamed on my ring finger. "What's mine is his, and what's his is mine. Isn't that part of the vows we took?"

"Yes, it is." Reid nodded swiftly, shooting me a reassuring look, before glaring at Madame Labelle. "She's welcome to anything I own."

"Of course, son." She flashed her own tight-lipped smile. "Though I do feel obligated to point out the two of you were never legally wed. Louise used a false name on the marriage license, therefore nullifying the contract. Of course, if you still choose to share your possessions with her, you are free to do so, but do not feel obligated in any way. Especially if she insists on endangering your life—*all* our lives—with her impulsive, reckless behavior."

My smile finally slipped. "The hood of your cloak hid my face. The woman didn't recognize me."

"And if she did? If the Chasseurs or Dames Blanches ambush us tonight? What then?" When I made no move to answer her, she sighed and continued softly, "I understand your reluctance to confront this, Louise, but closing your eyes will not make it so the monsters can't see you. It will only make you blind." Then, softer still: "You've hidden long enough."

Suddenly unable to look at anyone, I dropped my arms from Reid's neck. They immediately missed his warmth. Though he stepped closer as if to draw me back to him, I took another drink of wine instead. "All right," I finally said, forcing myself to meet her flinty gaze, "I shouldn't have left camp, but I couldn't ask Ansel to buy his own birthday present. Birthdays are sacred. We'll strategize tomorrow."

"Really," Ansel said earnestly, "it isn't my birthday until next month. This isn't necessary."

"It *is* necessary. We might not be here—" I stopped short, biting my errant tongue, but it was too late. Though I hadn't spoken the words aloud, they reverberated through camp all the same. *We might not be here next month.* Shoving the wine back at him, I tried again. "Let us celebrate you, Ansel. It's not every day you turn seventeen."

His eyes cut to Madame Labelle's as if seeking permission. She nodded stiffly. "*Tomorrow*, Louise."

"Of course." I accepted Reid's hand, allowing him to pull me close as I feigned another horrible smile. "Tomorrow."

Reid kissed me again—harder, fiercer this time, like he had something to prove. Or something to lose. "Tonight, we celebrate."

The wind picked up as the sun dipped below the trees, and the clouds continued to thicken.

STOLEN MOMENTS

Reid

Lou slept like the dead. Cheek pressed to my chest and hair sprawled across my shoulder, she breathed deeply. Rhythmically. It was a peace she rarely achieved while awake. I stroked her spine. Savored her warmth. Willed my mind to remain blank, my eyes to remain open. I didn't even blink. Just stared, unending, as the trees swayed overhead. Seeing nothing. *Feeling* nothing. Numb.

Sleep had evaded me since Modraniht. When it didn't, I wished it had.

My dreams had twisted into dark and disturbing things.

A small shadow detached from the pines to sit beside me, tail flicking. Absalon, Lou had named him. I'd once thought him a simple black cat. She'd quickly corrected me. He wasn't a cat at all, but a matagot. A restless spirit, unable to pass on, that took the shape of an animal. "They're drawn to like creatures," Lou had informed me, frowning. "Troubled souls. Someone here must have attracted him."

Her pointed look had made it clear who she thought that *some-one* was.

"Go away." I nudged the unnatural creature with my elbow now. "Shoo."

He blinked baleful amber eyes at me. When I sighed, relenting, he curled into my side and slept.

Absalon. I stroked a finger down his back, disgruntled when he began to purr. *I am not troubled.*

I stared up at the trees once more, convincing no one.

Lost in the paralysis of my thoughts, I didn't notice when Lou began to stir several moments later. Her hair tickled my face as she rose up on an elbow, leaning over me. Her voice was low. Soft with sleep, sweet from wine. "You're awake."

"Yes."

Her eyes searched mine—hesitant, concerned—and my throat tightened inexplicably. When she opened her mouth to speak, to ask, I interrupted with the first words that popped into my head. "What happened to your mother?"

She blinked. "What do you mean?"

"Was she always so . . . ?"

With a sigh, she rested her chin on my chest. Twisted the mother-of-pearl ring around her finger. "No. I don't know. Can people be born evil?" I shook my head. "I don't think so either. I think she lost herself somewhere along the way. It's easy to do with magic." When I tensed, she turned to face me. "It's not like you think. Magic isn't . . . well, it's like anything else. Too much of a good thing is a bad thing. It can be addictive. My mother, she—she loved the power, I suppose." She chuckled once. It was bitter. "And when *everything* is a matter of life and death for us, the stakes are higher. The more we gain, the more we lose."

The more we gain, the more we lose.

"I see," I said, but I didn't. Nothing about this canon appealed to me. Why risk magic at all?

As if sensing my distaste, she rose again to better see me. "It's a gift, Reid. There's so much more to it than what you've seen. Magic is beautiful and wild and free. I understand your reluctance, but you can't hide from it forever. It's part of you."

I couldn't form a reply. The words caught in my throat.

"Are you ready to talk about what happened?" she asked softly.

I brushed my fingers through her hair, my lips against her forehead. "Not tonight."

"Reid . . ."

"Tomorrow."

She heaved another sigh, but thankfully didn't press the issue. After reaching over to scratch Absalon's head, she lay back down, and together, we stared up at the patches of sky through the trees. I drifted back into my mind, into its careful, empty silence. Whether moments or hours passed, I didn't know.

"Do you think . . ." Lou's soft voice startled me back to the present. "Do you think there'll be a funeral?"

"Yes."

I didn't ask whose she meant. I didn't need to.

"Even with everything at the end?"

A beautiful witch, cloaked in guise of damsel, soon lured the man down the path to Hell. My chest ached as I remembered Ye Olde Sisters' performance. The fair-haired narrator. Thirteen, fourteen at most—the devil herself, cloaked not as a damsel, but a maiden. She'd looked so innocent as she'd delivered our sentence. Almost angelic.

A visit soon came from the witch he reviled with the worst news of all . . . she'd borne his child.

"Yes."

"But . . . he was my father." Hearing her swallow, I turned, wrapped a hand around the nape of her neck. Held her close as emotion threatened to choke me. Desperately, I struggled to reclaim the fortress I'd constructed, to retreat back into its blissfully hollow depths. "He slept with La Dame des Sorcières. A witch. The king can't possibly honor him."

"No one will be able to prove anything. King Auguste won't condemn a dead man on the word of a witch."

The words slipped out before I could stop them. *A dead man.* My grip tightened on Lou, and she cupped my cheek—not to coerce me into facing her, but simply to touch me. To tether me. I leaned into her palm.

She stared at me for a long moment, her touch infinitely gentle. Infinitely patient. "Reid."

The word was heavy. Expectant.

I couldn't look at her. Couldn't face the devotion I'd see in those familiar eyes. *His* eyes. Even if she didn't yet realize—even if she didn't yet care—she would someday hate me for what I'd done. He was her father.

And I'd killed him.

"Look at me, Reid."

The memory flashed, unbidden. My knife embedding in his ribs. His blood streaming down my wrist. Warm and thick and wet. When I turned to face her, those blue-green eyes were steady. Determined.

"Please," I whispered. To my shame—my humiliation—my voice broke on the word. Heat flooded my face. Even I didn't know what I wanted from her. *Please don't ask me. Please don't make me say it.* And then, louder than the rest, a keening wail rising sharply through the pain—

Please make it go away.

A ripple of emotion flashed in her expression—almost too quick for me to see. Then she set her chin. A devious glint lit her eyes. In the next second, she whirled to straddle me, brushing a single finger across my mouth. Her own parted, and her tongue flicked out to wet her bottom lip. "*Mon petit oiseau*, you've seemed . . . frustrated these last few days." She leaned lower, brushing her nose against my ear. Distracting me. Answering my unspoken plea. "I could help with that, you know."

Absalon hissed indignantly and dematerialized.

When she began to touch me, to move against me—lightly, maddeningly—the blood in my face pitched lower, and I closed my eyes, clenching my jaw against the sensation. The heat. My fingers dug into her hips to hold her in place.

Behind us, someone sighed softly in their sleep.

"We can't do this here." My strained whisper echoed too loud in the silence. Despite my words, she grinned and pressed closer—*everywhere*—until my own hips rolled in response, grinding her against me. Once. Twice. Three times. Slowly at first, then faster. I dropped my head back to the cold ground, breathing ragged, eyes still clenched shut. A low groan built in my throat. "Someone might see."

She tugged at my belt in answer. My eyes flew open to watch, and I flexed into her touch, reveling in it. In *her*. "Let them," she said, each breath a pant. Another cough sounded. "I don't care."

"Lou—"

"Do you want me to stop?"

"No." My hands tightened on her hips, and I sat forward swiftly, crushing her lips against mine.

Another cough, louder this time. I didn't register it. With her hand slipping into my undone trousers—her tongue hot against mine—I couldn't have stopped if I tried. That is, until—

"*Stop.*" The word tore from my throat, and I lurched backward, wrenching her hips in the air, away from my own. I hadn't meant for it to go this far, this fast, with *this* many people around us. When I cursed, low and vicious, she blinked in confusion, hands shooting to my shoulders for balance. Her lips swollen. Her cheeks flushed. I clamped my eyes shut once more—clenching, clenching, *clenching*—thinking of anything and everything but Lou. Spoiled meat. Flesh-eating locusts. Wrinkled, saggy skin and the word *moist* or *curd* or *phlegm*. Dripping phlegm, or, or—

My mother.

The memory of our first night here flashed with crystalline focus.

"I'm serious," Madame Labelle warns, pulling us aside, "absolutely no sneaking away for any secret rendezvous. The forest is dangerous. The trees have eyes."

Lou's laughter rings out, clear and bright, while I splutter with mortification.

"I know the two of you are physically involved—don't try to deny it," Madame Labelle adds when my face flushes scarlet, "but no matter your bodily urges, the danger outside this camp is too great. I must ask you to restrain yourselves for the time being."

I stalk off without a word, Lou's laughter still ringing in my ears. Madame Labelle follows, undeterred. "It's perfectly natural to have such impulses." She hurries to keep up, skirting around Beau. He too shakes with laughter. "Really, Reid, this immaturity is most off-putting. You are *being careful, aren't you? Perhaps we should have a frank discussion about contraceptives—"*

Right. That did it.

The building pressure faded to a dull ache.

Exhaling hard, I slowly lowered Lou back to my lap. Another cough sounded from Beau's direction. Louder this time. Pointed. But Lou persevered. Her hand slid downward once more. "Something wrong, husband?"

I caught her hand at my navel and glared. Nose to nose. Lips to lips. "Minx."

"I'll *show* you minx—"

With an aggrieved sigh, Beau pitched upright and interrupted loudly, "Hello! Yes, pardon! As it seems to have escaped your notice, *there are other people here!*" In a low grumble, he added,

"Though clearly those other people will soon shrivel up and die from abstinence."

Lou's grin turned wicked. Her gaze flicked to the sky—now pitched the eerie gray before dawn—before she looped her arms around my neck. "It's almost sunrise," she whispered into my ear. The hair on my neck rose. "Shall we find the stream and . . . have a bath?"

Reluctantly, I glanced at Madame Labelle. She hadn't woken from our tryst, nor from Beau's outburst. Even in sleep, she exuded regal grace. A queen disguised as a madam, presiding over not a kingdom, but a brothel. Would her life have been different if she'd met my father before he'd married? Would *mine*? I looked away, disgusted with myself. "Madame Labelle forbade us from leaving camp."

Lou sucked softly on my earlobe, and I shuddered. "What Madame Labelle doesn't know won't hurt her. Besides . . ." She touched a finger to the dried blood behind my ear, on my wrist— the same as the marks on my elbows, my knees, my throat. The same marks we'd all worn since Modraniht. A precaution. "Coco's blood will hide us."

"The water will wash it away."

"I have magic too, you know—and so do you. We can protect ourselves if necessary."

And so do you.

Though I tried to repress my flinch, she still saw. Her eyes shuttered. "You'll have to learn to use it eventually. Promise me."

I forced a smile, squeezing her lightly. "It's not a problem."

Unconvinced, she slid from my lap and flung open her

bedroll. "Good. You heard your mother. Tomorrow, all of this ends."

An ominous wave swept through me at her words, at her expression. Though I knew we couldn't stay here indefinitely—knew we couldn't simply wait for Morgane or the Chasseurs to find us—we had no plan. No allies. And despite my mother's confidence, I couldn't imagine finding some. Why would anyone join us in a fight against Morgane? Her agenda was theirs—the death of all who had persecuted them.

Sighing heavily, Lou turned away and curled into a tight ball. Her hair fanned out in a trail of chestnut and gold behind her. I slid my fingers through it, attempting to soothe her. To release the sudden tension in her shoulders, the hopelessness in her voice. A hopeless Lou just didn't make sense—like a worldly Ansel or an ugly Cosette.

"I wish . . . ," she whispered. "I wish we could live here forever. But the longer we stay, the more it's like—like we're stealing moments of happiness. Like these moments aren't ours at all." Her hands clenched to fists at her sides. "She'll reclaim them eventually. Even if she has to cut them from our hearts."

My fingers stilled in her hair. Taking slow, measured breaths—swallowing the fury that erupted whenever I thought of Morgane—I wrapped a hand around Lou's chin, forcing her to meet my gaze. To *feel* my words. My promise. "You don't need to fear her. We won't let anything happen to you."

She scoffed in a self-deprecating way. "I don't fear her. I—" Abruptly, she twisted her chin from my grasp. "Never mind. It's pathetic."

"Lou." I kneaded her neck, willing her to relax. "You can tell me."

"Reid." She matched my soft tone, casting a sweet smile over her shoulder. I returned it, nodding in encouragement. Still smiling, she elbowed me sharply in the ribs. "Piss off."

My voice hardened. "Lou—"

"Just leave it alone," she snapped. "I don't want to talk about it." We glared at each other for a long moment—me rubbing my bruised rib mutinously—before she visibly deflated. "Look, forget I said anything. It's not important right now. The others will be up soon, and we can start planning. I'm fine. Really."

But she wasn't fine. And neither was I.

God. I just wanted to hold her.

I scrubbed an agitated hand down my face before glancing at Madame Labelle. She still slept. Even Beau had burrowed back into his bedroll, oblivious to the world once more. Right. Before I could change my mind, I hauled Lou into my arms. The stream wasn't far. We could be there and back before anyone realized we'd gone. "It's not tomorrow yet."

A WARNING BELL

Reid

Lou floated atop the water in lazy contentment. Her eyes shut. Her arms spread wide. Her hair thick and heavy around her. Snowflakes fell gently. They gathered in her eyelashes, on her cheeks. Though I'd never seen a melusine—only read of them in Saint-Cécile's ancient tombs—I imagined they looked like her in this moment. Beautiful. Ethereal.

Naked.

We'd shed our clothing at the icy banks of the pool. Absalon had materialized shortly after, burrowing into them. We didn't know where he went when he lost corporeal form. Lou cared more than I did.

"Magic has its advantages, doesn't it?" she murmured, trailing a finger through the water. Steam curled at the contact. "All of our fun bits should be frozen right now." She grinned and peeked an eye open. "Do you want me to show you?"

I arched a brow. "I have quite the view from here."

She smirked. "Pig. I meant magic." When I said nothing, she tipped forward, treading water. She couldn't touch the bottom of the pool, not as I could. The water lapped at my throat. "Do you want to learn how to heat water?" she asked.

This time, I was ready for it. I didn't flinch. I didn't hesitate. I did, however, swallow hard. "Sure."

She studied me through narrowed eyes. "You aren't exactly emanating enthusiasm over there, Chass."

"My mistake." I sank lower in the water, swimming toward her slowly. Wolfishly. "Please, O Radiant One, exhibit your great magical prowess. I cannot wait another moment to witness it, or I'll surely die. Will that suffice?"

"That's more like it," she sniffed, lifting her chin. "Now, what do you know about magic?"

"The same as I did last month." Had it only been a month since she'd last asked that question? It felt like a lifetime. Everything was different now. Part of me wished it wasn't. "Nothing."

"Rubbish." She opened her arms as I went to her, and I brought them around my neck. Her legs locked around my waist. The position should've been carnal, but it wasn't. It was just...intimate. This close, I could count every freckle on her nose. I could see the water droplets clinging to her lashes. It took all my resolve not to kiss her again. "You know more than you think. You've been around your mother, Coco, and me for the greater part of a fortnight, and on Modraniht, you—" She stopped abruptly, then faked an elaborate bout of coughing. My heart plummeted to my feet. *And on Modraniht, you killed the Archbishop with magic.* She cleared her throat. "I—I just know you've been paying attention. Your mind is a steel trap."

"A steel trap," I echoed, retreating into that fortress once more.

She didn't know how right she was.

It took several seconds to realize she was waiting for my response. I looked away, unable to face those eyes. They were blue now. Almost gray. So familiar. So . . . betrayed.

As if reading my thoughts, the trees rustled around us, and on the wind, I swore I heard his whispered voice—

You were like a son to me, Reid.

Gooseflesh erupted across my skin.

"Did you hear that?" I whipped my head around, clutching Lou closer. No gooseflesh marred her skin. "Did you hear him?"

She stopped talking mid-sentence. Her entire body tensed, and she looked around with wide eyes. "Who?"

"I—I thought I heard—" I shook my head. It couldn't have been. The Archbishop was dead. A figment of my imagination come to life to haunt me. Between one blink and the next, the trees fell resolutely still, and the breeze—if there'd been one at all—fell silent. "Nothing." I shook my head harder, repeating the word as if that would make it true. "It was nothing."

And yet . . . in the sharp pine-scented air . . . a presence lingered. A sentience. It watched us.

You're being ridiculous, I chided myself.

I didn't release my hold on Lou.

"The trees in this forest have eyes," she whispered, repeating Madame Labelle's earlier words. She still looked around warily. "They can . . . see things, inside your head, and twist them. Manifest fears into monsters." She shuddered. "When I fled the first time—the night of my sixteenth birthday—I thought I was going mad. The things I saw . . ."

She trailed off, her gaze turning inward.

I hardly dared breathe. She'd never told me this before. Never told me anything about her past outside Cesarine. Despite her bare skin against mine, she wore secrets like armor, and she shed them for no one. Not even me. *Especially* not me. The rest of the scene fell away—the pool, the trees, the wind—and there was only Lou's face, her voice, as she lost herself in the memory. "What did you see?" I asked softly.

She hesitated. "Your brothers and sisters."

A sharp intake of breath.

My own.

"It was horrible," she continued after a moment. "I was blind with panic, bleeding everywhere. My mother was stalking me. I could hear her voice through the trees—her spies, she'd once laughed—but I didn't know what was real and what wasn't. I just knew I had to get away. The screams started then. Bloodcurdling ones. A hand shot out of the ground and grabbed my ankle. I fell, and this—this corpse climbed out on top of me." A wave of nausea rolled through me at the imagery, but I didn't dare interrupt. "He had golden hair, and his throat—it looked like mine. He clawed at me, begged me to help him—except his voice wasn't right, of course, because of the"—she touched her hand to her scar—"the blood. I managed to get away from him, but there were others. So many others." Her hands fell from my neck to float between us. "I'll spare you the gory details. None of it was real, anyway."

I stared at her palms faceup in the water. "You said the trees are Morgane's spies."

"That's what she claimed." She lifted an absent hand. "Don't worry, though. Madame Labelle hides us inside camp, and Coco—"

"But they still saw us just now. The trees." I seized her wrist, examining the smear of blood. Already, the water had eroded it in places. I glanced at my own wrists. "We need to leave. Right away."

Lou stared at my clean skin in horror. "Shit. I *told* you to keep an eye on—"

"Believe it or not, I had other things on my mind," I snapped, hauling her toward the bank. Stupid. We'd been so *stupid*. Too distracted, too wrapped up in each other—in *today*—to realize the danger. She squirmed as she tried to free herself. "Stop it!" I tried to hold her flailing limbs. "Keep your wrists and throat above the water, or we're both—"

She stilled in my arms.

"*Thank* you—"

"Shut up," she hissed, staring intently over my shoulder. I'd barely turned—just glimpsing patches of blue coats through the trees—before she shoved my head underwater.

It was dark at the bottom of the pool. Too dark to see anything but Lou's face—muted and pale in the water. She held my shoulders in a bruising grip, cutting off the circulation. When I shrugged beneath her touch, uncomfortable, she clung tighter, shaking her head. She still stared over my shoulder, her eyes wide and—and empty. Combined with her pale skin and floating hair, the effect was . . . eerie.

I shook her slightly. Her eyes didn't focus.

I shook her again. She scowled, her hands biting deeper into my skin.

If I could've managed, I would've breathed a sigh of relief. But I couldn't.

My lungs were screaming.

I hadn't had time to draw breath before she'd pushed me under, hadn't been able to brace myself against the sudden, piercing cold. Icy fingers raked my skin, stunning my senses. *Stealing* my senses. Whatever magic Lou had cast to warm the water had vanished. Debilitating numbness crept up my fingers. My toes. Panic swiftly followed.

And then—just as suddenly—my eyesight blinked out.

The world went black.

I thrashed against Lou's hold, loosening the little breath I had left, but she clung to me, wrapping her limbs around my torso and squeezing, anchoring us to the bottom of the pool. Bubbles exploded around us as I fought. She held me with unnatural strength, rubbing her cheek against mine like she meant to—to calm me. To comfort me.

But she was drowning us both, and my chest was too tight, my throat closing. There was no calm. There was no comfort. My limbs grew heavier with each passing second. In a last, desperate attempt, I pushed upward from the ground with all my strength. At the jerk of Lou's body, the silt solidified around my feet. Trapping me.

Then she punched me in the mouth.

I rocked backward—bewildered, my thoughts fading to

black—and prepared for the water to rush in, to fill my lungs and end this agony. Perhaps it'd be peaceful, to drown. I'd never given it thought. When I'd imagined my own death, it'd been at the end of a sword. Perhaps twisted and broken by a witch's hand. Violent, painful endings. Drowning would be better. Easier.

At the breaking point, my body inhaled involuntarily. I closed my sightless eyes. Wrapped my arms around Lou, buried my nose in her neck. At least Morgane wouldn't have us. At least I wouldn't know life without her. Small victories. Important ones.

But the water never came. Instead, impossibly crisp air flooded my mouth, and with it, the sweetest relief. Though I still couldn't see—though the cold remained debilitating—I could *breathe*. I could *think*. Coherency returned in a disorienting wave. I took another deep breath. Then another, and another. This—this was impossible. I was *breathing underwater*. Like Jonah's fish. Like the melusines. Like—

Like magic.

A sliver of disappointment pierced my chest. Inexplicable and swift. Despite the water around me, I felt . . . dirty, somehow. Sordid. I'd loathed magic my entire life, and now—now it was the only thing saving me from those I'd once called brothers. How had it come to this?

Voices broke around us, interrupting my thoughts. Clear ones. Each rang out as if we stood beside its owner on the shore, not moored beneath feet of water. More magic.

"God, I need a piss."

"Not in the pool, you idiot! Go downstream!"

"Be quick about it." A third voice, this one impatient. "Captain Toussaint expects us in the village soon. One last search, and we leave at first light."

"Thank God he's eager to return to his girl." One of them rubbed his palms together against the cold. My brow furrowed. *His girl?* "Can't say I'm sorry to leave this wretched place. Days of patrols with nothing to show for them except frostbite and—"

A fourth voice. "Are those . . . clothes?"

Lou's fingernails drew blood now. I barely felt it. My heartbeat roared in my ears. If they examined the clothing, if they lifted my coat and shirt, they'd find my bandolier.

They'd find my Balisarda.

The voices grew louder as the men drew closer. "Two piles, it looks like."

A pause.

"Well, they can't be in there. The water is too cold."

"They'd freeze to death."

Behind sightless eyes, I imagined them inching closer to the water, searching its shallow blue depths for signs of life. But trees kept the pool shaded—even in the rising sun—and silt kept the water clouded. The snowfall would've covered our footsteps.

Finally, the first muttered, "No one can hold their breath this long."

"A witch could."

Another pause, this one longer than the last. More ominous. I held my breath, counted each rapid beat of my heart.

Tha-thump.

Tha-thump.

Tha-thump.

"But ... these are men's clothes. Look. Trousers."

A haze of red cut through the unending blackness. If they found my Balisarda, I'd tear my feet from the silt by force. Even if it meant losing said feet.

Tha-thump.

Tha-thump.

I would not yield my Balisarda.

Tha-thump.

I'd incapacitate them all.

Tha-thump.

I would not lose it.

"Do you think they drowned?"

"Without their clothes?"

"You're right. The more logical explanation is that they're wandering around naked in the snow."

Tha-thump.

"Perhaps a witch pulled them under."

"By all means, go in and check."

An indignant snort. "It's freezing. And who knows what could be lurking in there? Anyway, if a witch *did* pull them under, they'll have drowned by now. No sense in adding my corpse to the pile."

"Some Chasseur you are."

"I don't see you volunteering."

Tha-thump.

A distant part of my brain realized my heartbeat was slowing. It recognized the creeping cold down my arms, up my legs. It pealed a warning bell. Lou's grip around my chest slowly loosened. I tightened my arms on her in response. Whatever she was doing to keep us breathing, to strengthen our hearing—it was draining her. Or perhaps it was the cold. Either way, I could feel her fading. I had to do something.

Instinctively, I sought the darkness I'd felt only once before. The chasm. The void. That place where I'd fallen as Lou lay dying, that place I'd carefully locked away and ignored. I fumbled to free it now, reaching blindly through my subconscious. But it wasn't there. I couldn't find it. Panic escalating, I tipped Lou's head back and brought my mouth to hers. Forced my breath into her lungs. Still I searched, but there were no golden cords here. There were no *patterns*. There was only freezing water and sightless eyes and Lou—Lou's head drooping against my arm, her grip slipping from my shoulders, her chest stilling against mine.

I shook her, my panic transforming to raw, debilitating fear, and wracked my brain for something—*anything*—I could do. Madame Labelle had mentioned balance. Perhaps—perhaps I could—

Pain knifed through my lungs before I could finish the thought, and I gasped. Water flooded my mouth. My vision returned abruptly, and the silt around my feet disbanded, which meant—

Lou had lost consciousness.

I didn't pause to think, to watch the gold flickering in my periphery take shape. Clutching her limp body, I launched to the surface.

PRETTY PORCELAIN

Lou

Heat radiated through my body. Slowly at first, then all at once. My limbs tingled almost painfully, nagging me back into consciousness. Cursing the pinpricks—and the snow, and the wind, and the coppery stench in the air—I groaned and opened my eyes. My throat felt raw, tight. Like someone had shoved a hot poker down it while I slept. "Reid?" The word came out a croak. I coughed—horrible, wet sounds that rattled my chest—and tried again. "Reid?"

Cursing when he didn't respond, I rolled over.

A strangled shriek tore from my throat, and I reeled backward.

A lifeless Chasseur stared back at me. His skin was bloodless against the icy shore of the pool, as most of said blood had melted the snow beneath him, seeping into the earth and water. His three companions hadn't fared much better. Their corpses littered the bank, surrounded by Reid's discarded knives.

Reid.

"Fuck!" I scrambled to my knees, hands fluttering over the

enormous, copper-haired figure on my other side. He lay face-down against the snow with his pants haphazardly laced, his arm and head shoved through his shirt as if he'd collapsed before he could finish dressing.

I rolled him over with another curse. His hair had frozen against his blood-spattered face, and his skin had turned an ashen blue-gray. Oh god.

Oh god oh god oh god

Pressing a frantic ear against his chest, I nearly wept with relief when I heard a heartbeat. It was weak, but it was there. My own heart pounded a traitorous beat in my ears—healthy and strong—and my own hair and skin were impossibly warm and dry. Realization swept through me in a wave of nausea. The idiot had almost killed himself trying to save me.

I flattened my palms against his chest, and gold exploded before me in a web of infinite possibilities. I skipped through them hastily—too panicked to delay, to think about the consequences—and stopped when a memory unfolded in my mind's eye: my mother brushing my hair the night before my sixteenth birthday, the tenderness in her gaze, the warmth of her smile.

Warmth.

Be safe, my darling, while we part. Be safe until we meet again.

Will you remember me, Maman?

I could never forget you, Louise. I love you.

Flinching at her words, I yanked at the golden cord, and it twisted beneath my touch. The memory changed within my mind. Her eyes hardened into chips of emerald ice, and she sneered at the hope in my expression, the desperation in my voice. My sixteen-year-old face fell. Tears welled.

Of course I do not love you, Louise. You are the daughter of my enemy. You were conceived for a higher purpose, and I will not poison that purpose with love.

Of course. Of course she hadn't loved me, even then. I shook my head, disoriented, and clenched my fist. The memory dissolved into golden dust, and its warmth flooded over and into Reid. His hair and clothing dried in a burst of heat. Color returned to his skin, and his breathing deepened. His eyes drifted open as I attempted to shove his other arm through his sleeve.

"Stop giving me your body heat," I snapped, tugging his shirt down his abdomen viciously. "You're killing yourself."

"I—" Dazed, he blinked several times, taking in the bloody scene around us. The color he'd regained in his skin vanished at the sight of his dead brethren.

I turned his face toward mine, cupping his cheeks and forcing him to hold my gaze. "Focus on me, Reid. Not them. You need to break the pattern."

His eyes widened as he stared at me. "I—I don't know how."

"Just relax," I coaxed, pushing his hair off his forehead. "Visualize the cord linking us in your mind, and let it go."

"Let it go." He laughed, but the sound was strangled. It held no mirth. "Right."

Shaking his head, he closed his eyes in concentration. After a long moment, the heat pulsing between us ceased, replaced by the bitter bite of cold, wintry air. "Good," I said, feeling that cold deep down in my bones. "Now tell me what happened."

His eyes snapped open, and in that brief second, I saw a flash of raw, unadulterated pain. It made my breath catch in my throat. "They wouldn't stop." He swallowed hard and averted his gaze. "You were dying. I had to get you to the surface. But they recognized us, and they wouldn't listen—" Just as quickly as it'd come, the pain in his eyes vanished, snuffed out as the flame of a candle. An unsettling emptiness replaced it. "I didn't have a choice," he finished in a voice as hollow as his eyes. "It was you or them."

Silence descended as realization clubbed me over the head.

This wasn't the first time he'd been forced to choose between me and another. This wasn't the first time he'd stained his hands with his family's blood to save mine. *Oh god.*

"Of course." I nodded too quickly, my voice horribly light. My smile horribly bright. "It's fine. This is fine." I pushed to my feet, offering him a hand. He eyed it for a second, hesitating, and my stomach dropped to somewhere around my ankles. I smiled harder. Of course he would hesitate to touch me. To touch anyone. He'd just undergone a traumatic experience. He'd cast his first magic since Modraniht, and he'd used it to harm his brethren. *Of course* he felt conflicted. *Of course* he didn't want me—

I flung the unbidden thought aside, cringing away as if it'd bitten me. But it was too late. The poison had already set in. Doubt oozed from the punctures of its fangs, and I watched—disconnected—as my hand fell back to my side. He caught it at the last second, gripping it firmly. "Don't," he said.

"Don't what?"

"Whatever you're thinking. Don't."

I gave a harsh laugh, casting about for a witty reply but finding none. I helped him to his feet instead. "Let's get back to camp. I'd hate to disappoint your mother. At this point, she's probably salivating to roast us both on a spit. I might welcome it, actually. It's freezing out here."

He nodded, still frighteningly impassive, and tugged on his boots in silence. We'd just started back for the Hollow when a small movement in my periphery made me pause.

His gaze cut around us. "What is it?"

"Nothing. Why don't you go on ahead?"

"You aren't serious."

Another movement, this one more pronounced. My smile—still too bright, too cheerful—vanished. "I need to take a piss," I said flatly. "Would you like to watch?"

Reid's cheeks flamed, and he coughed, ducking his head. "Er—no. I'll wait right—right over there." He fled behind the thick foliage of a fir tree without a backward glance. I watched him go, craning my neck to ensure he was out of sight, before turning to study the source of movement.

At the edge of the pool, not quite dead, the last of the Chasseurs watched me with pleading eyes. He still clutched his Balisarda. I knelt beside him, nausea churning as I pried it from his stiff, frozen fingers. Of course Reid hadn't taken it from him—from any of them. It would've been a violation. It didn't matter that witches would likely happen upon these bodies and steal the enchanted blades for themselves. To Reid, robbing his brethren of their identities in their final moments would've been an unthinkable betrayal, worse even than killing them.

The Chasseur's pale lips moved, but no sound came out. Gently, I rolled him onto his stomach. Morgane had once taught me how to kill a man instantly. "At the base of the head," she'd instructed, touching the tip of her knife to my own neck, "where the spine meets the skull. Sever the two, and there can be no resuscitation."

I mimicked Morgane's movement against the Chasseur's neck. His fingers twitched in agitation. In fear. But it was too late for him now, and even if it weren't, he'd seen our faces. Perhaps he'd seen Reid use magic as well. This was the only gift I could give either of them.

Taking a deep, steadying breath, I plunged the Balisarda into the base of the Chasseur's skull. His fingers stopped twitching abruptly. After a moment's hesitation, I rolled him back over, clasped his hands across his chest, and replaced his Balisarda between them.

As predicted, Madame Labelle waited for us on the edge of the Hollow, her cheeks flushed and her eyes bright with anger. Fire practically spewed from her nostrils. "*Where* have you—" She stopped short, eyes widening as she took in our rumpled hair and state of undress. Reid still hadn't laced his trousers. He hastened to do so now. "Imbeciles!" Madame Labelle cried, her voice so loud—so shrill and unpleasant—that a couple of turtle doves fled into the sky. "Cretins! Stupid, *asinine* children. Are you capable of thinking with the northernmost regions of your bodies, or are you ruled entirely by sex?"

"It's a toss-up on any given day." Marching to my bedroll, pulling Reid along in tow, I threw my blanket over his shoulders. His skin was still too ashen for my taste, his breathing too shallow. He pulled me under his shoulder, thanking me with a brush of his lips to my ear. "Though I am surprised to hear a madam being so prudish."

"Oh, I don't know." Sitting up in his bedroll, Beau dragged a hand through his rumpled hair. Sleep still clung to his face. "Just this once, I might call it prudence instead. And that's saying something from me." He arched a brow in my direction. "Was it good, at least? Wait—scratch that. If it was with anyone *other* than my brother, maybe—"

"Shut up, Beau, and stoke the fire while you're at it," Coco snapped, her eyes raking every inch of my skin. She frowned at whatever she saw there. "Is that blood? Are you hurt?"

Beau cocked his head to study me before nodding in agreement. He made no move to stoke the fire. "Not your best look, sister mine."

"She's not your sister," Reid snarled.

"And she looks better than you on her worst day," Coco added.

He chuckled and shook his head. "I suppose you're both entitled to your wrong opinions—"

"Enough!" Madame Labelle threw her hands in the air, wearisome in her exasperation, and glared between all of us. "What *happened*?"

With a glance up at Reid—he'd tensed as if Madame Labelle had stuck him with a fire poker—I quickly recounted the events at the pool. Though I skimmed the intimate parts, Beau groaned and fell backward anyway, pulling a blanket over his face. Madame Labelle's expression grew stonier with each word. "I was trying to maintain four patterns all at once," I said, prickling with defensiveness at her narrowed eyes, at the spots of color rising to her cheeks. "Two patterns to help us breathe and two patterns to help us hear. It was too much to control the temperature of the water too. I'd hoped I could last long enough for the Chasseurs to leave." I looked reluctantly at Reid, who stared determinedly at his feet. Though he'd returned his Balisarda to his bandolier, he still gripped its handle with his free hand. His knuckles were white around it. "I'm sorry I couldn't."

"It wasn't your fault," he mumbled.

Madame Labelle plowed onward, heedless of any and all emotional cues. "What happened to the Chasseurs?"

Again, I glanced at Reid, prepared to lie if necessary.

He answered for me, his voice hollow. "I killed them. They're dead."

Finally, *finally*, Madame Labelle's face softened.

"Then he gave me his body heat on the bank." I hurried to continue the story, suddenly anxious to end this conversation, to pull Reid aside and comfort him somehow. He looked so— so *wooden*. Like one of the trees growing around us, strange and unfamiliar and hard. I loathed it. "It was a clever bit of magic, but he almost died from the cold himself. I had to leech warmth from a memory to revive—"

"You *what*?" Madame Labelle drew herself up to her full height and stared down her nose at me, fists clenched in a gesture so familiar that I paused, staring. "You foolish girl—"

I lifted my chin defiantly. "Would you have preferred I let him die?"

"Of course not! Still, such *recklessness* must be checked, Louise. You know good and well how dangerous it is to tamper with memory—"

"I'm aware," I said through gritted teeth.

"Why is it dangerous?" Reid asked quietly.

I turned my head toward him, lowering my voice to match his. "Memories are sort of . . . sacred. Our experiences in life shape who we are—it's like nurture over nature—and if we change our memories of those experiences, well . . . we might change who we are too."

"There's no telling how that memory she altered has affected her values, her beliefs, her expectations." Madame Labelle sank in a huff onto her favorite tree stump. Breathing deeply, she straightened her spine and clasped her hands as if trying to focus on something else—anything else—than her anger. "Personality is nuanced. There are some who believe nature—our lineage, our inherited characteristics—influences who we are, regardless of the lives we lead. They believe we become who we are born to be. Many witches, Morgane included, use this philosophy to excuse their heinous behavior. It's nonsense, of course."

Every eye and ear in the Hollow fixed solely on her. Even

Beau poked his head out in interest.

Reid's brows furrowed. "So . . . you believe nurture holds greater sway than nature."

"Of course it does. The slightest changes in memory can have profound and unseen consequences." Her gaze flicked to me, and those familiar eyes tightened almost infinitesimally. "I've seen it happen."

Ansel gave a tentative smile—an instinctive reaction—in the awkward silence that followed. "I didn't know witchcraft could be so academic."

"What you know about witchcraft couldn't fill a walnut shell," Madame Labelle said irritably.

Coco snapped something in reply, to which Beau fired back. I didn't hear any of it, as Reid had lifted his hand to the small of my back. He leaned low to whisper, "You shouldn't have done that for me."

"I would do far worse for you."

He pulled back at my tone, his eyes searching mine. "What do you mean?"

"Nothing. Don't worry about it." I stroked his cheek, inordinately relieved when he didn't pull away. "What's done is done."

"Lou." He grabbed my fingers, squeezing gently before returning them to my side. My heart dropped at the rejection, however polite. "Tell me."

"No."

"Tell me."

"No."

He exhaled hard through his nose, jaw clenching. "*Please.*"

I stared at him, deliberating, as Coco and Beau's bickering escalated. This was a bad idea. A very bad idea, indeed. "You already know some of it," I said at last. "To gain, you must give. I tampered with a memory to revive you on the shore. I exchanged our sight for enhanced hearing, and I—"

To be perfectly honest, I wanted to lie. Again. I wanted to grin and tell him everything would be all right, but there was little sense in hiding what I'd done. This was the nature of the beast. Magic required sacrifice. Nature demanded balance. Reid would need to learn this sooner rather than later if we were to survive.

"You?" he prompted impatiently.

I met his hard, unflinching gaze head-on. "I traded a few moments from my life for those moments underwater. It was the only way I could think to keep us breathing."

He recoiled from me then—physically recoiled—but Madame Labelle leapt to her feet, raising her voice to be heard over Coco and Beau. Ansel watched the chaos unfold with palpable anxiety. "I said that's enough!" The color in her cheeks had deepened, and she trembled visibly. Reid's temper had obviously been inherited. "By the Crone's missing eyetooth, you lot—*all* of you—need to stop behaving like children, or the Dames Blanches will dance atop your ashes." She cut a sharp look to Reid and me. "You're sure the Chasseurs are dead? All of them?"

Reid's silence should've been answer enough. When Madame Labelle still glared expectantly, however, waiting for confirmation, I scowled and said the words aloud. "Yes. They're gone."

"Good," she spat.

Reid still said nothing. He didn't react to her cruel sentiment at all. He was hiding, I realized. Hiding from them, hiding from himself... hiding from me. Madame Labelle tore three crumpled pieces of parchment from her bodice and thrust them toward us. I recognized Coco's handwriting on them, the pleas she'd penned to her aunt. Below the last, an unfamiliar hand had inked a brusque refusal—*Your huntsman is unwelcome here.* That was it. No other explanations or courtesies. No *ifs*, *ands*, or *buts*.

It seemed La Voisin had finally given her answer.

I crushed the last note in my fist before Reid could read it, blood roaring in my ears.

"Can we all agree it is now time to face the monsters," Madame Labelle said, "or shall we continue to close our eyes and hope for the best?"

My irritation with Madame Labelle veered dangerously close to distaste. I didn't care that she was Reid's mother. In that moment, I wished her not *death*, per se, but—an itch. Yes. An eternal itch in her nether regions that she could never quite scratch. A fitting punishment for one who kept ruining everything.

And yet, despite her cruel insensitivity, I knew deep down she was right. Our stolen moments had passed.

The time had come to move on.

"You said yesterday we need allies." I stuck my hand into Reid's, squeezing his fingers tight. It was the only comfort I could offer him here. When he didn't return the pressure, however, an old fissure opened in my heart. Bitter words spilled forth from it before I could stop them. "Who would we even ask? The blood witches clearly aren't with us. The people of Belterra certainly won't be rallying to our cause. We're witches. We're evil. We've strung up their sisters and brothers and mothers in the street."

"*Morgane* has done those things," Coco argued. "*We* have done nothing."

"That's the point, though, isn't it? We let it happen." I paused, exhaling hard. "*I* let it happen."

"Stop it," Coco said fiercely, shaking her head. "The only crime you committed was wanting to live."

"It matters not." Madame Labelle returned to her stump with a pensive expression. Though her cheeks were still pink, she'd mercifully lowered her voice. My ears rejoiced. "Where the king leads, the people will follow."

"You're mad if you think my father will align with you," Beau said from his bedroll. "He already has money on Lou's head."

Madame Labelle sniffed. "We have a common enemy in Morgane. Your father might be more amenable than you think."

Beau rolled his eyes. "Look, I know you think he still loves you or whatever, but he—"

"—is not the only ally we'll be pursuing," Madame Labelle said curtly. "Obviously, our chances of success are far greater if we persuade King Auguste to join us, as he will undoubtedly command the Chasseurs until the Church appoints new leadership, but there are other equally powerful players in this world. The loup garou, for example, and the melusines. Perhaps even Josephine would be amenable under the right circumstances."

Coco laughed. "If my aunt refused to *host* us with an ex-Chasseur involved, what makes you think she'll agree to *ally* with the real things? She isn't particularly fond of werewolves or mermaids, either."

Reid blinked, the only outward sign he'd gleaned the content of La Voisin's note.

"Nonsense." Madame Labelle shook her head. "We must simply show Josephine that she has more to gain from an alliance than from petty politics."

"Petty politics?" Coco's lip curled. "My aunt's *politics* are life and death for my people. When the Dames Blanches cast my ancestors from the Chateau, both the loup garou and melusines refused to offer aid. But you didn't know that, did you? Dames Blanches think only of themselves. Except for you, Lou," she added.

"No offense taken." I stalked to the nearest root, hauled myself atop it, and glared down at Madame Labelle. My feet dangled several inches above the ground, however, rather diminishing my menacing pose. "If we're living in fantasy land, why don't we add the Woodwose and Tarasque to the list? I'm sure a mythical goat man and dragon would add nice color to this great battle you're dreaming up."

"I'm not dreaming up anything, Louise. You know as well as I that your mother hasn't been idle in her silence. She is planning *something*, and we must be ready for whatever it is."

"It won't be a battle." I swung my feet in a show of nonchalance, despite the trepidation prickling beneath my skin. "Not in the traditional sense. That's not her style. My mother is an anarchist, not a soldier. She attacks from the shadows, hides within crowds. It's how she incites fear—in chaos. She won't risk uniting her enemies by presenting an outright attack."

"Even so," Madame Labelle said coolly, "we number six against scores of Dames Blanches. We *need* allies."

"For the sake of your argument, let's say all parties *do* form a miraculous alliance." I swung my feet harder, faster. "The king, Chasseurs, Dames Rouges, loup garou, and melusines all working together like one big happy family. What happens after we defeat Morgane? Do we resume killing each other over her corpse? We're *enemies*, Helene. Werewolves and mermaids aren't going to become bosom buddies on the battlefield. Huntsmen aren't going to forsake centuries of teaching to befriend witches. The hurt is too long and too great on all sides. You can't heal a disease with a bandage."

"So give them the cure," Ansel said quietly. He met my gaze with a steady fortitude beyond his years. "You're a witch. He's a huntsman."

Reid's reply was low, flat. "Not anymore."

"But you were," Ansel insisted. "When you fell in love, you were enemies."

"He didn't know I was his enemy—" I started.

"But you knew he was yours." Ansel's eyes, the color of whiskey, flicked from me to Reid. "Would it have mattered?"

It doesn't matter you're a witch, he'd told me after Modraniht. His hands had cupped mine, and tears had welled in his eyes. They'd been so expressive, brimming with emotion. With love. *The way you see the world . . . I want to see it that way too.*

Holding my breath, I waited for his validation, but it never came. Madame Labelle spoke instead. "I believe a similar approach will work on the others. Uniting them against a common enemy—forcing them to work together—might change each side's perceptions. It could be the push we all need."

"And you called me a fool." I kicked harder to emphasize my skepticism, and my boot—still unlaced in my haste to leave the pool—slipped from my foot. A scrap of paper fluttered from it. Frowning, I leapt to the ground to retrieve it. Unlike the cheap, blood-spattered parchment Coco had stolen from the village, *this* note had been written on crisp, clean linen that smelled like— like eucalyptus. My blood ran cold.

Pretty porcelain, pretty doll, with hair as black as night,
She cries alone within her pall, her tears so green and bright.

Coco strode to my side, leaning closer to read the words. "This isn't from my aunt."

The linen slipped through numb fingers.

Ansel stooped to pick it up, and he too skimmed the contents. "I didn't know you liked poetry." When his eyes met mine, his smile faltered. "It's beautiful. In a sad sort of way, I guess."

He tried to hand the linen back to me, but my fingers still refused to work. Reid took it instead. "You didn't write this, did you?" he asked, except it wasn't a question.

Mutely, I shook my head anyway.

He studied me for a moment before returning his attention to the note. "It was in your boot. Whoever wrote it must've been there at the pool." His frown deepened, and he passed it to Madame Labelle, who'd extended an impatient hand. "Do you think a Chasseur—?"

"No." The disbelief that'd held me frozen finally ruptured in a hot wave of panic. I snatched the note from Madame Labelle—heedless of her protest—and stuffed it back into my boot. "It was Morgane."

THE WISEST COURSE OF ACTION

Reid

An ominous silence settled over camp. Everyone stared at Lou as she took a deep breath to collect herself. Finally, she gave our silence a voice. "How did she find us?"

It was a good question. It wasn't the right one.

I stared at the crackling fire, envisioning Morgane's pale hand—her writing curved and elegant—as she spelled out destruction and doom.

I had a decision to make.

"You left camp, remember?" Madame Labelle snapped. "To take a *bath*, of all things."

"Chateau le Blanc is miles from here," Lou said. I could tell she was struggling to keep her voice reasonable. "Even if the water washed away Coco's protection, even if the trees whispered our whereabouts, she couldn't have gotten here so quickly. She can't *fly*."

"Of course she could. If properly motivated, you could too. It's simply a matter of finding the right pattern."

"Or maybe she was already here, watching us. Maybe she's

been watching us all this time."

"Impossible." I glanced up to see Madame Labelle's eyes darken. "I enchanted this hollow myself."

"Either way," Coco said, planting her hands on her hips, "why didn't she just snatch you from the pool?"

I returned my attention to the fire. That was a better question. Still not the right one.

Morgane's words floated back through my mind. *She cries alone within her pall, her tears so green and bright.* The answer was right in front of us. I swallowed hard around the word. *Pall.* Of course this was Morgane's plan. Grief thundered against the door of my fortress, but I kept it at bay, ignored the shard of longing that threatened to cut me open.

Slowly, methodically, I marshaled my thoughts—my emotions—back into order.

"I don't know." Lou answered Coco's question with a sound of frustration and started to pace. "This is so—so *her.* And until we know how she found me—or what she wants—we aren't safe here." She pivoted abruptly to face Madame Labelle. "You're right. We need to leave immediately. Today."

She wasn't wrong.

"But she knows we're here," Coco said. "Won't she just follow us?"

Lou resumed pacing, didn't look up from the path she wore in the ground. "She'll try to follow. Of course she will. But her game isn't ready yet, or she would've already taken me. We have until then to lose her."

"Marvelous." Beau rolled his eyes skyward, flopping gracelessly to his bedroll. "We have an invisible axe hanging over our heads."

I took a deep breath.

"It's not invisible."

Every eye in the clearing turned to stare at me. I hesitated. I still hadn't decided what to do. If I was right—and I knew I was—many lives would be lost if we didn't act. And if we *did* act . . . well, we'd be walking into a trap. Which meant Lou . . .

I glanced at her, my heart twisting.

Lou would be in danger.

"Good God, man," Beau exclaimed, "now is not the time to play brooding hero. Out with it!"

"It was all in the note." Gesturing to the embers of the fire, I shrugged. The movement felt brittle. "Crying, tears, pall. It's a funeral." When I shot Lou a meaningful look, she gasped.

"The Archbishop's funeral."

I nodded. "She's baiting us."

Her brows dipped, and she tilted her head. "But—"

"That's only one line," Ansel finished. "What about the rest of it?"

I forced myself to remain calm. Collected. Empty of the emotion thrashing outside my mental fortress. "I don't know. But whatever she's planning, it's for his funeral. I'm sure of it."

If I was right, could I endanger Lou to save hundreds, perhaps thousands, of innocent people? Did risking her life to save the others make me any different than Morgane? One for the sake of many. It was a wise sentiment, but wrong, somehow. Even if it hadn't been Lou. The ends didn't justify the means.

And yet . . . I knew Morgane better than anyone here. Better than Madame Labelle. Better than even Lou. They knew La Dame des Sorcières as the woman. The mother. The friend. I knew her as the enemy. It had been my duty to study her strategy, to predict her attacks. I'd spent the last several years of my life growing intimately acquainted with her movements. Whatever she had planned for the Archbishop's funeral, it reeked of death.

But I couldn't risk Lou. I couldn't. If those few, terrible moments on Modraniht had taught me anything—when her throat had gaped open, when her blood had filled the basin—it was that I wasn't interested in a life without her. Not that it mattered. If she died, I would too. Literally. Along with dozens of others, like Beau and—and the rest of them.

My family.

The thought shook me to the core.

No longer faceless strangers, Morgane's targets were now the brothers and sisters I hadn't yet met. The brothers and sisters I hadn't yet allowed myself to dream about, to even think about. They were out there, somewhere. And they were in danger. I couldn't just abandon them. Morgane had as good as told us where she would be. If I could be there too—if I could somehow stop her, if I could cut off the viper's head to save my family, to save Lou, if I could prevent her from defiling my patriarch's last rites—

I was too distracted to notice the silence around me.

"You're reaching," Beau finally said, shaking his head. "You're drawing conclusions that aren't there. You want to attend the funeral. I understand. But that doesn't mean Morgane will be present too."

"What I *want* is to stop whatever she's planning."

"We don't *know* what she's planning."

I shook my head. "We *do*. She isn't going to spell it out for us, but the threat is clear—"

"Reid, darling," Madame Labelle interrupted gently, "I know you loved the Archbishop deeply, and perhaps you need closure, but now is not the time to charge heedlessly forth—"

"It wouldn't be heedlessly." My hands curled into fists of their own volition, and I struggled to control my breathing. My chest was tight. Too tight. Of course they didn't understand. This wasn't about me. This wasn't about—about *closure*. It was about justice. And if—if I could start to atone for what I'd done, if I could say goodbye . . .

The shard of longing burrowed deeper. Painful now.

I could still protect Lou. I could keep her from harm.

"You're the one who wanted to gather allies," I continued, voice stronger. "Tell us how to do that. Tell us how to—to persuade werewolves and mermaids to fight alongside each other. To fight alongside Chasseurs. This could work. Together, we'll be strong enough to confront her when she makes her move."

They all exchanged glances. Reluctant glances. Meaningful glances. Except for Lou. She watched me with an inscrutable expression. I didn't like it. I couldn't read it, and I could always read Lou. This look—it reminded me of a time when she kept secrets. But there were no more secrets between us. She'd promised.

"Do we . . ." Ansel rubbed the back of his neck, staring at his feet. "Do we even know if there'll be a funeral?"

"Or where it is?" said Beau.

"Or *when* it is?" said Coco.

"We'll find out," I insisted. "We'll be ready for her."

Beau sighed. "Reid, don't be stupid. If you're correct about this note—which I'm not convinced you are, by the way—we'd be playing right into her hands. This is what she *wants*—"

Absalon materialized at my feet just as I opened my mouth to argue—to explode—but Lou interrupted.

"It's true. This is what she wants." Her voice was quiet, contemplative, as she gestured between us. "It's exactly the sort of game she likes to play. Manipulative, cruel, divisive. She expects a response. She *craves* a response. The wisest course of action is to stay away."

The last she spoke directly to me.

"Thank the Maiden's flower." Madame Labelle heaved a sigh of relief, wiping a hand across her brow and gifting Lou a rare smile. "I knew you couldn't have survived this long without some common sense. *If* there is indeed a funeral and *if* Morgane indeed plans to sabotage it, we wouldn't have the necessary time to prepare. Travel along the road would be slow and dangerous with the entire kingdom searching for us. It would take nearly a fortnight to reach the Beast of Gévaudan's packland, and the melusines' home in L'Eau Mélancolique would be at least a week's journey in the opposite direction." She wiped her brow in agitation. "Beyond that, we'd need *weeks* at each place to foster the necessary relationships. I'm sorry, Reid. The logistics just don't work."

Lou watched me, waiting.

I didn't disappoint.

"Please, Lou," I whispered, stepping closer. "The wisest course of action isn't always the right one. This was my job. I've dealt with Morgane and the Dames Blanches all my life. I know how they operate. You were right before—Morgane incites chaos. Think about it. The day we met, she made an attempt on the king's life during his homecoming parade." I jerked my chin toward Beau at the memory. "She attacked the cathedral during the last of Saint Nicolas Day celebrations. Always, it's amidst a crowd. It's how she protects herself. It's how she slips away." I took her hand, surprised to feel her fingers trembling. "The Archbishop's funeral will have an assembly like the kingdom has never seen. People from all over the world will come to pay homage to him. The havoc she'll wreak will be devastating. But we have a real chance to stop her."

"And if no one joins us against her?"

"They will." Guilt ripped at my resolve, but I pushed it away. For now, I needed her to agree. I'd reveal this last bit of information when lives weren't at stake. "We don't need the blood witches or mermaids. The werewolves' land isn't far from Cesarine—a day or two's ride at most. We'll concentrate our efforts, focus on King Auguste and the Beast of—*Blaise*. We'll do whatever is necessary to persuade them. You said it yourself. Morgane isn't a soldier. She won't battle if we have equal footing." My thoughts raced faster, chasing different strategies. "She won't expect an alliance between the Chasseurs and werewolves. We'll ambush her . . . no. We'll create a diversion with the Chasseurs, drive her out of the city while the werewolves lie in wait. This could work," I repeated, louder now than before.

"Reid. You know this is a trap."

"I would never let anything happen to you."

"It's not me I'm worried about." With her free hand, she reached up to touch my cheek. "Did you know my mother threatened to feed me your heart if I escaped again?"

"That won't happen."

"No. It won't."

She dropped her hand, and everyone stilled, waiting. No one even breathed. In that moment, something shifted in our camp. Inadvertently, we'd looked to Lou for the final decision. Not Madame Labelle. Lou. I stared at her in dawning realization. She was the daughter of La Dame des Sorcières. I knew that. Of course I did. But I hadn't yet realized the implication. If all went according to plan . . . Lou would inherit the crown. The title. The power.

Lou would become a queen.

Lou would become the Maiden, the Mother, and the Crone.

She startled as if realizing this at the same moment I did. Her eyes widened, and her mouth twisted. It was an unpleasant realization, then. An unwelcome one. When she glanced at

Coco, looking deeply uncomfortable, Coco dipped her chin in a small nod.

"Right." Lou bent to crook a finger toward the cat at our feet. "Absalon, can you deliver a message to Josephine Monvoisin?" She shot an apologetic look at Coco. "This one should come from me."

"What are you doing?" Confusion laced my voice as I caught her hand, tugging her upright. "We should focus on Auguste and Blaise—"

"Listen, Chass." She patted my chest once before pulling away and crouching by Absalon once more. "If we're going to do this, we need all the help we can get. The mermaids *are* too far away, but the blood witches—maybe your mother is right. Maybe Josephine will be amenable under the right circumstances." To Coco, she added, "You said the blood camp is near?"

Coco nodded. "They usually camp in this area at this time of year."

Suspicion unfurled in my stomach as Lou nodded, whispering something to Absalon. "You said she wouldn't host an ex-Chasseur," I said.

Coco arched a brow pointedly. A smirk pulled at her lips. "She won't."

"Then what . . . ?"

Slowly, Lou rose to her feet, dusting mud from her knees as the cat vanished in a cloud of black smoke. "We're going to have to split up, Reid."

PAINTED HAIR

Lou

"White wine and honey, followed by a mixture of celandine roots, olive-madder, oil of cumin seed, box shavings, and a sprinkle of saffron." Madame Labelle carefully arranged the bottles on the rock we'd fashioned into a table. "If applied and left to alchemize for a full sun cycle, it will transform your locks to gold."

I stared at the many bottles, aghast. "We don't have a full sun cycle."

Her eyes cut to mine. "Yes, *obviously*, but with the raw ingredients, perhaps we could . . . speed the process." As one, we glanced across camp to Reid, who sulked by himself, sharpening his Balisarda and refusing to speak to anyone.

"No." I shook my head, pushing the bottles aside. The entire purpose of this futile exercise was to disguise myself *without* magic. After what had happened with Reid at the pool . . . well, we needn't poke the bear without reason. "Were there no wigs?"

Madame Labelle scoffed, reaching into her bag once more. "As inconceivable as it sounds, Louise, there were no costume shops in the small farming village of Saint-Loire." She slammed another jar on the rock. Inside it, *things* wriggled. "Might I interest you instead in a jar of pickled leeches? If allowed to bake into your hair on a sunny day, I'm told they yield a rich raven color."

Leeches? Coco and I exchanged horrified glances. "That is disgusting," she said flatly.

"Agreed."

"How about this as an alternative?" Madame Labelle fished two more bottles from her bag, throwing one to both Coco and me—or rather, *at* Coco and me. I managed to catch mine before it broke my nose. "The paste of lead oxide and slaked lime will dye your hair black as night. But be warned, the clerk informed me the side effects can be quite unpleasant."

They couldn't have been more unpleasant than her smile.

Beau paused in rummaging through Coco's rucksack. "Side effects?"

"Death, mostly. Nothing to fret about." Madame Labelle shrugged, unamused, and sarcasm dripped from her words. I didn't quite appreciate it. "Far safer than using *magic*, I'm sure."

Eyes narrowing, I knelt to inspect the contents of her rucksack myself. "It's just a precaution, all right? I'm *trying* to be nice. Reid and magic aren't exactly amicable at the moment."

"Have they ever been?" Ansel murmured.

Fair point.

"Can you blame him?" I pulled bottles out at random, examining their labels before tossing them aside. Madame Labelle must've bought the entire apothecary. "He's used magic twice, and both times, people have ended up dead. He just needs . . . time to reconcile everything. He'll make peace with himself."

"*Will* he?" Coco arched a dubious brow, casting him another long look. "I mean . . . the matagot showed for a reason."

The matagot in question lounged within the lower boughs of a fir, peering out at us with yellow eyes.

Madame Labelle snatched her rucksack from me. In a single, agitated motion, she swept the bottles inside. "We don't *know* the matagot is here because of Reid. My son is hardly the only troubled one in this camp." Her blue eyes flashed to mine, and she shoved a piece of ribbon in my hand. Thicker than what I'd once worn, but still . . . the black satin would barely cover my new scar. "Twice now your mother has attempted to murder you. For all we know, Absalon could be here because of *you*."

"Me?" I snorted in disbelief, lifting my hair for Coco to tie the ribbon around my throat. "Don't be stupid. I'm fine."

"You're mad if you think ribbon and hair dye will hide you from Morgane."

"Not from *Morgane*. She could already be here now, watching us." I flipped my middle finger over my head just in case. "But ribbon and hair dye might hide me from anyone who sees those wretched wanted posters—might even hide me from the Chasseurs."

Finished with the bow, Coco tapped my arm, and I let my hair fall, thick and heavy, down my back. I could hear the smirk in her voice. "Those posters *are* an uncanny likeness. The care with which the artist drew your scar—"

I snorted despite myself, turning to face her. "It looked like another appendage."

"A rather large one."

"A rather *phallic* one."

When we burst into a fit of cackles, Madame Labelle huffed impatiently. Muttering something about *children*, she stalked off to join Reid. Good riddance. Coco and I laughed anew. Though Ansel tried to play along with us, his smile seemed somewhat pained—a suspicion confirmed when he said, "Do you think we'll be safe in La Voisin's camp?"

Coco's response came instantly. "Yes."

"What about the others?"

Laughter fading, she glanced at Beau, who'd surreptitiously started digging through her pack once more. She knocked his hand away but said nothing.

"I don't like it," Ansel continued, bouncing his foot, growing more and more agitated. "If Madame Labelle's magic couldn't hide us here, it won't hide them on the road." He turned his pleading gaze to me. "You said Morgane threatened to cut out Reid's heart. After we separate, she could take him, force you back to the Chateau."

Reid had said as much an hour ago—or rather, shouted it.

As it turned out, he was much less keen on his *gather allies to confront Morgane at the Archbishop's funeral* plan when it meant we'd have to separate. But we needed the blood witches for this insane plan to work, and La Voisin had made it clear Reid wasn't welcome in her camp. Though small in number, their reputations were formidable. Fearsome enough that Morgane had denied their annual petitions to rejoin us in the Chateau.

I hoped it'd be enough for them to consider moving against her.

La Voisin was willing to listen, at least. Absalon had returned almost instantaneously with her consent. If we came without Reid, she'd allow us to enter her camp. It wasn't much, but it was a start. At midnight, Coco, Ansel, and I would meet her outside Saint-Loire, and she would escort us to the blood camp. In her presence, we'd be relatively safe, but the others—

"I don't know." When I shrugged helplessly, Coco's lips pressed tight. "We can only hope Helene's magic is enough. They'll have Coco's blood as well. And if worse comes to worst . . . Reid has his Balisarda. He can defend himself."

"It's not enough," Coco murmured.

"I know."

There was nothing else to say. If Reid, Madame Labelle, and Beau managed to survive the Chasseurs, Dames Blanches, cutthroats, and bandits of La Rivière des Dents—the only road through the forest, named as such for the teeth of the dead it collected—the danger would increase tenfold when they reached packland.

It was hard to say who the werewolves loathed more— huntsmen, witches, or princes.

Still, Reid knew those lands better than anyone in our company. He knew *Blaise* better than anyone in our company. I could only hope Madame Labelle's and Beau's diplomacy would serve them well. From what I'd heard of Blaise—which admittedly wasn't much—he ruled with a fair hand. Perhaps he'd surprise us all.

Either way, we didn't have time to visit both peoples together.

Tonight, we'd reconnoiter at a local pub to learn the exact date of the Archbishop's funeral. With luck, we'd be able to reunite in Cesarine before the services to approach King Auguste together. Madame Labelle maintained he could be swayed into a third alliance. We'd find out—for better or for worse—when we visited his castle.

Like Ansel, I didn't like it. I didn't like *any* of it. There was still too much to do, too much of the puzzle missing. Too little time. We'd piece together the rest at the pub tonight, but before we could do that . . .

"Aha!" Triumphant, Beau pulled two bottles from Coco's bag. She'd packed a motley assortment of ingredients to aid in her blood magic: some recognizable, such as herbs and spices, and some not, such as the gray powder and clear liquid Beau currently held aloft. "Wood ash and vinegar," he explained. When we stared at him blankly, he heaved an impatient sigh. "For your *hair*. You still want to dye it the old-fashioned way, correct?"

"Oh." Of their own volition, my hands shot up, covering my hair as if it protect it. "Yes—yes, of course."

Coco clutched my shoulder for moral support, shooting daggers at Beau with her eyes. "You're sure you know what you're doing?"

"I've helped many a paramour dye their hair, Cosette. Indeed, before you, there was a buxom blonde by the name of Evonne." He leaned closer, winking. "She wasn't naturally blond, of course, but her other natural assets more than made up for it." When Coco's gaze flattened—and her fingers tightened painfully on my shoulder—Beau smirked. "Whatever is wrong, *ma chatte*? You aren't . . . jealous?"

"You—"

I patted her hand, wincing. "I'll dismember him for you after we've finished."

"Slowly?"

"Piece by piece."

With a satisfied nod, she strode after Madame Labelle, leaving me alone with Ansel and Beau. Awkwardness loomed between us, but I cut through it—literally—with an anxious swipe of my hand. "You *do* actually know what you're doing, right?"

Beau ran his fingers through the length of my hair. Without Coco to goad him, he seemed to wilt, eyeing the bottles of wood ash and vinegar warily. "Never once did I claim to know what I'm doing."

My stomach rose. "But you said—"

"What I *said* is that I helped a paramour dye her hair, but that was only to piss off Cosette. What I actually *did* was *watch* a paramour dye her hair, while feeding her strawberries. Naked."

"If you fuck this up, I will skin you alive and wear your hide as a cape."

He arched a brow, lifting the bottles to examine their labels. "Noted."

Honestly, if a naked paramour didn't start feeding *me* strawberries soon, I'd burn the world down.

After pouring equal parts of ash and vinegar into Coco's mortar, he poked at it hopefully for several seconds, and an ominous gray sludge formed. Ansel eyed it in alarm. "How *would* you do it, though? If you magicked it a different color instead?"

Sweat broke out along my palms as Beau parted my hair into sections.

"That depends." I cast about for a pattern, and sure enough, several tendrils of gold rose to meet me. Touching one, I watched it curl up my arm like a snake. "I'd be changing something about myself on the outside. I could change something on the inside to match. Or—depending on the end color—I could take the hue, depth, or tone of my current shade and manipulate it somehow. Maybe transfer the brown to my eyes instead."

Ansel's gaze shifted to Reid. "Don't do that. I think Reid likes your eyes." As if afraid he'd offended me somehow, he hastily added, "And I do too. They're pretty."

I chuckled, and the tension knotting my stomach eased a bit. "Thanks, Ansel."

Beau leaned over my shoulder to look at me. "Are you ready?"

Nodding, I closed my eyes as he painted the first strand and kept my focus on Ansel. "Why are you so interested?"

"No reason," he said quickly.

"Ansel." I peeked an eye open to glare at him. "Out with it."

He wouldn't look at me, instead nudging a pine cone with

his toe. Several seconds passed. Then several seconds more. I'd just opened my mouth to prod him along when he said, "I don't remember much of my mother."

My mouth closed with a snap.

Behind me, Beau's hand stilled on my hair.

"She and my father died in a fire when I was three. Sometimes I think—" His eyes darted to Beau, who quickly resumed smearing the gray paste on my hair. Relieved, Ansel continued his dance with the pine cone. "Sometimes I think I can remember her laugh, or—or maybe his smile. I know it's stupid." He laughed in a self-deprecating way that I loathed. "I don't even know their names. I was too frightened of Father Thomas to ask. He did once tell me *Maman* was an obedient, God-fearing woman, but for all I know, she could've been a witch." He hesitated, swallowing hard, and finally met my eyes. "Just like—just like Reid's mother. Just like you."

My chest tightened at the hopefulness in his expression. Somehow, I knew what he was implying. I knew where this conversation was headed, and I knew what he wanted me to say—what he wanted, no, *needed*, to hear.

I hated disappointing him.

When I said nothing, his expression fell, but he continued determinedly. "If that's the case, maybe . . . maybe I have magic too. It's possible."

"Ansel . . ." I took his hand, deliberating. If he'd lived with his mother—*and* father—until he was three, it was highly unlikely the woman had been a Dame Blanche. True, she could've lived outside the Chateau—many Dames Blanches did—but even they rarely kept their sons, who were considered burdens, unable to inherit their mothers' magic or enhance their family's lineage.

Unbidden, my eyes cut to Reid. He whet his Balisarda on a stone with short, angry strokes.

How very wrong we'd been.

"It's possible," Ansel repeated, lifting his chin in an uncharacteristic display of stubbornness. "You said the blood witches keep their sons."

"The blood witches don't live in Cesarine. They live with their covens."

"Coco doesn't."

"Coco is an exception."

"Maybe I am too."

"Where is this coming from, Ansel?"

"I want to learn how to fight, Lou. I want to learn magic. You can teach me both."

"I'm hardly the person to—"

"We're headed into danger, aren't we?" He didn't pause for me to confirm the obvious answer. "You and Coco have lived on the streets. You're both survivors. You're both strong. Reid has his training and his Balisarda. Madame Labelle has her magic, and even Beau was quick-witted enough to distract the other witches on Modraniht."

The man in question scoffed. "Thanks."

Ansel ignored him, shoulders slumping. "But I was worthless in that fight, just like I'll be worthless in the blood camp."

I frowned at him. "Don't talk about yourself like that."

"Why not? It's true."

"No, it isn't." I squeezed his hand and leaned forward. "I understand that you might think you need to earn a place amongst us, but you don't. You already have one. If your mother was a witch, fine, but if she wasn't . . ." He slipped his hand from mine, and I sighed, longing to cut out my own tongue. Perhaps then I wouldn't need to eat my words so often. "You aren't worthless, Ansel. Never think you're worthless."

"I'm sick and tired of everyone needing to protect me. I'd like to protect myself for a change, or even—" When my frown deepened, he sighed and dropped his face into his hands, grinding his palms into his eyes. "I just want to contribute to the group. I don't want to be the bumbling idiot anymore. Is that so much to ask? I just . . . I don't want to be a liability."

"*Who* said you're a bumbling idiot—"

"Lou." He peered up at me, eyes lined with red. Pleading. "Help me. Please."

I stared at him.

The men in my life really needed to stop using that word on me. Disasters always followed. The thought of changing a single thing about Ansel—of hardening him, of teaching him to fight, to kill—made my heart twist, but if he felt uncomfortable in his skin, if I could help ease that discomfort in any way . . .

I could train him in physical combat. Surely no harm—and no bitter disappointment—would come from teaching him to defend himself with a blade. As for lessons in magic, we could simply . . . postpone them. Indefinitely. He'd never need to feel inferior in that regard.

"Of course I'll help you," I finally said. "If—if that's really what you want."

A smile broke across his face, and the sun dimmed in comparison. "It is. Thank you, Lou."

"This'll be good," Beau muttered.

I elbowed him, eager to change the subject. "How's it looking?"

He lifted a gummy strand and wrinkled his nose. "Hard to tell. I imagine the longer we let it sit, the stronger the color will be."

"How long did Evonne let it sit?"

"The hell if I know."

A half hour later—after Beau had finished coating each strand—Ansel left us to join Coco. With a dramatic sigh, Beau dropped to the ground across from me, heedless of his velvet pants, and watched him go. "I was perfectly content to loathe the little mouth breather—"

"He's not a mouth—"

"—but *of course* he's an orphan with no self-worth," Beau continued, unfettered. "Someone should burn that tower to the ground. Preferably with the huntsmen inside it."

A peculiar warmth started at my neck. "I don't know. At least the Chasseurs gave him some semblance of a family. A home. As someone who's lived without both, I can confidently say a kid like Ansel wouldn't have survived long without them."

"Are my ears deceiving me, or are you actually *commending* the Chasseurs?"

"Of course I'm not—" I stopped short, startled at the truth of his accusation, and shook my head incredulously. "Hag's teeth. I have to stop hanging out with Ansel. He's a terrible influence."

Beau snorted. "Hag's teeth?"

"You know." I shrugged, the uncomfortable warmth at my neck radiating across the rest of my scalp. Growing hotter by the second. "The hag's eyeteeth?" When he looked on, bemused, I explained, "A woman gains her wisdom when she loses her teeth."

He laughed out loud at that, but it didn't seem remotely funny to me now, not when my scalp was on fire. I tugged at a strand of hair, wincing at the sharp pain that followed. This wasn't normal, was it? Something had to be wrong. "Beau, get some water—" The word ended in a strangled cry as the strand of hair came away in my hand. "No." I stared at it, horrified. "No, no, *NO*."

Reid was at my side in an instant. "What is it? What's—?"

Shrieking, I hurled the gooey clump of hair at Beau's face. "You *idiot*! Look what you've—WHAT HAVE YOU *DONE*?"

He pawed the slime from his face, eyes wide and alarmed, and scrambled backward as I advanced. "I *told* you I didn't know what I was doing!"

Coco appeared between us with a flask of water. Without a word, she dumped it over my head, dousing me from head to toe, washing away the gray goop. I spluttered, cursing violently, and nearly drowned all over again when Ansel stepped forward to repeat the offense. "*Don't*," I snarled when Madame Labelle joined the group, her own flask poised for action. "Or I'll light you on fire."

She rolled her eyes and snapped her fingers, and with a puff of hot air, the water on my body evaporated. Reid flinched. "Such melodramatics," she said. "This is completely fixable—" But she stopped abruptly as I lifted a strand of too-brittle hair. We all stared at it together, realizing the worst in a heavy beat of silence.

My hair wasn't blond. It wasn't red or black or even the brassy color in between.

It was . . . white.

The strand broke off, crumbling in my fingers.

"We can fix this," Madame Labelle insisted, lifting a hand. "All will be as before."

"Don't." The tears in my eyes burned hotter than even my scalp. "No one else is going to lay a *fucking finger* on my hair." If I dyed it with another round of chemicals, the remaining strands would likely catch on fire, and if I used magic, I risked even graver consequences. The pattern required to change my hair from—from *this*—would be unpleasant. Not because of the color. Because of what the color represented. *Who* it represented. On anyone else, white, moonbeam hair could've been beautiful, but on *me* . . .

Chin quivering, nose in the air, I turned to Reid and slid a knife from his bandolier. I wanted to rage at him, to fling my damaged hair in his anxious face. But this wasn't his fault. Not truly. *I* was the one who'd trusted fucking *Beau* over magic, the one who'd thought to shield Reid from it. What a stupid notion. Reid was a witch. There would be no *shielding him* from magic— not now and certainly not ever again.

Though he watched me apprehensively, Reid didn't follow as I stalked across the Hollow. Hot tears—irrational tears, embarrassed tears—gathered in my eyes. I wiped them away angrily. Part of me knew I was overreacting, knew it was just *hair*.

That part could piss right off.

Snip.

Snip.

Snip.

My hair fluttered to the ground like strands of spider silk, pale and foreign. Delicate as gossamer. A strand floated to my boot as if teasing me, and I swore I heard my mother's laugh.

Jittery energy coursed through me as we waited for the sun to set.

We couldn't enter Saint-Loire for our reconnaissance until the sun went down. There was little reason to sneak into the pub if no villagers would be there. No villagers meant no gossip. No gossip meant no information.

And no information meant we still knew nothing about the world outside the Hollow.

I pushed abruptly to my feet, stalking toward Ansel. He'd said he wanted to train, and I still had Reid's knife from earlier. I flipped it from hand to hand. Anything to keep me from reaching up—*again*—to tug at my hair. The shorn ends just brushed the tops of my shoulders.

I'd thrown the rest of it into the fire.

Ansel sat with the others around the dying embers. Their conversation stalled as I neared them, and I had little trouble guessing what they'd been discussing. *Who* they'd been discussing. Fantastic. Reid, who'd been leaning against the nearest tree, approached cautiously. He'd been waiting for me, I realized. Waiting for permission to engage. I cracked a smile.

"How are you feeling?" He planted a kiss on top of my head, lingering on the white strands. For now, it seemed my tantrum trumped his own. "Better?"

"I think my scalp is still bleeding, but otherwise, yes."

"You're beautiful."

"You're a liar."

"I'm serious."

"I'm plotting to shave everyone's head tonight."

His lips twitched, and he looked suddenly sheepish. "I grew out my hair when I was fourteen. Alexandre has long hair, you know, in—"

"*La Vie Éphémère*," I finished, envisioning Reid with long, luscious locks that blew in the wind. I snorted despite myself. "Are you telling me you were a teenage heartthrob?"

One side of his mouth quirked up. "So what if I was?"

"*So* it's a pity we didn't meet as teenagers."

"You're still a teenager."

I lifted my knife. "And I'm still pissed." When he laughed in my face, I asked, "Why did you cut it?"

"Long hair is a liability in the training yard." He rubbed a rueful hand over his head. "Jean Luc got hold of it in a sparring session and nearly made *my* scalp bleed."

"He pulled your hair?" At my gasp, he nodded grimly, and I scowled. "That little *bitch*."

"I cut it afterward. I haven't worn it long since. Now"—his hands landed on his hips, his eyes glinting—"do I need to confiscate the knife?"

I tossed it in the air, catching it by the blade before sending it upward once more. "You can certainly try."

Quick as a flash—without breaking my gaze—he snatched the knife from above my head, holding it there out of reach. His eyes burned into mine, and a slow, arrogant grin touched his lips. "You were saying?"

Suppressing a delicious shiver—which he still felt, given his rumble of laughter—I spun and elbowed him in the gut. With an *oof*, he bent double, his chest falling hard against my back, and I pried the knife from his fingers. Craning my neck, I planted a kiss on his jaw. "That was cute."

His arms came around my chest, trapping me. Locking me in his embrace. "Cute," he repeated ominously. Still bowed, our bodies fit together like a glove. "*Cute.*"

Without warning, he lifted me into the air, and I shrieked, kicking my feet and gasping with laughter. He only released me after Beau sighed loudly, turned to Madame Labelle, and asked if we could depart ahead of schedule to spare his eardrums. "Will I need them in Les Dents, do you think? Or can I go without?"

Feet on the ground once more, I tried to ignore him—tried to keep playing, tried to poke Reid in the ribs—but his smile wasn't quite as wide now. The tension returned to his jaw. The moment had passed.

Someday, I wouldn't need to hoard Reid's smiles, and someday, he wouldn't need to ration them.

Today was not that day.

Straightening my shirt, I extended the knife to Ansel. "Shall we get started?"

His eyes widened. "What? *Now?*"

"Why not?" I shrugged, plucking another knife from Reid's bandolier. He remained wooden. "We have a few hours until sundown. You *do* still want to train, don't you?"

Ansel nearly tripped in his haste to stand. "*Yes*, I do, but—" Those brown eyes flicked first to Coco and Beau, then to Reid. Madame Labelle paused in dealing the former their cards. Instead of *couronnes*, they'd used rocks and sticks as bids. Pink colored Ansel's cheeks. "Should we—not do it here?"

Beau didn't look up from his cards. Indeed, he stared at them a bit too fixedly to be natural. "Don't presume we care what you're doing, Ansel."

Following Beau's lead, Coco offered Ansel a reassuring smile before she too returned to their game. Even Reid took the hint, squeezing my hand briefly before joining them without a word. No one turned in our direction again.

An hour later, however, they couldn't help but watch covertly.

"Stop, stop! You're flailing, and you're focusing too much on your upper body, anyway. You aren't Reid." I ducked beneath Ansel's outstretched arm, disarming him before he could sever a limb. Likely his own. "Your feet are for more than just footwork. Use them. Every strike should utilize both your upper- *and* lower-body strength."

His shoulders drooped in misery.

I lifted his chin with the tip of his sword. "None of that, *mon petit chou*. Again!"

Readjusting his form once more—twice more, a hundred times more—we parried through the greater part of the afternoon and into the evening. Though he showed little improvement, I didn't have the heart to end his lesson, even as the shadows around us deepened. When the sun touched the pines, he finally managed to knock my blade away out of sheer determination—and nick his own arm in the process. His blood flecked the snow.

"That was—you did—"

"Horrible," he finished bitterly, throwing his sword to the ground to examine his wound. Face still flushed—only partly from exertion—he shot a quick look in the others' direction. They all hastened to appear busy, gathering the makeshift plates they'd used for dinner. At Ansel's request, we'd trained right through it. My stomach grumbled irritably. "I was horrible."

Sighing, I sheathed my knife in my boot. "Let me see your arm."

He shook his sleeve down with a scowl. "It's fine."

"Ansel—"

"I said it's *fine*."

At his uncharacteristically sharp tone, I paused. "Do you not want to do this again?"

His face softened, and he dropped his head. "I'm sorry. I shouldn't have snapped at you. I just—I wanted this to go differently." The admission was quiet. This time, he looked to his own hands instead of the others. I gripped one of them firmly.

"This was your first attempt. You'll get better—"

"It wasn't." Reluctantly, he met my gaze. I hated that reluctance. That shame. I *hated* it. "I trained with the Chasseurs. They made sure I knew how terrible I was."

Anger washed through me, hot and consuming. As much as they'd given him, they'd taken even more. "The Chasseurs can eat a bag of dicks—"

"It's fine, Lou." He pulled his hand away to retrieve his fallen knife, but paused halfway down, gifting me a smile. Though weary, that smile was also hopeful—undeniably and unapologetically so. I stared at him, struck momentarily speechless. Though often naive and occasionally petulant, he'd remained so . . . pure. Some days I couldn't believe he was real. "Nothing worth having is easy, right?"

Nothing worth having is easy.

Right.

Heart lodged in my throat, I glanced instinctively at Reid's back across camp. As if sensing me, he stilled, and our eyes met over his shoulder. I looked away hastily, looping my arm through Ansel's and squeezing tight, ignoring the cold fist of dread in my chest. "Come on, Ansel. Let's end this wretched day with a drink."

CLAUD DEVERAUX

Reid

"I'm not drinking that."

I eyed the tumbler of liquid Lou offered me. The glass was dirty, the liquid brown. Murky. It suited the oily barkeep, the disheveled patrons who laughed, danced, and spilled beer down their shirts. A troupe had performed this evening as it passed through Saint-Loire, and the actors had congregated at the local tavern afterward. A crowd had soon followed.

"Oh, come on." She wafted the whiskey under my nose. It smelled foul. "You need to loosen up. We all do."

I pushed the whiskey away, still furious with myself. I'd been so hell-bent on convincing the others to gather allies, to confront Morgane—so blinded by my pathetic emotions—I hadn't considered the specifics.

"We aren't here to drink, *Lucida*."

The thought of leaving her filled me with visceral panic.

"Excuse me, Raoul, but *you* are the one who insisted we reconnoiter at a *tavern*. Not that I'm complaining."

It was the kind of panic that consumed everything, required every bit of my focus to contain. I wanted to scream. I wanted to rage. But I couldn't breathe.

It felt a lot like drowning.

"It's the best place to gather information." With a twitch in my jaw, I glanced across the room to where Madame Labelle, Coco, and Beau sat amidst the raucous traveling troupe. Like Lou and me, Beau had hidden his face within the deep hood of his cloak. No one paid us any notice. Our ensembles were nothing compared to those of the performers. "We can't—" I shook my head, unable to collect my thoughts. The closer we drew to midnight, the wilder they ran. The more riotous. My eyes sought anything but Lou. When I looked at her, the panic sharpened, knifed through my chest and threatened to cut me in two. I tried again, mumbling to my fingertips. "We can't continue with Madame Labelle's plan until we assess the situation outside camp. Alcohol loosens lips."

"Does it, now?" She leaned forward as if to kiss me, and I recoiled, panic rising like bile. Thank God I couldn't see her face properly, or I might've done something stupid—like carry her into the back room, bar the door, and kiss her for so long she forgot her inane plan to leave me. As it was, I kept my muscles locked, clenched, to prevent me from doing it anyway. She slumped back in her seat with disappointment.

"Right. I forgot you're still being an ass."

Now I wanted to kiss her for a different reason.

Night had fully fallen outside. Only the fire in the grate

illuminated the grubby room. Though we sat as far away from it as possible, masked in the deepest shadows, its dim light hadn't hidden the wanted posters tacked to the door. Two of them. One with a sketch of my face, one with a sketch of Lou's. Duplicates of the ones littering the village streets.

Louise le Blanc, under suspicion of witchcraft, her sign had said. *Wanted dead or alive. Reward.*

Lou had laughed, but we'd all heard it for what it was. Forced. And under my picture—

Reid Diggory, under suspicion of murder and conspiracy. Wanted alive. Reward.

Wanted *alive.* It still didn't make sense in light of my crimes.

"See? All hope isn't lost." Lou had elbowed me halfheartedly upon seeing my indictment. In a moment of weakness, I'd suggested fleeing for the nearest seaport, leaving this all behind. She hadn't laughed then. "No. My magic lives here."

"You lived without magic for years."

"That wasn't living. That was surviving. Besides, without . . . all of this"—she gestured around us—"who am I?"

The urge to seize her had been overwhelming. Instead, I'd leaned low—until we were eye to eye and nose to nose—and said fiercely, "You are everything."

"Even if witches weren't watching the ports, even if we somehow managed to escape, who knows what Morgane would do to those left behind. We'd live, yes, but we couldn't leave everyone else to such a fate. Could we?"

Phrased like that, the answer had sunk like dead weight in

my stomach. Of course we couldn't leave them. But she'd still searched my eyes hopefully, as if awaiting a different answer. It'd made me pause, a hard knot twisting in my stomach. If I'd maintained we should leave, would she have agreed? Would she have subjected an entire kingdom to Morgane's wrath, just so we might live?

A small voice in my head had answered. An unwelcome one.

She's already done that.

I'd pushed it away viciously.

Now—with her body angling toward mine, her hood slipping—my hands trembled, and I resisted the urge to continue our argument. Too soon, she would leave for the blood camp. Though she wouldn't be alone, she *would* be without me. It was unacceptable. It couldn't happen. Not with both Morgane and Auguste after her head.

She can look after herself, the voice said.

Yes. But I can look after her too.

Sighing, she slumped back in her chair, and regret cleaved my panic. She thought I'd rejected her. I hadn't missed the way her eyes had tightened by the pool, then again in camp. But I wasn't rejecting her. I was protecting her.

I made stupid decisions when she touched me.

"How about you, Antoine?" Lou thrust the tumbler toward Ansel instead. "You wouldn't let a lady drink alone, would you?"

"Of course I wouldn't." He looked solemnly to the left and right. "But I don't see a lady here. Do you?"

Lou mustered a cackle and dumped the amber liquid over his head.

"Stop it," I growled, tugging her hood back in place. For just a moment, her hair had been visible to the pub. Though she'd sheared it, the color remained startlingly white. Distinct. It wasn't a common color, but it was a notorious one. An iconic one. None would recognize it on Lou, but they might mistake her for someone altogether worse. Even Lou had to see the similarities between her and her mother's features now.

Snatching my hand away before I could caress her cheek, I mopped up the whiskey with my cloak. "This is exactly why Madame Labelle didn't want you out in public. You draw too much attention."

"You've known your mother for approximately three and a half seconds, and already she's the authority. I can't tell you how exciting this is for me."

I rolled my eyes. Before I could correct her, a group of men seated themselves at the table next to us. Dirty. Disheveled. Desperate for a drink. "Fifi, love," the loudest and dirtiest of them called, "bring us a pint and keep 'em comin'. That's my girl."

The barmaid—equally filthy, missing her two front teeth—bustled off to comply.

Across the bar, Beau mouthed something to Lou, tapping his own teeth, and she snickered. Jealousy radiated through me. I moved closer instinctively, stopped, and scooted back once more. Forced myself to sweep the perimeter of the room instead.

"Migh' wan' a take it easy, Roy," one of his companions said. "Early morn tomorrow, and all."

Behind the disheveled group, three men in dark clothing played cards. Swords at their hips. Mead in their cups. Beyond them, a young couple chatted animatedly with Madame Labelle, Coco, and Beau. Fifi and a powerfully built barkeep tended the counter. Actors and actresses danced by the door. More villagers spilled in from outside, eyes bright with excitement and noses red with cold.

People everywhere, blissfully unaware of who hid in their midst.

"Bah." Roy spat on the floor. A bit of the spittle dripped down his chin. Lou—seated closest to him—scooted her chair away, nose wrinkling. "Horse broke 'er leg yesterday eve. We won' be goin' ta Cesarine after all."

At this, the three of us grew still. Unnaturally still. When I nudged Lou, she nodded and took a sip of her drink. Ansel followed suit, grimacing when the liquid hit his tongue. He tipped it toward me. I declined, quickly tallying the distance from Saint-Loire to Cesarine. If these men planned on leaving in the morning, the Archbishop's funeral was in a fortnight.

"Lucky, you are," another said as Fifi returned with their mead. They drank greedily. "Wife won' let me outta it. Says we have ta *pay our respects*. Bleedin' 'alfwit, she is. Old Florin never did me nothin' but peeve the wee ones durin' harvest."

The sound of his name hit me like a brick. These were farmers, then. Several weeks ago, we'd been dispatched to deal with another lutin infestation outside Cesarine. But we'd been *helping* the farmers, not hindering them.

As if reading my mind, one said, "His blue pigs did kill 'em, though, Gilles. That's somethin'."

Blue pigs. Fury coiled in my throat at the slur. These men didn't realize all the Chasseurs did to ensure their safety. The sacrifices they made. The integrity they held. I eyed the men's rumpled clothing in distaste. Perhaps they lived too far north to understand, or perhaps their farms sat too far removed from polite society. None but simpletons and criminals referred to my brotherhood—I winced internally, correcting myself—the *Chasseurs'* brotherhood as anything but virtuous, noble, and true.

"Not all o' them," Gilles replied gruffly. "We had a righ' proper riot after they lef'. The little devils dug up their friends' corpses and shredded my wheat in one nigh'. We leave out a weekly offerin' now. The blues would burn us if they knew, but wha' can we do? Cheaper than losin' another field to the creatures. We're caught between the rock and the hard place. Can hardly put food in our bellies as it is."

He turned to order another round from Fifi.

"Aye," his friend said, shaking his head. "Damned if we do, and damned if we don'." He returned his attention to Roy. "Migh' be for the best, though. My sister lives in Cesarine with 'er whelps, an' she said Auguste 'as set a curfew. People ain't allowed out after sundown, an' women ain't allowed out at all without gentlemanly chaperones. He's got his soldiers patrollin' the streets day an' nigh' lookin' for suspicious womenfolk after wha' happened to the Archbishop."

Chaperones? Patrols?

Lou and I exchanged looks, and she cursed softly. It'd be harder to navigate the city than we expected.

Gilles shuddered. "Can't say I rightly mind it. Wee folk are one thing. Witches are another. Evil, they is. Unnatural."

The other men mumbled their agreement while Roy ordered another round. When one of them diverted the conversation to his hernia, however, Lou shot me a quick glance. I didn't like the gleam in her eye. Didn't like the determined set in her jaw. "Don't," I warned, voice low, but she took a hearty swig and spoke over me.

"Oi, you 'ear what that lummox Toussaint was claimin'?"

Every eye at the neighboring table swiveled toward her. Disbelief kept me rooted to my chair, gaping along with the rest of them. Ansel let out a nervous chuckle. More squeak than anything. Lou kicked him under the table.

After another tense second, Roy belched and patted his stomach. "Who're you, then? Why're you hidin' yer face?"

"Bad 'air day, boy-o. Sheared the whole o' it off in a fit o' rage, and now I can' stand the sight of meself."

Ansel choked on his whiskey. Instinctively, I pounded him on the back. Neither of us tore our eyes from Lou. I couldn't see her grin, but I could sense it. She was enjoying herself.

I wanted to strangle her.

"Plus, there's the wart on me chin," she added conspiratorially, lifting a finger to tap her face. It disappeared within the shadows of her hood. "No amount o' powder can cover it up. It's the size o' Belterra, it is."

"Aye." The man who'd spoken before nodded sagely, deep in his cups, and peered at her through bleary eyes. "Me sister 'as a wart on 'er nose. I reckon yer all right."

Lou couldn't contain her snort. "These are me brothers"—she gestured to Ansel and me—"Antoine and Raoul."

"'Ello, friends." Grinning, Ansel raised his hand in a stupid little wave. "Pleased ter meet yeh."

I stared at him. Though sheepish, his smile didn't falter.

"Anyhoo," Lou said, tossing back the rest of her whiskey, "Antoine and Raoul 'ere can right empathize wit' yer lutin problems. Farmers, we are. Them blue pigs is ruinin' life fer us as well, and Toussaint is the worst o' them."

With a grunt, Roy shook his head. "He was just 'ere with 'is damn pigs this morn, and *they* said old Toussaint gutted Morgane on Christmas Eve."

"Shit o' the bull!" Lou slapped the table for emphasis. I pressed my foot over hers in warning, but she kicked my shin in response. Her shoulders shook with silent laughter.

"*But*—" Roy belched again before leaning in, gesturing for us to do the same. "—they said they 'ad ta leave for Cesarine right away because o' the tournament."

My stomach dropped. "The tournament?"

"That's right," Roy said, cheeks growing ruddier by the second. Voice growing louder. "They have ta refill their ranks. Apparently the witches took ou' a few of their own. People are callin' it Noël Rouge." He leered and wiped his mouth on his sleeve. "Because o' all the blood."

When Ansel passed me his drink this time, I accepted.

The whiskey burned all the way down.

The one with the warty sister nodded. "They're havin' it before the Archbishop's services. Tryin' to make a festival outta it, I think. Bit morbid."

Gilles downed his third pint. "Maybe I should enter."

The man laughed. "Maybe I should enter yer wife while yer gone."

"I'll swap 'er for yer sister!"

The conversation deteriorated from there. I tried and failed to extricate Lou from an argument about who was uglier—the man's sister or the witch in the wanted posters—when an unfamiliar voice interrupted. "Claptrap and balderdash, all of it. There is nothing so venerable as a wart on the visage."

We turned as one to look at the man who plunked into the empty seat at our table. Brown eyes twinkled above an unruly mustache and beard. The troupe's fiddler. He extended a weathered hand to me. Lifted his other in a cheery wave. "Salutations. Claud Deveraux, at your service."

Roy and his companions turned away in disgust, muttering about charlatans.

I stared at his hand while Lou readjusted her hood. Ansel's eyes darted to Madame Labelle, Coco, and Beau. Though they watched us surreptitiously, they continued chatting with the couple beside them. Madame Labelle dipped her chin in a subtle nod.

"Right, then." Claud Deveraux dropped his hand but not his smile. "You don't mind the company, do you? I must confess, I need a respite from all the revelry. Ah, you have libations." He waved a hand to his troupe before helping himself to the rest of Ansel's drink. "I am indebted to you, good sir. Truly, my deepest gratitude." Winking at me, he dabbed at his mouth with a plaid pocket square. "Where was I? Oh, yes. Claud Deveraux. That's me. I am, of course, musician and manager of Troupe de Fortune. Did you perchance attend our performance this evening?"

I kept my foot pressed on Lou's, beseeching her to keep quiet. Unlike Roy, this man had sought us out. I didn't like it. With a grudging sigh, she sat back and crossed her arms. "No," I said brusquely, rudely. "We didn't."

"It was a splendid affair." He continued his one-sided conversation with relish, beaming at each of us in turn. I inspected him closer. Pinstriped pants. Paisley coat. Checkered bow tie. He'd thrown his top hat—tattered and maroon—on the table in front of him. Even to me, his outfit seemed . . . bizarre. "I do love these quaint little villages along the road. One meets the most interesting people."

Clearly.

"It is unfortunate indeed we leave this very night, spurred southward by the siren call of crowds and *couronnes* at our Holy Father's committal." He waved an absent hand. Black polish gleamed on his fingernails. "Such a tragic affair. Such an ungodly sum."

My lip curled. I liked Claud Deveraux less and less.

"And what of you? Might I inquire as to your names?" Oblivious to the tense, awkward silence, he tapped his fingers against the table in a jaunty rhythm. "Though I do love a good intrigue. Perhaps I could instead hazard a guess?"

"That won't be necessary." My words fell leaden between us. Roy had given us all the information we needed. It was time to go. Standing, I caught Beau's eye across the room and nodded toward the exit. He nudged my mother and Coco. "My name is Raoul, and these are my friends Lucida and Antoine. We're leaving."

"Friends! Oh, how delightful!" He drummed his fingers louder in delight, completely ignoring my dismissal. "And such marvelous names they possess! Alas, I'm not *quite* as fond of the name Raoul, but do let me explain. I knew a man once, a big burly bear of a man—though perhaps he was a small surly man of a bear—and the poor dear caught a splinter in his foot—"

"Monsieur Deveraux," Lou said, sounding equal parts irritated and intrigued. Probably irritated *because* she was intrigued. His smile slipped when she spoke, and he blinked slowly. Just once. Then his smile returned—wider now, genuine—and he leaned forward to clutch her hand.

"Please, Lucida, you must call me Claud."

At the sudden warmth in his voice, at the way his eyes shone brighter than before, the muted panic in my chest roared back to life, hardened into suspicion. But he couldn't have recognized her. Her face remained hidden. This familiarity—perhaps it was another quirk of his personality. An inappropriate one.

Lou stiffened beneath his touch. "*Monsieur Deveraux.* While I usually welcome a complete stranger drinking my whiskey and fondling my hand, it's been a rough few days. If you could kindly *piss off*, I'd greatly appreciate it."

Roy—who'd never quite stopped eavesdropping—lifted his head and frowned. I winced.

Lou had dropped her accent.

Releasing her hand, Deveraux tipped his head back and laughed. Loudly. "Oh, Lucida, what a *delight* you are. I can't begin to convey how I've missed such black humor—the kind that bites your hand if you move too close—which, incidentally, I am appropriately and grievously contrite about—"

"Cut the shit." Lou shoved to her feet, unaccountably flustered. Her voice rang out sharp and loud. Too loud. "What do you *want*?"

But her hood slipped at the sudden movement, and whatever words Claud Deveraux had planned fell away with it. He gazed at her raptly. All pretense gone. "I simply wanted to meet you, dear girl, and to offer help should you ever have need." His eyes dropped to her throat. The new ribbon—slicker, larger than usual, harder to tie in a bow—had loosened from its knot, sliding down to reveal her grisly scar.

Fuck.

"What's happened ta you, then?" Roy asked loudly.

Beside him, Gilles narrowed his eyes to slits. He turned toward the wanted posters on the door. "That's a nasty scar you've got there."

Deveraux tugged her hood back in place, but it was too late.

The damage was done.

Roy heaved himself to his feet. He waved his glass tankard at Lou, swaying and trying to keep his balance. Mead spilled down his trousers. "You don't have no wart, *Lucida*. No accent neither. But you do look an awful lot like that girl everyone's lookin' for. That *witch*."

A hush fell over the tavern.

"I'm not—" Lou spluttered, looking around wildly. "That's ridiculous—"

Unsheathing my Balisarda, I rose with deadly purpose. Ansel followed with his own knife. The two of us towered behind her as the rest of Roy's companions lurched to their feet.

"Oh, it's 'er, all right." Gilles stumbled into the table, pointing at the poster. He grinned in triumph. "She cut 'er hair, dyed it, but she can't hide that scar. Saw it clear as day. That girl there is Louise le Blanc."

And in a clumsy, terrifying movement, Roy lifted his glass tankard and shattered it into a jagged blade.

MARIONETTE

Reid

Despite the nightmare our lives had become, I still hadn't fought alongside Lou in physical combat. At Modraniht, she'd been unconscious. At Ye Olde Sisters' performance, she'd been hiding her magic. And at the smithy, she'd killed the criminals before I could intervene. I hadn't been able to fathom how someone so small could kill two fully grown men with such efficiency. Such brutality.

Now I understood.

The woman was a menace.

She moved with unexpected speed, feinting and striking with both hands. When her knife missed its mark, her fingers flexed and her opponent toppled. Or stiffened. Or smashed into the bar, shattering tumblers and dousing the room with whiskey. Glass rained down on our heads, but she didn't slow. Again and again she struck.

Even so, Roy and his friends sobered quickly, and they outnumbered four to her one. Five when the barkeep joined the fray.

Coco ran to meet him, but I caught her, pushing her toward the door. "Take the others and go. They don't know your faces yet, but they will if you stay and fight."

"I'm not leaving L—"

"Yes"—I seized the back of her dress and hurled her out the door—"you are."

Eyes huge, Beau raced after her. Both Ansel and Madame Labelle looked likely to argue, but I cut them off, throwing a knife to pin Roy's sleeve to the wall. He'd swiped his tankard at Lou while her back was turned. "We'll meet you at camp. *Go.*"

They hastened after Coco and Beau.

Lou called something to me—parrying three men at once—but I couldn't hear her over the villagers' shrieks. They trampled each other in their haste to flee the witch with magic, but the men with makeshift swords proved equally frightening. Laughing, yelling, the three strode through the crowd toward the exit. One tore down Lou's wanted poster and pocketed it. He seized mine next. Grinning at me over his shoulder, he tapped his hair.

My hand shot to my fallen hood.

"Take your time." His voice reverberated through the panic, and he swiped a tankard from the nearest table, drinking deeply. His companions had successfully barricaded the door, trapping the remaining villagers. Trapping us. "We can wait."

Bounty hunters.

"Husband!" Lou thrust her palm out, and Gilles's and his friends' skulls cracked together. Moaning, they crumpled to the floor. "I *try* not to be needy, really, but a little help over here would be *grand*—"

Roy freed himself and tackled her. I sliced through the bar-keep's leg, vaulting over him as he staggered, and sprinted toward them.

"Ugh, Roy, *mon ami*." Lou wrinkled her nose beneath him. "I hate to be indelicate, but when did you last bathe? You smell a bit ripe under here." With a retching sound, she bit the underside of his bicep. He reared backward, and I clubbed him in the head, hooking Lou's elbow and flipping her over my back before he could collapse on her. She kicked Gilles—who'd been trying to rise—neatly on her way down.

"You can't imagine how *toothsome* you look right now, Reid." Grinning wickedly, elbow still linked with mine, she spun into my arms and kissed me full on the mouth. I must've been insane because I kissed her back, until—

"Toothsome?" I pulled away, frowning. Adrenaline pounded in my chest. "Not sure I like that—"

"Why not? It means I want to eat you alive." She slashed at the last of Roy's friends as we dashed for the door. "Have you tried any patterns yet?"

The mountainous barkeep rose to block our path, roaring loudly enough to shake the rafters. Blood painted his leg crimson. "*Witch*," he seethed, swinging a club the size of Lou's body.

I blocked the blow with my Balisarda, gritting my teeth against the impact. "This is hardly the time—"

"But have you?"

"*No.*"

With an impatient sigh, Lou ducked beneath us to stab at Roy, who refused to stay down.

"I suspected as much." This time when Roy charged her, she rolled over his back and kicked him in the rear. He toppled over his friends' bodies, and Lou knocked away his sword. "Magic in combat can be tricky, but it doesn't have to end like this morning. The trick is to get creative—"

She broke off abruptly as Gilles seized her ankle. Winking at me, she stomped on his face. He crumpled against his friends and moved no more. Smashing my head into the barkeep's nose, I caught his club when he collapsed. The very foundation trembled on impact.

Breathing hard, I looked behind us. Five down. Three to go.

"Try to see beyond this disgusting little room to what lies beneath." Lou gestured wildly with her knife. Screaming anew, the trapped villagers scattered to hide behind overturned tables and chairs. "Go ahead. *Look*. Tell me what you see."

I returned my attention to the men at the door instead. True to their word, they'd waited. Pushing languidly from the wall, they drew their swords as we approached. "I suppose this means you aren't willing to simply step aside," Lou said with a sigh. "Are you sure that's wise? I am a witch, you know."

The one with the tankard finished his beer. "Did you know your head is worth one hundred thousand *couronnes*?"

She sniffed and came to a stop. "Frankly, I'm insulted. It's worth at least twice that. Have you spoken with La Dame des Sorcières? I'm sure she'd pay triple. For me, though. Not my head. I'd have to be *alive*, of course, which could present a problem for you—"

"Shut up." The man dropped the tankard, and it shattered at his feet. "Or I'll cut it off while you're still breathing."

"The king wants my *actual* head? How . . . barbaric. Are you sure you won't consider taking me to La Dame des Sorcières instead? I'm suddenly feeling quite sympathetic to her cause."

"If you surrender, we'll kill you quick," his companion promised. "Save the nasty business for after."

Lou grimaced. "How magnanimous of you." To me, she whispered, "They don't have Balisardas. Focus on the outcome, and the patterns will appear. Choose the one with the least collateral damage, but make sure you *choose*. Otherwise nature will choose for you. That's what happened this morning, isn't it?"

I gripped my own Balisarda tighter. "I won't need it."

"I'm trying to be patient, Chass, but we don't exactly have the luxury of time here—"

The first man's smile slipped, and he lifted his sword. "I said *shut up*. We have you outnumbered. Now, do you surrender or not?"

"Not." Lou lifted her own knife. It looked pathetically small in comparison. *She* looked pathetically small in comparison. Despite my deep, steadying breaths, the tension in my body built—built and built until I radiated with it, trembling with anticipation. "Wait, no, let me think." She tapped her chin. "*Definitely* not."

The man launched himself at her. I exploded, smashing my Balisarda into his gut, spinning as his companion attempted to maneuver past. My foot connected with his knee, and he buckled, driving his blade into my foot. Black spotted my vision as I wrenched the sword free.

With a feral cry, Lou darted toward the third, but he caught her wrist and twisted. Her knife clattered to the floor. She flicked a finger in response, and he crashed into the bar with enough force to splinter the wood. Coughing, she bent double. "Teachable moment," she choked. "I should've just killed the miserable bastard, but"—another cough—"I used the air around us to knock him backward instead, tried to—stick him on the wood. It knocked me pretty good in—in return. Make sense? I could've taken the air straight from my lungs instead, but he—he's too big. It would've taken too much air to move him. Probably would've killed me." She grinned to herself then, wider and wider until she was cackling. Blood trickled down her chin from her mouth. "And *then* how could I have claimed your father's hundred thousand *couronnes*—"

A knife flew at her from the wreckage of the bar.

She didn't have time to duck.

With a man on each arm, I watched in slow motion as she flinched, lifting a hand to stop the blade from piercing her heart. But the strength of the throw—the man's close proximity, his uncanny aim—was insurmountable. The blade would find its mark. There was nothing she could do to stop it. Nothing *I* could do.

Her fingers twitched.

And with that twitch, her eyes grew less focused, less—human. Between one blink and the next, the knife reversed direction and impaled its owner's throat.

Lou stared down at him, still smiling, her eyes shining with unfamiliar malice.

Except it wasn't unfamiliar. I'd seen it many times.

Just never on her.

"Lou?"

When I touched her, that terrible smile finally broke, and she gasped, clutching her chest. I pulled her behind me as the two men charged. She couldn't breathe, I realized in alarm. Despite her own warning, she'd given the air from her lungs to throw that knife—not as much as it would've taken to throw the man. Enough that red splotches had appeared in her eyes, enough that her chest worked furiously to replenish what it'd lost. "I'm fine," she said, struggling to rejoin me. Her voice was raw. Weak. I stepped in front of her. "I said I'm *fine*."

Ignoring her, I swung my Balisarda wide—unnerved by her ragged breathing, the thick stench of magic in the air, the blood roaring in my ears—to drive the other two back, to shield her. But my foot throbbed, and I stumbled. "Let us leave," I said, voice low and desperate, terrified for them. No—not for them. For Lou. "Let us leave, and we'll let you live."

The first rose from beside his companion's corpse. His smile had vanished. Eyeing my injured foot, he pressed closer. "There are rumors, you know. In the city. They say you're the king's bastard son."

My thoughts scattered at this new information. How could they know? The only ones privy to that information were those in our own company: Lou, Ansel, Coco, Beau, and—

The last piece clicked into place.

Madame Labelle.

"We can help you," the second coaxed, shadowing the first's

steps. "We can free you from this witch's spell."

Every instinct screamed at me to engage. To fight, to *protect*. But those weren't the same things right now. I retreated faster, stumbling again. Lou steadied me.

"Please," she sneered. "He practically sleeps with his Balisarda, you idiots. I couldn't enchant him if I tried."

"Shut your mouth, *witch*."

"What of your dead friend?" she asked silkily. "Should he speak for me instead?"

I pushed her behind me again.

My eyes darted to the door, the windows. Too far. Though the rational part of my brain knew I maintained the advantage— knew my wanted poster said *alive*, knew they couldn't risk killing me—the same wasn't true for Lou. Her life was forfeit in this fight, which meant theirs were too. I'd have to kill them before they could touch her, before she could retaliate. Even outnumbered, I could dispatch them. Even injured. But if I engaged, Lou would too. She wouldn't let me fight alone.

Once more, she tried to move to my side, and once more, I moved her behind.

I couldn't allow her to fight. Not with magic. Not after what I'd just seen. She could damage herself irrevocably. Yet I couldn't leave her defenseless either. Clutching her hand, I backed her against the wall. Caged her with my body. "Reach inside my coat," I whispered as the men closed in. "Get a knife."

She knocked my Balisarda from my hand instead.

"What're you—?" I leapt after it, incredulous, but she beat me to it, sliding it under her foot as the men charged.

"Trust me!" she cried.

With no time to argue, I pulled two knives from my bandolier and met them strike for strike. My mind anticipated their every movement. My weapons became extensions of my arms. Even the sharp pain in my foot receded to a dull ache. Inexplicably agitated, I watched—disconnected—as my body feinted, dipped, and twisted with unnatural speed. Jabbing here. Kicking there. Soon the men slowed, bloody and winded. Hatred twisted their faces as they gazed at Lou. But she'd remained behind me, hadn't entered the fray—

I glanced back. My vision tunneled on her contorted fingers, and shock punched through me, stealing my breath. No. Not shock. Fury. Yes, I'd seen this before. I'd seen it many times.

She was using me like a fucking marionette.

At my expression, her fingers faltered, and my arms dropped to my sides, strings cut. Limp. "Reid," she whispered. "Don't—"

The men finally saw their opportunity.

The quickest of them spun around me, slashing my hands and knocking my knives to the ground. Before I could stop him, his companion had thrust his blade to my chin. The first quickly followed with a sword in my rib.

"Don't make this difficult, Diggory," one of them panted, punching me hard in the stomach when I struggled. "The king wants you alive, and we'd hate to disappoint him."

They jerked me around to face Lou, who'd swooped to retrieve my Balisarda.

"Easy, love." They pushed their blades deeper. Warning her. Warning me. A rivulet of blood ran down my throat. Slowly, Lou rose to her feet. Her expression was murderous. "That's right. No sudden movements. You can go ahead and slide that knife over here."

She kicked it toward the door instead, eyes flickering at something she saw there. I didn't dare look. Didn't dare draw attention.

She took a deep breath. Before our eyes, her expression transformed. Batting her lashes, she gave the men a saccharine smile. My stomach dropped. With her white hair—her eyes green tonight instead of blue—she looked like someone else entirely. "Did you know," she said, holding her hands erect, motionless, "that physical gesticulation is necessary to perform magic? We have to signal intent, otherwise we risk channeling patterns with errant thought. Gesticulation is manifestation." She recited the last as if from a textbook. Another smile. This one wider than the last. Sweeter. They stared at her in bewilderment. I stared at her with dread. "The smallest gesture will do. As you witnessed, I impaled your friend with a twitch of my finger. Took less than a second."

Their grip on me tightened.

"Lou." My voice was low, strained. "Don't do this. If manipulating mere memory is dangerous, you don't want the consequences of manipulating lives. Trust me." Her eyes flicked to the door and back. I swallowed hard, grimacing against the blade. She was stalling. That's all this was. But that smile—it unnerved me. I tried again. "There are two of them. Even if you kill one, the other—"

"—will slit his throat," the man on my left finished, pressing his knife deeper for emphasis. His hand was clammy. Cold. I could smell the perspiration through his clothes. She frightened them. Under pretense of struggling, I glanced behind us. My heart leapt to my throat. Ansel, Coco, Madame Labelle, and Beau were dragging Roy and his unconscious friends out the door. Why hadn't they listened to me? Why hadn't they *left*? Instead, they helped the last of the trapped villagers to safety. Claud Deveraux sifted frantically through the wreckage at the bar.

"I suppose you're right." Lou winked at me, and the facade cracked. Relief flooded my system. "But I certainly enjoy watching you squirm."

Losing his patience, the one on the right barreled toward her. "And *I'll* enjoy cutting off your mouthy—"

A crow of triumph sounded behind us, and the men finally turned.

Standing behind the bar—holding a lit match—Deveraux grinned. "Good evening, *messieurs*. I do hate to interrupt, but I believe it's in poor taste to discuss beheading a lady in front of her."

He flicked the match toward us, and the entire building exploded.

WHITE SHADOWS

Lou

Fire is such bullshit.

I'd already burned once—burned and burned on a metaphysical stake until I was nothing but a husk—but it seemed the flames hadn't gotten enough of me. They wanted another taste.

Well, too fucking bad.

I dove toward Reid as the pub detonated around us, flinging a hand toward the pattern that shimmered between us and the flames. The golden cord siphoned the icy fear from my chest—wrapping a protective barrier around us in cold, glittering crystals—before bursting into dust. We clung to each other, untouched, as the fire raged.

The bounty hunters weren't so lucky.

I tried not to enjoy watching them burn to a crisp. Really, I did. Without the fear I'd just sacrificed, however, there was only rage—a rage that burned hotter and brighter than even the flames around us. Blood from Reid's throat still trickled onto his collar, staining it. Even amidst our heinous trek through the wilderness—our week-long stay in the Hollow—he'd managed to keep his clothing immaculate. But not now. A couple of bounty hunters would've bested us if not for Claud Deveraux.

Speaking of which . . . where *was* Claud Deveraux?

Still fuming, I scanned the blazing pub for any sign of him, but he was gone.

Reid clutched me tighter as the bottles of whiskey behind the bar exploded. Glass pelted against our melting shield, and black, noxious smoke began to curl beneath it. I coughed, tugging his ear to my mouth. "We need to move! The shield won't hold much longer!"

Nodding swiftly, his eyes darted to the exit. "Will the shield move with us?"

"I don't know!"

He grabbed my hand, bolting through the flames toward the door. I hurtled after him—scooping up his Balisarda as I went—and forced myself to breathe. One thready gasp after another. My chest ached from earlier, and my head still pounded. My vision quickly blurred. Smoke burned my nose and throat, and I choked, the first tendril of heat licking up my spine. It razed my shoulders and neck, and my panic finally returned as the last of the shield melted.

Memory of another fire razed through me.

"Reid!" I shoved his back with all my might, and he tumbled out the door, sprawling in a heap on the ground outside. I collapsed beside him and buried myself in the frigid mud, heedless of decorum, rolling side to side like a pig wallowing in a sty. A sob tore from my throat.

"We have to move!" Reid's hands seized my own, and he

wrenched me to my feet. Already, more men had surrounded us, drawing makeshift weapons. Pitchforks. Hammers. The flames of the pub reflected in their hateful eyes as they loomed above me, and their shouts echoed through the fog steadily clouding my mind.

Witch!

Hold her!

Fetch the Chasseurs!

A heavy weight settled in my limbs. Groaning, I stumbled into Reid's side and stayed there, trusting him to support my weight. He didn't disappoint. My voice sounded muffled as I said, "My back hurts."

He didn't answer, instead prying his Balisarda from me and swinging it at the men, clearing a path. The world began to drift in a pleasant, distracting sort of way, like one's thoughts the moment before one falls asleep. Was that Claud watching us from the crowd? Somewhere in the back of my mind, I realized perhaps I'd caught on fire. But the realization was quiet and far away, and the only thing that mattered were Reid's arms around me, the weight of his body against mine . . .

"*Lou.*" His eyes appeared directly in front of me, wide and anxious and perfectly blue. Except—there shouldn't have been four of them, should there? I chuckled, though it came out a rasp, and reached up to smooth the furrow between his brows. He caught my hands. His voice drifted in and out of focus. "Stay awake . . . back to camp . . . the Chasseurs . . . coming."

Coming.

I'm coming for you, darling.

Panic punched through my stomach, and my laughter died abruptly. Shuddering against him, I tried to wrap my arms around his waist, but my limbs wouldn't cooperate. They dangled limply at my sides, heavy and useless, as I collapsed against him. "She's coming for me, Reid."

Vaguely aware of him hoisting me upward—of his mouth moving reassuringly against my ear—I struggled to collect my nonsensical thoughts, to banish the shadows in my vision.

But shadows weren't white—and this shadow was blinding, incandescent, as it tore through my throat and feasted on my blood—

"I won't let her hurt you again."

"I wish I was your wife."

He stiffened at the unexpected confession, but I'd already forgotten I'd spoken. With one last drowsy inhalation—of pine and smoke and *him*—I slipped into darkness.

CROSSES TO BEAR

Lou

I woke to voices arguing. Though the pain in my back had miraculously vanished, my chest still felt tight, heavy. Honey coated my tongue, so I almost missed the sharper, coppery taste hiding amidst its sweetness. I should've been apologetic, but exhaustion made it difficult to muster anything but apathy. As such, I didn't open my eyes right away, content to feign sleep and cherish the breath in my lungs.

They'd laid me on my stomach, and night air caressed the skin of my back. The *bare* skin of my back. I almost laughed and gave myself away.

The deviants had cut open my shirt.

"Why isn't it working?" Reid snapped. A hot presence beside me, he clenched my hand in his own. "Shouldn't she have woken up by now?"

"Use your eyes, Diggory." Coco's voice cut equally sharp. "Her burns have obviously healed. Give her internal injuries time to do the same."

"*Internal* injuries?"

I imagined his face turning puce.

Coco sighed impatiently. "It isn't humanly possible to move a knife—let alone throw one—with only the air in our lungs. She compensated by using the air from her blood, her tissues—"

"She did what?" His voice was dangerously soft now. Deceptively soft. It did little to hide his ire, however, as his grip nearly broke my fingers. "That could've killed her."

"There's always a cost."

Reid scoffed. It was an ugly, unfamiliar sound. "Except for you, it seems."

"Excuse me?"

I fought a groan, resisting the urge to insert myself between them. Reid was an idiot, but today, he would learn.

"You heard me," he said, undeterred by Coco's proximity to his arteries. "Lou is different when she uses magic. Her emotions, her judgment—she's been erratic since the pool yesterday. Tonight was worse. Yet you use magic without consequence."

All desire to shield him from Coco disappeared. *Erratic?* It took a great deal of effort to keep my breathing slow and steady. Indignation seared away the last of my fatigue, and my heart pounded at the small betrayal. Here I was—lying injured beside him—and he had the gall to insult me? All I'd done at the pool and pub was keep his ungrateful ass *alive*.

Eviscerate him, Coco.

"Give me specific examples."

I frowned into my bedroll. That wasn't quite the response

I'd expected. And was that—was that *concern* I detected? Surely Coco didn't *agree* with this nonsense.

"She dyed her hair with little to no forethought. She tried to strangle Beau when it went wrong." Reid sounded as if he were ticking items from a carefully constructed list. "She wept afterward—genuinely wept—"

"She dyed her hair like that for *you*." Coco's voice dripped with disdain and dislike, and I peeked an eye open, slightly mollified. She glared at him. "And she's allowed to cry. We don't all suffer from your emotional constipation."

He waved a curt hand. "It's more than that. At the pub, she snapped on Claud Deveraux. She laughed when she hurt the bounty hunter—even though she hurt herself in the process. You saw the bruise on her ribs. She was coughing up *blood*." He raked a hand through his hair in agitation, shaking his head. "And that was before she killed his friend and nearly herself in the process. I'm worried about her. After she killed him, there was a moment when she looked—she looked almost exactly like—"

"Don't you dare finish that sentence."

"I didn't mean—"

"*Stop*." Blood still beaded Coco's hand, which clutched an empty vial of honey. Her fingers shook. "I don't have any comforting words for you. There is nothing comfortable about our situation. This sort of magic—the sort that balances life and death on a knife point—requires sacrifice. Nature *demands* balance."

"There's nothing natural about it." Reid's cheeks flushed as he spoke, and his voice grew harder and harder with each word. "It's aberrant. It's—it's like a sickness. A poison."

"It's our cross to bear. I would tell you there's more to magic than death, but you wouldn't hear it. You have your own poison running through your blood—which, incidentally, I'll boil if you ever speak like this in front of Lou. She has enough steaming shit to sort through without adding yours to the pile." Exhaling deeply, Coco's shoulders slumped. "But you're right. There's nothing natural about a mother killing her child. Lou is going to get worse before she gets better. Much, much worse."

Reid's fingers tightened around mine, and they both peered down at me. I slammed my eye shut. "I know," he said.

I took a deep breath to collect myself. Then another. But I couldn't ignore the sharp burst of anger their words had evoked, nor the hurt underlying it. This was not a flattering conversation. These were not the words one hoped to overhear from loved ones.

She's going to get worse before she gets better. Much, much worse.

My mother's face tugged at my memory. When I was fourteen, she'd procured a consort for me, insistent that I live a full life in only a handful of years. His name had been Alec, and his face had been so beautiful I'd wanted to weep. When I'd suspected Alec had favored another witch, I'd followed him to the banks of L'Eau Mélancolique one night . . . and watched as he'd laid with his lover. Afterward, my mother had cradled me to sleep, murmuring, "If you are unafraid to look, darling, you are unafraid to find."

Perhaps I wasn't as unafraid as I thought.

But they were wrong. I felt *fine*. My emotions weren't *erratic*. To prove it, I cleared my throat, opened my eyes, and—stared straight into the face of a cat. "*Ack*, Absalon—!" I lurched backward, startled and coughing anew at the sudden movement. My shirt—cut from my back in ribbons—fluttered at my sides.

"You're awake." Relief lit Reid's face as he sat forward, tentatively touching my face, sweeping a thumb across my cheek. "How do you feel?"

"Like garbage."

Coco knelt next to me as well. "I hope you nicked more clothing from that peddler. Your others quite literally melted into your back tonight. They were fun to remove."

"If by fun, you mean grotesque," Beau said, sidling up beside us. "I wouldn't look over there"—he waved a hand over his shoulder—"unless you'd like to see your love child of flesh and fabric. And Ansel's dinner. He parted with it shortly after seeing your injuries."

I glanced across the Hollow to where Ansel sat, looking miserable, while Madame Labelle fussed over him.

"You should change," Coco said. "It's near midnight. My aunt will be here soon."

Reid glared at her, shifting to block me from view. "I told you. Lou comes with me."

Coco fired up at once. "And I told *you*—"

"Shut up, both of you." The words leapt from me before I could stop them, and I cringed at their shocked expressions. They shared a quick glance, communicating without a word. But

I still heard it. *Erratic.* I forced a smile and stepped around Reid. "Sorry. I shouldn't have said that."

"Yes, you should've." Beau arched a brow, studying the three of us with unabashed interest. When he tilted his head, frowning as if he could *see* the tension in the air, I scowled. Maybe Reid had been right. Maybe I *wasn't* myself. Never before had I felt the need to apologize for telling him to shut the hell up. "They're incredibly annoying."

"Pot, meet kettle," Coco snapped.

"For the last time, I *go* wherever I want," I said. "Tonight was a disaster, but at least now we know the Archbishop's funeral is in a fortnight. It takes ten days of hard travel to reach Cesarine. That gives us only a couple of days with the blood witches and werewolves." I skewered Reid with a glare when he tried to interrupt. "We have to proceed with the plan as discussed. We go to the blood camp. You go to Le Ventre. We'll meet back in Cesarine on the eve of the funeral. You'll send Absalon along with the time and place—"

"I don't trust the matagot," Reid said darkly.

Absalon flicked his tail at him in response.

"He certainly likes you." I bent down to scratch his ears. "And he saved us on Modraniht by delivering Madame Labelle's message to the Chasseurs. If I remember correctly, you didn't like that plan either."

Reid said nothing, jaw clenched.

"Le Ventre?" Beau asked, puzzled.

"It's packland," I said shortly. Of course he'd never journeyed into that murky corner of his kingdom. Most avoided it if possible. Including me. "La Rivière des Dents empties into a cold-water swamp in the southernmost part of Belterra. The loup garou have claimed it as their territory."

"And *why* is it called the stomach?"

"The teeth lead to the stomach—plus the loup garou eat anyone who trespasses."

"Not everyone," Reid muttered.

"This is a shit plan," Beau said. "We'll hardly reach Cesarine in time for the funeral, yet we're also expected to journey to Le Ventre? Not to mention the *insanity* that is approaching my father about an alliance. You *were* in the pub, weren't you? You saw the wanted posters? Those men were going to cut off your head—"

"*My* head. Not Reid's. For whatever reason, your father doesn't want him dead. Maybe he already knows about their connection, but if he doesn't, he'll soon find out. You're going to introduce them." I slipped back behind Reid to change into my new clothing. He was wide enough to block three of me from view. "Just so you know," I added to him, "the only reason I'm allowing this brute show of possessiveness is because your brother hasn't seen my tits yet, and I'm going to keep it that way."

"You break my heart, sister mine," Beau said.

"Shut up." Blood crept up Reid's neck. "Not another word."

Interesting. *He* didn't feel the need to apologize. A peculiar bitterness settled on my tongue, and I didn't particularly enjoy the taste—like regret and uncertainty and . . . something else. I couldn't name it.

"You should think about leaving soon," I told them. "After our rather spectacular excursion in Saint-Loire, the road will be crawling with bounty hunters. The Chasseurs might've turned around too. I know you're still uncomfortable with magic, Reid, but Madame Labelle will have to disguise you again. We can also ask to—"

I stopped short at Coco's laughter. She looked expectantly at Reid. "I can't wait to hear this."

Peeking at her from beneath Reid's arm, I asked, "Can't wait to hear what?"

She nodded to Reid. "Go on. Tell her."

He craned his neck to look down his shoulder at me as I slipped the scarlet shirt over my head and leather tights up my legs. I bent to lace my boots. Finally, he muttered, "I can't do it, Lou."

Frowning up at him, I straightened. "Can't do what?"

He shook his head slowly, the flush in his throat creeping up his cheeks. He clenched his jaw and lifted his chin. "I can't be around it. Magic. I won't."

I stared at him, and between one breath and another, the pieces clicked into place. His standoffishness, his disloyalty, his *concern*—it all made sense now.

Lou is different when she uses magic. Her emotions, her judgment— she's been erratic.

I'm worried about her.

There was a moment when she looked—she looked almost exactly like—

Like her mother. He hadn't needed to finish the sentence.

It's aberrant, he'd said.

Aberrant.

The bitterness coated my throat now, threatening to choke me, and I finally recognized it for what is was. Shame. "Well, isn't that convenient."

From beneath Reid's arm, I caught a glimpse of Coco hooking Beau's elbow and dragging him away. He didn't protest. When they'd disappeared from my view, Reid turned to face me, bending low to meet my eyes directly. "I know what you're thinking. It's not that."

"People don't really change, do they?"

"Lou—"

"Are you going to start calling me *it*? I wouldn't blame you." I bared my teeth at him, leaning close enough to bite. Never once in my eighteen years had I allowed anyone to make me feel the way I felt now. I resented the tears pooling in my eyes, the nausea rolling in my belly. "I'm aberrant, after all. *Erratic*."

He cursed softly, his eyes fluttering closed. "You were listening."

"Of course I was listening. How *dare* you insult me to justify your own twisted narrative—"

"Stop. *Stop*." His eyes snapped open as he reached for me, gripping my arms, but his hands were gentle. "I told you it doesn't matter that you're a witch. I meant it."

"Bullshit." I jerked away from him, watching in acute misery as his hands fell. The next second, I tackled him around the waist, burying my face in his chest. My voice was muffled, broken, as I squeezed him tight. "You didn't even give me a chance."

He held me tighter still, wrapping his body around mine like he could shield me from the world. "This is about magic, not you."

"Magic *is* me. And it's you too."

"No, it isn't. All those pieces you're giving up—I want them. I want *you*. Whole and unharmed." He pulled away to look at me, those blue eyes blazing with intensity. "I know I can't ask you to stop using magic, so I won't. But I can ask it of my mother. I can ask it of myself. And I can"—he brushed a strand of hair from my cheek—"I can ask you to be careful."

"You can't be serious." Finally, *finally*, I recoiled from his touch, my heart catching up with my head. "You're acting like I'm suddenly damaged goods, or—or a piece of glass about to shatter. News flash—I've practiced magic all my life. I know what I'm doing."

"Lou." He reached for me again, but I swatted his hand away. Those eyes burned brighter, hotter. "You haven't been yourself."

"You see what you want to see."

"Do you think I *want* to see you as—"

"As what? As *evil*?"

He gripped my shoulders hard. "You are *not* evil."

"Of course I'm not." I wiped a tear from my eye before it could fall, before he could see. Never before had I allowed myself to feel small, to feel *ashamed*, and I refused to start now. "You would willingly endanger your life—your mother's life, your *brother's* life—by refusing to use magic on the road?"

"I'm damned either way."

I stared at him for a long moment. The conviction in his eyes shone brutally clear, and it cut deeper than I'd anticipated. That wounded part of me wanted him to suffer for his foolishness. As they were, they'd all die on the road without magic, and if they didn't, they certainly would in Le Ventre. He was crippling them with prejudice, weakening them with fear. The weak didn't survive war.

Reid had to survive.

"No, you aren't." I stepped away from him, resigned, and squared my shoulders. His life was worth more than my wounded pride. Later—when all of this was over—I'd show him how wrong he was about magic. About me. "Before the pub exploded, Claud Deveraux offered help if I should ever need it. His traveling troupe leaves for Cesarine tonight. You'll join him."

TROUPE DE FORTUNE

Reid

The others protested little to Lou's *solution*.

I wished they would. Perhaps she'd listen to them. She certainly hadn't listened to me. When we'd packed our belongings—a whirlwind of mud, snow, and blood—I'd tried to reason with her to no avail.

This entire scheme, albeit clever, depended on one thing: Claud Deveraux.

We didn't know Claud Deveraux. More important, *he* knew *us*—or at least he seemed to know Lou. He'd been infatuated with her at the pub. He'd also seen her use magic. He knew she was a witch. Though I'd learned witches weren't inherently evil, the rest of the kingdom had not. If he helped us, what sort of person did that make him?

"Your salvation," Lou had said, stuffing my bedroll into my pack. "Look, he saved our asses tonight. He could've let us die, but he didn't. He obviously doesn't wish us harm, which is more than we can say about anyone else—and no one will think to look for you in a troupe of actors. You'll be hidden without magic."

She hurried down the hill toward Saint-Loire now. The others followed. I lingered behind, glancing back at the forest's edge. A single snowflake fell from the sky—still thick and heavy with clouds—and landed on my cheek. An eerie silence fell over the forest in its wake. Like the calm before the storm. As I turned away, two luminescent eyes reflected in my periphery. Large. Silver. I spun, the hair on my neck rising, but there was nothing except trees and shadows.

I strode after the others.

Actors bustled around the village square, hauling trunks, instruments, and props in preparation for departure. Claud Deveraux directed them. He flitted to and fro, clapping his hands in delight. As if there were nothing bizarre about packing in the dead of night, nor leaving before a storm.

Lou hesitated in the alley, watching. We all stopped with her.

"What is it?" I murmured, but she shushed me as Claud Deveraux spoke.

"Come, Zenna!" He bounded toward a plump woman with lavender hair. "We must depart before sunrise! Dame Fortune favors only those who begin their journeys under the new moon!"

I blinked more snowflakes from my eyes.

"Right," Zenna muttered, tossing an instrument into the smaller wagon. She wore a peculiar cloak. Deep purple. Perhaps blue. It glittered with what looked like stars. Constellations. "Except Dame Fortune abandoned Cesarine years ago."

"Ah, ah." Monsieur Deveraux waggled his finger at her reprovingly. "Never despair. Perhaps she will join us there."

"Or perhaps we'll be burned at the stake."

"*Absurdité!* The people of Cesarine need their spirits lifted. Who better to lift them than we? Soon, we shall whisk the patrons of La Mascarade des Crânes away to a world of frivolity and fantasy."

"Brilliant." Zenna pinched the bridge of her nose. Though her coloring resembled Coco's, her skin was scarless. She might've been attractive, but heavy cosmetics—kohl around her eyes, rouge on her lips—hid her true features.

"Seraphine and I deserve three percent of the cover to make this worth our while, Claud," she continued. "We're walking straight into Hell for this funeral, flames and all."

"Of course, of course." He waved his hand, already turning away to hurrah another actor. "But let's make it four."

Coco nudged Lou. This time, Lou didn't hesitate. "*Bonjour,* Monsieur Deveraux. You already know me from this evening, but my name isn't Lucida. It's Louise le Blanc, and these are my friends, Reid and Ansel Diggory, Cosette Monvoisin, Beauregard Lyon, and Helene Labelle."

Louise le Blanc. Not Louise Diggory. I kept my gaze forward. Impassive.

His brows lifted, and his eyes sparked with recognition. With surprise. They flitted over each of us before landing again on Lou. "Well, well, we meet again, little one! How delightfully unexpected."

The other actors paused in loading their luggage to watch us. Only two trunks remained on the ground, one too full to properly latch. Glittering fabric spilled out of it. Fuchsia feathers fluttered to the snow.

Lou flashed him a charming smile. "I'm here to accept your offer of help if it still stands."

"Oh?"

"Oh." She nodded and extended her arms to the wanted posters tacked around us. To the smoking remains of the pub. "You may not have noticed earlier, but my friends and I have made *quite* the impression on His Royal Majesty."

"Killing the Holy Father will do that," the young woman behind Deveraux said softly. She'd woven flowers through her curly hair and clutched a cross pendant at her throat. I averted my eyes, struggled against the rising emotion. It clawed through my chest, abrupt and untethered.

Lou's smile sharpened on the woman. "Do you know how many of my sisters your Holy Father killed?"

The woman shrank into herself. "I—I—"

Ansel touched Lou's arm, shaking his head. I stared at the feathers. Watched as the snow seeped into the delicate pink filaments. Just another moment. I just needed another moment to regain control, to master myself. Then my hand would replace Ansel's. I would help Lou remember. I would forget this withering, thrashing *creature* in my chest—

The curly-haired woman drew herself up to her full height. She was taller than Lou. Nearly as tall as Madame Labelle. "He still didn't deserve what happened to him."

You were like a son to me, Reid.

My breath caught, and the beast raged. I retreated further. As if sensing my distress, Lou stepped in front of me. "Oh? What *did* he deserve?"

"Lou," Ansel murmured. A part of me registered his glance in my direction. "Don't."

"Right. Of course, you're right." Shaking her head, Lou patted his hand and returned her attention to Deveraux. The curly-haired woman watched us with wide eyes. "We need transport into Cesarine, *monsieur*. Certain complications have arisen, and the road is no longer safe to travel alone. Do you have room in your wagons for a few more?"

"Why, of *course* we—"

"Only actors ride in the wagons." Zenna crossed her arms and skewered Claud with a glare. "That's the rule, isn't it? That you can't afford to feed and house us if we don't perform?" To Lou, she added, "Claud is a collector of sorts. He adds only the best and brightest talent to his troupe. The rare and unusual. The exceptional."

Fingerless gingham mittens covered Deveraux's hands, which he clasped with a smile. "Zenna, my sweet, the exceptional come in all shapes and sizes. Let us discount no one." He turned to Lou apologetically. "Unfortunately, however nettlesome, a rule is a rule, and a shoe is a shoe. Zenna is correct. I only allow actors to ride with the troupe." He swayed his head slightly, pursing his lips. "*If*, however, you and your *charming* companions take to the stage—in full costume, of course—you would become, in fact, actors—"

"Claud," Zenna hissed, "they're *fugitives*. The huntsmen will have our heads if we shelter them."

He patted her lavender hair airily. "Ah, poppet, aren't we all? Liars and cheats and poets and dreamers and schemers, every last one."

"But not murderers." A young man stepped forward, tilting his head at me curiously. Tall. Russet-skinned. Long black hair. Beside him stood a man with an uncannily similar face. No— identical. Twins. "Did you do it? Did you kill the Archbishop?"

My jaw locked. Lou answered for me, arching a brow. "Does it matter? He's gone either way."

He studied her for several seconds before murmuring, "Good riddance."

They hated him. Emotion thrashed, demanding admission, but I felt nothing. I felt nothing.

Deveraux, who watched the exchange—who watched *me*— with an inscrutable expression, smiled brightly once more. "So, what do you say? Are you, in fact, *actors*?"

Lou looked back at me. I nodded. A reflex.

"Excellent!" Claud parted his hands to the sky in celebration. The snow fell thicker now. Heavier. "And precisely what is your act, Monsieur Diggory? A handsome, gargantuan fellow like yourself is sure to please a crowd, especially"—he leapt to the smaller wagon, pulling forth a pair of leather pants—"in an ensemble such as this. With a fetching wig and top hat, perhaps a bit of kohl around the eyes, you are sure to enthrall the crowd no matter your performance."

I stared at him for a second too long. "Er—"

"He's a storyteller," Lou said quickly, loudly, stepping backward to clutch my hand. I recognized her shift in posture. The subtle lilt in her voice. She'd started her performance already. Distracting them from—from me. "He loves stories. And you're right. He'll look ravishing in those pants. Shirtless, of course."

She smirked and squeezed my fingers.

"Inspired!" Deveraux tapped his chin as he considered us. "Alas, I'm afraid we already have a storyteller in sweet, sweet Zenna." He nodded to the lavender-haired woman, who seized this fresh opportunity to protest. Sweetly.

"See? He's useless. If it were meant to be, Dame Fortune would've sent someone—"

"Can you use those knives?" Deveraux's kohl-rimmed eyes fell to my open coat, to the knives strapped beneath it. "We latterly lost our knife thrower to a troupe in Amandine, and"—he leaned closer, winking—"though I myself am disinclined to choose favorites, the audience is not."

"Oh, you *cannot* be serious, Claud." Eyes sparking, Zenna planted a hand on each of her hips. "Nadine's act was mediocre at best—*certainly* not better than mine—and even if it weren't, I'm not splitting tips with this lot. We don't even *know* them. They could murder us in our sleep. They could turn us into toads. They could—"

"Tell you that you have lipstick on your teeth," Lou finished.

Zenna glared at her.

"It's true," Beau said helpfully. "Right there at the side."

Scowling, Zenna turned to rub at her incisors.

Lou grinned and returned her attention to Deveraux. "Reid's knives are practically extensions of his limbs, *monsieur*. He'll hit any target you put in front of him."

"How marvelous!" With a last, lingering look at said knives, Deveraux turned to Madame Labelle. "And you, *chérie* . . . ?"

"I'm—"

"His assistant." Lou grinned wider. "Why don't we strap her to a board and give you a demonstration?"

Deveraux's brows climbed up his forehead. "I'm sure that's unnecessary, but I do appreciate your enthusiasm. Quite infectious, I tell you." He turned to Beau, sweeping into a ridiculous bow. His nose touched the tip of his boot. "If I might divulge, Your Highness, it is an exceptional and unparalleled delight to make your acquaintance. I'm positively *expiring* with suspense at the prospect of learning your myriad talents. Tell us one, if you please. How will you dazzle us on the stage?"

Beau didn't return his smile. His lip curled. "I won't be on the stage, and I certainly won't be wearing anything feathered nor fuchsia." At Deveraux's expectant look, he sighed. "I'll do your sums."

Deveraux clapped his mittened hands together. "Just so! For royalty, we shall make an exception!"

"And you?" Zenna asked, sneering at Lou. "Any special talents for the stage?"

"If you must know, I play the mandolin. Quite well, in fact, because—" She hesitated, dipping her chin in an uncharacteristic display of insecurity. Though small—nearly indiscernible—the movement unsettled me. Pierced the haze of my thoughts. "It doesn't matter."

"Tell us," I said softly.

"Well . . . my mother insisted I learn to play. The harp, the clavichord, the rebec—but the mandolin was her favorite."

I frowned. I hadn't known Lou could play a single instrument, let alone many. She'd once told me she couldn't sing, and I'd assumed . . . but no. Those calluses on her fingers weren't from swordplay. The *mandolin*. I wracked my brain, trying to picture the instrument, to remember the sound, but I couldn't. The only instrument I'd heard in childhood had been an organ. I hadn't cared to make time for others.

"Ha!" Zenna laughed in triumph. "We already have a musician. Claud is a virtuoso. The best in the kingdom."

"Bully for him," Lou muttered, stooping to save the fuchsia feathers from the snow. She didn't meet anyone's eyes. "I said it doesn't matter, anyway. I'm not joining the troupe."

"I do beg your pardon?" Claud accepted the feathers with a scandalized expression. The wind picked up around us. It nearly blew his hat to the rooftops. "I believe I misheard you in this gale."

"You didn't." Lou gestured to Ansel and Coco, raising her voice. Snow soaked her new cloak. She clutched it under her chin to keep herself concealed. "The three of us will be traveling in a different direction."

Deveraux flapped his hands, and the feathers scattered once

more. "Nonsense! Preposterous! As you have so succinctly surmised, the road is not safe for you. You must come with us!" He shook his head too vigorously, and the wind snatched his hat. It spiraled upward and disappeared into the snow. "No. No, I fear there is no question that our little rendezvous at the pub was fated by none other than Dame Fortune herself. Furthermore, I cannot abide you traveling the road alone. Nay, I refuse to have that on my conscience."

"They will not be alone."

An unfamiliar voice. An inexplicable chill.

Lou and I stepped together, turning as one to the dark figure beside us.

A woman.

I hadn't heard her approach, hadn't seen her draw near. Yet she stood no more than a hand's breadth away, staring up at me with eerie, colorless eyes. Uncommonly thin—almost skeletal— with alabaster skin and black hair, she looked more wraith than human. My hand shot to my Balisarda. She tilted her head in response, the movement too quick, too bestial, to be natural.

Absalon wound between her emaciated ankles.

"Nicholina." Coco bared her teeth in a snarl. "Where's my aunt?"

The woman's face split into a slow, cruel grin, revealing bloodstained teeth. I pulled Lou backward, away from her. "Not here," she sang, her voice strange and high-pitched. Girlish. "Not here, not here, but always near. We come to answer your call."

I felt her strange eyes on me as I heaved the last trunk into the wagon.

The others hastened to secure belongings, calm horses, check knots. Deveraux had pulled Lou aside, and they appeared to be arguing over the strange woman's arrival. I couldn't tell. Snow blew around us in a tempest now, eliminating visibility. Only two of the torches lining the street remained. The rest had succumbed to the storm.

Scowling, I finally turned to face her—*Nicholina*—but she was gone.

"Hello, huntsman."

I jumped at her voice directly behind me, startled by her close proximity. Heat flushed my throat, my face. "Who are you?" I asked. "How do you keep doing that?"

She lifted a skeletal finger to my cheek, tilting her head as if fascinated. The torchlight flickered over her scars. They disfigured her skin, twisted it into a macabre lattice of silver and blood. I refused to flinch away.

"I am Nicholina le Claire, La Voisin's personal attendant." Trailing a sharpened nail along my jaw, her lip curled. The girlish cadence of her voice vanished, deepening unexpectedly to a guttural snarl. "And I will not explain the secrecies of blood craft to a huntsman." Darkness stirred in those colorless eyes as she gazed past me to Lou. Her grip on my chin hardened, and her nails bit deep. Nearly drawing blood. "Or his little mouse."

Coco stepped between us. "Careful, Nicholina. Lou is under my aunt's protection. Reid is under mine."

"Mmm . . . *Reid.*" Nicholina licked her lips salaciously. "Your name on my tongue tastes like salt and copper and warm, wet things—"

"Stop it." I stepped away from her, alarmed, disgusted, and glanced at Lou. She watched us from beyond the wagons, eyes narrowed. Deveraux waved his hands at her emphatically. I strode toward them—determined to remove myself from this situation—but Nicholina shadowed my footsteps. Still too close. Much, *much* too close. The childlike lilt returned to her voice.

"My mice whisper such naughty things about you, Reid. Such wicked, *naughty* things. *Cosette, regret, and forget,* they cry. *Cosette, regret, and forget.* I can't attest, as I've never tasted huntsman—"

"And you won't start with this one." Coco hurried after us as Lou extricated herself from Deveraux. "He's married."

"Is he?"

"Yes." I lurched to a stop, whirling to glare at her. "So please maintain the appropriate distance, *mademoiselle.*"

She grinned wickedly, arching a thin brow. "Perhaps my mice were misinformed. They do love to whisper. *Whisper, whisper, whisper.* Always whispering." She leaned closer, and her lips tickled the shell of my ear. Again, I refused to react. Refused to give this insane woman the satisfaction. "They say you hate your wife. They say you hate yourself. They say you taste *delicious.*" Before I realized her intention, she'd dragged her tongue down my cheek in a long, wet movement.

Lou reached us at the same moment. Her eyes flashed with turquoise fire.

"What the hell are you doing?" With both hands, she moved to shove Nicholina away, but Nicholina had already floated backward. The way she moved . . . it was like she wasn't entirely corporeal. But her nails on my chin had been real enough, as was her saliva on my cheek. I jerked up my shirt collar, wiping at the moisture, heat razing my ears. Lou's fists clenched. She squared up to the taller woman. Vibrated with anger. "Keep your hands to yourself, Nicholina."

"*Keep them, keep them.*" Her eyes roved the exposed skin of my throat, dropped lower to my chest. Hungry. I tensed instinctively. Resisted the urge to clasp shut my coat. "He can keep them for me. Keep them and sweep them and slowly creep them—"

A low, menacing sound tore from Lou, and she stepped closer. Their toes nearly touched. "If you touch him again, *I'll* keep them for you. Each"—she took another step, closing the distance between them—"bloody"—she leaned closer still, body taut with anticipation—"stump."

Nicholina grinned down at her, unaffected, despite the way the wind rose and the temperature plummeted. Coco glanced around. Alarmed. "Silly mouse," Nicholina purred. "He hunts even now. Even now, he hunts. He knows his own mind, didn't tell me to stop."

"You lie." Even I heard the defensiveness in my voice. Lou stood rooted in front of me. She didn't turn around when I touched her shoulder. "Lou, she's a—"

"But *can* he stop?" Nicholina circled us now, like a predator scenting blood. "Hunt and stop? Or stop and hunt? Soon we'll taste the noises on his tongue, oh yes, each moan and sigh and grunt—"

"Nicholina," Coco said sharply, seizing Lou's arm when she lunged. "Enough."

"The snake and her bird, the bird and his snake, they take and they break and they ache, ache, *ache*—"

"I said that's enough." Something in Coco's voice changed, deepened, and Nicholina's smile vanished. She stopped circling. The two stared at each other for several seconds—something unspoken passing between them, something dark—before Nicholina bared her throat. Coco watched this bizarre display of submission for a moment longer. Impassive. Cold. Finally, she nodded in satisfaction. "Wait for us at the forest's edge. Go now."

"As you wish, *princesse*." Nicholina lifted her head. Paused. Looked not to Lou, but to me. Her grin returned. This time, it was a promise. "Your little mouse will not always be here to protect you, huntsman. Take care."

The wind caught her words, blowing them around us with the snow. They bit at my cheeks, at Lou's cloak, Coco's hair. I took Lou's hand in silent reassurance—and startled. Her fingers were colder than expected. Unnaturally cold. Colder than the wind, the snow. Colder than Nicholina's smile.

Take care take care take care.

"Don't let her rile you," Coco murmured to Lou after she'd gone. "It's what she wants."

Nodding, Lou closed her eyes and took a deep breath. When she exhaled, the tension left her shoulders, and she glanced up at me. Smiled. I crushed her against me in relief.

"She seems like a real treat," Lou said, voice muffled by my coat.

"She is." Coco stared down the alley where Nicholina had disappeared. "The sort of treat that rots your soul instead of your teeth."

Deveraux approached through the snow. With a resigned sigh, he laid a hand on my arm. "The wagons are packed, *mon ami*. We must depart with the tempest, lest we miss our opportunity. Dame Fortune is a fickle mistress, indeed."

Though he waited expectantly, my arms refused to move. They held Lou in a vise, and I couldn't persuade them to let her go. I buried my nose in her shoulder instead, holding her tighter. Her cloak smelled unfamiliar. New. Like fur, damp earth, and the sweet, bitter scent of . . . something. Not magic. Perhaps wine. I frowned and pushed her hood aside, seeking her skin, the warmth I'd find there. But the unnatural cold in her hands had crept upward. It froze my lips as I brushed them against her throat. Alarmed, I met her eyes. Green now. So green.

"Be careful, Lou." I kept her cocooned within my arms, blocking the others from sight. Trying and failing to warm her. "Please. Promise me."

She kissed me instead. Gently disentangled herself. "I love you, Reid."

"It isn't supposed to be like this," I said helplessly, still reaching for her. "I should come with you—"

But she'd already stepped back, turned away. Clutched Coco's hand like she should've clutched mine. Her other reached for Ansel. "I'll see you soon," she promised, but it wasn't the one I wanted. The one I *needed*.

Without another word, she turned and vanished into the storm. I stared after her with a creeping sense of dread.

Absalon had followed.

THE MISSING PRINCE

Lou

The trees watched us, waiting, listening to our footsteps in the snow. They even seemed to breathe, inhaling and exhaling with each faint touch of wind in our hair. As sentient and curious as the shadows that crept ever closer.

"Can you feel them?" I whispered, cringing when my voice reverberated in the eerie quiet. The pines grew thicker in this part of the forest. Older. We could barely walk through their boughs, and with each step, they touched us, dusting our hair, our clothing, with glittering crystals of snow.

"Yes." Coco blew air into her hands, rubbing them together against the chill. "Don't worry. The trees here are loyal to my aunt."

I shivered in response. It had nothing to do with the cold. "Why?"

"Pretty lies or ugly truth?"

"The uglier, the better."

She didn't smile. "She feeds them her blood."

We smelled the camp before we saw it—hints of smoke and sage on the breeze hiding a sharper, acrid scent within them. At close range, however, one couldn't mistake the bite of blood magic. It overpowered my senses, burning my nose and throat, stinging my eyes. The tears froze in my lashes. Gritting my teeth against the bitter wind, I trudged onward, following Nicholina through snow drifts as high as my knees. "How much farther?" I called to her, but she ignored me. A blessing and a curse. She hadn't spoken a word since we'd left Troupe de Fortune in Saint-Loire. It seemed even she feared the forest after dark.

Coco inhaled the blood scent deeply, closing her eyes. She too had grown quieter over the past couple of hours—tenser, moodier—but when I'd questioned her, she'd insisted she was fine.

She was fine.

I was fine.

Reid was fine.

We were all *fine.*

A moment later, Nicholina halted outside a thick copse of pines and glanced back at us. Her eyes—so pale a blue they shone almost silver—lingered on my face before flicking to Coco. "Welcome home."

Coco rolled her eyes and moved to shove past her, but Nicholina had vanished. Literally.

"A real treat," I repeated, grinning despite myself at Coco's irritation. "Are all your sisters this charming?"

"She isn't my sister." Without looking back, Coco swept aside a branch and plunged into the trees, effectively ending the conversation. My grin slipped as I stared after her.

Ansel patted my arm as he passed, offering me a small smile. "Don't worry. She's just nervous."

It took every bit of my restraint not to snap at him. Since when did Ansel know more about Coco's feelings than I did? As if sensing my uncharitable thoughts, he sighed and hooked my elbow, dragging me after her. "Come on. You'll feel better after you've eaten."

My stomach growled in response.

The trees thinned abruptly, and we found ourselves on the edge of a rocky clearing. Campfires illuminated threadbare tents stitched together from bits of animal skin. Despite the inordinately early hour—and the cold and the darkness—a handful of witches huddled around the flames, clutching thick, matted furs for warmth. At the sound of our footsteps, they turned to watch us suspiciously. Though they ranged in age and ethnicity, all wore identical haunted expressions. Cheeks gaunt. Eyes hungry. One woman even gripped her auburn hair in her fists, weeping softly.

Ansel stumbled to a halt. "I didn't expect there to be so many males here." He stared at a young man roughly his age with undisguised yearning. "Are they . . . like Reid?"

His name cut through me like a knife, painful and sharp. I missed him. Without his steady presence, I felt . . . out of sorts. As if part of me was missing. In a way, I supposed that was true.

"Maybe. But if they are, I doubt they realize it. We've grown up believing only women possess magic. Our dear Chasseur . . . changes things."

Nodding, he tore his gaze away, cheeks pink. Coco didn't look at us as we approached, though she did murmur, "I should probably speak with my aunt alone."

I fought the urge to poke her in the cheek and *make* her look at me. When she'd spoken of her aunt's protection, of an alliance with her powerful kin, this was *not* what I'd envisioned. These witches looked as if they'd keel over from a strong wind, or perhaps even a sneeze. "Of course," I said instead. "We'll wait for you here."

"That won't be necessary." We all jumped as Nicholina materialized beside us once more. Her voice had lost its girlish pitch, and those silver eyes were flat, expressionless. Whatever show she'd performed for Reid's benefit, she didn't care to continue for us. "Josephine awaits the three of you in her tent."

"Can you stop doing that?" I demanded.

She twitched, every muscle in her face spasming, as if in physical protest to my question. Or perhaps to my mere voice. "Never address us, little mouse. Never, never, *ever*." Sudden life flared in her gaze, and she lunged, snapping her teeth viciously. Ansel reeled backward—pulling me with him—and nearly toppled us both. Though Coco stopped her with a quick, forceful hand, she'd still drawn near enough for me to feel the phantom brush of her teeth, to see the sharpened tips of her incisors. Waving skeletal fingers in my direction, she crooned as to a baby. "Or we will gobble you up whole. Yes, yes, we will—"

"*Enough*," Coco said impatiently, shoving her away. "Show us to our tents. It's late. We'll speak with my aunt after we've slept. That's an order, Nicholina."

"Tent."

"Pardon?"

"*Tent*," Nicholina repeated. She bobbed her head, resuming her maniacal performance. "Tent, tent, tent. A single tent is what I meant. One tent to share without dissent—"

"Share?" Ansel's eyes widened in alarm, darting to Coco. He released me to run a nervous hand through his hair, to tug at the hem of his coat. "We're sharing a tent? To—to sleep?"

"No, to fu—" I started cheerfully, but Coco interrupted.

"Why one tent?"

Shrugging, Nicholina wafted backward, away from us. We had no choice but to follow. The blood witches' gazes fell hard upon me as we passed, but all bared their throats to Coco in a gesture identical to Nicholina's earlier one. I'd seen this submission only once before tonight—when La Voisin had caught Coco and me playing together on the shore of L'Eau Mélancolique. She'd been furious, nearly dislocating Coco's shoulder in her haste to drag her away from me. Coco had showed her throat quicker than an omega showed its belly.

It'd unsettled me then, and it unsettled me now.

Echoing my thoughts, Ansel whispered, "Why do they do that?"

"It's a sign of respect and submission." We trailed several paces behind Coco and Nicholina. "Sort of like how you bow to royalty. When they bare their throats, they're offering Coco their blood."

"But . . . submission?"

After Coco had passed, the witches resumed glaring at our backs. I couldn't say I blamed them. I was a Dame Blanche, and Ansel had trained to be a Chasseur. Though La Voisin had allowed us to enter her camp, we were no more welcome than Reid had been.

"If Coco drank your blood right now," I explained, "she'd be able to control you. Temporarily, of course. But the Dames Rouges offer it to her and La Voisin freely. They're royalty here."

"Right." Ansel swallowed hard. "Royalty."

"*La princesse.*" Winking, I pinched his arm. "But still Coco."

He didn't look convinced.

"Why one tent, Nicholina?" Coco's hands curled into fists when Nicholina continued to hum under her breath. Apparently, her position as La Voisin's *personal attendant* afforded her more defiance. "*Tell me.*"

"You left us, *princesse.* Left us to rot. Now there's not enough food or blankets or cots. We die by the hour from cold or hunger. 'Tis a pity you couldn't have stayed away longer."

At Nicholina's chilling smile, Coco missed a step, but I steadied her with a hand on her back. When she pulled me to her side, lacing her fingers through mine, relief flooded through me. "Why does my aunt need to see us right now?" she asked, her frown deepening. "What can't wait?"

Nicholina cackled. "The son disappeared with the sun, went to rest below the rock. But he didn't come home, his body is gone, and vultures have started to flock."

"We don't speak wraith," I said flatly.

Coco—who possessed patience vastly superior to my own—didn't ask for clarification. Instead, her face twisted. "Who is it?"

"Who *was* it," Nicholina corrected her, her mouth still contorted in that disturbing smile. It was too large, too fixed, too—bloody. "*He's dead, he's dead*, my mice have said. Dead, dead, dead, dead, dead, dead, *dead*."

Well. I supposed that explained the weeping woman.

Nicholina drifted to a halt outside a small, threadbare tent at the edge of camp, separate from the rest. It overlooked the cliff's edge. In daylight, the sun's rays would warm this place, bathing the snow in a golden glow. With the uninhibited view of the mountains behind, the scene could've been beautiful, even in darkness.

Except for the vultures circling above.

We watched them dip lower and lower in ominous silence— until Coco tore her hand from mine and planted it on her hip. "You said he's missing," she said fiercely. "*Missing*, not dead. We'll speak with my aunt now. If she's organizing search parties, we'll join them. He might still be out there somewhere."

Nicholina nodded with glee. "Freezing to death slowly. Sloooowly."

"Right." Coco tossed her bag into our tent without looking inside. "Who is it, Nicholina? How long has he been missing?" Without warning, her bag came sailing back at her, knocking into the side of her head. She spun and swore violently. "What the——?"

From our tent stepped Babette Dubuisson.

Virtually unrecognizable without her thick makeup—and with her golden hair piled atop her head—she'd lost weight since we'd last seen her in Cesarine. Her scars shone silver against her ivory skin. Though fondness warmed her expression as she gazed at Coco, she did not smile. "We have known him as Etienne Gilly after his darling mother, Ismay Gilly."

Coco stepped forward, her relief palpable as they embraced. "Babette. You're here."

I frowned, feeling a bit as if I'd missed the bottom step on a staircase. Though Roy and his friends had confirmed our suspicions, muttering about *curfews* and *suspicious womenfolk* in Cesarine, I hadn't spared a thought for Babette or her safety. But Coco obviously had. My frown deepened. I considered Babette a friend—albeit in the loosest definition of the word—and I cared about what happened to her.

Didn't I?

"*Bonjour, mon amour.*" Babette kissed Coco's cheek before resting her forehead against hers. "I have missed you." When they parted, Babette eyed the fresh slash at my throat. I hadn't been able to salvage my ribbon. "And *bonjour* to you too, Louise. Your hair is *répugnant*, but I am happy to see you alive and well."

I offered her a wary smile, Reid's words returning with frightful clarity. *You haven't been yourself.* "Alive, indeed," I mused, smile fading. "But perhaps not well."

"Nonsense. In times such as these, if you are alive, you are well." Returning her attention to Coco, she sighed deeply. The sound lacked her signature melodrama. No, this sober, barefaced woman—with her tattered clothing and tangled hair—was not the Babette I'd always known. "But perhaps more than we can say of poor Etienne. You believe he still lives, *mon amour,* but I fear for his life—and *not* from the cold. Though we have known him by his mother, to the rest of the kingdom, Etienne Gilly would be known as Etienne Lyon. He is the king's bastard son, and he never returned from the morning hunt."

Larger than the others, La Voisin's tent had been pitched in the center of the clearing. Several wooden cages circled the ground around it, and glowing eyes reflected back at us. A fox lunged at the bars as we passed, snarling, and Ansel leapt into me with a squeak. When Babette snickered, Ansel blushed to the roots of his hair.

"Are these . . . pets?" he asked weakly.

"They're for blood," Coco said shortly. "And divination."

Nicholina glowered at Coco's explanation—probably a betrayal in her mind—before parting the bundles of dried sage hanging from the tent entrance. Babette pecked each of Coco's cheeks.

"I will find you after, *mon amour*. We have much to discuss."

Coco held her a second longer than necessary before they parted.

Inside, La Voisin stood behind a makeshift table, a smudge stick smoldering gently before her. Nicholina drifted to her side, picking up a rabbit's skin in one hand and a bloody knife in the other. The poor creature's various organs had been spread across most of the table. I tried to ignore her licking its blood from her fingers.

La Voisin looked up from the book she'd been studying and

fixed me with a cold stare. I blinked, startled at the smoothness of her face. She hadn't aged a day since I'd last seen her. Though she must've been thrice our age, no lines marred her brow or lips, and her hair—pinned back in a severe chignon—remained as black as the moonless night sky.

My scalp prickled as I remembered the wicked rumors about her at Chateau le Blanc: how she ate the hearts of babies to stay young, how she journeyed to L'Eau Mélancolique each year to drink the blood of a melusine—no, to *bathe* in it.

A long moment of silence passed as she studied Coco and me, her dark eyes glittering in the candlelight. Just as Nicholina's had done, her gaze lingered on me, tracing the contours of my face, the scar at my throat. I stared resolutely back at her.

She didn't acknowledge Ansel.

Coco finally cleared her throat. "*Bonjour, tante.*"

"Cosette." La Voisin closed the book with a snap. "You deign to visit at last. I see the circumstances finally suit you."

I watched in disbelief as Coco stared at her feet, immediately contrite. "*Je suis désolée.* I would've come sooner, but I ... I couldn't leave my friends."

La Voisin strode around the table, parting the smudge smoke in waves. She halted in front of Coco, grasping her chin and tilting her face toward the candlelight. Coco met her gaze reluctantly, and La Voisin frowned at whatever she saw there. "Your kin have been dying while you cavorted with your *friends.*"

"Babette told me of Etienne. We can—"

"I do not speak of Etienne."

"Then who ... ?"

"Sickness took Delphine and Marie. Only last week, Denys passed from exposure. His mother left him to forage for food. He tried to follow." Her eyes hardened to glittering chips of obsidian. She dropped Coco's chin. "Do you remember him? He was not yet two years old."

Coco's breath hitched, and nausea churned in my own belly.

"I'm—" Coco stopped then, reconsidering. A wise decision. La Voisin didn't want her apology. She wanted her to suffer. To stew. Abruptly, Coco turned to me. "Lou, you—you remember my aunt, Josephine Monvoisin." She gestured between us helplessly. Taking pity on her, I nodded and forced a smile. It felt disrespectful after such a revelation.

"*Bonjour*, Madame Monvoisin." I didn't extend my throat. As children, Coco's first lesson to me had been simple: never offer my blood to a Dame Rouge. Especially her aunt, who loathed Morgane and the Dames Blanches perhaps even more than I did. "Thank you for granting us an audience."

She stared at me for another long moment. "You look like your mother."

Coco quickly charged onward. "And this—this is Ansel Diggory. He's—"

La Voisin still didn't acknowledge him. Her eyes never strayed from mine. "I know who he is."

"A *baby* huntsman." Licking her bottom lip, Nicholina edged closer, her eyes hungry and bright. "He is pretty, oh yes."

"He's not a huntsman." Coco's voice cut sharp enough to draw blood. "He never was."

"And that"—La Voisin's lip curled in unconcealed disdain—"is the only reason he remains alive."

At her aunt's black look, Coco cleared her throat hastily. "You . . . you said Etienne isn't dead. Does that mean you've found him?"

"We have not." If possible, La Voisin's expression further darkened, and the shadows in the tent seemed to press closer. The candles flickered. And her book—it *moved*. I stared at it with wide eyes. Though barely perceptible, the black cover had *definitely* twitched. La Voisin stroked its spine before reaching inside to remove a piece of parchment. On it, someone had drawn a crude map of La Fôret des Yeux. I leaned closer to examine it, despite my unease. Blood spatters dotted the trees of ink. "Our tracking spell revealed he is alive, but something—or someone—has cloaked his exact location." When her black eyes fixed on mine, my chest tightened inexplicably. "We searched the general area in shifts yesterday, but he was not there. We have expanded our search tonight."

I crossed my arms to keep from fidgeting. "Could he not have left on his own?"

"His mother and sister reside here. He would not have left without saying goodbye."

"We all know filial relationships can be fraught—"

"He disappeared just after I agreed to meet with you."

"A weird coincidence—"

"I don't believe in coincidences." She studied us impassively as we shuffled shoulder to shoulder in front of her—like naughty schoolchildren. A situation made worse by Coco and

Ansel towering over me on either side. I tried and failed to stand a little taller. "Your message said you seek an alliance with our coven," she continued. I nodded. "It said Reid Labelle journeys to Le Ventre as we speak, seeking a similar alliance with the loup garou. From there, you plan to approach the king in Cesarine."

A tendril of satisfaction curled through me. Reid Labelle. Not Reid Diggory or Reid Lyon. The name felt . . . right. Of course, if we adhered to the customs of our kin, he'd have the choice of becoming Reid le Blanc instead. If . . . if we handfasted properly, this time.

"That's correct."

"My answer is no."

I blinked, startled at her abrupt dismissal, but she'd already returned her attention to the map, tucking it back within her creepy little book. Nicholina giggled. In my periphery, she held the dead rabbit by its front paws, making its limp body dance. Heat washed through me, and my hands curled into fists. "I don't understand."

"It is simple." Her black eyes met mine with a calm that made me want to scream. "You will fail. I will not jeopardize my kin for your foolish quest."

"Aunt Josephine—" Coco started, pleading, but La Voisin waved a curt hand.

"I read the portents. I will not concede."

I struggled to keep my voice even. "Was it the rabbit's bladder that convinced you?"

"I do not expect you to understand the burden of ruling a

people. *Either* of you." She glanced at Coco, arching a brow, and Coco ducked her chin. I wanted to claw out La Voisin's eyes. "Every death in this camp is on my hands, and I cannot risk evoking Morgane's wrath. Not for you. Not even for my niece."

The heat in my belly built, growing hotter and hotter until I nearly burst. My voice, however, remained cold. "Why did you bring us here if you aren't even willing to listen?"

"I owe you nothing, Louise le Blanc. Do not mistake me. You stand here—*alive* and *well*—only by my benevolence. That benevolence is quickly waning. My people and I will not join you. Knowing this, you may now leave. Cosette, however, will stay."

And there it was. The real reason she'd brought us here—to forbid Coco from leaving.

Coco stiffened as if her aunt's black eyes had quite literally pinned her there. "Too long you have forsaken your duties, Cosette," La Voisin said. "Too long you have protected your *enemies* over your *people*." She spat the last, planting her palms against the table. Her nails bit into the wood. Beside her, the black book seemed to quiver in anticipation. "It ends now. You are the Princesse Rouge, and you will act as such from this moment onward. Begin by escorting Louise and her companion from our camp."

My jaw unlocked. "We're not leaving—"

"Until they find Etienne," Coco finished, straightening her shoulders. Her arm brushed mine in the barest of touches. *Trust me*, it seemed to say. I clamped my mouth shut again. "They want to help, *tante*. They'll leave only after they've found him—and if they do, you'll give them your alliance."

"*And* Coco will come with us," I added, unable to help myself. "If she so chooses."

La Voisin's eyes narrowed. "I have given my final word."

Coco wouldn't hear it, however. Though her fingers trembled slightly, she approached the table, lowering her voice. We could all still hear her. "Our magic cannot find him. Maybe hers can." Her voice pitched lower still, but gained strength. "Together, we can defeat Morgane, *tante*. We can return to the Chateau. All of this—the cold, the sickness, the death—it'll end."

"I will not ally with enemies," La Voisin insisted, but she cast a quick glance in my direction. Her brows furrowed. "I will not ally with *werewolves* and *huntsmen*."

"We share a common enemy. That makes us friends." To my surprise, Coco reached out and clutched La Voisin's hand. Now it was the latter's turn to stiffen. "Accept our help. Let us find Etienne. Please."

La Voisin studied us for a moment that felt like eternity. At long last, she pulled her hand from Coco's grasp. "*If* you find Etienne," she said, lips pursing, "I will consider your proposition." At Ansel's and my sighs of relief, she added sharply, "You have until sunrise. If you have not found him by then, you will leave this camp without argument. Agreed?"

Indignant, I opened my mouth to argue such a ridiculous timeframe—less than a handful of hours—but something brushed my ankle. I glanced down in surprise. "Absalon? What are you . . . ?" Hardly daring to hope, I whirled toward the tent entrance, but there was no towering, copper-haired man standing there, no half smiles or clenched jaws or flushed cheeks. I frowned.

He wasn't here.

Disappointment bit deep. Then confusion. Matagots generally stayed with those who'd attracted them. Unless . . .

"Do you have a message for me?" I asked, frown deepening. A tendril of panic bloomed. Had something already gone wrong on the road? Had he been recognized, captured, discovered as a witch? A million possibilities sparked in my mind, spreading like wildfire. "What is it, Absalon? *Tell* me."

He merely meowed and wove between my ankles, human intelligence gleaming in his feline eyes. As I stared at him, bewildered, the last of my anger sizzled away. He hadn't stayed with Reid. He hadn't come to deliver a message. Instead, he'd simply . . . come. Here. He'd come *here*. And that meant—

"You named the matagot?" La Voisin blinked once, the only outward sign of her surprise.

"Everyone deserves a name," I said faintly. *They're drawn to like creatures. Troubled souls. Someone here must have attracted him.* Absalon stood on his hind paws, kneading the thick leather of my pants with his front. Instinctively, I knelt to scratch behind his ear. A low purr built in his throat. "He didn't tell me his, so I improvised."

Coco's brows knitted together as she glanced between me and Ansel—clearly trying to decide who the matagot had followed here—but La Voisin only smiled, small and suggestive. "You are not what I expected, Louise le Blanc."

I didn't like that smile. Straightening hastily, I nudged Absalon away with my foot. He didn't move. "Shoo," I hissed, but he merely gazed balefully back at me. Shit.

The auburn-haired woman from before interrupted us, peeking inside the tent. She held the hand of a child, a miniature version of herself. "The midnight search party has returned, my lady." Sniffing, she wiped away a fresh tear. "No sign of him. The next party has assembled."

"Do not fear, Ismay. We will find him." La Voisin clasped her hands, and her voice softened. "You must rest. Take Gabrielle back to your tent. We will wake you with developments."

"No, I—I must rejoin the party. Please do not ask me to sit idly while—while my son—" She broke off, overcome, before gritting her teeth. "I will not rest until he is found."

La Voisin sighed. "Very well." When Ismay nodded in thanks, guiding her daughter out of the tent, La Voisin inclined her head to me. "If you agree to my terms, you will join the next party in their search. They leave immediately. Nicholina will accompany you, as will Ismay and Gabrielle. You may also take your familiar and companion." She paused. "Cosette, you will attend me."

"*Tante*—" Coco started.

"He's *not* my familiar—" I snapped.

But La Voisin spoke over us, her eyes flashing. "You try my patience, child. If I am to consider this alliance, you will find Etienne before the first light of day. Do we have a deal?"

ONE STEP FORWARD

Reid

The weight of the knife was heavy in my palm. Solid. The blade balanced and sharp. I'd purchased it from one of the finest smiths in Cesarine—a smith who had later consorted to kill my wife with a couple of criminals. *Blue pig*, he'd spat after I'd given him to the authorities. In all our years of business, I hadn't known he despised me. Just like the farmers in Saint-Loire. All because of my uniform.

No. That wasn't true.

All because of *me*. My beliefs.

Golden stars took up most of the spinning board. Leather cuffs hung from four strategic points on the circular wood—two for an assistant's hands, and two for their feet. The top of the board had been stained with something that looked suspiciously like blood.

With a halfhearted flick of my wrist, I threw my knife. It lodged dead center.

Deveraux erupted into applause. "Well, that was quite—quite *extraordinary*, Monsieur Diggory! Really, Louise wasn't fibbing when she spoke of your bladed prowess!" He fanned himself for a moment. "Ah, the crowd will positively *exalt* your performance. The Dagger of Danger, we shall call you. No, no—Knife Strife."

I stared at him, alarmed. "I don't think—"

"Argh, you're right, you're *right*, of course. We have not yet found the perfect appellation. Never fear! Together, we shall—" His hands shot skyward abruptly, fingers splayed as if framing a portrait. "Three-Fingered Red? It takes three fingers to perform, yes?"

"Any more, and it would just be uncomfortable." Lounging behind us on a spangled blanket, Beau laughed. The remains of his lunch littered the ground beside him. "Might I suggest *Le Petit Jésus* as an alternative?"

"Stop." I took a deep breath through my nose. Heat worked up my throat, and even to me, the word sounded tired. I'd thought to use the break in travel to practice. An egregious lapse in judgment. "I don't need a stage name."

"My dear, dear boy!" Deveraux clutched his chest as if I'd insulted his mother. "Whatever else shall we call you? We cannot simply announce you as Reid Diggory." He flapped a hand, swatting away my protests. "The *couronnes*, dear boy, just think of the *couronnes*! You need a name, an *identity*, to whisk the audience into their fantas—" His hand stilled mid-swipe, and his eyes lit with excitement. "*The Red Death*," he said with relish. My heartbeat faltered. "That's it. The clear winner. The obvious selection. Come one, come all, to witness the horrible, the hellacious, the *handsome* Red Death!"

Beau doubled over with laughter. I nearly threw another knife at him.

"I prefer Raoul."

"Nonsense. I have *clearly* articulated my feelings on the name Raoul." Deveraux dropped his hands. The feather on his hat bobbed in agitation. "Never fear, I have every confidence the honorific shall grow on you. But perhaps a respite is in order in the meantime? We might instead outfit you both for your grand debut!"

Beau rose hastily to his elbows. "I told you I won't be onstage."

"Everyone in the company must model the appropriate attire, Your Highness. Even those collecting tickets and tips from the audience. You understand, I'm sure."

Beau fell backward with a groan.

"That's the spirit!" From his sleeve, Deveraux pulled a measuring tape. "Now, I'll just need a few measurements—a negligible amount, really—and all will be set. May I?" He gestured to my arm. When I nodded, he stepped into my space, engulfing me in the scent of wine.

That explained a lot.

"For the remainder of our journey," he prattled, unfurling his tape, "might I suggest you bunk with the twins in the amber wagon? Your mother may join you. Your brother, however, may better suit the scarlet wagon with Zenna and Seraphine. Though I sleep little, I will accompany him there." He chortled at an unspoken joke. "I've been told Zenna and Seraphine are the fiercest of snorers."

"I *would* be better suited to Zenna and Seraphine's wagon." I could hear the smirk in Beau's voice. "How perceptive you are, Claud."

He barked a laugh. "Oh no, dear boy, I fear if romance is what you seek, you shall be markedly disappointed. Zenna's and Seraphine's very souls are intertwined. *Cosmic*, I tell you."

Beau's expression flattened, and he looked away, muttering about piss poor luck.

"Why the sleeping arrangements?" I asked suspiciously. After bidding Lou goodbye, I'd spent the remainder of the night riding up front with Claud. He'd tried to pass the time with conversation. When I hadn't kept up my end, he'd started to sing, and I'd regretted my grave error. For *hours*.

"You're quite contrary, aren't you, Monsieur Diggory? Quite prickly." He peered up at me with a curious expression before dropping to measure my inseam. "'Tis nothing nefarious, I assure you. I simply think it wise for you to consider pursuing a friendship with our dear Toulouse and Thierry."

"Again, *why*?"

"You might have more in common with them than you think."

I glanced over my shoulder at Beau. He frowned at Deveraux. "That's not cryptic at all."

Deveraux sighed and stood once more, patting the mud from his corduroy trousers. *Violet* corduroy trousers. "If I might be frank, *messieurs*." He turned to me. "You have recently suffered a rather traumatic event and are in desperate need of platonic companionship. Your forefather is gone. Your brotherhood has abandoned you. Your self-loathing has cleaved a physical and emotional cleft between you and your wife. More important, it has cleaved a cleft within *yourself.*"

Sharp, hot anger spiked through me at the unexpected reprimand. "You don't even know me."

"Perhaps not. But I do know you don't know yourself. I know you cannot know another until you do." He snapped his fingers in front of my nose. "I know you need to wake up, young man, lest you leave this world without finding that which you truly seek."

I glared at him, the beginning of shame flushing my neck. My ears. "And what's that?"

"Connection," he said simply, spinning his tape into a tidy roll. "We all seek it. Accept yourself, accept *others*, and you just might find it. Now"—he turned on his booted heel, smiling cheerily over his shoulder—"I suggest you partake in your midday meal. We soon continue to Domaine-les-Roses, where you shall woo the crowd with your knife-wielding prowess. Ta-ta!"

He strode off whistling a merry tune.

Beau snorted in the ensuing silence. "I like him."

"He's *mad.*"

"All the best ones are."

His words sparked others—sharper ones now. Words that bit and snapped within my mind, seeking blood. *Claud is a collector of sorts*, Zenna had said. *He adds only the best and brightest talent to his troupe. The rare and unusual. The exceptional.*

My suspicion deepened. His curious look, his meaningful smile . . . was it possible he knew my secret? Did he know what I'd done on Modraniht? It wasn't likely. And yet—Morgane knew. I wasn't fool enough to believe she'd keep that knowledge to herself. When it best suited her purposes, she'd reveal it, and I would burn. And perhaps I deserved to burn. I'd taken life. I'd played God—

No. I retreated from my spiraling thoughts, breathing deeply. Marshaling my mind into order. Into silence. It lasted only seconds before another unwelcome question crept in.

If Deveraux *did* know, did that mean—were the twins also witches?

You might have more in common with them than you think.

Scoffing, I unsheathed another knife. In all my years around magic, in all *Lou's* years around it, we'd never heard of another male witch. To stumble upon two others this quickly after Modraniht was the least likely possibility of all. No. Less than unlikely. Absurd.

Claud is a collector of sorts.

Closing my eyes, I focused on emptying my mind of thought. Such speculation did little good. I had one purpose now—to protect Lou, to protect my unknown brothers and sisters. I couldn't know them if they were dead. I breathed in through my nose. Out through my mouth. Retreated to my fortress. Relished the darkness of my lids.

It didn't matter if the twins were witches.

It didn't matter if Deveraux knew I was one.

Because I wasn't a witch if I didn't practice.

I wasn't a witch.

Heedless of my conviction, gold flickered to life in the darkness, and there—soft at first, so soft I nearly missed them—voices began to hum.

Seek us, seek us, seek us.

My eyes snapped open.

When Beau cleared his throat behind me, I jumped, nearly dropping my knife. "You aren't seriously planning on strapping your mother to that board, are you?" he asked. "You could decapitate her."

In response, I hurled the knife—end over end—toward the center of the board. It sank deep beside the first one.

"Now you're just posturing." He rose from his blanket, stepped to my side for a better view. To my surprise, he tugged another knife from my bandolier, studying it in his hand. Then he threw it.

It thudded against the board like a dead fish before falling to the ground.

A beat of silence passed.

"It would seem"—Beau straightened his coat with as much dignity as he could muster—"I'm shit at this."

I snorted despite myself. The knot in my chest loosened. "Was there ever any doubt?"

A self-deprecating grin broke over his face, and he pushed my shoulder halfheartedly. Though tall, he stood a couple of inches shorter than me.

"When's your birthday?" I blurted.

He arched a black brow. So different from my own. "The ninth of August. I'm twenty-one years old. Why?"

"No reason."

"I'm older than you, if that's what you're wondering."

"I wasn't, and you're not."

"Come now, little brother, I told you my birthdate. It's only fair you reciprocate." When I didn't answer, his grin spread. "Your silence is damning. You really *are* younger, aren't you?"

Pushing his hand from my shoulder, I stalked toward the amber wagon. My neck burned.

Cots lined the walls inside, built above and below storage shelves like pieces of a puzzle. Pillows overflowed. Though threadbare, silk and velvet and satin covered each of them. Trunks had been shoved in the corners, along with a battered rack of costumes and a half-dressed mannequin. My chest twisted.

It reminded me of Soleil et Lune's attic.

Except for the incense. Frankincense and myrrh burned within a small porcelain pot. The smoke funneled out through a hole in the roof.

I hurled the entire pot outside into the snow.

"Easy there." Beau dodged the projectile, following me into the wagon. "Have the resins personally offended you?"

Again, I didn't answer. He didn't need to know it reminded me of the cathedral. Of . . . him.

I collapsed onto the nearest cot, tossing my bag to my feet. Rummaging for a dry shirt. When my hand caught instead on my journal, I pulled it out. Trailed my fingers across the worn cover. Flipped through the crinkled pages. Though perhaps I'd been foolish to pack such a sentimental token, I hadn't been able to leave it behind. Absently, I paused at my last entry—the evening I'd visited the king after burning Estelle.

My father.

I traced the words on the page, not truly seeing them. I'd done my best not to think of him, but now, his face crept back into my thoughts. Golden hair. Strong jaw. Piercing eyes. And a smile—a smile that disarmed all who looked upon it. He wielded it like a blade. No—a deadlier weapon still. A blade could not disarm his enemies, but his smile could.

As a Chasseur, I'd seen it from afar my entire life. Only when he'd invited me to dine with him had I witnessed it personally. He'd smiled at me the entire night, and despite Lou writhing alone in my bed—burning alive for her sister's sin—I'd felt . . . seen. Appreciated. *Special.*

Beau had inherited that smile. I had not.

Before I could lose my nerve, I asked, "What do our sisters look like? Violette and Victoire?"

Beau paused in examining the contents of the nearest trunk. I couldn't see his face. If my abrupt question surprised him, he didn't say. "They look like me, I suppose. Like our mother. She hails from an island across the sea. It's a beautiful kingdom. Tropical. Much warmer than this nonsense." He waved a hand toward the snow outside before plucking a crystal orb from the nearest trunk. "They're twins, you know. Prettier than my mother and me. Long black hair and blacker eyes, not a blemish on either of their faces. Like paintings—and my father treats them as such.

That's why you've never seen them. They're rarely allowed outside the castle walls."

"How old are they?"

"Thirteen."

"What do they"—I leaned forward eagerly—"what do they like? Do they read? Ride horses? Play with swords?"

He turned and smiled that smile, then. But it looked different on him. Genuine. "If by play, you mean bash their big brother over the head, then . . . yes. They like to *play* with swords." He eyed the journal in my hand. "And Violette likes to write and read. Victoire not so much. She prefers to chase cats and terrorize the staff."

A warmth I'd never known spread through me at the picture he painted. A warmth I hardly recognized. It wasn't anger or humiliation or—or shame. It was something else. Something . . . happy.

It hurt.

"And our father?" I asked quietly. "What's he like?"

Beau's smile faded then, and he dropped the lute he'd been plucking back into the trunk. His eyes narrowed as he faced me fully. "You know what he's like. Don't paint us like a fairy tale, Reid. We aren't one."

Closing my journal with more force than necessary, I pushed to my feet. "I know that. I just—I've—" I exhaled hard and threw caution to the winds. "I've never had a family."

"And you still don't." He shook his head in exasperation, eyeing me as if I were a stupid child in need of admonishment. "I should've known you'd do this. I should've known you'd want to *bond*." Stepping closer, he stuck a finger in my chest. "Listen carefully, *little brother*. This isn't a family. It's a noose. And if this brilliant plan of yours goes awry, we'll all swing from it—you, me, Violette, Victoire, and every other poor bastard our father has fucked into existence." He paused, and his expression softened infinitesimally before hardening once more. He kicked open the wagon door. "Make peace with it now, or we'll break your heart."

He left without another word.

The sway of wheels woke me. Groggy, disoriented, I jolted from my cot. My head pounded—doubly so when I cracked it against the shelf overhead—and my neck ached. I rubbed it with a muttered curse.

"Sleep well?" Madame Labelle regarded me over the brim of her teacup. Jade with gold filigree. The scent of spiced pears pervaded the wagon. Mulled perry, then. Not tea. It rippled with each roll of the wheels. Late afternoon sunlight filtered in through the window, as did Deveraux's cheery whistle.

"What time is it?" I asked.

"Around four o'clock. You've been asleep for hours. I didn't want to wake you." She offered me a second cup, along with a small smile. "Would you like some? I'm quite partial to perry after a long nap. Perhaps you are too?"

A hopeful question. A transparent one.

When I didn't answer, she prattled on, spinning her own cup

in her hands. Around and around. A restless gesture. "My mother brewed it for me when I was a girl. A grove of pear trees grew in the valley near the Chateau, and it was our secret place. We'd harvest the fruit at the end of summertime and hide them all over the Chateau, waiting for them to ripen." Her grin broadened as she looked up at me. "And we'd weave the blossoms into crowns, necklaces, rings. Once I even made Morgane a cape of them. It was glorious. Her mother—Louise's grandmother—organized a dance that May Day just so she could wear it."

"I'm allergic to pears."

I wasn't, but I'd heard enough. Her smile fell.

"Of course. Forgive me. Perhaps some tea instead?"

"I don't like tea."

Her eyes narrowed. "Coffee?"

"No."

"Wine? Mead? Beer?"

"I don't drink alcohol."

She set her cup down with an angry *clink*. "As you're sitting healthy and whole before me, I presume you drink *something*. Pray tell me what it is, so I might indulge you."

"Water."

She downright scowled then, abandoning her saccharine act. With a wave of her hand over the pot of perry, the spiced scent in the air vanished. The sharp bite of magic replaced it. Mouth pursed, she poured crystal-clear water into my cup. Pushed it roughly toward me.

My gut twisted, and I crushed my palms against my eyes. "I

told you. I don't want to be around—"

"Yes, yes," she snapped. "You've developed a renewed aversion to magic. I understand. One step forward, two steps back, and all that rubbish. I'm here to give you a gentle push back in the right direction—or a not so gentle one, if necessary."

I fell back to my pillow, turning away from her. "I'm not interested."

The next second, water doused the side of my face, my hair, my shoulder.

"And I am not finished," she said calmly.

Spluttering, pushing aside my sopping hair, I lurched upright once more to seize control of the conversation. "The men in the tavern knew I'm the king's bastard. How?"

She shrugged delicately. "I have contacts in the city. I requested they spread the word far and wide."

"*Why?*"

"To save your life." She arched a brow. "The more people who knew, the more likely it was to reach Auguste—and it did. You're wanted *alive*, not dead. Once he discovered the connection, I knew he'd want to see you again, to . . . study you. Your father is nothing if not vain, and children make impeccable mirrors."

"You're *insane*."

"That is not a polite word." She sniffed and smoothed her skirts, folded her hands in her lap. "Especially in light of Louise's new situation. Do you call *her* insane?"

"No." I forced my clenched teeth apart. "And you don't either."

She waved her hand. "Enough. You've made it perfectly clear

you don't desire a friendship with me—which is fortunate, indeed, as you're in desperate need of not a friend, but a parent. It is to that end I now speak: we will not defeat Morgane without magic. I understand you've had two less than ideal experiences with it, but the whole is greater than the sum of its parts. You must put aside your fear, or you will kill us all. Do you understand?"

At her tone—imperious, *sanctimonious*—anger tore through me, sharp and jagged as shattered glass. How dare she speak to me like a petulant child? How dare she presume to *parent* me?

"Magic is death and madness." I wrung out my shirt, stalking to join her at the table, tripping over my bag in the process. Swearing viciously at the tight quarters. "I want no part of it."

"There is more in this earth than in all your Heaven and Hell, yet you remain blind. I have said it before, and I will say it again. *Open your eyes*, Reid. Magic is not your enemy. Indeed, if we are to persuade Toulouse and Thierry into an alliance, I dare say you'll need to be rather less critical."

I paused with a fresh cup of water to my lips. "What?"

She regarded me shrewdly over her own cup. "The entire purpose of this endeavor is to procure allies, and two powerful ones have just landed in our lap. Morgane will not expect them. What Morgane does not expect, Morgane cannot manipulate."

"We don't know they're witches," I muttered.

"Use that thick head of yours, son, before it falls from your shoulders."

"*Don't* call me son—"

"I've heard of Claud Deveraux in my travels. What lovely Zenna professed is true—he surrounds himself with the exceptional, the talented, the *powerful*. I met a woman in Amandine years ago who'd performed with Troupe de Fortune. Rumor had it she could—"

"Is there a point to this?"

"The *point* is that Toulouse and Thierry St. Martin—probably even Zenna and Seraphine—are not what they appear. No one batted an eye when Lou revealed herself as a witch. They were far more concerned with *you* as a Chasseur, which means someone in this troupe practices magic. Claud wants you to befriend Toulouse and Thierry, yes?"

You might have more in common with them than you think.

I forced a nod.

"Excellent. Do it."

Shaking my head, I downed the rest of the water. As if it were that simple. As if I could disguise my disdain for magic and—and *charm* them into a false friendship. Lou could've done it. The thought curdled in my gut. But I could neither forget that look in her eye at the pub, nor the way she'd removed my Balisarda to control me. I couldn't forget the feel of the Archbishop's blood on my hand. My ex-brethrens' blood. My chest tightened.

Magic.

"I don't care if the St. Martins are witches." My lip curled, and I pushed away from the table. We'd stop for dinner soon. I'd suffer even Deveraux's singing to escape this conversation. "I have no intention of bonding with any of you."

"Oh?" Her eyes flashed. She too sprang to her feet. "You seemed intent on bonding with Beauregard. You seemed to care a great deal about Violette and Victoire. How do I earn such coveted treatment?"

I cursed my own carelessness. She'd been listening. Of course she'd been listening—filthy eavesdropper—and I'd shown her my soft underbelly. "You don't. You abandoned me."

In her eyes, our last moment on Modraniht unfolded. Those thousand moments. I shoved them all aside. "I thought we'd moved past this," she said softly.

I stared at her in disgust. Yes, I'd given her peace with her last breath, but that gift—it'd been for me too. She'd been dying. I couldn't spend the rest of my life haunting a ghost, so I'd let her go. I'd let it *all* go. The pain. The bitterness. The regret. Except she hadn't died, she hadn't *left*, and now she haunted me instead.

And some hurt couldn't stay buried.

"How does one move past being left to die in a garbage bin?"

"How many times must I tell you? *I* didn't—" She shook her head, color heightened and eyes overbright. Tearful. Whether angry or sad, I didn't know. Her voice was small, however, as she continued. "I am sorry, Reid. You've led a tumultuous life, and the blame in part is mine. I know this. I understand my role in your suffering." Catching my hand, she rose to her feet. I told myself to pull away. I didn't. "Now *you* must understand that, if given the choice, I never would've left you. I would've forsaken everything—my home, my sisters, my *life*—to keep you, but I cannot change the past. I cannot protect you from its pain. I *can* protect you here and now, however, if you let me."

If you let me.

The words were living things in my ears. Though I tried to bury them, they took root, suffocating my anger. Swathing my sorrow. Enveloping it. Enveloping *me.* I felt—warm, unsteady. Like lashing out and railing against her. Like falling down and clutching her skirt. How many times had I wished for a parent to protect me? To love me? Though I'd never admitted it—never *would* admit it—the Archbishop, he hadn't been—

No. It was too much.

I pulled away from her, sinking onto my cot. Staring at nothing. A moment of silence passed. It might've been uncomfortable. It might've been tense. I didn't notice. "I love pears," I finally mumbled, near incoherent. She still heard. The next second, she'd pressed a hot cup of perry into my hands.

Then she went for the kill.

"If you wish to defeat Morgane, Reid—if you wish to protect Louise—you must do what is necessary. I am not asking you to practice magic. I am asking you to tolerate it. Toulouse and Thierry will never join us if you scorn their very existence. Just—get to know them." After a second of hesitation, she added, "For Louise."

For yourself, she'd wanted to say.

I stared into the perry, feeling sick, before lifting it to my lips. The steaming liquid burned all the way down.

THE WHITE PATTERN

Lou

After two hours of trudging through the shadows of La Fôret des Yeux—pretending not to jump at small noises—a sudden realization clubbed me in the head.

Gabrielle Gilly was Reid's half sister.

I studied the little girl's back through the pines. With her auburn hair and brown eyes, she clearly favored her mother, but when she glanced at me over her shoulder—for the hundredth time, no less—there was something in her smile, the slight dimple in her cheek, that reminded me of Reid.

"She keeps looking at you." Ansel tripped over a stray limb, nearly landing face-first in the snow. Absalon leapt sleekly from his path.

"Of course she does. I'm objectively beautiful. A masterpiece made flesh."

Ansel snorted.

"Excuse me?" Offended, I kicked snow in his direction, and he nearly tumbled again. "I don't think I heard you correctly. The *proper* response was, 'Goddess Divine, of course thy beauty is a sacred gift from Heaven, and we mortals are blessed to even gaze upon thy face.'"

"Goddess Divine." He laughed harder now, brushing the snow from his coat. "Right."

Pushing him away with a snort of my own, I bounded atop a fallen log to walk beside him. "You can laugh, but if this plan of ours doesn't go tits up, that'll be my title someday."

Pink crept into his cheeks at my vulgarity. "What do you mean?"

"You know—" When the log ended, I hopped down, shooing Absalon away again. "—if we kill Morgane, I'll inherit the Triple Goddess's powers in her stead."

Ansel stopped walking abruptly, like I'd clubbed him in the back of the head. "You'll become the Maiden, Mother, and Crone."

"Goddess Divine." I smirked, stooping to pick up a handful of snow, but he didn't share my humor any longer. A furrow appeared between his brows. "What's with the face?" I asked, packing the snow between my palms. "That's how it works. La Dame des Sorcières possesses divine power as a blessing from the Triple Goddess."

"Do you *want* to become La Dame des Sorcières?"

I hurled the snowball at a tree, watching as it exploded on the limbs. What an unexpected question. Certainly no one had ever asked it before. "I . . . I don't know. I never thought I'd live past my sixteenth birthday, let alone plot a revolt against my mother.

Inheriting her divine power seemed far-fetched, even as a child."

He resumed walking, albeit slower than before. I fell into step beside him. But after several instances of him glancing at me, looking away, opening his mouth, and shutting it again, I'd had enough. I made another snowball and chucked it at his head. "Out with it."

With a disgruntled look, he knocked the snow from his curls. "Do you think you'll be able to kill your own mother?"

My stomach twisted unpleasantly. As if answering some unspoken call, Absalon dropped from a pine overhead to saunter along behind me. I didn't look at him—didn't look at anyone or anything but my own boots in the snow. My toes had gone numb. "She hasn't given me a choice."

It wasn't an answer, and Ansel knew it. We lapsed into silence.

The moon peeked out overhead as we continued our search, dappling the forest floor in light. The wind gradually ceased. If not for Nicholina floating along like a specter beside Ismay and Gabrielle, it would've been peaceful. As it was, however, a bone-deep chill settled within me.

There'd been no sign of Etienne.

If I am to consider this alliance, you will find Etienne before the first light of day. Do we have a deal?

As if I'd had a choice.

When I'd called for a pattern to find Etienne—standing at the edge of camp with everyone's eyes on my back—the golden threads had tangled, coiling and shifting like snakes in a nest. I hadn't been able to follow them. At La Voisin's expectant look, however, I'd lied my ass off—which was why I now wandered through a random copse of spruces, trying and failing not to watch the sky. Sunrise couldn't be too far away.

I took a deep breath and examined the patterns again. They remained hopelessly knotted, spiraling out of control in every direction. There was no give. No take. Just . . . confusion. It was like my third eye—that sixth sense enabling me to see and manipulate the threads of the universe—had . . . blurred, somehow. I'd never known such a thing was possible.

La Voisin had said someone was shielding Etienne's location from us. Someone powerful. I had a sick suspicion who that might be.

After another quarter hour, Ansel sighed. "Should we maybe . . . call out for him?"

"You *should*." Nicholina cackled in front of us. "Call him, call him, let the trees *maul* him, boil and butter and split and saw him—"

"Nicholina," I said brusquely, still keeping one eye on the patterns. "I think I speak for everyone here when I say to *shut up*."

But she only drifted backward, clutching the inky hair on either side of her face. "No, no, no. We're going to be the best of friends, the three of us. The very best of friends." When I arched an incredulous brow at Ansel, she cackled louder. "Not him, silly mouse. Not him."

A branch snapped ahead, and if possible, she laughed all the louder. "The trees in this forest have eyes, little mouse. She spies, she spies, she spies, little mouse—"

"*Or* it could be a wounded Etienne." I unsheathed my knife

in a single, fluid movement—unnerved despite myself—and whirled toward the noise. "You should go investigate."

Still leering, Nicholina vanished between one blink and the next. Ismay stared ahead, visibly torn between investigating the source of the noise and protecting her daughter. She clutched Gabrielle's hand tightly.

"Go." I approached them with caution, but I didn't sheathe my weapon. The hair on my neck still prickled with unease. *She spies, she spies, she spies, little mouse.* "We'll take care of your daughter."

Though Ismay pressed her lips together, she nodded once and slipped into the trees. Gabrielle waited until she'd gone before sticking her hand out to me, wriggling with excitement.

Then she opened her mouth.

"My name is Gabrielle Gilly, and *you* are even shorter than they said. Practically elfin! Tell me, how do you kiss my brother? I heard he's as tall as this evergreen!" I tried to answer—or perhaps laugh—but she continued without breath. "I suppose I should call him my half brother, though, shouldn't I? *Maman* doesn't like you being here. She doesn't like me knowing about him, but she's gone for the moment and I don't really care what she thinks, anyway. What's he like? Does he have red hair? Nicholina told me he has red hair, but I *don't* like Nicholina very much. She thinks she's so clever, but really, she's just weird. Too many hearts, you know—"

"Hearts?" Ansel shot me a bewildered look. As if realizing his poor manners, he hastened to add, "I'm Ansel, by the way. Ansel Diggory."

"The hearts keep her young." Gabrielle continued like he

hadn't spoken, nodding in a matter-of-fact way. "*Maman* says I shouldn't speak of such things, but I *know* what I saw, and Bellamy's chest was stitched shut on his pyre—"

"Wait." I felt a bit out of breath myself listening to her. "Slow down. Who's Bellamy?"

"Bellamy was my best friend, but he died last winter. He lost his *maman* a few years before that. His sister was born a white witch, see, so his *maman* sent her to live at the Chateau to have a better life. But then his *maman* went and died of a broken heart because Bellamy wasn't enough for her. He was enough for me, though, until he died too. Now he's not enough at all."

"I'm sor—" Ansel started, but Gabrielle shook her head, sending her auburn hair rippling around her shoulders in an agitated wave.

"Strangers always says that. They always say they're sorry, like they're the ones who killed him, but they didn't kill him. The snow did, and then Nicholina ate his heart." Finally—*finally*—she paused to draw breath, blinking once, twice, three times, as her eyes focused on Ansel at last. "Oh. Hello, Ansel Diggory. Are you related to my brother too?"

Ansel gaped at her. A laugh built in my throat at his gobsmacked expression, at her inquisitive one, and when it finally burst free—brilliant and clear and bright as the moon—Absalon darted into the boughs for cover. Birds in their nests took flight. Even the trees seemed to rustle in agitation.

As for me, however, I felt lighter than I had in weeks.

Still chuckling, I knelt before her. Her brown eyes met mine with familiar intensity. "I cannot *wait* for your brother to meet you, Gabrielle."

She beamed. "You can call me Gaby."

When Nicholina and Ismay returned a moment later—Nicholina trilling about naughty trees—Gaby scoffed and whispered, "I told you she's weird. Too many hearts."

Ansel swallowed hard, casting a dubious look at Nicholina's back as she drifted farther and farther ahead, leaving the rest of us behind. Ismay walked much closer than before. Her rigid spine radiated disapproval.

"You really think she—*eats* hearts?" he asked.

"Why would she do that?" I asked. "And how would they keep her young?"

"Your magic lives outside your body, right?" Gaby asked. "You get it from your ancestors' ashes in the land?" She plowed ahead with her explanation before I could answer. "Our magic is different. It lives within us—right inside our hearts. The heart *is* the physical and emotional center of a blood witch, after all. Everyone knows that."

Ansel nodded, but he didn't seem to know at all. "Because your magic is only accessible through blood?"

"Gabrielle," Ismay said sharply, lurching to a stop. She didn't turn. "Enough. Speak no more of this."

Gaby ignored her. "*Technically*, our magic is in every part of us—our bones, our sweat, our tears—but blood is the easiest way."

"Why?" Ansel asked. "Why blood over the others?"

In a burst of clarity, I remembered the tour he'd given me of

Cathédral Saint-Cécile d'Cesarine. He'd known every detail of that unholy place. And what's more—he'd spent much of our time in the Tower poring over leather-bound books and illuminated manuscripts from the library.

If Gaby's curious nature served, he'd found himself a like-minded friend.

"I said *enough*, Gabrielle." Ismay finally turned, planting her fists on her hips to block our path. She took care not to look at me. "No more. This conversation is inappropriate. If Josephine knew—"

Gaby narrowed her eyes and stepped around her, pulling us along with her. "How much do you know about Dames Blanches' magic, Ansel Diggory?"

Ismay closed her eyes, lips moving as if praying for patience. Ansel gave her an apologetic smile as we passed. "Not much, I'm afraid. Not yet."

"I figured." Tossing her hair over her shoulder, Gaby harrumphed, but a smug smile played on her lips. "Dames Blanches' and Dames Rouges' magic might be different, but it's also the same because each requires balance. When we spill our blood, we weaken our bodies, which limits us. We surrender little pieces of ourselves with each enchantment, and eventually, we *die* from it." She said the last with relish, swinging our hands once more. "Well, if we don't die from exposure first. Or starvation. Or huntsmen."

Ansel frowned, casting me a confused look over her head. I watched as the implication sank in.

Coco.

When I nodded sadly, his face crumpled.

Ismay hurried after us. "Gabrielle, *please*, we cannot discuss such things with—"

"*That* is why blood is the most powerful way," Gaby continued, determinedly ignoring her. "Because we must sacrifice with each cut, and that makes the enchantments stronger."

"*Gabrielle*—"

"Blood is easily given." The words left my mouth before I could catch them. When Gaby peered up at me, surprised, I hesitated. Though she was clearly intelligent, she was also still a child—perhaps only seven or eight years old. And yet . . . she'd also clearly known pain. I repeated the words Coco had told me years ago. "Tears—the pain that causes them—aren't."

They both gazed at me in silence.

"You—" Behind us, Ismay's voice faltered. "You know our magic?"

"Not really." I stopped walking with a sigh, and Ansel and Gabrielle followed suit. They watched with transparent curiosity as I turned to face Ismay. "But I've known Coco for most of my life. When I met her, she was—well, she was trying not to cry." The memory of her six-year-old face flared in my mind's eye: the quivering chin, the determined expression, the crumpled sea lily. She'd clutched it with both hands as she'd recounted the argument with her aunt. "But we were six, and the tears fell anyway. When they touched the ground, they sort of multiplied until we were standing in a pond, ankle-deep in mud."

Ansel stared at me with wide eyes.

At long last, Ismay's hostility seemed to fracture. She sighed and extended a hand to Gabrielle, who took it without complaint. "Long ago, we *did* experiment with tear magic, but it proved too volatile. The tears often overpowered the additives and transformed them into something else entirely. A simple sleeping solution could send the drinker into a peaceful slumber or . . . a more permanent one. We concluded it depended on the *emotions* of the witch when she shed the tears in question."

As fascinating as her conjecture would've been, an inexplicable tugging sensation had started in my chest, distracting me. I glanced around. Nothing seemed amiss. Though we still hadn't found Etienne, there'd been no signs of foul play—no signs of life anywhere, in fact. Except—

A crow alighted on a branch in front of us. It tilted its head, curious, and stared directly at me.

Unease crept down my spine.

"What is it?" Ansel asked, following my gaze. The crow cawed in response, and the sound echoed loudly around us, reverberating through the trees. Through my bones. Frowning, Ismay drew Gabrielle closer. Nicholina had disappeared.

"It's—" I rubbed my chest as the tugging sensation grew stronger. It seemed to be pulling me . . . inward. I dug in my feet, bewildered, and glanced at the sky. Gray light filtered toward us from the east. My heart sank.

Our time was almost up.

In one last effort, I called the patterns back to sight. They

remained as chaotic as ever. In a spectacular show of temper—
or perhaps desperation—I waded through them, determined to
find something, *anything*, that could help locate him before the
sun truly rose. Vaguely, I heard Ansel's concerned voice in the
background, but I ignored it. The pressure in my chest built to a
breaking point. With each pattern I touched, I gasped, startled by
an innate sense of *wrongness*. It felt ... it felt as if these weren't my
patterns at all. But that was ludicrous, impossible—

A speck of white glinted amidst the golden cords.

As soon as I touched it, a single white cord pulsed to life—
wrapping around my fingers, my wrist, my arm—and my sixth
sense sharpened to crystal clarity. *Finally.* With a sigh of relief, I
whipped my head east once more, gauging the time we had left.

"What's happening?" Ansel asked, alarmed.

"I found him."

Without another word, I tore into the forest, following the
white blaze of light. Racing against the sunrise. The others
crashed after me, and the crow careened from its branch with an
indignant *caw!* Snow flew everywhere. Fiercely hopeful, invigo-
rated, I couldn't help but smile.

"Where is he?" Ismay cried, struggling to keep up.

"How does it work?" Gaby soon outpaced her. "Your—your
pattern?"

Ansel tripped on a root, nearly decapitating himself on a lower
bough. "Why now?"

I ignored them all, ignoring the burn in my lungs and running faster. We had a chance now—a real chance to procure this

alliance. The white pattern continued to pulse, leading me closer and closer to victory, and I nearly crowed in triumph. La Voisin hadn't expected me to find him. I'd prove her wrong, prove them *all* wrong.

My certainty punctured slightly as the trees thinned around us and the first tents of camp came into view.

"He's—he's here?" Face flushed and breath heavy, Ismay looked around wildly. "Where? I don't see him."

I slowed as the pattern wove through the campsite—between firepits and caged animals, past Coco and Babette—before curving down the slope toward . . .

Toward our tent.

I stumbled those last few steps, rounding the corner and skidding to a halt. The pattern burst in a cloud of glittering white dust, and my blood ran cold. Ismay's scream confirmed what I already knew.

Propped against the pole of our tent was the corpse of a young man with auburn hair.

THE FOOL

Reid

"Er—" Toulouse blinked at me the next morning, his baguette still caught between his teeth. Hastily, he tore off a chunk, chewed, and swallowed—then choked. Thierry thumped his back with silent laughter. I still hadn't heard him speak a word. "Come again?"

"Your tattoo," I repeated stiffly. Heat crept up my neck at the awkwardness. I'd never needed to make friends before. I'd never even needed to *get to know* someone. I'd simply always known Célie and Jean Luc. And Lou . . . suffice it to say, there'd never been any awkward silences in our relationship. She always filled them. "What does it mean?"

Toulouse's black eyes still watered. "Straight to the personal questions, eh?"

"It's on your face."

"*Touché.*" He grinned, contorting the tattoo on his cheek. Small. Golden. A rose. It gleamed metallic. When I'd sat next to him and his brother to break my fast, it'd been the first thing I'd seen. The first question out of my mouth. My neck still burned. Perhaps it hadn't been the right question to ask. Perhaps it'd been too . . . *personal*. How could I have known? He'd inked the thing right on his cheek.

Across the fire, Madame Labelle ate her morning meal—cantal cheese and salted ham—with Zenna and Seraphine. Clearly, she hoped to befriend them like she hoped I'd befriend the St. Martins. Her attempts had been met with more enthusiasm than my own; Zenna preened under her praise, swelling like a peacock. Even Seraphine seemed reluctantly pleased at the attention. Behind them, Beau cursed. Deveraux had coerced him into helping with the horses, and it sounded as though he'd just stepped in dung.

My morning could've been worse.

Slightly mollified, I returned my attention to Toulouse and Thierry.

When they'd entered the amber wagon last night, I'd feigned sleep, torn with indecision. It still didn't sit right, my mother's plan. It still felt deceitful to feign friendship. But if deceit would defeat Morgane, if it would help Lou, I could pretend. I could tolerate magic.

I could befriend whoever wielded it here.

Toulouse drew a deck from his pocket, flicking a single card toward me. I caught it instinctively. In thick paints of black, white, and gold, the card depicted a boy standing on a cliff. He held a rose in his hand. A dog stood at his feet.

My first instinct was to recoil. The Church had never tolerated tarot cards. The Archbishop had counseled King Auguste to ban all variety of them from Cesarine years ago. He'd claimed their divination mocked the omniscience of God. He'd claimed those who partook in them would be damned to Hell.

He'd claimed so many things.

I cleared my throat, feigning interest. "What is it?"

"The Fool." Toulouse tapped the rose on his cheek. "First card I ever drew. I inked it as a reminder of my innocence." My eyes honed in on his hands. Black symbols decorated the skin there— one tattoo on each of his knuckles. I vaguely recognized a bolt of lightning. A shield. "The Major Arcana cards," he explained. "Twenty-two in all. Ten on my fingers. Ten on my toes. One on my cheek, and one . . . elsewhere."

He expected a laugh at that. Too late, I forced a chuckle. The sound came out dry, rough, like a cough. He and Thierry exchanged an amused glance at my expense, and I ground my teeth in frustration. I didn't know what to say. Didn't know how to transition smoothly to another topic. God, why wouldn't they *say* something? Another silence threatened to loom. Panicked, I glanced at my mother, who stared at me in disbelief. When she waved her hand impatiently, mouthing, *Go on*, Zenna didn't hide her snicker. Seraphine, however, pulled a Bible from her bag and started reading.

My stomach clenched.

"Uh . . ." I trailed off, not quite sure how to finish. *Are you both witches? How long have you known? Did your powers manifest after brutally killing your patriarch? Will you join us in a battle to the death against*

Morgane? Each question rattled around my brain, but somehow, I didn't think they'd appreciate them. Unfortunately, they didn't seem inclined to end my suffering, either. And their smiles—they were almost *too* benign. Like they enjoyed watching me squirm.

I'd probably tried to kill them at some point.

Turning quickly to Thierry, I blurted, "What's your act?"

Thierry's eyes, black and fathomless, bore into my own. He didn't answer. I cringed in the silence. My voice had been too loud, too curt. A shout instead of a civil question. At least Beau hadn't yet returned to witness my failure. He would've laughed himself hoarse. The mighty Reid Diggory—youngest captain of the Chasseurs, recipient of *four* Medals of Honor for bravery and outstanding service—laid low at last by small talk with strangers. What a joke.

"He doesn't speak," Toulouse said after another painful moment. "Not like you and I do."

I latched onto his answer like a lifeline. "Why not?"

"Curiosity killed the cat, you know." With a flick of his wrist, he cut the cards, shuffling them with lightning speed.

I returned his polite smile with one of my own. "I'm not a cat."

"Fair enough." He bridged the deck together. "My brother and I are resident psychics here at Troupe de Fortune."

"Psychics?"

"That's right. I'm reading your thoughts at this very moment, but I promise not to share. Spilling a person's secrets is a lot like spilling their blood. Once it's done, it's done. There's no going back."

I frowned. They weren't the same thing at all. "Have you ever spilled blood?"

His gaze flicked to Thierry for half a second—less than half a second—but I still saw. He kept smiling. "That's none of your business, friend."

I stared at him. *Psychics.* That sounded like magic to me. My gaze flicked surreptitiously over their clothes. Unlike the others', theirs were dark. Simple. Unremarkable. The clothing of men who didn't want to be remembered. I leaned closer under the pretense of examining Toulouse's deck. This close, I could smell the faint earth on his shirt. The even fainter sweetness on his skin. His hair.

"You admit it, then," I said carefully. The scent itself wasn't proof. It could've lingered on him from another. Claud himself had a peculiar smell. "You use . . . magic."

Toulouse stopped shuffling. If possible, his smile grew—like he'd been waiting for this. Wariness tightened my neck, my shoulders, as he resumed snapping his cards. "An interesting question from a Chasseur."

"I'm not a Chasseur." The tightness built. "Not anymore."

"Really?" He held a card in the air, its face pointed away from me. "Tell me, what card is this?"

I stared at him, confused.

"Your reputation proceeds you, Captain Diggory." He slipped it back into the deck. Still smiling. Always smiling. "I was there, you know. In Gévaudan."

My heart skipped a painful beat.

"Troupe de Fortune had just finished our last performance of the season. There was one boy in the audience—couldn't have been more than sixteen—who just *adored* the cards. He must've visited us—what—three times that night?" He looked to Thierry, who nodded. "He couldn't afford a full spread, so I pulled a single card for him each time. The *same* card for him each time." His smile hardened into a grimace, as did mine. My shoulders ached with tension. In the next second, however, he brightened once more. "I couldn't show it to him, of course. It would've frightened him out of his wits. The next morning, we found him dead along the side of Les Dents, left to rot in the sun like roadkill. A Chasseur had cut off his head. I heard he leveraged it for a pretty captaincy."

"Let me tell you"—Toulouse shook his head, scratched his neck absently—"the Beast of Gévaudan didn't take it well. A friend of mine said you could hear his howls of rage and grief all the way in Cesarine."

I cast a furtive glance at my mother. He still saw.

Leaning forward on his elbows, he spoke softly. "She doesn't know, does she? None of them do. For someone who has never performed, you're doing a fine job of it."

Significance laced his voice. I didn't like his implication.

Thierry watched us impassively.

"They think Blaise will help you kill Morgane," Toulouse said, leaning closer still. "But I don't think Blaise will ever ally with the man who killed his son. Perhaps I'm wrong, though. It's happened before. For instance, I thought only Chasseurs were in the business of killing witches, yet here you are." His eyes fell to the Balisarda still strapped to my chest. "*Not* a Chasseur."

My fingers curled around the hilt protectively. "It's a powerful weapon. It'd be foolish to stop carrying it." The words sounded defensive, even to me. At his superior expression, I added, "And killing Morgane is different. She wants to kill us too."

"So much killing," he mused, flipping the card between his fingers. I still couldn't see its face. Only the gold and black paints on its back. They swirled together into the shape of a skull—a leering skull with roses in its eyes and a snake twined between its teeth. "You say you're no longer a Chasseur. Prove it. What card am I holding in my hand?"

Jaw clenched, I ignored the soft hiss in my ear. "You're the psychic. How should I know?"

Seek us, seek us, seek us.

His smile finally slipped. A cold stare replaced it, chilling me to the bone. "Let me be clear. Claud may trust you, but I don't. It's nothing personal," he added, shrugging. "I don't trust anyone— it's how people like us stay alive, isn't it?"

People like us.

The words hung between us, sentient, and the hiss in my ear grew louder, more insistent. *We have found the lost ones. The lost ones are here. Seek us, seek us, seek us—*

"I know what you want from me," he said, voice hard with finality, "so I'll ask you one last time: What card am I holding?"

"I don't know," I ground out, slamming the door on the voices, retreating from their unholy shrieks. My hands shook with the effort. Sweat beaded my brow.

"Tell me if you figure it out." Toulouse's lips pressed tight in disappointment. He returned the card to his deck, rising to his feet. Thierry shadowed his movements. "Until then, I'd appreciate if you stay away from me, Captain. Oh, and"—he flashed another smile, casting a sly look in my mother's direction—"good luck with your performance."

BLOOD DROPS

Lou

The blood witches called it *pendency*—the time between this life and the next. "The soul remains earthbound until the ashes ascend," Gabrielle murmured, holding a cup of her mother's blood. Identical in their grief, their cheeks were pale, their eyes wet and swollen. I couldn't fathom their pain.

Etienne Gilly hadn't died of exposure or starvation.

His body had been burned beyond recognition, except—

Except for his head.

Ansel had vomited when it'd tumbled from Etienne's charred shoulders, rolling to touch my boots. I'd nearly succumbed as well. The hacked flesh of his throat communicated unspeakable torment, and I didn't want to imagine which horror he'd suffered first—being burned or decapitated alive. Worse still, the witches' horrified whispers had confirmed Etienne hadn't been the first. A handful of similar tales had plagued the countryside since Modraniht, and all the victims shared a common thread: rumors of their mothers once dallying with the king.

Someone was targeting the king's children. Torturing them.

My hands stilled in Gaby's hair, my eyes flicking to where Coco and Babette stood watch over Etienne's pyre. He was little more than ashes now.

Upon finding his body, La Voisin hadn't been kind.

Coco bore the worst of it, though her aunt had made it clear she blamed *me*. After all, Etienne had disappeared when she'd agreed to harbor me. His body had been placed at my tent. And I'd—I'd been led to him, somehow, by the white pattern. In the ensuing chaos—the panic, the screams—I'd quickly realized it wasn't mine. It'd been inside my head, inside my *sight*, yet it hadn't belonged to me. My stomach still rolled at the violation.

This was my mother's handiwork. All of it. But *why*?

The question plagued me, consuming my thoughts. Why here? Why *now*? Had she abandoned her plan to sacrifice me? Had she decided to make the kingdom suffer bit by bit, child by child, instead of killing them all at once?

A small, ugly part of me wept with relief at the possibility, but . . . she'd cut off Etienne's head. She'd burned him and left him at my tent. It couldn't be a coincidence.

It was a message—another sick move in a game I didn't understand.

She'd wanted me to know he'd suffered. She'd wanted me to know it was my fault. *Should you attempt to flee*, she'd told me, *I will butcher your huntsman and feed you his heart.* I hadn't heeded her warning. I'd fled anyway, and I'd taken my huntsman with me. Could this be her retaliation?

Could this heinous evil be less for the king and more for me?

With a deep breath, I resumed braiding Gaby's hair. My questions could wait just a few more hours. *Morgane* could wait. After the ascension this evening, we'd leave to rejoin Reid on the road in the morning—with or without La Voisin's alliance. The plan had changed. If Morgane was actively hunting the king's children, Reid and Beau were in graver danger than we'd anticipated. I needed to find them, tell them her plan, but first . . .

Gaby watched in silence as Ismay dipped a finger into the blood, as she added a strange symbol to the whitewashed pot in her lap. Though I didn't understand the ritual, the marks she painted felt ancient and pure and . . . mournful. No—more than mournful. Anguished. Completely and irrevocably heartbroken. Gaby sniffed, wiping her eyes.

I couldn't leave her. Not yet—and not just because of her grief.

If Reid and Beau were in danger, she was too. Morgane had just proved she could slip through La Voisin's defenses.

Ansel tucked his knees to his chin, watching in silence as Ismay continued to cover the white pot with blood. When they'd finished, Ismay excused herself, and Gaby turned to me. "Did you get your alliance?"

"Gaby, don't worry about—"

"*Did* you?"

I finished her braid, tying it with a scarlet ribbon. "La Voisin hasn't decided."

Her brown eyes were earnest. "But you made a deal."

I didn't have the heart to tell her there'd been quite a bit of gray area in that deal—like whether I'd found her brother dead or alive, for instance. I flicked her braid over her shoulder. "It'll all work out."

Satisfied with my answer, she fixed her attention on Ansel next. "I can read their lips, if you like." Startled from his reverie, he blushed and tore his gaze from Coco. "They aren't talking about anything exciting, though." She leaned forward, pursing her lips in concentration. "Something about Chasseurs burning down a brothel. Whatever that is." Sitting back once more, she patted Ansel's knee. "I like the *princesse*, even though some people don't. I hope she kisses you. That's what you want, isn't it? I only want it to happen if you want it to happen—and if she wants it to happen too. My *maman* says that's called *consent*—"

"Why do some people dislike Coco?" I asked, ignoring Ansel's wide-eyed mortification. Irritation pricked dangerously close to anger at her implication, and I glared at the few blood witches around us. "They should revere her. She's their *princesse*."

Gaby toyed with her ribbon. "Oh, it's because her mother betrayed us, and we've wandered the wilderness ever since. It happened a long time ago, though, before I was born. Probably even before Cosette was born."

A sickening wave of regret swept through me.

In all the years Coco and I had known each other, we'd never spoken of her mother. I'd always assumed the woman was a Dame Blanche—Dames Rouges were incredibly rare, born as unpredictably as those with color blindness or albinism—but I'd never sought her out at the Chateau as a child. I hadn't wanted to look upon a mother who could abandon her own daughter.

The irony of my own situation wasn't lost on me.

"La Voisin always goes on and on about how *we ruled this land from its conception, long before the gods poisoned it with dead magic*," Gaby continued. Her imitation of La Voisin's low voice and rigid calm was uncanny. "I'm assuming that means she's ancient. *I* think she eats the hearts with Nicholina, but *Maman* forbids me from saying so." When she glanced after her mother, her chin wobbled a bit.

"Do it again," I said quickly, hoping to distract her. "Another impression. You were wonderful."

She brightened slightly before twisting her face in an exaggerated scowl. "*Gabrielle*, I do not expect you to understand the *legacy* of *what has always been* and *what will always be*, but *please*, refrain from collaring my auguries and taking them for walks. They are not *pets*."

I stifled a snort and tugged on her braid. "Go on, then. Join your mother. Perhaps she needs a laugh too."

She left with little more convincing, and I laid my head on Ansel's shoulder. His gaze had returned to Coco and Babette. "Chin up," I said softly. "The game isn't over yet. She's just a new piece on the board."

"This isn't the time."

"Why not? Ismay's and Gabrielle's suffering doesn't lessen your own. We need to talk about this."

While we still can, I didn't add.

Resting his head atop my own, he sighed. The sound tugged on my heartstrings. Such naked vulnerability required strength. It required courage. "There are already too many pieces on the board, Lou. And I'm not playing a game," he finished miserably.

"If you don't play, you can't win."

"You also can't lose."

"Now you just sound petulant." I lifted my head to look at him. "Have you told her how you feel?"

"She sees me like a kid brother—"

"*Have you*"—I ducked to catch his eye when he looked away—"*told her*"—I leaned closer—"*how you feel?*"

He huffed another sigh, this one impatient. "She already knows. I haven't hidden it."

"You haven't addressed it, either. If you want her to see you as a man, *act* like a man. Have the conversation."

He glanced again to Coco and Babette, who'd cuddled close together against the cold.

I wasn't surprised. This wasn't the first time Coco had revisited Babette, her oldest friend and lover, for comfort in times of strain. It never ended well, but who was I to question Coco's choices? I'd fallen in love with a Chasseur, for God's sake. Still, I hated this for Ansel. Truly. And though I also hated myself for the part I now played in his eventual heartbreak, I couldn't watch as he pined away from unrequited love. He needed to ask. He needed to know.

"What if she says no?" he breathed, so quietly now that I read his lips rather than heard his voice. He searched my face helplessly.

"You'll have your answer. You move on."

If it was possible to see a heart break, I saw it then in Ansel's eyes. He said nothing more, however, and neither did I. Together, we waited for the sun to set.

The blood witches didn't gather at the pyres all at once; they collected gradually, standing in melancholic silence, joining hands with each new mourner as they came. Ismay and Gabrielle stood at the front, weeping softly.

All wore scarlet—whether a cloak or hat or shirt, as mine.

"To honor their blood," Coco had told Ansel and me before we'd joined the vigil, wrapping a red scarf around his neck. "And its magic."

She and La Voisin had donned thick woolen gowns of scarlet with matching fur-lined cloaks. Though the silhouettes were simple, the ensembles painted them as a striking portrait. Woven circlets adorned their brows, and within the silver vines, drops of rubies glittered. *Blood drops*, Coco had called them. As I watched the two stand together at the pyres—tall, regal, and proud—I could envision the time of which Gaby had spoken. A time when the Dames Rouges had been omnipotent and everlasting. Immortals among men.

We ruled this land from its conception, long before the gods poisoned it with dead magic.

I suppressed a shiver. If La Voisin ate the hearts of the dead to live eternal, it wasn't my business. I was an outsider here. An interloper. This vigil itself proved I didn't understand their customs. I was probably reading too much into her persona, anyway. True, La Voisin could be intimidating, and that book of hers was certainly creepy, but—rumors. That's all they were. Surely this coven would know if their leader harvested hearts. Surely they'd object. Surely Coco would've told me—

Not your business.

I focused on the embers of Etienne's pyre.

But what did *dead* magic mean?

When the sun touched the pines, Ismay and Gaby moved in sync, sweeping the ashes into their whitewashed pot. Gabrielle clutched it to her chest, and a sob escaped her. Though Ismay hugged her tightly, she murmured no words of comfort. Indeed, no one said a word as the two started into the forest. A sort of ritualistic procession formed—first Ismay and Gaby, second La Voisin and Coco, third Nicholina and Babette. The other mourners fell into place behind them until the entire camp trod an unspoken path through the trees—a path they knew well, it seemed. Still no one spoke.

"A soul caught between this life and the next is agitated," Coco had explained. "Confused. They see us here but can't touch us, can't speak with us. We soothe them with silence and lead them to the nearest grove."

A grove. The final resting place of a blood witch.

Ansel and I waited until the last mourner had passed before joining the procession, journeying deeper into the forest. Absalon's tail soon brushed my boots. To my dismay, a black fox joined him. She stalked through the shadows nearest me, her pointed nose swiveling in my direction with every few steps, her amber eyes gleaming. Ansel hadn't noticed her yet, but he soon would. Everyone would.

I'd never heard of a person attracting *two* matagots.

Miserable, I focused on Gaby's auburn braid through a gap in the procession. She and Ismay slowed as we entered a copse of silver birch trees. Snow coated their spindly branches, illuminated by soft white light as feu follet winked into existence around us. Legend claimed they led to the deepest desires of one's heart.

My mother had once told me about a witchling who'd followed them. She'd never been seen again.

Clutching Ansel tighter when he gazed at them, I murmured, "Don't look."

He blinked and halted mid-step, shaking his head. "Thank you."

From the spindly branches of the birch trees, a dozen clay pots blew gently in the wind. Reddish-brown symbols had been painted on each in unique designs, and wind chimes—complete with feathers and beads—hung from most. The few unadorned pots appeared to be so old that their markings had chipped and flaked from the elements. In unison, La Voisin and Coco drew twin daggers from their cloaks, pulled down their collars, and drew the blades across their bare chests, using fresh blood to paint over the faded symbols. When they'd finished, Ismay joined them, accepting a dagger and making an identical cut on her own chest.

I watched in fascination as she painted one last symbol on her son's pot. When she hung it with the others, La Voisin clasped her hands and faced the procession. Every eye turned to her. "His ashes and spirit ascend. Etienne, know peace."

A sob escaped Ismay when La Voisin inclined her head, ending the simple ceremony. Her kin rushed to console her.

Coco extricated herself from the crowd and found us a moment later, her eyes silvered with tears. She rolled them determinedly toward the sky and heaved a great sigh. "I will not cry. I won't."

I offered her my free elbow, and she linked hers through mine, forming a human chain. The cut at her chest still bled freely, staining the neck of her gown. "It's perfectly acceptable to cry at funerals, Coco. Or anytime you like, for that matter."

"That's easy for you to say. Your tears won't set the world on fire."

"That is so badass." She gave a weak chuckle, and warmth spread through me at the sound. It'd been too long since we'd done this. Too long since we'd spoken so simply. "This place is beautiful."

Ansel nodded to Etienne's pot, where Ismay's blood still gleamed against the white clay. "What do the markings mean?"

"They're spells."

"Spells?"

"Yes, Ansel. Spells. They protect our remains from those who'd use them for foul purposes. Our magic lives on with our ashes," she explained at his furrowed brow. "If we scattered them across the land, we'd only strengthen our enemies." Here, she gave me an apologetic look, but I merely shrugged. Our kin might've been enemies, but we were not them.

Fresh tears gathered as her gaze returned to the pots. To Ismay keening beneath them.

"I hardly even knew him," she whispered. "It's just—all of this—" She waved a hand around us and hung her head. Her arm went slack. "It's my fault."

"What?" Dropping Ansel's elbow, I spun to grip her shoulders. "Coco, no. *None* of this is your fault. Your people—they would never blame you for what happened here."

"That's exactly the point, isn't it?" She wiped her eyes furiously. "They should. I abandoned them. *Twice.* They're freezing and starving and *so* afraid, yet their own *princesse* couldn't be bothered to care. I should've been here, Lou. I should've—I don't know—"

"Controlled the weather?" My hands joined hers, wiping at her tears. Though they burned my skin, I didn't pull away, blinking rapidly against the moisture in my own eyes. "Single-handedly defeated Morgane? You didn't know, Coco. Don't blame yourself."

"Yes, I did." She wrenched the crown from her head, glaring at the glittering rubies. "How can I lead them? How can I even *look* at them? I knew their suffering, and I fled anyway, while their conditions only worsened." She tossed the crown into the snow. "I am no *princesse.*"

To my surprise—perhaps because I'd forgotten he still stood with us—Ansel bent to retrieve it. With impossibly gentle hands, he placed it back on her head. "You're here now. That's what matters."

"And you are our *princesse, mon amour,*" Babette said, appearing at her side. She smiled at Ansel, not guileful but genuine, and straightened Coco's crown. "If it wasn't in your blood, it is in your heart. No other cares so much. You are better than us all."

They both stared at her with such warm affection—such *adoration*—that my heart twisted. I did not envy her this choice.

And Beau . . . he wasn't even here to offer his handsome, sneering face as an alternative. Taking pity on her, I turned her shoulders to face me. "They're right. You're doing everything you can to help them now. When Morgane is dead—when I—afterward, your people will be welcome in the Chateau again. We just need to keep focus."

Though she nodded swiftly, instinctively, her face remained grim. "I'm not sure she'll join us, Lou. She—"

A scream overpowered the rest of her words, and Ismay bolted through the crowd, face wild. "Where is Gabrielle? Where is she?" She whirled, shrieking, "*Gabrielle!*" Though hands reached out to her—though La Voisin herself attempted to calm her with steady words and soothing touches—Ismay ignored them all, darting toward me with frantic eyes. She gripped my arms hard enough to bruise. "Have you seen my daughter?"

Panic closed my throat. "I—"

"Could she have followed the feu follet?" Placing a hand on Ismay's, Coco tried and failed to pry me free. "When was the last time you saw her?"

Tears spilled down Ismay's cheeks, peppering the snow with black flowers. Begonias. I'd learned their meaning from a naturalist tutor at the Chateau. "I—I don't remember. She was with me during the procession, but I let go of her hand to finish Etienne's pot."

Beware.

They meant *beware.*

"Don't panic," another witch said. "This isn't the first time

Gabrielle has run off. It won't be the last."

"I'm sure she's fine," another added. "Overwhelmed, perhaps. So much grief is hard on one so young."

"We were all right here," said a third, voicing what everyone else was thinking. "Surely none could have stolen her from the heart of our coven. We would have seen."

"They're right." Coco finally succeeded in loosening Ismay's grip, and blood rushed back into my arms. "We'll find her, Ismay." When she looked at me, however, her eyes said what her mouth did not: *one way or another.*

I only half listened as the blood witches spread out across the grove in search of her.

I knew in my bones what had happened here. Morgane must've rejoiced when she'd discovered not one but *two* of the king's children hidden in this camp. Her timing, as always, had been unerring. She'd planned this.

Twenty-seven children, Madame Labelle had said. The king had sired twenty-seven children at her last count. Surely finding them would be like finding needles in a haystack. But Morgane was nothing if not tenacious. She would find them, she would torture them, and she would kill them. And it was all because of me.

"Look here!" an unfamiliar witch cried after several long moments. Every person in the clearing turned to stare at what she held in her hands.

A scarlet ribbon.

And there—staining the witch's palms on contact—
Blood.

I closed my eyes in defeat. The memory of Etienne's head on my boot soon rose up to meet me, however, forcing them open once more. It would be Gabrielle's head next. Even now—at this very second—Morgane could be mutilating her tiny body. She would shear her auburn braid and slice her pale throat—

Ismay's cries turned hysterical, and the others soon took up her panicked call.

Gabrielle! Gabrielle! Gabrielle!

Her name echoed within the grove, between the trees. Inside my mind. As if in response, the feu follet flickered out one by one, leaving us in darkness. Despite their frantic attempts to conjure a tracking spell, they knew her fate as well as I did. We all knew.

Gabrielle didn't answer.

She never would.

At long last, Ismay fell to her knees, weeping, pounding the snow in anguish.

I wrapped my arms around my waist, doubling over against the nausea, but a hand caught my nape, forcing me upright. Cold, dark eyes met my own. "Compose yourself." La Voisin's grip hardened. When I tried to wriggle away, biting back a cry of pain, she watched me struggle with grim determination. "Your wish has been granted, Louise le Blanc. The Dames Rouges will join you in Cesarine, and I myself will rend your mother's beating heart from her chest."

THE FIRST PERFORMANCE

Reid

Twilight had settled over Domaine-les-Roses when Claud took to his stage the next evening—a cracked fountain in town square, its basin filled with leaves and snow. Ice coated the rim, but he didn't slip as he danced along it. With fingers as deft as his feet, he plucked a mandolin in a lively rhythm. The audience shouted their approval. Some divided into couples, laughing and spinning wildly, while others showered Seraphine's feet with petals. Her voice rose above the crowd. Unearthly. Passionate. Too beautiful to be human.

When I pulled at my leather trousers, sullen, my mother tipped her cup toward me. Inside, a pink-colored liquid swirled. The villagers of Domaine-les-Roses fermented their own rose petal wine. "This might help, you know."

I arched a brow, readjusting my pants again. "I doubt it."

She'd donned a new dress for our performance tonight. Black and white. Garish. The edges of her mask had been trimmed with ludicrous poms. Still, no one had assaulted *her* with kohl. My eyes burned. Itched.

Zenna hadn't told me how to remove it without blinding myself.

Worse still—Deveraux hadn't provided a shirt with my costume. I'd been forced to strap my bandolier to my bare chest. Though I'd thrown on a coat for modesty's sake—and to protect against the bitter wind—I doubted he'd allow it during *The Red Death's* performance.

I told myself it was for the best. If a Chasseur hid in the audience, he wouldn't recognize me. He wouldn't suspect his once great captain of parading shirtless. Of flinging knives or lining his eyes with cosmetics. Of wearing a mask that extended into horns. I was ridiculous. Debased. Heat burned my throat, my ears, as a memory surfaced.

It won't kill you to live a little, you know.

I'm a Chasseur, Lou. We don't . . . frolic.

Glaring out at the festivities from the stoop of a boulangerie, I watched as Beau wove through the audience with a tin can and hooded cloak. In his free hand, he held a wooden scythe. Deveraux had thought it a fitting addition to the sinister costume. In the alley beside us, Toulouse and Thierry had set up a tent to peddle their services. To lure the weak with promises of fame and fortune-filled futures. Women paraded past them, batting their lashes. Blowing kisses. I couldn't fathom it.

"They're handsome," Madame Labelle explained, smirking as Toulouse caught a girl's hand and kissed it. "You can't fault them for that."

I could, and I did. If the villagers' feathered ensembles were any indication, Domaine-les-Roses was a bizarre town.

"Being young and beautiful isn't a crime, Reid." She pointed to the young woman nearest us, who'd been watching me for the last quarter hour. Bold. Blond. Buxom. "You have many admirers yourself."

"I'm not interested."

"Ah, yes." She winked at her own admirers. "For a moment, I forgot I spoke to the inexorable Saint Reid."

"I'm not a saint. I'm married."

"To whom? Louise Larue? I'm afraid the girl doesn't exist."

My fingers stilled around the knife in my hand. "And what's *my* name, *Maman*?" She stiffened at the word, her eyes flying wide. Vicious satisfaction stole through me. "Diggory, Lyon, or Labelle? Should I choose one arbitrarily?" When she didn't answer, opening and closing her mouth—spots of color blooming high on her cheeks—I turned away. Resumed rotating my knife. "A name isn't a person. I don't care what a stupid piece of paper says hers is. I made a vow, and I will honor it. Besides," I muttered, "these girls look like birds."

These girls aren't Lou.

"You think Louise has never worn feathers in her hair?" Madame Labelle returned to herself with a thready laugh. "Those are swan feathers, dear boy, and we wear them to honor the Maiden. See that bonfire? The villagers will light it for Imbolc next month—as Louise has done every year since her birth, I assure you."

My eyes sharpened with newfound interest on the girl, on the revelers near her. They clapped and stamped their feet to Claud's mandolin, shouting praises. Fingers sticky from honey almond fritters. Rosemary biscuits. Seeded rolls. I frowned. The entire square reeked of vitality. *Vitality*—not fear. "They dare celebrate Imbolc?"

"You are far from Cesarine, my dear." She patted my knee. Belatedly, I glanced at the door behind me, at the doors of all the shops lining the street. Not a single wanted poster. Whether Claud or the villagers had removed them, I didn't know. "In the north, the old ways are still more common than you think. But don't fret. Your brethren are too thick-witted to realize what swan feathers and bonfires mean."

"They aren't thick-witted." A knee-jerk response. I ducked my head when she chuckled.

"I had to enlighten *you*, didn't I? How can you condemn your culture if you don't know your culture?"

"I don't want to know my culture."

Sighing heavily, she rolled her eyes. "Mother's tits, you *are* petulant."

I whirled to face her, incredulous. "*What* did you just say?"

She lifted her chin, hands clasped in her lap. The picture of poise and grace. "Mother's tits. It's a common enough expletive at the Chateau. I could tell you all about life there if you'd unclog the wax from your ears."

"I—I don't want to hear about my mother's tits!" Cheeks flaming, I stood, determined to put as much distance between myself and *that* disturbing image as possible.

"Not *mine*, you blathering ingrate. *The* Mother's. As in the *Triple Goddess*. When a woman grows a child in her womb, her breasts swell in preparation for feeding—"

"No." I shook my head vehemently. "No, no, no, no, *no*. We aren't discussing this."

"Honestly, Reid, it's the most natural thing in the world." She patted the spot beside her. "You've been raised in a grossly masculine environment, however, so I'll forgive your immaturity just this—oh, for goodness' sake, *sit*." She caught my wrist as I tried to flee, pulling me down beside her. "I know I'm in dangerous territory, but I've been meaning to discuss this with you."

I forced myself to look at her. "Breasts?"

She rolled her eyes. "No. Louise." At my bewildered expression, she said, "Are you . . . *sure* about her?"

The question—so unexpected, so *absurd*—jarred me to my senses. "You're kidding."

"No, I'm afraid not." Tilting her chin, she seemed to think hard on her next words. A wise decision. She *was* in dangerous territory. "You met only a few months ago. How well can you really know her?"

"Better than you could," I growled.

"I doubt that very much. Morgane was my dearest childhood friend. I loved her, and she loved me. We were closer than sisters."

"So?"

"So I know how alluring the le Blanc women can be." As if sensing the rising tide in me, she plucked my knife away and sheathed it in her boot. "To be near them is to love them. They're wild and free and excessive. Addictive. They consume us. They make us feel *alive*." My hands trembled. I clenched them into fists. "But they're also dangerous. This will always be your life with her—running, hiding, fighting. You will never know peace. You will never know family. You will never grow old with her, son. One way or another, Morgane will not allow it."

Her words knocked the breath from me. A second passed as I regained it. "No. We'll kill Morgane."

"Louise loves her mother, Reid."

I shook my head vehemently. "*No*—"

"*Every* child loves their mother. Even those with complicated relationships." She didn't look at me, intent on sipping her wine. On watching Deveraux dance. His music faded to a dull roar in my ears. "But we aren't discussing Lou and her mother, or her mother and me. We're discussing the two of you. Louise has started her descent. I know the signs." She nodded at my unspoken question. "Yes. The same thing happened to Morgane. You cannot stop it, and you cannot slow it down. It will consume you both if you try."

"You're wrong." Vitriolic anger coated the words, but Madame Labelle didn't recoil. Her voice only strengthened, sharpened.

"I hope so. I don't want this darkness for her—and I certainly don't want it for you. Think hard on your choice, son."

"I've made my choice."

"There are very few choices in life that can't be unmade."

Deveraux and Seraphine ended their song to roars of applause.

A small part of me recognized it was our turn to take the stage, but I didn't move. I wanted to shake her, to make her understand. *There are very few choices in life that can't be unmade*, she'd said. But I'd already killed the Archbishop. That was one choice I couldn't *unmake*—and even if I could, I wouldn't.

I'd lied when I'd said I'd made my choice.

In truth, there'd been no choice at all. There never had been.

I loved her.

And if I had to run, hide, and fight for that love, I would. For the rest of my life, I would.

"I implore you to choose carefully," Madame Labelle repeated, rising to her feet. Her face was grave. "Louise's story does not end in happiness. It ends in death. Whether at her mother's hands or her own, she will not remain the girl with whom you fell in love."

Pressure built behind my eyes. "I'll love her anyway."

"A noble sentiment. But you owe no one unconditional love. Take it from someone who knows—when a person brings you more hurt than happiness, you're allowed to let them go. You do not have to follow them into the dark." She smoothed her skirts before extending a hand to me. Her fingers were warm, steady, as she led me toward the stage. "Let her go, Reid, before she takes you with her."

I managed not to impale my mother.

Sweat curled my hair, slicked my skin, as I threw my last knife, untethered her from the board, and pushed through the horde of women who'd gathered to watch our performance. They giggled. Tittered. The blonde seemed to be following me. Everywhere I turned, she appeared, dragging two friends in tow. Batting her lashes. Angling her body to brush mine. Irritated, I spotted Beau through the crowd and beelined toward him.

"Here." I hooked his arm and wheeled him in their direction. "Distract them."

A roguish chuckle sounded beneath his hood. "With pleasure."

I slipped away before the girls could follow.

Claud had parked the wagons in the alley behind the St. Martins' tent. No one would bother me there. I'd have a moment alone to think, to *change*. To scrub my face. I half listened to Zenna as I wove through the crowd, cursing her and her stick of kohl. At least she hadn't painted my lips blue, as her own. Beneath her extraordinary cloak, a silver dress rippled as she lifted her arms to begin her performance. Bangles glittered on her wrists.

"Herald! Hark! Hold dear ones close!" The cadence of her voice deepened, turned rich and melodic. A hush fell over the audience. "For this, a tale most grandiose of maiden fair and dragon dire—and their love, which ends in fire."

Oi. Verse.

I kept walking. As suspected, Deveraux had confiscated my coat. The wind cut across my bare skin.

"Tarasque, a fearsome beast was he, but Martha, gentler far was she." Enraptured, the crowd stilled as she continued her story. Even the children. I snorted and walked faster, shivering.

"Tarasque a mighty fire sprayed, but Martha closed her eyes and prayed."

At the last, my footsteps slowed. Halted. Against my better judgment, I turned.

Torchlight cast half of Zenna's face in shadow as she tipped her chin to the sky, clasping her hands in prayer. "'Suffer not for me, O Lord, but spare my kin the dragon's hoard!' And as her cry did pierce the sky, Tarasque looked down from kingdom high." Zenna spread her arms wide, fanning the cloak behind her. In this flickering light, the fabric became wings. Even her eyes seemed to glow. "'Who is this morsel, luscious treat, who calls to me with voice so sweet? I shall eat her, bones and all!' And so Tarasque began to fall."

Despite the cold, there was something in her voice, her expression, that held me there. My mother's words echoed around Zenna's. *Toulouse and Thierry St. Martin—probably even Zenna and Seraphine—are not what they appear.*

Like the others, I listened, rapt, as she wove her tale of woe: how Martha's family—crazed with fear—offered her up to the dragon for slaughter, how Tarasque took her as his bride and the two fell in love. How, eventually, Martha longed to return to her homeland, where her father secretly lay in wait with a magic chain. How he used it to fell Tarasque, to hold him while he burned his own daughter at the stake.

At this, Zenna's eyes found mine. Unadulterated hatred simmered within them. I felt it in my own chest.

Her voice grew louder, stronger, as she finished the story.

"Mighty was the dragon's roar, as he broke the magic ore. And from their heads did bodies part, those men who stole his love—his heart." Across the square, the blonde wept into Beau's shoulder. Actually *wept*. And yet—I couldn't scorn her. "To this day, he roves above, still grieving for his lady love. He withers crops and salts the earth and slaughters men, who rue their birth. Herald! Hark! Hold dear ones close, for this a tale of tears and woe, of maiden dead and dragon dire . . . and his wrath, which ends in fire."

She heaved one last, tremendous exhale, and her breath in the cold night air billowed like smoke from her lips. Absolute silence descended in its wake. Undeterred, she swept to the ground in a magnificent bow. Her cloak pooled around her as liquid starlight. She remained that way, posed, until the audience finally found their voice. They erupted in cheers—louder even than they'd given Deveraux and Seraphine.

I gaped at her. What she'd done with her words—it shouldn't have been possible. When she'd told me Claud collected only the exceptional, I hadn't quite believed her. Now I knew. Now I *felt*. Though I didn't examine the emotion too closely, it wasn't a comfortable one. My face burned. My throat tightened. For those brief moments, Tarasque had felt real—more than real. And I'd felt sorry for a monster who'd kidnapped his bride and beheaded her kin.

Her kin who had burned her.

Never before had I thought of the women I'd burned. Not even Estelle. I'd thought only of Lou, who wasn't like them. Lou, who wasn't like other witches. *How convenient*, she'd told me before we'd parted. *You see what you want to see.*

Had I burned my own kin? I had no way of knowing, but even if I did . . . I couldn't handle such knowledge. Couldn't bear the consequences I'd reap, atone for the pain I'd inflicted. For the love I'd stolen. Once I would've argued such creatures weren't capable of love. But Lou had proved otherwise. Madame Labelle and Coco had proved otherwise.

Perhaps Lou *wasn't* like other witches.

Perhaps they were like her.

Unnerved by the realization, I barreled toward the wagons, heedless of those around me. But when I almost knocked a small boy to his knees, I lurched to a halt, catching his collar to steady him. "*Je suis désolé*," I murmured, dusting off his tattered coat. His shoulders felt thin under my hands. Malnourished.

He clutched a wooden doll to his chest and nodded, keeping his eyes downcast.

Reluctant to release him, I asked, "Where are your parents?"

He gestured back toward the fountain, where Zenna had started an encore. "I don't like dragons," he whispered.

"Smart child." I glanced behind him toward Toulouse and Thierry's tent. "Are you . . . in line?"

Again, he nodded. Perhaps not so smart, after all. I let him go.

When I reached the amber wagon, however, I couldn't help but turn to watch him enter their tent. Though I couldn't see Toulouse's face, I could still see the boy's. He requested the crystal ball. When Toulouse set it on the table between them—right next to a pot of incense—I tensed.

The boy clearly had little coin. He shouldn't be spending it on *magic*.

A hand caught my arm before I could intervene. My free hand flew to my bandolier, but I stopped mid-motion, recognizing Thierry. He'd tied his hair away from his face. The style emphasized his harsh cheekbones. His black eyes. With the hint of a smile, he released me, jerking his chin toward the tent. I frowned as the boy handed Toulouse his doll—a wooden carving, I realized. It had horns. Hooves. Peering closer, I vaguely recognized the shape of it from Lou's bottle of wine. I wracked my brain, failing to remember its name.

Toulouse accepted it carefully with one hand. He stroked the crystal ball with his other.

Within the mist of the glass, shapes began to form: the familiar horned man ruling over flora and fauna, a winged woman crowned with clouds. A third woman with fins soon joined them. The boy clapped in delight as she flitted through ocean waves. His laughter, it sounded . . . wholesome.

My frown deepened.

When he scampered from the tent a moment later, he still clutched his coin in hand—no. A *stack* of coins. Toulouse hadn't taken from the boy. He'd *given* to him. I stared, incredulous, as an elderly woman stepped up to the table.

"Why don't you speak, Thierry?" I asked.

He didn't answer me right away, but I felt his eyes upon my face. I sensed his deliberation. I said nothing more, however, watching as Toulouse gestured to the crystal ball. The woman extended her hand instead, and Toulouse traced the lines on her palm. Her withered mouth lifted in a smile.

At long last, Thierry sighed.

Then—impossibly—I heard a voice in my head. An *actual* voice. Like Toulouse's, but softer. Exceedingly gentle.

Toulouse and I grew up in the streets of Amandine.

I should've been surprised, but I wasn't. Not after everything I'd seen. After everything I'd *done*. Part of me rejoiced at having been right—Toulouse and Thierry St. Martin had magic. The other part couldn't celebrate. Couldn't do anything but study the elderly woman in Toulouse's tent. With each stroke of his fingers, the woman seemed to grow younger, though her features never changed. Her skin rosier. Her eyes clearer. Her hair brighter.

We stole what we needed to survive. Thierry too watched his brother help an old woman feel beautiful again. *At first, we were only pickpockets. A* couronne *here and there to purchase food, clothing. But it was never good enough for Toulouse. He eventually set his sights on wealthier marks—comtes, marquises, even a duc or two.*

He gave me a mournful smile. *By then, Toulouse had learned real wealth didn't come from stolen trinkets, but from knowledge. We stole secrets instead of gems, sold them to the highest bidder. It didn't take long for us to gain a reputation. A man named Gris eventually recruited us to join his crew.* He sighed then, looking down at his hands. *Toulouse and Gris got into an argument. Toulouse threatened to spill his secrets, and Gris retaliated by cutting out my tongue.*

I stared at him in horror. "He cut out your tongue."

In response, Thierry slowly opened his mouth, revealing a hollow circle of teeth. At the back of his throat, the stump of his tongue moved uselessly. Bile rose in my own throat. "But you did nothing. Why were you punished?"

The streets are cruel, huntsman. You're lucky you never knew them. They change you. Harden you. The secrets, the lies necessary to survive... they aren't easily unlearned. His eyes flicked back to his brother. *I don't hold Toulouse responsible for what happened. He did what he felt was necessary.*

"He's the reason you don't have a *tongue*."

Gris knew the best way to keep my brother silent was to threaten me. And it worked. The night I lost my voice is the night he lost his. Toulouse has been a secret keeper ever since. And a better man.

Unable to wrap my head around such fortitude—such acceptance, such steady calm—I changed courses. "You said you lost your voice, yet I can hear it clearly in my mind."

We found our magic that night—and I'd already paid the price of silence. Our ancestors allowed me to communicate a different way.

That caught my attention. "You didn't know you had magic?"

To my surprise, it wasn't Thierry who answered. It was Deveraux. He ambled toward us from the scarlet wagon, hands in his pinstriped pockets. His paisley coat gaped open over a shirt riddled with polka dots, and the peacock feather in his hat bounced with each step. "Tell me, Reid, if you'd never seen the color red, would you know what it looks like? Would you recognize it on that cardinal?" He gestured to the roof of the boulangerie, where a crimson bird had perched. As if sensing our attention, it took flight.

"Er . . . no?"

"And do you think it could fly if it spent its entire life believing it couldn't?"

At my frown, he said, "You've spent a lifetime subconsciously repressing your magic, dear boy. Such an undertaking is not easily undone. It seems only the sight of your wife's lifeless body was powerful enough to release it."

My eyes narrowed. "How do you know who I am?"

"You'll soon find out I know a great deal of things I shouldn't. A rather obnoxious corollary of making my acquaintance, I'm afraid."

Thierry's laughter echoed inside my mind. *It's true.*

"And . . . and you?" I asked, throwing caution to the winds. He knew who I was. *What* I was. There was no sense pretending otherwise. "Are *you* a witch, Monsieur Deveraux?"

"From one honest man to another?" He gave a cheery wink and continued toward the square. "I am not. Does that answer your question?"

A nagging sensation pricked the back of my skull as he disappeared into the crowd.

"No, it doesn't," I muttered bitterly. The old woman rose to leave as well, drawing Toulouse into a bone-crushing hug. If I hadn't seen her transformation myself, I would've sworn she was a different person. When he kissed her cheek in return, she blushed. The gesture—so innocent, so *pure*—twisted sharp in my chest. Combined with Deveraux's enigmatic exit, I felt . . . off balance. Adrift. Such magic wasn't done. This—*all* of this—it wasn't right.

Thierry's hand came down on my shoulder. *You see magic as a weapon, Reid, but you're wrong. It simply . . . is. If you wish to use it for harm, it harms, and if you wish to use it to save . . .* Together, we looked to Toulouse, who tucked a flower behind the woman's ear. She beamed at him before rejoining the crowd. *It saves.*

PART II

Quand le vin est tiré, il faut le boire.
When the wine is drawn, one must drink it.
—French proverb

RED DEATH AND HIS BRIDE,
SLEEP ETERNAL

Reid

Zenna's necklace—large, gold, its diamond pendant the size of my fist—battered my face as she leaned over my hair. She'd lathered her hands in a putrid paste to style the waves. I pushed her necklace away irritably. Eyes stinging. If I tossed her kohl out of the wagon, would she notice?

"Don't even think about it," she said, swatting my hand away from the death stick.

Beau had conveniently disappeared when Zenna brought forth her pouch of cosmetics. I hadn't seen my mother since we'd parked in this field, either. The villagers of Beauchêne, a hamlet on the outskirts of La Fôret des Yeux, had constructed an actual stage for troupes passing through—much different from the town squares and pubs in which we'd been performing. They'd set it up here this afternoon. Merchant and food carts had followed. As the sun gradually slipped out of sight, laughter and music drifted into the amber wagon.

My chest ached inexplicably. Six days had passed since my

first performance. Beauchêne was the last stop on Troupe de Fortune's official tour. Within Cesarine, Deveraux and his actors would disappear into the catacombs beneath the city, where the privileged of society mingled with the dregs. Uninhibited, wanton, and masked.

La Mascarade des Crânes, Madame Labelle called it.

The Skull Masquerade.

I'd never heard of such a spectacle. She hadn't been surprised.

Deveraux finished buttoning his vest. "A little more volume on top if you please, Zenna. Ah, yes. That's the ticket!" He winked at me. "You look *resplendissant*, Monsieur Red Death. Absolutely *resplendent*—and as you well should! Tonight is a special night, indeed."

"It is?"

Zenna's eyes narrowed to slits. She wore an emerald gown this evening—or perhaps purple. It shimmered iridescent in the candlelight. She'd painted her lips black. "*Every* night is a special night on the stage, huntsman. If you're bored out there, the audience will be able to tell. A bored audience is a tightfisted audience, and if they don't tip *me* because of *you*, I'm going to be upset." She leveled her gilded brush at my face. "You don't want me to be upset, do you?"

I pushed her brush aside slowly. She brought it right back. "You're always upset," I said.

"Oh, no." She flashed a menacing grin. "You haven't seen me upset."

Deveraux chuckled as the voices outside grew louder. The

shadows longer. "I do not imagine *anyone* will be bored tonight, sweet Zenna."

When they shared a meaningful look, I frowned, certain I'd missed something. "Has there been a change of schedule?"

"How very astute." He flicked my horned mask to me, waggling his brows. "As it so happens, dear boy, *you* are the change of schedule. Tonight, you shall replace Seraphine and me as Troupe de Fortune's opening act."

"And you'd better not foul it up," Zenna warned, threatening me with her hairbrush once more.

"What?" I narrowed my eyes as I slipped on my mask. "Why? And where is my mother?"

"Awaiting you, of course. Never fear, I have already alerted her to the change in schedule. Beau is affixing her to the board as we speak." His eyes glittered with mischief. "Shall we?"

"Wait!" Zenna pulled me back to her cot and carefully arranged a lock of hair over my mask. When I stared at her, bewildered, she shoved me toward the door. "You'll thank me later."

Though there was nothing inherently suspicious in her words—in *either* of their words—my stomach rolled and fluttered as I stepped from the wagon. The sun had almost set, and anticipation thrummed in the evening air. It shone in the faces of those nearest me. In how they bounced on their toes, turned to whisper to their neighbors.

My frown deepened.

Tonight was different.

I didn't know why—I didn't know how—but I felt it.

Still grinning like a cat with cream, humming under his breath, Deveraux ushered me to the stage. A wooden square in the center of the field. Lanterns flickered along its perimeter, casting faint light on the hard-packed snow. On the coats and scarves and mittens. Someone had turned my throwing board away from the audience. I couldn't see my mother, but Beau stood slightly apart, bickering with her. I moved to join them.

Deveraux caught my arm. "Ah, ah, ah." He shook his head, spinning me forward and stripping me of my cloak simultaneously. I scowled. Then shivered. Eyes bright with excitement, the crowd watched me expectantly, clutching goblets of mead and spiced wine. "Are you ready?" Deveraux murmured. Instinctively, I checked the knives in my bandolier, the sword strapped down my back. I straightened my mask.

"Yes."

"Excellent." He cleared his throat then, and a hush fell over the field. He spread his arms wide. His smile spread wider. "Lords and ladies, butchers and bakers, plebeians and patricians—*bonsoir*! Salutations! Drink up, drink up, if you please, and allow me to kindly express my deepest gratitude for your hospitality." The crowd cheered. "If you delight in our performances this evening, please consider gifting the actors a small token of appreciation. Your generosity enables Troupe de Fortune to continue providing Beauchêne with that which we all love—unbridled frivolity and wholesome entertainment."

I glanced down at my leather pants.

Wholesome.

As if reading my mind, someone in the crowd catcalled. Ears burning, I squinted in their general direction, but in the semi-darkness, I couldn't discern the culprit. Just shadows. Silhouettes. A shapely woman and lanky man waved back at me. Scoffing, I looked away and—

My eyes flew open.

"Hear me, all, and hear me true!" Deveraux's voice rang out, but I hardly heard him, inching closer to the stage's edge, searching for the familiar woman and man. They'd disappeared. My heartbeat pounded thunderously in my ears. "Honored guests, tonight and tonight only, we shall witness a singular experience on this stage. A wholly and completely *new* act, a saga—a *paragon*—of dangerous intrigue and deadly romance."

New act? Alarmed, I caught his eye, but he only winked, striding past me to the throwing board. Beau grinned and stepped aside. "And now, without further ado, I present to you our very own *Mort Rouge*"—Deveraux gestured to me before wheeling the board around— "and his bride, *Sommeil Éternel!*"

My jaw dropped.

Strapped to the board, Lou grinned back at me. White butterflies—no, *moths*—covered the upper corner of her face, their wings disappearing into her pale hair. But her dress . . . my mouth went dry. It wasn't a dress at all—more like strands of spider silk. Gossamer sleeves trailed down her shoulders. The neckline plunged to the curve of her waist. From there, the delicate fabric of the skirt—sheer, shredded—blew gently in the wind, revealing her legs. Her *bare* legs. I stared at her, transfixed.

Deveraux coughed pointedly.

My face burned at the sound, and I moved without thinking, tearing my cloak from his hands as I went. Lou snorted when I lifted it to shield her, to cover all that smooth, golden skin—

"Hello, Chass."

Blood roared in my ears. "Hello, *wife*."

She glanced behind me, and this close, her grin seemed . . . arranged, somehow. Fixed. At my frown, she smiled all the brighter, lashes fluttering against the silver dust on her cheeks. Perhaps she was just tired. "We have an audience."

"I *know*."

She eyed my hair, following it to the line of my jaw before straying to my throat. My chest. My arms. "I have to admit," she said with a wink, "the eyeliner works for me."

My stomach contracted. Unsure whether I was angry or ecstatic or—or something else—I stepped closer, tossing the cloak aside. Another step. Close enough now to feel the warmth emanating from her skin. I pretended to check the straps on her wrists. Trailed my fingers down the inside of her thighs, her calves, to tighten the ones on her ankles. "*Where* did you get this dress?"

"Zenna, of course. She likes beautiful things."

Of course. *Fucking* Zenna. Still, relief quickly overwhelmed my disbelief. Lou was here. She was *safe*. Slowly, I dragged my gaze up to hers, lingering at her mouth, before rising. "What are you doing here?" When she moved her chin toward Ansel and Coco, who now hovered beside the stage, I shook my head, interrupting.

"No. *You*. What are *you* doing strapped to this board? It's too dangerous."

"I wanted to surprise you." Her smile stretched farther. "And only actors ride in the wagons."

"I can't throw *knives* at you."

"Why not?" When my frown deepened, she wriggled her hips against the board. Distracting me. Always trying to distract me. "Have I exaggerated your prowess?"

Reluctantly, I took a step back. "No."

Her eyes gleamed wicked. "Prove it."

I don't know what made me do it. Perhaps it was the open challenge in her grin. The feverish flush on her cheeks. The hushed whispers of the audience. Unsheathing a knife from my Balisarda, I walked backward, tossing it in the air and catching it with a muted thud. Before I could rethink—before I could hesitate—I hurled it at the board.

It embedded deep in the wood between her legs. The whole board reverberated from the impact.

The crowd roared their delight.

And Lou—she dropped her head back and laughed.

The sound filled me, bolstered me, and the audience fell away. There was only Lou and her laugh. Her smile. Her *dress*. "Is that it?" she called. I drew another knife in response. And another. And another. Flinging them faster and faster as I closed the distance between us, kissing the lines of her body with each blade.

When I'd thrown the last, I rushed forward, breathless with my own adrenaline. I wrenched the knives from the wood amidst the audience's applause. "How did you reach us so quickly?"

She dropped her head on my shoulder. Her own still shook. "Not magic, if that's what you're asking. Your Sleep Eternal hasn't slept in a week."

"And did you—did you get the alliance?"

Lifting her face, she grinned anew. "We did."

"*How?*"

"We—" Something shifted in her eyes, in her smile, and she planted a kiss on the sensitive skin between my neck and shoulder. "It was Coco. You should've seen her. She was brilliant—a natural leader. It took her no time at all to convince her aunt to join us."

"Really?" I paused in pulling another knife free. "La Voisin wouldn't even let me *enter* her camp. How did Coco persuade her to work with us so quickly?"

"She just—the advantages of an alliance outweighed the disadvantages. That's all."

"But she would've known the advantages beforehand." A shard of confusion pierced my thoughts. Too late, I realized Lou had tensed in the straps. "She still refused."

"Maybe she didn't know. Maybe someone enlightened her."

"Who?"

"I already *told* you." Her smile vanished now, and her expression hardened abruptly, all pretenses gone. "It was Coco. *Coco* enlightened her." When I balked at her tone, drawing back, she sighed and looked away. "They're meeting us in Cesarine in two days. I thought you'd be happy."

My brows furrowed. "I am happy, it just—"

It doesn't make sense.

Something had happened at the blood camp. Something Lou wouldn't tell me.

When she finally returned my gaze, her eyes were unreadable. Carefully blank. Controlled. Like she'd pulled shutters between us, blocking me out. She jerked her chin to my knives. "Are we done here?"

As if he'd been listening, Deveraux descended upon us, his gaze darting across the audience. "Is something wrong, poppets?"

I tugged the last knife from the wood, struggling to keep my voice even. "Everything is fine."

"Shall—shall we continue with the grand finale, then?"

Walking backward once more, I drew the sword from its sheath down my spine. "Yes."

A ghost of a smile touched Lou's lips. "Aren't you going to set it on fire?"

"No." I stared at her, thinking hard, as Deveraux wrapped the blindfold around my mask. My eyes. Without my vision, I saw another scene clearly within my mind. The dust. The costumes. The blue velvet. I smelled the cedar wood and oil lamps. I heard her voice. *I'm not hiding anything, Reid.*

It had snowed that evening. Her hair had been damp beneath my fingertips. *If you aren't comfortable enough to tell me, it's my fault, not yours.*

Lou was keeping secrets again.

I forced myself to focus, to listen as Deveraux pulled the

handle, and the board began to move. With each soft *whisk*, I counted its rotation, established its speed, visualized the location of Lou's body in relation to each spin. I'd been nervous throwing this sword at my mother the first time, but I'd known trust was critical to success. I had to trust her, and she had to trust me.

We never missed.

Now—standing before Lou—I visualized the point above her head. Just a few scant inches of wood. Five, to be precise. There was no room for error. Taking a deep breath, I waited. I waited.

I let my sword fly.

The audience gasped, and the sound of sword striking board vibrated in my bones. I tore off my blindfold.

Chest heaving, mouth parted, Lou stared back at me with wide eyes. The sword had lodged not atop her head, but beside it—so close it'd drawn a thin line of blood on her cheek. One of her moth wings fluttered to the stage, severed, as she slowed to a stop. The audience cheered wildly. Their shouts, their praise, their laughter—it made little sense to me.

I'd missed.

And Lou was keeping secrets again.

SHE LOVES ME NOT

Lou

When the last villagers retreated to their homes, bleary-eyed and stumbling, Claud Deveraux broke out the Boisaîné to celebrate our reunion. "We should dance," I murmured, dropping my head to Reid's shoulder. He rested his cheek on my hair. Together, we sat on the amber wagon's steps, huddled beneath a patchwork quilt, and watched as Coco and Ansel joined hands with Zenna and Toulouse. They staggered round and round in a frenzied circle to Deveraux's mandolin. Each tried and failed to remember the lyrics to "Big Titty Liddy." With every bottle of wine at their feet, their laughter grew louder, and their song grew stupider.

I wanted to join them.

When I yawned, however—my eyelids impossibly heavy from exhaustion and wine—Reid brushed a kiss to my temple. "You're exhausted."

"They're butchering Liddy's song."

"*You* butcher Liddy's song."

"Excuse me?" I leaned forward, turning to glare at him. A

smile still tugged at my lips. "Thank you *very* much, but my enthusiasm is everything."

"Except a full vocal range."

Delighted, I widened my eyes in mock outrage. "All right, then. Fine. Let's hear your *full vocal range*." When he said nothing—only smirked—I poked him in the ribs. "Go on. Show me how it's done, O Melodious One. The plebeians await your instruction."

Sighing, he rolled his eyes and scooted away from my finger. "Forget it, Lou. I'm not singing."

"Oh no!" I followed like a plague, poking and prodding every inch of him I could reach. He dodged my attempts, however, and surged to his feet. I bounded to the top step in response, leaning forward until we were nearly nose to nose. The blanket fell to the ground, forgotten. "I'm prepared for shock and awe here, Chass. Your voice had better hypnotize snakes and charm the pants from virgins. It'd better be the love child of Jesus and—"

His kiss swallowed the rest of my words. When we broke apart, he murmured, "I have no interest in charming the pants from virgins."

Smirking, I wound my arms around his neck. He hadn't mentioned our spat onstage or the black fox that slept in our wagon. I hadn't mentioned the cut on my cheek or that said fox's name was Brigitte. "Not even Ansel?" I asked.

After our performance, Coco and Ansel had cornered me, asking how Reid had received the news of his siblings' murders. My ensuing silence had exasperated them. *Their* ensuing silence had exasperated me. It wasn't that I—that I didn't *want* to tell Reid the whole truth, but what purpose would it serve? He didn't *know* Etienne and Gabrielle. Why should he mourn them? Why should he take responsibility for their deaths? And he *would* take responsibility. Of that much, I was certain. If he knew my mother had started targeting his individual siblings, his focus would shift to protecting them instead of defeating Morgane—an illogical strategy, as her death was the *only* way of ensuring their safety.

No, this wasn't a lie. I hadn't *lied* to him. This was just . . . a secret.

Everyone had secrets.

Reid shook his head. "Ansel isn't really my type."

"No?" I pressed closer, the word a breath against his lips, and he climbed the steps slowly, backing me against the wagon door. His hands braced on either side of my face. Caging me there. "What *is* your type?"

He trailed his nose along my shoulder. "I *love* girls who can't sing."

Scoffing, I planted my hands on his chest and shoved. "You *ass*."

"What?" he asked innocently, stumbling backward, nearly busting said ass in the snow. "It's the truth. When your voice cracks on a high note, it gets me—"

"BIG WILLY BILLY TALKED SORT OF SILLY," I bellowed, thrusting a hand on each hip. I stalked toward him, trying and failing to repress my laughter. "BUT HIS KNOB WAS AS LONG AS HIS ARM." When he spluttered, glancing behind toward the others, I said loudly, "Is this what you like, Chass? Does this make you hot?"

The revelry behind us ceased at my words. Every eye fell upon us.

A flush crept up Reid's cheeks, and he lifted a placating hand. "All right, Lou. You've made your point—"

"ITS SHAPE DOWN HIS THIGH SOON CAUGHT LIDDY'S EYE—"

"*Lou.*" Darting forward when Madame Labelle giggled, he attempted to cover my mouth, but I danced out of reach, looping elbows with Beau and spinning wildly.

"—AND IN NINE MONTHS, A NIPPER WAS BORN!" Over my shoulder, I called, "Did you hear that, Reid? A *nipper.* Because *sex*—"

Deveraux clapped his hands together and cackled. "Excellent, excellent! I knew Liddy, you know, and a lovelier creature I will never again meet. Such a vivacious spirit. She would have quite enjoyed knowing she is now beloved by the entire kingdom."

"Wait." I pivoted toward Deveraux, dragging Beau with me as I went. "Big Titty Liddy was a real person?"

"And you *knew* her?" Beau asked incredulously.

"Of course she was. And young William. It's an unfortunate fact the two didn't remain together after the birth of their dear daughter, but such is the nature of relationships nourished solely by appetites of passion."

Reid and I exchanged a glance.

We both looked away quickly.

And *that* is when I saw Coco and Ansel slipping away together.

Unfortunately, Beau saw it too. Scoffing, he shook his head and marched back to the campfire, bending low to snag a bottle of wine as he went. Reid stared after him with an inscrutable expression. As for me, I tried to discern Coco's and Ansel's silhouettes across the field, where they stood near a stream on the edge of the forest. They looked . . . close. *Suspiciously* close. *Alarmingly* close.

Deveraux interrupted my furtive observation. "You fear for your friend's heart."

"I—what?" I tore my gaze from them. "What are you talking about?"

"Your friend." Sagely, he nodded to Ansel. "*La jeunesse éternelle.* He will remain eternally young. There are some who do not appreciate such innocence in a man."

"There are some who are stupid," I said, craning my neck to watch as Ansel—

My eyes widened.

Oh my god.

Oh my god, oh my god, oh my *god*.

They were kissing. They were *kissing*. Coco had—she'd leaned in, and Ansel—he was actually doing it. He was playing the game, making his move. I inched closer, pride and fear swelling within me in equal measure.

Deveraux smirked and arched a brow. "Obviously, there are also some who *do* appreciate it."

Reid dragged me back to his side. "It's none of our business."

I cast him an incredulous look. "You're kidding, right?"

"No—"

But I didn't listen to the rest of his reprimand. Shaking off his hand, I slipped around the wagons. Perhaps it was the wine that compelled me, or perhaps it was the way Coco held herself—stiff and awkward—like . . . like she . . .

Like she was kissing her kid brother. Shit.

She withdrew for one second, two, *three*, before leaning in to try again.

I crept around the stage, hiding within its shadows, close enough to hear her murmur for him to stop. Shaking her head, she wrapped her arms around her waist as if trying to make herself as small as possible. As if trying to disappear. "Ansel, please." She struggled to look at him. "Don't cry. This isn't—I didn't mean—"

Shit, shit, *shit*.

I pressed closer to the stage, straining to hear her whispered explanation. When a hand touched my back, I nearly leapt out of my skin. Reid crouched behind me, radiating disapproval. "I'm serious, Lou," he repeated, voice low. "This is their business, not ours."

"Speak for yourself." Peeking back around the corner of the stage, I watched as Ansel wiped a tear from his cheek. My heart twisted. "Those are my best friends out there. If things get messy between them, I'm the one who'll have to clean it up. It is absolutely my business."

"Lou—"

Coco's head whipped in our direction, and I lurched backward, knocking straight into Reid. He managed to catch himself before he toppled the entire stage, grabbing my shoulders for balance and pulling us both to the ground. I turned my head to whisper against his cheek. "Shhh."

His breath at my ear sent chills down my spine. "This is wrong."

"By all means, then, go back to the wagons."

He didn't, and together, we leaned forward, hanging on Coco's every word.

"I didn't mean for this happen, Ansel." She buried her face in her hands. "I'm so sorry, but this was a mistake. I shouldn't have—I didn't mean for it to happen."

"A mistake?" Ansel's voice broke on the word, and he stepped closer to clutch her hand. Fresh tears trickled down his cheeks. "You kissed me. *You* kissed *me*. How can you say it was a mistake? Why did you kiss me again if it was?"

"Because I needed to know!" Wincing at her outburst, she dropped his hand and started to pace. "Look," she whispered furiously, "I'm a little drunk—"

His face hardened. "You aren't that drunk."

"Yes, I am." She pushed the hair away from her face in agitation. "I'm drunk, and I'm acting like an idiot. I don't want to give you the wrong impression." She clutched his hands then, winging them. "You're a good person, Ansel. Better than me. Better than everyone. You're—you're *perfect*. Anyone would be lucky to have you. I just—I—"

"Don't love me."

"No! I mean *yes*." When he pulled away, turning his face from hers, she visibly wilted. Her voice dropped so low that Reid and I strained forward in our desperation to hear. "I know you think you're in love with me, Ansel, and I—I wanted to be in love with you too. I kissed you because I needed to know if I ever could be. I kissed you again because I needed to be sure."

"You needed to be sure," he repeated. "So . . . each time you touched me . . . made me blush, made me *feel* like you—like you might want me too . . . you didn't know. You gave me hope, but you weren't *sure*."

"Ansel, I—"

"So which is it?" Ansel held himself rigid, his back to us. Though I couldn't see his face, his voice sounded sharper than I'd ever heard it. Meaner. In its pitch, I could almost *see* his anguish, a living thing that tormented them both. "Do you love me or not?"

Coco didn't answer for a long while. Reid and I waited with bated breath, not daring to speak. To even move. Finally, she laid a gentle hand on his back.

"I do love you, Ansel. I just . . . don't love you the same way you love me." When he flinched, violent in his reaction, she dropped her hand and backed away. "I'm so sorry."

Without another word, she turned and fled down the stream.

Ansel's shoulders drooped in her absence, and I moved to approach him—to fold him in my arms and hold him until his tears subsided—but Reid's arms tightened on my waist. "Don't," he said, voice low. "Let him process."

I stilled beneath his touch, listening as Deveraux announced it was time for bed. Ansel wiped his tears, hurrying to help him clean up. "Typical Ansel," I whispered, feeling physically sick. "Why does he have to be so—so—"

At last, Reid released me. "He didn't deserve what she did to him."

Conflicting emotions warred within me. "She didn't *do* anything. Flirtation is hardly a cardinal sin."

"She led him on."

"She—" I struggled to articulate my thoughts. "She can't change the way she feels. She doesn't *owe* him anything."

"It wasn't just harmless flirtation, Lou. She knew Ansel's feelings. She used them to make Beau jealous."

I shook my head. "I don't think she meant to. You have to understand . . . Coco has always been beautiful. She grew up with suitors flocking to her, even as a child, which means she grew up quickly. She's confident and vain and guileful because of it—and I *love* her—but she isn't cruel. She didn't mean to hurt Ansel. She just . . . didn't understand the depth of his emotion."

Reid scoffed and shoved to his feet, extending a hand to me. "No. She didn't."

While the others prepared for bed, dousing the fire and gathering empty bottles of wine, I snuck down the stream to find Coco. It didn't take long. Within a few yards, I found her sitting beside a holly tree, face buried in her arms. I sat next to her without a word. The water trickled gently before us, counting the seconds. It would've been peaceful if not for the snow soaking through my pants.

"I'm a piece of shit," she finally mumbled, not lifting her head.

"Nonsense." In a practiced movement, I parted her hair, dividing each half into three sections near her crown. "You smell much better than shit."

"Did you hear us?"

"Yes."

She groaned and lifted her head, teary-eyed. "Did I ruin everything?"

My fingers maintained their deft movements, adding new strands of hair to each section as I braided. "He'll be fine, Coco. He won't die of a broken heart. It's actually a rite of passage for most." I finished the first braid, leaving the tail loose. "Alec broke mine, and I lived. Babette broke yours. Without them, we wouldn't have found the next one. I wouldn't have found Reid."

She stared out at the water. "You're saying it's fine I broke his heart."

"I'm *saying* if you hadn't done it, someone else would have. Very few of us settle down with our first loves."

She groaned again, tipping her head back in my hands. "Oh, *god*. I was his first love."

"Tragic, isn't it? I suppose there's no accounting for taste." When I finished the second braid, I snapped a sprig of holly from the nearest branch, stripping the berries and tucking them into her hair. She sat in silence while I worked. At last, I crawled around to sit in front of her. "Give him time, Coco. He'll come around."

"No." She shook her head, and her braids came undone. The berries sprinkled the snow around us. "He'll hate me. He might've forgiven the flirtation, but I never should have kissed him."

I said nothing. It would do little good to tell her what she already knew.

"I *wanted* to love him, you know?" She gripped her elbows against the cold, hunching slightly. "That's why I did it. That's why I never shut him down when he *looked* at me like that—all doe-eyed and smitten. It's why I kissed him twice. Maybe I should've tried a third."

"Coco."

"I feel *terrible*." Fresh tears brimmed in her eyes, but she stared determinedly at the sky. Not a single one escaped. "I never wanted to hurt him. Maybe—maybe this ache in my chest means I'm wrong." She looked up abruptly and clutched my hand. "I've never hurt over romance like this in my entire life, not even when Babette abandoned me. Maybe that means I *do* care for him. Maybe—Lou, maybe I'm misinterpreting my feelings!"

"No, I don't think—"

"He's certainly handsome enough." She spoke over me now, her desperation bordering on hysteria. "I *need* someone like him, Lou—someone who's kind and caring and *good*. Why don't I ever like the good ones? *Why?*" Her face crumpled, and her hands relaxed around mine. She dropped her chin in defeat. "We need mothers for this kind of shit."

With a snort, I leaned back on my hands and closed my eyes, savoring the icy bite of snow between my fingers. The moonlight on my cheeks. "Isn't that the truth."

We lapsed into silence, each caught in the tempest of our

thoughts. Though I'd never admitted it to anyone before this moment, I yearned for my mother. Not the scheming Morgane le Blanc. Not the all-powerful La Dame des Sorcières. Just . . . my mother. The one who'd played with me. Listened to me. Wiped my tears when I'd thought I would die of a broken heart.

When I opened my eyes, I caught her staring at the water once more. "Aunt Josephine says I look like her," she said, emotion thick in her voice. "That's why she can't stand the sight of me." She tucked her knees to her chest, resting her chin on them. "She hates me."

I didn't ask her to clarify between La Voisin or her mother. The pain in her eyes would be there with either.

Sensing silence would comfort her more than words, I didn't speak. She'd waited a long time for the right moment to tell me this, I realized. Besides—what words could I possibly offer her? The Dames Blanches' practice of forsaking their children—their sons without magic and their daughters with the wrong kind— was aberrant. No words could ever make it right.

When she finally spoke again, a wistful smile touched her lips. "I can't remember much of her, but sometimes—when I really concentrate—I catch glimpses of blue, or light shining through water. The smell of lilies. I like to think it was her perfume." Her smile faded, and she swallowed hard, as if the pleasant memory had turned sour on her tongue. "It's all ridiculous, of course. I've been with Aunt Josephine since I was six."

"Did she ever visit you? Your mother?"

"Not once." Again, I waited, knowing she had more to say. "On my tenth birthday, I asked Aunt Josephine if *Maman* would come to celebrate." She clutched her knees tighter against the wind. Or perhaps the memory. "I still remember Aunt Josephine's face. I've never seen such loathing before. She . . . she told me my mother was dead."

The confession struck me with unexpected force. I frowned, blinking rapidly against the stinging in my eyes, and looked away to compose myself. "Is she?"

"I don't know. I haven't had the nerve to ask about her since."

"Shit, Coco." Eager to distract her, to distract myself, I shook my head, casting about for a change of subject. *Anything* would be preferable to this distressing conversation. I'd thought Morgane to be cruel. Perspective was a curious thing. "What was the book in your aunt's tent?"

She turned her head to face me, frowning. "Her grimoire."

"Do you know what's in it?"

"Spells, mostly. A record of her experiments. Our family tree."

I repressed a shudder. "What sort of spells? It seemed . . . alive."

She snorted. "That's because it's creepy as hell. I've only flipped through it once in secret, but some of the spells in there are evil—curses, possession, sickness, and the like. Only a fool would cross my aunt."

Now I couldn't repress my shudder, no matter how hard I tried. Mercifully, Claud chose that moment to approach. "*Mes chéries*, though I am loath to interrupt, the hour has grown late. Might I suggest you both retire to the amber wagon? You are undoubtedly exhausted from your travels, and it is unwise to linger alone here at night."

I climbed to my feet. "Where is Reid?"

Claud cleared his throat delicately. "Alas, Monsieur Diggory finds himself otherwise occupied at the moment." At my arched brow, he sighed. "After a poorly timed jest from His Royal Highness, the young master Ansel has succumbed to tears. Reid is comforting him."

Coco sprang to her feet, hissing like an incredulous, angry cat. When she at last found her words, she snarled, "I'm going to kill him." Then she stormed back toward camp with a violent stream of curses. Beau—who spotted her coming across the way—changed directions abruptly, fleeing into a wagon.

"Do it slowly!" I called after her, adding a curse or two of my own. Poor Ansel. Though he'd be mortified if he saw Coco sweeping in to save him, *someone* needed to kick Beau's ass.

Claud chuckled as a shout rent the air behind us. I turned, startled—and perhaps a bit pleased, expecting to see Beau wetting down his leg—and froze.

It wasn't Beau at all.

A half dozen men spilled into the clearing, swords and knives drawn.

AN UNEXPECTED REUNION

Lou

"Get down," Claud ordered, his voice abruptly deeper, more assertive. He pushed me flat to the ground behind him, angling his body to shield mine. But I still peeked beneath his arm, frantically searching for the blue coats of Chasseurs. There were none. Dressed in tattered rags and fraying coats, these men reeked instead of bandits. Literally *reeked*. I could smell them from where we lay, thirty paces away.

Claud had warned us about the danger of the road, but I hadn't taken him seriously. The thought of mere men accosting us had been laughable in light of witches and huntsmen. But that realization wasn't what made me gape. It wasn't what made me struggle to rise, to race *toward* the thieves instead of away from them.

No. It was something else. *Someone* else.

At their back—wielding a blade as black as the dirt on his face—stood Bas.

"*Shit*." Horrified, I elbowed Claud in the side as Bas's and Reid's eyes met. He didn't budge. "Let me up! Let me up *now*!"

"Do not draw attention to yourself, Louise." He held me down with a single arm, implausibly strong. "Remain still and quiet, or I'll throw you in the creek—a most unpleasant experience, I assure you."

"What the hell are you talking about? That's *Bas*. He's an old friend. He won't harm me, but he and Reid look like they're about to tear each other to pieces—"

"Let them," he said simply.

Helpless, I watched as Reid drew his Balisarda from his bandolier. The last of his knives. The rest remained embedded in his turning board from our performance. Bas's face twisted into a sneer. "*You*," he spat.

His companions continued herding the others into the center of the campsite. We were woefully outnumbered. Though Ansel brandished his knife, they disarmed him within seconds. Four more men erupted from the wagon, dragging Coco and Beau out with them. Already, they'd tied their wrists and ankles with rope, and both struggled in vain to free themselves. Madame Labelle, however, didn't fight her captor. She acquiesced calmly, making casual eye contact with Toulouse and Thierry.

A short man with bone-white skin strolled toward Reid and Bas, picking his teeth with a dagger.

"And just who might this be, eh, Bas?"

"This is the man who killed the Archbishop." Bas's voice was unrecognizable, hard as the steel in his hands. His hair had grown long and matted in the months since I'd last seen him, and a wicked scar forked down his left cheek. He looked . . . sharp.

Hungry. The opposite of the soft, cosseted boy I'd known. "This is the man who killed the Archbishop. Fifty thousand *couronnes* for his capture."

Bone White's eyes lit up in recognition. "Reid Diggory. How 'bout that?" He laughed—a jarring, ugly sound—before slapping one of the wagons in delight. "Dame Fortune's right, innit? Here we was thinking we'd pinch a few coins, maybe cop a touch wit' a pretty actress, and friggin' *Reid Diggory* falls in our lap!"

Another bandit—this one tall and balding—stepped forward, tugging Coco along with him. His knife remained at her throat. "Innit there another one travelin' wit' him, boss? A girl wit' a nasty scar at her throat? Posters say she's a witch."

Shit, shit, *shit*.

"Keep quiet," Claud breathed. "Do not move."

But that was stupid. We were in plain sight. All the idiots had to do was glance down the stream, and they'd spot us—

"Yer right." Bone White scanned the rest of the troupe eagerly. "Hundred thousand *couronnes* for the head o' that one."

Reid's hand tensed on his Balisarda, and Bone White smiled, revealing brown teeth. "I'd hand that over if I was you, sonny. Don't be gettin' no delusions of grandeur." He gestured to Coco, and Baldy tightened his hold. "'Less you wanna see this pretty little thing without her head too."

To my shock, Bas laughed. "Take her head. I'd like to see everything else, though."

"*What* did you just say?" Coco spluttered, indignant. "Did you just—*Bas*. It's *me*. It's Coco."

Grin slipping, he tilted his head to study her. He gripped her chin between his thumb and finger. "How do you know my name, *belle fille?*"

"Unhand her," Beau commanded in a valiant attempt at gallantry. "By order of your crown prince."

Bone White's eyes lit up. "What's this, then? The crown prince?" He crowed with delight. "I didn't recognize yeh, Yer Highness. Yer an awful long way from home."

Beau glared down at him. "My father will hear about this, I assure you. You will be punished."

"Will I, now?" Bone White circled him with a leer. "By my reckonin', I'd wager *yer* the one who'll be punished, Yer Highness. Been gone weeks now, haven' yeh? The city's all in an uproar. Yer dad is tryin' to keep it quiet-like, but rumors spread. His precious boy has taken up with *witches.* Can yeh imagine? No, I don' think I'll be punished for returnin' yeh home to him. I think I'll be rewarded." To Reid, he added, "The *knife.* Hand it over. Now."

Reid didn't move.

Baldy's blade left a thin line of blood at Coco's throat. "Bas—" she said sharply.

"How do you know my *name?*" he repeated.

"Because I know *you.*" Coco struggled harder, and the blade bit deeper. Bas's frown deepened inexplicably, as did my own. What was he doing? Why was he pretending not to know her? "We're friends. Now let me *go.*"

"D'yeh smell that, then?" Distracted, Bone White stepped toward her, staring at her blood with a peculiar, hungry expression. "Smells like somethin's burnin'." He nodded to himself. A pleased smile stretched across his face. "Y'know I've heard rumors o' a witch o' the blood. They don' cast wit' their hands like the others. Swore I saw one meself once. Smelled it, more like. Nearly singed my nostrils off."

Bas's voice hardened with conviction. "I've never heard of such a thing, and I've never seen this woman before in my life."

Coco's eyes widened. "You *asshole*. We practically lived together for a *year*—"

Baldy clubbed her in the head. Seizing his opportunity, Reid lunged—at the exact same second Coco twisted, trying to coat Baldy's wrist with her blood. Skin sizzling, the man shrieked, and all three collided in a mass of tangled limbs. More men sprang forward amidst the tussle, wrenching away Reid's Balisarda and pinning them both to the ground. Coco's blood hissed where it touched the snow. Smoke curled around her face.

Madame Labelle looked on with an anxious expression, but still she didn't move.

"Well," Bone White said pleasantly, still grinning, "that solves that, then, dinnit? She'll fetch a right nice price wit' the Chasseurs. We passed some o' them just up the road. Smarmy bastards. They've been scourin' the forest for weeks, makin' a right mess for us, haven't they? O'course, I might just keep 'er blood for meself. Near priceless it is, to the right buyer." Bone White scratched his chin thoughtfully before gesturing to Reid. "And this one? How abouts do you be knowin' Reid Diggory, son?"

Bas's grip on his knife tightened. "He arrested me in Cesarine."

Trembling with rage, he knelt beside Reid, sticking his knife in his face. "It's because of you that my cousin disinherited me. It's because of *you* that he left me for dead in the streets."

Reid stared at him impassively. "I didn't murder those guards."

"It was an accident. I only did it because—" Bas spasmed abruptly. Blinking rapidly, he shook his head to clear it. "Because—" He glanced at Coco in confusion. She frowned back at him. "I—why—?"

"Stop yer blatherin', boy, and get to the point!"

"I—I don't . . . remember," Bas finished, brow furrowed. He shook his head once more. "I don't remember."

Baldy regarded Coco warily. "Witchcraft, it is. Eerie stuff."

Bone White snorted in disgust. "I don't give a damn about witchcraft. All I care about is my *couronnes*. Now, Bas, tell me—is the other one here? The one they're all after?" He rubbed his hands together greedily. "Just think what we can do wit' a hundred thousand *couronnes*."

"There are stilts in the wagon, if you're thinking prosthetics." Coco bared her teeth in a smile, jerking her chin toward his diminutive legs. The men tried and failed to force her face into the ground. "I'm sure with the right pants, no one would ever know."

"Shut yer face," Bone White snarled, his cheeks flushing crimson. "A'fore I shut it for you."

Coco's grin vanished. "Please do."

But it seemed Bone White—despite claiming he didn't care about witches—had a healthy respect for them. Or perhaps fear.

He merely grunted and turned back to Bas. "Well? Is she here?"

I held my breath.

"I don't—" Bas's eyes flicked over the troupe members. "I don't know."

"What d'ya mean, *you don't know*? She's supposed to be travelin' wit this one, innit she?" He pointed his knife at Reid.

Bas shrugged weakly. "I've never seen her before."

Relief surged through me, and I closed my eyes, expelling a sigh. Beneath his rather unfortunate new exterior, perhaps Bas was still in there. My old friend. My confidant. I *had* saved his skin in the Tower, after all. It would've been poor repayment for him to watch as his friends chopped off my head. This—this thing with Coco—it was merely an act. He was trying to help us, to save us.

Bone White growled in frustration. "Search the area."

At the command, my eyes snapped open—just in time to see Reid glance in my direction. When Bone White followed his gaze, I suppressed a groan. "Is she hidin' behind that tree, then?" he asked eagerly, pointing his knife straight at us. "Over there, boys! She's over there! Find her!"

"Quiet." Claud's whisper sent a tingle down my spine. The air around us felt heavy, thick with spring rains and storm clouds, pine sap and lichen. "Do not move."

I obeyed his command—hardly daring to breathe—as Bas and one other bandit stalked toward us. The rest remained poised in a circle around the troupe, watching as Baldy began to tie Coco's hands and feet. She eyed his knife as if contemplating whether to impale herself on it. With a bit more blood, these idiots would rue the day they'd been born.

"I don't see nothin'," Bas's companion muttered, circling us with a frown.

Bas peered into the holly branches, his eyes skipping past us as if we weren't there at all. "Me either."

Claud's hand tightened on my shoulder, silently warning me not to move.

"Anythin'?" Bone White called.

"Nothin'!"

"Well, go on and check down the creek then, Knotty! We'll find her."

Bas's companion grunted and hobbled away. Without a backward glance in our direction, Bas rejoined Bone White.

"What was that?" I whispered, confusion heightening to panic. None of this made sense. Even Bas wasn't this good of an actor. He'd stared at me—*through* me—without giving a single indication he saw me. Not a wink or brush of his hand. Not even *eye contact*, for shit's sake. And *why* hadn't Madame Labelle yet trounced these idiots? "What just happened?"

The pressure at my back relented slightly, though Claud still didn't release me. "Illusion."

"What? They—they think we're part of the tree?"

"Yes."

"*How?*"

He fixed me with his gaze, uncharacteristically serious. "Shall I explain now, or shall we wait until the imminent danger has passed?"

I scowled at him, returning my attention to the others. Bas had started helping Baldy with the ropes. When Baldy moved to bind Reid, Bas stopped him with a nasty smile. "I'll take that one."

Reid returned the smile. In the next second, he thrust his head backward—breaking his first captor's nose—and rolled to his back, kicking the second in the knees. I almost cheered. With uncanny speed, he snatched his Balisarda from the howling man and exploded to his feet. Bas reacted with equal swiftness—as if he'd expected the attack—and used Reid's momentum against him.

Though I cried out a warning—though Reid tried to correct—it was too late.

Bas plunged his knife into Reid's belly.

"No," I breathed.

Stunned, Reid staggered sideways, his blood spattering the snow. Bas grinned triumphantly, twisting the knife deeper, slicing upward through skin and muscle and sinew until white glinted through crimson. Bone. Bas had gutted him to the bone.

I moved without thinking.

"Louise!" Claud hissed, but I ignored him, throwing off his arm and scrambling to my feet, racing to where Reid fell to his knees. "Louise, *no*!"

The thieves gawked as I sprinted toward them—probably stupefied at seeing a tree transform into a human—but I couldn't think past the blood roaring in my ears.

If Reid didn't—if Coco couldn't heal—

I would kill Bas. I would *kill* him.

Throwing my dagger at Coco's feet—praying she could reach it—I dropped to my knees in front of Reid. Mayhem erupted around us. Finally, *finally*, Madame Labelle burst free of her ropes. With each flick of her hand, bodies flew. A small part of my brain realized Toulouse and Thierry had joined her, but I couldn't focus, couldn't hear anything but the thieves' panicked cries, couldn't *see* anything but Reid. *Reid.*

Even injured, he still tried to push me behind him. The movement was weak, however. Too much of his blood had been lost. *Decidedly* too many of his innards were on display. "Don't be stupid," I said, trying to hold pieces of his flesh together. Bile rose in my throat as more blood spilled from his mouth. "Keep still. Just—just—"

But the words wouldn't come. I glanced to Coco helplessly, trying to summon a pattern. *Any* pattern. But this wound was mortal. Only another's death would heal it, and I couldn't—I *couldn't* trade Coco. It'd be like ripping out my own heart. And Ansel—

Ansel. Could I—?

Lou is different when she uses magic. Her emotions, her judgment—she's been erratic.

No. I shook my head vehemently against the thought, but it lodged there like a growth, a tumor, poisoning my mind. Reid's blood soaked my front, and he slumped forward in my arms, pressing his Balisarda into my hand. His eyes closed.

No no no—

"Well, looky 'ere." Bone White's snarl sounded behind me.

Too close. His hand fisted in my hair, ripping my head back, and his other tugged aside the ribbon at my throat. He traced my scar. "My little witch has finally come out o' hidin'. Yeh might've changed yer hair, but yeh can' change yer scar. Yer comin' wit' me."

"I don't think so." Coco descended on him like a bat out of Hell, my knife flashing, slashing his wrist.

"You stupid bitch." With a howl, he released my hair and swiped furiously at her. His fingers caught her shirt, and he pulled her to him, forcing her back against his chest. "I'll drain yeh like I drained yer kin, sell all this pretty blood to the highest bidder at the Skull Masquerade—"

Coco's eyes widened, and her face contorted with rage. Bringing her own dagger up sharply, she plunged it deep into his eye. He crumpled instantly, screaming and clutching his face. Blood poured between his fingers. She kicked him once for good measure before dropping to her knees beside Reid. "Can you heal him?" I asked desperately.

"I can try."

BLOOD AND HONEY

Reid

I slammed back into my body with excruciating pain. Gasping for breath, I clung to the first thing I touched—brown hands, scarred. Distantly, the sounds of men shouting and swords clashing met my ears.

"We have to move," Coco said urgently. She pulled at my arms, trying to lift me. Blood trickled from the crook of her elbow, and charred, bitter magic burned my nose. I glanced down to my stomach, where the flesh had begun knitting itself back together. "Come *on*. My blood won't hold it closed without honey. You have to help me. We have to get to the wagons before the Chasseurs show up."

I looked up, disoriented, and took in the field for the first time. Chaos reigned. Someone had freed my throwing knives, and everywhere I turned, actors and thieves battled.

Deveraux chased one into the trees with a bejeweled rapier. Toulouse and Zenna fought back-to-back against three others. Toulouse's hands blurred in the air, and the thieves fell to the ground instantly. Ansel tackled the knees of another—this one descending on Seraphine. When the man disarmed him, Thierry rushed in, but he needn't have. Ansel nearly bit off the man's ear, and Seraphine kicked in his teeth. Madame Labelle and Beau fought together against the others, the former incapacitating them and the latter slitting their throats.

I tried to sit up, stopping short when my elbow met something soft. Warm.

Beside me, their leader lay still with a bloody hole where his eye should've been.

I pushed him away, scoured the scene for Lou. Found her mere feet away.

She and Bas circled each other like wolves. Though blood oozed from Bas's nose, it soon became clear Lou was on the defensive. "I don't want to hurt you, Bas," she hissed, deflecting yet another of his attacks with my Balisarda. "But you *need* to stop being an idiot. It's *me*. It's *Lou*—"

"I've never met you before in my life, *madame*." He lunged once more, and his blade caught her shoulder.

Her mouth flew open in disbelief as she clutched the wound. "Are you *kidding* me? I saved your fucking skin in the Tower, and this is how you repay me?"

"I escaped the Tower on my own—"

With a shriek of rage, she launched herself at him, swinging up and around until she clung to his back. Her legs encircled his waist. Her arms encircled his throat. "This *isn't funny*. We're trouncing your motley crew. It's over. It's finished. There's no reason to keep pretending—"

"*I'm. Not. Pretending.*"

She tightened her hold until his eyes bulged, and he jerked his knife upward, aiming for her eye. Releasing him hastily—too hastily—she fell on her back in the snow. He was on top of her within seconds, his knife poised at her throat.

Again, I struggled to rise, but Coco pinned me in place. "Let me go," I snarled.

"You're too weak." She shook her head, eyes wide as she watched them. "Lou can handle him."

"Bas. Bas, *stop.*" Lou's hand closed around his wrist. Her chest rose and fell rapidly, as if fighting back panic. "*How* do you not remember me?" He pressed his knife harder in response. Her arms trembled against his strength. "You're not pretending. Shit. *Shit.*"

He hesitated, as if her curses had sparked something in him. A memory. "How do you know me?" he asked fiercely.

"I've known you for years. You're one of my best friends." When she reached up to touch his face, his jaw, his hand eased on the knife. "But I—did I do something to you in the Tower?" Her brows furrowed as she strained to remember. "You were locked away. They were going to kill you unless—" Realization dawned in her turquoise eyes. "Unless you gave them the names of the witches at Tremblay's. That's it."

"You—you know about Tremblay's?"

"I was there."

"You couldn't have been. I would remember."

Finally, she pushed his knife away. He didn't stop her. "Bastien St. Pierre," she said, "we met backstage at Soleil et Lune two summers ago. A rehearsal for *La Barbe Bleue* had just ended, and you hoped to steal a moment or two with the leading lady. You were courting her at the time. A week later, you"—her face contorted with pain against some unseen force, and the scent of fresh magic burst through the air—"you started courting me."

"How do you—?" He lurched away from her abruptly, clutching his head as if she'd cleaved it in two. "Stop it! Stop it, please!"

"I stole your memories from you. I'm simply returning them."

"Whatever you're doing, please, *please* just stop—"

Falling to his knees, Bas begged and pleaded, but Lou did not stop. Soon his wails drew the attention of the others. Madame Labelle—who'd just dispatched the last of the thieves—froze. Her eyes widened. "Louise, stop it. *Stop*," she said sharply, tripping over her skirts in her haste to reach them. "You'll kill yourself!"

But Lou didn't listen. Her and Bas's eyes rolled back simultaneously, and together, they collapsed.

I succeeded in pushing away Coco's hands, in staggering to Lou's side. The smell of incense choked me—sharp and sweet— and I coughed violently. Pain lanced through my stomach at the movement. "Lou." I cupped her neck as Bas regained consciousness. "Can you hear me?"

"Louey?" Bas bolted upright, clutching her hand with sudden urgency. He patted her cheek. "Louey, wake up. *Wake up.*"

Nausea churned as her eyes fluttered open, as she blinked up at me. As she turned to face him.

As I realized the truth.

Lou had lied. Again. She *had* rescued her lover from the Tower.

Right under my nose. It shouldn't have surprised me—shouldn't have *mattered*—but the deception still cut deep. Deeper than it should have, deeper than any flesh wound ever could. I felt raw, exposed, cut past muscle and bone to my very soul.

I dropped my hands, collapsing on the ground beside her. Breathing heavily.

With all eyes on us, none saw the thieves' leader climb to his feet behind Coco. None except Lou. She tensed, and I turned to see him raise his knife with deadly intent, aiming for the spot between Coco's shoulders. A death blow.

"Look out!" Bas cried.

Coco whirled, but the man was already upon her, the tip of his blade poised to pierce her chest—

Lou threw my Balisarda.

End over end, it soared between them, but the man moved at the last second, jerking his arm out of its path. And so it continued to fly, unimpeded, straight past. It didn't stop until it sank deep into the tree behind them.

And then the tree ate it.

My mouth fell open. My breath abandoned me. I could do nothing but watch as the whole trunk shuddered, swallowing the precious steel inch by inch until nothing remained. Nothing but the sapphire on its hilt. And the tree—it *changed*. Veins of silver spread through its bark—once black—until the entire tree glinted in the moonlight. Midnight fruit bloomed on stark branches. Thorns enveloped each bud. Sharp. Metallic.

The kites nesting in its boughs took flight with startled cries, shattering the silence.

Coco moved quickly. With brutal efficiency, she stabbed the man in his heart. This time, he didn't rise.

But I did.

"Reid," Lou said placatingly, but I couldn't hear her. A ringing had started in my ears. A numbness had crept through my limbs. Pain should've razed my body with each step, but it didn't. Agony should've destroyed my heart with each beat. *Gone*, it should've thumped. *Gone-gone, gone-gone, gone-gone.* But it didn't.

I felt nothing.

Without my Balisarda, *I* was nothing.

As if floating above, I watched myself reach out to touch the sapphire, but Lou's hand descended on mine. "Don't touch it," she said breathlessly. "The tree could suck you in too." I didn't drop my hand. It kept reaching, reaching, until Lou managed to wrestle it to my side. "Reid, *stop*. It's—it's—it's gone. But don't worry. We'll—we'll get you another one. All right? We'll—" She broke off when I turned to look at her. Pink tinged her cheeks. Her nose. Alarm widened her eyes.

"Let him go, Louise," Madame Labelle said sternly. "You've done quite enough damage for one day."

"Excuse me?" Lou whirled to face her, lip curling. "*You* don't get to speak about damage done."

Coco stepped to Lou's side. "None of this would've happened if you hadn't waited so long to intervene. These men didn't know you had magic. You could've ended this as soon as it began. Why didn't you?"

Madame Labelle lifted her chin. "I do not answer to you."

"Then answer to me."

At my strained words, everyone in the camp turned in my direction. The troupe members huddled close, watching with wide eyes. Deveraux looked aghast. When Ansel took a tentative step forward, Beau pulled him back with a shake of his head. I ignored them all, locking eyes with my mother. She blanched. "I—"

"Isn't it obvious?" Lou's laughter held an ugly edge. "She wants you to use magic, Reid. She waited until the last possible moment to see if your defense mechanisms would kick in. Isn't that right, mother dear?"

I waited for my mother to deny such an outrageous accusation. When she didn't, I felt myself stumble back a step. Away from her. Away from Lou.

Away from my Balisarda.

"I almost died," I said simply.

Madame Labelle's face crumpled, and she stepped closer, lifting a mournful hand. "I never would've let you—"

"You almost didn't have a choice." Turning on my heel, I strode toward the amber wagon. Lou moved behind, but I couldn't look at her. Couldn't trust myself to speak.

"Reid—"

Without a word, I shut the door in her face.

The door couldn't keep Coco away.

She wasted no time in following me, in accosting me with honey. With jerky movements, she pulled the jar of amber liquid from her bag and tossed it to me. "You're bleeding."

My eyes dropped to my stomach, where my wound had pulled open. I hadn't noticed it. Even now—as fresh blood seeped through my shirt—a bone-deep weariness settled within me. Lou's and my mother's voices rose outside. Still arguing. I closed my eyes.

This will always be your life with her—running, hiding, fighting.

No. My eyes snapped open, and I pushed the thought away.

Coco crossed the wagon to kneel at my side. Dipping a bloody finger into the jar of honey, she rubbed the mixture over my wound. The flesh drew together almost instantly.

"Why did your blood burn that man?" I asked, voice hollow.

"A Dame Rouge's blood is poison to her enemies."

"Oh." I nodded mechanically. As if it made sense. "Right."

Finished, she rose to her feet, staring at me as if deliberating. After several awkward seconds, she pressed a fresh vial of blood and honey into my palm. "What happened out there wasn't fair to anyone, least of all you." She closed my fingers around the vial. It was still warm. "Take it. I think you'll need it before all of this is over."

I glanced back at my stomach in confusion. The wound had already healed.

She gave me a grim smile. "It isn't for your flesh. It's for your heart."

DAGGER OF BONE

Lou

Deveraux insisted we keep moving. With bodies piled up outside of Beauchêne, it would only be a matter of time before someone alerted the local authorities. We needed to be far, *far* away before that happened. Fortunately, Deveraux didn't seem to sleep like a normal person, so he harnessed the horses immediately.

Unfortunately, he suggested I join him.

The wagon rocked beneath us as he eased the horses into motion.

One of the twins drove the wagon behind us. The *amber wagon*, Claud had called it. I didn't care about its name. I only cared that Reid was currently inside it, and I was not.

Reid *and* Coco. I should've been grateful they were getting along.

I wasn't.

Burrowing deeper in my blanket, I glared up at the stars. Claud chuckled. "*Couronne* for your thoughts, little one?"

"Do you have a family, Monsieur Deveraux?" The words

popped out of their own volition, and I resisted the urge to clap a hand over my mouth.

With a knowing look—as if he'd been expecting such a question—he coaxed the horses into a trot. "As a matter of fact, I do. Two elder sisters. Terrifying creatures, to be sure."

"And . . . parents?" I asked, curious despite myself.

"If I ever did, I no longer recall them."

"How old are you?"

He chuckled, his eyes cutting to mine. "What an impolite question."

"What a frustratingly vague answer." When his chuckle deepened to a laugh, I switched tactics, narrowing my eyes. "Why are you so interested in me, Deveraux? You know I'm married, right?"

He wiped a tear from his eye. "Dear child, a pervert I am not—"

"What is it, then? Why are you helping us?"

Pursing his lips, he considered. "Perhaps because the world needs a whit less hate and a trifle more love. Does that answer suffice?"

"No." I rolled my eyes, crossing my arms and feeling petulant. A second later, my eyes drifted back to him of their own accord. "Have *you* ever been in love?"

"Ah." He shook his head, eyes turning inward. "Love. The most elusive of mistresses. In all my years, I must confess to finding her only twice. The first was a headstrong young shepherd much like your Reid, and the second . . . well, that wound is not quite healed. It would be foolish to reopen it."

In all my years. It was an odd turn of phrase for someone who appeared to be in his forties.

"How old *are* you?" I asked again, louder this time.

"Very old."

Odd, indeed. I stared at him. "*What* are you?"

He chuckled, his eyes cutting to mine. "I simply . . . am."

"That's not an answer."

"Of course it is. Why must I bind myself to fit your expectations?"

The rest of the conversation—indeed, the rest of the *night*—passed in a similarly frustrating fashion. When the sky had lightened from pitch black to dusky gray to dazzling pink, I was no closer to figuring out the mystery of Claud Deveraux.

"We near Cesarine, little one." He nudged my shoulder and motioned to the east, where wisps of chimney smoke curled into the golden light of dawn. Pulling gently on the reins, he slowed the horses. "I dare venture no closer. Wake your companions. Though her own lodgings have burned, I believe Madame Labelle has contacts within the city. Together, we shall procure a safe place for your return, but we must say *adieu* for now."

For now.

I studied his placid face in bemusement. It made no sense, him helping us. None at all. The suspicious side of my nature cried foul—surely he had hidden motives—but the practical side told it to shut the hell up and thank him.

So I did.

He merely clasped my hand in both of his own, staring me directly in the eye. "Be safe, my darling, while we part. Be safe until we meet again."

I knocked softly on the wagon door.

"Reid?" When he didn't answer, I heaved a sigh, resting my forehead against the wood. "It's time to go."

No response.

Despair threatened to swallow me whole.

Once, when I was a child, my mother took an influential lover—a man from *la noblesse*. When she tired of him, she banished him from the Chateau, but he didn't leave easily. No, this was a man unaccustomed to rejection, with nearly infinite funds and power at his disposal. He soon hired men to haunt the forest, capturing our sisters and torturing them to reveal the Chateau's location. My mother's location.

He was an idiot. I hadn't been sorry when she'd killed him.

I *had* been sorry when she'd cut open his chest and filled him with rocks, dumping his corpse into L'Eau Mélancolique. I'd watched him sink out of sight with a sense of shame. His wife would never know what had happened to him. Or his children.

"Fret not, darling," Morgane had whispered, her bloody fingers squeezing mine in reassurance. "Though a secret is a lie in pretty clothing, some secrets must be kept."

But I hadn't been reassured. I'd been sick.

This silence between Reid and me felt something like that— like leaping into the sea with rocks in my chest, helpless to stop sinking. To stop bleeding. Only it wasn't my mother who had cut me open this time.

It was me.

I knocked harder. "Reid. I know you're there. Can I come in? Please?"

The door finally cracked open, and there he stood, staring down at me. I offered a tentative smile. He didn't return it—which was *fine*. Really. It was. If I kept saying it, maybe it'd become true. After several awkward seconds, Coco swung the door open and stepped outside. Ansel followed. "We'll be right back," she promised, touching my arm as she passed. "We just need to . . . be somewhere else."

Reid closed the door behind me.

"I should pack too," I said, my voice overly bright. Cursing internally, I cleared my throat and adopted a more natural tone. "I mean—there isn't much to pack, but still. The quicker we're on the road again, the better, right? The funeral *is* tomorrow. We only have today to convince Blaise to join us." I cringed into the silence. "If you need more time here, though, one of Claud's horses threw a shoe, so they aren't waiting on *us*, per se. More like Thierry. I think he's the troupe farrier, something about apprenticing for a man up in Amandine . . ." Hunched over his bag, Reid gave no indication he was listening. I kept talking anyway, incapable of stopping. "He might be the only person alive who speaks less than you do." I gave a weak chuckle. "He's quite the brooding hero. Did—did I see him using magic against the bandits last night? Are he and his brother—?"

Reid gave a terse nod.

"And . . . did you *happen* to persuade them into joining us against Morgane?"

Though his entire body tensed, he still didn't turn. "No."

My nausea intensified to something akin to guilt. "Reid . . ." Something in my voice finally made him turn. "Last night was my fault. Sometimes I just *react*—" I blew out a frustrated breath, worrying a strand of my hair. "I didn't mean to lose your Balisarda. I'm so sorry."

For everything.

He caught the strand of my hair, and we both watched it slide through his fingers. I willed him to hold me, to kiss away this tension between us. He handed me a clean shirt instead. "I know."

The rigidity of his shoulders said what he did not.

But it's still gone.

I wanted to shake him. I wanted to scream and rage until I shattered the reproachful silence he cloaked himself in like armor. I wanted to tie us together until we bruised from the binds and *force* him to talk to me.

Of course, I did none of those things.

Whistling low, I trailed my fingers across the lowest shelf. Unable to sit still. Baskets of dried fruit, eggs, and bread cluttered the space, along with wooden toy soldiers and peacock feathers. An odd coalition. "I can't believe you found others so quickly. I'd gone my entire life without meeting a single one." I shrugged and slid a peacock feather behind my ear. "*True*, most of that life I spent sequestered in the Chateau—where no one would believe such a thing—and the rest I spent thieving in the streets, but still." Whirling to face him, I stuck a feather behind his ear as well. He grumbled irritably but didn't remove it. "I know I'm the first to flip fate the bird, but what are the chances?"

Reid stuffed the last of his clothing in his bag. "Deveraux collects things."

I eyed the cluttered shelves. "I can see that."

"No. He collects *us*."

"Oh." I grimaced. "And no one thinks that's weird?"

"Everything about Deveraux is weird." He cinched his bag shut, throwing it over his shoulder—then stilled, gaze falling to the table. Mine followed. A book lay open there. A journal. We both stared at it for a split second.

Then we lunged.

"Ah ah ah." Snatching the book from beneath his fingers, I cackled and danced away. "You're getting slow, old man. Now— where were we? Ah, yes." I pointed at the leather cover. "Another delicious journal. One would *think* you'd have learned your lesson about leaving these lying about." He sprang at me, but I leapt atop his cot, swinging the pages out of reach. He didn't return my grin. A small voice in my head warned I should stop—warned this behavior, once entertaining, was now decidedly not—even as I opened my mouth to continue. "What shall we find in this one? Sonnets praising my wit and charm? Portraits immortalizing my beauty?"

I was still laughing when a leaf of parchment shook free.

I caught it absently, turning it over to examine it.

It was a drawing of his face—a masterful charcoal portrait of Reid Diggory. Clad in full Chasseur regalia, he stared up at me with an intensity that transcended the page, unnerving in its depth. I leaned closer in fascination. He seemed younger here, the lines of his face smoother, rounder. The cut of his hair short and neat. Save the four angry gashes peeking above his collar, he looked as immaculate as the man I'd married.

"How old were you here?" I traced the captain's medal on his coat, vaguely recognizing it from our time together at the Tower. It'd been nondescript then, a simple piece of his uniform. I'd hardly noticed it. Now, however, it seemed to consume the entire portrait. I couldn't tear my eyes away.

Abruptly, Reid stepped backward, dropping his arms. "I'd just turned sixteen."

"How can you tell?"

"The wounds at my neck."

"Which are from . . . ?"

He tugged the portrait away and shoved it into his bag. "I told you how." His hands moved swiftly now, gathering my own bag and tossing it to me. I caught it without a word. The beginning of a memory took shape in my mind, blurry around the edges. Sharpening with every second.

How did you become captain?

Are you sure you want to know?

Yes.

"Are you ready?" Reid threw his bag over his shoulder, eyes sweeping the clutter of the cot for any forgotten belongings. "If we're going to reach Le Ventre by nightfall, we need to leave now. Les Dents is treacherous, but at least it's a road. We're venturing into the wild."

I stepped down from his cot on wooden legs. "You've been to Le Ventre before, haven't you?"

He nodded tersely.

A few months after I joined the Chasseurs, I found a pack of loup garou outside the city.

"There won't be any bounty hunters or thieves there," he added. "No witches either."

We killed them.

I grew roots at the realization.

Glancing at me over his shoulder, he pushed open the door. "What is it?"

"The werewolves you found outside the city . . . the ones you killed to become captain . . . were they—?"

Reid's expression shuttered. He didn't move for a long moment. Then, curiously, he drew a peculiar knife from his bandolier. Its handle had been carved from bone into the shape of a howling—

The breath left my chest in a rush.

A howling wolf.

"Oh, god," I whispered, acid coating my tongue.

"A gift from the"—Reid's throat bobbed—"from the Archbishop. To celebrate my first kill. He gave it to me at my captain ceremony."

I retreated a step, knocking into the table. The teacups there shuddered. "Tell me that isn't what I think it is, Reid. Tell me that isn't the bone of a *werewolf.*"

"I can't tell you that."

"*Shit*, man." I charged toward him now, reaching behind to wrench the door shut. The others couldn't overhear this. Not when we were moments away from journeying deep into the belly of the beast—a beast that'd be much less amenable to an alliance while we carried around the bones of its *dead*. "Whose bone was it? Fuck. What if it belonged to one of Blaise's relatives? What if he remembers?"

"He will."

"*What?*"

"He'll remember." Reid's voice resumed that irritating steadiness, that deadly calm. "I slaughtered his son."

I gaped at him. "You cannot be serious."

"You think I'd joke about this?"

"I think it'd *better* be a joke. I think a piss poor joke would be a hell of a lot better than a piss poor plan." I sank onto his cot, eyes still wide with disbelief. "I can't believe you. This—this was your plan. *You* were the one who wanted to tear across the kingdom in a mad dash to gather allies. Do you really think Blaise will want to cozy up with the murderer of his child? Why didn't you mention this earlier?"

"Would it have changed anything?"

"Of course it would have!" I pinched the bridge of my nose, squeezing my eyes shut tight. "All right. We'll adapt. We can—we can ride into Cesarine with Claud. Auguste might still join us, and La Voisin has already agreed—"

"No." Though he knelt between my knees, he took care not to touch me. Tension still radiated from his shoulders, his clenched jaw. He hadn't yet forgiven me. "We need Blaise as an ally."

"Now isn't the time for one of your principled stands, Reid."

"I'll accept the consequences of my actions."

I barely resisted the urge to stamp my foot. Just *barely*. "Well, I'm sure he'll appreciate your gallantry. You know—when he's tearing out your throat."

"He won't tear out my throat." Now Reid did touch me, the slightest brush of his fingers across my knee. My skin there tingled. "The werewolves value strength. I'll challenge Blaise to a duel to fulfill my blood debt. He won't be able to resist the opportunity to avenge his son. If I win, we'll have demonstrated we're strong allies—perhaps stronger than even Morgane."

A beat of silence.

"And if you lose?"

"I'll die."

UNTIL ONE OF US IS DEAD

Reid

The forest swallowed us when we left the road. Trees grew thicker, the terrain rugged. In some places, the canopy above blocked all sunlight. Only our footsteps broke the silence. It was slightly warmer here. Muddier. From experience, I knew the farther south we traveled, the wetter the ground would become. With luck, it would be low tide when we reached the cold-water swamp of Le Ventre.

"What an absolute armpit of a place." Beau blew into his hands to warm them. "It's been woefully misnamed."

When no one answered him, he heaved a dramatic sigh.

Coco had taken shelter beside me. Ansel didn't return her covert glances. With the threat of imminent death no longer upon them, their rift had reopened. He hadn't spoken a word since our departure. Neither had Lou. Her silence weighed upon me heavily, but I couldn't bring myself to assuage it. Shame and anger still smoldered deep in my gut.

"It's a real pity," Beau finally muttered, shaking his head and looking at each of us in turn. His eyes shone with disappointment. "I know you're all too preoccupied with your pining to notice, but I just caught my reflection in that last puddle—and *damn*, I look good."

Coco smacked him upside the head. "Do you ever think of anyone but yourself?"

He rubbed the spot ruefully. "Not really, no."

Lou grinned.

"Enough." I hung my bag on a low-lying limb. "We can stop here for midday meal."

"And *eat*." Lou pulled out a hunk of cheese with a moan. Deveraux had kindly supplied us with rations for the journey. Breaking off a piece, she offered it to Ansel. He didn't accept.

"When you're finished," he murmured, sitting on the root beside her, "I thought maybe we could train. We skipped yesterday." To me, he added, "It'll only take a moment."

Lou barked a laugh. "We don't need his permission, Ansel."

Beau helped himself to Lou's cheese instead. "I hope this isn't alluding to his not-so-valiant attempt at swordplay last night."

"He *was* valiant," Lou snapped.

"Don't forget I was there when the men burst into our wagon, Beau," Coco said sweetly. His eyes narrowed. "You almost pissed down your leg."

"Stop it." Voice low, Ansel stared determinedly at Coco's feet. "I don't need you to defend me."

"That's rich." Beau pointed to Ansel's arm. "You're still bleeding. You tripped and cut yourself during the fight, didn't you?

You're lucky the brigands disarmed you."

"Shut your mouth, Beau, before I shut it for you." Lou shoved to her feet, dragging Ansel up as well. She examined the cut on his arm before handing him her knife. "Of course we can train. Just ignore that bastard."

"I don't think *I* am the—"

I interrupted before he could finish. "We don't have time for this. The Chasseurs were near last night. Ansel will be fine. He trained with us in the Tower."

"Yes." Lou knelt over me, tugging another blade from my bandolier. The sheath by my heart remained painfully empty. "That's the problem."

My lip curled of its own volition. "Excuse me?"

"It's just that—how do I put this—" She tilted her head to consider me, puffing air from her cheeks with a crude sound. "Don't be offended, but Chasseurs have a certain reputation for being, well . . . archaic. *Gallant.*"

"Gallant," I repeated stiffly.

"Don't get me wrong, those injections of yours were a vicious step in the right direction, but historically, your brotherhood seems to suffer from delusions of grandeur. Knight errantry and the like. Protectors of the meek and defenseless, operating under a strict code of moral conduct."

"And that's wrong?" Ansel asked.

"There's no place for morality in a fight, Ansel. Not with bandits or bounty hunters. Not with witches." Her gaze hardened. "And not with Chasseurs, either. You're one of us now.

That means you're no longer meek *or* defenseless. Those men you called brothers won't hesitate to burn you. It's life or death—yours or theirs."

I scoffed. "Ridiculous."

Yes, Lou had cut down the bounty hunters with relative ease. She'd slaughtered the criminals in the smithy and defeated the witch in the Tower. But if she thought she knew better than generations of Chasseurs . . . if she thought she could teach Ansel more than the best fighters in the kingdom . . .

She knew nothing. Trickery might work against bounty hunters and common criminals, but against Chasseurs, skill and strategy were necessary. Fundamentals built upon through years of careful study and training. Patience. Strength. Discipline. For all her skill, Lou possessed none of these. And why would she? She was a witch, trained in darker arts than *patience*. Her time in the streets—clearly her only education in combat—had been short and furtive. She'd spent more time hiding in attics than fighting.

"Ridiculous," I repeated.

"You seem quite confident, Chass." She lifted my knife slowly, angling the blade to reflect the afternoon sunlight. "Perhaps we should give Ansel a demonstration."

"Very funny."

"I'm not laughing."

I stared at her. "I can't fight you. It wouldn't be fair."

Her eyes flashed. "I agree. Not fair in the slightest. But I fear Ansel isn't the only one in need of a lesson today. I would hate for either of you to walk away with the wrong impression."

"No." Rising, I crossed my arms and glared at her. "I won't do it. Don't ask me."

"Why not? You have nothing to fear. You *are* the strongest of us, after all. Aren't you?"

She stepped closer, her chest brushing my stomach, and stroked a finger down my cheek. Her skin flickered, and her voice deepened. Multiplied. Just like it had in the pub. Blood pounded in my ears. Without my Balisarda, I could feel the pull of her magic beneath my skin. Already, my muscles began to relax, my blood to cool. A pleasant numbness crept down my spine.

"You're curious." Her voice was a purr as she circled me, her breath warm against my neck. Ansel, Beau, and Coco watched with wide eyes. "Admit it. You want to know what it feels like. You want to see it—this part of me. This part of *you*. It scares you, but you're curious. So, so curious." Her tongue flicked out, licking the shell of my ear. Heat spiked through my belly. "Don't you trust me?"

She was right. I *did* want to see. I wanted to know. This emptiness on her face was foreign and strange, yet I—

No. I shook my head fiercely. I didn't want to see it at all. Only yesterday, I'd watched her nearly kill herself with magic. She shouldn't do this. *We* shouldn't do this. It wasn't right. It wasn't Lou. It wasn't—

Surrender.

Those strange, unfamiliar voices brushed against my innermost thoughts once more, caressing me. Coaxing me. "Of course I trust you."

"Prove it." She reached up to run her fingers through my

hair. I shuddered at the touch. At the intrusion in my head. "Do as I say."

Surrender.

"I—that's enough. What are you doing?" I tore her hand away and stumbled backward. Knocked my bag from the tree. No one moved to retrieve it. "Stop it!"

But her skin only shone brighter as she reached for me—her eyes full of longing—and suddenly, I wasn't sure I wanted her to stop at all.

Surrender. Touch her.

"Reid." She extended her arms to me in supplication, and I felt myself step forward, felt myself bury my face in her hair. But she smelled wrong. All wrong. Like smoke and fur and—and something else. Something sharp. It pierced through the haze in my mind. "Embrace me, Reid. Embrace *this*. You don't have to be afraid. Let me show you how powerful you can be. Let me show you how weak you are."

Too sharp. Sickly sweet. Burning.

My hands came down on her shoulders, and I forced her back a step, tearing my gaze away. "Stop it. Now." Unwilling to risk her eyes again, I stared instead at her throat. At her scar. Slowly, her skin dimmed beneath my hands. "This isn't you."

She snorted at that, and her skin flickered out abruptly. She shoved away from me. "Quit telling me who I am." When I hazarded a glance at her, she glared back, lips pursed and brows drawn. One hand on her narrow hip. Expectant. "So? Are we doing this or not?"

"Lou . . . ," Ansel warned.

My entire body trembled. "That's twice you've used magic to control me," I said quietly. "Never do it again. Do you understand? *Never.*"

"You're being dramatic."

"You're out of control."

A wicked grin curved her lips. Jezebel incarnate. "So punish me. I prefer chains and a whip, but a sword will do."

Unbelievable. She was—she—

I sucked in a harsh breath. "You really want to do this?"

Her grin widened, feral, and in that instant, I no longer recognized her. She was no longer Lou, but a true white lady. Beautiful, cold, and strange. "I really do."

You met only a few months ago. How well can you really know her? Madame Labelle's words tormented me. Louder and louder they grew. *Louise has started her descent. I know the signs. I've seen it happen before. You cannot stop it, and you cannot slow it down.*

"If I agree to this," I said slowly, "I have a condition."

"I'm listening."

"If I win, no more magic. I'm serious, Lou. You stop using it. I don't want to see it. I don't want to smell it. I don't want to *think* about it until all this is over."

"And if I win?" She trailed a finger across my chest. The unnatural luster returned to her skin. The unfamiliar gleam in her eye. "What then, darling?"

"I learn to use it. I let you teach me."

Her skin guttered abruptly, and her smile slipped. "Deal."

Throat tight, I nodded and stepped back. Finally, we could end this—this madness between us. This tension. This *impasse*. I would disable her quickly, efficiently. Despite her taunting, I didn't wish to harm her. I *never* wished to harm her. I just wanted to protect her. From Morgane. From Auguste.

From herself.

And now I finally could.

Drawing a second knife, I rolled my shoulders back. Stretched my neck. Flexed my wrist.

A sensation akin to giddiness overwhelmed me as we faced each other, as she twirled my knife between her fingers. But I didn't let my emotions betray me. Unlike Lou, I could control them. I could master them. I *would* master them.

"Are you ready?" Her smirk had returned, and her posture remained relaxed. Arrogant. Ansel scrambled to the cover of the nearest tree. Cypress. Even Coco backed away, tugging Beau with her. "Shall we count to three?"

I kept my own grip on my knife light. "One."

She tossed her knife in the air. "Two."

We locked eyes.

"Three," I breathed.

She sprang immediately, surprising me, and attacked with unexpected strength. I blocked her easily enough, countering with a strike of my own. Half force. I just needed to subdue her, not bludgeon her, and she was so small—

Darting around me, she used my momentum to kick the back of my knee and send me sprawling forward. Worse, she half tackled, half rode me to the ground, ensuring I landed face-first in the snow. Her knife touched my throat as my own skidded out of reach. Chuckling, she dug her knees into my back and brushed a kiss to my neck.

"First lesson, Ansel: find your opponent's weaknesses and exploit them."

Furious, I spat snow from my mouth and shoved her knife away. "Get off me."

She laughed again and rolled to the side, freeing me, before springing to her feet. "So, what did Reid do wrong? Besides falling on his face *and* losing his weapon?" Winking, she plucked it from the ground and returned it to me.

Ansel fidgeted under the tree, refusing to make eye contact. "He—he didn't want to hurt you. He held back."

I pushed to my feet. Heat burned up my neck and ears as I beat the snow and mud from my coat, my pants. *Fuck.* "A mistake I won't make twice."

Lou's eyes danced. "Shall we try for round two?"

"Yes."

"On your count."

I took the offensive this time, striking hard and fast. I'd underestimated her quickness before, but not again. Maintaining my momentum and balance, I kept my movements controlled, forceful. She might've been faster, but I was stronger. Much, much stronger.

Her smirk vanished after a particularly powerful blow to her sword arm. I didn't hesitate. Again and again I struck, driving her back toward the cypress tree. Trapping her. *Exploiting her weakness.* Her arms shook with effort, but she could scarcely deflect my attacks, let alone counter. I didn't stop.

With one last strike, I knocked away her knife, pinning her against the tree with my forearm. Panting. Grinning. Triumphant. "Yield."

She bared her teeth and lifted her hands. "Never."

The blast came before I could react. And the smell. The *smell.* It singed my nose and burned my throat, following me as I soared through the air—as I smashed into a branch and slid into the snow. Something warm and wet burst from my crown. I touched the spot gingerly, and my fingers came away red. Bloody.

"You—" My throat tightened with disbelief. With rage. "You cheated."

"Second lesson," she snarled, swooping down to retrieve our fallen knives. "There's no such thing as cheating. Use every weapon in your arsenal."

Ansel watched with wide, terrified eyes. Pale and motionless.

I rose slowly. Deliberately. My voice shook. "Give me a knife."

"No." She lifted her chin, eyes overbright, and slid it through her belt loop. "That's twice you've lost yours. Win it back."

"Lou." Ansel stepped forward tentatively, hands outstretched between us as if placating wild animals. "Maybe—maybe you should just give it—"

His words ended in a cry as I tackled her to the ground. Rolling to my back, I absorbed the worst of the impact, seizing her wrists and tearing her own knife away. She clawed at me, shrieking, but

I kept her hands pinned together with one of my own, using the other to reach—to *search*—

Her teeth sank into my wrist before I could find her belt.

"Shit!" I released her with a snarl, welts forming from the teeth marks. "Are you *crazy*—?"

"*Pathetic.* Surely the great captain can do better than *this*—"

Vaguely, I could hear Ansel shouting something in the distance, but the roaring in my ears drowned out everything but Lou. *Lou.* I rolled, diving for her discarded knife, but she leapt after me.

I reached it first.

Instinctively, I swung out in a wide, vicious arc, defending my back. Lou should've danced out of reach. She should've anticipated the move and countered, ducked beneath my outstretched arm and charged.

But she didn't.

My knife connected.

I watched in slow motion—bile rising in my throat—as the blade tore through her coat, as her mouth widened in a surprised O. As she tripped, clutching her chest, and tumbled to the ground.

"No." I gasped the word before dropping to my knees beside her. The roaring in my ears went abruptly silent. "Lou—"

"Reid!" Ansel's voice shattered the silence as he raced toward us, splattering snow and mud in every direction. He skidded to a stop and fell forward, hands fluttering wildly over the gash in her coat. He sat back with a sigh. "Thank God—"

"Coco," I said.

"But she isn't—"

"COCO!"

A quiet chuckle sounded below us. My vision tunneled on Lou's pale form. A grin touched her lips, wicked, and she rose to her elbows.

"Stay down," I pleaded, my voice cracking. "Please. Coco will heal you—"

But she didn't stay down. No, she continued to rise, lifting her hands in a peculiar gesture. My mind—sluggish and slow with panic—didn't comprehend the movement, didn't understand her intent until it was too late—

The blast lifted me into the air. I didn't stop until my back slammed into the tree once more. Doubling over, I choked and tried to regain my breath.

Another chuckle, this one louder than the last. She strode toward me, opening her coat to reveal her shirt, her skin. Both intact. Not even a scratch. "Third lesson: the fight isn't over until one of you is dead. Even then, check twice. Always kick them when they're down."

A DEBT OF BLOOD

Reid

If the tension between us had been thick before, now it was impassable. Each step a brick between us. Each moment a wall.

We walked for a long time.

Though Lou sent the black fox—*Brigitte*, she had named it—ahead with our request to meet, the Beast of Gévaudan didn't answer.

No one said another word until dusk fell. Cypress trees had gradually replaced pine and birch, and the ground beneath us had softened. It squelched underfoot, more mud now than moss and lichen. Brine flavored the cold winter air, and above us, a lone seagull cawed. Though water soaked my boots, luck was on our side—the tide hadn't yet risen.

"It'll be dark soon," Beau whispered. "Do you know where they live?"

Lou pressed closer to my side. Gooseflesh steepled her skin. "I doubt they invited him in for tea."

I resisted the urge to wrap an arm around her, to hold her

tight. She hadn't apologized this time. I hadn't expected it. "We caught strays unaware last time. I . . . don't know where the pack resides."

"Strays unaware?" Lou looked up at me sharply. "You told me you found the pack."

"I wanted to impress you."

"It doesn't matter." Coco glanced at the sky, at the ghost of the moon in the purple sunset. Full tonight. Growing brighter by the minute. "They'll find us."

Beau followed her gaze, paling. "And until then?"

A howl pierced the night.

Now I did take Lou's hand. "We keep going."

True darkness fell within the hour. With it, deeper shadows materialized, flitting through the trees. "They're here." Voice soft, Lou tipped her head to our left, where a silver wolf slipped out of sight. Another streaked ahead without a sound. More howls echoed the first until a chorus of cries surrounded us. We drew together collectively.

"Stay calm," I breathed. Though anxious to draw a blade, I kept my hand firmly in Lou's. This first moment was critical. If they suspected danger, they wouldn't hesitate. "They haven't attacked yet."

Beau's voice heightened to a squeak. "*Yet?*"

"Everyone kneel." Slowly, warily, I sank into a crouch, bowing my head, guiding Lou down with me. Our fingers threaded together in the mire. With each of her breaths, I synchronized my own. Centered myself. Anticipation corded my neck, my arms. Perhaps Blaise wouldn't listen to me. Despite what I'd told Lou, perhaps he wouldn't accept my challenge. Perhaps he'd just kill us. "Make eye contact with only those you wish to challenge."

As if awaiting my words, the wolves descended. Three dozen of them, at least. They emerged from every direction, as silent as the moon overhead. Surrounding us. Lou's face went white. Beside her, Ansel trembled.

We were outnumbered.

Alarmingly outnumbered.

"What's happening?" Beau asked on a ragged breath. He'd pressed his forehead into Coco's shoulder, clenching his eyes shut.

I struggled to keep my own voice steady. "We're requesting an audience with the alpha."

Directly in front of us, an enormous yellow-eyed wolf stepped into view. I recognized him immediately—his fur the color of smoke, his maw grizzled and misshapen. A chunk of his nose had been torn away. I still remembered the sight of it falling to the ground. The feel, the smell, of his blood on my hands. The sound of his tortured cries.

When he curled his lip, revealing teeth as long as my fingers, I forced myself to speak.

"Blaise. We need to talk."

When I moved to rise, Lou stopped me with a curt shake of her head. She rose instead, addressing Blaise directly. Only I could feel her hand trembling. "My name is Louise le Blanc, and I seek an audience with the Beast of Gévaudan, leader of this pack. Can I assume you're him?"

Blaise snarled softly. He didn't look away from me.

"We're here to negotiate a partnership against La Dame des Sorcières," Lou continued, her voice stronger now. "We don't want to fight."

"You are very brave." A sturdy young woman slipped out from between the trees, dressed in only a shift. Copper skin. Black hair. Deep brown eyes. Behind her, a miniature, male version followed. "Bringing a prince and a Chasseur into Le Ventre."

Beau glanced at me. When I nodded, he too stood. Though cautious, his posture shifted subtly, transforming him before our eyes. He straightened his shoulders. Planted his feet. Gazed down at the woman with an impassive expression. "I'm afraid you have us at the disadvantage, Mademoiselle . . . ?"

She glared at him. "Liana. I am the Beast of Gévaudan's daughter."

Beau nodded. "Mademoiselle Liana. It is a pleasure to meet you." When she didn't return the sentiment, he continued, undeterred. "My companion spoke truth. We are here to make peace with the loup garou. We believe an alliance could benefit all parties involved."

Lou cast him a grateful look.

"And what party do *you* represent?" Liana asked silkily, stalking closer. Beau's eyes shifted as a handful of wolves shadowed her movements. "Your *Highness.*"

Beau gave a strained smile. "Unfortunately, I am not here in an official capacity, though I maintain hope my father is also amenable to an alliance."

"Before or after he sends his huntsmen to slaughter my family?"

"We don't want to fight," Lou repeated.

"That's too bad." Liana grinned, and her incisors lengthened, sharpening to lethal points. "Because we do."

Her little brother—perhaps five years younger than Ansel—bared his teeth. "Take them."

"Wait!" Beau cried, and the wolf nearest him startled, snapping at his hand. He tumbled to the ground with a curse.

"Please, listen!" Lou darted between them, lifting her hands in a placating gesture. Heedless of her pleas, the wolves charged. I scrambled after them, drawing twin knives from my bandolier, preparing to throw—

"We just want to talk!" Her voice rose desperately. "We don't want to fi—"

The first wolf slammed into her, and she staggered back, hand extending to me. Eyes seeking mine. I adjusted my aim instinctively, throwing the knife straight and true. Catching the hilt as it turned, she slashed at the wolf in a single, continuous movement. When it yelped and leapt aside, bleeding, its kin skidded to a halt all around. Snarls and howls filled the night.

"We don't mean any harm." Lou's hand no longer trembled. "But we will defend ourselves if necessary." At her back, I lifted my own knife for emphasis. Coco and Ansel joined with theirs. Even Beau unsheathed his dagger, completing our circle.

"Well," Coco said bitterly. The wolves prowled around us, searching for a weak point to attack. "This spiraled out of control even quicker than I thought it would."

I swung at a wolf who edged too close. "You know what I need to do, Lou."

She shook her head vehemently. "No. No, we can still negotiate—"

"You have an interesting way of *negotiating*," Liana snarled, gesturing to her wounded kin, "bringing knives and enemies into our home and cutting us open."

"I didn't want for that to happen." Another wolf lunged while Lou spoke, hoping to catch her off guard. To her credit, she didn't stab it. She kicked it in the nose. "We have information on your enemy, La Dame des Sorcières. Together, we might finally defeat her."

"Ah. I understand now." A small smile played on Liana's lips. She lifted a hand, and the wolves stopped circling abruptly. "You've come to beg for the pack's help."

"To ask for it," Coco said sharply. She lifted her chin. "We will not beg."

The two stared at each other for several seconds. Neither flinching. Neither looking away. Finally, Liana inclined her head. "I acknowledge your bravery, Cosette Monvoisin, but the pack will never help a prince, a huntsman, and their whore." When she nodded toward Beau, me, and Lou, I saw red. Gripping my knives with deadly intent, I stepped forward. Coco's arm came across my chest. Liana laughed, the sound fierce. Feral. "You shouldn't have come here, Reid Diggory. I'll enjoy tearing out your throat."

"Enough, Liana." Deep and hoarse, Blaise's voice cut through the din of eager growls. I hadn't seen him slip away. He stood before us now as a man, clothed only in a pair of loose-fitting pants. His chest was as scarred as his face. His shoulders as broad as my own. Perhaps broader. Like his wolf's coat, his hair grew long and stormy gray, streaked with silver. "Morgane le Blanc visited us earlier this week with a similar proposition. She spoke of war."

"And freedom from the Chasseurs," Liana spat.

"All we must do is deliver her daughter—your wife"—Blaise's yellow eyes bored into mine, filled with hatred—"and my people's persecution will end."

"She's going to sacrifice me." Lou's hand clenched on her knife. Blaise tracked the movement. Predatory. Assessing any weaknesses, even now. "I'm her *daughter*," Lou continued, her voice rising in pitch. A glance confirmed that her pupils had dilated. Her body was also preparing to fight, even if her mind hadn't yet grasped the danger of our situation. "Yet she only conceived me—raised me—to die. She never loved me. Surely you see how evil that is?"

Blaise bared his teeth at her. His incisors were still sharp. Pointed. "Do not speak to me of family, Louise le Blanc, when you have never known one. Do not talk of killing children. Not with the company you keep."

Lou grimaced, a note of desperation lacing her voice. "He's a changed man—"

"He owes us blood. His debt will be paid."

"We never should've come here," Beau whispered.

He was right. Our plan had been half-assed at best, and this—this had been a suicide mission from the start. The Beast of Gévaudan would never join us. Because of me.

"Morgane won't hesitate to slaughter you after you've fulfilled her purpose." Lou abandoned all attempts at civility, planting her feet wide in front of me. Defending me against an entire pack of werewolves. "Dames Blanches loathe loup garou. They loathe anything different from themselves."

"She can try." Blaise's canines extended past his lip, and his eyes gleamed in the darkness. The wolves around him snarled and began to circle us again. Hackles raised. "But she will quickly discover that loup garou savor the blood of our enemies most. You were foolish to venture into Le Ventre, Louise le Blanc. Now your huntsman will pay with his life." His bones began to crack and shift, and his eyes rolled back in his head. Liana grinned. The wolves inched closer, licking their lips.

Lou lifted her hands once more. This time, the gesture wasn't placating. "You will not touch him."

"Lou." I touched her elbow, shaking my head. "Stop."

She knocked my hand aside and lifted her own higher. "*No*, Reid."

"I knew what would happen when I came here." Before she could protest, before Blaise could complete his transition to wolf, I took a deep breath and stepped forward. "I challenge you, Blaise, the Beast of Gévaudan and alpha of this pack, to a duel. On your honor, and my own." His bones stopped snapping abruptly, and he stared at me, frozen between two forms. Lupine and human-oid. A grotesque blend of wolf and man. "Just the two of us. One weapon of our choice. If I win, you and your pack will join us in the upcoming battle. You will help us defeat La Dame des Sor-cières and her Dames Blanches."

"And if I win?" Blaise's voice was distorted, disjointed, from his elongated mouth. More snarls than words.

"You kill me."

He snorted, his lips pulling back from his teeth. "No."

I blinked. "No?"

"I refuse your challenge, Reid Diggory." He nodded to his daughter and son before surrendering himself to the change completely. Within seconds, he landed on all fours, panting in the cold night air. A wolf once more. Liana stood behind him. In her eyes shone a hatred I recognized. A hatred that had once stolen my own breath and hardened my own heart.

"This time, Captain Diggory," she said softly, "we will hunt you. If you reach the village on the other side of our land, you escape with your life. If not . . ." She inhaled deeply, smiling as if scenting our fear, before extending her arms to her pack mem-bers. "Glory to the loup garou who kills you."

Lou's face twisted in horror.

"The village, Gévaudan, is due south from here. We will give you a head start."

"How much of a head start?" Beau asked, eyes tight and anx-ious.

She only grinned in response.

"Weapons?" Lou asked.

"He may keep the weapons on his person," Liana said. "No more and no less."

I quickly tallied my inventory. Four knives in my bandolier. Two in my boots. One down my spine. Seven teeth of my own. Though I prayed I wouldn't need them, I wasn't naive. This would not end well. It would end bloody.

"If any of *you* intervene in the hunt," her little brother added, looking between Lou, Coco, Ansel, and Beau, "with magic or otherwise, your lives will be forfeit."

"What about Morgane?" Coco asked quickly. "If Reid wins, you'll ally with us against her?"

"Never," Liana snarled.

"This is bullshit!" Lou advanced toward them, hands still lifted, but I caught her arm. To my surprise, so did Beau.

"Little sister," he said, eyes wide as the wolves closed in around us, "I think we ought to play their game."

"He'll *die*."

Coco's eyes darted everywhere as if searching for an escape. There was none. "We'll all die unless he agrees." She looked to me for confirmation. Waiting. In that look, I understood. If I chose not to do this, she would join me in fighting our way out. They all would. But the cost—the risk—

As if pulled by an invisible force, my eyes drifted again to Lou. To her face. I memorized the curve of her nose, the slope of her cheek. The line of her neck. If we fought, they would take her. There were too many of them to kill, even with magic on our side.

They would take her, and she would be gone.

"Don't do this," she said, her distress palpable. My chest ached. "Please."

My thumb brushed her arm. Just once. "I have to."

When I turned back to Liana, she was already halfway through the change. Black fur covered her lupine face, and her lips curled in a horrifying smile. "Run."

THE WOLVES DESCEND

Reid

A sense of calm enveloped me as I entered the swamp. South. Due south. I knew of Gévaudan. The Chasseurs and I had stayed there the night after our werewolf raid—the night before I'd become Captain Diggory. If I remembered the terrain correctly, the river that powered Gévaudan's mill flowed into this estuary. If I could find that river, I could lose my scent in the waters. Traverse them into the village.

If I didn't drown first.

I glanced down. The tide was rising. It'd soon flood the estuary, which would in turn flood the river. The current would be dangerous, especially while I was laden with heavy weaponry. Still—better the devil I knew than the devil I didn't. I'd rather drown than feel Blaise's teeth in my stomach.

Hurtling around the trees—taking care to mark each one with my scent—I doubled back, diluting my trail as much as possible. I dropped to a crouch. Loup garou were faster than regular wolves, faster than even horses. I couldn't outrun them. The water was my only hope. That, and—

Clawing at the ground, I scooped handfuls of mud and slathered them onto my skin. My clothes. My hair. Beyond strength and speed, the werewolves' noses were their greatest weapons. I needed to disappear in every sense.

Somewhere behind me, a howl shattered the silence.

I looked up, the first knot of fear making me hesitate.

My time was up. They were coming.

I cursed silently, sprinting south and listening—*listening*—for the telltale rush of water. Searching for thick trunks and hanging moss amidst the other muted greens and browns of the forest. The river had taken shape within a thick copse of bald cypresses. It had to be near here. I remembered this place. Each landmark that rose up before me refreshed my memory. Jean Luc had stopped to rest against that gnarled trunk. The Archbishop—stubbornly clad in his choral robes—had nearly fallen over that rock.

Which meant the cypresses should be right . . . *there.*

Triumphant, I raced toward them, slipping through the trunks as another howl sounded, breathing a sigh of relief as I finally, *finally* found the—

I stopped short. My relief withered.

There was nothing here.

Where the river had been, only a cluster of ferns remained. Their leaves—brown and dead—fluttered gently in the wind. The ground beneath them was muddy, wet, covered in lichen and moss. But none of the riverbed remained. Not one grain of sand. Not a single river rock. It was as if the entire river had simply . . .

disappeared. As if I'd imagined the whole thing.

My hands curled into fists.

I hadn't imagined anything. I'd drunk from the damn thing myself.

Around me, the trees' branches rustled in the wind, whispering together. Laughing. Watching. Another howl pierced the night—this one closer than the last—and the hair on my neck rose.

The forest is dangerous. My pulse quickened at my mother's words. *The trees have eyes.*

I shook my head—unwilling to acknowledge them—and peered up at the sky to recalculate my bearings. South. Due south. I just had to reach Gévaudan's gate, and the mud on my skin ensured that the werewolves couldn't track me by scent. I could still do this. I could make it.

But when I stepped backward—my boot sinking in a particularly wet pocket of earth—I realized the glaring flaw in my plan. Stopping abruptly, I turned to look behind me. My panic deepened to dread. The werewolves didn't *need* their noses to track me. I'd left them a path of footprints to follow instead. I hadn't calculated the soft terrain into my plan, nor the rising tide. There was no way I could flee for Gévaudan—or the river, or anywhere—without the werewolves seeing exactly where I'd gone.

Come on. My heart beat a frantic rhythm now, thundering inside my head. I forced myself to think around it. Could I magic my way out? I instantly rejected the impulse, unwilling to risk it. The last time I'd used magic, I'd nearly killed myself, freezing to death on the bank of a pool. More than likely, I'd do more harm than good, and I had no room for error now. Lou wasn't here to save me. *Think think think.* I wracked my brain for another plan, another means of hiding my trail. As shitty as Lou was at strategizing, she would've known exactly what to do. She always escaped. Always. But I wasn't her, and I didn't know.

Still . . . I'd chased her long enough to guess what she'd do in this situation. What she did in every situation.

Swallowing hard, I looked up.

Breathe. Just breathe.

Wading back into the cypresses, I heaved myself onto the lowest branch.

Another.

The trees grew close together in this part of the forest. If I could navigate the canopy far enough, I'd break my trail. I climbed faster, forcing my gaze skyward. Not down. Never down.

Another.

When the branches began thinning, I stopped climbing, crawling slowly—too slowly—to the end of the limb. I stood on shaky legs. Counting to three, I leapt onto the next branch as far as I could. It bowed precariously under my weight, and I crumpled, wrapping my arms around it with deep, gasping breaths. My vision swam. I forced myself to crawl forward once more. I couldn't stop. I had to move faster. I'd never reach Gévaudan at this pace, and the wolves grew louder with each howl.

After the third tree, however, my breathing came easier. My muscles relaxed infinitesimally. I moved faster. Faster still. Confident now. The trees still grew thick, and hope swelled in my chest. Again and again I leapt, until—

A splintering crack.

No.

Spine seizing, mind reeling, I swiped desperately at the nearest branch, hurtling toward the ground at alarming speed. The wood snapped under my momentum, and sharp pain lanced up my arm. The next branch smashed into my head. Stars burst behind my eyes, and I landed—hard—on my back. The impact knocked the breath from my throat. Water flooded my ears. I wheezed, blinking rapidly, clutching my bloody palm, and tried to stand.

Blaise stepped over me.

Teeth gleaming, he snarled when I squelched backward—eyes too intelligent, too eager, too *human* for my liking. Slowly, cautiously, I lifted my hands and rose to my feet. His nostrils flared at the scent of my blood. Instinct screamed for me to reach for my knives. To assume the offensive. But if I drew first blood—if I killed the alpha—the werewolves would never join us. Never. And those eyes—

Things had been much simpler when I'd been a Chasseur. When the wolves had been only beasts. Demons.

"It doesn't have to be this way." Head throbbing, I whispered, "Please."

His lips rose over his teeth, and he lunged.

I dodged his strike, circled him as he pivoted. My hands remained outstretched. Conciliatory. "You have a choice. The Chasseurs will kill you, yes, but so will Morgane. After you've served her purpose. After you've helped her murder innocent children."

Mid-charge, Blaise stopped abruptly. He cocked his head, ears twitching.

So Morgane hadn't told him the intricacies of her plan.

"When Lou dies, all of the king's children will die with her." I didn't mention my own death. That would only fortify the were-wolves' resolve to join Morgane. "Dozens of them, most of whom don't even know their father. Should they pay for his sins?"

Shifting his weight, he glanced behind as if uneasy.

"No one else has to die." I hardly dared breathe as I stepped toward him. "Join us. Help us. Together, we can defeat Morgane and restore order—"

Hackles rising, ears flattening, he snapped a warning to stay back. Revulsion twisted my stomach as his bones began to crack. As his joints popped and shifted just enough for him to stand on two legs. Smoky fur still covered his misshapen body. His hands and feet remained elongated, his back hunched. Grotesque. His face contracted in on itself until his mouth could form words.

"Restore order?" he snarled, the words guttural. "You said the Chasseurs will"—he struggled to move his jaw, grimacing in pain—"kill us. How will you defeat them?" Neck straining, he rescinded his teeth farther. "Can you kill—your own brothers? Your own"—another grimace—"father?"

"I'll convince him. I'll convince them all. We can show them another way."

"Too much—hate in their hearts. They'll refuse. What—then?"

I stared at him, thinking quickly.

"As I thought." His teeth snapped again. He started to shift back. "You would watch us—*bleed*—either way. A huntsman—through and through."

Then he lunged.

Though I dove aside, his teeth still caught my arm and buried deep. Tearing muscle. Shredding tendon. I wrenched away with a cry, dizzy with pain, with *anger*. Gold flickered wildly in my mind's eye. It blinded me, disorienting, as voices hissed, *seek us seek us seek us.*

I almost reached for them.

Instinct raged at me to attack, to protect, to tear this wolf's head off by any means necessary. Even magic.

But—no. I couldn't.

When everything is life and death, the stakes are higher, Lou said, chiding me in my memories. *The more we gain, the more we lose.*

I wouldn't.

Blaise readied to spring once more. Gritting my teeth, I leapt straight into the air and caught the branch overhead. My arm screamed in pain, as did my hand. I ignored both, swinging back as he rose to snap at my heels—and kicked him hard in the chest. He yelped and fell to the ground. I dropped beside him, drawing a dagger from my bandolier and stabbing it through his paw into the ground below. His yelps turned to shrieks. The other wolves' answering howls were murderous.

Arm dangling uselessly, I tore at my coat with my good hand. I needed to bind the wound. To stem the bleeding. The mud on my skin wouldn't mask the scent of fresh blood. The others would soon smell my injuries. They'd find me within moments. But my hand refused to cooperate, shaking with pain and fear and adrenaline.

Too late, I realized Blaise's screams had transformed.

Human now, naked, he wrenched the knife from his hand and snarled, "What was his name?"

FROZEN HEART

Lou

My footsteps wore a path in the ground as I paced. I hated this feeling—this *helplessness*. Reid was in there, fleeing for his *life*, and there was nothing I could do to help him. The three wolves Blaise had left to guard us—one of them Blaise's own son, Terrance—made sure of that. Judging by their size, Terrance's companions were equally young. Each of them stared at the tree line, giving us their backs, and whined softly. Their rigid shoulders and pinned ears said what they no longer could.

They wanted to join the hunt.

I wanted to skin them alive and wear their fur like a mantle.

"We have to do something," I muttered to Coco, glaring at Terrance's dark back. Though he and the others were smaller than the rest, I had no doubt their teeth were still sharp. "How will we know if he reaches Gévaudan? What if Blaise kills him anyway?"

I felt Coco's gaze, but I didn't look away from the wolves, longing to embed my knife in their rib cages. Restless energy hummed beneath my skin. "We don't have a choice," she murmured. "We just have to wait."

"There's always a choice. For example, we could *choose* to slit these little imps' throats and be on our way."

"Can they understand us?" Ansel whispered anxiously from beside Beau. "You know"—he dropped his voice further—"in their wolf form?"

"I don't give a shit."

Coco snorted, and I glanced at her. She smiled without humor. Her eyes were as drawn as mine, her skin paler than usual. It seemed I wasn't the only one worried about Reid. The thought warmed me unexpectedly. "Trust him, Lou. He can do this."

"I *know*," I snapped, said warmth freezing as I whirled to face her. "If anyone can out-beast the Beast of Gévaudan, it's Reid. But what if something goes wrong? What if they ambush him? Wolves hunt as a pack. It's highly unlikely they'll attack unless they have him outnumbered, and the idiot spurns magic—"

"He's armed to the teeth with knives," Beau reminded me.

"He was a Chasseur, Lou." Coco's voice gentled, so unbearably patient that I wanted to scream. "He knows how to hunt, which means he also knows how to hide. He'll cover his tracks."

Ansel nodded in agreement.

But Ansel—bless him—was a *child*, and neither he nor Coco knew what the hell they were talking about.

"Reid isn't the type to hide." I resumed pacing, cursing bitterly at the thick mud coating my boots. Water sloshed up my legs. "And even if he was, this entire godforsaken place is knee-deep in mud—"

Beau chuckled. "Better than snow—"

"Says who?" His eyes narrowed at my tone, and I scoffed,

kicking at the water angrily. "Stop looking at me like that. They're equally shitty, okay? The only real advantage in the middle of winter would be ice, but *of course* the dogs live in a goddamn swamp."

Howls erupted in the distance—eager now, tainted with unmistakable purpose—and our guards stood, panting with feverish excitement. Terrance licked his lips in anticipation. Horror twisted my chest like a vise. "They've found him."

"We don't know that," Coco said quickly. "Don't do anything stupid—"

Reid's cry rent the night.

"Lou." Eyes wide, Ansel swiped for my wrist. "Lou, he doesn't want you to—"

I slammed my palm into the ground.

Ice shot from my fingertips across the swamp floor, the very ground crackling with hoarfrost. I urged it onward, faster, *faster*, even as tendrils of bone-deep cold latched around my heart. My pulse slowed. My breathing faltered. I didn't care. I stabbed my fingers deeper into the spongy soil, urging the ice as far as the pattern would take it. Farther still. The gold cord around my body pulsed—attacking my mind, my body, my very *soul* with deep and boundless cold—but I didn't release it.

Vaguely, I heard Coco shouting behind me, heard Beau cursing, but I couldn't distinguish individual sounds. Black edged my vision, and the wolves in front of me faded to three snarling shadows. The world tilted. The ground rushed up to meet me. Still I held on. I would freeze the entire sea to ice—the entire world—before I let go. Because Reid needed help. Reid needed . . .

Frozen ground. He needed frozen ground. Ice. It would . . . it would give him . . . something. Advantage. It would give him . . . an advantage. Advantage against . . .

But delicious numbness crept through my body, stealing my thoughts, and I couldn't remember. Couldn't remember his name. Couldn't remember my own. I blinked once, twice, and everything went black.

Pain cracked across my cheek, and I jerked awake with a start.

"Holy hell." Coco dragged me to my feet before slipping on something and plummeting back to the ground. We landed in an angry heap. Swearing viciously, she rolled me off her. I felt . . . odd. "You're lucky you aren't *dead*. I don't know how you did it. You *should* be dead." She struggled upward once more. "What the hell were you *thinking*?"

I rubbed my face, wincing slightly at the sharp scent of magic. It burned my nose, brought tears to my eyes. I hadn't smelled it this concentrated since the temple at Modraniht. "What do you mean?"

"Ice, Lou," Coco said, gesturing around us. "*Ice.*"

Thick, crystalline rime coated every inch of our surroundings, from the blades of dead grass, ferns, and lichen on the forest floor to the boughs of cypress in the canopy. I gasped. As far as the eye could see, Le Ventre was no longer green. No longer wet and heavy and *alive*. No. Now it was white, hard, and glistening, even in darkness. I took a step, testing the ice under my foot. It didn't yield beneath my weight. When I stepped again, checking behind, my footprint left no impression on its surface.

I smiled.

A snarl to my left jerked me back to attention. A wolf had just launched himself at Beau and Ansel, who lifted his knife in an attempt to defend them. Coco darted forward to help, dodging Terrance, who slid right past her in his haste. The third wolf loped toward me, teeth first.

I grinned wider. It seemed I'd broken the rules.

With a snort of amusement, I twirled my fingers, and the wolf spun out of control on the ice. The pattern dissolved into golden dust. I wobbled but kept my feet, fighting a rush of vertigo. When the sensation passed, the wolf regained his footing. I bounced a finger off his nose as he careened past once more, slipped, and fell in a tangled heap.

Though my vision swam, I laughed—then clenched my fist, guiding the ice up and over his paws.

He yelped as it devoured his legs, his chest, edging steadily toward his throat. I watched in fascination, even as my laughter turned colder. Chilling.

More more more.

I wanted to watch the light leave his eyes.

"Lou!" Coco cried. "Look out!"

With hollow compulsion, I turned and flicked my wrist— catching a pattern easily—as Terrance leapt for my throat. The bones on the right side of his body shattered, and he fell to the ice with a piercing cry. But I felt no pain. Stepping over him, I lifted my hands toward his remaining companion. He backed away from Ansel and Coco slowly.

"You will leave my friends alone," I said, following him with a smile. Gold winked all around me with infinite possibilities—so many more now than ever before. So much pain. So much suffering. The wolf deserved it. He would've killed them.

His kin might've already killed Reid, a voice whispered.

My smile vanished.

Ansel stepped in front of me, looking alarmed. "What are you doing?"

"Ansel." Coco eased between us, gripping his hand and maneuvering him behind her. "Stay back." Her eyes never left mine. "Enough, Lou. You control your magic. It doesn't control you." When I didn't answer, when I didn't lower my hands, she stepped closer still. "This ice. Melt it. The price was too much."

"But Reid needs the ice. He'll die without it."

She grasped my hands gently, guiding them down between us. "There are worse things than death. Undo it, Lou. Come back to us. Don't continue down this path."

I stared at her.

Witches willing to sacrifice everything are powerful, the voice reminded me.

And dangerous, a distant corner of my mind argued. *And changed.*

"You aren't your mother," Coco whispered.

"I'm not my mother," I repeated, uncertain. Ansel and Beau watched with wide eyes.

She nodded and touched my cheek. "Undo it."

My ancestors kept silent now, waiting. Despite what Coco thought, they wouldn't urge me to do anything I didn't want to do. They only amplified my desires, carried me away in order to fulfill them. But desire was a heady thing, as addictive as it was deadly.

Reid's voice reverberated from that distant corner. *Reckless.*

"This isn't you, Lou," Coco said, coaxing. "Undo it."

If I'd trusted her any less, I might not have listened. But that distant corner of my mind seemed to believe her words. Kneeling, I placed my hand on the ground. A single pattern arose in my mind's eye, drifting out from the frozen wasteland of my chest toward the ice. I took a shuddering breath.

And a blue-tipped arrow nicked my leg.

"No!" Coco cried, flinging herself over me. "Stop! Don't shoot!"

But it was too late.

We passed some o' them just up the road. Bone White's eyes had gleamed with hunger. *Smarmy bastards. They've been scourin' the forest for weeks, makin' a right mess for us, haven't they?*

Reid's face now, drawn with fatigue. *The Chasseurs were near last night.*

Nearer than we'd thought, it seemed. Pushing Coco aside, I rose to my feet. My body thrummed with anticipation. My fingers flexed. It'd only been a matter of time before they found us—and what spectacular timing too.

At last, they were here.

Chasseurs.

Bows and Balisardas drawn, Jean Luc led a squadron from behind the trees. Surprise lit his eyes when he saw me, replaced quickly with resolve. Lifting a hand to halt the others, he approached slowly. "If it isn't Louise le Blanc. You can't imagine how pleased I am to see you."

I smiled, staring at his Balisarda. "Likewise, Jean Luc. What took you so long?"

"We buried the corpses you left on the road." Those pale eyes took in the ice around us before flicking to my face, my hair. He whistled low. "The facade has cracked, I see. The surface finally reflects the rot within." He gestured to the half-frozen wolf. "Though I'll thank you for making our jobs easier. Blaise's pack has never been easily tracked. His Majesty will be pleased."

I bowed low, extending my arms. "We are ever his servants."

Jean Luc spotted Beau then. "Your Highness. I should've known you'd be here. Your father has been in an uproar for weeks."

Though he still looked uneasy, Beau rose to his full height, staring down his nose at him. "Because you told him about my involvement on Modraniht."

Jean Luc sneered. "Your indiscretions shall not go unpunished. Truly, it disgusts me to one day call you king."

"Never fear. You won't be alive to witness that crowning achievement. Not if you continue to threaten my friends."

"Your *friends*." Jean Luc stepped closer, his knuckles white on silver and sapphire. I grinned. I'd told Reid I'd get him another Balisarda. How *delightful* that Balisarda would be Jean Luc's.

"Understand me, Your Highness. This time, there will be no escape. These witches"—he jerked his chin toward Coco and me—"and their conspirators will burn. *Your friends* will burn. I will light their pyres myself when we return to Cesarine. One for Cosette Monvoisin. One for Louise le Blanc. One for Ansel Diggory"—he bared his teeth—"and one for Reid Diggory."

He was wrong, of course. So very, very wrong.

"A fitting way to honor our late forefather. Don't you agree?"

"Célie will hate you if you burn Reid," Beau spat.

I twirled a lock of hair around my finger. "Tell me, Jean, have you fucked her yet?"

A beat of silence, then—

"I don't—" His eyes flew wide, and he spluttered incoherently. "What—"

"That's a yes, then." I sauntered closer, just out of his blade's reach. "Reid never fucked her himself, in case you were wondering. Poor girl. He did love her, but I suppose he took his vows seriously." My grin widened. "That, or he was saving himself for marriage."

He lashed out with his Balisarda. "Shut your mouth—"

I met him with a blade of ice. The other men tensed, edging closer, and Coco, Ansel, and Beau lifted their knives in turn.

"I can't imagine he'll be pleased when he learns his best friend loved his girlfriend in secret for all those years. So *naughty* of you, Jean. Did you at least wait to sow your seed until Reid moved to greener pastures?"

He jutted his face over our clashed blades. "Do not speak of Célie."

I continued undeterred. "One can't help but notice your new circumstances with Reid out of the picture. He always had the life you wanted, didn't he? Now you get to pretend at his. Secondhand title, secondhand power." I shrugged with a saccharine grin, sliding my blade along his slowly. The ice touched his hand. "Secondhand girl."

With a snarl, he pushed away from me. A vein throbbed in his forehead. "Where is Reid?"

"How disappointed she must be now. Though I suppose a secondhand girl deserves a secondhand boy—"

He launched himself at me again. I sidestepped easily. "That *murderer* didn't deserve to breathe her air. When she heard what he'd done, it nearly killed her. She's been in seclusion for *weeks* because of some misplaced emotion for him. If not for me, he would've *ruined* her. Just as you've ruined him. Now *where is he?*"

"Not here," I sang, still smiling sweetly as we circled each other. Beneath me, the ice thickened, and the foliage cracked audibly. "You're a thief, Jean Luc—a damn good one, of course—but I'm better. You have something I need."

"Witch, tell me where he is, or I'll—"

"You'll what? If your history is any indication, soon you'll be begging me to ruin *you* too."

With a snarl, he signaled to his men, but I jerked my hand upward before they could reach us. Shards of ice spiked up behind him, around him, until we stood in a circle of jagged icicles. Trapped, he shouted panicked orders—eyes darting, searching for a gap—while the Chasseurs hit and hacked at the ice.

"Cut it down!"

"Captain!"

"Get him *out*—"

One of the icicles shattered, raining ice on our heads. Capitalizing on the distraction, I lunged, slicing Jean Luc's sword hand. He cried out but kept hold of his Balisarda. His other hand seized my wrist, twisting, and that—well, that just wouldn't do.

I spat directly in his eye.

Rearing back, he loosened his hold on me, and I dug my fingers into his wound, pulling and tearing the skin there. He roared with pain. "You *bitch*—"

"Oh dear." I flipped his Balisarda into my hand, the ice sword poised at his throat. Then I laughed. Laughed and laughed until Coco, Ansel, and Beau joined the Chasseurs in beating against the ice. *Lou Lou Lou* came their anxious cries, reverberating around me. Through me. The moon reflected in Jean Luc's wide eyes. He backed away slowly. "It seems you've misplaced something, Captain." I hurled the ice sword into the icicle by his head before raising my free hand. "This is going to be fun."

SANCTUARY

Reid

"His—his name?"

Blaise bared his teeth, the first flicker of emotion flashing through his eyes. Blood dripped down his hand. "My *son*. Do you even know his name?"

I unsheathed a second blade, shame congealing in my gut. Though he made no further move to attack, I would not be caught unaware. "No."

"Adrien." He said the word on a whisper. Reverential. "His name was Adrien. My eldest son. I still remember the moment I first held him in my arms." He paused. "Do you have children, Captain Diggory?"

Distinctly uncomfortable now, I shook my head. Gripped my knives tighter.

"I thought not." He stepped closer. I stepped back. "Most loup garou mate with progeny in mind. We cherish our pups. They are everything." Another pause, longer this time. "My mate and I were no different, but we were incapable of reproduction. He came from a pack across the sea." Another step. We stood nearly nose to nose now. "When your brethren slew Adrien's biological parents, we adopted him as our own. When you slew Adrien, my mate took his own life." His eyes—once unbearably soft, lost in memory—now hardened. "He never met Liana or Terrance. He would've loved them. They *deserved* his love."

Self-loathing burned up my throat. I opened my mouth to say something—to say anything—but closed it just as quickly, fighting the urge to vomit. No words could ever erase what I'd done to him. What I'd taken.

"So you see," Blaise said, voice rough with emotion, "you owe me blood."

I still couldn't speak. When he began to shift once more, however, I choked, "I don't want to fight you."

"Nor I you," he growled, bones shuddering, "but fight we shall."

He'd just fallen back to all fours when the temperature plummeted, and ice—*ice*—shot across the ground beneath us. Stumbling, I stared as it devoured the path ahead, engulfing each tree and ravaging each leaf. Each needle. When it reached the tip of the tallest branches, it burst into a cloud of white, showering us with snow that stank of magic. Of *rage*. Blaise yelped in surprise and lost his footing.

Horror gripped my heart in a fist.

What had Lou done?

"Powerful—isn't she?" Blaise's body continued to snap and twist, his eyes gleaming in the darkness. His teeth glinting. "Her mother's daughter, after all."

A piercing howl erupted over the trees then. Higher than the others. Anguished. Blaise's head snapped up, and he gave a panicked whine. "Terrance." The word was garbled, barely discernible through his maw. He bolted without finishing his transition.

Lou.

Knives in hand, I hurried after him, slipping and sliding on the ice. It didn't matter. I didn't stop. Neither did Blaise. When we finally burst through the trees at the edge of the loup garou territory, I lurched to a halt at the sight before me.

A handful of Chasseurs hung midair, revolving slowly—necks taut, muscles seizing—while even more loup garou struggled to free themselves from the ice trapping their paws. Their legs. The Chasseurs and wolves who weren't debilitated hacked at one another with steel and teeth. When the bodies shifted—revealing a slight, pale-haired figure in the center of a shattered ice cage— my heart dropped like a stone.

Lou.

Eyes hollow, smile cold, she contorted her fingers like a maestro. Coco shouted beside her, tugging fruitlessly on her arms, while Beau and Ansel tried their best to defend them. Tears spilled down Ansel's cheeks. Blaise lunged forward with a snarl. I tackled him from behind, wrapping my arms around his ribs, and we rolled.

"Lou!" My shout made Lou pause. Made her turn. My blood ran cold at her grin. "Lou, stop!"

"I know I lost your Balisarda, Reid," she called, her voice sickeningly sweet, "but I found you a new one."

She lifted a bloody Balisarda into the air.

Jean Luc—I did a double take—*Jean Luc* dove at her.

"Watch out!" I cried, and she spun gracefully, lifting him with the sweep of her hand. He landed hard on a shard of ice, nearly impaling himself. Realization dawned swift and brutal.

She'd taken his Balisarda.

Spotting his father, Terrance whined and tried to drag himself toward us. Half of his body looked—limp. The angles wrong. Distorted. Blaise thrashed in my arms, twisting around to bite the wound on my arm, and I dropped him. He shot forward like a flash, gripping Terrance's ruff between his teeth and dragging him to safety.

I dodged around a Chasseur, sprinting toward Lou. When I took her in my arms, she cackled. And the look in her eyes . . . I squeezed her tighter. "What is this?"

"She has to melt the ice!" Coco cried, now locked in battle with Jean Luc. He fought viciously despite his injuries—or perhaps because of them. Within seconds, I realized he didn't just want to hurt Coco. He wanted to kill her. "She won't listen to—" She ducked as he swung a piece of ice savagely, but it still caught her chest. Her words ended in a gasp.

Bewildered, still horrified—torn between helping Coco or Lou—I took Lou's face in my hands. "Hello, you," she breathed, leaning into my embrace. Her eyes were still horribly empty. "Did the ice save you?"

"Yes, it did," I lied quickly, "but now you need to melt it. Can you do that for me? Can you melt the ice?"

She tilted her head, and confusion stirred within those lifeless eyes. I held my breath. "Of course." She blinked. "I'll do anything for the ones I love, Reid. You know that."

The words, spoken so simply, sent a chill down my spine. Yes, I did know that. I knew she would freeze to death to put breath in my lungs, twist up her very memory to give my body heat.

I knew she would sacrifice her warmth—her humanity—to protect me from loup garou.

"Melt the ice, Lou," I said. "Do it now."

Nodding, she sank to her knees. When she pressed her hands against the ground, I moved to defend her back. Punched a Chasseur who came too close. Prayed the pattern was reversible. That it wasn't too late.

The world seemed to still as Lou closed her eyes, and warmth pulsed outward in a wave. The ground melted to mud beneath her fingers. The suspended Chasseurs drifted back to their feet, and the trapped werewolves licked their newly freed paws. I prayed. I prayed and prayed and prayed.

Bring her back. Please.

Seek us.

When she rose, shaking her head, I crushed her in my arms. "Lou."

"What—" She leaned back, eyes widening at the carnage around us. The Chasseurs and werewolves watched her warily, unsure how to proceed without orders. No one appeared eager to approach her again. Not even those with Balisardas. Jean Luc's hung limp at Lou's side. "What happened?"

"You saved us," Coco said firmly. Though she swayed on her feet—face ashen, shirt bloody—she still looked better than Jean Luc. He'd collapsed, panting, at her boots. When he struggled to rise, she kicked him in the face. "And you will never . . . *ever* do it again. Do you hear me? I don't care if Reid is . . . bound and gagged . . . at the stake—" She broke off with a wince, applying pressure to her wound.

Lou sprang forward just in time, and Coco collapsed in her arms.

"I'm fine," Coco said, voice faint. "It'll heal. Don't use your magic."

"You stupid—bitches." Clutching his nose, Jean Luc crawled toward them. Blood poured through his fingers. "I'm going to cut you both to pieces. Give it back to me. Give me back my Balisarda—"

"Enough." Blaise's deep, terrible voice preceded him into view, and the werewolves shifted anxiously. In his arms, he held Terrance. Sweat coated the boy's brow, and his breathing came quick. Labored. He'd shifted back. In this form, it was clear his entire right side had collapsed. A brown wolf near Ansel yelped sharply. After the telltale crack of bones, Liana raced forward. Though I averted my eyes from her naked skin, I couldn't ignore her cries.

"Terrance! No, no, *no*. Mother moon, please. *Terrance*."

Blaise's yellow eyes flashed from the Chasseurs to Lou. "Who did this?"

Jean Luc spat blood. "*Magic*."

Every eye in the vicinity turned to Lou. She paled.

"I can heal him." Coco lifted her head from Lou's shoulders. Her eyes were glazed. Pained. "Bring him here."

"No." I stepped in front of them, and Blaise snarled. "Peace, Blaise. I—I can heal your son." Reaching into my pocket, I withdrew the vial of blood and honey.

A ghost of a smile touched Coco's lips. She nodded. "His injuries are internal. He needs to drink it."

Blaise didn't stop me when I approached. He didn't halt my wrist when I lifted the vial to Terrance's lips.

"Drink," I urged, tipping the liquid down the boy's throat. He struggled weakly against me, but Blaise held him firm. When he swallowed the last of it, we all waited. Even Jean Luc. He watched with an expression of fascination and disgust as Terrance's breathing grew stronger. As the color returned to his cheeks. One by one, the bones of his ribs snapped back into their proper places. Though he gasped in pain, Blaise stroked his hair, whispering comforts.

Tears poured down the old man's cheeks.

"*Père?*" Terrance's eyes fluttered open, and Blaise wept harder.

"Yes, son. I am here."

The boy groaned. "The witch, she—"

"Will not be harmed," I finished. Blaise and I locked eyes. After a tense moment, he dipped his chin in a nod.

"You have saved my son's life, Reid Diggory. I am indebted to you."

"No. I am indebted to you." My gaze dropped to Terrance, and my gut twisted once more. "I know it changes nothing, but

I am sorry. Truly. I wish—" I swallowed hard and looked away. Lou clutched my hand. "I wish I could bring Adrien back."

"Oh, good Lord." Jean Luc rolled his eyes and motioned to the Chasseurs from his position on the ground. "I've heard enough. Round them all up—even the Beast. They can bond in the Tower dungeon before they burn." He turned his glare on Lou. "Kill that one now."

Blaise's lip curled. He stepped beside me, and the wolves stepped beside him. Growls built deep in their throats. Their hackles rose. I drew my own knives, as did Ansel, and though her face was still pale, Lou lifted her free hand. The other supported Coco. "I think not," Blaise said.

Beau sauntered in front of us. "Consider me on their side. And as my father isn't here to throw his weight, I'll speak for him too. Which means . . . I outrank you." He grinned and nodded curtly to the Chasseurs. "Stand down, men. That's an order."

Jean Luc glared at him, trembling with rage. "They don't answer to you."

"Without your Balisarda, they don't answer to you either."

The Chasseurs hesitated.

"We have a proposition," Lou said.

I tensed, wary once more. We'd just defused the greatest danger. A single word from Lou could exacerbate it again.

At the sound of her voice, Blaise's lip curled over his teeth. One of the werewolves growled. Lou ignored them both, focusing only on Jean Luc. He laughed bitterly. "Does it end with you on the stake?"

"It ends with Morgane on one."

Surprise stole the scowl from his face. "What?"

"We know where she is."

His eyes narrowed. "Why should I believe you?"

"I hardly have reason to lie." She gestured around us with his Balisarda. "It's not like you're in any position to arrest me now. You're outnumbered. Vulnerable. But if you return to Cesarine with us, you'll have a good chance of finishing what you started on Modraniht. Just think—she's still injured. If she dies, King Auguste is safe, and *you* become the kingdom's new hero."

"Morgane is in Cesarine?" Jean Luc asked sharply.

"Yes." She glanced at me. "We . . . think she's planning an attack during the Archbishop's funeral."

Heavy silence descended. At last, Blaise asked coldly, "Why do you think this?"

"We received a note." She bent to retrieve it from her boot. "It's in my mother's handwriting, and it mentions a pall, and tears."

Blaise regarded her with suspicion. "If your mother delivered this note, why did she not take you then?"

"She's playing with us. Baiting us. This is her idea of a game. It's also why we believe she'll strike amidst the Archbishop's funeral—to make a statement. To rub salt in the wound of the kingdom's grief. La Voisin and the Dames Rouges have already agreed to stand with us. With all of your help, we can finally defeat her."

"We need your help, *frère*." I hesitated before finally extending a hand to him. "You're . . . you're a captain of the Chasseurs now.

Your support might sway King Auguste to our cause."

He knocked my hand away. Bared his teeth. "You are no brother of mine. My brother died with my father. My *brother* would not defend one witch to condemn another—he would kill them both. And you're a fool to believe the king will ever join your *cause*."

"I'm still the same person, Jean. I'm still *me*. Help us. We can be as we were once more. We can honor our father *together*."

He stared at me a beat.

Then he punched me in the face.

I staggered backward, eyes and nose streaming, as Lou snarled and tried to leap forward, caught beneath Coco. Ansel and Beau stepped to my side instead. The former attempted to subdue Jean, who lunged for another attack, while the latter bent to check my nose. "It's not broken," he muttered.

"I *will* honor our father"—Jean Luc struggled to free himself from Ansel, who held him with surprising strength—"when I lash you to the stake for conspiracy. As God is my witness, you will burn for what you've done. I will light your pyre myself."

Blood poured down my mouth, my chin. "Jean—"

He finally shoved Ansel away. "How disappointed he would be to see how far you've fallen, Reid. His golden son."

"Oh, get over it, Jean Luc," Lou snapped. "You can't win a dead man's affection. Even alive, the Archbishop saw you for the sniveling little rat you are—"

He launched himself at her now, completely out of control, but Blaise rose up to meet him, his expression hard as flint. Liana,

Terrance, and a handful of others closed in behind him. Some bared their teeth, incisors sharp and gleaming. Others shifted their eyes yellow. "I have offered Reid Diggory and his companions sanctuary," Blaise said, voice steady. Calm. "Leave now in peace, or do not leave at all."

Lou shook her head vehemently, eyes wide. "Blaise, no. They can't leave—"

Jean Luc swiped at her. "*Give me my Balisarda*—"

The wolves around us growled in agitation. In anticipation.

"Captain . . ." A Chasseur I didn't recognize touched Jean Luc's elbow. "Perhaps we should go."

"I will not leave without—"

"Yes," Blaise said, lifting a hand to his wolves. They pressed closer. Too close now. Close enough to bite. To kill. Their snarls multiplied to a din. "You will."

The Chasseurs needed no further encouragement. Eyes darting, they seized Jean Luc before he could damn them all. Though he roared his protests, they pulled him backward. They kept pulling. His shouts echoed through the trees even after they'd disappeared.

Lou whirled to face Blaise. "What have you done?"

"I have saved you."

"No." Lou stared at him in horror. "You let them *go*. You let them go after we told them our plan. They know now we're traveling to Cesarine. They know we're planning to visit the king. If Jean Luc tips him off, Auguste will arrest us the moment we step foot in the castle."

Grimacing, Coco readjusted her arm on Lou's shoulders. "She's right. Auguste won't want to listen. We've just lost the element of surprise."

"Maybe"—Lou's eyes swept the pack—"maybe if we show up in numbers, we can *make* him listen."

But Blaise shook his head. "Your fight is not our fight. Reid Diggory saved my second son after taking the life of my first. He has fulfilled his debt. My kin will no longer hunt him, and you will leave our homeland in peace. I do not owe him an alliance. I do not owe him anything."

Lou stabbed the air with her finger. "That's horseshit, and you know it—"

His eyes narrowed. "After what you've done, be grateful I do not demand *your* blood, Louise le Blanc."

"He's right." I took her hand in mine, squeezing gently when she opened her mouth to argue. "And we need to leave now if we have any hope of beating Jean Luc to Cesarine."

"What? But—"

"Wait." To my surprise, Liana stepped forward. She'd set her chin in a determined expression. "You may owe him nothing, *Père*, but he saved my brother's life. I owe him everything."

"As do I." Terrance joined her. Though young, his flinty countenance reflected his father's as he nodded in my direction. He didn't make eye contact. "We will join you."

"No." With the curt shake of his head, Blaise lowered his voice to a whisper. "Children, I have already told you, our debt is fulfilled—"

Liana clasped his hands together, holding them between her own. "Our debt is not yours. Adrien was your son, *Père*, but we didn't know him. He's a stranger to Terrance and to me. We must honor this debt—especially now, beneath the face of our mother." She glanced up at the full moon. "Would you have us spurn this obligation? Would you disavow Terrance's life so quickly after she restored him to us?"

Blaise stared down at them both for several seconds. Finally, his facade cracked, and beneath it, his resolve crumbled. He kissed both their foreheads with tears in his eyes. "Yours are the brightest of souls. Of course you must go, and I—I will join you. Though my debt as a man is fulfilled, my duties as a father are not." His eyes cut to mine. "My pack will remain here. You will never step foot in our lands again."

I nodded curtly. "Understood."

We turned and raced toward Cesarine.

A PROMISE

Reid

Blaise, Liana, and Terrance outdistanced us by the next morning, promising to return with reconnaissance of the city landscape. When they found us again—a mere mile outside of Cesarine, hidden within the trees near Les Dents—they delivered our worst fear: the Chasseurs had formed a blockade to enter the city. They checked each wagon, each cart, without bothering to hide their intentions.

"They're searching for you." Liana emerged from behind a juniper in fresh clothes. She joined her father and brother with a grim expression. "I recognized some of them, but I didn't see Jean Luc. He isn't here."

"I assume he went straight to my father." Beau readjusted the hood of his cloak, eyeing the thick congestion of the road. Though his expression remained cool and unaffected, his hands shook. "Hence the blockade."

Lou kicked the juniper's branches in frustration. When snow fell into her boots, she cursed viciously. "That sniveling little *shit.*

Of course he isn't here. He wouldn't want an audience to watch him piss down his leg when he sees me. An appropriate response, mind you."

Despite her brazen words, this crowd made me uncomfortable. It'd grown worse the nearer we'd drawn to the city, as Les Dents was the only road into Cesarine. Part of me rejoiced so many had come to honor the Archbishop. The rest didn't know how to feel. Here—with every face and every voice a reminder—I couldn't properly dissociate. The doors to my fortress rattled. The walls shook. But I couldn't focus on that now. Couldn't focus on anything but Lou. "Are you all right?" she'd whispered earlier when we'd hidden amongst these trees.

I'd studied her face. It seemed she'd reversed her disastrous pattern, yes, but appearances could be deceiving. Memory lasted forever. I'd certainly never forget the sight of her braced within that frozen swamp, fingers contorted, expression cold and hard as the ice at her feet. I doubted she would either. "Are *you?*" I'd whispered back.

She hadn't answered.

She whispered to her matagots now. A third had joined us overnight. A black rat. It perched on her shoulder, eyes beady and bright. No one mentioned it. No one dared look in its direction—as if our willful disregard could somehow make it less real. But the set of Coco's shoulders said the words she didn't, as did the shadow in Ansel's eyes. Even Beau cast me a worried glance.

As for the wolves, they wouldn't go near them. Blaise's lip curled when Absalon sauntered too close.

"What is it?" Taking her hand, I pulled her apart from the others. The matagots followed like shadows. If I knocked the rat from her shoulder—if I wrapped my hands around the necks of the cat and fox—would they leave her in peace? Would they haunt me instead?

"I'm sending word to Claud," she said, and the fox disappeared in a cloud of smoke. "He might know how to get through this blockade undetected."

Beau craned his neck, eavesdropping unapologetically. "That's your plan?" Skepticism laced his voice. "I know Claud somehow... shielded you in Beauchêne, but these aren't bandits."

"You're right." An edge clipped Lou's voice as she faced him. "These are huntsmen armed with Balisardas. I got lucky with Jean Luc—I knew his buttons, and I pressed them. I distracted him, disarmed him. His men didn't dare hurt me while he was under my power. But he isn't here now, and I doubt I'll be able to disarm all two dozen of them without quite literally setting the world on fire." She exhaled impatiently, stroking the rat's nose, as if to—as if to calm down. My stomach twisted. "Even then, we're trying *not* to raise the alarm. We need a quick and quiet entrance."

"They'll be expecting magic," I hurried to add. Anything to keep her from changing strategy. Anything to keep her from the alternative. "And Claud Deveraux hid us along Les Dents. Maybe he can hide us here too."

Beau threw his hands in the air. "This is a completely different situation! These men *know* we're here. They're searching every wagon. For Claud Deveraux to hide us, he'd need to *quite literally* make us disappear."

"Do you have another plan?" Both Lou and the rat glared at him. "If so, by all means, please share with the class." When he didn't answer, she scoffed bitterly. "That's what I thought. Now can you do everyone a favor and shut the hell up? We're anxious enough as it is."

"Lou," Coco admonished in a low voice, but Lou only turned away, crossing her arms and scowling at the snow. Of their own volition, my feet moved—my body angled—to shield her from the others' disapproving looks. She might've deserved them. I didn't care.

"If you're going to reprimand me, you can piss off too." Though she wiped furiously at her eyes, a tear still escaped. I brushed it away with my thumb. Instinctive. "Don't." She jerked, swatting my hand, and turned her back on me too. Absalon hissed at her feet. "I'm *fine*."

I didn't move. Didn't react. Inside, however, I reeled as if she'd struck me—as if the two of us hurtled toward a cliff, heedless, each pulling at the other. Each pushing. Both desperate to save ourselves, and both helpless to stop our trajectory. We were careening toward that edge, Lou and I.

I'd never felt so powerless in my life.

"I'm sorry," I whispered, but she didn't acknowledge me, instead shoving Jean Luc's Balisarda into my hand.

"We didn't have time earlier, but while we're waiting . . . I stole it for you. To replace the one I lost." She pressed it harder. My fingers curled around the hilt reflexively. The silver felt different. Wrong. Though Jean Luc had clearly cared for the blade—it'd been recently cleaned and sharpened—it wasn't *mine*. It didn't smooth the jagged edge in my chest. Didn't fill the empty hole there. I slid it into my bandolier anyway, unsure of what else to do. She continued without enthusiasm. "I know I might've gotten a little carried away in the process. With—with the ice. I'm sorry. I promise it won't happen again."

I promise.

For days I'd waited to hear those words, yet now they rang hollow in my ears. Empty. She didn't understand the meaning of them. Perhaps couldn't. They implied truth, trust. I doubted she'd ever known either. Still—I wanted to believe her. Desperately. And an apology from her didn't come lightly.

I swallowed against the sudden tightness in my throat. "Thank you."

We stayed quiet for a long time after that. Though the sun crept across the sky, the queue hardly moved. And the others' eyes—I felt them on us. Especially the wolves'. Heat prickled along my neck. My ears. I didn't like the way they looked at Lou. They knew her only as she was now. They didn't know her warmth, her compassion. Her love.

After what you've done, be grateful I do not demand your *blood, Louise le Blanc.*

Though I trusted they wouldn't harm *me*, they'd made no such promise to her. Whatever madness this day inevitably brought, I wouldn't leave them alone with her. I would give them no opportunity to retaliate. Forlorn, I traced the curve of Lou's neck with my gaze. She'd knotted her white hair at her nape. Tied another ribbon around her throat. All at once so familiar yet so different.

I had to fix her.

When the sun crested the trees, the fox at last returned to us. She nosed Lou's boot, staring up at her intently. Communicating silently with her eyes. "Does she . . . speak to you?" I asked.

Lou frowned. "Not with words. It's more like a feeling. Like—like her consciousness touches mine, and I *understand*." Her head snapped up. "Toulouse and Thierry are coming."

Within minutes, two familiar black heads parted the crowd, proving her right. With a crutch under his arm, Toulouse whistled one of Deveraux's tunes. He grinned at Liana, tipping his hat, before grasping my shoulder.

"*Bonjour à vous*," he told her. "Good morrow, good morrow. And fancy meeting you here, Monsieur Diggory."

"Shhh." I ducked my head, but no one on the road paid us any notice. "Are you daft?"

"Some days." His gaze fell behind us to the werewolves, and he grinned wider. "I see I was mistaken. How unexpected. I'll admit, I doubted your powers of persuasion, but I've never been more pleased to be wrong." He elbowed Thierry with a chuckle. "Perhaps I should try it more often, eh, brother?" His grin faded slightly as he turned back to me. "Would you like to try that card now?"

I nodded to his crutch instead. "Are you injured?"

"Of course not." He tossed it to me. "I'm fit as Deveraux's fiddle. That's one of his stilts, by the way. He sends his assistance."

Thierry swung a bag from his shoulder and handed it to Lou.

"Spectacles?" Beau leaned over her, incredulous, withdrawing a pair of wire frames. She pushed him away. "Mustaches? Wigs? *This* is his assistance? Costumery?"

"Without magic, there's little other way to trick the huntsmen, is there?" Toulouse's eyes gleamed with mischief. "I mistook you for intelligent along Les Dents, Beauregard. It seems I'm wrong *twice* in one day. It's absolutely thrilling."

I ignored them both as Thierry's voice resounded in my head. *I am sorry. Claud wishes he could've come himself, but he won't leave Zenna and Seraphine alone.*

My thoughts sharpened. *Has something happened to them?*

It's dangerous inside the city, Reid. Worse even than usual. Jean Luc warned the king of Morgane's threat, and the Chasseurs have arrested three women this morning alone. The rest guard him and his daughters inside the castle. Toulouse has requested we not assist you further.

I startled. *What?*

The card, Reid. Prove him wrong a third time.

What does the card *have to do with anything?*

Everything. He sighed as Lou pushed Beau out of her personal space again, shaking his head. *I like you, huntsman, so I will help you one last time: Morgane can't touch the king in his castle, but he will join the funeral procession this afternoon. It's his duty as sovereign to honor the Holy Father. If Morgane is to strike, it will be then. Though Jean Luc resides with him, he no longer holds his Balisarda.* His black eyes dipped to the sapphire in my bandolier. *A dozen others are new. Inexperienced. They took their vows only this morning.*

The tournament. I closed my eyes in resignation. Amidst the horrors of Les Dents, I'd forgotten about the Chasseurs' tournament. If there'd been any doubt Morgane would attack at the funeral, it vanished with the realization. The brotherhood had never been weaker. The crowd had never been larger. And the stakes—they'd never been higher. It was the perfect stage for Morgane, grander even than that on Saint Nicolas Day. We needed to get into the city. Now. *Is there nothing else Claud can do?*

You do not need Claud. You need only trust yourself.

My gaze cut to Lou. She still bickered with Beau. Toulouse looked on with amusement. *If you're suggesting I use magic, I won't.*

It is not your enemy, Reid.

It's not a friend, either.

Your fear is irrational. You are not Louise. You are reason, where she is impulse. You are earth. She is fire.

Anger sparked. More riddles. More convolution. *What are you talking about?*

Your choices are not her choices, friend. Do not condemn yourself to her fate. My brother and I have used magic for years, and we remain in control of ourselves. So too does Cosette. With temperance, magic is a powerful ally.

But I heard only some of his words. *Her fate?*

As if in answer, Beau muttered, "I never thought I'd die dressed as a hag. I suppose there are less interesting ways to go." He made to throw the spectacles back into the bag, raising his voice at my uncertain glance. "What? You know how this ends. We're arming ourselves with scraps of lace against blades of steel. We're—we're playing dress-up, for Christ's sake. The Chasseurs will kill us out of spite for the insult."

"You forget I sprinkle spite into my tea every morning." Lou snatched the spectacles from his hand and shoved them on her nose. "Besides, playing dress-up hasn't failed me yet. What could possibly go wrong?"

TRIAL BY FIRE

Reid

Everything went wrong.

"That wagon there." Crouched in the boughs of a pine, Lou pointed to a wagon apart from the crowd. Its horse was bony. Old. A middle-aged man held the reins. His leathery skin and gnarled hands marked him a farmer, and his gaunt face marked him poor. Hungry.

"No." I shook my head abruptly, voice brusque. "I won't prey on the weak."

"You will if you want to live." At my silence, she sighed impatiently. "Look, those are the only two covered transports within a mile. I'll be preying on that one"—she pointed to the gilded carriage in front of the farmer's wagon—"so I'll be close, in case you need help. Just give me a shout, but remember—it's Lucida, not Lou."

"This is madness." My chest constricted at the thought of what I was about to do. "It'll never work."

"Not with that attitude!" Gripping my shoulders, she turned

me to face her. Nausea rolled through my stomach. Disguised in Deveraux's velvet suit and hat, she looked at me from behind gold spectacles. An aristocrat's scholarly son on his return home from Amandine. "Remember your story. You were set upon by bandits, and they broke your nose." She adjusted the bloody bandage on my face for good measure. "And your leg." She tapped the makeshift crutch we'd fashioned out of the stilt. "Just knock on the door. The wife will take pity on you after one look."

"And if she doesn't?"

"Knock her out. Drag her inside. Enchant her." She didn't flinch at the prospect of bludgeoning an innocent woman. "Do whatever is necessary to get inside that wagon."

"I thought you said no magic."

She snorted impatiently. "This isn't the time for a principled stand, Reid. We can't risk magic out in the open, but within the confines of her wagon, do whatever is necessary. If even one person recognizes us, we're dead."

"And when the Chasseur arrives to search the wagon?"

"You're in a wig. Your face is covered. You might be worrying for nothing. But if he recognizes you—if he suspects—you'll have to disarm him while keeping him conscious. Otherwise he can't wave you through the blockade."

"Even if I threaten to slit his throat, a Chasseur will never wave me through that blockade."

"He will if he's enchanted." I opened my mouth to refuse— or to vomit—but she continued, undeterred. "Whatever you do, don't cause a scene. Be quick and quiet. That's the only way we survive this."

Saliva coated my mouth, and I struggled to breathe, clutching my bandolier for support. I didn't fear meeting my brethren. I didn't fear exchanging blows or obtaining injury. I didn't even fear capture, but if that happened—if the Chasseurs arrested me here—Lou would intervene. They'd call in reinforcements. They would hunt her, and this time, she wouldn't escape.

That could not happen.

Even if—even if that meant using magic.

It is not your enemy, Reid.

With temperance, magic is a powerful ally.

"I won't. I *can't*." I nearly choked on the words. "Someone will smell it. They'll know we're here."

She tugged my coat closed over my bandolier. "Maybe. But this road is teeming with people. It'll take them time to distinguish who's casting it. You can force the enchanted Chasseur to wave you through before they figure it out."

"Lou." The word was desperate, pleading, but I didn't care. "There are too many things that could go wrong—"

She kissed my cheek swiftly. "You can do this. And if you can't—if something *does* go wrong—just punch the Chasseur in the nose and run like hell."

"Great plan."

She chuckled, but the sound was strained. "It worked for Coco and Ansel."

Pretending to be newlyweds, they'd already slipped through the convoy on foot. The Chasseur who'd inspected them had been new, and they'd passed into Cesarine unscathed. Beau had forgone costume completely, instead finding a pretty young widow to smuggle him inside. She'd nearly fainted at the sight of his royal face. Blaise and his kin hadn't revealed how they planned to slip into the city. As there'd been no commotion, I assumed they made it in undetected.

I doubted Lou and I would be so lucky.

"Reid. *Reid.*" I snapped to attention. Lou spoke faster now. "The enchantment should come naturally, but if you need a pattern, focus with specific intent. Visualize your objectives. And remember, it's always, *always* about balance."

"Nothing about magic comes easily to me."

Liar.

"Because you're incapacitating yourself with hate," Lou said. "Open yourself up to your magic. Accept it, welcome it, and it'll come to you. Are you ready?"

Seek us.

My lips were numb. "No."

But there was little time to argue. The wagon and carriage were almost upon us.

She squeezed my hand, tearing her gaze from the carriage to look at me. "I know things have changed between us. But I want *you* to know that I love you. Nothing can ever change that. And if you die today, I will find you in the afterlife and kick your ass for leaving me. Understand?"

My voice was weak. "I—"

"Good."

And then she was gone, tugging a book from her pack and dashing toward the carriage. "*Excusez-moi, monsieur!*" she called to the driver, pushing her spectacles up her nose. "But my horse has thrown a shoe. . . ."

A hollow pit opened in my stomach as her voice faded into the crowd.

I love you. Nothing can ever change that.

Damn it.

I didn't get to say it back.

Adopting a limp, leaning heavily on my crutch, I navigated the crowd to the wagon. The convoy was at a standstill, and the farmer—preoccupied with a dirty child throwing rocks at his horse—didn't see me. I knocked once, twice, on the frame. Nothing. I knocked louder.

"What d'yeh want?" A reedy woman with sharp cheekbones and horselike teeth finally poked her head out. A cross dangled from her throat, and a cap covered her hair. Pious, then. Probably traveling to Cesarine to pay her respects. Hope swelled in my chest. Perhaps she *would* take pity on me. It was the mandate of our Lord to help the helpless.

Her scowl quickly punctured that hope. "We don't 'ave no food fer beggars, so clear off!"

"Apologies, *madame*," I said hastily, catching the flap when she moved to yank it shut, "but I don't need food. Bandits set upon me down the road"—I rapped my crutch against the wagon for emphasis—"and I cannot continue my journey on foot. Do you have room in your wagon for one more?"

"No," she snapped, trying to wrestle the flap from my hand.

No hesitation. No remorse. "Not fer the likes o' you. Yer the third one oo's come knockin' at our wagon this mornin', and I'll be tellin' you the same as I told them: we won't be takin' no chances wif strange folk today. Not wif His Eminence's funeral this evenin'." She clutched the cross at her throat with spindly fingers and closed her eyes. "May God keep 'is soul." When she cracked an eye open and saw me still standing there, she added, "Now shove off."

The wagon inched forward, but I held firm, forcing myself to remain calm. To think like Lou would think. To lie. "I'm not a witch, *madame*, and I'm in desperate need of aid."

Her mouth—deeply lined—twisted in confusion. "O course yer not a witch. D'yeh think I'm daft? Everyone knows menfolk can't have magic."

At the word, those nearest us turned to stare. Eyes wide and wary.

I cursed inwardly.

"Bernadette?" The farmer's voice rose above the din of the crowd. More heads swiveled in our direction. "Is this lad botherin' you?"

Before she could answer—before she could seal my fate—I hissed, "'He that despiseth his neighbor sinneth, but he that hath mercy on the poor, happy is he.'"

Her eyes narrowed. "What did you just say?"

"'He that giveth unto the poor shall not lack: but he that hideth his eyes shall have many a curse.'"

"Are you quotin' scripture at me, boy?"

"'Withhold not good from them to whom it is due, when it is in the power of thine hand to do it.'"

"Bernadette!" The farmer stood from his box. "Did you hear me, love? Shall I fetch a Chasseur?"

"Should I continue?" White-knuckled on the wagon flap, my fingers trembled. I fisted them tighter, glaring at her. "For as the Lord commands—"

"That's enough o' you." Though her wrinkled lip curled, she surveyed me with grudging appreciation. "I don't be needin' no lessons in 'oliness from guttersnipes." To her husband, she called, "Everythin's fine, Lyle! This one 'ere busted 'is ankle and needs a lift is all."

"Well, tell 'im we don't want no—"

"I'll tell 'im what I want to tell him!" Jerking her head behind her, she drew the wagon flap aside. "Come inside, then, Yer Holiness, a'fore I change me mind."

The inside of Bernadette's wagon looked nothing like the inside of Troupe de Fortune's. Every inch of the troupe's wagons had been crammed full. Trunks of costumes and trinkets. Crates of food. Props. Lanterns. Cots and bedrolls.

This wagon was bare save a single blanket and a near empty satchel of food. A lonely pot sat beside it.

"Like I said," Bernadette muttered, hunkering down on the floor. "No food fer beggars here."

We waited in stony silence as the wagon crept closer to the Chasseurs. "You look familiar," she said after several moments. She peered at me suspiciously, eyes sharper than I would've liked.

They studied my black wig, my charcoal-dark eyebrows. The bloody bandage on my nose. I readjusted it involuntarily. "'Ave we met a'fore?"

"No."

"Why is you goin' to Cesarine, then?"

I stared at my hands without seeing them. *To attend the funeral of the man I killed. To fraternize with blood witches and werewolves. To kill the mother of the woman I love.* "Same as you."

"You don't strike me as the religious type."

I pinned her with a glare. "Likewise."

She harrumphed and crossed her arms. "Mouthy lit'le imp, isn't you? Ungrateful too. Should've made you walk like all the rest, busted ankle an' all."

"We're comin' up on 'em now!" Lyle called from outside. "City's straight ahead!"

Bernadette rose and marched to the front of the wagon, sticking her head out once more. I strode after her.

Framed by the gray skyline of Cesarine, a dozen Chasseurs rode through the crowd, slowing traffic. Some inspected the faces of those on foot. Some dismounted to check wagons and carriages intermittently. I recognized eight of them. Eight out of twelve. When one of those eight—Philippe—started toward our wagon, I cursed.

"Watch yer mouth!" Bernadette said in outrage, elbowing me sharply. "And budge over, would you—" She stopped short when she saw my face. "Yer white as a sheet, you are."

Philippe's deep voice rumbled through the procession, and he pointed toward us. "Have we cleared this one yet?"

Older than me by several decades, he wore a beard streaked through with silver. It did nothing to diminish the breadth of his chest or heavy muscle of his arms. A scar still disfigured his throat from his battle with Adrien's kin in the werewolf raid.

He'd hated me for stealing his glory that day. For stealing his advancement.

Shit.

Jean Luc's Balisarda weighed heavier than the other knives in my bandolier. If Philippe recognized me, I'd need to kill or disarm him. And I couldn't kill him. I couldn't kill another brother. But if I disarmed him instead, I'd have to—

No. My mind raged against the thought.

This isn't the time for a principled stand, Reid, Lou had said. *If even one person recognizes us, we're dead.*

She was right. Of course she was right. And even if it made me a hypocrite—even if it condemned me to Hell—I would channel those insidious voices. I would hang myself with their golden patterns. If it meant Lou would live, I would do it. Damn the consequences. I would do it.

But how?

Open yourself up to your magic. Accept it, welcome it, and it'll come to you.

I hadn't welcomed anything on Modraniht, yet the pattern had still appeared. The same had happened at the pool near the Hollow. In both situations, I'd been desperate. Hopeless. Morgane had just cut Lou's throat, and I'd watched as her blood poured into the basin, draining her life by the second. The golden cord had risen from my pit of despair, and I'd reacted instinctively. There hadn't been time for anything else. And—and at the pool—

The memory of Lou's blue lips surfaced. Her ashen skin.

But this wasn't like that. Lou wasn't dying in front of me now. I tried to summon the same sense of urgency. If Philippe caught me, Lou *would* die. Surely that possibility should trigger something. I waited anxiously for the floodgates to burst open, for gold to explode in my vision.

It didn't.

It seemed imagining Lou dying wasn't the same as watching it happen.

Philippe continued toward us, close enough now to touch the horses. I nearly roared in frustration. What was I supposed to *do*?

You could ask. A small, sinister voice echoed through my thoughts at last, reverberating as if legion. The hair on my neck rose. *You need only seek us, lost one, and you shall find.*

Panicking, I shoved at it instinctively.

An unearthly chuckle. *You cannot escape us, Reid Labelle. We are part of you.* As if to prove its words, it latched tighter, the pressure in my head building—painful now—as tendrils of gold snaked outward, stabbing deep and taking root. Into my mind. My heart. My lungs. I choked on them, struggling to breathe, but they only pressed closer. Consuming me. *For so long we have slept in the darkness, but now, we are awake. We will protect you. We will not let you go. Seek us.*

Black threatened the edges of my vision. My panic intensified. I had to get out, had to stop this—

Staggering backward, I faintly registered Bernadette and Lyle's alarm. "What's the matter wif you, eh?" Bernadette asked. When I didn't answer—couldn't answer—she moved slowly to her bag. My eyes struggled to focus on her, to remain open. I dropped to my knees, fighting desperately to repress this growing *thing* inside me—this monster clawing through my skin. Inexplicable light flickered around us.

He approaches, child. He is coming. The voice turned hungry now. Anticipatory. The pressure in my head built with each word. Blinding me. Tormenting me. My nightmares made flesh. I clutched my head against the pain, a scream rising in my throat. *He will burn us if you let him.*

"What's happenin' wif yer head?"

No. My mind warred against itself. The pain cleaved me in two. *This isn't right. This isn't—*

"I'm talkin' to you, imp!"

He will burn Louise.

No—

"Oi!" A whistle cut through the air, and fresh pain exploded behind my ear. I crumpled to the wagon floor. Groaning softly, I could just distinguish Bernadette's blurred form above me. She lifted her frying pan to strike again. "Bleedin' mad, aren't yeh? I knew it. And today o' all days—"

"Wait." I held up a weak hand. The peculiar light shone brighter now. "Please."

She lurched backward, face twisting in alarm. "What's this happenin' with yer skin, then, eh? What's goin' on?"

"I don't—" My vision sharpened on my hand. On the soft light emanating from it. Hideous despair swept through me. Hideous relief.

Seek us seek us seek us.

"P-Put down the frying pan, *madame*."

She shook her head frantically, struggling to keep her arm raised. "Wha' witchcraft is this?"

I tried again, louder now. A strange humming filled my ears, and the inexplicable desire to soothe her overwhelmed me—to soothe and be soothed. "It's going to be all right." My voice sounded strange, even to my own ears. Layered. Resonant. Part of me still raged against it, but that part was useless now. I left it behind. "Put down the frying pan."

The frying pan fell to the floor.

"Lyle!" Her eyes boggled from her head, and her nostrils flared. "Lyle, help—!"

The wagon flap burst open in response. We turned as one to see Philippe standing in the entrance, his Balisarda drawn. Despite the bandage—the wig, the cosmetics—he recognized me immediately. Hatred burned in his eyes. "Reid Diggory."

Kill him.

This time, I heeded the voice without hesitation.

With lethal speed, I charged, seizing his wrist and dragging him into the wagon. His eyes widened—shocked—for a split second. Then he attacked. I laughed, evading his blade easily.

When the sound reverberated through the wagon, infectious and strange, he recoiled.

"It can't be," he breathed. "You can't be a—a—"

He lunged, but again, I moved too quick, sidestepping at the last moment. He barreled into Bernadette instead, and the two careened into the wall of the wagon. My skin erupted with light at her shrieks.

Silence her!

"Be quiet!" The words tore through me of their own volition, and she slumped—mercifully quiet—with her mouth closed and her eyes glazed. Philippe launched to his feet just as Lyle entered the wagon, bellowing at the top of his lungs.

"Bernadette! Bernadette!"

I struggled to look at him, prying Philippe's fingers from my throat with one hand and holding his Balisarda off with the other. My wig tumbled to the floor. "Qui—et—" I said, voice strangled, as Philippe and I crashed through the wagon. But Lyle didn't quiet. He continued shouting, lunging forward to grab Bernadette beneath the arms and drag her from the wagon.

"Wait!" I flung a hand out blindly to stop him, but no patterns emerged. Not even a flicker. Anger erupted at my own ineptitude, and the light emanating from my skin vanished abruptly. "Stop!"

"Help us!" Lyle dove from the wagon. "It's Reid Diggory! He's a witch! HELP!"

New voices sounded outside as Chasseurs converged. Blood roaring in my ears—the voices in my mind damnably silent—I wrenched away from Philippe, flinging the blanket in his face. A quiet entrance into the city was no longer possible. I had to flee. To *run*. Disentangling himself from the blanket, he slipped on the food satchel and flailed backward. I dove for the frying pan.

Before he could regain his footing—before I could reconsider—I swung it at his head.

The crack reverberated through my bones, and he toppled to the wagon floor, unconscious. I dropped to make sure his chest moved. Up and down. Up and down. The other Chasseurs tore aside the wagon's flap just as I leapt through the front, vaulting over the box to the horse's back. It reared, braying indignantly, and the wagon's front wheels lifted from the ground, tipping the structure precariously. Inside, the Chasseurs shouted in alarm. Their bodies thudded into the canvas.

I fumbled with the horse's harness, cursing as more Chasseurs sprinted toward me. Slick with sweat, my fingers slipped over the buckles. I cursed and tried again.

"It's Reid Diggory!" someone shouted. More voices took up the call. Blood roared in my ears.

"Murderer!"

"Witch!"

"Arrest him!"

"ARREST HIM!"

Losing any semblance of control, I tore at the last buckle with frantic fingers. A Chasseur I didn't recognize reached me first. I kicked him in the face—finally, *finally* loosening the clasp—and urged the horse forward with a violent squeeze of my legs. It bolted, and I held on for dear life.

"Out of the way!" I roared. People dove sideways, dragging children with them, as the horse careened toward the city. One man was too slow, and a hoof caught his leg, breaking it. The Chasseurs on horseback pounded after me. They gained ground quickly. Theirs were stallions, bred for speed and strength, and mine was an emaciated mare on her last leg. I urged her on anyway.

If I could clear the city limits, perhaps I could lose them in the streets—

The crowd thickened as the road narrowed, transitioning from dirt to cobblestone. The first buildings rose up to swallow me. Above, a shadow leapt lithely from rooftop to rooftop, following the shouts that chased me. It pointed frantically to the dormer looming ahead.

I nearly wept with relief.

Lou.

Then I realized what she wanted me to do.

No. No, I couldn't—

"Got you!" A Chasseur's hand snaked out and caught the back of my coat. The others closed in behind him. Legs cinching the mare like a vise, I twisted to break his grip, but the mare had had enough.

Braying wildly, she reared once more, and I saw my opportunity.

Climbing up her neck—praying to whoever might be listening—I caught the metal sign overhead with the tips of my fingers. It splintered under my weight, but I kicked hard, leveraging myself against the mare's back and leaping onto the dormer. The mare and Chasseurs' stallions cantered past below.

"STOP HIM!"

Gasping for air, I scrabbled for purchase against the rooftop. My vision pitched and rolled.

"Just keep climbing!" Lou's voice rang out above me, and my head snapped up. She leaned over the roof's edge, fingers splayed and straining to reach me. But her hand was so small. So far away. "Don't look down! Just look at me, Reid! Keep looking at me!"

Below, the Chasseurs roared orders, urging the crowd to part as they turned their horses around.

"AT ME, REID!"

Right. Swallowing hard, I set to finding pockmarks in the stone wall. I inched higher. My head spun.

Higher.

My breath caught.

Higher.

My muscles seized.

Higher.

The Chasseurs had maneuvered back to me. I heard them dismounting. Heard them starting to climb.

Lou's hand caught my wrist and heaved. I focused on her face, on her freckles. Through sheer willpower alone, I clambered over the eave and collapsed. But we didn't have time to relax. She pulled me to my feet, already sprinting for the next rooftop. "What *happened?*"

I followed her. Concentrated on my breathing. It was easier now, with her here. "Your plan was shit."

She had the gall to laugh, but quickly stopped when an arrow whizzed past her face. "C'mon. I'll lose these jackasses within three blocks."

I didn't reply. It was best I kept my mouth closed.

THE DROWNING

Lou

Always aiming to please, I lost them in two.

Their voices faded as we ran, dipping into shadowy alcoves and dropping behind ramshackle dormers. The key was breaking their line of sight. Once that happened, it was too easy to slip into the boundlessness of the city.

No one could disappear like I could.

No one had the practice.

I dropped to a forgotten backstreet in East End. Reid landed a second later, collapsing against me. Though I tried to hold him steady, we both tumbled to the dirty cobblestones. He kept his arms locked around my waist, however, and buried his face in my lap. His heart pulsed a frantic rhythm against my thigh. "I can't do that again."

Throat suddenly thick, I stroked his hair. "That's fine. They're gone." His breathing gradually slowed, and finally, he sat up. I let him go reluctantly. "Before your fiasco, I sent Charles to find Madame Labelle. She booked us rooms at an inn called Léviathan."

"Charles?"

"The rat."

He expelled a harsh breath. "Oh."

Shame—now familiar—washed through me all over again. Though sharp words rose to my tongue in response, I bit down on them hard, drawing blood, and offered him a hand. "I already sent Absalon and Brigitte to fetch Coco, Ansel, and Beau. Charles went to the werewolves and blood witches. We'll all need to strategize before the funeral this afternoon."

We climbed to our feet together, and he kissed the back of my hand before releasing it. "It'll be difficult to gain an audience with the king. Thierry said all Chasseurs who aren't at the blockade are inside the castle. Maybe Beau can—"

"Wait." Though I forced a chuckle, there was nothing funny about that obstinate gleam in his eyes. "You can't seriously mean to still speak with Auguste? Jean Luc tipped him off. He knows you're coming. He—he knows Madame Labelle's a witch, and if those Chasseurs' shouts were any indication, he'll soon know *you're* one too." Reid's face blanched at the last. *Ah.* It seemed he hadn't yet drawn *that* conclusion. I hurried to press my advantage. "He knows you're a witch," I repeated. "He won't help you. He certainly won't help me. We don't *need* him, Reid. The Dames Rouges and loup garou are powerful allies."

His lips pursed as he considered this—his jaw clenched—and I waited for him to see the sense in my plan. But he shook his head and muttered, "No. I'll still speak with him. We need a united front against Morgane."

I gaped at him. "Reid—"

A group of children raced past our alley at that moment, chasing a snarling cat. The slowest of them hesitated when he saw us. I jerked my brim lower on my forehead, and Reid hastily retied the bandage over his eye. "We need to get off the streets," he said. "Our entrance into the city wasn't exactly subtle—"

"Thanks for that—"

"And East End will be crawling with Chasseurs and constabulary soon."

I waved to the child, who grinned and took off after his friends, before slipping my elbow through Reid's. I poked my head into the street. It was less crowded here, the majority of funeral visitors congregating in the wealthier West district. The shops lining the streets were closed. "Léviathan is a few blocks past Soleil et Lune."

Reid quickened his pace, adopting a limp once more. "Given our history, the theater will be the first place the Chasseurs look."

Something in his voice made me pause. I frowned up at him. "That wasn't intentional, by the way. My little stunt in the theater. I don't think I ever told you."

"You're kidding."

"I'm not." With nonchalance, I tipped my hat to a nearby woman. Her mouth parted at my velvet suit. Not exactly mourning attire, but at least it was a nice deep shade of aubergine. Knowing Claud, it could've been canary yellow. "Completely accidental, but what could I do? It's not my fault you couldn't keep your hands off my breasts." When he sputtered indignantly, I pressed on, smirking. "I don't blame you in the slightest."

Careful to keep my brim low, I kept a sharp eye on passersby. A familiar air of trepidation hung heavy and thick overhead, as it always did when a crowd this size gathered in Cesarine. People from every walk of life had come to honor the late Archbishop: aristocrats, clergymen, and peasants held vigil together as we neared the cathedral, where the Archbishop's body waited to receive burial rites. Dressed all in black, they leeched the color from an already dreary city. Even the sky was overcast today, as if it too mourned the fate of the wrong man.

The Archbishop didn't deserve anyone's grief.

The only color in the streets came from the fanfare. The usual Lyon flags had been replaced with brilliant red banners depicting the Archbishop's coat of arms: a bear spouting a fountain of stars. Drops of blood in a sea of black and gray.

"Stop." Reid's eyes widened with horror at something in the distance. He pivoted in front of me, clutching my arms as if to shield me from it. "Turn around. Let's go a different way—"

I shook him off, rising to my toes to see over the crowd.

There, at the base of the cathedral, stood three wooden stakes. And chained to those stakes—

"Oh my god," I breathed.

Chained to those stakes were three charred bodies.

Limbs crumbling—hair gone—the corpses were near indistinguishable. Behind them, ash coated the cathedral steps, thicker than the snow on the street. Bile rose in my throat. There had been others before these women. Many others. And recently. The wind hadn't yet carried away their ashes.

But true witches were careful and clever. Surely so many hadn't been caught since Modraniht.

"These women"—I shook my head in disbelief—"they can't all have been witches."

"No." Cradling the back of my head, Reid pulled me to his chest. I inhaled deeply, ignoring the sting of pain in my eyes. "No, they probably weren't."

"Then what—?"

"After the Archbishop, the king would've needed a show of power. He would've needed to reestablish control. Anyone suspicious would have burned."

"Without proof?" I leaned back, searching his face for answers. His eyes were pained. "Without trial?"

He clenched his jaw, looking back at the blackened corpses. "He doesn't need proof. He's the king."

I spotted her the moment Reid and I turned away—thin as a reed with ebony skin and onyx eyes, standing so still she could've been the statue of Saint-Cécile if not for her hair blowing in the breeze. Though I'd known her my entire life, I couldn't read the emotion in her eyes as she stared at the women's remains.

As she turned on her heel and fled into the crowd.

Manon.

"Léviathan is that way." I craned my neck to keep her in my sights, jerking my chin westward. A golden-haired man had followed her, catching her hand and spinning her into his arms. Instead of protesting—of spitting in his face—she gave him a tight smile. That arcane emotion in her eyes melted to unmistakable warmth as she gazed at him. Just as unmistakable, however, was her sorrow. As if trying to banish the emotion, he peppered her cheeks with kisses. When the two started forward once more, I hurried after them. "I'll meet you there in a quarter hour."

"Hold on." Reid seized my arm with an incredulous expression. "We aren't separating."

"I'll be fine. If you keep to the side streets and maybe hunch a bit, you will be too—"

"Not a chance, Lou." His eyes followed mine, narrowing as they searched the crowd, and he slid his grip from my elbow to my hand. "What is it? What did you see?"

"You are the most obstinate—" I stopped short with an impatient huff. "*Fine.* Come with me. But stay low and stay quiet." Without another word, fingers still entwined with his, I slipped through the crowd. No one spared us a second glance, their eyes rapt on the three burning women. Their fascination sickened me.

Manon appeared to be leading the golden-haired man to a less congested area. We followed as quickly and noiselessly as we could, but twice we were forced to duck out of sight to avoid Chasseurs. By the time we found them again, Manon had steered the man down a deserted alley. Smoke from a nearby trash pile nearly obscured its entrance. If not for the man's panicked cry, we might've walked straight past.

"You don't have to do this," he said, voice cracking. Exchanging a wary glance, Reid and I crouched behind the trash and peered through the smoke. Manon had cornered him against a wall. Hands raised, she wept openly, her tears flowing so thick and so fast that she struggled to breathe. "We can find another way."

"You don't understand." Though her entire body spasmed, she lifted her hands higher. "Three more burned this morning. She'll be wild—crazed. And if she finds out about us—"

"How can she?"

"She has eyes everywhere, Gilles! If she even suspects I'm attached to you, she'll—she'll do horrible things. She tortured the others for no other reason than their parentage. She'll do worse to you. She'll *enjoy* it. And if—if I return to her again today empty-handed, she'll know. She'll come for you herself, and I would rather *die* than see you in her hands." She pulled a blade from her cloak. "I promise you won't suffer."

He extended his hands, beseeching, reaching to hold her even as she threatened his life. "So we run away. We leave this place. I have some money saved from cobbling. We can sail to Lustere or—or anywhere. We can build a new life far, far away from here. Somewhere Morgane's influence doesn't reach."

At my mother's name, Reid stiffened. I glanced at him, watching as he finally placed Manon's face.

Head thrashing, she wept harder. "No. No, stop. Please. I *can't*."

"You *can*, Manon. *We* can. Together."

"She gave me orders, Gilles. If—if I don't do this, she will."

"Manon, please—"

"This wasn't supposed to happen." Her hands shook around the blade. "*None* of this was supposed to happen. I—I was supposed to find you and kill you. I wasn't supposed to—to—" A strangled sound tore from her throat as she stepped closer. "They killed my sister, Gilles. They killed her. I—I swore on her pyre I'd avenge her death. I swore to *end* this. I—I—" Her face crumpled, and she lifted the blade to his throat. "I love you."

To his credit, Gilles didn't flinch. He merely dropped his hands, eyes tracing her face as if trying to memorize it, and brushed his lips to her forehead. "I love you too."

They stared at each other. "Turn around," Manon whispered.

"I have to stop her." Tension radiated from every muscle in Reid's body. Unsheathing Jean Luc's Balisarda, he rose to charge forward, but I leapt in front of him—tears streaming down my own cheeks—and pressed my hands against his chest. Manon couldn't know he was here. I had to hide him. I had to make sure she never saw. "What are you doing?" he asked, incredulity twisting his face, but I only shoved him backward.

"Move, Reid." Panic stole the heat from my voice, made it breathless, desperate. I pushed him harder. "*Please*. You have to move. You have to go—"

"*No.*" His hands pried my wrists away. "I have to *help*—"

Behind us, something thudded to the ground. It was a horrible, final sound.

Too late—locked in our own sick embrace—we turned as one to see Gilles lying facedown on the cobblestones. Manon's knife protruded from the base of his skull.

My breath left me in a painful rush, and suddenly, only Reid's hands kept me upright. Blood roared in my ears. "Oh my god."

Manon sank to her knees, pulling him into her lap and closing her eyes. His blood soaked her dress. Her hands. She cradled him to her neck anyway. Though her tears had finally stopped, she gasped as she rocked him, as she slid the knife free of his flesh and dropped it to the ground. It landed in the pool of Gilles's blood. "This isn't God, Louise." Her voice was wooden. Hollow. "This isn't Goddess, either. No divinity smiles upon us now."

I stepped toward her despite myself, but Reid held me back. "Manon—"

"Morgane says sacrifice is necessary." She clutched Gilles tighter, shoulders shaking and fresh tears spilling down her cheeks. "She says we must give before we receive, but my sister is still dead."

Acid coated my tongue. I said the words anyway. "Did killing him bring her back?"

Her eyes snapped to mine. Instead of fury, they filled with a hopelessness so deep I could've drowned in it. I *wanted* to drown in it—to sink beneath its depths and never resurface, to leave this hell behind. But I couldn't, and neither could she. Reaching slowly for the knife, her fingers swam instead through her lover's blood. "Run, Louise. Run far and run fast, so we never find you."

MADAME SAUVAGE'S
CABINET OF CURIOSITIES

Lou

Heart still racing from Manon's warning, I dragged Reid down the nearest alleyway—through a narrow, shadowed arch—and into the first shop I saw. If Manon had followed us, we couldn't risk staying on the street. A bell tinkled at our entrance, and the sign above the door swayed.

MADAME SAUVAGE'S CABINET OF CURIOSITIES

I skidded to a halt, regarding the little shop warily. Stuffed rats danced in the window display, alongside glass beetles and dusty books with gold-painted edges. The shelves nearest us—teetering between black-and-white floors and starry ceilings—had been crammed with a motley assortment of animal skulls, gemstones, pointed teeth, and amber bottles. Pinned along the far wall, barely visible beneath all the clutter, were cerulean-blue butterfly wings.

Reid's silence cracked at the queerness of the place. "What . . . what is this?"

"It's an emporium." My voice came out a whisper, yet it still seemed to echo all around us. The hair on my neck rose. If we left now, Manon might see us—or worse, follow us to Léviathan. Grabbing a brown wig from a particularly hideous marionette, I tossed it to him. "Put this on. The Chasseurs recognized you earlier. You need a new disguise."

He crumpled the wig in his fist. "Your disguises don't work, Lou. They never have."

I paused in rifling through a basket of woven fabrics. "Would you prefer we use magic instead? I noticed you used it earlier to get yourself out of that little bind with the Chasseurs. How does that work? You're allowed to use it when you deem necessary, but I'm not?"

He clenched his jaw, refusing to look at me. "I used it responsibly."

They were the simplest words—perhaps spoken innocently—yet anger cracked open in my stomach all the same, like a rotten egg that'd been waiting to hatch. I felt it rising to my cheeks, enflaming me. I didn't care that we were standing in a house of horrors. I didn't care that the clerk was probably listening out of sight, that Manon was likely closing in at this very moment.

Slowly, I removed my spectacles and placed them on the shelf. "Say what you need to say, Reid, and say it now."

He didn't hesitate. "Who was the man, Lou? Why didn't you let me save him?"

My heart dropped like a stone. Though I'd expected the question—though I'd known this conversation to be inevitable after what we'd witnessed—I was less prepared to address it now than I'd been in Beauchêne. I swallowed hard, tugging on my cravat, trying and failing to articulate the situation without causing irreparable damage. I didn't want to lie. I *certainly* didn't want to tell the truth. "We've been fighting for days, Reid," I deflected. "Those aren't the right questions."

"Answer them anyway."

I opened my mouth to do exactly that—unsure what words would spill out—but an elderly woman with deep, leathery skin hobbled toward us, swathed in a burgundy cloak three times her size. Golden rings glinted on her every finger, and a maroon scarf enveloped her hair. She smiled at us, brown eyes crinkling at the corners. "Hello, dearies. Welcome to my cabinet of curiosities. How may I serve you today?"

I willed the old woman to go away with every fiber of my being. "We're just browsing."

She laughed, the sound throaty and rich, and began rifling through the shelf nearest her. This one held a collection of buttons and pins, with the occasional shrunken head. "Are you quite sure? I couldn't help but overhear terse words." She plucked two dried flowers from a bin. "Might I interest you in calla lilies? They're said to symbolize humility and devotion. The perfect blooms to end any lovers' quarrel."

Reid accepted his in a reflexive movement, too polite to decline. I knocked it from his hand to the floor. "They also mean death."

"Ah." Her dark eyes glittered with mischief. "Yes, I suppose that is one interpretation."

"We're sorry if we disturbed you, *madame*," Reid muttered, his lips hardly moving, his jaw still clenched. He stooped to retrieve the flower and handed it back to her. "We'll leave now."

"Nonsense, Reid." She winked cheerily, returning the lilies to the shelf. "Manon won't find you here. You and Louise may stay as long as you like—though *do* lock the door when you're finished, won't you?"

We both stared at her, alarmed, but she simply spun with unnatural grace and . . . *vanished*.

I turned to Reid incredulously, mouth parted, but he'd resumed glaring at me with a single-minded intensity that immediately roused my defenses.

"What?" I asked warily.

"Who was that?" He articulated the words slowly, precisely, as if expending extraordinary effort to keep his temper in check. "And how do you know her? How does she know us?"

When I opened my mouth to answer him—to tell him I hadn't the faintest idea—he cut across me abruptly, voice harsh. "Don't lie to me."

I blinked. The implication of his words stung more than I cared to admit, rekindling my anger. I'd only lied to him when absolutely necessary—like when the alternative had been him burning me alive. Or Morgane chopping off his head. *Don't lie to me*, he said. Just as sanctimonious and arrogant as he'd always been. As if *I* were the problem. As if *I* were the one who'd spent the last fortnight lying to myself about who and what I was.

"You can't handle the truth, Reid." I stalked past him toward the door, a flush creeping up my cheeks. "You couldn't handle it then, and you can't handle it now."

His hand caught my arm. "Let me decide that."

"Why? You don't have a problem making decisions for me." Jerking away, I pressed a hand against the door, fighting to prevent the words from spilling out of me. To swallow the bitter vitriol that had settled in my bones after weeks of his disapproval. His hatred. *Aberrant*, he'd called me. *Like a sickness. A poison.* And his face—after I'd saved his ass with the ice in Le Ventre—

"I'm clearly not making decisions for you," he said dryly, dropping my arm. "Or we wouldn't be in this mess."

Hateful tears welled in my eyes. "You're right. You'd be dead at the bottom of a pool with a frozen dick." My hand curled into a fist against the wood. "Or you'd be dead in the remains of a pub with a burnt one. Or bleeding out in La Fôret des Yeux from a thief's blade. Or in Le Ventre from werewolves' teeth." I laughed then—wild, perhaps hysterical—my nails biting into the door hard enough to leave marks in the wood. "Let's pick a death, shall we? God forbid I take the decision away from you."

He pressed forward, so close now I felt his chest against my back. "What happened in the blood camp, Lou?"

I couldn't look at him. Wouldn't look at him. Never before had I felt so stupid—so stupid and callow and unappreciated. "A funeral," I said, voice wooden. "For Etienne Gilly."

"A funeral," he repeated softly, planting his hand on the wood above my head, "for Etienne Gilly."

"Yes."

"Why didn't you tell me?"

"Because you didn't need to know."

His head dropped to my shoulder. "Lou—"

"Forgive me, husband, for trying to keep you *happy*—"

Snapping his head up, he snarled, "If you want to make me *happy*, you'd treat me like your partner. Your *spouse*. You wouldn't keep secrets from me like a foolish child. You wouldn't play with memories or steal Balisardas. You wouldn't turn yourself to *ice*. Are you—are you *trying* to get yourself killed? I don't—I just—" He pushed away, and I turned, watching him drag a hand through his hair. "What is it going to *take*, Lou? When are you going to *see* how reckless you're being—"

"You churlish *ass*." My voice rose, and I fought the urge to pound my fists and stomp my feet, to *show* him what a foolish child I could be. "I have sacrificed *everything* to keep your ungrateful ass alive, and you've scorned me at every turn."

"I never asked you to sacrifice anything—"

I lifted my hands to his face. "Perhaps I can find a pattern to reverse time. Is that what you want? Would you rather have died in that pool than lived to see me become who I truly am? I'm a *witch*, Reid. A *witch*. I have the power to protect the ones I love, and I will sacrifice *anything* for them. If that makes me a monster—if that makes me *aberrant*—I'll don the teeth and claws to make it easier for you. I'll get worse, if that justifies your twisted rhetoric. Much, much worse."

"Goddamn it, I'm trying to *protect* you," he said angrily, flinging my hands out of his face. "Don't turn this into something it's not. I *love* you, Lou. I *know* you're not a monster. Look around." He extended his arms, eyes widening. "I'm still here. But if you don't stop sacrificing pieces of yourself to save us, there won't be anything left. You don't owe us those pieces—not me, not Coco, not Ansel. We don't want them. We want *you*."

"You can cut the shit, Reid."

"It's not shit."

"No? Tell me something, then—that night when I robbed Tremblay's townhouse, you thought I was a criminal, not a witch. Why?"

"Because you *were* a criminal."

"Answer the question."

"I don't know." He scoffed, the sound harsh and jarring in the stillness of the shop. "You were wearing a suit three sizes too big and a mustache, for God's sake. You looked like a little girl playing dress-up."

"So that's it. I was too human. You couldn't fathom me being a witch because I wasn't inherently evil enough. I wore pants and ate sticky buns and sang pub songs, and a witch could never do those things. But you knew, didn't you? Deep down, you *knew* what I was. All the signs were there. I called the witch at Tremblay's a friend. And Estelle—I mourned her. I knew more about magic than anyone in the Tower, loathed the books in the library that denounced it. I bathed twice a day to wash away the scent, and our room smelled permanently of the candles I stole from the sanctuary. But your prejudices ran deep. Too deep. You didn't want to see it—didn't want to admit that you were falling in love with a witch."

He shook his head in vehement denial. It was as good as a condemnation.

A sick sort of satisfaction swept through me. I was right, after all. My magic hadn't twisted *me*; it'd twisted *him*, taking root in the space between us and wrapping around his heart. "After everything, I thought you could change—could learn, could grow—but I was wrong. You're still the same as you were then— a scared little boy who thinks all things that roam the night are monsters, and all things that rule the day are gods."

"That's not true. You *know* that's not true—"

But with one realization came another. This one bit deeper, its thorns drawing blood. "You're never going to accept me." I stared up at him. "No matter how hard I try, no matter how much I wish it weren't so ... you're not my husband, and I'm not your wife. Our marriage—our entire relationship—it was a lie. A hoax. A trick. We're natural enemies, Reid. You'll always be a witch hunter. I'll always be a witch. And we'll always bring each other pain."

A beat of silence passed, as deep and dark as the pit opening in my chest. The mother-of-pearl ring burned a circle of fire into my finger, and I tore at the golden band, desperately trying to remove it—to *return* it. It wasn't mine. It'd never been mine. Reid hadn't been the only one playing pretend.

He marched forward, ignoring my struggle and gripping my face between his hands. "Stop this. Stop. You need to listen to me."

"Stop telling me what I *need* to do." Why wouldn't he just admit it? Why couldn't he say the words that would set me free? That would set *him* free? It wasn't fair to either of us to continue this way, aching and yearning and pining after something that could never be. Not like this.

"You're doing it again." His thumbs stroked my cheeks anxiously, desperately, as my hysteria built. "Don't make a rash decision. Stop and think, Lou. Feel the truth in my words. I'm here. I'm not leaving."

My gaze sharpened on his face, and I reached deep, searching for something—anything—that'd force him to admit he thought me a monster. To admit the *truth*. I thrust the ring into his pocket. "You wanted to know about the man. Gilles." Though somewhere inside that pit a voice warned me to stop, I couldn't. It *hurt*. That revulsion in his eyes when he'd seen me in Le Ventre—I could never forget it. I'd done *everything* for him, and now I—I was scared. Scared he was right. Scared he wasn't.

Scared I'd get worse before I got better. Much, much worse.

Reid's thumbs stilled on my cheeks. I forced myself to meet his eyes, to speak each word to them.

"He was your brother, Reid. Gilles was your brother. Morgane has been hunting your siblings, torturing them to send me a message. She murdered two more at the blood camp while I was there—Etienne and Gabrielle Gilly. *That* is why La Voisin joined us—because Morgane murdered your brother and sister. I didn't tell you because I didn't want to distract you from our plan. I didn't want you to feel pain—*guilt*—for two people you've never known. I stopped you from saving Gilles because it didn't matter if he died, so long as you lived. I did it for the greater good—*my* greater good. Do you understand now? Does that make me a monster?"

He stared at me for a long moment, white-faced and trembling. At last, he dropped his hands and stepped back. The anguish in his eyes cleaved my chest in two, and fresh tears trickled down my cheeks. "No," he finally murmured, brushing them away one last time. A farewell. "It makes you your mother."

I waited several minutes after Reid left the shop to break down. To sob and scream and smash the glass beetles from their shelves, crush the calla lilies beneath my boot. When I finally cracked the door open a half hour later, the shadows of the alley had vanished in the afternoon sun, and he was nowhere in sight. Instead, Charles waited at the threshold. I breathed a sigh of relief—then stopped short.

A small piece of paper had been tacked to the door. It fluttered in the breeze.

Pretty porcelain, pretty doll, forgotten and alone,
Trapped within a mirrored grave, she wears a mask of bone.

I tore it from the door with shaking fingers, peering down the alley behind me. Whoever had left this here had done it while I was still inside the shop—either when Reid and I had argued or after Reid had left. Perhaps Manon had found me, after all. I didn't question why she hadn't attacked, however. I didn't question the morbid words of her riddle. It didn't matter. They didn't matter.

Nothing mattered at all.

A CHANGE OF PLANS

Reid

My heart beat a painful rhythm outside Léviathan. Though I could hear the others inside, I paused at the back entrance, hidden from the street beyond. Breathing heavily. Light-headed with words. They careened into my defenses like bats out of Hell, wings tipped with steel. With razors. Bit by bit, they sliced.

Lou is going to get worse before she gets better. Much, much worse.

Deeper now. They found each crack and cut deeper.

This will always be your life with her—running, hiding, fighting. You will never know peace.

We were supposed to be partners.

Louise has started her descent. You cannot stop it, and you cannot slow it down. It will consume you both if you try.

God, I'd tried.

She will not remain the girl with whom you fell in love.

My hands curled into fists.

I'll don the teeth and claws to make it easier for you. I'll get worse, if that justifies your twisted rhetoric. Much, much worse.

Tendrils of anger curled around the words now, charring them. Setting fire to their sharp tips. I welcomed each flame. Relished them. The smoke didn't damage the fortress—it added to it. Swathed it in heat and darkness. Time and time again, I'd trusted her. And time and time again, she'd proven herself unworthy of my trust.

Did I not deserve her respect?

Did she truly think so little of me?

I'd given her everything. *Everything.* My protection, my love, my *life*. And she'd tossed each aside as if they meant nothing. She'd stripped me of my name, my identity. My *family*. Every word from her mouth since the day we'd met had been a lie—who she was, *what* she was, her relationship with Coco, with Bas. I'd thought I'd moved past them. I'd thought I'd forgiven her. But that hole . . . it hadn't healed quite right. The skin had grown over infection. And hiding my siblings from me, preventing me from saving them . . .

She'd torn me back open.

I couldn't trust her. She obviously didn't trust me.

Our entire relationship had been built on lies.

The fury, the betrayal, burned up my throat. This anger was visceral, a living thing clawing from my chest—

I pounded a fist against the stone wall, sinking to my knees. The others—they couldn't see me like this. Alliance or not, if they scented blood in the water, they'd attack. I had to master myself. I had to—to—

You are in control. Another voice—this one unbidden, still painful—echoed through my mind. *This anger cannot govern you, Reid.*

I'd—I'd killed the Archbishop to save her, for Christ's sake. How could she say I'd scorned her?

Breathing deeply, I knelt in silence for another moment. The anger still burned. The betrayal still ached. But a deadly sense of purpose overpowered both of them. Lou no longer wanted me. She'd made that perfectly clear. I still loved her—I always would—but she'd been right: we could not continue as we were now. Though ironic, though cruel, we'd fit together as witch and witch hunter. As husband and wife. But she'd changed. *I'd* changed.

I wanted to help her. Desperately. But I couldn't force her to help herself.

On steadier feet, I rose, pushing open the door to Léviathan.

What I *could* do was kill a witch. It's what I knew. It's what I'd trained for my entire life. At this very moment, Morgane hid within the city. She hunted my family. If I did nothing—if I sat in this alley and wept over things I could not change—Morgane would find them. She would torture them. She would kill them.

I would kill her first.

To do that, I needed to visit my father.

When I stepped over the threshold, Charles, Brigitte, and Absalon turned and fled upstairs. She was here, then. Lou. As if reading my thoughts, Madame Labelle touched my forearm and murmured, "She came in a few moments before you did. Coco and Ansel followed her up."

Something in her eyes spoke further, but I didn't ask. Didn't want to know.

Small and unremarkable—contrary to its namesake— Léviathan sat tucked within the farthest reach of Cesarine, overlooking the cemetery. Gaps in the floorboards. Cobwebs in the corners. Cauldron in the hearth.

No patrons beyond our own group.

At the bar, Deveraux sat with Toulouse and Thierry. Déjà vu swept through me at the sight of them together. Of another time and another place. Another tavern. That one hadn't housed blood witches and werewolves, though. It'd caught fire instead. "There's a joke here somewhere," Beau muttered, nursing a pint at the table nearest me. His hood still shadowed his face. Beside him sat Nicholina and a woman I didn't recognize. No—a woman I *did*. Tall and striking, she had Coco's face. But her eyes gleamed with unfamiliar malice. She held her spine rigid. Her mouth pursed.

"Good evening, Captain." She inclined her neck stiffly. "At last we meet."

"La Voisin."

At the name, Blaise and his children bared their teeth, snarling softly.

Heedless of the tense silence—of the palpable antagonism—Deveraux laughed and waved me over. "Reid, how *splendid* to see you again! Come hither, come hither!"

"What are you doing here?"

"La Mascarade des Crânes, dear boy! Surely you haven't forgotten? One of the entrances lies below this very—"

I turned away, ignoring the rest of his words. I didn't have time for a happy reunion. Didn't have time to make peace between blood witches and werewolves. To entertain them.

"We're lucky he's here," Madame Labelle murmured, though her voice held more strain than reproach. "After Auguste burned the Bellerose, my contacts in the city are too frightened to speak with me. I would've had a devil of a time procuring a safe place for us if Claud hadn't stepped in. Apparently, the innkeeper owes him a favor. We're the only patrons of Léviathan tonight."

I didn't care. Instead of answering, I nodded to Beau, who plunked his tankard down with a sigh. He joined Madame Labelle and me at the door. "If you're still planning what I think you're planning, you're an idiot of the highest order—"

"What's the timetable?" I asked brusquely.

He blinked at me. "I assume the priests are finishing preparation of the body now. They'll administer last rites soon. Mass will commence in under an hour, and afterward, the Chasseurs will escort my family in the burial procession. They'll lay it to rest around four o'clock this afternoon."

It. The implication of the word stung. *It.* Not *him.*

I forced the thought away. "That gives us an hour to breach the castle. Where will Auguste be?"

Though Beau and Madame Labelle shared an anxious look, neither protested further. "The throne room," he said. "He, my mother, and my sisters will be in the throne room. It's tradition to hold court before ceremonial events."

"Can you get us in?"

He nodded. "Like Claud said, there is a system of tunnels that span the entire city. I used to play in them as a child. They connect the castle, the catacombs, the cathedral—"

"The Bellerose," Madame Labelle added, arching a wry brow. "This pub."

Beau dipped his head with a chuckle. "There's also a passage behind a tapestry in the throne room. You and your mother can hide while I approach my father. After Jean Luc's explanation of events in Le Ventre—and your own rather unfortunate entrance to the city—I think it best I speak with him first. It'll prevent him from arresting you on sight." He leaned in, lowering his voice. "But word will have spread, Reid. He'll know you're a witch now. They all will. I don't know what he'll do. Approaching him on the day of the Archbishop's funeral is a huge risk, especially since you're—" He broke off with an apologetic sigh. "Since you're the one who killed him."

Emotion choked my throat, but I swallowed it down. I could not dwell. I had to move forward. "I understand."

"If I judge him to be amenable, I'll summon you forth. If I don't, you'll run like hell." He looked me in the eye then, squaring his shoulders. "I won't concede that point, brother. If I tell you to run, you will run."

"Perhaps you should have a code word for when things go wrong." With a skeletal grin, Nicholina slipped her face between Beau's and mine. "I suggest flibbertigibbet. Or bumfuzzle. *Bumfuzzle, bumfuzzle, meaning to puzzle—*"

Beau pushed her face away without hesitation. "If for some reason we're separated, take the left-hand tunnel at each fork you meet. It'll take you to La Mascarade des Crânes. Find Claud, and he'll lead you back here."

My brow furrowed. "Won't taking the left-hand tunnel lead us in a circle?"

"Not underground it won't. The left-hand tunnel is the only way to reach the Skull Masquerade." He nodded again, this time to himself. "Right. The entrance is in the storeroom behind the bar, and the castle is a twenty-minute walk from here. If we're going to do this, we need to leave now."

"What's this, then?" Nicholina's brows wriggled as she circled us. Her girlish voice pitched higher. "*To the castle, to the snare, you rush to save your lady fair—*"

"Would you *shut up*, woman?" Beau whirled, incredulous, and tried to shoo her back toward La Voisin. "She's been doing this since I arrived." To her, he added, "Go on, now. Go. Back to your—your master, or whoever—"

Nicholina giggled. "Flibbertigibbet."

"What an odd creature," Madame Labelle murmured, staring after her with a frown. "Quite touched in the head. She called Louise a *mouse* earlier. Do you have any idea what that means?"

I ignored her, signaling for Beau to lead the way. He hesitated. "Should someone—fetch her? Lou? I thought she'd planned on joining us?"

And I thought she'd planned on loving me forever.

I stepped around him, around the counter, disregarding the barkeep's objections. "Plans change."

THE KING'S COURT

Reid

I had a rock in my boot.

It'd lodged there immediately upon entering the tunnels. Small enough for me to endure. Large enough for me to fixate. With each step, it jostled against my foot. Curling my toes. Setting my teeth on edge.

Or perhaps that was Beau.

He'd thrown back his hood in the semidarkness, and he strolled through the earthen tunnels with hands in his pockets. Torchlight flickered over his smirk. "So many rendezvous down here. So many memories."

The rock slid under my heel. I shook my foot irritably. "I don't want to know."

Apparently, however, Madame Labelle did. She arched a brow. Lifted her skirt to step over a divot in the earth. "Come now, Your Highness. I've heard rumors your exploits are *grossly* exaggerated."

His eyes widened. "Excuse me?"

"I owned a brothel." She fixed him with a pointed look. "Word spread."

"*What* word?"

"I don't want to hear," I repeated.

It was her turn to smirk. "You forget I knew you as a child, Beauregard. I remember the gap in your teeth and the spots on your chin. And then—when you developed that unfortunate stutter—"

Cheeks flushing, he thrust out his chest, nearly stumbling on another rock. I hoped it found quarter in *his* heel. "I didn't develop a stutter," he said, indignant. "That was a complete and utter misunderstanding—"

I kicked at the air surreptitiously, and the rock caught between my toes. "You had a stutter?"

"*No*—"

Madame Labelle cackled. "Tell him the story, dear. I'd quite like to hear it again."

"How do you—?"

"I told you—brothels are hotbeds of information." She winked at him. "And I *do* intend that pun."

He looked mutinous. Though pink still tinged his cheeks, he expelled a breath, blowing a limp strand of hair from his eye. Madame Labelle's smile broadened with expectation. "Fine," he snapped. "As I'm sure you heard the *incorrect* story, I will set the matter straight. I lost my virginity to a psellismophiliac."

I stared at him, the rock in my boot forgotten. "A what?"

"A psellismophiliac," he repeated irritably. "Someone who is *aroused* by *stuttering.* Her name was Apollinia. She was a chamber-maid in the castle and several years older than me, the beautiful hag."

I blinked once. Twice. Madame Labelle cackled louder. Gleeful. "Go on," she said.

He glared at her. "You can imagine how our encounter proceeded. I thought her fetish normal. I thought *everyone* enjoyed stuttering in the bedchamber." Recognizing the horror in my eyes, he nodded fervently. "Yes. You see the problem, don't you? When I found my next lover—a *peer* in my father's court—I'm sure you can imagine how *that* encounter proceeded, as well." He lifted a hand to his eyes. "God. I've never been so mortified in my entire life. I was forced to flee to these very tunnels to escape his laughter. I couldn't look him in the eye for a year." He snapped his hand to his side in agitation. "A *year.*"

An unfamiliar tickle built in my throat. I pursed my lips against it. Bit my cheek.

It escaped anyway, and I laughed, sharp and clear, for the first time in a long time.

"It's *not funny,*" Beau snapped as Madame Labelle joined in. She bent double, clutching her ribs, her shoulders shaking. "Stop laughing! Stop it now!"

At long last, she wiped a tear from her eye. "Oh, *Your Majesty.* I shall never tire of that story—which is, in fact, the story my girls thought so amusing. If it soothes your wounded pride, I'll confess I too have experienced my share of humiliating encounters. I often perused these tunnels myself as a younger woman. Why, there was a time your father spirited me down here—"

"No." Beau shook his head swiftly, waving a hand. "No. Do not finish that sentence."

"—but there was a feral cat." She chuckled to herself, lost in memory. "We didn't notice him until it was too late. He, ah, *mistook* part of your father's anatomy—or rather, *two* parts of your father's anatomy—"

The laughter died in my own throat. "Stop."

"—for a plaything! Oh, you should've heard Auguste's shrieks. One would've thought the cat had gutted his liver instead of scratched his—"

"*Enough.*" Horrified, wide-eyed with disbelief, Beau physically clapped a hand over her mouth. She snorted against his fingers. "Never, *ever* tell that story again. Do you understand me? *Ever.*" He shook his head sharply, clenching his eyes shut. "The psychological *scars* you've just inflicted, woman. I cannot unsee what my mind's eye has conjured."

She knocked his hand away, still laughing. "Don't be such a prude, Beauregard. Surely you understand your father's extracurricular activities, given the situation we're all—" Her smile slipped, and the playful atmosphere between us vanished instantly. She cleared her throat. "What I mean to say is—"

"We shouldn't talk anymore." With a grim expression, mouth drawn, Beau pointed ahead to a northward tunnel. "We're nearing the castle. Listen."

Sure enough, in the quiet that followed, muffled footsteps could be heard overhead. Right. I knelt to wrench off my boot. Shook the damn rock free and replaced it. No more distractions. Though I appreciated Madame Labelle's attempt to lift our spirits, this wasn't the time or the place.

It hadn't been the time or place in weeks.

We walked the rest of the way in silence. As the tunnel sloped gradually upward, the voices grew louder. As did my heartbeat. I shouldn't have been nervous. I'd seen the king before. Seen him, talked to him, dined with him. But I'd been a huntsman then, esteemed, celebrated, and he'd been my king. Everything had changed.

Now I was a witch—reviled—and he was my father.

"Everything will be fine," Madame Labelle whispered as if reading my thoughts. She nodded to me. To herself. "You are his child. He will not harm you. Even the Archbishop did not burn his child, and Auguste is twice the man the Archbishop was."

I flinched at the words, but she'd already turned to the cavernous fissure in the wall. The warp and weft of a muted tapestry covered it. I recognized it from my brief time in the castle—a man and a woman in the Garden of Eden, naked, fallen before the Tree of the Knowledge of Good and Evil. In their hands, each held a golden fruit. Above them, a giant serpent coiled.

I stared at the reverse of its black coils now, feeling sick.

"Watch through here," Beau breathed, pointing to a thin gap between the wall and tapestry. Less than an inch. Bodies shifted beyond it. Aristocrats and clergymen from all over the kingdom—all over the world. An assemblage of black caps, veils, and lace. Their low voices reverberated in a steady hum. And there—raised on a stone dais, draped over a colossal throne—sat Auguste Lyon.

From the window directly behind, a shaft of sunlight traced

his silhouette. His gilded crown and golden hair. His fur cape and broad shoulders. The placement of the window, the throne . . . they'd been arranged intentionally. An optical illusion to trick the eye into believing his very body emitted light.

Backlit, however, his face remained shadowed.

But I could still see his smile. He laughed with three young women, heedless of Queen Oliana beside him. She stared determinedly at nothing, expression as stony as the steps beneath her. In the corner of the room, a handful of aristocrats in foreign clothing shared her features. Shared her anger. Theirs were the only sober faces in the room.

Resentment prickled beneath my skin as I took in the bards, the wine, the food.

These people did not mourn the Archbishop. How dare they mock his death with their revelry? How dare they speak idly beneath black hoods? No mourning veil could hide their apathy. Their hedonism. These people—these *animals*—did not deserve to grieve him.

On the heels of that thought, however, came another. Shame burned away my righteousness.

Neither did I.

Beau beat the dust from his cloak, smoothed his hair as best he could. It did little to help his travel-worn appearance. "Right. I'll enter the proper way and request an audience. If he's amenable—"

"You'll call us forward," I finished, mouth dry.

"Right." He nodded. Kept nodding. "Right. And if he's not . . . ?" He waited expectantly, brows climbing upward each second I didn't answer. "I need to hear a confirmation, Reid."

My lips barely moved. "We run."

Madame Labelle clasped my forearms. "Everything will be fine," she repeated. Beau didn't look convinced. With one last nod, he strode in the opposite direction from whence we'd come. Unconsciously, I stepped closer to the gap between wall and tapestry. Waited for him to reappear. Watched as two familiar figures cut toward the dais.

Pierre Tremblay and Jean Luc.

Expression drawn, stricken, Jean Luc pushed Tremblay forward with inappropriate force. Those nearest the king stilled. Tremblay was a *vicomte*. Jean Luc assaulting him—in public, no less—was a punishable offense. Frowning, Auguste waved the women away, and the two climbed the dais steps. They leaned close to whisper in Auguste's ear. Though I couldn't hear their hasty words, I watched as Auguste's frown deepened. As Oliana leaned forward, concerned.

The throne room doors burst open a moment later, and Beau strode in.

Audible gasps filled the chamber. All conversation ceased. One woman even emitted a small shriek. He winked at her. "*Bonjour*, everyone. I am sorry if I kept you waiting." To his mother's family in the corner, he added in a softer voice, "*Ia orana.*"

Tears filled Oliana's eyes as she leapt to her feet. "*Arava.*"

"*Metua vahine.*" Upon seeing her, Beau's smile warmed to something genuine. He tilted his head to peer behind her at someone I couldn't see. "*Mau tuahine iti.*" When delighted squeals answered him, my heart stuttered painfully. Two someones. Violette and Victoire. I pressed closer, trying in vain to see them, but Madame Labelle pulled me back.

Auguste stiffened visibly at his son's arrival. His eyes never left Beau's face. "The prodigal son returns."

"*Père.*" Beau's smirk reappeared. His armor, I realized. "Did you miss me?"

Absolute silence reigned as Auguste studied his son's rumpled hair, his filthy clothes. "You disappoint me."

"I assure you, the sentiment is mutual."

Auguste smiled. It held more promise than a knife. "Do you think you're clever?" he asked softly. He still didn't bother to rise. "Do you mean to embarrass me with this tawdry display?" With a lazy flick of his wrist, he gestured around the chamber. "By all means, do continue. Your audience is rapt. Tell them of how disappointed you are in your father, the man who ravaged the countryside for weeks to find his son. Tell them of how your mother wept herself to sleep all those nights, waiting for word. Tell them of how she prayed to her gods and mine for your return." Now he did stand. "*Tell them*, Beauregard, of how your sisters slipped out of the castle to find you, how a witch nearly cut off their heads."

Fresh gasps sounded as Beau's eyes widened.

Auguste descended the steps slowly. "They're all waiting to hear, son. Tell them of your new companions. Tell them of the witches and werewolves you call *friends*. Perhaps they're already acquainted. Perhaps your companions have murdered their families." His lip curled. "Tell them of how you abandoned *your* family to help the daughter of La Dame des Sorcières—the daughter whose blood could kill not only you, but also your sisters. Tell them of how you freed her." He reached Beau at last, and the two stared at each other. For a second. For an eternity. Auguste's voice quieted. "I have long tolerated your *indiscretions*, but this time, you go too far."

Beau tried to sneer. "You haven't tolerated them. You've ignored them. Your opinion means less to me now than it ever has—"

"My *opinion*," Auguste snarled, fisting the front of Beau's shirt, "is the only reason you haven't been lashed to a stake. You dare to dismiss me? You dare to challenge your father for the sake of a witch's dirty cunt?" Auguste shoved him away, and Beau stumbled, blanching. No one lifted a hand to steady him.

"It isn't like that—"

"You are a *child*." At the venom in Auguste's voice, the aristocrats drew back further. "A cosseted child in a gilded tower, who has never tasted the blood of war or smelled the stench of death. Do you fancy yourself a hero now, son? After a fortnight of playing pretend with your friends, do you call yourself a warrior? Do you plan to *save* us?" He shoved him again. "Have you ever seen a loup garou feast on the intestines of a soldier?" And again. "Have you ever watched a Dame Blanche desiccate a newborn babe?"

Beau struggled to his feet. "They—they wouldn't do that. Lou wouldn't—"

"You are a child *and* a fool," Auguste said coldly, "and you have humiliated me for the last time." Expelling a hard breath from his nose, he straightened to his full height. *My* height. "But I am not without mercy. Captain Toussaint told me of your grand plan to defeat La Dame des Sorcières. Tell me the location of her daughter, and all will be forgiven."

No. Panic caught in my throat. I forgot to breathe. To think. I could only watch as Beau's eyes widened. As he yielded a step to his father. "I can't do that."

Auguste's face hardened. "You will tell me where she is, or I will strip you of your title and inheritance." Shocked whispers erupted, but Auguste ignored them, his voice growing louder with each word. With each step. Oliana touched a hand to her mouth in horror. "I will banish you from my castle and my life. I will condemn you as a criminal, a conspirator, and when you burn beside your friends, I will think of you no more."

"Father," Beau said, aghast, but Auguste did not stop.

"*Where is she?*"

"I—" Beau's gaze darted helplessly to his mother, but she merely closed her eyes, weeping softly. He cleared his throat and tried again. I held my breath. "I can't tell you where she is because I—I don't know."

"*Frère!*" From behind Oliana, a beautiful girl with Beau's black hair and tawny skin darted forward. My chest seized as she wrung her hands, as Auguste swept her backward, away from Beau. "*Frère*, please, tell him where she is. Tell him!"

Her twin raced to join them. Though she glared, her chin quivered. "You don't need to *beg*, Violette. Of course he'll tell him. The witches tried to *kill* us."

Beau's voice turned strangled. "Victoire—"

Auguste's eyes narrowed. "You would protect a witch over your own sisters?"

"We should go." Madame Labelle tugged fruitlessly on my arm, her breathing shallow. Panicked. "This was a mistake. Clearly Auguste won't help us."

"We can't just *leave* him—"

Beau lifted his hands, gesturing to the aristocrats. "It doesn't have to *be* this way. They aren't all evil. If you'd just *help* us, we can eliminate Morgane. She's in the city—here, *now*—and she's planning something terrible for the Archbishop's funeral—"

Madame Labelle pulled more insistently. "Reid—"

"You truly are a fool." Auguste wrapped a possessive arm around each of his daughters, dragging them backward. "I must confess, however, I am not surprised. Though you loathe me, I know you, son. I know your habits. I know your haunts. For fear of losing your newfound friends, I knew you would visit me on this foolish errand."

Vaguely, I recognized the sound of footsteps behind me. Of voices. Madame Labelle clawed at my arm now, shouting my name, but my mind followed too slow, sluggish. The realization came too late. I turned just as Auguste said, "And I knew you would use the tunnels to do it."

"Flibbertigibbet!" Beau's shouts filled the chamber as he whirled toward us with wild eyes. "Bumfuzzle!"

The hilt of a Balisarda smashed into my temple, and I saw no more.

PRIDE GOETH BEFORE THE FALL

Lou

He'd left without me. I stared into my whiskey, tipping it sideways, pouring it slowly onto the wooden bar. Coco took the tumbler from me without missing a beat in her conversation with Liana. Across the tavern, Ansel sat between Toulouse and Thierry. They all laughed at a joke I couldn't hear.

One big, happy family.

Except they all stared at me, whispering, like I was a cannon about to explode.

And that bastard had left without a word.

I don't know what I'd expected—I'd practically doused *him* in whiskey and lit the match. But I hadn't lied. I hadn't said anything *untrue*. That's what he'd wanted, right? He'd wanted the *truth*.

Don't lie to me, he'd said.

I shoved away from the bar, stalking to the filthy window up front and staring through its dirt-streaked panes. He should've been back by now. If he'd left when Deveraux said he'd left—when I'd been sulking upstairs in misery—he should've climbed back through the tunnel a half hour ago. Something must've happened. Perhaps he'd found trouble—

Do you understand now? Does that make me a monster?

No. It makes you your mother.

A fresh wave of anger washed over me. Perhaps he *had* found trouble. And—this time—perhaps he could sort it out without me. Without magic.

Breath tickled my neck, and I whirled, coming face-to-face with Nicholina. When she grinned at me, I scowled. Blood had stained her teeth yellow. Indeed, her paper-thin skin was now her palest feature, brighter and whiter than the moon. I shouldered past her to an empty table in the corner. "I want to be alone, Nicholina."

"Shouldn't be too hard, *souris*." She drifted around me, whispering, gesturing to Coco and Ansel, to Blaise and Liana, to Toulouse and Thierry. "*They* certainly don't want our company." She leaned closer. Her lips brushed my ear. "We make them uncomfortable."

I swatted her away. "Don't touch me."

When I plunked down, turning my back to her, she floated to the chair opposite. She didn't sit, however. I supposed wraiths didn't sit. One couldn't look sinister and uncanny with one's ass on a barstool. "We aren't so very different," she breathed. "People don't like us either."

"People like me just fine," I snapped.

"Do they?" Her colorless eyes flicked to Blaise, where he watched me from the bar. "We can sense his thoughts, oh yes, and he hasn't forgotten how you crushed his son's bones. He longs to feast on your flesh, make you whimper and groan."

My own gaze cut to his. His lip curled over sharp incisors. Fuck.

"But you won't whimper, will you?" Nicholina canted her face closer to mine. "You'll fight, and you'll bite with teeth of your own." She laughed then—the sound skittered down my spine—and repeated, "We aren't so very different. For years, our people have been persecuted, and *we* have been persecuted among even them."

For some reason, I doubted she referred to *we* as her and me, the two of us. No. It seemed Nicholina wasn't the only one living inside her head these days. Perhaps there were ... others. *I told you she's weird*, Gabrielle had confided. *Too many hearts*. My own heart twisted at the memory. Poor Gaby. I hoped she hadn't suffered.

Ismay sat at a table with La Voisin, eyes red-rimmed and glassy. A handful of their sisters joined them. Babette had remained in the blood camp to care for those too young, too old, too weak, or too sick to fight.

They hadn't recovered Gaby's body.

"We'll tell you a secret, little mouse," Nicholina whispered, drawing my attention back to her. "It isn't on us to make them comfortable. No, no, no it's not. It's not, it's not, it's not. It's on *them*."

I stared at her. "How did you become like this, Nicholina?"

She grinned again—a too-wide grin that nearly split her face in half. "How did *you* become like this, Louise? We all make choices. We all suffer consequences."

"I'm done with this conversation." Expelling a harsh breath, I returned Blaise's glare with one of my own. If he didn't blink soon, he'd lose an eye. Nicholina—though clearly demented—was right about one thing: I *would* bite back. When Terrance murmured in his ear, he finally shifted his gaze away from me toward the storeroom door. I tensed immediately. Had they heard something I hadn't? Had Reid returned?

Without hesitating, I curled a finger, and my eyesight clouded. My hearing, however, heightened, and Terrance's low voice echoed as if he stood beside me. "Do you think he's dead? The huntsman?"

Blaise shook his head. "Perhaps. There is no peace in the human king's heart. Reid was foolish to approach him."

"If he *is* dead . . . when can we leave this place?" Terrance cast a sidelong look at La Voisin and Ismay, at the blood witches around them. "We owe these demons no loyalty."

A twitch started in my cheek. Before I realized my feet had moved, I was standing, pressing my fists against the table. The pattern dissolved. "It seems you owe Reid no loyalty either." They both looked up, startled—angry—but theirs was a flicker to my rage. Nicholina clapped her hands together in delight. Coco, Ansel, and Claud all rose tentatively. "If you suspect he's in danger, why are you still here?" My voice rose, grew into something beyond me. Though I heard myself speaking, I did not form these words. "You owe him a life debt, you mangy *dogs*. Or would you like me to reclaim Terrance's?" I lifted my hands.

Blaise's teeth flashed as he rose from his chair. "You dare threaten us?"

"Louise...," Claud said, his voice conciliatory. "What are you doing?"

"They think Reid is dead," I spat. "They're debating when they can leave us."

Though La Voisin chuckled, her eyes remained flat and cold. "Of course they are. At the first sign of trouble, they tuck their tails and flee back to their swamp. They're cowards. I told you not to trust them, Louise."

When Liana moved toward the door, I slammed it shut with an easy flick of my wrist. My eyes never left Blaise's. "You aren't going anywhere. Not until you bring him back to me."

Snarling, Blaise's face began to shift. "You do not control the loup garou, witch. We did not harm you for your mate's sake. If he dies, so too does our benevolence. Be very careful."

La Voisin stepped to my side, hands clasped. "Perhaps it is *you* who should be careful, Blaise. If you invoke the wrath of this witch, you invoke the wrath of us all." She lifted a hand, and the blood witches stood as one—at least a dozen of them. Four times as many as Blaise, Liana, and Terrance, who edged back-to-back, growling low in their throats. Their fingernails extended to lethal points.

"We will leave here in peace." Despite his words, Blaise met La Voisin's gaze in open challenge. "No blood must be drawn."

"How easily you forget." La Voisin smiled, and it was a cruel, chilling thing. When she lowered her collar, revealing three jagged scars across her chest—claw marks—the blood witches hummed with anticipation. And so did I. *God*, so did I. "We *like* blood. Especially our own."

Tension in the room taut to explode, they stared at each other.

Ansel started to step between them—*Ansel*, of all people—but Claud stopped him with a hand on his shoulder. "Stand down, lad. Before you get hurt." To La Voisin and Blaise, he said, "Let us not forget the grander purpose here. We have a common enemy. We can all play nice until Monsieur Diggory returns, can't we?" With a pointed glance first at Blaise, then at me, he added, "Because he *will* return."

Not a breath sounded in the long, tense silence that followed. We all waited for someone to move. To strike.

At last, Blaise sighed heavily. "You speak wisdom, Claud Deveraux. We will await Monsieur Diggory's return. If he does not, my children and I will leave this place—and its inhabitants"—his yellow eyes found mine—"unharmed. You have my word."

"Ah, excellent—"

But La Voisin only smirked. "Coward."

That was all it took.

With a snarl, Terrance launched himself at her, but Nicholina appeared, seizing his half-shifted throat and twisting. He yelped, flying through the air, and landed at Blaise's feet. Liana had already shifted. She tore after Nicholina. Blaise quickly followed, as did Ansel and Claud when they realized the blood witches were after, well—*blood*. Knives in hand, Ismay and her sisters attacked the wolves' jugulars, but the wolves moved faster, leaping atop the bar to gain higher ground. Though cornered, though outnumbered, Terrance managed to knock away Ismay's knife, pinning her beneath his paw. When his other slashed open her face, she screamed. Coco rushed to intervene.

And I . . . I touched a finger to the whiskey on the bar. Just a finger. One simple spark—so similar, yet so different from that pub fire long ago. Had it only been a fortnight?

It felt like years.

The flames chased the whiskey down the bar to where Terrance—

No. Not Terrance. I tilted my head, bemused, as the flames instead found another, climbing up her feet, her legs, her chest. Soon she screamed in terror, in pain—trying desperately to draw blood, to claw magic from her wrists—but I only laughed. I laughed and laughed until my eyes stung and my throat ached, laughed until her voice finally pierced the smoke in my mind. Until I realized to whom that voice belonged.

"Coco," I breathed.

I stared at her in disbelief, releasing the pattern. The flames died instantly, and she crumpled to the floor. Smoke curled from her clothing, her *skin*, and she gasped between sobs, struggling to catch her breath. The rest of the room came back in pieces— Ansel's horrified expression, Terrance's frantic shout, Ismay's mad dash to find honey. When I stumbled forward to help her, a hand caught my throat.

"No closer," La Voisin snarled, her nails biting into my skin.

"Enough, Josephine." Deveraux loomed over us, graver than I'd ever seen him. "Release her."

La Voisin's eyes bulged slightly as she glared at him, but—one by one—her fingers gradually loosened. I sucked in a harsh breath and staggered forward. "*Coco.*"

But both blood witches and werewolves shielded her as I approached, and I could see little more than her eye above Ansel's arm. He too had positioned himself between us. My breath caught at the hostility in their gazes. At the fear. "Coco, I'm so sorry—"

She struggled to rise. "I'll be fine, Lou," she said weakly.

"It was an accident. You have to believe me." My voice broke on the last, but my heart—it broke at the tears welling in her eyes as she looked at me. She pressed a hand to her mouth to stem her sobs. "Coco, please. You *know* I never would've—would've never intentionally—"

Behind her, Nicholina grinned. Her inflection deepened, changed, as she said, "The Lord doth say, 'Come, heed him, all. Pride goeth before the fall.'"

The finality of what I'd done cleaved through me, and I heard his voice. Felt his soft touch on my hair.

You haven't been yourself.

You see what you want to see.

Do you think I want to see you as—

As what? As evil?

Burying my face in my hands, I sank to my knees and wept.

PROPER KNIGHTS

Reid

A face.

I woke to a face. Though mere inches from my own, I struggled to bring its features into focus. They remained shapeless, dark, as if I stood in heavy fog. But I wasn't standing. I couldn't move my limbs. They felt heavier than normal—impossibly heavy and cold. Except my wrists. My wrists burned with black fire.

Eyes closing, opening—lethargic, each blink enormous effort—I tried to lift my head. It slumped uselessly against my shoulder. I thought the shape of lips might've moved. Thought a voice might've rumbled. I closed my eyes again. Someone pried my jaw apart, forced something bitter down my throat. I vomited instantly.

I vomited until my head pounded. My throat ached.

When something hard struck my face, I spat blood. The taste of copper, of salt, jarred my senses. Blinking faster now, I shook my head to clear it. The room swam. At last, the face before me took shape. Golden hair and gray eyes—like a wolf—with straight nose and chiseled jaw.

"You're awake," Auguste said. "Good."

Beside me, Madame Labelle sat with her wrists bound behind her chair. It forced her shoulders out of socket. Though blood trickled from a puncture at the side of her throat, her eyes remained clear. It was then I noticed the metal syringes in Auguste's hand. The bloody quills.

Injections.

He'd drugged us—drugged *me*—like I was a—a—

Bile burned up my throat.

Like I was a witch.

Madame Labelle struggled against her binds. "Really, Auguste, this isn't necessary—"

"You dare address His Majesty so informally?" Oliana asked. Her voice pitched and rolled with my consciousness.

"Forgive me," Madame Labelle snapped. "After birthing a man's child—and all that predicates such a happy occasion—I assumed formalities would cease. An egregious mistake."

I vomited again, unable to hear Oliana's reply.

When I reopened my eyes, the room sharpened. Mahogany shelves filled with books. A carved mantel. Portraits of stern-lipped kings and embroidered carpet beneath booted feet. I blinked, vision honing in on the Chasseurs lining the walls. At least a dozen. Each held a hand to the Balisarda at his waist.

Except the Chasseur who stood behind me. He held his at my throat.

A second moved to stand behind Madame Labelle. His blade

drew blood, and she stilled. "At least clean him up," she said weakly. "He isn't an animal. He is your *son*."

"You insult me, Helene." Auguste crouched before me, tracking a hand in front of my face. My eyes struggled to follow it. "As if I'd allow even my hounds to sit in their own spew." He snapped his fingers. "I need you to focus, Reid. Mass starts in a quarter hour, and I cannot be late. The kingdom expects me to mourn that sanctimonious prick. I shan't disappoint them."

Hatred burned through the haze of my thoughts.

"But you understand the importance of keeping up pretenses, don't you?" He arched a golden brow. "You had all of us fooled, after all. Including him." My stomach heaved again, but he leapt backward just in time, lip curling. "Between the two of us, I'm pleased you killed him. I cannot count the times that filthy hypocrite presumed to admonish me—*me*—when all this time, he'd stuck his cock in Morgane le Blanc."

"Yes, a filthy hypocrite," Madame Labelle echoed pointedly. The Chasseur behind her ripped her hair backward, pressing his blade deeper into her throat. She said no more.

Auguste ignored her, tilting his head to study me. "Your body reacted to the injection. I suppose that proves Philippe's claim. You are a witch."

I forced my head upright through sheer power of will. For one second. Two seconds. "I would like to see . . . *your* body . . . react to hemlock . . . Your Majesty."

"You poisoned them?" Beau asked in disbelief. Another Chasseur held him in the corner of the room. Though his mother shook her head desperately, he didn't acknowledge her. "You put *hemlock* in those injections?"

"A fucking gilded tower." Auguste rolled his eyes. "I have little patience for your voice at the moment, Beauregard—or yours, Oliana," he added when she tried to interrupt. "If either of you speak again, you will regret it." To me, he said, "Now, tell me. How is it possible? How did you come to exist, Reid Diggory?"

A grin rose, unbidden, and I heard Lou's voice in my head. Even then—trapped backstage with two of her mortal enemies— she'd been fearless. Or perhaps stupid. Either way, she hadn't known how right she was. "I believe," I gasped, "when a man and a . . . witch . . . love each other very much—"

I anticipated his strike. When it came, my head thudded against the chair and stayed there. A laugh bubbled from my lips, and he stared at me like I was an insect. Something to quash beneath his boot. Perhaps I was. I laughed again at the irony. How many times had I drugged a witch? How many times had I worn his exact expression?

He grabbed my chin, crushing it between his fingers. "Tell me where she is, and I promise you a quick death."

My grin receded slowly. I said nothing.

His fingers bit harder. Hard enough to bruise. "Are you fond of rats, Reid Diggory? They're ugly little creatures, to be sure, but beneath their beastly hides, I must admit to sharing a certain kinship with them."

"I'm not surprised."

He smiled then. It was cold. "They're intelligent, rats.

Resourceful. They value their own survival. Perhaps you should heed their good instinct." When still I said nothing, his smile grew. "It's a curious thing when you trap a rat atop a man's stomach—let's say, for example, with a pot. Now, when you apply heat to said pot, do you know how the rat responds?" He shook my head for me when I didn't answer. "It burrows through the man's stomach, Reid Diggory. It bites and claws through skin and flesh and bone to escape the heat. It *kills* the man, so it might survive."

At last, he released me, standing and flicking a handkerchief from his pocket. He wiped the vomit from his fingers in distaste. "Unless you desire to be that man, I suggest you answer my question."

We stared at each other. The shape of his face wavered. "I won't," I said simply.

The words echoed in the silence of the room.

"Hmm." He picked something up from his desk. Small. Black. Cast iron. "I see."

A pot, I realized.

I should've felt fear. Perhaps the hemlock prevented it. Perhaps the rolling nausea or splitting headache. He *wanted* me to fear him. I could see it in his eyes. In his smile. He wanted me to tremble, to beg. This was a man who relished dominance. Control. I'd helped him, once. As his huntsman. I'd sought his approval as my king. Even after—when I'd learned his role in my conception, my suffering—I'd wanted to know him, deep down.

I'd dreamed up a version of him from my mother's stories. I'd accepted her rose glasses. But this man was not him.

This man was real.

This man was ugly.

And—looking at him now—all I felt was disappointment.

Slowly, he placed the pot on a rack above the fire. "I shall ask you one more time—where is Louise le Blanc?"

"Father—" Beau started, pleading, but with the wave of Auguste's hand, the Chasseur struck him in the head. When he slumped, dazed, Oliana's shrieks filled the cabinet. She rushed toward him, but Auguste caught her around the waist, flinging her against his desk. She collapsed to the ground with a sob.

"I said *be silent,*" Auguste snarled.

Madame Labelle's eyes widened.

"Who are you?" Her voice climbed higher with disbelief. "The man I loved would *never* have treated his family this way. That is your *wife.* These are your *sons—*"

"They are no sons of mine." Auguste's face flushed as he gripped the arms of Madame Labelle's chair. As he bent low in her face, eyes burning with wild intensity. "And I shall have another son, Helene. I shall have a *hundred* more sons to spite that heinous, white-haired bitch. My legacy will live on. Do you understand me? I don't care if I have to fuck every woman in this godforsaken spit of land, I will not yield." He lifted a hand to her face, but he didn't touch her. His fingers clenched with hatred. With longing. "You beautiful, fucking *liar.* What am I going to do with you?"

"Please, stop this. It's me. It's Helene—"

"You think I loved you, *Helene?* You think you're any different from the others?"

"I know I was." Her eyes shone with fierce conviction. "I could not tell you I was a witch—and for that, I apologize—but you knew me, Auguste. As one soul knows another, you *knew* me, and I knew you. What we shared was real. Our child was born from love, not from lust or—or obligation. You must rethink this blind hatred and remember. I am the same now as I was then. *See* me, *mon amour*, and see him. He needs our help—"

Auguste did touch her now, twisting her lips between his fingers. He pulled them a hair's breadth from his own. "Perhaps I shall torture you too," he whispered. "Perhaps I shall see which of you breaks first."

When she glared back at him, resolute, pride swelled in my chest.

Love.

"Why doesn't the hemlock work on you, *mon amour*?" He released her lips to stroke her cheek. They could've been the only two people in the room. "How do you remain unaffected?"

She lifted her chin. "I've injected myself with hemlock every day since the day we met."

"Ah." His fingers tightened, clawing her skin. "So much for it being real."

The door to the cabinet burst open, and a liveried man swept in. "Your Majesty, I've delayed the priests as long as possible. They insist we begin Mass immediately."

Auguste stared at my mother for a second longer. With a sigh, he released her and straightened his coat. Smoothed back his hair. "Alas, it seems our conversation must wait until after the festivities." Donning black gloves with practiced efficiency, he slid his mask back into place. His persona. "I shall call for the two of you when they're over—if she hasn't arrived by then."

"We've told you." I closed my eyes to stop the spinning. To stop the nausea. When the darkness made it worse, I forced them open once more. "Morgane is already in the city."

"I speak not of Morgane, but of her daughter." His smile emanated through the room, casting shadows in my heart. The first flicker of fear. "If you love her as you say, she will come for you. And I"—he patted my cheek as he strode past—"I will be waiting."

If possible, the dungeons were colder than even the air outside. Icicles had formed in the corner of our cell where water had dripped down the stone. Pooled on the earthen floor. I slumped against the iron bars, muscles weak and useless. Though Madame Labelle's hands remained bound, she rubbed her sleeve against the ice to wet the fabric. Knelt beside me to clean my face as best she could.

"With the emetic and your body mass," she said, trying and failing to soothe, "the effects of the injection should wane soon. You'll be fit as a fiddle when Louise comes to rescue us. We can only hope she realizes what has happened before we're eaten by rats."

"She isn't coming." My voice rang hollow. Dull. "We had a fight. I told her she was like her mother."

Beau broke off an icicle and shattered it against the wall. "Brilliant. That's just *brilliant*. Well done, brother. I can't wait to see how your spleen looks when a rat opens you up." He whirled to

Madame Labelle. "Can't you—I don't know—magic us out of here somehow? I know you're bound, but all it takes is a twitch of your finger, right?"

"They've coated our irons in some sort of numbing agent. I can't move my hands."

"Can you use your elbow instead? Perhaps a toe?"

"Of course I could, but the magic would be clumsy. I'd likely do more harm than good if I attempted it."

"What are you talking about?"

"Manipulating patterns requires dexterity, Your Highness. Imagine tying a knot with your elbows or toes, and you might grasp the difficulty. Our hands—our fingers—enable us to signify intent with much greater specificity." Color rose on her cheeks as she scrubbed my own. "Also, though it has *clearly* escaped your great mental prowess, there are four huntsmen standing guard at the end of this corridor."

He prowled the cell like an angry cat. Hackles raised. "So?"

"Mother's tits." She dragged her forehead across her shoulder in exasperation. "*So* I realize that I've accomplished *many* extraordinary magical feats in our time together, Beauregard, but even I must admit defeat when confronted with escaping prison, defeating four huntsmen, and fleeing the city with only my damned *elbow*."

"Well, what are we supposed to do, then?" Beau flung his hands in the air. "Sit here and wait for my father to feed us to his rats? Excellent plan, approaching him, by the way," he added with a snarl. "*He loved me once*, my ass."

"Beau," I said when Madame Labelle flinched. "Shut up."

"He isn't going to feed *you* to his rats, Your Highness," she said. "Despite his bluster, I don't think he means you any real harm. You're his only legitimate heir. The law dictates he cannot pass the kingdom to Violette or Victoire."

Beau whirled to face the corridor, crossing his arms angrily. "Yes, well, forgive me for no longer trusting your instincts." I stared at his profile as the pieces clicked into place. Her rose-colored glasses. He'd worn them too. Despite their unhappy relationship, Beau had still dreamed of more with his father. Those dreams had publicly shattered on the floor of the throne room.

I'd lost the idea of my father. Beau had lost the real thing.

"Hang on." Beau gripped the bars abruptly, his eyes fixating on something at the end of the corridor. I turned my head. Eased myself up the bars as panicked cries resounded from behind the door. Hope swelled, sharp and unexpected. Could it be . . . ? Had Lou come for us, after all? Beau grinned. "I know that voice. Those little *shits*."

Footsteps pounded away from us, and with them, the shouts faded. The corridor door creaked open.

A mischievous face poked through. Violette. I didn't know *how* I knew it was her rather than her sister, but I did. Instinctively. She skipped down the corridor toward us with a smirk. In her hand, she swung the guards' keys. "Hello, *taeae*. Did you miss me?"

"Violette." Beau thrust his face between the bars. "How are you here? Why aren't you at Mass?"

She rolled her eyes. "Like Papa would let us outside the castle with Morgane on the loose."

"Thank God for small mercies. Right. We need to hurry." He held his hand out insistently. "The huntsmen could be back any second. Give me the keys."

She settled a hand on her narrow hip. "They *won't* be back any second. I told them Victoire accidentally impaled herself on her blade, and the idiots dashed upstairs to help her." She scoffed. "As if Victoire would ever *accidentally* impale someone."

"Yes," he said impatiently, "but when they don't find Victoire bleeding to death, they'll know you tricked them. They'll come back down—"

"No, they won't. There's quite a bit of blood."

"*What?*"

"We snuck into the apothecary's stores and stole his lamb's blood. Victoire was a bit heavy-handed with it on the carpets, but she has several more vials. She's leading the huntsmen on a wild-goose chase. It should keep them busy for a few moments at least."

"You gave Victoire blood?" Beau blinked at her. "You just . . . gave it to her? To play with?"

Violette shrugged. "Couldn't be helped. Now"—she dangled the keys in front of his nose—"do you want to be rescued or not?" When he swiped for them, she snatched them out of reach. "Ah, ah, ah. Not so fast. You owe us an apology."

"Yes." A second voice joined hers, and Victoire material- ized. Her eyes gleamed in the semidarkness, and blood coated her hands. She extended her sword to the tip of Beau's nose. "Apologize for leaving us, *taeae*, and we shall free you." Her nose wrinkled when she looked at me. At Madame Labelle. "*You*. Not them. Papa says they deserve to burn."

Beau swung for the keys again. Missed. "Do me a favor, girls. When Father opens his mouth, close your ears. His voice will rot your brains."

"I think it's awfully romantic." Violette tilted her head to study me in an eerie impression of Auguste. Whereas his gaze had been cold, however—calculating—hers was shyly curious. "*Metua vahine* said he sacrificed everything to save the girl he loves. She doesn't like you much," she added to me, "or your *maman*, but I think she respects you."

"It's not romantic. It's *stupid*." Victoire kicked the bar closest to me before turning to Beau. "How could you choose this son of a whore over us?"

"Don't say that word," Beau said sharply. "Don't say it ever again."

She ducked her head, glowering but chastised. "You left us, *taeae*. You didn't tell us where you'd gone. We could've come with you. We could've fought the witches by your side."

He lifted her chin with his finger. "Not all witches are bad, *tuahine, tou*. I found some good ones. I intend to help them."

"But Papa said he'd disinherit you!" Violette interjected.

"Then I suppose you'll be queen."

Her eyes widened.

"I'm sorry I didn't say goodbye," Beau said softly, "but I'm not sorry I left. I have a chance to be part of something extraordinary. Together, all of us—humans, witches, werewolves, maybe even mermaids—we have a chance to change the world."

Violette gasped. "Mermaids?"

"Oh, shut it, Violette." Victoire snatched the keys from her and tossed them to Beau. "Do it." She nodded to him curtly. "Break it. Make it better. And at the end of it—when you put the pieces back together—I want to be a huntsman."

"Oh, me too!" Violette cried. "Except I want to wear a dress."

Beau fumbled to unlock the cell. "Huntsmen will be part of the broken pieces, girls."

"No." Victoire shook her head. "Not a huntsman like they are now. We want to be huntsmen like they should be—proper knights, riding forth to vanquish the forces of evil. *True* evil." She waved a hand at me—at the sick covering my front—as Beau slid the cell open. "Not whatever this is."

I couldn't help but grin.

To my surprise, she grinned back. Small. Hesitant. But still there. Emotion reared at the sight, and I stumbled at the strength of it. Violette wrapped an arm around my waist to steady me. To lead me down the corridor. "You stink, *taeae*. And proper knights don't stink. How can you rescue your fair maiden if she can't stand the smell of you?"

Fighting her own grin, Madame Labelle braced my other side. "Perhaps his fair maiden doesn't need rescuing."

"Perhaps *she* will rescue him," Victoire called over her shoulder.

"Perhaps *they* will rescue each other," Violette snapped back.

"Perhaps we will," I murmured, feeling lighter than I'd felt in ages. Perhaps we could. Together. In a swift burst of realization, I saw things clearly for perhaps the first time: she wasn't the only broken one. I'd closed my eyes to hide from the monsters—*my* monsters—hoping they couldn't see me. Hoping if I buried them deep enough, they'd disappear.

But they hadn't disappeared, and I'd hidden long enough.

Anxious now, I walked faster, ignored the pounding in my head. I had to find Lou. I had to find her, to *talk* to her—

Then several things happened at once.

The door flew open with a cataclysmic *bang*, and the four huntsmen charged back into the corridor. Madame Labelle yelled "RUN!" at the same time Victoire sliced through her binds. Chaos reigned. With the pulse of Madame Labelle's hands, rock from the ceiling rained on the Chasseurs' heads. A stone the size of my fists connected with one, and he collapsed. The others shouted in panic—in *fury*—trying to coordinate, to subdue her. Two tackled her while the third leapt in front of us. Shrieking a battle cry, Victoire stomped on his toes. When he reeled backward, swinging the blade of his Balisarda away from her, Violette punched him in the nose.

"Get out of here!" Victoire shoved him, and—already off balance—he tumbled to the floor. Beau cut his binds on her sword. "Before it's too late!"

I struggled to reach Madame Labelle. "I can't leave her—"

"GO!" Madame Labelle flung an arm out beneath the

Chasseurs' bodies, blasting the door apart. "NOW!"

Beau didn't give me a choice. Flinging his arms around me, he dragged my weakened, useless body down the corridor. More footsteps pounded above us, but we took a sharp left down another corridor, disappearing within a half-concealed crag in the wall. "Hurry," Beau said desperately, pulling me faster. "Mass has started, but the Chasseurs who remained in the castle will be here soon. They'll search these tunnels. Come on, *come on.*"

"But my mother, our *sisters*—"

"Our sisters will be fine. He'll never hurt them—"

Still I struggled. "And Madame Labelle?"

He didn't hesitate, forcing me down another tunnel. "She can take care of herself."

"NO—"

"*Reid.*" He spun me to face him, gripping my arms when I thrashed. His eyes were wide. Wild. "She made a choice, all right? She chose to save you. If you go back now, you won't be helping her. You'll be spiting her." He shook me harder. "Live today, Reid, so you can fight tomorrow. We'll get her back. If I have to burn down this castle myself, we *will* get her back. Do you trust me?"

I felt myself nod, felt him pull me along once more.

Behind us, her screams echoed in the distance.

WHEN A SNAKE SHEDS HER SKIN

Lou

Wrapping my arms around my legs, I rested my chin on my knees and gazed up at the afternoon sky. Thick, heavy clouds had gathered overhead, shrouding the sunshine and promising precipitation. Though my eyes still stung, I postponed closing them just a little longer. Below me, Coco and Ansel waited in my room. I could hear their murmurs from where I sat atop the roof.

At least something good had come from this nightmarish day. At least they were speaking again—even if it was about me.

"What can we do?" Ansel said anxiously.

"We can't do anything." Coco's voice was hoarse from tears— or perhaps smoke. The honey had healed her burns, but it hadn't repaired the bar. Claud had promised to pay the innkeeper for damages. "At least she knows now. She'll be more careful."

"And Reid?"

"He'll come back to her. He always does."

I didn't deserve any of them.

As if trying to lift my spirits, the wind caressed my face,

grasping tendrils of my hair in its wintry grip. Or maybe it wasn't the wind at all. Maybe it was something else. *Someone* else. Feeling slightly ridiculous, I looked to the vast, ubiquitous clouds and whispered, "I need your help."

The wind stopped teasing my hair.

Encouraged, I sat up and squared my shoulders, letting my feet dangle from the eave. "Fathers shouldn't abandon their children. Mine was a shitty excuse for a human being—give him a kick from me if he's up there—but even he tried to protect me in his own twisted way. You, though . . . you should do better. You're supposed to be the father of all fathers, aren't you? Or maybe—maybe you're the mother of all mothers, and it's like my own *maman* said." I shook my head, defeated. "Maybe she's right. Maybe you *do* want me dead."

A bird shot from a window below me with a startled cry, and I tensed, peering down the edge of the building, searching for what had disturbed it. There was nothing. All was quiet and calm. Remnants of the last snowfall still clung to the corners of the rooftop, but now the sky couldn't seem to decide between snow and rain. Aimless flakes drifted through the air. Though a few mourners gathered in the damp, narrow street below, most wouldn't arrive until they finished with Requiem Mass.

Coco's and Ansel's voices had tapered off a few moments ago. Perhaps they'd gone to her room to resolve their own problems. I hoped they did. Whether together or apart, they each deserved happiness.

"Reid says I'm . . . lost," I breathed. Though the words unfurled gently, softly, I couldn't have stemmed them if I'd tried. It's as if they'd been floating just beneath my skin, waiting patiently for this moment. For this last, desperate window of opportunity to open. For this . . . prayer. "He says I'm changing—that I'm different. And maybe he's right. Maybe I just don't want to see it, or—or maybe I can't. I've certainly made a piss poor mess here. The werewolves left, and if my mother doesn't kill me, they will. Worse, La Voisin keeps—keeps *watching* me like she's waiting for something, Nicholina thinks we're great pals, and I—I don't know what to do. I don't have the answers. That's supposed to be your job."

I snorted and turned away, anger spiking sharp and sudden in my heart. The words spewed faster. Less a trickle, more a torrent. "I read your book, you know. You said you knitted us together in our mothers' wombs. If that's true, I guess that joke was on me, huh? I really am the arrow in her hand. She wants to use me to destroy the world. She thinks it's my purpose to die at the altar, and you—you *gave* me to her. I'm not innocent now, but I was once. I was a baby. A *child*. You gave me to a woman who would kill me, to a woman who would never love me—" I broke off, breathing hard and grinding my palms against my eyes, trying to relieve the building pressure. "And now I'm trying not to break, but I *am*. I'm broken. I don't know how to fix it—to fix me or Reid or *us*. And he—he *hates* me—" Again, I choked on the words. An absurd bubble of laughter rose in my throat.

"I don't even know if you're real," I whispered, laughing and crying and feeling infinitely foolish. My hands trembled. "I'm probably talking to myself right now like a madwoman. And maybe I am mad. But—but if you *are* real, if you *are* listening, please, *please...*"

I dropped my head and closed my eyes. "Don't abandon me."

I sat there, head bowed, for several long minutes. Long enough for my tears to freeze on my cheeks. Long enough for my fingers to stop trembling. Long enough for that window in my soul to slowly, quietly click closed. Was I waiting for something? I didn't know. Either way, the only answer I received was silence.

Time slipped away from me. Only Claud Deveraux's whistle— it preceded him to the rooftop—drew me from my reverie. I almost laughed. Almost. I'd never met a person so attuned to melancholy; at the first sign of introspection, he seemed to just *appear* like a starving man before a buffet of pastries and sweets. "I could not help but overhear," he said lightly, dropping to the eave beside me, "your rather magnificent conversation with the celestial sphere."

I rolled my eyes. "You absolutely could've."

"You're right. I'm a filthy eavesdropper, and I have no intention of apologizing." He nudged my shoulder with a small smile. "I thought you should know Reid just arrived, whole if not unharmed."

A beat passed as his words sank in.

Whole if not unharmed.

Lurching to my feet, I nearly slipped and fell to my death in my haste to reach the stairwell. When Claud caught my hand with the gentle shake of his head, my heart plummeted. "Give him a few moments to collect himself, *chérie*. He's been through an ordeal."

"What happened?" I demanded, snatching my hand away.

"I did not ask. He will tell us when he's ready."

"Oh." That one simple word echoed my heartache better than a hundred others ever could. I was part of that *us* now, an outsider, no longer privy to his innermost thoughts or secrets. I'd pushed him away, frightened—no, nearly crazed—that he would do it first. He hadn't, of course, but the effect remained the same. And it was my fault—*all* my fault. Slowly, I sank back onto the eave. "I see."

Claud raised a brow. "Do you?"

"No," I said miserably. "But you already knew that."

A moment passed as I watched mourners—the poor and bereft, mostly, with their tattered black clothes—trickle into the street. The bell tower had chimed half past a quarter hour ago. Soon, Requiem Mass would end, and the burial procession would wind through these streets, allowing commoners to say their goodbyes. The Archbishop's body would pass directly beneath us on its way to the cemetery, to the Church's tomb in the catacombs and its final resting place. Though I still didn't *like* Madame Labelle, I appreciated her forethought in this location. If there was one person in the entire kingdom who'd loved the Archbishop, it was Reid. He should've been the one to prepare the body this morning. He should've been the one to speak over it. Even now, he should've been the one holding vigil beside it.

Instead, he was forced to hide in a dirty inn.

He would miss the Archbishop's last rites. He would miss lowering his forefather into the earth. He would miss his final goodbye. I forced the thought away, tears threatening once more. It seemed all I did was cry these days.

At least here, Reid would have one last glimpse of him.

If Morgane didn't kill us all first.

I felt rather than saw Claud studying me. He had the air of someone trapped in paralyzing indecision. Taking pity on him, I turned to tell him to stop, to tell him it was okay, but his resolve seemed to harden at something in my eyes. He removed his top hat with a sigh. "I know you are troubled. Though I have long debated the time and place to tell you this, perhaps I might ease your conscience by freeing my own." He looked to the sky with a wistful expression. "I knew your mother, and you are nothing like her."

I blinked at him. Of all the things I'd been expecting, that wasn't one. "What?"

"You're the best parts of her, of course. The vitality. The cleverness. The charm. But you are not her, Louise."

"How do you know her?"

"I don't know her. Not anymore." The wistfulness in his gaze faded, replaced by something akin to sorrow. "In a different time—a thousand years ago, it seems—I loved her with a passion unequal to any I've ever known. I thought she loved me too."

"Holy hell." I lifted a hand to my brow and closed my eyes. It made sense now, his strange and unsettling fascination with me.

The white hair probably hadn't helped. "Look, Claud, if you're about to tell me you—you empathize with her, or you still love her, or you've been secretly plotting with her all along, can you wait? I've had the shittiest of all days, and I don't think I can handle a betrayal right now."

His chuckle did little to reassure me. "Dear girl, do you really think I'd admit such a connection if I were in league with her? No, no, no. I knew Morgane before she . . . changed."

"Oh." There was that word again. It plagued me, full of unspoken pain and unacknowledged truths. "No offense, but you're hardly my mother's type."

He laughed then, louder and more genuine than before. "Appearances can be deceiving, child."

I fixed him with a pointed look and repeated my earlier question. It seemed important now. "What *are* you, Claud?"

He didn't hesitate. His brown eyes—warm, concerned— might've pierced my soul. "What are *you*, Louise?"

I stared at my hands, deliberating. I'd been called many impolite things in my life. Most didn't bear repeating, but one had stuck with me, slipping beneath my skin and moldering my flesh. He'd called me a liar. He'd called me—

"A snake," I replied, breath hitching. "I suppose . . . I'm a snake. A liar. A deceiver. Cursed to crawl on my belly and eat dust all the days of my life."

"Ah." To my surprise, Claud's face didn't twist in disgust or revulsion. He nodded instead, a knowing smile playing on his lips. "Yes, I would agree with that assessment."

Humiliation hung my head. "Right. Thanks."

"Louise." A single finger lifted my chin, forcing me to look at him. Those eyes, once warm, now blazed with intensity, with conviction. "What you are now is not what you've always been, nor is it what you always will be. You *are* a snake. Shed your skin if it no longer serves you. Transform into something different. Something better."

He tapped my nose before rising and offering me his hand. "Both blood witch and werewolf will stay until after the funeral. Cosette spoke rather passionately to the former on your behalf, and with Reid's return, the latter are eager to repay their blood debt. However, I wouldn't expect a bouquet of roses from either party in the foreseeable future, and—well, I might also avoid Le Ventre for the entirety of my life if I were you."

I accepted his hand, rising heavily. "Reid."

"Ah, yes. Reid. I'm afraid I might have omitted the teensiest, tiniest of details in his regard."

"What? What do you—"

He pressed a kiss to my forehead. Though the gesture should've been jarring in its intimacy, it felt . . . comforting. Like a kiss my father might've given if . . . well, if things had been different. "He asked for you. Quite insistently, in fact, but our stalwart Cosette insisted he bathe before seeing you. He was covered in vomit, of all things."

"Vomit?" Each rapid blink only heightened my confusion. "But—"

The door to the stairwell burst open, and there—filling up

every inch of the frame—stood Reid.

"Lou." His face crumpled when he looked at me, and he crossed the rooftop in two strides, crushing me into his arms. I buried my face in his coat, fresh tears dampening the fabric, and held him tighter still. His frame trembled. "They took her, Lou. They took my mother, and she's not coming back."

THE FUNERAL

Reid

The first drops of rain signaled the start of the burial procession. The droplets stung my hand. Icy. Sharp. Like tiny knives. Lou had flung open our room's window to watch as the crowd thickened. A sea of black. Of tears. Few bothered with umbrellas, even as the rain fell harder. Faster.

Constabulary lined the street in somber uniforms, their faces and weapons drawn. Chasseurs swathed in black stood rigid among them. Some I recognized. Others I didn't.

Somewhere down there, the Dames Blanches and loup garou lay in wait for any sign of Morgane. Toulouse and Thierry hadn't joined them. My fault. My own stubborn pride. Deveraux, however, had insisted on helping. He'd also insisted Lou and I remain out of sight. Though he claimed our absence might dissuade her from foolish action, I knew better. He'd gifted us privacy—*me* privacy—to watch the procession. To . . . mourn.

"Therewithal," he'd said, matter-of-fact, "we can't very well allow the king or Chasseurs to spot you in the crowd. Chaos would ensue, and our dear Lady *thrives* in chaos."

In the room beside us, water gurgled through the pipes. I assumed it was for Coco's bath. Like us, Deveraux had banished her, Beau, and Ansel to their rooms, asserting, "Your faces are known." It felt silly, after everything, to hide away while the others endangered themselves. This hadn't been part of the plan.

I couldn't bring myself to protest.

Ansel probably watched the procession from his window. I hoped he did. He wasn't a Chasseur, but he might have been, once. He might've grown to love the Archbishop. If not loved . . . he certainly would've respected him. Feared him.

I wondered if anyone below had truly loved our patriarch.

He'd had no siblings, no parents. No wife. At least, not in the legal sense. In the biblical, however, his had been a woman who'd tricked him into bed, into conceiving a child destined to destroy him—

No. I stopped the thought before it could form. Morgane was to blame, yes, but so was he. She hadn't forced him. He'd made a decision. He wasn't perfect.

As if reading my thoughts, Lou squeezed my hand. "Sometimes it hurts to remember the dead as who they were, rather than who we wanted them to be."

I returned the pressure but said nothing. Though I knew she longed for a bath—for a change of clothes—the tub remained empty. The fresh clothing Deveraux had procured for her remained folded on the bed. Untouched. Instead, she stood beside me, with me, staring down at the street below. Listening to the rain, to the faint chants of liturgy from Saint-Cécile. Waiting for the procession to pass through East End to the cemetery beyond.

I couldn't imagine what she felt. Did she too mourn him? Did she too feel the keen loss of a father?

Will there be a funeral?

Yes.

But . . . he was my father. I remembered her wide eyes back in the Hollow. Her hesitance. Her guilt. Yes, she'd felt something. Not grief, exactly, but perhaps . . . regret.

He slept with La Dame des Sorcières. A witch.

I couldn't blame her. I couldn't hate her for what had happened. I'd made a choice, same as the Archbishop. Lou might've lied. She might've deceived me. But when I'd followed her to the Chateau, I'd chosen my fate, and I'd done it with my eyes wide open. I'd chosen this life. This love. And with my fingers trembling in hers, with her heart beating alongside mine, I still chose it.

I still chose her.

The king can't possibly honor him.

Once, I would've agreed with her. A man tainted by witchcraft deserved no honor. He deserved only judgment—only hatred. But now . . . now I tired of hating that man. Of hating myself. That hatred could crush a person. Even now, it weighed heavily, a millstone around my neck. Strangling me. I couldn't hold it much longer. I didn't want to.

Perhaps . . . perhaps Lou had been right. Perhaps a small part of me *did* resent her magic. My magic. The small part of me still connected to the man below. After seeing what I'd seen, it'd be easy to disparage magic. I couldn't deny its effects on Lou. And yet . . . Lou had proven time and time again she wasn't evil. Despite those changes, despite the hurt between us, she was still here—holding my hand, comforting me—as I mourned the father she'd never know. The father I'd taken from her.

Magic was just one part of her.

It was part of me.

And we would find a way forward together.

The voices outside grew louder, rising over the crowd, and an assemblage of clergymen turned down our street. They moved slowly, regally, and incanted the Song of Farewell, their holy vestments soaked through from rain. Behind them, a small army of Chasseurs surrounded the royal carriage. Auguste and Oliana had changed into full mourning regalia. Their faces solemn. False.

Between just the two of us, I'm pleased you killed him.

More carriages rounded the corner, bringing with them notable members of the aristocracy. At the end of the line, the Tremblay carriage appeared. The grief on Pierre's face seemed genuine, at least. I couldn't see beyond him to Célie, but her tears would've been too. The Archbishop had doted on her.

"Reid." Lou's voice lowered to a whisper, and she stared at the last carriage as it appeared around the corner. "It's him."

Crafted from gold brighter than even the king's crown—engraved with angels and skulls and crossbones, his name and reign of service—the Archbishop's casket remained closed. Of course it did. My chest ached. He'd been unrecognizable, in the end. I didn't want to imagine him, didn't want to remember—

My hand slips, and Morgane hisses as blood trickles down her throat. The ebony witch steps closer. "Let her go, or he dies."

"Manon," Lou pleads. "Don't do this. Please—"

"Be quiet, Lou." Her eyes glow manic and crazed—beyond reason. The Archbishop continues screaming. The veins beneath his skin blacken, as do his nails and tongue. I stare at him in horror.

No. I shook my head, dropping Lou's hand and reeling backward. He'd once been immortal in my eyes. Strong and unbreakable. A god in himself.

"I know it hurts," Lou whispered. "But you need to grieve him, Reid, or you'll never be able to let him go. You need to *feel*."

At her words, another memory surfaced, uninvited:

Blood drips from my nose. Father Thomas says I'm a hateful child for brawling with the local street rats. They resent me for my situation in the Church, for the hot food in my belly and the soft bed in my room. Father Thomas says I was found in the trash. He says I should've been one of them, should've grown up in their hovel of poverty and violence. But I didn't, and the Church's hot food made me tall and the Church's soft bed made me strong.

And I taught them for attacking when my back was turned.

"Come back here!" Father Thomas chases me through the cathedral with a switch. But he's old and slow, and I outrun him, laughing. He doubles

over to catch his breath. "Wicked boy, I shall inform the Archbishop this time, mark my words!"

"Inform me of what?"

That voice makes me stumble, makes me fall. When I look up, the Archbishop looms over me. I've only seen him from afar. From the pulpit. After the priests force me to wash my hands and face. After they thrash my backside so I can't sit during Mass.

I sit anyway.

Father Thomas draws himself up, struggles to breathe. "The boy nearly crippled a child in East End this morning, Your Eminence."

"I was provoked!" I wipe the blood from my nose, glaring at them. I am not afraid of the switch. I am not afraid of anything. "He and his friends ambushed me."

The Archbishop raises a brow at my insolence. At my defiance. "And you dealt their punishment?"

"They deserved what they got."

"Indeed." He circles me now, assessing. Despite my anger, I am uneasy. I've heard of his soldiers. His huntsmen. Perhaps I have grown too tall. Too strong. "'Let justice roll on like a river, and righteousness like a never-failing stream.'"

I blink at him. "What?"

"What is your name, young man?"

"Reid Diggory."

He repeats my name. Tastes it. "You have a very bright future ahead of you, Reid Diggory." To Father Thomas, he nods curtly. "After you've finished with the boy, bring him to my study. We begin his training immediately."

In the street below, Jean Luc marched in my place beside the casket. Beside the Archbishop. Even from afar—even in the rain—I could see his eyes were red. Raw. Hot tears spilled down my own cheeks. I wiped them away furiously. Once, we would've comforted each other. We would've mourned together. But no longer.

"Again, Reid."

The Archbishop's voice cuts through the din of the training yard. I pick up my sword and face my friend. Jean Luc nods encouragingly. "You can do it," he whispers, lifting his sword again. But I can't do it. My arm trembles. My fingers ache. Blood runs from a cut on my shoulder.

Jean Luc is better than me.

Part of me wonders why we're here. The initiates around us are older. They are men, and we are boys. And fourteen-year-olds have no hope of becoming Chasseurs.

"But you're growing stronger every day." Inside my head, the Archbishop reminds me. "Channel your anger. Sharpen it. Hone it into a weapon."

Anger. Yes. Jean Luc and I are very angry.

This morning, Julien cornered us in the commissary. Captain Aurand had left with the others. We were alone.

"I don't care if you are the Archbishop's pet," he said, lifting his blade to my throat. Though he's several years older than Jean Luc and me, his head only brushes my chin. "When Chasseur Delcour retires, his position is mine. No trash boy will carry a Balisarda."

Trash boy. That is my name in this place.

Jean Luc punched him in the stomach, and we ran.

Now, I turn my blade on Jean Luc, determined. I am no trash boy. I am worthy of the Archbishop's attention. Of his love. I am worthy of the Chasseurs. And I will show them all.

Small hands touched my shoulder, easing me onto the bed. I sat without thinking. My lips trembled, but I fought viciously against the despair rising inside me. The hopelessness. He was gone. The Archbishop was gone, and he was never coming back.

I'd killed him.

The crowd's cheers drown out Jean Luc's roar of pain. I do not stop. I do not hesitate. Despite my too-small coat, the bile on my tongue, I strike swift and sure, knocking his sword from his hand. Disabling him. "Yield," I say, lifting my boot to his chest. Adrenaline makes me dizzy. Clouds my thoughts.

I have won.

Jean Luc bares his teeth, clutching his wounded leg. "I yield."

Captain Aurand steps between us. Lifts my arm. "The winner!"

The crowd goes wild, and Célie cheers loudest of all.

I think I love her.

"Congratulations," the Archbishop says, striding into the arena. He draws me into a tight embrace. "I am so proud of you, my son."

My son.

The pride in his eyes makes my own prick and sting. My heart threatens to burst. I am no longer trash boy. I am the Archbishop's son—Chasseur Diggory—and I belong. I hug him so tightly that he gasps, laughing.

"Thank you, Father."

Behind us, Jean Luc spits blood.

"I killed my father," I whispered.

Lou stroked my back. "I know."

Heat washes over me as her lips touch mine. Slowly, at first, and tentative. As if fearful of my reaction. But she has nothing to fear from me. "Célie," I breathe, looking at her in wonder.

She smiles, and the entire world lurches to a halt at her beauty. "I love you, Reid."

When her lips descend once more, I forget the bench in this dark confessional. I forget the empty sanctuary beyond. There is only Célie. Célie, standing between my legs. Célie, twining her fingers in my hair. Célie—

The door bursts open, and we break apart.

"What is going on here?" the Archbishop asks, appalled.

With a horrified squeak, Célie covers her mouth and ducks beneath his arm, fleeing into the sanctuary and out of sight. The Archbishop watches her go incredulously. Finally, he turns back to me. Scrutinizes my rumpled hair. My flushed cheeks. My swollen lips.

Sighing, he extends a hand to help me up. "Come, Reid. It seems we have much to discuss."

He was the only man who'd ever cared for me. The tears fell faster now, soaking my shirt. My hands. My tarnished, *ugly* hands. Gently, Lou wrapped her arms around me.

The loup garou's blood coats the grass in the clearing. It stains the wildflower petals, the riverbank. My Balisarda. My hands. I rub them on my pants as inconspicuously as possible, but he still sees. He approaches warily. My brothers part for him, bowing low.

"To mourn them would be a waste of your compassion, son."

I stare at the corpse at my feet. The body, once lupine, reverted back to humanoid after death. His dark eyes stare at the summer sky without seeing. "He's my age."

"It," the Archbishop corrects me, voice gentle. "It was *your age. These creatures are not as you and me."*

The next morning, he presses a medal into my palm. Though the red is gone, the blood remains. "You have done the kingdom a great service," he says. "Captain Diggory.*"*

"I'm sorry, Reid." Despite my shaking shoulders, Lou held me tightly. Tears streamed down her own cheeks. I crushed her against me, breath shuddering—each gasp painful, burning—as I buried my face in the crook of her neck. As I finally, *finally* allowed the grief to win. To consume me. In great, heaving sobs, it burst forth—a torrent of hurt and bitterness, of shame and regret—and I choked on it, helpless to stop its wrath. Helpless to do anything but cling to Lou. My friend. My shelter. My home. "I'm so sorry."

I don't hesitate. I don't think. Moving quickly, I sweep a second knife from my bandolier and charge past Morgane. She lifts her hands—fire lashing from her fingertips—but I don't feel the flames. The gold light wraps around my skin, protecting me. But my thoughts scatter. Whatever strength my body claimed, my mind now forfeits. I stumble, but the gold cord marks my path. I vault over the altar after it.

The Archbishop's eyes fly open as he realizes my intent. A small, pleading noise escapes him, but he can do little else before I fall upon him.

Before I drive my knife home in his heart.

The Archbishop's eyes are still wide—confused—as he slumps forward in my arms.

"I did it all for you too, Lou."

And with that—as his casket faded from view in the cemetery beyond, as the crowd swallowed up my last memory of him—I let the Archbishop go.

SOMETHING NEW

Lou

I didn't know how much time passed as Reid and I held each other on that bed. Though my limbs ached from sitting still for so long—from the cold creeping into the room—I didn't dare let go. He needed this. He needed someone to love him. To comfort him. To honor and keep him. I would've laughed at the irony of the situation if it hadn't been so heartbreaking.

How many people in this world had truly loved Reid? A lost little boy in a trash can grown into a hardened young man in a uniform. Two? Maybe three? I knew I loved him. I knew Ansel did too. Madame Labelle was his mother, and Jean Luc had cared once. But our love was fleeting, all things considered. Ansel had only grown to love him in the last few months. Madame Labelle had abandoned him. Jean Luc had grown to resent him. And I . . . I'd given up on him at the first opportunity. No, for all his hypocrisy and hatred, the Archbishop had loved him most and loved him longest. And I would always be grateful to him for it—that he'd been a father to Reid when he hadn't been one to me.

But now he was dead.

Reid's shoulders stopped shaking as the sun dipped below the windowsill—his sobs gradually quieting—but still he didn't loosen his grip. "He would've hated me," he finally said. More tears leaked onto my shoulder. "If he'd known, he would've hated me."

I stroked his back. "It wouldn't have been possible for him to hate you, Reid. He adored you."

A beat of silence passed.

"He hated himself."

"Yes," I said grimly. "I think he did."

"I'm not like him, Lou." He leaned back to look at me, though his arms didn't leave my waist. His poor face was splotched with color, and his eyes were nearly swollen shut. Tears clung to his lashes. But there—resolving behind the sorrow—was a hope so keen and sharp I might've cut my finger on it. "I don't hate myself. I don't hate you either."

I gave him a wary smile but said nothing.

Releasing my waist, he lifted a hand to cup my jaw, brushing a tentative thumb across my lips. "You still don't believe me."

I opened my mouth to argue, but the words died in my throat when he lifted his hand to the open window. The temperature had fallen with the sun, and the raindrops had solidified to snow-flakes. They drifted into the room on a gentle breeze. At the coaxing of his fingers, they transformed into fireflies.

I exhaled in delight as they floated toward me, as they landed on my hair. "How are you . . . ?"

"You said it yourself." Their glow reflected in his eyes. "Magic isn't good or evil. It heeds those who summon it. When life is a choice between fighting or fleeing—every moment life or death—everything becomes a weapon. It doesn't matter who holds them. Weapons harm. I've seen it. I've experienced it first-hand."

He touched the dingy, floral paper on the walls, and the blooms exploded upward, *outward*, until he reached up to pluck one, tucking it behind my ear. The scent of winter jasmine filled the room. "But life is more than those moments, Lou. We're more than those moments."

When he dropped his hands, the flowers returned to their paper, and the fireflies dimmed, white and wet once more. But I didn't feel the cold. I stared at him for a while, memorizing the lines of his face with a sense of wonder. I'd been wrong about him. About everything. I'd been so very, very wrong.

A tremble of my lips betrayed me. "I'm sorry, Reid. I *am* out of control. I—I set Coco on fire this afternoon. Maybe . . . maybe you were right, and I shouldn't use magic at all."

"I spoke with Coco earlier. She told me what happened. She also said she'd exsanguinate me if I judged you for it." He brushed the snow from my hair, swallowing hard. "Not that I ever would. Lou . . . we've both made mistakes. You're a witch. I shouldn't have resented you using magic. Just—don't let it take you somewhere I can't follow." When he glanced out the window, my gaze followed instinctively, and I saw what he saw.

A cemetery.

He shook his head. "Where you go, I go, remember? You're all I have now. I can't lose you too."

I crept into his lap. "What am I, Reid? Say it again."

"You're a witch."

"And what are you?"

He didn't hesitate, and my heart swelled. "I am too."

"Only partly right, I'm afraid." My smile—now genuine—grew at his confusion, and I leaned forward, rubbing my nose against his. He closed his eyes. "Allow me to fill in the gaps for you." I kissed his nose. "You are a huntsman." Though he recoiled slightly, I didn't let him escape, kissing his cheek. "You are a son." I kissed his other cheek. "You are a brother." His forehead. "You are a husband." His eyelids and his chin. "You are brave and strong and *good*." And, finally, his lips. "But most important, you are *loved*."

A fresh tear trickled down his face. I kissed it too. "You're also sanctimonious and stubborn and short-tempered." His eyes flicked open, and he frowned. I kissed his lips again. Gentle and slow. "Not to mention brooding, with a shit sense of humor." When he opened his mouth to argue, I spoke over him. "But despite all that, you aren't alone, Reid. You'll never be alone."

He stared at me for a long moment.

And then he was kissing me.

"I'm sorry too," he breathed, hands cradling my face as he lowered me to the bed. Gently. So, so gently. But those hands burned as they trailed down my throat, down my chest. Burned and trembled. "I'm so sorry—"

I caught them before they could reach my belt. "Reid. Reid, we don't have to do this. If it's too soon—"

"Please." When he looked at me, the longing in his eyes made my breath catch in my throat. I'd never seen anything so beautiful. "I can't—I've never been good with words. Just—please. Let me touch you. Let me *show* you."

Swallowing hard, I released his hands.

Slowly—so slowly I wanted to scream—he slid the velvet jacket from my shoulders, untucking my shirt and inching it up my torso, revealing the skin of my belly. My ribs. My chest. When I lifted my arms for him to continue, however, he carefully rolled the hem over my eyes and left it there. Blinding me. Trapping my arms in the sleeves.

When I wriggled in protest, he splayed a hand across my hip, stilling me. His lips moved lightly against my neck. "Don't you trust me?"

The word rose to my lips, unbidden. "Always."

"Prove it."

I stopped straining abruptly. A chill swept through my entire body, lifting the hair on my arms, my neck, as I remembered.

Do as I say.

"Embrace me, Lou," he repeated my own words back to me, trailing feather-light kisses on my throat, catching my earlobe gently in his teeth. I gasped. Though his body pinned mine to the mattress, he was careful to support his weight with his elbows. I wished he wouldn't. I wanted to feel him. All of him. "Embrace *us*."

Let me show you how powerful you could be. My hateful words seemed to echo around us. *Let me show you how weak you are.*

"You don't have to be afraid." If possible, his touch—his lips—turned even gentler. He trailed a finger between my breasts, and fresh gooseflesh erupted in his wake. I shivered, my knees shaking. "Let me show you how much you mean to me. Let me show you how loved *you* are." His lips followed after his hand, each kiss reverent. Each a vow. "I'll never take you for granted. I'll want you every day for the rest of my life, and I'll love you even after."

"Reid—"

"Do you want to kiss me?" His finger stilled on my waistband, and I nodded, breathless. I knew the next words before he spoke them. I reveled in them. "Show me."

In a single, smooth motion, he pulled the shirt over my head.

I was on him in a second. He landed on his back with a soft laugh, which I captured in a kiss. He laughed again at my enthusiasm, arms tightening around me, before rising up to his elbows to help me tear his shirt from his pants. I shucked it over his head and to the floor, pushed him back against the bed and straddled his waist.

"Have I told you," I said, bending low to whisper in his ear, "how beautiful you are when you smile?"

He smiled then, the kind of smile that dimpled his cheek and set my heart on fire. "Tell me."

"Sometimes when I look at you, I can't breathe." My hand moved to his belt. "I can't think. I can't function until you look back. And when you give me this smile"—I brushed my knuckle against his dimple—"it's like a secret just for the two of us. I don't think I ever love you more than when you smile at me."

He chuckled in disbelief at the words, but the sound faded into nothing as we stared at each other. As he slowly realized their truth. And they *were* true. Each of Reid's smiles—so rare, so genuine—was a gift to me. He couldn't know how much I cherished them, how I wished I could keep them in my pocket to pull out whenever he felt sad. He felt sad so often.

After all this was over, I'd make sure he never felt sad again.

He ran his fingertips down my ribs, lingering on my waist. "I want to know all your secrets."

"My secrets are ugly, Reid."

"Not to me." He swallowed hard when I inched my hand beneath his belt. Lower still. "I meant what I said after Modraniht. I've never met anyone like you. You make me feel alive, and I just"—he gasped at my touch—"I want to share everything with you."

I pressed my free fingers to his lips. "And you will."

I released him only to ease his pants down his hips, his thighs, his ankles, trailing kisses down every inch of pale skin I revealed. He shuddered beneath me but mostly kept still . . . until I took him in my mouth. His hips bucked involuntarily then, and he lurched upright. "Lou—"

I placed a hand against his chest to still him. "Do you want me to stop?"

He groaned, falling backward and clenching his eyes shut. "No."

"Then open your eyes. Don't hide from me."

Though he seemed to have difficulty drawing breath, he did as I asked. Slowly, his eyes fluttering open and shut, he flexed into me. Every muscle in his body went taut. He flexed again. A fine sheen of sweat coated his skin. Again. His throat worked, and his mouth parted. Again and again and again. He fisted his hands in the bedsheets and threw his head back, breathing ragged, body on the edge of losing control—

Lunging forward suddenly, he yanked at my pants, and I twisted to oblige, helping him drag them down my legs. When they caught on my shoes, he made a low, impatient sound, and my stomach knotted with anticipation. I shucked each boot off hastily, ignoring the notes that fluttered to the floor. Ignoring everything but his hard body on mine. When we fell back to the bed, tangled in every possible way, I clung to him, reveling in the way he moved, in the way his hips fitted between my legs and his hands braced against the headboard. In the heat of his skin. Of his gaze.

He didn't hide from me.

Each emotion played in his eyes, uninhibited, and I consumed them all, kissing every part of his damp face between breaths, between gasps. Desire. Joy. Wonder. He moved faster, determined—chasing each raw emotion as it came—and I followed, digging my fingertips into the hard muscle of his back. Though I was desperate to close my eyes—to revel in the sensation—I couldn't stop looking at him. He couldn't stop looking at me. Trapped in each other's eyes, helpless to stop ourselves, we built and built until we shattered, baring ourselves to each other at last.

Not just our bodies.

Our souls.

And in that moment when we fell apart . . . we came together again as something new.

PART III

Qui vivra verra.
He who lives, shall see.
—French proverb

THE LAST NOTE

Lou

I descended the steps that night feeling lighter than I'd felt in weeks—and perhaps a bit foolish. Coco had knocked on our door only moments ago to tell us there'd been no sign of Morgane during the procession. Not a single sighting. Not even a hint of magic on the breeze. It seemed after everything—after suffering blood camps and cold swamps, Les Dents and Le Ventre—we'd come here for nothing. I couldn't say I was exactly *disappointed* she hadn't wreaked havoc and mayhem. Indeed, her inaction had quite made my night. Her notes burned holes in my boot, but I ignored them, pinching Reid's backside as we entered the bar.

Though I knew he still grieved—as he should, as he would for the rest of his life—he shot me an indulgent, slightly exasperated smile before looping his arm around my neck and kissing my temple. "Insatiable as ever, *mademoiselle*."

"That's Madame Diggory to you."

His free hand slipped into his pocket. "About that. I think we should—"

"At last!" At a table near the stairs, Claud applauded as we arrived. The dim candlelight couldn't conceal the impatience on La Voisin's and Blaise's faces. Both sat with their respective parties as far from one another as the small room allowed. Coco, Ansel, Toulouse, and Thierry acted as a buffer between them— as did Zenna and Seraphine. They'd donned glittering costumes quite at odds with the others' travel clothing. "The lovebirds have flown. How wonderful, how *marvelous*—"

"Where's Beau?" I interrupted, scanning the room again.

"He stepped out for a moment." Coco's expression turned grim. "He said he needed air."

I frowned but Reid shook his head and murmured, "I'll explain later."

"You lied to us." La Voisin didn't raise her voice, despite the wrath in her eyes. It seemed she hadn't yet forgiven me for Coco's sake. "You said Morgane would attack today. I brought my people here to claim vengeance, yet all we've received"—those eyes flicked to Blaise—"is disrespect and disappointment."

I hurried to correct her. "We didn't lie. We said we *thought* Morgane would attack today—"

"We too have been disrespected." Blaise stood, and Liana and Terrance followed. "Though our debt remains unfulfilled, we will leave this place. Nothing more can be done."

When both parties looked to us expectantly, Reid and I shared a surreptitious glance.

What do we do now? his eyes seemed to ask.

The hell if I know, mine replied.

Before either of us could bumble a plea, Coco spoke instead. Bless her. "Clearly, we misinterpreted the notes, but that doesn't mean our window of opportunity has passed. Manon is in the city, which means Morgane likely is too. Perhaps we shouldn't have hidden Lou and Reid away. Maybe we could use them to draw her out—"

"No, no." Deveraux shook his head vehemently. Tonight, his clothes were uncharacteristically simple in head-to-toe black. Even the paint on his fingernails and kohl around his eyes matched. His lips, however, he'd daubed with bloodred rouge. "'Tis never a good idea to play cat and mouse with Morgane. She is never the mouse. Inherently feline, that one—"

Coco's eyes narrowed. "Then what do you suggest?"

"I suggest"—he pulled a white mask from his cloak and tied it around his face—"that you all take a breath and attend our performance tonight. Yes, even you, Josephine. Some levity in La Mascarade des Crânes might do wonders for those crinkles between your brows."

I froze, staring at him.

His mask was shaped like a skull.

Though Claud continued to babble about Dame Fortune, delighted when La Voisin snapped back, Reid didn't miss the abrupt change in my manner. "What is it?" he asked. With cold fingers, I reached down into my boot, and his smile faltered. "What are you—?"

Without a word, I handed him the scraps of paper I'd hastily replaced after my bath this evening. He accepted them with a frown. I watched his lips shape the words to himself.

Pretty porcelain, pretty doll, with hair as black as night,
She cries alone within her pall, her tears so green and bright.

Pretty porcelain, pretty doll, forgotten and alone,
Trapped within a mirrored grave, she wears a mask of bone.

"I don't understand." Reid's eyes shot to mine, searching, as Claud finally stopped talking. As he stood to read the lines over Reid's shoulder. "We still don't know what these mean—"

"Mask of bone," I whispered. "La Mascarade des Crânes. It can't be coincidence."

"*What* can't be a coincidence?" He took my face in his hands. The papers fluttered to the dirty floor. "These are just bits of gibberish, Lou. We came to the Archbishop's funeral. She wasn't—"

"Oh dear." Claud's eyes widened as he bent to retrieve them, finally catching sight of the ominous words. "Feline, indeed."

Reid spun to face him, but a knock sounded on Léviathan's door. Frowning, I crossed the room to pull it open, but Reid stopped me with a hand on my arm. Straightening his coat, Claud opened the door instead. A small, unfamiliar girl stood on the threshold. "For you, *mademoiselle*," she said, stuffing a third scrap of paper in my palm before scurrying away. I unfolded it cautiously, dread seeping into my stomach.

Pretty porcelain, pretty doll, your pretty clock doth start

Come rescue her by midnight, or I shall eat her heart.

All my love,
Maman

With shaking fingers, I showed the note to Reid. He skimmed it quickly, face paling, before hurtling after the girl. Blaise followed with a snarl.

"Oh dear," Claud said again, taking the note from me. He shook his head, reading through it once, twice, three times. "Oh dear, oh dear, oh dear. Who is this poor soul? This—this porcelain doll?"

I stared at him in dawning horror.

Yes. We'd misinterpreted the notes.

Mistaking my silence, he patted my shoulder consolingly. "Not to worry, dear. We shall solve this mystery. Now, it seems to me the greatest clues to learning her identity lie in this first note . . ."

"What's going on?" Coco joined us now, Ansel following on her heels. She plucked the note from Claud, skimming the words before passing it to Liana, who in turn handed it to Terrance. La Voisin stood behind them, watching with an inscrutable expression. Nicholina, as always, smiled.

"Perhaps her skin could be described as porcelain?" Claud mused, stroking his beard. "Her features doll-like? The black hair is quite clear, but the—"

"Green tears?" Terrance scoffed. "No one has green tears."

"It's symbolic," Ismay said, rolling her eyes. "Green is a metaphor for envy."

Oh no.

I took the note from her, rereading the lines and thinking hard—praying, *praying* I was wrong. But no. It was all here. Porcelain skin. Black hair. Envious tears. Forgotten, alone . . . even the goddamn *pall* fit. How could we have missed it? How could we have been so *stupid?*

But that last line . . . eating her *heart* . . .

Feeling sick, I glanced at La Voisin and Nicholina, but Reid soon emerged beside me—red-faced and panting—and scattered my train of thought. "She's gone. She just—vanished."

"Of course she did," Coco muttered bitterly. "Morgane wouldn't have wanted her to stick around and play."

"Who was taken?" Blaise asked, voice deep and insistent. "Who is the girl?"

A commotion sounded at the door, and Jean Luc plowed inside, holding Beau by the collar. The former's eyes were wild, crazed, as they found mine. Found Reid's. He pushed toward us with single-minded determination. "Reid! Where is she? *Where?*"

When she heard what he'd done, it nearly killed her. She's been in seclusion for weeks—weeks—and all because of some misplaced emotion for him.

Lips numb, I crumpled the note in my fist, taking a deep breath and steeling myself for the pain to come—for the emotions I'd see in Reid's uncharacteristically open expression, in those newly vulnerable eyes. I could've kicked myself. I'd encouraged him to stop hiding, to *feel*. And now he would. And now I didn't want to see.

And my mother had known exactly how to play with us.

I turned toward him anyway.

"It's Célie, Reid. She's taken Célie."

COCO'S VISION

Lou

Until the day I died, I'd never forget the look on Reid's face.

The disbelief.

The horror.

The rage.

And in that moment, I knew—deep down in my bones—that I would save Célie's life or die trying.

Our motley crew glanced back and forth between where I paced at the window and Reid stood at the door. Heedless of the chairs, Claud had plunked down on the floor by the bar, crossing his legs as if he intended to stay awhile. But we didn't have awhile. Already our clock had started. *Come rescue her by midnight, or I shall eat her heart.*

Reid stared at his hands, transfixed and unmoving.

"She's trying to lure you out," Beau insisted. "Don't let her."

"She'll kill Célie," Jean Luc snarled, still clutching the notes I'd handed him. When Monsieur Tremblay had finally revealed Célie's *weeks of seclusion* hadn't been seclusion at all, but abduction,

Jean Luc had combed through every inch of East End to find us after the funeral. It'd been a happy coincidence indeed that Beau had stepped out tonight, or Jean Luc never might've found us. What a tragedy that would've been. "We have to rescue her."

"*You* do not speak." La Voisin's eyes held vicious promise. "Make no mistake, huntsman. Your holy stick will not prevent me from cutting out your tongue."

"*How does he taste, he taste, he taste?*" Nicholina edged forward, licking her lips. "*Let's tear off his face, his face, his face.*"

Blaise growled low in agreement.

Claud persuading the innkeeper to let his rooms to witches and werewolves had been nothing. Claud persuading the blood witches and werewolves not to tear a huntsman limb from limb, however, was proving more difficult. Jean Luc didn't seem to realize the precariousness of his situation—especially as his *holy stick* remained tucked out of sight in Reid's bandolier. To Reid's credit, he didn't reveal his old friend's secret. If the blood witches suspected Jean Luc defenseless, they wouldn't hesitate to attack.

Terrance knew, however. His lip curled in anticipation as he looked between Reid and Jean Luc.

"And where *is* she, exactly?" Coco had gravitated back to her kin, standing between La Voisin and Nicholina. "Have you managed to divine her location from Morgane's riddles?"

Jean Luc gestured to the rumpled papers. "She's—she's in the tunnels. In this Skull Masquerade."

"The tunnels are vast, Captain." Claud turned a tarot card over in his fingers again and again. At my repeated glances, he extended it to me. It wasn't a tarot card at all. Upon closer inspection, this card was crimson, not black, and painted with a leering skull. Gold letters that read *Nous Tombons Tous* curled into the shape of its mouth and teeth. At the top, *Claud Deveraux and his Troupe de Fortune* had been inked in meticulous calligraphy. An invitation. I handed it back with an ominous feeling. "They traverse the entire city," Claud continued. "Our search will continue long after midnight without proper direction."

"She's given us direction," Zenna pointed out. "*She cries alone within her pall* and *trapped within a mirrored grave* couldn't be more obvious. She's in the catacombs."

The catacombs. Shit.

"She has given *us* nothing," Claud said sharply. When Zenna's eyes flashed, his voice softened. "Alas, we must cancel our performance, *mes chers.* The world below is not safe tonight. I fear you must return to your rooms, where you might escape Morgane's notice. Toulouse and Thierry will join you there."

Zenna's eyes flashed. "The witch does not scare me."

Claud's face grew grave. "She should." To Seraphine, he added, "Perhaps you could . . . ruminate on the situation."

She clutched the cross at her throat, staring at him with wide eyes.

Once again, I turned to Reid, but he remained as if carved from stone. A statue. I sighed. "The catacombs will still take several hours to search. Does anyone have the time?"

Deveraux pulled out his pocket watch—a silly, gilded contraption. "Just shy of nine o'clock in the evening."

"Three hours." I nodded to myself, trying to infuse optimism into my words. "We can find her in three hours."

"I can perhaps buy you an extra hour or two," Claud offered, "if I find Morgane before we find this Célie. We have much to debate, La Dame des Sorcières and I." He ambled to his feet, abruptly relaxed once more—as if we discussed the weather and not abduction and murder. "The hour draws late, Monsieur Diggory. It is clear none wish to proceed without your blessing. A decision must be made. Will we ignore La Dame des Sorcières' threat, or will we venture into La Mascarade des Crânes to rescue your lady fair? All paths involve considerable risk to those you love."

Your lady fair. I couldn't help a grimace. *Those you love.*

Reid's eyes snapped to mine, not missing the movement. Neither did Jean Luc. He pressed closer to Reid, unwilling or unable to hide his desperation. "Reid." He touched a hand to Reid's chest, tapping insistently. "Reid, this is Célie. You aren't going to leave her in the hands of that madwoman, are you?"

If Reid wondered about Jean Luc's sudden interest in Célie, he didn't show it. Perhaps he'd known. Perhaps he'd known all along. He didn't break eye contact with me. "No."

"Thank God." Jean Luc allowed himself a brief second of relief before nodding. "We haven't a moment to lose. Let's go—"

Reid stepped around him to face me. I forced myself to return his gaze, knowing his next words before he even opened his mouth. "Lou, I . . . I don't think you should come. This is a trap."

"Of course it's a trap. It's always been a trap."

At last, La Voisin broke her silence. "If you need reassurance of her safety, huntsman, I can provide it." If Nicholina had been capable, she might've bounced on the balls of her feet. As it was, she tittered girlishly. "A bit of Louise's blood will show me her future." She extended her hand to me with an inscrutable expression. "If she dares."

The werewolves looked on uneasily, shifting their feet. Though they remained in their human forms, their nails had sharpened amidst the panic. An instinctive reaction, I presumed.

"No." Coco slapped her aunt's hand away—actually *slapped* it—and stepped in front of her. "If *anyone* tastes Lou's blood, it'll be me."

La Voisin's lip curled. "You do not have my skill with divination, niece."

"I don't care." Coco squared her shoulders before asking me silent permission with her eyes. If I said no, she wouldn't ask again. She wouldn't let the others ask either. She'd accept my decision, and we would find another way forward. "It's me or no one."

Inexplicably nervous, I placed my hand in hers. I didn't fear Coco. She wouldn't abuse my blood in her system. She wouldn't attempt to control me. No, I feared what she might see. When she lifted my finger to her mouth, the blood witches—even the werewolves—seemed to press closer in response. In anticipation. Reid seized my wrist. "You don't have to do this." Panic laced his voice. "Whatever *this* is."

I gave a grim smile. "It's better to know, isn't it?"

"Rarely," Claud cautioned.

"Just do it," I said.

Without another word, Coco pierced the pad of my finger with her incisor, drawing a single bead of blood into her mouth. I didn't turn to see the others' reactions, instead watching as Coco closed her eyes in concentration. After several tense seconds, I whispered, "Coco?"

Her eyes snapped open, rolling to the back of her head. Though I'd seen her scour the future countless times before, I still shivered at the way those white, sightless eyes studied my face. At least I'd been prepared for it. The others gasped audibly—some cursing, some retching—as Ansel darted forward. His hands fluttered around her, helpless, as if he was unsure whether or not he could touch her. "What's happening? What's wrong?"

"Shut up, and she'll tell us," Beau said, watching her with rapt attention.

"Lou . . ." Reid edged closer, his hand slipping into mine. "What is this?"

"She's fine." I glanced back at the werewolves, who—standing in the tavern of a dirty inn, watching a witch divine the future— seemed to be questioning their life choices. Jean Luc's face contorted with disgust. "Just give her a moment."

When Coco touched my cheek, everyone drew a collective breath. "I see death," she said, voice deep and strange.

A beat passed as we all stared at her.

"I see death," she repeated, tilting her head, "but not your own." Reid exhaled in a sigh of relief. The movement attracted

Coco. Her eerie gaze flicked between us, through us. My chest tightened at that look. This wasn't over. This wasn't good, and Reid didn't seem to understand—

"By the stroke of midnight, a man close to your heart will die."

My hand slipped from Reid's.

"What?" Ansel whispered, horrified.

"Who?" Pushing past us, Beau gripped Coco's shoulder with sudden urgency. "What man?"

"I cannot see his face."

"Damn it, Coco—"

"Let her go." Through numb lips, I forced the words out, remembering her explanation from so long ago. Before the heist. Before Reid. Before everything. "All she can see is what my blood shows her."

Beau stumbled back, crestfallen, before whirling to look at Reid. "We don't know it's you. It could be Ansel or Deveraux or—or that Bas fellow. Or the heart could be symbolic," he added quickly, nodding. "*You* are her heart. Maybe—maybe it could mean a man close to *you* like—like Jean Luc or our father, or—"

"Or you," Reid admitted quietly.

Beau whirled to face me. "Are there any other ex-boyfriends who—"

"Beau." I shook my head, and he broke off, staring at his boots. I swallowed hard. My throat ached with unshed emotion, but only a fool cried over what hadn't yet happened—what *would not* happen. A small voice in my head warned it unwise to poke fate in the nose, so I gave her the finger instead. Because I wouldn't allow this. I wouldn't accept it.

"Can you see anything else, Cosette?" More than one head turned at the cool, detached voice of La Voisin. She surveyed Coco dispassionately. "Ground yourself in the vision. Touch it. Taste it. Hone your focus however you can."

But Coco's hand merely fell from my cheek. Her eyelids fluttered shut. "You will lose the one you love."

Absolute silence descended as Coco gradually came back to herself.

Though Beau dropped his head in defeat, Reid turned me to face him with gentle hands. "Are you ... okay? Lou?"

You will lose the one you love.

I supposed that cleared it up nicely.

"Of course. Why wouldn't I be?" At his concerned look, I said, "Oh, I won't be losing you anytime soon. Coco's visions are changeable, subjective to the user's current path. You see?"

"I—" He glanced at Coco, whose eyes sharpened as they returned to normal. Ansel held her steady. "No, I don't."

"It's simple, really. If I continue on the path as planned, you'll die, but if I change my path, you'll live. Which means you aren't coming with me."

Reid fixed me with a flat, incredulous look, while Deveraux tilted his head. "I'm not sure that logic tracks, my dear. He can expire in this inn quite as easily as he can expire in the tunnels."

"Yes, but Morgane is down there," Beau insisted. Our eyes locked in understanding. "At least he has a chance up here."

I stared at the door to the storeroom, unable to meet anyone's eye.

Blaise shook his head. "We cannot afford for Reid to hide

above. We need numbers in this battle. Strength."

"You owe him a *life debt*," Beau said, uncharacteristically emphatic. "How can you fulfill it if he dies?"

"She said *someone* would die." Liana crossed her arms, shooting an unapologetic look in my direction. "You were right. We don't know if it'll be Reid."

Beau threw his hands in the air. "Except Coco then followed with—and I quote—*you will lose the one you love*. How the hell are we supposed to interpret that? Morgane told her once that she'd cut out his heart. How do we know that won't happen tonight?"

Coco clamped her jaw and exhaled hard through her nose. "We don't know. We don't know what's going to happen down in those tunnels. But I *do* know that my visions are rarely what they seem. I had one before we robbed Tremblay too. I thought it meant something ominous, but Angelica's Ring ended up saving Lou's ass—"

Jean Luc looked likely to die from apoplexy then and there. "I don't care about rings and blood visions. Célie is down there now—trapped in a *crypt*—and we're wasting time."

"You *do not speak*—" La Voisin hissed.

"He's right," Reid said curtly. "I'm going into those tunnels. The more people searching, the faster we'll find her." Though he gave me a cursory glance, lips pursed with genuine remorse, his voice brooked no argument. Heart pounding, still numb, I felt myself nod.

Beau slumped in his chair, defeated, and cursed bitterly. "The crypts are nearly as expansive as the tunnels—and they're creepy as shit, in case you were wondering."

Reid nodded. "We'll split into groups to cover more ground." With a subtle change in posture, he shifted seamlessly into captain once more. Jean Luc didn't even gnash his teeth. "Josephine, divide your kin into groups of three. You can search the northern and eastern crypts. Blaise, you and your children can take the southern. Deveraux and his troupe can take the Skull Masquerade."

Ansel stepped forward tentatively. "What about me? Where should I go?"

"I need you to stay here, Ansel. The patrons of La Mascarade des Crânes won't know the danger that awaits them. If anyone enters Léviathan seeking this entrance through the tunnels, warn them away."

It was a thinly veiled excuse, and Ansel knew it. His face fell. There would be no patrons in Léviathan tonight. Claud had assured it. Though Reid sighed, he continued, undeterred. "Coco and I will take the western crypts . . ."

His voice dimmed into background noise as Nicholina caught my eye from behind him. She looked pointedly to the storeroom door. For once, she wasn't smiling. I stared at her. She couldn't possibly be helping me. She couldn't possibly care. . . .

Soon we'll taste the noises on his tongue, oh yes, each moan and sigh and grunt.

A sharp pain spiked through my chest.

Perhaps she didn't want Reid to die either.

I didn't stop to consider her nefarious purposes for wanting him alive. When she glided toward him, weightless, I shifted subtly, making room for her beside him. She took full advantage, draping herself across his chest. "Do you wish to die, Monsieur Diggory?" He shot me an anxious glance, but I shrugged, adopting my best nonplussed expression. *"Death comes swiftly on this night,"* she sang sweetly, *"cloaked not in black, but eerie white."*

I inched backward.

Coco scowled. "Get off him, Nicholina—"

"She is his bride, his maiden fair, who feasts upon flesh and despair."

"Just ignore her," Beau said, rolling his eyes. "I do."

The wood of the storeroom door touched my fingertips as he tried to push her away. His hands couldn't quite connect, however, as if her form consisted of more vapor than flesh. It clung to him like mist.

"As she eats, her bridegroom moans, come to gather skin and bones—"

I turned the handle. Reid struggled helplessly as Nicholina brought her lips toward his.

Swallowing bile, I hesitated, but La Voisin slid into place before the door, blocking me from view. She didn't look at me. The slight dip of her chin was my only indication she'd seen me at all.

With one last, lingering look at Reid's back—the breadth of his shoulders, the coppery waves at his neck—I slipped through the door and out of sight. This was the only way. Though they'd deliberated, Coco's vision had been clear: *you will lose the one you love.* I let the words flow through me, strengthening my resolve, as I glanced around the storeroom, searching for the tunnel entrance.

A thick layer of dust coated the rotting shelves, the amber bottles, and the oaken barrels. I stepped carefully over shards of shattered glass, my boots sticking to the tacky floor around them. A single lantern bathed everything in flickering, eerie light. But—*there.*

I rolled a whiskey cask away from the darkest corner, revealing a trapdoor. Its hinges made not a sound as I swung it open. They were well oiled, then. Well used. Beneath the trapdoor, a narrow staircase disappeared into complete and utter darkness. I peered into it warily. The only things missing were weeping and gnashing of teeth.

After bending to retrieve the dagger from my boot, I stepped down, closed the door overhead, and shoved the blade through the handle. I pushed up once experimentally. It didn't budge.

Good.

I turned away. He couldn't follow me—not easily, at least. Not without magic.

When life is a choice between fighting or fleeing—every moment life or death—everything becomes a weapon. It doesn't matter who holds them. Weapons harm.

Weapons harm.

If we lived through this, I refused to be a weapon any longer.

But until then . . . I glanced up at the trapdoor, torn with indecision.

You're a witch. I shouldn't have resented you using magic. Just—don't let it take you somewhere I can't follow.

This time, however, that was exactly what I needed to do. A

simple knife wouldn't keep Reid away. Despite Coco's vision, he would do everything in his power to follow, to protect me from Morgane. From myself. If ever there was a moment of life and death, this was it—and it was mine.

I slipped my dagger from the handle, sheathing it in my boot once more. Then I lifted trembling hands. "Just once more," I promised him, taking a deep breath. "One last time."

I heard their shouts—the storeroom door rattle—as I turned and descended into Hell.

NOUS TOMBONS TOUS

Reid

"Lou! LOU!" I pounded on the trapdoor, roaring her name, but she didn't answer. There was only silence. Silence and panic—raw, visceral panic that closed my throat. Narrowed my vision. I beat on the door again. Tore at the handle. "Don't do this, Lou. Let us in. LET US IN."

Deveraux, Beau, Coco, and Ansel gathered around me. The others watched from the tavern door. "If you're determined to continue on this rather fruitless course of action, I will not stop you." Deveraux touched a gentle hand to my forearm. "I will, however, point out this door has been barred with magic and suggest we journey to a secondary entrance. The closest resides within the cemetery, perhaps a quarter hour walk from here."

Jean Luc pushed past Nicholina, who stroked a pale hand down his back. He leapt away. "East End is brimming with Chasseurs. The rest are down those tunnels. If we're seen, I can't protect you. I won't."

"Your loyalty inspires," Liana snapped.

"I'm not *loyal* to any of you. I'm *loyal* to Célie—"

"Jean Luc," Beau said, clapping a hand to his shoulder. Bracing. "Everyone here wants to kill or possibly eat you. Shut up, good man, before you lose your spleen."

Jean Luc fell into mutinous silence. I turned to Coco. "Open the door. Please."

She stared at me for several tense seconds. "No," she said at last. "You could die. I know you don't care, but Lou does. To everyone's surprise, *I* do. I won't supersede her efforts to protect you—and even if I wanted to, I can't open this door. No one can but the witch who cast the enchantment."

A snarl to rival the werewolves' tore from my throat. "I'll do it myself."

When I willed the patterns to emerge, however, none did. Not a single strand of gold. Not a single voice in my head. Furious, desperate, I turned to Toulouse, ripping the tarot deck from his shirt pocket. I shoved a card into his chest, and now, *now*, gold finally flared in my vision.

To know the unknown, you must unknow the known, the voices whispered.

Nonsense. Riddles. I didn't care. Choosing a pattern at random, I watched as it exploded into dust. "Reverse Strength," I snapped, and Toulouse grinned, glancing down at the card. "It means intense anger. Fear. A lack of confidence in one's own abilities, a loss of faith in oneself. In some cases—"

"—it is a loss of one's identity altogether." He chuckled and flipped the card to face me, revealing an upside-down woman and lion. Despite the horrific circumstances, triumph burst in my chest. Toulouse's grin spread. "It's about time too. You had me worried for a moment."

I jerked my chin toward the door. "Can you help me?"

His eyes dimmed. "Only Lou can open that door. I'm sorry."

Fuck.

"On to the cemetery, is it?" Deveraux clapped his hands. "Marvelous! Might I suggest we tarry forth? Time continues slipping away from us."

I nodded, breathing deeply. Forcing myself to calm. He was right. Each moment I'd bickered was a moment wasted—a moment Morgane tormented Célie, a moment Lou slipped farther away. Two desperate problems. One potential solution? I wracked my brain, thinking quickly. Analytically.

Lou would find Célie. Of that, I was sure. She had a head start. She had knowledge. She had incentive. No, there wasn't a force in Heaven or Hell—including Morgane—that would prevent her from succeeding in this. I didn't need to find Célie. If I found Lou, I'd find them both.

Lou was the target.

And if a small part of me hesitated, remembering Coco's premonition, I ignored it. I moved forward. I threw an arm across Ansel's chest when he followed the others to the door, shaking my head. "I told you to guard the tunnel."

His brows furrowed. "But the tunnel is locked. No one is going through it."

"Just stay here." Impatience sharpened my voice. I didn't care to soften it. Too much was at stake. At Modraniht, he'd proved more hindrance than help, and now we'd allied with enemies. Any one of them could turn on us in the tunnels. Ansel proved the easiest prey. I tried again. "Look, Zenna and Seraphine are staying behind too. Look after them. Keep them safe."

Ansel's chest caved, and he turned his burning gaze to the ground. Pink tinged his cheeks, his ears. Though he looked as if he wanted to protest, I was out of time. I could humor him no longer. Without another word, I turned on my heel and left.

There was nothing stiller than a cemetery at night. This one was small, the oldest in the city. The Church had stopped burying citizens in its soil long ago, favoring the newer, larger plot beyond Saint-Cécile. Now only the most powerful and affluent members of the aristocracy rested here—but even they weren't buried, instead joining their ancestors in the catacombs below.

"The entrance is there." Deveraux nodded to a statue of an angel. Moss grew on half her face. The wind had effaced her nose, the feathers on her wings. Still, she was beautiful. Words engraved onto the crypt beside her read *Nous Tombons Tous*. I didn't know what it meant. Fortunately, Deveraux did. "We all fall down," he said softly.

When I swung open the door, a gust of stale air rose to meet me. A single torch lit the narrow, earthen steps.

Beau stepped too close behind, peering into the darkness with unabashed apprehension. "Does the plan remain the same? Do we separate?"

Instead of looking below, Deveraux gazed upward at the night sky. Moonless tonight. "I don't think that's wise."

"We'll cover more ground if we do," Jean Luc insisted.

Foreboding lifted the hair on my neck as I climbed down the first step. "We stay together. Blaise, Liana, and Terrance can lead us to Lou. They know her scent. She'll be with Célie."

"You place an awful lot of confidence in that witch." Jean Luc shoved past me, tugging the torch from the wall and lifting it higher. Illuminating the path. The ceiling pressed down on us, forcing me to stoop. "What makes you so sure she'll find her?"

"She will."

Behind me, Beau and Coco struggled to walk side by side. "Let's hope the Chasseurs don't find *her*," she muttered.

The rest filed in after them, their footsteps the only sounds in the silence. So many footsteps. Jean Luc. Coco and Beau. Deveraux, Toulouse, and Thierry. La Voisin and her blood witches. Blaise and his children. Each equipped. Each powerful. Each ready and willing to destroy Morgane.

A tendril of hope unfurled in my chest. Perhaps that would be enough.

The first passage wore on interminably. Though I thought the tight space inconvenient, it didn't bring the sweat to my skin as it did Jean Luc. It didn't make my hands tremble, my breath catch. He refused to slow, however, walking faster and faster until we reached our first split in the tunnel. He hesitated. "Which way?"

"The crypts should be just past the eastern tunnel," Beau whispered.

"Why are you whispering?" Despite her objection, Coco whispered too. "And which direction is that?"

"East."

"*Left* or *right*, jackass?"

"Cosette," Beau said in mock surprise, "do you not know your—?"

A sudden wind doused the torch, plunging us into absolute darkness. Panicked voices rose. Swiftly, I reached for the wall, but it wasn't where it should've been. It wasn't *there*. "What the hell is going on?" Beau cried, but Liana interrupted, cursing violently.

"Something just *cut* me. Someone—"

Nicholina's scream splintered the tunnel.

"*Nicholina*." La Voisin's voice pitched high and sharp. My own throat felt tight. When I brushed wool in front of me—Jean Luc's coat—his fingers seized my arm and held on. "Nicholina, where are you?"

"Everyone stay calm," Deveraux commanded. "There is strange magic here. It plays tricks—"

The torch sprang back to life abruptly.

Blood spattered the tunnel floor. A handful of panicked faces blinked back at me in the light. Too few. *Far* too few.

"Where is Nicholina?" La Voisin seized Blaise's coat and slammed him against the wall, baring her teeth. I'd never seen her exhibit such uncontrolled emotion. Such fear. "*Where is she?*"

Blaise shoved her away with a snap of his teeth, charging down the tunnel and shouting for Liana and Terrance. A quick glance confirmed they too had vanished—along with the majority of blood witches. I searched the remaining faces, weak with relief when Beau and Coco nodded back at me, clutching each other. With a start, I realized Jean Luc still held my arm. He released me at the same instant.

Deveraux's face was drawn. "Thierry has disappeared as well."

"I swear I saw—" Toulouse started, but the torch extinguished again. His voice went with it. Forcibly. When Deveraux called after him, he didn't answer. Blaise's snarls echoed through the narrow tunnel, amplifying, heightening our frenzy, and something—something snarled *back*. La Voisin shouted, but I couldn't hear over the blood roaring in my ears, my own shouts for Beau and Coco—

Then she and Deveraux went silent too.

Forcing myself to focus, I summoned the patterns. Sifted through them on instinct, discarded them at the slightest touch. I needed fire. Not as a weapon. As *light*. Anger, hatred, bitter words—they'd all provide the expedient. I cast them aside without hesitation, searching for that single spark of energy. Something simple. Something . . . physical?

There.

I chafed my palms together—just once, with just enough pressure. Heat sparked. A flame flickered to life, illuminating the newfound blister on my finger. Like I'd rubbed actual kindling instead of skin. The air took care of the rest, and the fire grew in my hand.

Only Beau, Coco, Blaise, and Jean Luc remained in the tunnel with me.

The latter stared at the fire with an inscrutable expression. He hadn't seen it yet. My magic.

"They're gone." Beau loosened his grip on Coco, face pale. "They're just *gone*." He glanced up and down the tunnel with wide eyes, hesitating at the blood by our feet. "What do we do?"

Jean Luc answered for me, relighting his torch with my fire. Turning to the eastern tunnel. "We continue."

PARADISE LOST

Lou

Torches lined the earthen passages, casting the faces of passersby in shadow. Fortunately, few wandered this part, and those who did walked purposefully toward something—La Mascarade des Crânes, if their jewel-toned masks were any indication. They took the left-hand tunnels. On a whim, I took the right. The floors sloped gradually at first—the stone below smooth and slippery from the tread of many feet—before dipping unexpectedly. I stumbled, and a man lurched from the shadows, knocking into me and clutching my shoulders. I let out an undignified squeak.

"Where's your mask, pretty lady?" he slurred, his breath nearly burning the hair from my nose. His own mask covered the upper part of his face, jutting out in a cruel black beak. A crow. In the center of his forehead, a third eye stared down at me. It couldn't have been coincidence.

And I swore it just blinked.

Scowling—face hot with embarrassment, shoulders tense with unease—I pushed him away. "I'm already wearing one. Can't you tell?" I resisted the urge to flick my wrist, to lengthen my nails into razor-edged knives and score the porcelain at his cheek. Though the magic to lock Reid out physically had also locked him out emotionally—temporarily, until I lifted the pattern—I still heard his voice within my mind, if not my heart. I needn't harm this man. I needn't harm myself. Forcing a wicked grin instead, I whispered, "It's the skin of my enemies. Shall I add yours?"

He yelped and scrambled away.

Exhaling hard, I continued.

The tunnels wound in a labyrinth of stone. I wandered them in silence for several more minutes, my heart pounding a wild beat in my chest. It grew louder with each step. I walked faster, the hair on my neck lifting. Someone watched me. I could feel it. "Come out, come out, wherever you are," I breathed, hoping to bolster myself.

At my words, however, a strange wind rose in the tunnel, blowing out the torches and plunging me into darkness. Familiar laughter echoed from everywhere at once. Cursing, I grappled for my knife and tried to find a wall, tried to anchor myself in this insidious darkness—

When my fingertips brushed stone, the torchlight sprang back to life.

A flash of white hair disappeared around the bend.

I tore after it like a fool, unwilling to be caught alone in that darkness again, but it was gone. I kept running. When I burst into a long, shadowed room lined with coffins, I stopped short, panting and examining the nearest one in relief. "Father Lionnel Clément," I said, reading the faded name scratched into the stone. A yellow skull sat on a ledge above it. I glanced at the next name. *Father Jacques Fontaine.* "Clergymen."

I crept forward, pausing every so often to listen.

"Célie?" Though soft, my voice echoed unnaturally in the tomb. Unlike the absolute silence of the tunnels, this silence seemed to live and breathe, whispering against my neck, urging me to flee, flee, *flee*. I grew increasingly jumpy as the moments wore on, as the rooms grew in size. I didn't know what to look for—didn't know where even to start. Célie could've been in any one of these caskets, unconscious or worse, and I never would've known. Still . . . I couldn't shake the feeling Morgane *wanted* me to find Célie. There was less fun in a game I had no chance of winning. Morgane wouldn't have liked that. She wouldn't have just chosen an arbitrary grave, either. Her games were methodical, every move striking hard and true. Her notes had led me this far, each phrase a riddle, a clue, leading me deeper into her game.

Forlorn within her pall . . . alone but not alone.
Trapped within a mirrored grave, she wears a mask of bone.

It all pointed to *here*, now, this place. Only her use of the word *mirrored* made me pause.

Lost in thought—certain I'd missed something—I nearly didn't notice the dais in the next room, where hundreds of candles illuminated a gilded coffin. Winged angels and horned demons flickered in shadow on the lid, locked in an eternal embrace, while roses and skulls wove together in macabre beauty on each side. It was a masterpiece. A work of art.

Unbidden, I stepped closer, trailing my fingers along the cruel face of an angel. The petals of a rose. The letters of his name.

HIS EMINENCE, FLORIN CARDINAL CLÉMENT,
ARCHBISHOP OF BELTERRA
Verily I say unto thee, today shalt thou be with me in Paradise

Florin Clément. I'd laughed at the name once, not knowing it belonged to me. In a different world, I might've been Louise Clément, daughter of Florin and Morgane. Perhaps they would've loved each other, adored each other, filling our home in East End with sticky buns and potted eucalyptus—and children. Lots and lots of children. An entire house of them, little brothers and sisters with freckles and blue-green eyes. Just like me. I could've taught them how to climb trees and braid hair, how to sing off pitch outside our parents' room at dawn. We could've been happy. We could've been a family.

Now that—*that*—would've been Paradise.

With a wistful sigh, I lowered my hand and turned away.

It did little good to imagine such a life for myself. My wine had been drawn long ago, and it was not a bouquet of hearth and home, nor friends and family. No, mine smelled of death. Of secrets. Of rot. "Are you in there with him, Célie?" I asked bitterly, mostly to distract myself from such wallowing thoughts.

"Seems like the sort of thing Morgane would—" Gasping, I whirled around, eyes wide. "Mirrored grave," I whispered. *An entire house of them, little brothers and sisters with freckles and blue-green eyes. Just like me.*

Holy hell.

I knew where she was.

A NECESSARY EVIL

Reid

The others' disappearances became a presence of its own. It hung over us like a rope, tightening with each small noise. When Beau kicked a pebble, Jean Luc tensed. When Coco inhaled too sharply, Blaise growled. He'd half shifted, eyes glowing luminous in the semidarkness, to better scent Lou—and to better fight whatever roamed these tunnels.

"This doesn't end with Célie and Lou," Coco had said fiercely when he'd tried to leave, to search for his missing children. Curiously, he hadn't been able to smell where they'd gone. Where *any* of them had gone. They'd just . . . vanished. "It ends with Morgane. This has her clawed hands all over it. Wherever she is, Liana and Terrance will be too. Trust me."

No one voiced what that meant. Everyone knew.

Even a moment spent under Morgane's mercy was too long. Too late.

"*Are* her hands clawed?" Beau had muttered a few moments later.

Coco had raised her brows at him. "You were at Modraniht. You saw them."

"They weren't clawed."

"They should've been. She should have a wart and a hunchback too, the hackneyed bitch."

Even Jean Luc cracked a grin. His Balisarda weighed heavy against my chest. At last—when I could stand it no more—I unsheathed it, handing it to him. "Here. Take it."

His smile slipped, and he missed a step. "Why—why would you give this back to me?"

I curled his fingers around the hilt. "It's yours. Mine is gone." When I shrugged, the movement didn't feel forced. It felt . . . right. *Light.* A weight lifted from my shoulders. "Perhaps it's for the best. I'm not a huntsman anymore."

He stared at me. Then the dam broke. "You're a witch. You killed the Archbishop with . . . magic." His voice dripped with accusation. With betrayal. But there, in his eye, was a sliver of hope. He wanted me to deny it. He wanted to blame someone else—anyone else—for what had happened to our forefather. In that sliver, I recognized my old friend. He was still in there. Despite everything, he still wanted to trust me. The thought should've warmed me, but it didn't.

That sliver was a lie.

"Yes." I watched as his hope shriveled, as he physically recoiled from me. Blaise's gaze touched my cheek, curious—studying—but I ignored him. "I won't deny it, and I won't explain myself. I am a witch, and I killed our forefather. The Archbishop didn't deserve it, but he also wasn't the man we thought he was."

Visibly deflating, he scrubbed a hand down his face.

"Mother of God." When he looked up again, he met my gaze with not camaraderie, exactly, but a sense of resignation. "Have you known all this time?"

"No."

"Did you enchant him to receive your position?"

"Of course not."

"And does it . . . feel different?" At this, he swallowed visibly, but he did not look away. In that small act of defiance, I remembered the boy who'd befriended me, cared for me, the one who'd always pulled me up when I fell. The one who'd punched Julien for calling me trash boy. Before the greed had hardened us to each other. Before the envy.

"I'm not the same person I was, Jean." The words, so different than before—so true—fell heavy from my lips. Final. "But neither are you. We'll never be what we were. But here, now, I'm not asking for your friendship. Morgane is near, and together— regardless of our past—we have a real chance to finish her."

"You thought she'd attack at the funeral. You were wrong."

Unbidden, more truth spilled forth. I felt lighter with each word. "I thought whatever I needed to think to attend the Arch-bishop's funeral." I hadn't realized it at the time. Perhaps *couldn't* have realized it. And though I'd thought wrong, I didn't regret it. I couldn't. He started to argue, but I pushed forward before the next words died in my throat. Forced myself to meet his gaze directly. "Jean. I . . . I never knew about Célie."

He stiffened.

"If I'd known how you felt, I would've . . ." What? Not accepted her love? Not accepted the Archbishop's? Would I not have fought him in the tournament or taken my oath? Would I have given up my dreams because he wanted them too? "I'm sorry," I said simply.

And I was. I was sorry life had dealt us the same cards. I was sorry for his pain, for the suffering I'd inadvertently caused him. I couldn't take it away, but I could acknowledge it. I could open the door for us. I couldn't, however, force him to step through it.

A tense moment passed before he dipped his chin, but I recognized that nod for what it was—a single step.

Without another word, we continued our search. It took another half hour for Blaise to catch Lou's scent. "She is close." He frowned, creeping toward the tunnel ahead. "But there are others. I can hear their heartbeats, their breaths—" He skidded backward abruptly, eyes wide as he turned. "*Run.*"

Chasseurs rounded the corner.

Balisardas lifted, they recognized me immediately and charged. Philippe led them. When Jean Luc leapt in front of us, however—shoving me backward, out of their line of fire—they staggered to a halt. "What is this?" Philippe snarled. He didn't lower his blade. His eyes fell to Jean Luc's own Balisarda. "Where did you . . . ?"

"Reid returned it to me."

Those behind Philippe shifted uncomfortably. They disliked this new information. I was a witch. A murderer. Confusion, unease flitted across their faces as they took in Jean's protective stance. "Why are you here, Captain?" Philippe jerked his chin toward me. "He is our enemy. They all are."

"A necessary evil." After a single, hesitant look in my direction, Jean Luc straightened his shoulders. "We have new orders, men. Morgane is here. We find her, and we kill her."

THE MIRRORED GRAVE

Lou

In the middle of the catacombs, I found the Tremblay family tomb.

Never before had I hoped I was wrong as fervently as I did now—and never before had I felt so sick. As with the other tombs, skulls lined the shelves here, marking each ancestor's final resting place. It was a custom I'd never understood. Witches didn't decapitate their dead. Did one remove the deceased's head before or after decomposition? Or—or did they do it during the embalming process? And for that matter, *who* was responsible for doing it in the first place? Surely not the family. My stomach churned at the thought of sawing through a loved one's bones, and I decided I didn't want to know the answers after all.

My steps grew heavier, leaden, the farther I crept into the room until finally—*finally*—I found her name carved into a pretty rosewood casket.

FILIPPA ALLOUETTE TREMBLAY
Beloved daughter and sister

"Célie? Are you in there?"

There was no answer.

At least Filippa's skull hadn't yet been displayed.

Muscles straining, I pried at the casket's lid, but it didn't budge. After several moments of struggling in vain, I panted, "I don't know if you can hear me—and I really hope you're not in there, in which case I apologize *profusely* to your sister—but this isn't working. The damn thing is too heavy. I'll have to magic you out."

A rock skittered across the ground behind me, and I whirled, hands lifted.

"*Ansel?*" Mouth falling open, I dropped my hands. "What are you doing here? How did you *find* me?"

He took in the skulls with wide eyes. "When the others left, I tried the trapdoor again. I had a hunch." He gave me a tentative smile. "After what happened with Coco, I knew you'd try to be more careful with your magic, with the patterns you could safely maintain, and sealing the door against just Reid . . . it seemed simpler than sealing it against everyone else or sealing it permanently. I was right. When it opened, I followed the first tunnel. It led me straight here."

"That's impossible." I stared at him incredulously. "That tunnel is a dead end. You must've gotten turned around in the dark. Where are the others?"

"They went to a cemetery entrance."

"A cemetery entrance." Instinctively, I released the pattern keeping hold of my heart, and all the love I felt for Reid—all the despair, all the *panic*—surged through me in a disorienting wave. I stumbled slightly under its magnitude. "*Shit*. Did Reid—?"

He shrugged helplessly. "I don't know. He told me to stay behind, but I—I couldn't. I had to help you somehow. Please don't be mad."

"Mad? I'm not—" A sudden, terrible thought caught my throat in its fist. No. I shook my head, reeling at the complete absurdity of it. Choking with laughter. To him, to myself, I said, "No, no, no. I'm not mad."

No, no, no, my thoughts echoed, repeating the word like a talisman.

Pasting on a bright smile, I looped my elbow through his and tugged him to my side. "There's absolutely nothing to worry about. I just think, under the circumstances, Reid might've been right. It'd be better if you returned to the tavern and waited—"

He pulled away, eyes flashing with hurt. "It's almost midnight, and you haven't found Célie. I can help."

"Actually, I might've found her—"

"Where is she?" He glanced at the skulls and caskets, anxiety creasing his brow. "Is she alive?"

"I think so, but I'm having a little trouble—"

"Whatever it is, I can help."

"No, I think it's better if you—"

"What's the problem?" His voice rose. "Do you not think I can do it?"

"You *know* that's not what I—"

"Then what is it? I can help. I *want* to help."

"I know you do, but—"

"I'm not a *child*, Lou, and I'm sick and tired of everyone treating me like one! I'm almost *seventeen*! That's a year older than you were when you saved the kingdom—"

"When I *fled*," I said sharply, losing my patience. "Ansel, I *fled*, and now I'm asking you to do the same—"

"*Why?*" he exploded, throwing his hands in the air. Color bloomed on his cheeks, and his eyes burned overbright. "You once told me I'm not worthless, but I still don't believe you. I can't fight. I can't cast enchantments. Let me prove I can do *something*—"

I swore loudly. "How many times do I have to tell you, Ansel? You don't need to prove *anything* to me."

"Then let me prove it to myself." Voice breaking on the word, he cringed and dropped his gaze. Stared dejectedly at his fists. "Please."

My heart broke at the sight of him. He thought he was worthless. No, he *believed* it, deep down in his bones, and I—I could do nothing about it. Not now. Not with his life at stake. Perhaps he wasn't worth much to the world, to himself, but to me . . . to me, he was precious beyond value. If there was even a chance . . .

A man close to your heart will die.

I loathed myself for what I was about to do.

"You're right, Ansel." My voice hardened. If I told him the truth, he would balk. He'd refuse to leave. I needed to hurt him badly enough that he wouldn't—*couldn't*—stay. I nodded and crossed my arms. "You want me to say it? You're right. You wreck everything you touch. You can't even *walk* without stumbling, let alone wield a sword. You can't talk to a woman without blushing, so how could you save one? Honestly, it's—it's *tragic* how helpless you are."

With each word, he crumbled more, tears sparkling in his eyes, but I wasn't finished.

"You say you're not a child, Ansel, but you are. You *are*. It's like—you're a little boy playing pretend, dressing up with our coats and boots. We've let you tag along for laughs, but now the time for games is done. A woman's life is in danger—*my* life is in danger. We can't afford for you to mess this up. I'm sorry."

Face ashen, he said nothing.

"Now," I said, forcing myself to continue, to *breathe*, "you're going to turn around and march back up the tunnel. You're going to return to the tavern, and you're going to hide in your room until it's *safe*. Do you understand?"

He stared at me, pressing his lips together to stop their trembling. "No."

"No, you don't understand?"

"No." He stood a little taller, wiping an errant tear from his cheek. "I will not."

"Excuse me?"

"I said *no*, I will—"

My eyes narrowed. "I heard what you said. I'm giving you a chance to reconsider."

"What are you going to do?" He laughed scornfully, and the sound was so sad, so unnatural, it cut me at my core. "Freeze my heart? Shatter my bones? Make me forget I ever knew you?"

I brushed the rosewood with my fingertips, deliberating. This magic would hurt us both, but at least he'd be hurt and *alive*. "If you make me."

We stared at each other—him looking fiercer than I'd ever seen him—until something thumped beside us. We turned to look at Filippa's coffin, and I closed my eyes in shame. I'd forgotten about Célie.

"Is someone—" Ansel's lips parted on a horrified breath. "Is Célie in there? *Alive?*"

"Yes," I whispered, the fight leaving me abruptly. Coco had said her visions were rarely what they seemed. Perhaps this one could still play out differently. The future was fickle. If I sent him away, he could meet his death in the tunnels instead. At my side, perhaps I could . . . protect him, somehow. "Stay close to me, Ansel."

Between the two of us, we managed to slide Filippa's coffin to the floor. Opening the lid was another story. It took magic to unseal it. But I knew all about breaking locks, however, and fortunately for me, I'd just broken a relationship.

Another round in Morgane's game.

The lid opened easily after that.

When we saw Célie lying, unconscious, among her sister's remains, Ansel promptly vomited up the contents of his stomach. I nearly joined him, pressing a fist to my mouth to stem the bile. Filippa's corpse had not yet fully decomposed, and her rotted flesh oozed against Célie's skin. And the smell, it—

I vomited on Monique Priscille Tremblay's skull.

"She'll never recover from this," I said, wiping my mouth on my sleeve. "This—this is sick, even for Morgane."

At the sound of my voice, Célie lurched upright at the waist, her eyes snapping open. Tears spilled down her cheeks as she turned to stare at me. "Célie," I breathed, dropping down beside her. "I am so sorry—"

"You found me."

I wiped the slime from her face and hair the best I could. "Of course I did."

"I d-didn't think you'd c-come. I've been down here for w-weeks." Though she shivered violently, she didn't rise from the coffin. I slipped my cloak around her shoulders. "She—she visited me sometimes. Taunted me. S-said that I'd d-d-die here. Said—said Reid had f-forgotten about me."

"Shhh. You're safe now. Reid is the one who sent me. We'll get you out of here, and—"

"I can't leave." She sobbed harder when Ansel and I tried to lift her, but her body remained firmly in the coffin. We tugged harder. She didn't budge. "I c-c-can't m-move. Not unless I take you to—to her. She e-enchanted me." I smelled it then, the magic, almost indiscernible beneath the stench of decay. "If I d-don't, I'll have to s-s-stay here with—with Filippa—" A keening wail rose from her throat, and I hugged her closer, wishing desperately Reid were here. He'd know what to do. He'd know how to comfort her—

No. I slammed the door shut on the thought.

I hoped Reid *wasn't* here. Though I couldn't lock Ansel away—not alone in the catacombs with only Filippa's corpse for company—I could still prevent Reid from finding us, from following us to Morgane. In my mind, if I kept them separate, he'd be fine. I could still pray Coco's vision had been wrong, and everyone would survive the night.

"Can you stand at all?" I asked.

"I d-don't think so."

"Can you try? Ansel and I will help you."

She cringed away as if just realizing I'd been touching her. "N-No. You—you t-*took* Reid from me. She t-told me you *enchanted* him."

I tried to remain calm. This wasn't Célie's fault. It was Morgane's. If I knew my mother at all, everything she'd told Célie in their time together had been a lie. Once Célie's shock wore off, it'd be impossible to persuade her into leaving with me. I was the enemy. I was the witch who'd stolen Reid's heart. "We can't sit on this floor forever, Célie. Eventually, we have to move."

"Where's Reid?" Her breathing hitched once more, and she looked around wildly. "Where is he? I want Reid!"

"I can take you to him," I said patiently, motioning for Ansel to join me on the floor. She'd started keening again, rocking back and forth and clutching her face. "But I need you to step out of the coffin."

As predicted, her wailing ceased when she spotted Ansel through her fingers. "You," she whispered, clutching the edge of the casket. "I—I saw you in the Tower. You're an initiate."

Thank God Ansel had enough sense to lie. "Yes," he said smoothly, taking her hand. "I am. And I need you to trust me. I won't let anyone harm you, Célie, especially a witch."

She leaned closer. "You don't understand. I can f-feel her magic pulling at me. Right here." She tapped her chest, the movement fitful, frantic. Blood caked beneath her fingernails, as if she'd tried to scratch her way through the rosewood. "If I get up, I won't have a choice. S-She's *waiting* for us."

"Can you break the enchantment?" Ansel asked me.

"It doesn't work like that. I don't know how Reid did it at Modraniht, but it must've taken extraordinary focus, maybe a powerful surge of emotion while Morgane was distracted, and right now, I can't—" Faint voices echoed down the tunnel. Though I couldn't discern the words, the cadences, it wouldn't do for anyone to find us here. Especially Reid.

"Get up," I snapped to Célie. "Get up, and take us to Morgane before this night goes to complete hell." When she stared, dumbfounded at my sudden outburst, I tugged fiercely on her hand. It was no use. I couldn't break this bind. Célie would have to choose to rise herself. Which she did, after I grabbed her face and hissed, "If you don't get up, Reid will die."

LA MASCARADE DES CRÂNES

Lou

No longer in control of her body, Célie walked with mechanical footsteps down each left-hand tunnel, leading us into La Mascarade des Crânes. I nearly clipped her heels twice in my haste. Any second, Reid could march around the bend. I needed to deal with Morgane before that happened.

My mind raged against me, presenting fresh problems with each step—fresh problems and stale solutions. As usual, Morgane had played one move ahead. I'd gathered my allies—*and snuck away to face Morgane without them*, my mind sneered—persuaded powerful pieces onto the board, waited for her to strike. But she hadn't struck. At least, not in the way I'd planned. I stared at Célie's frail back, her soiled mourning gown. Now I was trapped like a rat in the sewers with only Ansel and Célie for help. Even if I hadn't vowed to keep both out of the fray, my chances of walking away from this encounter were nonexistent.

This was a disaster.

The path widened as we crept onward, more lanterns

illuminating this tunnel than the others. We'd walked for only a minute or so before voices echoed up the tunnel—many voices this time, carousing and loud. Unfamiliar. Some rose together in song, accompanied by the merry twang of mandolins, the dulcet chords of a harp, even the sharper notes of a rebec. When we rounded the corner, the first painted stalls rose to meet us. Here, masked merchants crooned to scandalously clad maidens, promising more than sweetmeat and pies, while others hawked wares such as bottled dreams and fairy dust. Bards wove through the shoppers. To the applause of passersby, a contortionist twisted his limbs into impossible shapes. Everywhere I looked, revelers danced, laughed, shouted, spilling wine on the tunnel floors. Coins spilled just as freely.

When a dirty-faced child—a cutpurse—slipped her hand into my pocket, I seized her wrist, clucking my tongue. "I think you'll find better luck over there," I whispered, pointing to a drunken couple who sat beside a cart of powdered *bugne*. The girl nodded appreciatively and crept toward them.

We couldn't stop to enjoy the sights, however, as Célie marched onward, weaving through the revelers like a snake being charmed. We hurried to keep up.

She ignored the infinite side tunnels and their unknown delights, keeping instead to the main path. Others joined us, whispering excitedly, their faces obscured by elaborate costumes: lions and lionesses with thick fur headpieces and claws of diamond; horned dragons with painted-on scales that gleamed metallic in the torchlight; peacocks with teal, gold, and turquoise feathers, their glittering masks carved into fashionable beaks. Even the poorer attendants had spared no expense, donning their finest suits and painting their faces. The man nearest me resembled the devil with his red face and black horns.

Each glanced at our bare faces curiously, but none commented. My apprehension mounted with each step. Morgane was nearby. She had to be. I could almost feel her breath on my neck now, hear her voice calling my name.

Sensing my distress, Ansel slipped his hand into mine and squeezed. "I'm here, Lou."

I returned the pressure with numb fingers. Perhaps I hadn't broken our relationship beyond repair. The thought bolstered me enough to whisper, "I'm scared, Ansel."

"So am I."

Too soon, the tunnel opened to cavernous, empty space—like the inside of a mountain growing down into earth instead of up into sky. Crude stone benches lined the sloping walls like rows of teeth, and steep stairs led down, down, down to an earthen mouth.

And there, in the center of that primitive stage, stood my mother.

She looked resplendent in robes of black velvet. Her arms remained bare despite the underground chill, and her moonbeam hair waved loose down her back. An intricate golden circlet sat atop her head, but the corpses floating above her in a circle—peaceful, eyes closed and hands clasped—they formed her true crown. Though I couldn't see the details of their faces, I *could* see their slashed throats. My stomach dropped with understanding. With dread. I shifted Ansel and Célie ever so subtly behind me.

She spread her arms wide, smiled broadly, and called, "Darling, welcome! I'm so happy you could join us!"

Around us, hundreds of people sat unnaturally still on the benches, silent and staring behind their masks. Magic coated the air, so thick and heavy my eyes watered, and I knew instinctively they couldn't move. The eyes of those who'd entered with us emptied, and without a word, they walked promptly to their seats. Seized by sudden panic, I searched for Reid, Coco, and Beau amidst the audience, but they were nowhere to be seen. I breathed a short-lived sigh of relief.

"Hello, *Maman*."

Her smile grew at my defensive stance. "You look beautiful. I must admit, I *did* chuckle when you melted your hair—classic mistake, darling—but I think you'll agree the new color suits you. Do come closer, so I might see it better."

My feet grew roots. "I'm here. Let Célie go."

"Oh, I don't think so. She'll miss all the fun." Flicking the train of her robes behind her, she stepped forward, revealing another body at her feet. My heart dropped. Even from afar, I recognized the slight build, the auburn curls.

"Gabrielle," I whispered in horror.

Ansel stiffened beside me. "Is she . . . ?"

"Dead?" Morgane supplied helpfully, nudging Gaby's face with her boot. Gaby moaned in response. "Not yet, but soon. With my daughter's help, of course." She stepped on Gabrielle's hand as she continued across the stage. "Where is your hunts-man, Louise? I had hoped he would join you. I have *much* to discuss with him, you see. A male witch! You cannot imagine my surprise after the little trick he pulled at Modraniht. Trading the Archbishop's life for yours? It was inspired."

I squared my shoulders. "Your note said you'd let her go."

"No. My note said I'd eat her heart if you didn't rescue her by midnight, which"—she licked her teeth salaciously—"is now. Perhaps you can offer a distraction in the meantime."

"But I rescued her—"

"No, Louise." Morgane's grin darkened. "You haven't. Now," she said, matter-of-fact, "tell me, are there more like your hunts-man? Perhaps I was foolish in sending away our sons. It has proved near impossible to track them, and those we found . . . well, they're quite terrified of me. It seems not *all* sons inherit our gifts." She looked lovingly to the corpses above her. "But I am not without reward. My labor yielded different fruit."

"We found no one," I lied, but she knew. She smiled.

"Come here, sweeting." She crooked a finger at Célie, who stood so close behind me I could feel her body shake. "Such a lovely little doll. Come here, so I may shatter you."

"Please," Célie whispered, clutching my arm as her feet moved of their own accord. "Please, help me."

I caught her hand and held it there. "Leave her alone, Mor-gane. You've tormented her enough."

Morgane cocked her head as if considering. "Perhaps you're right. It would be much less satisfying to simply kill her, wouldn't it?" She clapped her hands together and laughed. "Oh, how delightfully cruel you are. I must say I'm impressed. With her dead sister's flesh still fouling her skin, *of course* we must condemn her to live—to live and to never forget. The *torment*, as you say, will be delicious."

Tasting bile, I released Célie's hand. When her feet continued forward, however, she let out a sob. "What are you doing?" I snarled, leaping down the steps after her.

"Please, Louise," Morgane crooned, "I *desire* for you to come closer. Follow the doll." To Ansel, she added, "From the way you flit at her side, I assume you're some kind of pet. A bird, perhaps. Remain where you are, lest I pluck your feathers for a hat."

Ansel reached for the knife at his belt. I waved him back, hissing, "Stay here. Don't give her more reason to notice you."

His doe-like eyes blinked, confused. He still hadn't connected the dots.

"I'm waiting," she sang, her voice dripping with honey.

Witches lined the steps, watching as Célie and I descended. More than I'd expected. More than I recognized. Manon stood near the bottom, but she refused to look at me. Indifference smoothed her pointed features, turned her ebony face into a hard mask. But—she swallowed hard as I passed, mask cracking as her eyes flicked to one of the corpses.

It was the handsome, golden-haired man from earlier. Gilles.

Beside him, two girls with equally fair complexions drifted, their glassy eyes just as blue. An older brunette hovered on his other side, and a toddler—he couldn't have been older than three—completed the circle. Five bodies in all. Five perfect corpses.

"Do not let their expressions deceive you," Morgane murmured. This close, I could see the angry red scar on her chest from Jean Luc's blade. "Their deaths were not peaceful. They were not pretty or pleasant. But you know that already, don't you? You saw our sweet Etienne." Another smile twisted her lips. "You should've heard him scream, Louise. It was beautiful. Transcendent. And all because of you."

With the curl of her fingers, the bodies lowered, still circling, until they surrounded me at eye level. Their toes brushed the earth, and their heads—I swallowed a gag.

Their heads were clearly kept intact by magic.

Numb, I rose to my toes, closing first the toddler's eyes—his head wavered at the contact—then the brunette's, the twins', and finally, the handsome stranger's. Manon shifted in my peripheral vision. "You're sick, *Maman*," I said. "You've been sick for a long time."

"You would know, darling. You can't imagine my delight watching you these past weeks. I've never been so proud. Finally, my daughter realizes what must be done. She's on the wrong side, of course, but her sacrifices are still commendable. She has become the *weapon* I conceived her to be."

Bile rose in my throat at her emphasis, and I prayed—*prayed*—she hadn't been spying on us earlier, hadn't overheard Reid's words in our room at Léviathan. Our *bedroom*. Her presence would poison those moments between us.

Please, not those.

Her finger—cold and sharp—lifted my chin. But her eyes were colder. Her eyes were sharper. "Did you think you could save them?" When I said nothing, only stared, she pinched my chin harder. "You humiliated me on Modraniht. In front of all our sisters. In front of the Goddess herself. After you fled, I realized how blind I'd been. How fixated. I sent your sisters into the kingdom in search of Auguste's spawn." She backhanded Gilles's face, rupturing his skin. Stagnant blood oozed out of him. It dripped onto Gaby's hair. She moaned again. "And I found them—not all of them, no, not yet. But soon. You see, I do not need your wretched throat to exact my vengeance, Louise. My will shall be done, with or without you.

"Make no mistake," she added, seizing my chin once more, "you *will* die. But should you escape again, I will not chase you. Never again will I chase you. Instead, I will cherish dismembering your huntsman's brothers and sisters, and I will send you each piece. I will bottle their screams and poison your dreams. Each time you close your eyes, you will witness the end of their miserable lives. And—after the last child is slain—I will come for your huntsman, and I will cut the secrets from his mind, butchering him in front of you. Only *then* will I kill you, daughter. Only when you *beg* for death."

I stared at her. My mother. She was mad, wholly and completely crazed. She'd always been passionate, volatile, but this . . . this was different. In her quest for vengeance, she'd given away too much. *All those pieces you're giving up—I want them,* Reid had said. *I want* you. *Whole and unharmed.* I searched her face for any sign of the woman who'd raised me—who'd danced with me on the beach and taught me to value my worth—but there was nothing left. She was gone.

Do you think you'll be able to kill your own mother?

She hasn't given me a choice.

It hadn't been an answer then. It was now.

"Well?" She released my chin, her eyes blazing with fury. "Have you nothing to say?"

My hands were heavy, leaden, but I forced them upward anyway. "I think . . . if you plan to dismember *all* of his children, one by one . . . I have quite a bit of time to stop you." She bared her teeth, and I grinned at her, faking bravado. That stretch of my mouth cost everything. It also provided a distraction for the half step I took in Gabrielle's direction. "And I *will* stop you, *Maman*—especially if you blather about your plans every time we meet. You really love the sound of your voice, don't you? I never took you for narcissistic. Deranged and fanatical, yes, at times even vain, but never narciss—"

Morgane hauled Gaby to her feet before I could finish, and I cursed mentally. When she twisted a hand, a ball of fire bloomed atop her palm. "I had thought to offer you an ultimatum, *darling,* between Célie and Gabrielle—just a bit of fun—but it seems you've quite tested my patience. Now I will kill them both. Though I know you prefer ice, I'm partial to fire. It's rather poetic, don't you think?"

Célie whimpered behind me.

Shit.

At the stroke of Morgane's finger, Gaby's eyes snapped open—then widened, darting around us. "Lou." Her voice cracked on my name, and she thrashed in Morgane's arms. "Lou, she's a maniac. She and—"

She stopped talking on a scream when Morgane swept the fire against her face—when Morgane swept and kept sweeping, drawing the flames down her throat, her chest, her arms. Though she screamed and screamed, thrashing anew, Morgane didn't release her. Panicked, I cast about for a pattern, for *the* pattern, but before I could commit, a blade sliced through the air, through Morgane's *hand*.

Howling in outrage, she dropped Gaby and jerked toward—

My breath caught in my throat.

Ansel. She jerked toward Ansel.

He'd followed me again.

Eyes narrowing, she looked at him—*really* looked at him—for the first time. Her blood dripped onto the hem of her robes. One drop. Two drops. Three. "I remember you." When she smiled, her face twisted into something ugly and dark. She didn't stop Gaby as she scrambled backward, away from us, and disappeared into the tunnel below the aisles. "You were at Modraniht. Such a pretty little bird. You've finally found your wings."

He gripped his knives tighter, jaw set, and widened his stance, planting his feet and preparing to use both his upper- and lower-body strength. Pride and terror warred inside my heart. He'd saved Gaby. He'd drawn Morgane's blood.

He'd been marked.

The patterns came without hesitation as I stepped to his side. When I raised my hands, determined, he nudged the knife in my boot instead. I drew it swiftly. "First lesson," he breathed. "Find your opponent's weaknesses and exploit them."

"What are you whispering?" she hissed, drawing another fireball into her hand.

She'd chosen fire to make a statement, but fire could be stoked. It meant passion. *Emotions.* In combat, she'd react swiftly, without forethought, and that impulsivity could be her undoing. We'd have to be careful, quick. "I knew you'd choose fire." I smirked, tossing the blade in my hand with casual nonchalance. "You're growing predictable in your old age, *Maman.* And wrinkled." When she launched the first fireball, Ansel ducked swiftly. "It's a good thing your hair is naturally white. It hides the gray, yes?"

With a scream of indignation, she flung the second. This time, however, I moved swifter still, catching the flames on my blade and hurling them back at her. "Second lesson," I said, laughing as her cloak caught fire. "There's no such thing as cheating. Use every weapon in your arsenal."

"You think you're clever, don't you?" Morgane flung her cloak to the ground, panting. It smoldered gently, sending clouds of smoke to curl around her. "But I taught you how to fight, Louise. *Me.*" Barely discernible through the smoke, she gathered a third ball of fire between her palms, eyes glittering with malice. "Third lesson: the fight isn't over until one of you is dead." When she threw the fireball, it grew into a sword—a pillar—and neither Ansel nor I could move swiftly enough. It razed our skin as it passed, knocking us from our feet, and Morgane lunged.

Anticipating the movement—body screaming in pain—I swiped Ansel's knife and rolled over him, slashing his blade at her face. Her upper half reared backward, but the movement propelled her lower half toward me—toward *my* knife, which I drove through her stomach. She gasped. The flames vanished, and the bodies floating above thudded to the ground. Horrified gasps rose from the audience as her spell lifted. With Ansel's blade, I moved to finish the job, watching her every movement, every emotion, as if time had slowed. Memorizing her face. Her brows as they dipped in confusion. Her eyes as they widened in surprise. Her lips as they parted in fear.

Fear.

It was one emotion I'd never seen on my mother's face.

And it made me hesitate.

Above us, footsteps thundered, and Reid's shout splintered the silence.

No.

Faster than humanly possible, Morgane's hand snaked out, catching my wrist and twisting. The world rushed back into focus with vivid clarity, and I dropped the knife with a cry.

"You tried to kill me," she whispered. "*Me.* Your *mother.*" Wild, cackling laughter stole her breath, even as—as *Chasseurs* descended. Reid and Jean Luc led them with Blaise snarling behind, fully shifted. "And what if you'd succeeded, daughter? Is that why you came here? Did you think you'd become queen?"

She twisted brutally, and I heard my bone snap. Pain radiated up my arm, consuming everything, and I screamed. "A queen must do what is necessary, Louise. You were almost there, but you stopped. Shall I show you the path to continue? Shall I show you everything you lack?"

She dropped my wrist, and I staggered backward, watching through tears as Reid sprinted toward us, pulling away from the rest, knives drawn. I couldn't move fast enough. I couldn't stop him. "Reid, *NO*—!"

Morgane hurled a fourth and final ball of fire, and it exploded against his chest.

THE WOODWOSE

Reid

Smoke engulfed me, thick and billowing. It smothered my nose, my mouth, my eyes. Though I couldn't see her, I could still hear Lou as she screamed, as she raged against her mother, who laughed. Who laughed and laughed and laughed. I waded through the smoke to reach her, to tell her I was fine—

"Reid!" Ansel bellowed. Jean Luc's voice soon joined his, shouting over the din as audience members fled for safety. As witches shrieked and footsteps pounded, thick as the smoke in the air.

But where was the fire?

I patted my chest, searching for the sharp heat of flames, but there were none. Instead, there was—there was—

Claud Deveraux stood beside me, offering me a sly smile. In his hands, he held the ball of flames—shrinking now, smoking wildly—and in his eyes . . . I blinked rapidly through the smoke. For just a moment, his eyes seemed to flicker with something ancient and wild. Something *green*. I yielded a step in astonishment. The faint earthiness I'd smelled within Troupe de Fortune's wagons had returned tenfold. It overwhelmed the smoke, doused the cavern in the scent of pine sap and lichen, fresh soil and hay. "I thought—you said you weren't a witch."

"And I'm still not, dear boy."

"We couldn't find you. In the tunnels, we couldn't—"

"My ducklings had gone missing, hadn't they?" He straightened my coat with a tight smile. "Never fear. I *shall* find them." Beyond the smoke, Lou still screamed. It filled my ears, hindering all other thought. "And though *sweet* Zenna knew better, the temptation of violence proved too much to resist—such bloodlust in that one. I found her in the tunnels while I searched for the others. Poor Seraphine had no choice but to follow, and I couldn't very well leave them unprotected. I *had* hoped to return before the situation here escalated—better to prevent than to heal, you know—but alas." He looked over his shoulder toward Morgane's laughter. "Her sickness may consume us all. If you'll excuse me."

He parted the smoke with the flick of his wrist.

Lou and Morgane materialized, circling each other with their hands raised. Past them, Ansel shielded Célie in his arms, and Jean Luc and Coco fought back-to-back against a trio of witches. Above us, Beau ushered panicked revelers to the exits. The body of a witch cooled at Blaise's feet, throat torn open, but another had cornered him. Her hands contorted wildly.

Two Chasseurs reached her first.

When Deveraux stepped out of the smoke, Lou and Morgane both froze. I followed behind.

"*You*," Morgane snarled at him, and she stumbled—actually *stumbled*—backward.

Deveraux sighed. "Yes, darling. Me."

And with those words, Claud Deveraux began to change. Growing taller, broader, his form stretched over even me. Cloven hooves burst from his polished shoes. Stag antlers erupted from his styled curls. A crown of oaken branches wove around them. Pupils narrowing abruptly to slits, his eyes gleamed in the darkness like a cat's. He stared down at us in silence for several seconds.

I took a shaky breath.

"Holy *shit*." Lou gaped up at him in disbelief. In confusion. I edged toward her. "You're ... you're the Woodwose."

Winking, he tipped his hat to her. It vanished in a burst of lilacs, which he presented to her with a flourish. "'Tis a pleasure to meet you, little one." His voice was deeper now, ancient, as if it hailed from the earth itself. "I do apologize for not revealing myself sooner, but these are strange and difficult times."

"But you aren't *real*. You're a goddamn *fairy tale*."

"As are you, Louise." His yellow eyes crinkled. "As are you."

"You shouldn't have come here, Henri," Morgane said through tight lips. She still hadn't lowered her hands. "I'll kill all of them to spite you."

He smiled without warmth, revealing pointed fangs. "Tread carefully, darling. I am not a dog who must obey his master's summons." His voice grew harder, fiercer, at Morgane's grimace. "I am the Wild. I am all that inhabits the land, all things that are made and unmade. In my hand is the life of every creature and the breath of all mankind. The mountains bow to my whim. The wild animals honor me. I am the shepherd and the flock."

Despite herself, Morgane yielded a step. "You—you know the Old Laws. You cannot intervene."

"I cannot *directly* intervene." He drew to his full height, looming over her—over us all—his catlike eyes flashing. "But my sister . . . she is displeased with your recent exploits, Morgane. Very displeased."

"Your sister," Lou repeated faintly.

Morgan paled. "Everything I've done, I've done for her. Soon, her children will be free—"

"And your child will be dead." Frowning, he reached down to touch her cheek. She didn't recoil. Instead, she leaned into his touch. I wanted to look away. I couldn't. Not when profound sadness welled in this strange being's eyes, not when it slid as a tear down Morgane's cheek. "What has happened to you, my love? What evil poisons your spirit?"

Now she did recoil. The tear curled into smoke on her cheek. "You *left* me."

The word broke something in her, and she leapt into movement, thrusting her hands toward him. Lou lifted her own instinctively. I followed a second too late, dropping one of my knives, cursing as it skidded across the ground past Morgane. She didn't see it, thrusting her hands at Deveraux again and again. He only flicked his wrist and sighed. The sharp scent of cedar wood engulfed us.

"You know that won't work on me, darling," he said irritably. With another flick, Morgane sailed directly upward, suspended as if pinned to a tree. Her palms snapped together. The tumult around us quieted as everyone turned to stare. "I *am* the land. Your magic comes from *me.*"

When she screamed in frustration, flailing wildly, he ignored her. "But you're right," he continued. "I never should've left. It is a mistake I will not make twice." He paced before a line of corpses, growing steadily taller with each step. Nausea pitched violently in my stomach when I looked closer. When I recognized my mouth on one face. My nose on another. My jaw. My eyes.

Deveraux spotted the toddler, and his voice darkened. "For too long, I've sat quietly—watching you drown others, watching you founder yourself—but no longer. I will not let you do this, *ma chanson.*" He glanced at Lou, and the terrible fury in his eyes softened. "She could have been ours."

"But she's *not,*" Morgane spat, throat bulging with strain. "She's not mine, and she's not yours. She is *his.* She is *theirs.*" She pointed to me, to Ansel, to Coco and Jean Luc, to Beau and Blaise. "She was *never* mine. She has chosen her side. If it's the last thing I do, I will make her suffer as her sisters have suffered."

Several witches crept toward the main tunnel now. Blaise— face bloody, mouth dripping—blocked the entrance, but he numbered only one. When the witches engaged, streaking past, the Chasseurs gave chase, deserting us. Ansel edged back to guard the smaller actors' tunnel. Trembling beside the corpses, Célie stood alone. When she turned to look at me—alive, *terrified*—I beckoned her over. The slightest twitch of my fingers. Her face crumpled, and she raced toward us. Lou caught her, and I wrapped my arms around them both.

We would survive this. All of us. I didn't care what Coco's vision said.

Deveraux watched us for a moment, his expression wistful, before turning back to Morgane. He shook his head. "You are a fool, my love. She is your daughter. Of course she could have been yours." With the wave of his hand, Morgane floated back to the ground. Her hands broke apart. "This game is over. My sister has grown rather fond of Louise."

My arms tightened around her, and—shuddering with relief—she dropped her head to my shoulder. To my surprise, Célie stroked her hair. Just once. A simple gesture of comfort. Of hope. The unlikeliness of it startled me, shattered me, and warm relief swept in. My knees buckled. We really *would* survive this. All of us. With Deveraux and his sister on our side—a *god* and *goddess*—Morgane's hands were tied. For all her power, she was human. She couldn't hope to fight this war and win.

Panting and flexing her wrists, she glared at Deveraux with pure animosity. "Your sister is the fool."

His eyes flattened, and he motioned for Blaise and Ansel to step away from the tunnel entrances. "You try my patience, love. Leave now, before I change my mind. Undo what can be undone. Do not attempt to harm Louise again, or feel my sister's wrath— and mine. This is your final warning."

Morgane backed toward the tunnel slowly. Her eyes darted

upward, watching the last witches flee from sight and the last huntsmen follow. Deveraux let them go. Morgane would never surrender with an audience. Now the auditorium was nearly empty. Only our own remained—and Manon. She stared at Gilles's empty face, her own equally lifeless. Lou looked as if she might approach her, but I squeezed her waist. *Not yet.*

"My final warning," Morgane breathed. "The wrath of a goddess." When she lifted her hands, everyone tensed, but she only brought them together in applause. Each clap echoed in the empty auditorium. A truly frightening grin split her face. "Well done, Louise. It seems you have powerful pieces in our game, but do not forgot I have mine. You have outplayed me . . . for now."

Lou stepped away from Célie and me, swallowing hard. "I was never playing, *Maman*. I loved you."

"Oh, darling. Didn't I tell you love makes you weak?" A wild gleam lit Morgane's eyes as she inched backward. She was close to the tunnel now. Close to escape. Ansel hovered nearby with an anxious expression. It mirrored my own. I glanced to Deveraux, praying he'd change his mind—capture her—but he didn't move. He trusted her to leave, to obey her goddess's command. I didn't. "But the game isn't over yet. The rules have simply changed. That's all. I cannot use magic, not here. I cannot touch *you*, but . . ."

I realized her intent too late. We all did.

Cackling, she swooped up my fallen knife and lunged, driving it into the base of Ansel's skull.

THE END OF THE WORLD

Lou

The world didn't end in a scream.

It ended in a gasp. A single, startled exhalation. And then—

Nothing.

Nothing but silence.

SOMETHING DARK AND ANCIENT

Lou

I could do nothing but watch him fall.

He dropped to his knees first—eyes wide, unseeing—before falling forward. There was no one to catch him, no one to stop his face from hitting the ground with a sickening, definitive thud. He did not move again.

Ringing silence filled my ears, my mind, my *heart* as blood surrounded him in a scarlet halo. My feet wouldn't move. My eyes wouldn't blink. There was only Ansel and his crown, his beautiful limbs draped behind him as if—as if he were just sleeping—

By midnight, a man close to your heart will die.

A scream pierced the silence.

It was mine.

The world rushed back into focus then, and everyone was shouting, running, slipping in Ansel's blood—

Coco tore her arm open with one of Reid's knives, and her own blood spilled on Ansel's face. They turned him over on

Reid's lap, forcing his lips apart. His head lolled. Already, his skin had lost its color. It didn't matter how they shook him, how they sobbed. He wouldn't wake.

"Help him!" Coco lurched to her feet and took Claud by the coat. Tears streamed down her face, burning everything they touched, sparking tendrils of flame at our feet. And still they fell. She was breathless now, no longer shaking him, but clutching his shoulders. Keening. Drowning. "Please, *please*, bring him back—"

Claud removed her hands gently with a shake of his head. "I am sorry. I cannot interfere. He is . . . gone."

Gone.

Ansel was gone.

Gone gone gone. The word swirled around me, through me, whispering with finality. *Ansel is gone.*

Coco sank to the ground, and her tears fell thicker, faster. Fire curled around her like molten petals. I relished the heat. The pain. This place would burn for what it'd taken. I hoped the witches were still here. I hoped the red-faced devil and his friends had not yet escaped. Blowing each shimmering pattern, I fanned the flames higher, hotter. They would all die with Ansel. Each one of them would die.

Laughter echoed from the darkness of the tunnel.

With a guttural roar, I tore after it. Jean Luc said I'd rotted, but that wasn't true. Magic didn't rot. It cracked, like a splintering mirror. With each brush of magic, those cracks in the glass deepened. The slightest touch might shatter it. I hadn't corrected him at the time. I hadn't wanted to acknowledge what was happening to me—what we'd all known. But now—

"Did you *love* him, Louise?" Morgane's voice echoed in the darkness. "Did you watch as the light left those pretty brown eyes?"

Now I shattered.

Light exploded from my skin in every direction, illuminating the entire tunnel. The walls shook, the ceiling cracking and raining stones, collapsing beneath my wrath. I pushed harder, wrenching patterns blindly. I would bring the tunnel down on her head. I would break the world and tear down the sky to punish her for what she'd done. For what *I* had done. At a gap in the passage, Morgane stood frozen, mouth parted in surprise— in delight. "You are magnificent," she breathed. "*Finally.* We can have some fun."

Closing my eyes, I tipped my head back, holding all of their lives in my fingers. Reid. Coco. Claud. Beau. Célie. Jean Luc. Manon. I tested the weights of each one, searching for a thread to match Morgane's. She had to die. Whatever the cost.

And if another must die in return? the voice whispered.

So be it.

Before I could pluck the thread, however, a body slammed into me. Blood soaked his shirt. I tasted it in my mouth as he trapped me against the wall, as he lifted my hands above my head. "Stop, Lou. Don't do this."

"Let me *go*!" Half screaming, half sobbing, I fought Reid with all my strength. I spat out Ansel's blood. "It's my fault. I killed him. I told him he was *worthless*—he was *nothing*—"

At the mouth of the tunnel, Claud, Beau, and Jean Luc struggled to contain Coco. She must've followed me in. By her feral expression, she'd planned a similar fate for my mother. Fire roared behind her.

When I turned back to Morgane, she'd disappeared.

"Let her go," Reid pleaded. Tears and soot streaked his face. "You'll get another chance. We have to move, or this whole place will come down on top of us."

I slumped in his arms, defeated, and he exhaled hard, pressing me into his chest. "You don't get to leave me. Do you understand?" Cupping my face, he wrenched me backward and kissed me hard. His voice was fierce. His eyes were fiercer. They burned into mine, angry and anguished and *afraid*. "You don't get to do this alone. If you retreat into your mind—into your magic—I'll follow you, Lou." He shook me slightly, tears glistening in those frightened eyes. "I'll follow you into that darkness, and I'll bring you back. Do you hear me? Where *you* go, *I* will go."

I looked back to the auditorium. The flames burned too high now for us to retrieve Ansel's body. He would burn here. This dirty, deplorable place would be his pyre. I closed my eyes, expecting the pain to come, but there was only emptiness. I was hollow. Vacant. No matter what Reid claimed . . . this time, he wouldn't be able to bring me back.

Something dark and ancient slithered out of that pit.

OLD MAGIC

Lou

Late afternoon sunlight shone through the dusty window, illuminating the warm woods and thick carpets of Léviathan's dining room. La Voisin and Nicholina stared at me from across the table. They looked out of place in this ordinary, mundane room. With their scarred skin and haunting eyes, they were two creatures of a horror story who'd escaped their pages.

I would bring their horror story to life.

The innkeeper had assured me that we wouldn't be disturbed here.

"Where were you?"

"The tunnels separated us." La Voisin met my gaze impassively. We still hadn't found the others. Though Blaise and Claud searched relentlessly, Liana, Terrance, Toulouse, and Thierry remained lost. I assumed Morgane had killed them. I couldn't bring myself to care. "When we reached the Skull Masquerade, Cosette had already set it on fire. I instructed my kin to flee."

"*Sea of tears and lake of fire.*" Nicholina rocked back and forth on her chair. Her silver eyes never left mine. "*To drown our foes on their pyres.*"

"My niece tells me you've had a change of heart." La Voisin glanced toward the door, where the others waited in the tavern. All except one. "She says you wish to march on Chateau le Blanc."

I met Nicholina's unflinching stare with one of my own. "I don't want to march on Chateau le Blanc. I want to burn it to the ground."

La Voisin lifted her brows. "You must see how that upsets my agenda. Without the Chateau, my people remain homeless."

"Build a new home. Build it on my sisters' ashes."

A peculiar glint entered La Voisin's eyes. A smile touched her lips. "If we agree . . . if we burn your mother and sisters inside their ancestral home . . . it does not solve the larger problem. Though your mother's methods have grown erratic, we are still hunted. The royal family will not rest until every one of us is dead. Even now, Helene Labelle remains captive."

"So we kill them too." My voice sounded hollow to my own ears. "We kill them all."

La Voisin and Nicholina exchanged a glance, and La Voisin's smile grew. Nodding—as if I'd passed some sort of unspoken test—she drew her grimoire from her cloak and placed it on the table. "How . . . cruel."

Nicholina licked her teeth.

"They want death," I said simply. "I'll give them death."

La Voisin rested her hand atop her grimoire. "I appreciate your commitment, Louise, but such a feat is easier said than done.

The king has numbers in his Chasseurs, and the Chasseurs have strength in their Balisardas. Morgane is omniscient. She has . . . powerful pieces on her board."

It seems you have powerful pieces in our game, but do not forgot I have mine. I frowned at the turn of phrase.

"Did you never wonder how she found you in Cesarine?" La Voisin stood, and Nicholina followed. I rose with them, unease prickling my neck. The door behind them remained shut. Locked. "How she slipped a note into my own camp? How she knew you traveled with Troupe de Fortune? How she followed you to this very inn?"

"She has spies everywhere," I whispered.

"Yes." La Voisin nodded, moving around the table. I fought to remain still. I would not flee. I would not cower. "Yes, she does." When she stood only a hair's breadth from my shoulder, she stopped, staring down at me. "I warned Coco against her friendship with you. She knew I disliked you. She was always so careful to protect you from me, never revealing even a scrap of information about your whereabouts." Tilting her head, she considered me with predatory focus. "When she heard of your marriage to the Chasseur, she panicked. It made her careless. Reckless. We followed her trail back to Cesarine, and lo and behold—there you were. After two years of searching, we had found you."

I swallowed hard. "We?"

"Yes, Louise. We."

I bolted then, but Nicholina flashed in front of the door. In a sickeningly familiar movement, she pushed me into the wall, yanking my hands above my head with inhuman strength. When I smashed my forehead into her nose, she simply leaned closer, inhaling against the skin of my neck. Her blood sizzled against my skin, and I screamed. "Reid! REID! *COCO!*"

"They can't hear you." La Voisin flipped through the pages of her grimoire. "We've enchanted the door."

I watched, horrified, as Nicholina's nose shifted back into place. "It's the mice," she breathed, grinning like a fiend. "The mice, the mice, the mice. They keep us young, keep us *strong*."

"What the *hell* are you always talking about? Do you eat mice?"

"Don't be silly." She giggled and brushed her nose against mine. Her blood continued to boil my face. I thrashed away from her—from the pain—but she held strong. "We eat *hearts*."

"Oh my god." I retched violently, gasping for breath. "Gaby was right. You eat your dead."

La Voisin didn't look up from her grimoire. "Just their hearts. The heart is the core of a blood witch's power, and it lives on after one dies. The dead have no need for magic. We do." She pulled a bundle of herbs from her cloak next, setting each beside her grimoire and calling them by name. "Bayberry for illusion, eyebright for control, and belladonna"—she lifted the dried leaves to inspect them—"for spiritual projection."

Spiritual projection.

What was the book in your aunt's tent?

Her grimoire.

Do you know what's in it?

Curses, possession, sickness, and the like. Only a fool would cross my aunt.

Oh shit.

"Fang of an adder," Nicholina chanted, still leering at me. "Eye of an owl."

La Voisin set to crushing the herbs, the fang, the *eye* into powder on the table.

"Why are you doing this?" I kneed Nicholina in the stomach, but she pressed closer, laughing. "I agreed to *help* you. We want the same things, we want—"

"You are easier to kill than Morgane. Though the plan was to deliver you to La Mascarade des Crânes, we are flexible. We will deliver you to Chateau le Blanc instead."

I watched in horror as she slit her wrist open, as her blood poured into a goblet. When she added the powder, a plume of black smoke curled from the foul liquid. "So kill me, then," I choked. "Don't—don't do *this*. Please."

"By decree of the Goddess, Morgane can no longer hunt you. She cannot force you to do anything against your will. You must go to her willingly. You must *sacrifice* yourself willingly. I would simply feed you my blood to assume control, but the pure, unadulterated blood of an enemy kills." She gestured to Nicholina's blood on my face, to my ravaged skin. "Fortunately, I have an alternate solution. It's all thanks to you, Louise. The rules of old magic are absolute. An impure spirit such as Nicholina's cannot touch a pure one. This darkness in your heart . . . it calls to us."

Nicholina tapped my nose. "Pretty mouse. We shall taste your huntsman. We shall have our kiss."

I bared my teeth at her. "*You* won't."

She cackled as La Voisin crossed the room to lift the goblet to her lips. Drinking greedily, she relaxed her hands, and I bucked away from her, lunging for the door—

La Voisin caught my injured wrist. I arched away, screaming— screaming for Reid, for Coco, for *anyone*—but she caught my hair and forced my head back. My mouth open. When the black liquid touched my lips, I collapsed and saw no more.

EVIL SEEKS A FOOTHOLD

Reid

Deveraux's face was unusually grim as he sat down across the table in Léviathan. At least it was *human*. The Woodwose's face had been . . . unsettling. I shook my head, staring into my tankard of beer. It'd gone flat an hour ago. Jean Luc brought me another one. "Drink up. I have to leave soon. The king wants us in the catacombs within the hour."

"What will you tell him?" Deveraux asked.

"The truth." He chugged his own tankard before nodding to Beau, who'd draped an arm around Coco at the next table. Her eyes were red-rimmed and swollen, and she turned a glass of wine in her hand without seeing it. Beau coaxed her into taking a sip. "He's already after all of you," Jean Luc continued. "This changes nothing."

Deveraux frowned. "And your men? They won't reveal your involvement?"

"Which was what, exactly?" Jean Luc's eyes narrowed. "I took advantage of a poor situation to rescue the daughter of an aristocrat." He plunked his glass on the table and stood, straightening his coat. "Make no mistake—we are not allies. If you aren't gone by the time I return, I will arrest all of you, and I will lose no sleep tonight."

Deveraux looked down to conceal his grin. "Why not now? We are here. You are here."

Jean Luc scowled, leaning closer and lowering his voice. "Do not make me regret this, old man. After what I saw down there, I could see you burned. It is the fate that awaits every witch. You are no different."

"After what you saw down there," Deveraux mused, still examining his fingernails, "I assume you have many questions." When Jean Luc opened his mouth to argue, Deveraux spoke over him. "Your men certainly will. Make no mistake. Are you prepared to answer them? Are you prepared to paint us all with the same stroke as Morgane?"

"I—"

"Louise risked her life to save an innocent young woman last night, and she paid dearly for it."

As one, they turned to look at Célie. She sat beside me at the table, pale and trembling. She hadn't spoken since we'd left La Mascarade des Crânes. When I'd kindly suggested she return home, she'd broken down in tears. I hadn't mentioned it since. Still, I didn't know what to do with her. She couldn't stay with us. Her parents must've been worried sick, and even if they weren't... the road ahead would be dangerous. It was no place for someone like Célie.

She blushed under Deveraux's and Jean Luc's gazes, folding

her hands in her lap. Dirt still stained her mourning dress. And something else. Something—putrid.

I still didn't know what had happened to her down there. Lou had refused to tell me, and Ansel—

My mind viciously rejected the thought.

"Louise is the *reason* Célie was kidnapped," Jean Luc said through gritted teeth. "And I cannot discuss the matter any further. I must go. Célie"—he extended a hand toward her, face softening—"can you stand? I will escort you home. Your parents are waiting." Fresh tears welled in her eyes, but she wiped them away. Straightening her shoulders, she placed her trembling hand in his. Jean Luc moved to leave but stopped short, clutching my shoulder at the last second. His eyes were impenetrable. "I genuinely hope I don't see you again, Reid. Leave the kingdom. Take Louise and Coco with you if you must. Take the prince. Just—" Sighing heavily, he turned away. "Take care of yourself."

I watched the two of them walk out the door with a strange, pinching sensation. Though I no longer loved Célie romantically, it was . . . odd. Seeing her hand in Jean Luc's. Uncomfortable. Still, I wished them every happiness. Someone should have it.

"How is she?" Deveraux said after a moment. No one asked who he meant. "*Where* is she?"

I took my time answering, contemplating my beer again. After one enormous swallow and another, I wiped my mouth. "She's in the dining room with La Voisin and Nicholina. They're . . . planning."

"La Voisin? Nicholina?" Deveraux blinked between Coco and me, appalled. "These are the same women who abandoned us in the tunnels, are they not? What in the wilderness is Lou *planning* with them?"

Coco didn't look up from her wine. "Lou wants to march on Chateau le Blanc. It's all she's talked about since we escaped. She says she needs to kill Morgane."

"Oh dear." Deveraux's eyes widened, and he blew out a breath. "Oh dear, oh dear, oh dear. I must admit, that is . . . troubling."

Coco's hand tightened around her glass. Her eyes snapped up, burning with unshed emotion. "Why? We all want vengeance. She's taking the steps to get us there."

Deveraux appeared to choose his next words carefully. "Thoughts such as these could invite something very dark into your lives, Cosette. Something very dark, indeed. Evil always seeks a foothold. We must not give it one."

The stem of her glass snapped between her fingers, and a tear sizzled against the table. "She snuffed him out like a *candle*. You were there. You *saw*. And he—he—" She closed her eyes to regain her composure. When she opened them again, they were nearly black. Beau watched her with a wooden expression. Emotionless. Blank. "He was the best of us. Evil has more than a foothold here, Claud—thanks to you. You set it loose last night. You let it roam free. Now we all must suffer the consequences."

The door to the dining room flew open, and Lou stepped out. When her eyes met mine, she grinned and started toward me. I frowned. I hadn't seen her grin since—since—

Without a word, she swept me into a passionate kiss.

ACKNOWLEDGMENTS

People warned me about second books. They said the sophomore novel, whether sequel or standalone, was an entirely different beast than a debut. After a rather intense revision period with *Serpent & Dove*, I thought I could handle whatever *Blood & Honey* threw at me. Life doesn't come with voice-over narration, but if it did, my narrator would've laughed at this point—perhaps Jim would've deadpanned to the camera—and said, "How very wrong she was." For whatever reason, this book demanded my blood and sweat and tears. It gave me nightmares; my first panic attack. I nearly had a psychotic break in the coffee aisle of the grocery store. (I don't drink coffee. I started drinking coffee while rewriting this book.) Now, on the other side, I can't help but feel proud of this story. It's proof we're capable of doing hard things, even if we need to ask for help with them sometimes—which I did while writing this book. A lot.

RJ, I don't think I'll ever forgive you for the airball reference, but also, like . . . you made me laugh when I wanted to cry. That's a gift. It's also why I married you. Thanks for being a single parent the last few months while I wrote and rewrote and revised and re-revised. I love you.

Beau, James, and Rose, I hope when you read this someday, you'll know that while you don't owe anyone unconditional love, you certainly have mine. Even when you argue. Even when you scream. Even when you paint the bathroom with my favorite lipstick on the morning of my 7 o'clock flight.

Mom and Dad, words don't suffice when I think of how to thank you. Even as a writer, I can't quite describe the swell of emotions in my chest at everything you've done for me, so I won't even try. Just know I pretty much hero-worship both of you.

There's a passage near the end of *Blood & Honey* where Lou describes her childhood paradise as being surrounded by family and laughter. Jacob, Brooke, Justin, Chelsy, and Lewie, you guys inspired that paradise. I lived it then, and I live it now.

Pattie and Beth, those days you spent with the kids were invaluable. You gave a lot of time and energy—and probably food—for me to write this book, and I appreciate it. Truly.

Jordan, Spencer, Meghan, Aaron, Courtney, Austin, Adrianne, Chelsea, Jake, Jillian, Riley, Jon, and Aaron, writing has become a large part of my life, but you've never begrudged me it. You've kept me grounded while simultaneously allowing me to grow, all without judgment. Even for the black lipstick. I couldn't do life without you guys.

Jordan, if there's a single person I need to thank for helping me write *Blood & Honey*, it's you. The time and energy you've poured into both me and this story . . . honestly, it chokes me up a little. Thank you for listening as I cried in the coffee aisle of the grocery store. Thank you for talking me through my panic attack, for suggesting Beau's next joke, for loving these characters like I do, for sending TikTok videos to make me laugh, for enduring hours upon hours of Voxer messages when I just couldn't crack the plot. Most important, however, thank you for being so much more than my critique partner. I cherish our friendship.

Katie and Carolyn, your support through the years means more than you know. Buckle up. I'm never letting either of you go.

Isabel, thank you for welcoming me into your home—and life—with open arms. Also for feeding me delicious food. Adalyn, you've become both the angel and the devil on my shoulders, whispering my worth in both ears. Your Instagram feed looks great too. Adrienne, your drive and work ethic and knowledge inspire me daily. Like, you literally inspired me to order a carrot stick for my eyes the other day. That doesn't just happen. Kristin, you have great hair. And skin. And fierce, badger-like loyalty to the people you love. I'm so lucky to have you in my corner. Rachel, the support you've given me—someone you've never met who crashed the group chat on a random Tuesday—is overwhelming. I can't wait to crash your next writing retreat, too.

Agent extraordinaire, Sarah, none of this would be possible without your knowledge, guidance, and warmth. Erica, your vision for this series remains unerring. Thank you for keeping

Lou, Reid, and me in line, especially when we tend to stray in the middle. You have the patience of a saint. Louisa Currigan, Alison Donalty, Jessie Gang, Alexandra Rakaczki, Gwen Morton, Mitch Thorpe, Michael D'Angelo, Ebony LaDelle, Tyler Breitfeller, Jane Lee, and everyone else at HarperTeen, if someone would've asked what my dream team looked like before I sold *Serpent & Dove*, that team would've looked exactly like you. I can't thank you enough for the time and energy you've given to this series.

TURN THE PAGE FOR A
SNEAK PEEK AT THE NEXT
BOOK IN THE SERIES.

A NEST OF MICE

Nicholina

Bayberry, eyebright, belladonna
Fang of an adder, eye of an owl
Sprinkle of flora, spray of fauna
For purpose fair or possession foul.

Ichor of friend and ichor of foe
A soul stained black as starless night
For in the dark dost spirits flow
One to another in seamless flight.

The spell is familiar, oh yes, familiar indeed. Our favorite. She lets us read it often. The grimoire. The page. The spell. Our fingers trace each pen stroke, each faded letter, and they tingle with promise. They promise we'll never be alone, and we believe them. We believe *her*. Because we aren't alone—we're never alone—and mice live in nests with dozens of other mice, with *scores* of them. They burrow together to raise their pups, their children, and they find warm, dry nooks with plenty of food and magic. They find crannies without sickness, without death.

Our fingers curl on the parchment, gouging fresh tracks.

Death. Death, death, *death*, our friend and foe, as sure as breath, comes for us all.

But not me.

The dead should not remember. Beware the night they dream.

We tear at the paper now, shredding it to pieces. To angry bits. It scatters like ash in the snow. Like memory.

Mice burrow together, yes—they keep each other safe and warm—but when a pup in the litter sickens, the mice will eat it. Oh yes. They gobble it down, down, down to nourish the mother, the nest. The newest born is always sick. Always small. We shall devour the sick little mouse, and she shall nourish us.

She shall nourish us.

We shall prey on her friends, her *friends*—a snarl tears from my throat at the word, at the empty promise—and we shall feed them until they are fat with grief and guilt, with frustration and fear. Where we go, they will follow. Then we shall devour them too. And when we deliver the sick little mouse to her mother at Chateau le Blanc—when her body withers, when it *bleeds*—her soul shall stay with us forever.

She shall nourish us.

We will never be alone.

L'ENCHANTERESSE

Reid

Mist crept over the cemetery. The headstones—ancient, crumbling, their names long lost to the elements—pierced the sky from where we stood atop the cliff's edge. Even the sea below fell silent. In this eerie light before dawn, I finally understood the expression *silent as the grave.*

Coco brushed a hand across tired eyes before gesturing to the church beyond the mist. Small. Wooden. Part of the roof had caved in. No light flickered through the rectory windows. "It looks abandoned."

"What if it isn't?" Beau snorted, shaking his head, but stopped short with a yawn. He spoke around it. "It's a *church*, and our faces are plastered all over Belterra. Even a country priest will recognize us."

"Fine." Her tired voice held less bite than she probably intended. "Sleep outside with the dog."

As one, we turned to look at the spectral white dog that followed us. He'd shown up outside Cesarine, just before we'd agreed to travel the coast instead of the road. We'd all seen enough of La Fôret des Yeux to last a lifetime. For days, he'd trailed behind us, never coming near enough to touch. Wary, confused, the matagots had vanished shortly after his appearance. They hadn't returned. Perhaps the dog was a restless spirit himself—a new type of matagot. Perhaps he was merely an ill omen. Perhaps that was why Lou hadn't yet named him.

The creature watched us now, his eyes a phantom touch on my face. I gripped Lou's hand tighter. "We've been walking all night. No one will look for us inside a church. It's as good a place as any to hide. If it *isn't* abandoned"—I spoke over Beau, who started to interrupt—"we'll leave before anyone sees us. Agreed?"

Lou grinned at Beau, her mouth wide. So wide I could nearly count all her teeth. "Are you *afraid*?"

He shot her a dubious look. "After the tunnels, you should be too."

Her grin vanished, and Coco visibly stiffened, looking away. Tension straightened my own spine. Lou said nothing more, however, instead dropping my hand to stalk toward the door. She twisted the handle. "Unlocked."

Without a word, Coco and I followed her over the threshold. Beau joined us in the vestibule a moment later, eyeing the darkened room with unconcealed suspicion. A thick layer of dust coated the candelabra. Wax had dripped to the wooden floor, hardening among the dead leaves and debris. A draft swept through from the sanctuary beyond. It tasted of brine. Of decay.

"This place is haunted as shit," Beau whispered.

"Language." Scowling at him, I stepped into the sanctuary. My chest tightened at the dilapidated pews. At the loose hymnal pages collecting in the corner to rot. "This was once a holy place."

"It isn't haunted." Lou's voice echoed in the silence. She stilled behind me to stare up at a stained-glass window. The smooth face of Saint Magdaleine gazed back at her. The youngest saint in Belterra, Magdaleine had been venerated by the Church for gifting a man a blessed ring. With it, his negligent wife had fallen back in love with him, refusing to leave his side—even after he'd embarked on a perilous journey at sea. She'd followed him into the waves and drowned. Only Magdaleine's tears had revived her. "Spirits can't inhabit consecrated ground."

Beau's brows dipped. "How do you know that?"

"How do you *not*?" Lou countered.

"We should rest." I wrapped an arm around Lou's shoulders, leading her to a nearby pew. She looked paler than usual with dark shadows beneath her eyes, her hair wild and windswept from days of hard travel. More than once—when she didn't think I was looking—I'd seen her entire body convulse as if fighting sickness. It wouldn't surprise me. She'd been through a lot. We all had. "The villagers will wake soon. They'll investigate any noise."

Coco settled on a pew, closed her eyes, and pulled up the hood of her cloak. Shielding herself from us. "Someone should keep watch."

Though I opened my mouth to volunteer, Lou interrupted. "I'll do it."

"No." I shook my head, unable to recall the last time Lou had slept. Her skin felt cold, clammy, against mine. If she *was* fighting sickness, she needed the rest. "You sleep. I'll watch."

A sound reverberated from deep in her throat as she placed a hand on my cheek. Her thumb brushed my lips, lingering there. As did her eyes. "I'd much prefer to watch you. What will I see in your dreams, Chass? What will I hear in your—"

"I'll check the scullery for food," Beau muttered, shoving past us. He cast Lou a disgusted glance over his shoulder. My stomach rumbled as I watched him go. Swallowing hard, I ignored the ache of hunger. The sudden, unwelcome pressure in my chest. Gently, I removed her hand from my cheek and shrugged out of my coat. I handed it to her.

"Go to sleep, Lou. I'll wake you at sunset, and we can"—the words burned up my throat—"we can continue."

To the Chateau.

To Morgane.

To certain death.

I didn't voice my concerns again.

Lou had made it clear she'd journey to Chateau le Blanc whether or not we joined her. Despite my protests—despite reminding her *why* we'd sought allies in the first place, why we *needed* them—Lou maintained she could handle Morgane alone. *You heard Claud.* Maintained she wouldn't hesitate this time. *She can no longer touch me.* Maintained she would burn her ancestral home to the ground, along with all of her kin. *We'll build new.*

New what? I'd asked warily.

New everything.

I'd never seen her act with such single-minded intensity. No. Obsession. Most days, a ferocious glint lit her eyes—a feral sort of hunger—and others, no light touched them at all. Those days were infinitely worse. She'd watch the world with a deadened expression, refusing to acknowledge me or my weak attempts to comfort her.

Only one person could do that.

And he was gone.

She pulled me down beside her now, stroking my throat almost absently. At her cold touch, a shiver skittered down my spine and a sudden desire to shift away seized me. I ignored it. Silence blanketed the room, thick and heavy, except for the growls of my stomach. Hunger was a constant companion now. I couldn't remember the last time I'd eaten my fill. With Troupe de Fortune? In the Hollow? The Tower? Across the aisle, Coco's breathing gradually evened. I focused on the sound, on the beams of the ceiling, rather than Lou's frigid skin or the ache in my chest.

A moment later, however, shouts exploded from the scullery, and the sanctuary door burst open. Beau shot forward, hotfooting it past the pulpit. "Bumfuzzle!" He gestured wildly toward the exit as I vaulted to my feet. "Time to go! Right now, right *now*, let's *go*—"

"Stop!" A gnarled man in the vestments of a priest charged into the sanctuary, wielding a wooden spoon. Yellowish stew dripped from it. As if Beau had interrupted his morning meal. The flecks of vegetable in his beard—grizzled, unkempt, concealing most of his face—confirmed my suspicions. "I said get *back* here—"

He stopped abruptly, skidding to a halt when he saw the rest of us. Instinctively, I turned to hide my face in the shadows. Lou flung her hood over her white hair, and Coco stood, tensing to run. But it was too late. Recognition sparked in his dark eyes.

"Reid Diggory." His dark gaze swept from my head to my toes before shifting behind me. "Louise le Blanc." Unable to help himself, Beau cleared his throat from the foyer, and the priest considered him briefly before scoffing and shaking his head. "Yes, I know who you are too, boy. *And* you," he added to Coco, whose hood still cloaked her face in darkness. True to his word, Jean Luc had added her wanted poster beside ours. The priest's eyes narrowed on the blade she'd drawn. "Put that away before you hurt yourself."

"We're sorry for trespassing." I lifted my hands in supplication, glaring at Coco in warning. Slowly, I slid into the aisle, inched toward the exit. At my back, Lou matched my steps. "We didn't mean any harm."

The priest snorted but lowered his spoon. "You broke into my home."

"It's a church." Apathy dulled Coco's voice, and her hand dropped as if it suddenly couldn't bear the dagger's weight. "Not a private residence. And the door was unlocked."

"Perhaps to lure us in," Lou suggested with unexpected relish. Head tilted, she stared at the priest in fascination. "Like a spider to its web."

The priest's brows dipped at the abrupt shift in conversation, as did mine. Beau's voice reflected our confusion. "What?"

"In the darkest parts of the forest," she explained, arching a brow, "there lives a spider who hunts other spiders. L'Enchanteresse, we call her. The Enchantress. Isn't that right, Coco?" When Coco didn't respond, she continued undeterred. "L'Enchanteresse creeps into her enemies' webs, plucking their silk strands, tricking them into believing they've ensnared their prey. When the spiders arrive to feast, she attacks, poisoning them slowly with her unique venom. She savors them for days. Indeed, she's one of the few creatures in the animal kingdom who enjoy inflicting pain."

We all stared at her. Even Coco. "That's disturbing," Beau finally said.

"It's *clever.*"

"No." He grimaced, face twisting. "It's *cannibalism.*"

"We needed shelter," I interjected a touch too loudly. Too desperately. The priest, who'd been watching them bicker with a disconcerted frown, returned his attention to me. "We didn't realize the church was occupied. We'll leave now."

He continued to assess us in silence, his lip curling slightly. Gold swelled before me in response. Seeking. Probing. Protecting. I ignored its silent question. I wouldn't need magic here. The priest wielded only a spoon. Even if he'd brandished a sword, the lines on his face marked him elderly. Wizened. Despite his tall frame, time seemed to have withered his musculature, leaving a spindly old man in its wake. We could outrun him. I seized Lou's hand in preparation, cutting a glance to Coco and Beau. They both nodded once in understanding.

Scowling, the priest lifted his spoon as if to stop us, but at that moment, a fresh wave of hunger wracked my stomach. Its growl rumbled through the room like an earthquake. Impossible to ignore. Eyes tightening, the priest tore his gaze from me to glare at Saint Magdaleine in the silence that followed. After another beat, he grudgingly muttered, "When did you last eat?"

I didn't answer. Heat pricked my cheeks. "We'll leave now," I repeated.

His eyes met mine. "That's not what I asked."

"It's been . . . a few days."

"How many days?"

Beau answered for me. "Four."

Another rumble of my stomach rocked the silence. The priest shook his head. Looking as though he'd rather swallow the spoon whole, he asked, "And . . . when did you last sleep?"

Again, Beau couldn't seem to stop himself. "We dozed in some fishermen's boats two nights ago, but one of them caught us before sunrise. He tried to snare us in his net, the half-wit."

The priest's eyes flicked to the sanctuary doors. "Could he have followed you here?"

"I just said he was a half-wit. Reid snared him in the net instead."

Those eyes found mine again. "You didn't hurt him." It wasn't a question. I didn't answer it. Instead I tightened my grip on Lou's hand and prepared to run. This man—this *holy* man—would soon sound the alarm. We needed to put miles between us before Jean Luc arrived.

Lou didn't seem to share my concern.

"What's your name, cleric?" she asked curiously.

"Achille." His scowl returned. "Achille Altier."

Though the name sounded familiar, I couldn't place it. Perhaps he'd once journeyed to Cathédral Saint-Cécile d'Cesarine. Perhaps I'd met him while under oath as a Chasseur. I eyed him with suspicion. "Why haven't you summoned the huntsmen, Father Achille?"

He looked deeply uncomfortable. Shoulders radiating tension, he stared down at his spoon. "You should eat," he said gruffly. "There's stew in the back. Should be enough for everyone."

Beau didn't hesitate. "What kind?" When I shot a glare over my shoulder, he shrugged. "He could've woken the town the moment he recognized us—"

"He still could," I reminded him, voice hard.

"—and my stomach is about to eat itself," he finished. "Yours too, by the sound of it. We need food." He sniffed and asked Father Achille, "Are there potatoes in your stew? I'm not partial to them. It's a textural thing."

The priest's eyes narrowed, and he jabbed the spoon toward the scullery. "Get out of my sight, boy, before I change my mind."

Beau inclined his head in defeat before scooting past us. Lou, Coco, and I didn't move, however. We exchanged wary looks. After a long moment, Father Achille heaved a sigh. "You can sleep here too. Just for the day," he added irritably, "so long as you don't bother me."

"It's Sunday morning." At last, Coco lowered her hood. Her

lips were cracked, her face wan. "Shouldn't villagers be attending service soon?"

He scoffed. "I haven't held a service in years."

A reclusive priest. Of course. The disrepair of the chapel made sense now. Once, I would've scorned this man for his failure as a religious leader. For his failure as a man. I would've reprimanded him for turning his back on his vocation. On God.

How times had changed.

Beau reappeared with an earthen bowl and leaned casually against the doorway. Steam from the stew curled around his face. When my stomach rumbled again, he smirked. I spoke through gritted teeth. "Why would you help us, Father?"

Reluctantly, the priest's gaze trailed over my pale face, Lou's grisly scar, Coco's numb expression. The deep hollows beneath our eyes and the gaunt cut of our cheeks. Then he looked away, staring hard at the empty air above my shoulder. "What does it matter? You need food. I have food. You need a place to sleep. I have empty pews."

"Most in the Church wouldn't welcome us."

"Most in the Church wouldn't welcome their own mother if she was a sinner."

"No. But they'd burn her if she was a witch."

He arched a sardonic brow. "Is that what you're after, boy? The stake? You want me to mete out your divine punishment?"

"I believe," Beau drawled from the doorway, "he's simply pointing out that *you* are among the Church—unless you're actually the sinner of this story? Are you unwelcome amongst your peers, Father Achille?" He glanced pointedly at our dilapidated surroundings. "Though I abhor jumping to conclusions, our beloved patriarchs surely would've sent someone to repair this hovel otherwise."

Achille's eyes darkened. "Watch your tone."

I interrupted before Beau could provoke him further, spreading my arms wide. In disbelief. In frustration. In . . . everything. Pressure built in my throat at this man's unexpected kindness. It didn't make sense. It couldn't be real. As horrible a picture as Lou painted, a cannibal spider luring us into its web seemed likelier than a priest offering us sanctuary. "You know who we are. You know what we've done. You know what will happen if you're caught sheltering us."

He studied me for a long moment, expression inscrutable. "Let's not get caught, then." With a mighty *harrumph*, he stomped toward the scullery door. At the threshold, however, he paused, eyeing Beau's bowl. He seized it in the next second, ignoring Beau's protests and thrusting it at me. "You're just kids," he muttered, not meeting my eyes. When my fingers wrapped around the bowl—my stomach contracting painfully—he let go. Straightened his robes. Rubbed his neck. Nodded to the stew. "Won't be worth eating cold."

Then he turned and stormed from the room.

THE COMPLETE SIZZLING TRILOGY!

Bound as one to love, honor . . . or burn.

This book is a general guide only and should never be a substitute for the skill, knowledge,
and experience of a qualified medical professional dealing with the facts, circumstances, and
symptoms of a particular case.

The nutritional, medical, and health information presented in this book is based on the research,
training, and professional experience of the authors, and is true and complete to the best of
their knowledge. However, this book is intended only as an informative guide for those wishing
to know more about health, nutrition, and medicine; it is not intended to replace or
countermand the advice given by the reader's personal physician. Because each person and
situation is unique, the authors and the publisher urge the reader to check with a qualified
health-care professional before using any procedure where there is a question as to its
appropriateness. A physician should be consulted before beginning any exercise program. The
authors and the publisher are not responsible for any adverse effects or consequences resulting
from the use of the information in this book. It is the responsibility of the reader to consult
a physician or other qualified health-care professional regarding his or her personal care.

Library and Archives Canada Cataloguing in Publication
Kaur, Sat Dharam
    The complete natural medicine guide to women's health / Sat Dharam Kaur,
Mary Danylak-Arhanic, Carolyn Dean.

ISBN 10: 0-7788-0127-6
ISBN 13: 978-0-7788-0127-6

1. Women—Health and hygiene. 2. Women—Diseases—Alternative treatment.
3. Naturopathy. 4. Self-care, Health. I. Danylak-Arhanic, Mary II. Dean, Carolyn III. Title.

RA778.K39 2005   613'.04244   C2005-902586-7

Edited by Bob Hilderley, Senior Editor, Health.
Copyedited by Fina Scroppo.
Design and page composition by PageWave Graphics Inc.
Illustrations by Kveta.
Cover Photo: Rolf Bruderer/Masterfile.

The publisher acknowledges the financial support of the Government of Canada through
the Book Publishing Industry Development Program.

Published by Robert Rose Inc.
120 Eglinton Ave. E., Suite 800, Toronto, Ontario Canada M4P 1E2
Tel: (416) 322-6552 Fax: (416) 322-6936
www.robertrose.ca

Printed and bound in Canada.

3 4 5 6 7 8 9 FP 19 18 17 16 15 14 13

Contents

Section Four

Restoring Harmony with the Earth's Elements

Section Five

Seasonal Cleansing and Rejuvenation Program

Section Six

Women's Conditions

Preface

What you have in this book are tools for a lifetime of good health. Though the healing practices and information may seem like too much at first — just start with one thing. It might be five pieces of fruit a day, 40 minutes of exercise, or a sauna. Build slowly on your successes. Remember that your body regenerates itself over a period of years. By slowly integrating positive health practices into your lifestyle, you can create a healthier body, mind, and spirit as you age.

Good health and illness are not mysteries — the four basic steps we present prevent and heal almost every condition.

- Improve Nutrition
- Restore Balance
- Detoxify and Rejuvenate
- Integrate Body, Mind, and Spirit

We will be reinforcing the importance of these steps to healing the whole person throughout this book while providing the knowledge you need to step forward confidently.

Carry on this path until a healthy lifestyle is firmly established, but be patient. This may take several years. Keep re-reading the book — you'll get more out of it each time.

You can start by setting 3-month seasonal goals for yourself as you follow some of the guidelines in this book — for example, you could eliminate sugar from your diet, eat organic foods, balance your urine and saliva pH, and do a parasite cleanse for 3 months. Work with a natural medicine practitioner and keep moving along until you've taken care of the four steps we present for healing the whole person. If you have a serious illness, such as cancer, try to encompass all of the healing steps in the shortest time possible — it is possible for you to become well if you do so. Just begin and keep going with faith and commitment as your companions.

With this book, we have made the effort to meet a need in women's health literature for a comprehensive natural medicine approach by integrating many natural healing practices and traditions rather than focusing on one or two therapies to the exclusion of the others. Written by a trio of women trained as naturopathic and medical doctors, we also offer a unique complementary perspective on women's medicine.

The author of *The Complete Natural Medicine Guide to Breast Cancer*, Dr. Sat Dharam Kaur (ND) has practiced Kundalina yoga for 30 years and lectures in women's health at the Canadian College of Naturopathic Medicine. Dr. Mary Danylak-Arhanic (MD) is a leading holistic physician, well-seasoned in both conventional and natural medicine. Licensed in conventional medicine as well as naturopathic medicine, Dr. Carolyn Dean (MD & ND) has written several books, including *The Miracle of Magnesium, Natural Prescriptions for Common Ailments*, and *Menopause Naturally.* We feel our collective knowledge and skills are complementary and will serve you well.

What Is Natural Medicine?

*N*atural medicine can be a confusing term. As health-care practitioners have revived traditional healing systems and developed new treatments over the past few years, natural medicine has taken on many meanings. Natural medicine has been associated with homeopathy and naturopathy, osteopathy and hydrotherapy, vitamins and herbs, traditional Chinese medicine and traditional Indian (Ayurvedic) medicine. Add in the more unconventional dark-field microscopy, biological terrain ecology, iridology, reflexology, and auriculomedicine — and you can see how a host of health-care practices fall under the umbrella of natural medicine.

Natural medicine is flourishing, in part, because of a reaction to the apparent limitations of conventional surgical and pharmaceutical treatments for illness. For many women under our care, conventional medicine is not enough. They choose natural medicine to complement conventional medicine in their pursuit of optimum health.

Natural medicine practitioners believe that we are whole beings, integrated in body, mind, and spirit, with an inherent capacity to heal when healing mechanisms are supported and obstacles to healing are removed. We are proactive in preventing illness and ensuring lifelong well-being by supporting these healing mechanisms and removing these obstacles to cure.

Natural Medicine Traditions

Humans have used natural medicines to heal the sick and prevent illness for thousands of years. North American indigenous people used natural herbal medicine and healing rituals long before the European discovery of the continent. Ayurvedic medicine ("science of life") originated in India more than 5,000 years ago, using herbs, aromas, gems, colors, yoga, mantras, and surgery to heal. Considered the father of modern naturopathic medicine, the ancient Greek physician Hippocrates of Cos trained his medical students to suture wounds and to heal with herbs, fasting, and water treatments (hydrotherapy). Hippocrates believed in the body's innate capacity to heal itself and in the healing power of nature, two guiding principles that still govern natural medicine.

Let's look more closely at these and other natural healing traditions. Each tradition explains the origins of illness differently and recommends distinct therapies for restoring health. Each model contains pieces of the puzzle, contributing to a broader understanding of health, disease, and our relationship to the outer world.

Native American Medicine

Native American medicine encompasses the healing beliefs and practices of all the indigenous people of North America, combining herbal remedies, purification rituals, and spiritual ceremonies to treat a wide range of physical, mental, and emotional ailments — from the common cold to cancer. Native Americans believe that all things in nature are connected, with corresponding presences in the spiritual world. These spirits can promote health or cause illness.

Medicine men, medicine women, shamans, or healers prescribe herbs, oversee purification rituals, and conduct spiritual ceremonies. These are intended to call on or to appease the spirits, rid us of impurities, and restore our spiritual integrity.

Today, Native American medicine is used by both Native and non-Native Americans, either as a primary source of health care or as adjunct treatment to conventional medicine. In this book, we recommend Native American herbs (for example, black cohosh for menopausal hot flashes) and seasonal cleansing rituals. Like Native American medicine, our approach to women's health honors the cycles of nature.

Herbal Remedies

Herbal remedies are prescribed for various physical, emotional, and spiritual ailments, varying from tribe to tribe and depending upon what herbs are available in a particular area. Herbal medicines are administered fresh or dried, as a tea or mixed with another beverage or with food. Certain herbs, such as sage, sweet grass, or cedar, may be burned, using smoke to purify the patient.

Purification Rituals

The traditional Native American purification ritual takes place in a sweat lodge (the womb of Mother Earth), typically a small domed structure made of tree branches and covered by skins or blankets or sealed with mud or sod. The patient, the healer, and any helpers pray, sing, and sometimes drum together. A pipe is passed around and smoked to call on the spirits for healing. At the same time, water is sprinkled over hot stones (called grandfathers), as in a sauna, to create steam that cleanses the body of disease and purifies emotions.

Spiritual Ceremonies

Among the various tribal spiritual ceremonies, the use of the medicine wheel, the sacred hoop, and the 'sing' is most common. The community comes together to help the ailing individual, with patients often surrounded by praying or chanting family members

DID YOU KNOW...

Of the 10 top-selling herbs in North America today, seven of them have been used for centuries by Native American healers. Our current use of echinacea to bolster the immune system against common colds, goldenseal for treating infections and cancers, and black cohosh for 'cooling' menopausal hot flashes comes from Native American healers.

CASE STUDY: PURIFICATION

Native American medicine has proven to be especially effective in the treatment of breast cancer, primarily through the use of herbal formulas (often featuring goldenseal and bloodroot) and purification rituals (such as sweat lodges). One of our patients was diagnosed with breast cancer but postponed surgery while she participated in intensive Native healing ceremonies. She also began homeopathic treatment. Her breast cancer tumors receded, and two years later, she has no signs of cancer and feels as though she has given birth to a new self. While not all cases of serious disease resolve through Native American medical treatments, these practices should not be discounted, but rather considered in any treatment plan.

and friends, in contrast to the one-on-one, doctor-patient relationship emphasized in conventional Western medicine.

Members of the community dance, chant, and drum to align the body with the heartbeat of the earth, and use feathers and rattles to remove blockages and stagnant energy that may be contributing to ill health. Sometimes sacred stones are rubbed over the part of the person's body suspected to be diseased.

Ayurvedic Medicine

Ayurvedic medicine maintains and restores health by balancing the body's three fundamental energies or doshas — vata, pitta, and kapha. Like everything in the universe, we are created from five elements — ether, air, fire, water, and earth — and these five elements combine to form our particular dosha. Imbalanced doshas are treated with diet, exercise, rest, herbs, oils, detoxification and rejuvenation programs, mantra meditation, color therapy, gemstones, aromatherapy, and yoga.

THREE DOSHAS

Vata
The elements ether and air are dominant, which generate increased movement and a tendency to dryness. Imbalances in individuals with the vata dosha include constipation, gas, sciatica, arthritis, insomnia, excessive worry, fear, and anxiety.

Pitta
The elements fire and water are dominant, which govern digestion and metabolism. Imbalances in pitta individuals may manifest as increased anger, irritability, acid indigestion, heartburn, inflammation, hives, or acne.

Kapha
The elements water and earth are dominant; which form the body's structure and provide lubrication. Imbalances in kapha individuals lead to increased congestion and phlegm — colds, sneezing, allergies, cysts, asthma — and, on a psychological level, to the tendency to become overly attached to people and possessions.

Yoga and Meditation

The science of yoga originated more than 40,000 years ago and was incorporated into Ayurvedic medicine. Yoga postures, mantra meditation, and breathing exercises improve the flow of energy through the invisible pathways in the body. In yoga, this energy is called prana and the pathways are known as nadis. Prana is the life force that vibrates in every atom of the universe as well as in our minds and bodies, sustaining our existence. The practice of

yoga helps to distribute prana through the nadis, linking mind, body, and spirit. The ultimate goal of yoga and meditation is realization of our true divine nature and oneness with all. Kundalini Yoga, first brought to North America by Yogi Bhajan in 1968, will be used throughout this book to complement other treatment strategies. Exercise sequences are presented that help to enhance awareness, balance the glands and emotions, assist organ function, regulate the sympathetic and parasympathetic nervous system, and direct energy to a particular chakra.

CHAKRAS

Located along the spine and in the subtle body, the eight chakras are hubs of electrical and chemical activity that receive, process, and distribute prana or information, acting as bridges between the external world and the body. Each center is associated with specific organs, glands, hormones, nerve plexi, archetypal themes, and emotional states.

The chakras metabolize specific frequencies. After the energy from the magnetic field is drawn into a specific chakra, it is carried along the nadis and distributed first to the nerve plexi that are linked to each chakra, then to the glands, and finally to the organs, blood, and cells. The incoming information alters the expression of neuropeptides (information molecules) on the cell membranes, particularly where they are concentrated in the nerve plexi, which can then cause both a local and whole body shift in cellular function.

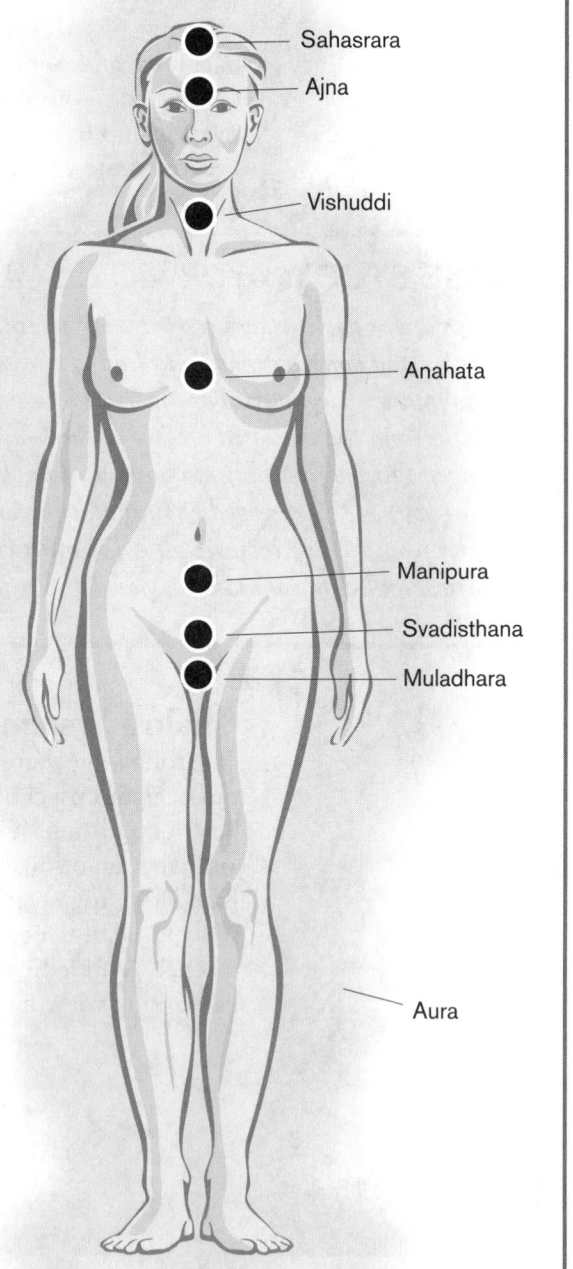

Energy Imbalance

Our belief systems, our thought patterns, our traumas, and our suppressed emotions, as well as the vibrational fields (an abusive partner, for example) and electromagnetic fields, may create imbalances in any of these energy centers. Illness can be caused by an imbalance of energy or a blockage in flow. A knot in the energetic body creates a corresponding physical dysfunction.

When the chakras are more open, there is greater energy flow and better health. Yoga, bodywork, mindfulness meditation, and breathing exercises are methods to release energetic contractions and blockages. Once obstructions are removed and the energy can flow, physical ailments may heal, emotions become better balanced, and our spiritual potential grows. We feel more connected to our unfolding life purpose and recognize our relationship to events, people, and the world around us. We become more whole.

CASE STUDY: AYURVEDIC SOLUTION

One of our patients was experiencing severe symptoms of menopause, including hot flashes and bone loss that could lead to osteoporosis. Using Ayurvedic medicine and the chakras, we diagnosed that she had excess pitta. The increased heat intensified hot flashes and the increased acidity in the body caused calcium to be pulled from the bones. Osteoporosis may also be caused by the increase in vata that normally occurs with aging. The Ayurvedic solution we recommended was to avoid hot drinks and spicy foods (which increase pitta), to practice left nostril breathing (which decreases pitta), and to use an alkaline powder to neutralize the body's acids.

Chakra System

The following chart gives an overview of the chakras and their physical and psychological associations. If you have a particular health condition, identify which chakra may be imbalanced and what emotional issues you may have to heal. Look for a Kundalini Yoga teacher in your area (a directory is listed at www.kundaliniyoga.com) or work with another skilled yoga teacher, Ayurvedic medicine practitioner, or bodyworker trained in working with the chakras.

Traditional Chinese Medicine

In traditional Chinese medicine, disease is viewed as a disorder or imbalance of energy in the body, while health is the harmonious balance between the complementary principles of yin and yang and the harmonious integration of five phases and organs, each one representing a category of related functions and qualities that together express the flowing cycle of life.

Treatment in Chinese medicine combines the use of herbal formulations with acupuncture to correct imbalances in the flow of energy or chi. Chi flows through energetic pathways called meridians, which are like invisible rivers that traverse the body, similar to the nadis. Acupuncture points exist along the meridians where the energy flow can be adjusted through tonification (strengthening the flow) or sedation (removing excess energy), using needling techniques or the application of heat, known as moxibustion. In addition, complex herbal formulas are compounded and prescribed to invigorate the organs.

DID YOU KNOW...

Written more than 2,000 years ago, *The Yellow Emperor's Classic of Medicine* forms the basis of current traditional Chinese medicine (TCM), featuring treatment strategies for 225 internal diseases using acupuncture and herbal formulas.

ACUPUNCTURE MERIDIANS

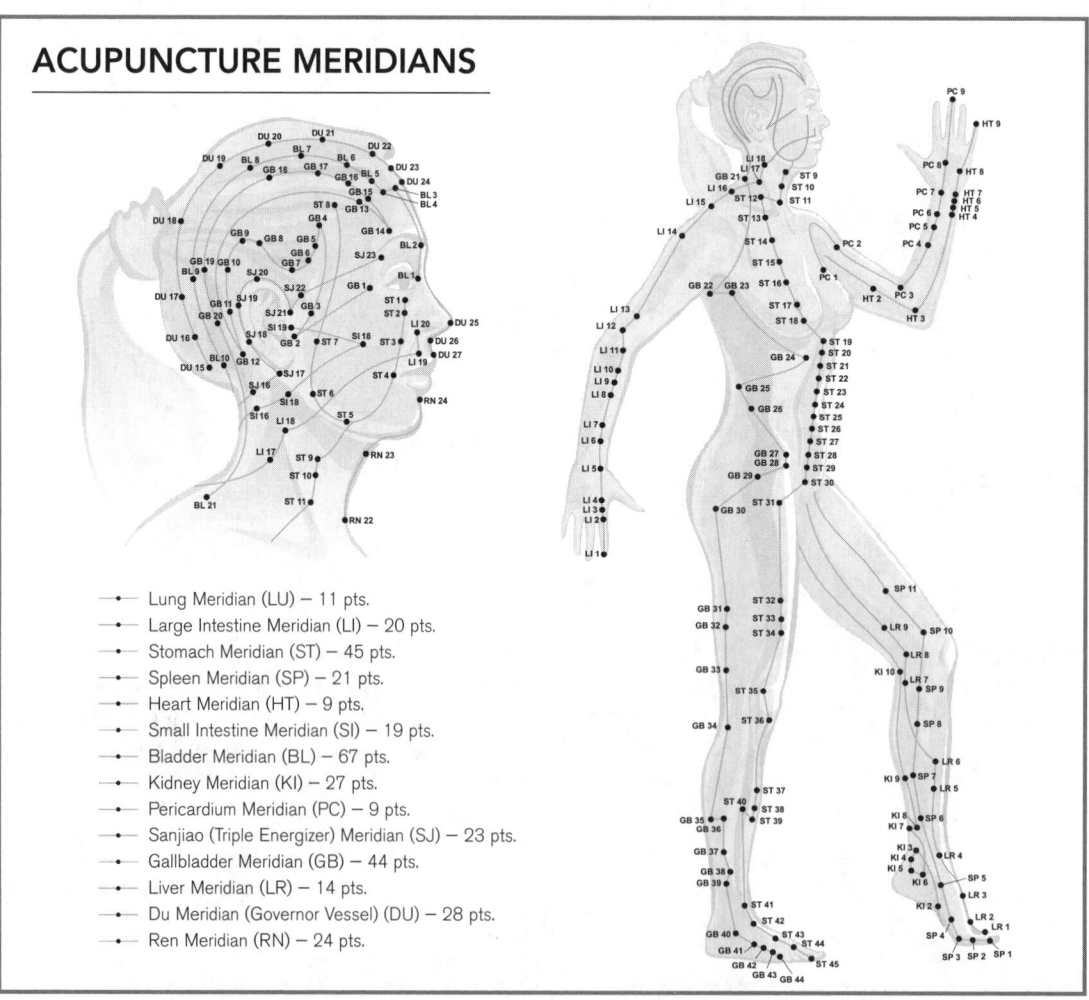

- Lung Meridian (LU) — 11 pts.
- Large Intestine Meridian (LI) — 20 pts.
- Stomach Meridian (ST) — 45 pts.
- Spleen Meridian (SP) — 21 pts.
- Heart Meridian (HT) — 9 pts.
- Small Intestine Meridian (SI) — 19 pts.
- Bladder Meridian (BL) — 67 pts.
- Kidney Meridian (KI) — 27 pts.
- Pericardium Meridian (PC) — 9 pts.
- Sanjiao (Triple Energizer) Meridian (SJ) — 23 pts.
- Gallbladder Meridian (GB) — 44 pts.
- Liver Meridian (LR) — 14 pts.
- Du Meridian (Governor Vessel) (DU) — 28 pts.
- Ren Meridian (RN) — 24 pts.

	FIRST CHAKRA (*Muladhara*)	SECOND CHAKRA (*Svadisthana*)
LOCATION	Base of the spine between the anus and vagina	Area just above pubic bone, sexual organs
COLOR	Red	Orange
ELEMENT	Earth	Water
PHYSICAL LINKS	Base of spine, rectum, and anus (anal sphincter muscle is rich in neuropeptide activity), hip joints, blood, legs and feet, adrenal medulla, elimination of solids, sense of smell, sacral nerve plexus	Uterus, ovaries, vagina, cervix, lumbar vertebrae, bladder, kidneys, appendix, sense of taste, elimination of fluids, male prostate, area where spinal cord innervates sexual organs
ARCHETYPAL THEMES	Connection to the earth, groundedness, strong foundation, basic instincts, safety and security, trust, loyalty, physical survival issues, ability to stand alone, ability to provide for oneself, balance between dependence and independence	Emotional life, creativity, relationship issues, healthy sensuality and sexuality, pleasure, being faithful to one's partner, feelings, passion, opinions, financial security
IMBALANCED TENDENCIES	Feeling victimized, impulse to escape, paranoia, phobias, timidity, panic disorders, feeling as if one doesn't belong on Earth or in one's culture or family, self-destructive Hostility, impulse to fight, "them or us attitude," sadism, aggressiveness, recklessness, acting as a perpetrator, compulsiveness, fixated behaviors, greed	Avoiding relationships, sexual repression, guilt, poor boundaries, shut down, denial of pleasure, flat expression, emotional delusion, excess sexual fantasy, fear of abandonment, history of sexual abuse, eating disorders Prostitution, compulsive sexuality, blocked creativity, disorders with gender identity, being unfaithful, irresponsible relationships without commitment, lust
PHYSICAL AILMENTS	Hemorrhoids, constipation, sciatica, low back pain, rectal tumors or cancer, ulcerative colitis, chronic fatigue syndrome, environmental sensitivities, fibromyalgia, autoimmune diseases	Uterine fibroids or cancer, ovarian cysts or cancer, infertility, sexual dysfunctions, vaginal infections, bladder infections, appendicitis, pelvic pain
YOGA EXERCISES	Crow pose, chair pose, body drops, frog pose, double leg front stretch, lying on stomach with feet kicking buttocks	Frog pose, cobra, cat-cow, pelvic lifts, spinal rock with knees apart, butterfly

THIRD CHAKRA (Manipura)	FOURTH CHAKRA (Anahata)
One inch below the navel	In the center of the sternum at the level of the nipples
Yellow	Green, rose-pink
Fire	Air
Liver, gallbladder, stomach, pancreas, small intestine, digestion, lower esophagus, spleen, midspine, adrenal cortex, sense of sight, solar plexus	Breasts, heart, dilation of blood vessels and circulation, lungs, thymus gland, upper esophagus, diaphragm, shoulders, sense of touch, immune system, cardiac plexus
Assertiveness, confidence, courage, cooperation, digestion, ability to "chew" life, linear thinking, power to accept or reject food, personal power, stamina, self-esteem, identity, judgment, warrior, entrepreneur, risk taker, ability to fight for a cause, area that stores the energy of the cosmos, follow-through with a goal or mission, fearlessness, initiator of change, action, discipline, will, control	Joy, sadness, giving and receiving, compassion, hope, empathy, forgiveness, love, service, devotion, kindness, consideration, healing, intimacy, nurturing, family relationships, self-love, acceptance, altruism, community, balance between heaven and earth, conscious relationship boundaries, integration between upper and lower chakras
Passive, oppressed, lethargic, submissive, self-defeatist, putting oneself down, despair, shame, conformist, putting aside one's wishes and emotions, fear of responsibility or irresponsible, poor boundaries, low stamina Angry, aggressive, domineering, controlling, overly ambitious, authoritarian, abusive, obsessive-compulsive, selfish, over-responsible	Martyr complex, serves others at the expense of oneself, gives too much, inability to receive, sentimental, easily hurt, smothering of others, co-dependent, need to "fix" others, overly sensitive, excessively dutiful, excess grief, attachment, relationship addictions, fear of rejection, overly sympathetic Uses others, always taking, irresponsible, no sense of duty, inability to feel, invulnerable, emotionally guarded, won't let others in, fear of intimacy, lack of joy, indecision, anxiety
Gastric or duodenal ulcers, difficulty with digestion and absorption, hepatitis, liver problems, pancreatitis, diabetes, heartburn, gastritis, anorexia, bulimia	Breast cysts and cancer, heart disease, hypertension, arrhythmia, circulatory problems, chest pain, bronchitis, pneumonia, asthma, lung cancer, breathing difficulties, allergies, upper back and shoulder pain
Stretch pose, bow pose, double leg lifts, breath of fire, locust pose, sat kriya	Side twists, spinal flex, ego eradicator, all arm exercises, cobra, bow pose, bridge pose, yoga mudra, breathing exercises (pranayams)

	FIFTH CHAKRA (*Vishuddi*)	SIXTH CHAKRA (*Ajna*)	
LOCATION	Throat	Between the eyebrows	
COLOR	Sky blue	Indigo	
ELEMENT	Ether	Light	
PHYSICAL LINKS	Throat, voice, neck, thyroid gland, parathyroid glands, ears, mouth, teeth and gums, laryngeal plexus	Brain, pituitary gland, frontal lobe, cavernous plexus	
ARCHETYPAL THEMES	Speaking one's truth, creative expression, communication, listening, surrender to one's destiny, embodying Divine Will, teaching, initiating a sequence of events through speaking precise words, honor, ability to command through speech, power of the word, speaking things into being, taking responsibility for one's actions	Intuition, clairvoyance, ability to visualize, wisdom, insight, fantasy, concentration, ability to focus, planning, intention, understanding one's life purpose, command center, seeing beyond duality, integration, holding a mental projection, maintaining goals, care and support for all life	
IMBALANCED TENDENCIES	Inability to voice one's feelings or creativity, writer's block, inability to take in what another is saying, inability to act out one's destiny, shyness, poor communication skills, fear of other's opinions and judgments, insecurity Being overly verbal, total disregard for other's beliefs and opinions	Confusion, depression, rejection of spirituality, inability to focus, over-intellectualizing, schizophrenia	
PHYSICAL AILMENTS	Recurrent sore throats, neck pain, laryngitis, hoarseness, speech problems, underactive or overactive thyroid, mouth sores, gum disease, ear infections, hearing problems, swollen glands in neck, temporomandibular joint (TMJ) problems	Glandular imbalances, vision problems, attention deficit disorder, multiple sclerosis, neurological diseases, brain tumor, epilepsy, learning disabilities	
YOGA EXERCISES	Chanting, plow pose, shoulder stand, cobra, neck rolls, nose to knees while on back, cat-cow	Focus at the third eye point, archer pose, baby pose, bowing from rock pose, yoga mudra	

SEVENTH CHAKRA *(Sahasrara)*	EIGHTH CHAKRA *(Aura)*
Top of head	Electromagnetic field, 9 feet in all directions from the physical body
Violet	White
Cosmic Sound	
Brain, pineal gland	Integration of all parts of the body
Seat of the soul, enlightenment, unity with all, connection to the highest self, merging with God or the source of creation, humility, surrender to a higher power, infinite vastness, transcendence, spiritual integration	Power of projection, radiance, presence, protection, integration
Alienation, suicidal thoughts, addictions to drugs and alcohol, fear of death, depression, lack of faith, disconnectedness	Poor boundaries, accident prone, vulnerable, shy, withdrawn, easily affected by negative influences
Life-threatening illness, neurological diseases, seasonal affective disorder, manic depression, schizophrenia, cancers, insomnia, disturbance of body rhythms	Environmental sensitivities and allergies
Meditation, ego eradicator, focus on tip of nose	Triangle pose, archer pose, arm exercises, horse pose with breath of fire, windmills

CASE STUDY: *WAKE-UP CALL*

Physical symptoms can be seen as a 'wake-up call' nudging us back to a more integrated life, where emotions are expressed and the spirit is nourished. For many, the journey through illness is accompanied by a profound psychological shift and spiritual awakening.

Take the case of Vanessa. She came to see us for help with PMS, hypothyroidism, and depression. She was a dancer, training several hours each day, hoping to audition for a major dance troupe. She also wanted to come off her antidepressants.

Within a month after we had begun treating her with Chinese herbs for her PMS symptoms, she called to say that her period had arrived with no warning — and no PMS symptoms. She was elated. The following week she had some bodywork sessions and afterward relived a scene from her childhood when she had been sexually abused. She had told no one about this before. She experienced a huge emotional and physical release in her pelvis, followed by greater ease of movement. Her dancing improved immediately. The experience also gave her the courage to wean herself off antidepressants.

Yin and Yang Balance

Yin and yang refer to the fundamental duality of the universe that also exists in the human body. Yin represents form and structure, while yang is associated with movement and energy. In the body, yin governs the inner aspect, the more solid organs (kidney, spleen, liver, heart, lung), the front of the body, the lower part of the body, the bones, and the blood. It is associated with conditions of deficiency. Yang relates to the outer aspect, the more hollow organs (bladder, stomach, gallbladder, small intestine, large intestine), the back of the body, the upper part of the body, the skin, and the flow of energy or chi. It is associated with conditions of excess.

Generative and Control Cycles

Disharmony in the five phases, expressed in the relationship between the organs, often follows one of two main sequences: the generative cycle or the control cycle.

Generative Cycle: The energy of one phase or organ promotes the strength and vitality of the organ ahead of it. They have a 'mother-son relationship': one phase or organ is the mother of the organ that follows it in the generative cycle. For example, the energy of the stomach/spleen nourishes the vitality of the lung/large intestine, while the kidney/bladder helps to sustain the liver/gallbladder. If the mother is weak, the son will become weak. If the son is excessive, it will draw too much energy from the mother.

FIVE PHASES AND ORGAN PAIRS

Like the five elements in Ayurvedic medicine, there are five phases in traditional Chinese medicine that correspond to paired organs. They are used as tools for diagnosis and treatment. One of the great strengths of Chinese medicine is its organization of the relationships between the organ systems and its understanding of the body/mind as an integrated system rather than as disjointed parts. The five phases and their associations are all clues to an overall pattern of disharmony that, once identified, will guide treatment.

If you have a particular health condition, identify which phase or phases may be imbalanced. Consult a practitioner of traditional Chinese medicine, an acupuncturist, or a naturopathic doctor to discuss diagnosis and treatment options.

Five Phases of Traditional Chinese Medicine and their Associations

	WOOD PHASE	FIRE PHASE	EARTH PHASE	METAL PHASE	WATER PHASE
Process	• Birth • Growth • Expansion	• Peak of expansion	• Balance • Neutrality • Transformation	• Declining functions	• Regeneration after decline
Yin Organ	Liver	Heart	Spleen	Lungs	Kidneys
Yang Organ	Gallbladder	Small intestine	Stomach	Large intestine	Bladder
Sense Organ	Eyes	Tongue	Mouth	Nose	Ears
Season	Spring	Summer	Late Summer	Fall	Winter
Climate	Wind	Heat	Dampness	Dryness	Cold
Direction	East	South	Center	West	North
Color	Green	Red	Yellow	White	Black
Taste	Sour	Bitter	Sweet	Pungent	Salty
Smell	Goatish	Scorched	Fragrant	Rank	Rotten
Tissue	Tendons	Blood vessels	Muscle	Skin/Body Hair	Bones/Head Hair
Emotion	Anger	Joy	Worry	Grief	Fear
Theme	Reactivity	Control	Nourishment	Rigidity	Instability
Sound	Shouting	Laughing	Singing	Weeping	Groaning

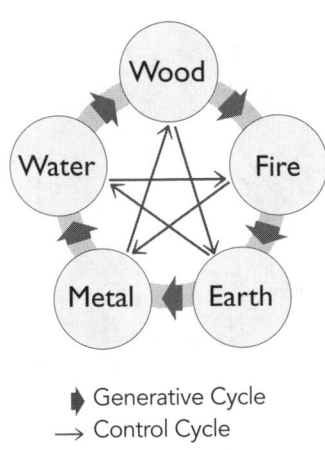

◗ Generative Cycle
→ Control Cycle

Control Cycle: The energy of one element helps keep the energy of the controlled element in check so that it does not become excessive. For example, the liver/gallbladder controls the stomach/spleen and if the liver/gallbladder weakens, the stomach/spleen energy may develop excessively. However, if the wood phase (liver/gallbladder) is too strong, then the earth phase (stomach/spleen) may be weakened. Energy can be shifted from one meridian to another to balance potential disharmonies.

Disease Conditions

Excessive or Deficient Constitutions

Acute diseases tend to result from excessive conditions in a person, while chronic diseases often occur with deficient conditions. Signs of an excessive condition are a normal or loud voice, heavy breathing, pain worse with pressure, thick fur on the tongue, and a strong pulse. Individuals with deficient conditions are quiet and withdrawn, have a soft, low voice, a pale complexion, shallow breathing, pain that improves with massage and pressure, little fur on the tongue, and a weak pulse.

Inherited, Internal, or External Causes of Disease

Chinese medicine recognizes that diseases can be inherited or arise from internally generated or externally generated causes. Internal causes include diet, lifestyle, smoking, alcohol, exercise, as well as unexpressed emotions, past traumas, beliefs, and attitudes. External causes include weather conditions, such as cold, heat, dampness, dryness, and wind; infectious agents; and toxic chemical exposure.

CASE STUDY: WOOD IMBALANCE

June is a chartered accountant in her mid-thirties who came to see us complaining of stress, with chronic neck and shoulder tension, irregular periods, and premenstrual irritability, accompanied by headaches behind her eyes. In listening to her speak, there was loudness in her voice (the equivalent of shouting). Her eyes had a slight green tinge around them (sign of wood imbalance). She stated that her headaches could also be brought on by exposure to wind. She had a craving for (sour) vinegar on French fries and green apples. The sour taste is associated with a disturbed liver/gallbladder. With herbs to circulate liver chi, daily breathing exercises, yoga exercises for her shoulders, a change in diet, and a daily walking program, her symptoms resolved within 2 months.

Conventional Western Medicine

The founder of the Western medical tradition in the 5th century BC, Hippocrates disproved the prevailing belief that disease was a punishment for sin and provided empirical proof that all illness has a natural cause. The emphasis on systematic clinical observation that prevails in modern medicine began with Hippocrates. In the 1st century AD, Claudius Galen developed natural treatments to restore balance to the four humors — blood, phlegm, yellow bile, and blood bile — not unlike the five phases in traditional Chinese medicine. Galen also dissected animals to gain understanding of anatomy. The ancient Greeks and Romans used herbal remedies, did minor surgery, and prescribed physical fitness, clean drinking water, and regular bathing to maintain health.

In the Middle Ages, Christianity dominated medicine, again promoting the view that disease was a punishment from God. This shifted back to the Hippocratic empirical tradition with the development of the scientific method by Rene Descartes in the 17th century, a process whereby phenomena are observed, hypotheses are created, results are predicted, and tests are conducted repeatedly to prove or disprove the hypotheses. This has become the backbone of medical research science.

At the same time, Leonardo da Vinci and others were exploring human anatomy, laying the groundwork for modern surgical procedures. Surgery saves lives, particularly when performed after accidental injury. The setting of bones, the suturing of wounds, hip and knee replacements, coronary bypasses and valve replacements, and cataract removal are some of the surgeries we have come to rely upon to prolong our lives or improve our quality of life.

Pharmaceutical Drugs

The scientific method has also led the way to the development of pharmaceutical drugs to treat the symptoms of disease. Drug therapy has come to dominate contemporary Western medicine.

Pharmaceuticals were first developed in ancient Egypt, Greece, Rome, India, and China from herbal medicine. Many pharmaceutical drugs, such as aspirin, quinine, Taxol and digitalis, were originally derived from active ingredients in herbs. Drugs are concentrated fractions of natural substances or original man-made chemical compounds 'proven' in clinical trials to alleviate the symptoms of disorders or disease. While antibiotic drugs can stop the spread of disease and anti-inflammatory drugs can dampen pain, they seldom address the cause of poor health and they have limited preventive effect. Unfortunately, they can also cause a battery of side effects that can be life threatening. This is in sharp

DID YOU KNOW...

The scientific method has steered research scientists into many life-saving discoveries, such as microorganisms being causative factors in diseases (for example, Helicobacter pylori linked to stomach cancer) and nutritional deficiencies causing certain illnesses (e.g., iodine deficiency linked to hypothyroidism).

DID YOU KNOW...

Even when properly prescribed and used, pharmaceutical drugs are the fourth leading cause of death in North America, after cardiovascular disease, cancer, and smoking.

contrast to a natural medicine practice, such as homeopathy, which only works when a remedy is precisely selected for an individual, based on her particular assortment of symptoms, and rarely causes harm.

Because drugs are largely fast acting, they have displaced traditional herbal and homeopathic remedies. Herbs are relatively slow acting, and because of the emphasis on 'proving' drugs, they have not been extensively tested in similar large controlled studies. Economic gain has driven the development of new drugs at the expense of herbal medicine. Because they are natural substances, herbs cannot be patented into drugs, so it is of little economic benefit to prove their medicinal value.

Psychiatry

Psychiatry has developed alongside surgery and drug therapy as a principal practice of contemporary Western medicine, first given systematic presentation in the work of Sigmund Freud. Psychiatrists are medical doctors who diagnose, prevent, and treat mental, emotional, and behavioral disorders, such as depression, attention deficit disorder, anxiety, schizophrenia, obsessive-compulsive disorder, phobias, addictions, and bipolar disorder, with 'talk' therapy and psychotropic drugs. These talk therapies range from classic psychotherapy to cognitive therapy. Drug therapy, especially antidepressants, have become ever more popular, despite their serious physical health side effects and failure to address the cause of the illness.

Compartmentalized Medicine

Western medicine has tended to view the body and the mind as separate entities whose parts can be 'fixed' individually rather than as pieces of a whole, integrated, cooperative system that includes body, mind, and spirit. Although honing in on individual body parts has yielded much useful information about how our body works, it has not promoted long-lasting healing of illness or prevention of disease.

Western medicine focuses on reducing illness to one causative factor that can be cut out (like a wart), killed (like a bacterial infection), or contained (like cancer), rather than identifying the many causative factors and imbalanced relationships between physical and energetic body systems and mental-emotional patterns that contribute to ill health. The underlying themes behind most medical practices are aggression (kill the cancer cells) and domination (suppress asthmatic symptoms with cortisone). These themes are vastly different from the themes of harmony and balance stressed in Chinese and Ayurvedic medicine.

Botanical Medicine

Contemporary botanical medical practice is an amalgam of Native American, Ayurvedic, Chinese, and Western herbal traditions that includes aromatherapy and gemmotherapy (the use of young plant growth). Plant substances are chosen from around the world for their healing effects and nutritional value.

Despite the popularity of drugs in contemporary Western medical practice, botanical medicine has gained credibility in recent years. Many of the herbs have now been 'proven' in clinical studies and are included in primary medical references, such as the German Commission E guide to the efficacy and safety of herbal medicines and the *PDR for Herbal Medicines.*

A combination of herbs is often chosen to alleviate a specific condition. The quality of the herbal source is important for the efficacy of treatment. Botanicals are most potent in their liquid form — as tincture or tea — but individuals sensitive to alcohol may require them in capsule or tablet form. Treatments are individualized to the patient's signs and symptoms in order to address the cause of the disorder. Herbs may also be prescribed as general tonics to prevent illness and support lifelong well-being.

DID YOU KNOW...

Herbs usually work more slowly than drugs, but unlike drugs, they seldom cause side effects, in part, because the active ingredients in herbs are small in comparison to drugs and they remain in their natural chemical form, balanced by other plant chemicals.

PROVEN PLANT POWERS

Botanical medicines and herbs are effective in preventing illness and restoring wellness for several reasons.

1. Plants contain vitamins, minerals, and phytochemicals that the body can utilize. For example, kelp is a rich source of iodine, needed by the thyroid; amla contains loads of vitamin C; and milk thistle contains silymarin, an aid to liver detoxification and repair.

2. Specific plants have an affinity for various organs and tissues. For example, hawthorne revitalizes the heart, calendula the skin, tang kuei the blood, phytolacca the breast.

3. Plants have energetic qualities that balance disharmony in the body. For example, the mucilaginous nature of slippery elm heals the intestinal lining; the bitter quality of goldenseal has drying and antibiotic effects; the warming nature of cinnamon dispels cold; the drying nature of juniper helps eliminate dampness in the joints.

4. Plants are imbued with a kind of energetic intelligence that can heal. When we feel a resonance with or affinity to a specific herb, we may be sensing the ability of that plant to protect us or heal us.

Aromatherapy

Aromatherapy utilizes the essential oils of plants to stimulate healing. Fragrance molecules attach to some of the 25 million receptors in the olfactory epithelium high in the roof of the nasal cavity, where they trigger electrical impulses that travel to the olfactory bulb in the brain. From there, the stimulus can travel to the gustatory center (where we perceive taste), the amygdala (where emotional memories are stored), and parts of the limbic system (the 'emotional' brain). The limbic system relays messages to the hypothalamus, which controls blood pressure, appetite, heart rate, and neurotransmitter levels, while helping to regulate the immune system and glandular system. Thus, smells can have powerful effects on our emotions and all aspects of health through their influence on the limbic system and hypothalamus.

CASE STUDY: *HOT FLASHES AT BAY*

This is a case involving one of us, Sat Dharam Kaur. A few months ago, at age 47, I experienced my first hot flashes — little ones that caused my face to flush but otherwise were innocuous. I was having three or four a day. One of my patients noticed and advised me to eat ground flaxseeds, advice I had given to her 5 years ago! I mixed up a combination of shou wu, black cohosh, and schizandra in tincture form, took one or two sips a day, and in less than a week they disappeared. I have only needed a sip of the tincture every couple of weeks or so to keep them at bay.

Homeopathic Medicine

Homeopathic medicine has likewise regained popularity. Developed in Germany by Dr. Samuel Hahnemann (1755–1843), this practice is based on the principle of "like cures like" — a substance capable of producing certain effects when taken by a healthy person is able to cure an illness that displays similar effects.

Homeopathic remedies are usually derived from various natural sources — plants, minerals, animals, glandular substances taken from animals (called sarcodes), diseased tissue (called nosodes) — or from immaterial substances, such as X-ray, magnet, and luna (a remedy made from moonlight).

Homeopathic remedies are manufactured in a series of dilutions, varying in concentration from the original crude substance (the mother tincture) to a substance that has been diluted a million times. Each potency is 100 times more dilute than the previous one. Often the more dilute a remedy is, the

HOMŒOPATHIC

DOMESTIC MEDICINE

BOERICKE AND TAFEL:

NEW YORK,
No. 145 GRAND STREET.

SAN FRANCISCO,
No. 234 SUTTER STREET

PHILADELPHIA:

F. E. BOERICKE.

1877.

THE CHANGE OR TURN OF LIFE.

The period which is well known by this term, is that at which the menstrual function ceases to be performed. But there is no precise limit to the age at which this may occur. Indeed the final cessation of the menstrual discharge is apt to occur at any period between five or six and thirty, and over sixty years of age. It is usually regulated by the original early or late appearance of the secretion. In the majority of cases, in this country, the cessation occurs between the fortieth and forty-eighth year.

TREATMENT.

The medicines which are generally appropriate for the treatment of the sufferings incidental to the *cessation* of the menstrual discharge are, in the generality of cases, the same as have been enumerated in the foregoing article on "Painful or Difficult Menstruation" (pp. 688–691). The following may, however, be additionally or more especially particularized.

Aconitum is to be employed, if indicated by a general fulness of blood, determination to the head, headache with buzzing in the ears, full, or small and accelerated pulse, sensation of heaviness in the forehead and temples, or sometimes stupefying headache, &c., all of which symptoms are aggravated by motion or by the least exertion.

Dose: Three globules in a teaspoonful of water, repeated after the lapse of six hours, and then (if yet requisite) at intervals of twelve hours, until decided amelioration or change.

Cocculus is doubly indicated by the sensation of nausea, or even by the occasional bilious vomiting which sometimes occurs, as well as by the violent spasmodic and cramp-like pains in the bowels, which are apt to ensue upon the cessation of the menstrual discharge.

Dose: Three globules in a teaspoonful of water, night and morning, until amelioration or change; or, if against severe *spasmodic* pains, at intervals of three hours, until these sufferings are allayed.

In homeopathic medicine, the patient's total symptoms are matched with the descriptions listed in various homeopathic *Materia Medica*, which contain hundreds of remedies, to find the single remedy that matches the patient's symptoms most precisely. Minute amounts of this substance are then used to stimulate the body's self-healing abilities.

Reproduced here is a page from an 1877 *Materia Medica*.

---

more profound its effects. The homeopathic practitioner must not only match the correct remedy to the patient but also choose the most suitable dilution.

Tissue Salts

Tissue salts are combinations of homeopathically prepared minerals that are normally found in healthy human blood and are necessary for cellular survival. A deficiency in any one of the salts can cause disease.

There are 12 tissue salts, and their effect is to balance mineral-related disorders, likely by improving absorption and utilization. The tissue salts are most often produced in a 6X potency, meaning that they have been diluted one part mineral to 10 parts water, in 6 sequential steps.

CASE STUDY: *SYMPTOM FREE*

Sheila came to see us complaining of frequent urinary tract infections and vaginal yeast infections occurring after intercourse, with outbreaks of genital herpes every 6 to 8 weeks, usually occurring before, during, or after her period. These had been afflicting her every couple of months for the past 11 years. She also had 8 days of spotting before her menstrual periods, which were every 28 days.

Sheila noticed constant vivid dreams at night during the week before the full moon. Every spring she experienced allergy symptoms, with burning, watery eyes. She had trouble digesting meat and bread, feeling as though it sat in her stomach, and craved watermelon and sweets. Generally, she felt chilly, with cold hands and feet, but kept her room cool at night because she disliked stuffy rooms.

After cross-checking her symptoms with remedies (a process called repertorization) and consulting the Materia Medica, we recommended taking the homeopathic remedy Thuja 200K, 3 pellets, once weekly for 6 weeks. Sheila's symptoms resolved. No more bladder infections, yeast infections, or genital herpes. She has remained free of these symptoms for 5 years.

HOMEOPATHIC REGIMENS

Classical Homeopathy

A classical homeopath uses only one remedy at a time — matching the totality of symptoms to the remedy — and patiently waits to see the effect. This follows the approach and teaching of Samuel Hahnemann and has very profound healing effects when the right remedy and potency are chosen.

Drainage Therapy

Other practitioners use what is called complex homeopathy, where different remedies in low potency have been blended together for a specific effect. For example, a blend of juniper, asparagus, and *Berberis vulgaris* may be employed daily for several weeks to improve the ability of the kidneys to cleanse the body of toxins. This process is also called drainage therapy.

Pulsed Therapy

Still another way of using homeopathic remedies is in a pulsed fashion several times a day. This technique is more common among French homeopaths. A small group of remedies may be used in sequence throughout the day, usually in low potency, to target a specific area of the body or disease process.

Tissue Salts Actions

- Calcarea fluor — Increases tissue elasticity
- Calcarea phos — Restorative tonic
- Calcarea sulph — Purifies the blood
- Ferrum phos — Improves oxygenation; decreases early inflammation
- Kali mur — Decreases congestion and swelling
- Kali phos — Tonifies the nervous system
- Kali sulph — Clears infection and chronic inflammation
- Magnesia phos — Calms nerves; decreases spasm
- Natrum mur — Distributes water properly
- Natrum phos — Neutralizes excess acid
- Natrum sulph — Eliminates excess water
- Silicea — Discharges pus and foreign material

Hydrotherapy

Hydrotherapy treatments may include alternating hot and cold showers, sitz baths, saunas, hot or cold foot baths, ice packs, steam inhalations, poultices, body wraps, colonic irrigation, and douches. These treatments are curative and restorative. This medical practice also has a long history in the West. The English physician John Floyer published *The History of Hot and Cold Bathing* in 1697, while the American physician Henry Lindlahr wrote a classic book called *Nature Cure* in 1913.

We highly recommend the regular use of saunas to detoxify and rejuvenate the body. Directions for taking saunas are given in the Seasonal Cleansing and Rejuvenation section of this book.

Bodywork

Loosely grouped under the heading of bodywork are the natural medicine practices of osteopathy, physiotherapy and massage therapy. These practices focus on the health of our musculoskeletal system, using manipulation and massage to restore physiological balance.

DID YOU KNOW...

Hydrotherapy has been used historically to treat disease in Egyptian, Babylonian, Assyrian, Persian, Greek, Roman, Hebrew, Hindu, and Chinese cultures.

Osteopathy

Founded by the American physician Andrew Still in the late 19th century, osteopathic medicine emphasizes structural balance of the musculoskeletal system using gentle joint manipulation, postural re-education, cranial-sacral therapy, organ adjustments, physical therapy, massage, and surgery. Distorted or imbalanced skeletal structures, as well as tension or restriction in the muscles, may contribute to other ailments. Corrections in structure and release of tension help to balance physiological function, preventing disease and promoting recovery.

Physiotherapy

Physiotherapy is the treatment of health conditions with physical agents and methods, such as massage, manipulation, exercise, hot and cold applications, electromagnetic frequencies (short-wave, microwave, ultrasound, infrared therapy), hydrotherapy, electrical stimulation, and light to restore normal movement and function after injury or illness. A physiotherapist may assist in resolving muscular pain or sports injuries, in alleviating tendon or ligament problems, in improving recovery after a stroke or hip replacement, in assisting a disabled child in learning to move or walk, or in suggesting exercises to improve posture or performance.

Massage Therapy

Most people are familiar with the benefits of massage therapy in assisting with muscle relaxation, relieving pain and headaches, and creating a feeling of well-being. Massage therapy can also connect us to the feelings and emotions we hold in different parts of our body. Regular massage provides a healthy antidote to accumulated stress.

Mind-Body Medicine

While traditional Ayurvedic and Chinese medicine are based on a holistic concept of the integration of mind, body, and spirit, only in the last decade have Western medical practitioners gained some scientific understanding of how our mental-emotional responses are linked to physical symptoms and ailments.

Therapies that bridge the gap between our thoughts, emotions, and physical body are crucial in establishing health. Some of these therapies include certain types of bodywork (massage, reiki, rolfing, and cranial-sacral therapy); yoga, tai chi, qi qong, and martial arts; meditation; and applied kinesiology (muscle testing) systems, such as TBM (Total Body Modification), NET (Neuroemotional Technique), NAET (Nambudripad Allergy Elimination Technique), and NMT (NeuroModulation Technique).

DID YOU KNOW...

Osteopathy is particularly effective for treating sports injuries, arthritis, chronic tension, pain, and decreased mobility. In many countries, Doctors of Osteopathy (DOs) also provide primary care, conduct minor surgery, and prescribe medications.

THE EMOTIONAL BRAIN

Our emotions affect every part of our body through the changing flow of neuropeptides. Neuropeptides circulate in the cerebrospinal fluid around the brain and spinal cord, as well as in the blood and extracellular fluid. They translate our emotional reality into cellular processes. In other words, our brains 'hear' how our body cells 'feel' through the language of the neuropeptide system, and our cells respond to our thoughts and feelings through the same psychosomatic network.

Receptors (docking stations for neuropeptides) exist throughout the body on the membranes of all types of cells. Neuropeptides attach to receptors and then pass into the cell, entering the nucleus, where they cause precise metabolic shifts, causing cells to divide or to stop dividing, opening and closing ion channels, activating specific genes, adding or subtracting chemical groups. Each of these shifts can change physiology, behavior, and mood.

When negative emotions are unacknowledged or unexpressed, the pattern of neuropeptide release can be disrupted or blocked, which leads to persistent psychosomatic symptoms. However, when emotions are recognized and expressed with fluidity, the neuropeptides flow and change, ever responsive to the shaping hand of our thoughts, feelings, and environment.

Health is linked to emotional responsiveness in the face of changing life circumstances and social interactions. The word "e-motion" tells it all — we need to keep our feelings and energy in motion, rather than locking them in our tissues.

Environmental Medicine

The medical outcome of the anti-nuclear protests and pollution consciousness of the 1960s, environmental medicine is now a comprehensive, proactive, and preventive approach to health care that evaluates, manages, and prevents ailments triggered by environmental toxins. Our bodies continuously adapt to our increasingly toxic environment, sometimes becoming destabilized by stressors in food, water, or air, resulting in symptoms or disease. External stressors can include inhalants, such as dust, mold, pollen and dander; man-made and naturally occurring chemicals; food sensitivities, preservatives, colorings, pesticides, and other items we ingest; infectious organisms; and physical agents, such as radiation, heat, cold, humidity, vibrations, noise, and electromagnetic fields.

Treatment of environmentally triggered illness may include elimination or decreased exposure to the environmental stressors; correction of abnormal nutritional, biochemical, and psychological dysfunctions; dietary changes and supplementation; and therapies that address the immune system.

DID YOU KNOW...

The entire gastrointestinal tract from the esophagus to the large intestine is rich with neuropeptide receptors. We truly do experience 'gut feelings' through these mind-body mechanisms.

Because of the proven deleterious effect of environmental toxins on women's health, we devote an entire section of this book to strategies for preventing, diagnosing, and treating environmental-related illnesses.

Naturopathic Medicine

Naturopathic medical practices encompass diverse natural healing traditions while complementing Western conventional or allopathic medicine. Naturopathic practices are sometimes called complementary and alternative medicine (CAM).

The current practice of naturopathic medicine evolved from alternative healing models developed first in Europe and then introduced to North America during the 19th century, where it was influenced by the herbal medicine of Native Americans. Dr. Benedict Lust founded the first American college of naturopathic medicine in New York City in 1902, while Dr. John Bastyr revived this medical and educational tradition with the founding of the National College of Naturopathic Medicine in 1956 (now located in Portland, Oregon). Subsequently, several other naturopathic colleges have been licensed in North America — Bastyr University (Seattle, Washington), Southwest College of Naturopathic Medicine (Tempe, Arizona), Bridgeport College of Naturopathic Medicine (Bridgeport, Connecticut), and The Canadian College of Naturopathic Medicine (Toronto, Ontario).

NATUROPATHIC MODALITIES

Naturopathic doctors are trained in seven core natural medicine practices or modalities:

- Clinical Nutrition
- Botanical Medicine
- Homeopathic Medicine
- Traditional Asian Medicine (Ayurvedic and Chinese)
- Physical Therapies
- Hydrotherapy
- Lifestyle Counseling

A unique contribution of naturopathic medicine is its focus on clinical nutrition and lifestyle counseling, which are often neglected in conventional medical school training. Naturopathic doctors also cooperate with supportive conventional medical doctors in an effort to create what is now called integrative medicine.

Clinical Nutrition

Clinical nutrition examines the relationship between diet and health. Specific diets are tailored to an individual's needs, and treatment may include nutritional supplements, such as vitamins, minerals, amino acids, essential fatty acids, and enzymes.

We stress the importance of a healthy diet, using food nutrients and nutritional supplements as medicine for preventing and treating health conditions and ensuring lifelong well-being. Good nutrition is the foundation of good health. We devote one section of this book to presenting a healthy diet for women of all ages.

Lifestyle Counseling

A trusting relationship between a health-care practitioner and a patient can be one of the most important components of a healing process. A naturopathic doctor is trained to listen closely to what her patient is saying, to observe body language, to intuit how much of an illness may be psychologically based, and then to address those issues. Stress management tools, such as relaxation, visualization, time management, and assertiveness training, are often used in naturopathic medicine. The underlying psychological or spiritual causes of addictions are addressed. By using mind-body therapies, the naturopathic practitioner can often help women get in touch with buried emotions and release them in order to accelerate healing and transformation. Lifestyle changes recommended include an exercise program, the strength to say "no" more often, regular meditation, journaling, and paying attention to one's dreams to gain insight into what the unconscious is telling us.

Integrative Medical Practice

For many women's health conditions, such as allergies, skin conditions, menstrual irregularities, menopausal symptoms, osteoporosis, benign breast ailments, and vaginal infections, naturopathic medicine is highly successful. Treatments can be curative and restorative, with minimal or no side effects. For other health ailments, like cervical dysplasia, uterine fibroids, and breast or ovarian cancers, naturopathic therapies are best combined with conventional medical treatments.

Many women with serious chronic disease require an interdisciplinary approach to healing — they may need acupuncture to resolve pain, psychotherapy to release trauma, clinical nutrition for dietary advice, medical laboratory science for ongoing diagnostic tests and monitoring, or surgery. Clinics and hospitals now exist where a range of practitioners work side-by-side and refer patients to one another for the best combination of treatments. Yoga and meditation are routinely taught in hospitals, something that would have been a rare event only 10 years ago.

DID YOU KNOW...

Many disorders and diseases are caused in part by nutritional deficiencies, the most celebrated being scurvy, caused by a deficiency of vitamin C, and pellagra, caused by a vitamin B-3 deficiency. While these diseases have been almost eradicated from Western culture through nutrient-rich diets and vitamin supplements, other disorders persist because of nutrient deficiencies and food toxicities.

DID YOU KNOW...

At this time in the history of medicine in Western culture, there is once more a merging of the natural and conventional streams of healing. Not only are women demanding access to both systems and the right to choose the type of treatment they want, they are also asking their caregivers to communicate with one another. Women are leading the way to an integrated health-care system, where, in an atmosphere of mutual respect, teamwork, and open dialog, practitioners and patients can work together with optimal health as our goal.

NATURAL MEDICINE PRINCIPLES & PRACTICES

Regardless of the tradition practiced, natural medicine doctors tend to follow standard principles and practices of care. The following principles comprise the naturopathic doctor's oath.

1. First, do no harm

The physician's challenge is to match the strength and frequency of the treatment to the vitality of the patient while determining the ideal duration of treatment. Carefully selected diets, nutritional supplements, herbs, homeopathic remedies, and even acupuncture rarely cause adverse reactions.

As the make-up of our bodies derives from the soil, food, water, and air in our environment, we can extend this principle to our relationship with the earth. If we did not harm the planet, diseases like asthma and cancer would be much less common because they are exacerbated by environmental toxins.

2. Cooperate with the healing power of nature

Natural medicine practitioners believe that the body has an innate capacity to heal, once the obstacles to healing are removed and the processes of healing are supported. The healing power of nature is heightened when we eat organic food; drink pure water; breathe clean air; balance the minerals in our bodies; spend time outdoors under the sun and the moon; synchronize our biological clocks to the rhythms of nature; take time to relax and exercise; acknowledge our feelings and beliefs; and use natural substances to support any areas of weakness. We also need to adopt an attitude that healing is possible.

The planet is currently in the midst of an environmental crisis. When we remove the obstacles to healing in the global environment, such as greenhouse gasses, hormone-disrupting chemicals, loss of soil nutrients, ionizing radiation contamination, and freshwater depletion, we not only heal ourselves but also our Mother Earth.

3. Address the fundamental causes of health disorders and disease

Most illnesses have several contributing causes. Natural medicine practitioners identify the causes of one woman's illness with a thorough history-taking that looks not only at past illnesses and genetic predispositions, but also at diet and nutrition, thought patterns and emotional traumas, as well as exposure to toxins in the environment and side effects of prescription drugs.

We listen to our patients, to what they are saying, what they are not saying, and what their symptoms are trying to tell us. Symptoms may be a way of communicating deeper unconscious issues that need to be addressed consciously.

4. Treat the whole person with individualized therapies

Health is a state of wellness, balance, and integration of body, mind, and spirit. Natural therapies may address any or all of these areas. Each of us is biochemically and psychologically unique. Natural therapies are individually customized to the needs of each patient.

We can nourish the body with good nutrition and herbal or homeopathic supplementation. We can nourish the mind by developing constructive thought patterns and by feeding our intellectual curiosity. We can nourish the spirit with meditation, prayer, love, service, and joy, creating a life brimming with meaning.

5. Prevent disease

We each have our constitutional weaknesses, determined by family history, mental-emotional factors, environment, and physiology. We attempt to prevent these weaknesses from becoming illnesses by designing supportive programs to decrease the likelihood of disease occurrence. Specific testing and keen observation can identify risk factors before they manifest as illness.

Primary prevention also includes efforts to maintain what is our birthright — pure drinking water, clean air, direct sunlight and moonlight, and nutrient-rich, uncontaminated food. We also need to preserve the natural environments where many of our healing plants are found so we have a steady supply of quality natural medicines.

6. Educate the patient

The natural medicine practitioner plays an important role in teaching patients how to heal themselves. We take the time to explain the causes of illness and to customize prevention and treatment strategies for each patient. We encourage our patients to participate in the creation and restoration of their health and well-being.

Education in the principles and practices of natural medicine extends beyond the individual to the community. We teach how our individual and collective actions affect planetary health. When we respect and protect the earth, we heal ourselves and protect subsequent generations from poor health.

For these educational reasons, we are writing this book. We encourage all women to take an active role in creating, protecting, and restoring their health and well-being — and the health and well-being of all women on our planet, now and for future generations.

Four Steps Toward Optimum Health

To establish optimum health and ensure lifelong well-being, women need to take four steps forward. We present these steps toward this goal now, with brief notes on each step that will be expanded throughout this Complete Natural Medicine Guide to Women's Health. Establishing good health is hard work, restoring health after illness even harder, but the joy of feeling well is its own reward.

If we define health as a state of balanced integration of body, mind, and spirit such that the whole person can actualize her potential, then wellness is a feeling of joyous contentment with this integration.

1. Improve Nutrition

- **Eat a healthy diet.** We are what we eat. Our food should be organic, as close to the way nature made it as possible — unprocessed, non-GMO, and additive-free. Primarily vegetarian is best. Focus on whole grains, legumes, fruits, vegetables, nuts and seeds, with some raw food daily. Limit or avoid dairy foods, meat, and fish because they are high in contaminants.

- **Strengthen digestion.** We are also what we digest. Poor digestion contributes to a toxic colon, which is often where illness begins. Digestion can be strengthened by avoiding food sensitivities, stimulating hydrochloric acid production, supplementing with digestive enzymes and friendly intestinal bacteria, as well as using herbal and homeopathic remedies.

- **Drink plenty of clean water.** Since water comprises 70% of our body weight, we should supply ourselves with the best quality of water possible. The best sources of water are from well-maintained reverse osmosis and carbon block-filtering systems. Aim to drink at least 8 glasses or 2.5 liters or quarts of water daily, taken between meals.

- **Supplement with antioxidants.** Antioxidant supplements will help to neutralize the production of free radicals, slow down the aging process, and decrease your risk of cancer, heart disease, Alzheimer's disease, arthritis, Parkinson's disease, cataracts, glaucoma, and inflammation. Antioxidants include vitamins C and E, beta carotene, zinc, selenium, grape seed extract, coenzyme Q10, alpha lipoic acid, N-acetyl cysteine, and reduced glutathione.

2. Restore Balance

- **Attune yourself to nature's rhythms.** The sun and the moon have powerful effects on our health. Our waking and sleeping cycles and our menstrual cycles are governed by these natural rhythms. When we disrupt these biorhythms, we expose ourselves to health risks. We can restore these rhythms with good nutrition, exercise, and habits that balance hormone levels affected by circadian, ultradian, lunar, menstrual, and breathing rhythms, reducing our risk of osteoporosis, breast cancer, colon cancer, ovarian cancer, multiple sclerosis, and Alzheimer's disease.

- **Balance your estrogen and other hormonal levels.** Imbalance in the level of hormones in the body can lead to estrogen dominance and serious health conditions, including breast cancer, infertility, adrenal exhaustion, and hyperthyroidism or hypothyroidism. We need to improve our nutrition, adjust our lifestyle, and detoxify our bodies to restore and maintain hormonal harmony.

- **Regulate your breath.** Good health is more easily retrieved when we consciously develop long, slow, deep breathing. The breath helps to regulate the pineal and pituitary glands, which synchronize other glands and biorhythms. Conscious breathing can help to dispel anxiety, depression, and fatigue, bring us in touch with our feelings, distribute energy, and decrease acidity in our body.

- **Exercise regularly.** Design an exercise program that you enjoy and can stick to. Include both stretching and aerobic exercises in your program. Aim for a total of 4 hours or more weekly. Walk as often as possible. Use the stairs rather than the elevator. Use more of your own physical energy and less energy derived from technology to decrease your impact on global warming.

- **Balance the pH (acid/alkaline) in your body.** The blood must be maintained at a pH of 7.35. Slight variations in this will cause sickness and death. The body has several mechanisms it uses to keep the blood slightly alkaline. Water intake reduces acidity, as do particular foods, minerals, and breathing techniques.

- **Regulate blood sugar metabolism.** Blood sugar is regulated by the liver, pancreas, and adrenal glands, which are taxed by chronic stress and consumption of sugar, refined carbohydrates, saturated fats, hydrogenated oils, caffeine, and alcohol, resulting in wide fluctuations in blood sugar levels. This can contribute to emotional swings, spaciness, dizziness, headaches, candidiasis, hypoglycemia, diabetes, weight gain, and even cancer. You can correct blood sugar metabolism through diet, relaxation, and supplementation.

- **Eliminate infectious organisms and balance the body's intestinal flora.** Chronic low-grade bacterial and parasitic infections cause inflammation that can lead to systemic diseases, such as arthritis, heart disease, Alzheimer's disease, and cancer. Root canals in your teeth are a common site of bacterial infection and often need to be removed for health improvement. Candidiasis is a prevalent condition because of the overuse of antibiotics and the birth control pill, chlorinated water, and excess consumption of sugar and refined foods. We need to cleanse our bodies of these toxic organisms and restore the balance of our intestinal, oral, and vaginal flora.

- **Maintain an ideal weight.** Since obesity strongly increases the risk of heart disease, diabetes, polycystic ovaries, osteoarthritis, breast cancer, and hypertension, we must include a weight-management program as part of our lifestyle. This will involve a dietary and exercise program most suited to our individual makeup.

- **Balance the body's energy to improve overall vitality.** The body has within it a sophisticated, intelligent network of conduits of energy and information. Blockages or disruptions within this energetic system can be removed through acupuncture, osteopathy, kinesiology, massage, homeopathy, bodywork, breathing practices, and exercises in yoga, qi qong, or tai chi.

- **Strengthen any weak organs or glands.** It is common for a particular organ or gland to be working at less than optimal function at times and at other times to be overfunctioning. Once identified, an imbalanced organ or gland can be helped through specific herbs, nutrients, homeopathy, foods, and exercises.

3. Detoxify and Rejuvenate

- **Remove the obstacles to healing.** These may include overuse of alcohol, sugar, caffeine, tobacco and drugs, exposure to toxic chemicals or metals, side effects of pharmaceutical treatments, harmful electromagnetic fields, radiation exposure, air pollution, exhaustion from overwork, lack of fresh air, sunlight or exercise, improper breathing, poor nutrition, chronic or acute infections, past trauma and repressed feelings, scars blocking the flow of chi, musculoskeletal imbalances, and unhealthy or self-destructive attitudes, emotions, and thought patterns.

- **Purge your body of toxic metals and chemicals.** Toxic metals and chemicals contribute to fatigue, neurological symptoms, hormonal imbalances, learning disabilities, cancer, uterine fibroids, endometriosis, hypothyroidism, PMS, progesterone deficiency and infertility. Ask a health-care professional to assess your personal body burden through hair, urine, or blood tests and implement specific detoxification regimens to remove them.

- **Improve drainage of the liver, kidneys, lymph, lungs, colon, and skin.** The toxic load on our organs has increased with chemicals, toxic metals, pollutants, drugs, and hormones that have infiltrated our soil, water, air, food, and bodies. Sauna therapy, sweat lodges, hydrotherapy, clay baths, breathing techniques, yoga exercises, nutritional supplements, herbs, homeopathic remedies, chelation therapy, and acupuncture can be used to support these organs.

- **Decrease inflammation.** Inflammation can result from toxic overload, chronic infection, food and environmental allergies, an over-acidic diet, nutritional deficiencies, long-term stress, physical overexertion, and poor liver function. Inflammation is a contributing cause in arthritis, fibromyalgia, endometriosis, dysmenorrhea, cancer, heart disease, Alzheimer's disease, and many other ailments. A vegetarian diet, supplemented with generous amounts of turmeric, ginger, flaxseed oil, and fish oil, can prevent and reverse inflammation.

- **Avoid sources of electromagnetic pollution.** Chronic exposure to electromagnetic fields (EMFs), 'dirty power', and radiation can lead to ill health. Places where EMFs are high include radio and cellular telephone towers, high tension power lines and transformers, the stack where wiring enters your house, and offices where electronic equipment (computers, fax machines, photocopiers, printers) is concentrated, and the kitchen microwave oven. We are also exposed to the toxic effects of increased gamma radiation from past nuclear testing, nuclear power plants, nuclear weapons, and missiles or ammunition coated with depleted uranium. Avoid EMFs and lobby for clean power.

- **Decrease stress.** Chronic, inescapable, or unpredictable stress is one of the primary causes of disease, contributing to lowered immunity, digestive difficulties, pain syndromes, inflammation, PMS, menopausal hot flashes, and cancer. Balance the sympathetic (yang) and parasympathetic (yin) nervous system to ensure restful sleep. Minerals, herbs, amino acids, and breathing exercises can balance the nervous system.

4. Integrate Body, Mind and Soul

- **Be aware of your thought patterns and emotions.** Our physical health is informed by our conscious and unconscious thought patterns, past traumas, mental pictures, beliefs, and emotions. These are encoded cellularly throughout the body by neuropeptides, which direct our biochemistry. Work with a psychotherapist or lifestyle counselor to make the unconscious conscious and purge unhealthy thoughts and emotions.

- **Change the vibrational energy in your environment.** We are profoundly affected by the sights, sounds, smells, tastes, and feelings we take in through our senses and by the types of people surrounding us. Surround yourself with uplifting people, music, art, and social environments that promote harmony, happiness, and spiritual contentment. Remove yourself from a career, relationship, or physical environment that generates negativity, causes chronic discomfort, or may be abusive.

- **Acknowledge your soul.** Body, mind, and spirit are intimately linked. A sense of purpose and feeling that you are following your destiny are powerful catalysts to personal healing. Prayer, meditation, yoga, martial arts, creative arts, nature, ceremony, ritual, and spiritual practice develop our connection to and experience of the divine. Create a sacred space in your home to use for personal prayer and meditation and establish regular times for spiritual practice.

- **Make efforts to promote the well-being of the planet.** We can only be as healthy as the air, water, soil, and food that nourish us. Do your part to protect the health of the earth by conserving energy and water, consuming less, composting, recycling, planting trees, and becoming involved in local environmental initiatives.

Looking Ahead

Since nutritious, clean food is fundamental for good health and lifelong well-being, we present a program to improve your nutrition in the next section of this book. Once we take this first step forward, we will be better prepared to take the remaining three steps toward optimum health.

NOTE ON SUPPLIERS:

Most of the nutrient supplements, herbs, homeopathic remedies, Chinese herbal formulas, and specialty products mentioned in the book are available at your local health-food store or naturopathic pharmacy. If not, consult the Resources section at the back of the book for reliable suppliers.

SECTION TWO

Food as Medicine

We are what we eat — and what we digest. A natural foods diet is a key to good health and lifelong well-being, while a nutrient poor diet and food contaminated with environmental toxins can lead to ill health and disease conditions.

Natural, clean food is the ideal way for us to get our daily nutrient supply, but, sadly, much of our food is deficient in nutrients because the soil is impoverished. When we live a fast-paced lifestyle and experience increased stress, we also use vital nutrients more quickly. For these reasons, we may need to take nutrient supplements — vitamins, minerals, amino acids, essential fatty acids, and digestive enzymes — to make up for dietary deficiencies. Supplements are also valuable in treating the conditions and the diseases their very deficiency has caused.

Natural foods and nutrient supplements are both preventive and therapeutic medicine. The study of our nutrient needs and the use of foods and supplements to heal us is called clinical nutrition.

Women's Health Diet

When we examine the dietary strategies that keep us healthy and prevent disease, some consistent principles stand out. The following recommendations are relatively easy to adapt to your daily eating habits, but take your time in doing so. Aim to add one recommendation to your diet per week over a 16-week or 4-month period. If you are more ambitious or if your health is poor, you might want to speed up the adoption process. You will be healthier for doing so.

If you have any concerns about these recommendations, be sure to consult a naturopathic doctor, clinical nutritionist, or registered dietitian. This is not a weight-loss diet but rather a good-health diet. Still, adopting these strategies should result in achieving a healthy natural weight after some time. Beware of fad weight-loss diets, high protein diets, or food restriction diets that may compromise your health.

DID YOU KNOW...

A recent clinical study showed that levels of antioxidants (such as vitamins C and E) and other cancer-fighting compounds were over 50% higher in organically grown food than in conventionally grown food.

Best Dietary Strategies for Optimum Health

❶ Eat Organic

Aim to eat certified organic food whenever possible or grow your own food without using pesticides.

Organic food has fewer hormone-disrupting and cancer-causing pesticides and higher levels of cancer-fighting nutrients. Organic crops contain significantly more vitamin C, iron, magnesium, and phosphorus than their chemically assisted cousins.

When we eat organic food, we promote the continuation of sustainable agriculture and protect our watersheds from pesticide pollution. Israel's breast cancer rate dropped 8% after they banned the use of three pesticides — lindane, DDT and alpha-BHC. Two or three pesticides acting together on our food can have a synergystic estrogenic effect 1000 times greater than either pesticide alone.

② Eat a Primarily Vegetarian Diet

Restrict or avoid consuming meat, poultry, fish, dairy, and eggs. Instead, build a diet around vegetables, fruit, whole grains, legumes, tofu, seaweeds, and a small amount of nuts and seeds.

The vitamins, minerals, fiber, and phytochemicals in vegetables and fruit offer significant protection from cancer, inflammation, and heart disease, particularly when eaten raw, because enzymes and vitamins are destroyed through heating, as are the indoles in the brassica family of foods. Eating lower on the food chain decreases the quantity of environmental chemicals that we ingest. A low-fat, high-fiber vegan diet is best for managing estrogen and insulin — both implicated in breast and uterine ailments.

③ Eat an Alkaline Diet

Monitor the pH of your urine and saliva and adjust your food intake to keep your pH in the range of about 6.8 to 7. Approximately 80% of your dietary intake should be alkaline-forming foods.

Fruits and vegetables increase alkalinity (raise pH), while animal protein and grains (except millet) increase acidity (lower pH). Increased acidity tends to promote fungal growth, accumulation of toxic metals, loss of the alkaline minerals calcium, magnesium, sodium and potassium, and degenerative diseases, including osteoporosis, heart disease, and cancer. An alkaline diet, combined with deep breathing and plenty of water, can create a healthy body pH.

Make vegetables the main part of your meals, with lesser amounts of grains and protein. Add seaweed whenever you can — nori sheets and dulse powder added to soups and other seaweed to salads. These foods are alkaline forming.

Acid and Alkaline Forming Foods and Activities

The following chart lists in descending order the acid- and alkaline-forming foods and activities that affect pH. Foods at the top of the acid group are the most acid-forming. Foods at the beginning of the alkaline group are the most alkalinizing. Aim to eat 20% acid-forming foods and 80% alkaline-forming.

ALKALINE-FORMING FOODS (80% OF DIET) AND ACTIVITIES

FRUITS & VEGETABLES		NUTS & BEANS	OTHER	ACTIVITIES
• Lemon	• Spinach	• Adzuki beans	• Greens+	• Sea salt baths
• Figs	• Kale	• String beans	• Pure Synergy	• Gentle stretching: tai chi, yoga, Qigong
• Apricots	• Carrots	• Tofu	• Barley Green	
• Bananas	• Mushrooms	• Flaxseeds	• Spirulina	
• Pineapple	• Potatoes	• Sunflower seeds	• All sprouts	• Deep breathing
• Strawberries	• Burdock root	• Pumpkin seeds	• Wheatgrass juice	• Massage
• Orange juice	• Cabbage	• Brazil nut	• Egg white	• Meditation
• Grapefruit	• Radish	• Coconut	• Organic milk	• Walking
• Cantelope	• Squash		• Organic yogurt	• Cold showers or baths
• Peaches	• Bamboo shoots		• Apple cider vinegar	• Magnetic field therapy with negative polarity magnets
• Apples	• Sweet potatoes		• Celtic sea salt	
• Cherries	• Endive		• Antioxidants	
• All berries	• Celery		• Sodium bicarbonate	
• Persimmons	• Lettuce		• Stevia	• More dietary fiber
• Pears	• Broccoli		• Cinnamon	• Antioxidants
• Grape juice	• Turnip		• Good water	• Enzymes
• Watermelon	• Dill pickles		• Flaxseed oil	
• Wakame	• Dulse		• Olive oil	
• Kombu	• Swiss chard			
• Ginger	• Pumpkin			
• Raw rhubarb	• Zucchini			
• Kelp	• Cucumbers			
• Irish moss	• Tomatoes			
• Nori	• Eggplant			
• Mustard greens	• Cauliflower			
• Shiitake mushrooms	• Asparagus			
• Maitake mushrooms	• Avocado			
• Reishi mushrooms	• Onions			
	• Soybeans			
	• Tempeh			
	• Almonds			
	• Chestnuts			

Alkalinizing Powder

Ask a compounding pharmacist to make up a blend of 40% potassium bicarbonate, 26% calcium carbonate, 14% magnesium carbonate and 20% sodium bicarbonate. Use $\frac{1}{2}$ tsp in warm water twice daily, away from meals, to balance pH, prevent calcium loss from the bones, and to help prevent absorption of toxic metals.

ACID-FORMING FOODS (20% OF DIET) AND ACTIVITIES

ANIMAL	GRAINS	NUTS & BEANS	OTHER	ACTIVITIES
• Dried squid	• Buckwheat	• Peanuts	• Beer	• Vigorous exercise: jogging, rebounding, dancing, sports
• Dried fish	• Rice bran	• Cashews	• Coffee	
• Egg yolk	• Oatmeal	• Pecans	• Sugar	• Hot showers or baths
• Tuna	• Brown rice	• Walnuts	• Honey	
• Octopus	• Pearl barley	• Black beans	• Maple syrup	• Shallow breathing
• Liver	• Buckwheat flour	• Chick peas	• Alcohol	
• Chicken	• White rice	• Fava beans	• Soft drinks	• Aging
• Carp	• White flour	• Kidney beans	• Chocolate	
• Oysters	• Wheat gluten	• Pinto beans	• White vinegar	
• Veal	• Bread	• Lima beans	• Wine	
• Salmon	• Pasta	• Lentils	• Cranberry juice	
• Clam	• Cornmeal	• Peas	• Fried foods	
• Scallops	• Millet (can be considered alkaline)		• Saturated fats	
• Pork			• Pesticides	
• Beef			• Chemicals, drugs	
• Cheese			• Free radical damage	
• Abalone				
• Shrimp				
• Whole egg				
• Butter				

④ Eat Low-Glycemic Carbohydrates

Aim to eat low to medium glycemic index carbohydrates. Become familiar with the glycemic index of carbohydrates and choose those that do not sharply elevate insulin and blood sugar levels.

When we eat carbohydrates, they are broken down into glucose, a form of sugar that provides energy to our cells. However, certain carbohydrates sharply raise blood sugar levels after we eat them, which elevates insulin, increasing the risk of diabetes, heart disease, and cancer.

The degree to which a carbohydrate raises blood sugar 2 to 3 hours after eating is called its glycemic index and has been measured for different foods. A diet high in carbohydrates with a high glycemic index will cause consistently high blood levels of the hormones insulin and insulin-like growth factor (IGF-1), which lead to increased fat deposition and promotion of breast and uterine cell growth, predisposing us to cysts, fibroids, and cancer. When carbohydrates are combined with fiber, protein, or flaxseed oil in the same meal, the glycemic index is lowered.

GLYCEMIC INDEX OF COMMON FOODS

LOW GLYCEMIC INDEX (7–45)		MEDIUM GLYCEMIC INDEX (46–60)		HIGH GLYCEMIC INDEX (61–115)	
GRAINS & PASTA					
Burgen soy lin bread	19	Macaroni	46	Rye bread	64
Pearl barley	25	Linguini	46	Semolina bread	64
Rice bran	27	Bulgur	47	Couscous	65
Chickpea flour chapati	27	Red River Cereal	49	Rolled barley	66
Fettucine	32	Pumpernickel bread	50	Crackers	67
Vermicelli	35	Cracked barley	50	Gnocchi	67
Spaghetti	6	Special K	54	Taco shells	68
Whole rye	37	Corn	55	Cornmeal	69
Barley kernel bread	39	Brown rice	55	Melba toast	70
Wheat bran	42	Oatbran	55	Cream of Wheat	70
Barley chapati	43	Buckwheat	55	Shredded Wheat	70
		Linseed rye bread	55	White flour products	71
		Popcorn	55	English muffins	71
		Muesli	56	Millet	71
		Wild rice	57	White bagels	72
		Pita bread, white	57	Puffed Wheat	74
		White rice	58	Cheerios	74
		Rice vermicelli	58	Puffed cereals	74
		Oatmeal	60	Rice cakes	77
				Rice Krispies	82
				Corn chips/Cornflakes	83
				Brown rice pasta	92
				French baguette	95
BEANS					
Chana daal	8	Romano beans	46	Broad beans (fava)	79
Soybeans	17	Baked beans	48		
Red lentils	25				
Kidney beans	29				
Green lentils	29				
Butter beans	30				
Black beans	31				
Chickpeas	33				
Navy beans	38				
Mung beans	38				
Pinto beans	38				
Black-eyed beans	41				

GLYCEMIC INDEX OF COMMON FOODS

LOW GLYCEMIC INDEX (7–45)		MEDIUM GLYCEMIC INDEX (46–60)		HIGH GLYCEMIC INDEX (61–115)	
PROTEIN					
Plain yogurt	14			Ice cream	61
Nuts	15				
Skim milk	32				
FRUIT					
Cherries	22	Canned peaches	47	Raisins	64
Grapefruit	25	Orange juice	52	Pineapple	66
Dried apricot	31	Kiwi	53	Dried fruit	70
Pear	37	Banana	54	Watermelon	72
Plum	38	Mango	56		
Apple	38	Blueberry	57		
Peach	42				
Orange	44				
VEGETABLES					
Peas	<15	Raw carrots	49	Beets	64
Green beans	<15	Yams	51	Mashed potatoes	70
Tomato	<15	Sweet potatoes	54	Rutabaga	72
Brassica family	<15	White potatoes, boiled	56	French fries	75
Sea vegetables	<15			Pumpkin	75
Herbs	<15			Cooked carrots	85
Powdered greens	<15			Parsnips	98
Green vegetables	<15				
OTHER					
Fructose	22	Lactose	46	Sucrose	65
Stevia	N/A	Chocolate	49	Soft drinks	68
Licorice root	N/A	Honey	58	Glucose	100
				Maltose	105
				Alcohol	>100

Glycemic Index of Common Foods

Glycemic index numbers refer to how fast the carbohydrate of a particular food is converted to glucose and enters the bloodstream, compared to the action of glucose itself. For example, legumes, pearl barley, and bran have a low glycemic index, while white rice, corn, and potatoes have a high glycemic index.

On the scale, pure glucose equals 100, so anything above 100 raises blood sugar faster than glucose, and any food below 100 does it that much slower.

(Most of these values are extrapolated from the book *The G.I. Factor: The Glycaemic Index Solution* by Dr. Jennie Brand Miller, Kaye Foster-Powell, and Stephen Colagiuri.)

⑤ Eat High-Fiber Foods

Aim to consume 45 to 60 grams (1½–2 ounces) of dietary fiber daily, using beans, bran, psyllium, ground flaxseed, raw fruits and vegetables, and whole grains to do so. This is equivalent, for example, to the combination of 1 cup of beans, 2 tbsp ground flaxseed, 1 tbsp psyllium, 6 servings of fruits and vegetables, and 2 servings of whole grain. Minimize white flour products, such as bread, baked goods, and pasta.

Fiber is present in legumes, bran, psyllium, fruits and vegetables, grains, nuts, and seeds.

A high fiber diet has a lower content of fat and a higher content of antioxidant vitamins, which slow down the aging process and protect us from cancer. Diets high in fiber and complex carbohydrates stabilize blood sugar, lower cholesterol, decrease heart disease risk, and improve insulin sensitivity, which is associated with a drop in circulating estrogen.

A high-fiber diet modifies the composition of flora in the bowel, promoting more of the good bacteria that create a strong immune system, improve mineral absorption, and decrease osteoporosis risk. Fiber speeds up elimination and decreases toxicity, while improving bowel disorders, such as irritable bowel syndrome and colitis.

HIGH-FIBER MENU SUGGESTIONS

◕ Breakfast

You can create a high-fiber diet by eating a cooked cereal for breakfast, such as oatmeal, quinoa, buckwheat, amaranth, rye flakes, seven-grain, or millet meal, with added oat bran and freshly ground flaxseeds. Psyllium can be taken in powdered or capsule form for additional benefit and bowel cleansing.

◕ Lunch and Dinner

Grains that can be included in lunch or dinner are brown or basmati rice, wild rice, millet, quinoa, buckwheat, barley, and kamut. Because wheat (other than the bran variety) and corn are common food allergens, they should be eaten infrequently, perhaps once weekly, or not at all. However, wheat bran, if tolerated, can lower estrogen and detoxify mercury excess. Beans are a wonderful source of fiber and can be consumed daily in soups, spreads, or grain dishes.

Health Tip Worksheet

Evaluating the Fiber Content of Your Diet

Using the following chart, estimate what your daily fiber intake has been each day over the last 3 days. My average daily fiber intake is: _____ grams or ounces. How close do you come to 45 grams or $1\frac{1}{2}$ ounces?

FIBER CONTENT OF YOUR DIET

GRAMS/OZ FIBER	FOOD ITEM	*Day 1*	*Day 2*	*Day 3*
15 g / 0.53 oz	1 cup kidney beans			
10 g / 0.35 oz	$\frac{1}{2}$ cup wheat or oat bran			
10 g / 0.35 oz	$2\frac{1}{2}$ tbsp psyllium			
10 g / 0.35 oz	1 cup split peas			
10 g / 0.35 oz	$1\frac{1}{4}$ cup lentils			
10 g / 0.35 oz	$\frac{3}{4}$ cup navy beans			
10 g / 0.35 oz	$\frac{1}{4}$ cup ground flaxseed			
5 g / 0.18 oz	$\frac{1}{2}$ cup cooked dried beans, peas, or lentils			
5 g / 0.18 oz	1 serving of a high fiber wheat bran cereal			
2 g / 0.07 oz	1 serving of a fruit or vegetable			
2 g / 0.07 oz	1 serving of any whole grain food			
2 g / 0.07 oz	1 cup oatmeal			
2 g / 0.07 oz	1 slice of whole-grain bread			
2 g / 0.07 oz	$\frac{1}{2}$ cup whole-grain pasta			
2 g / 0.07 oz	$\frac{1}{2}$ whole-grain bagel			
2 g / 0.07 oz	1 slice rye crisp cracker			
2 g / 0.07 oz	$\frac{1}{2}$ cup cooked brown rice			
1 g / 0.035 oz	1 serving of refined grain			
1 g / 0.035 oz	10 almonds			
1 g / 0.035 oz	20 filberts			
		Total:	Total:	Total:
		3-day Average:		

⑥ Eat at Least 8 Servings of Fruits and Vegetables Daily

Fruits and vegetables contain vitamins, minerals, and phytochemicals that prevent heart disease and cancer. One serving is equal to ½ cup of vegetables or 1 cup of salad or one large piece of fruit.

Particularly good vegetable choices are those in the brassica family (cabbage, broccoli, kale), as well as onions, garlic, leeks, sprouts, and sea vegetables. These should be consumed daily. Foods high in beta carotene are protective and include orange fruits and vegetables and leafy greens. These foods are also rich in phytochemicals, which are highly protective against health disorders and diseases.

Phytochemical Sources
The following chart lists many of the protective phytochemicals present in fruits, vegetables, and other foods.

PHYTOCHEMICAL SOURCES AND HEALTH VALUES

PHYTOCHEMICAL	EFFECT	FOOD SOURCES
ALLYL SULFIDES	Increases liver enzymes to detoxify carcinogens	Garlic, onions, leeks
CAPSAICIN	Prevents carcinogens from binding to DNA	Chili peppers
CAROTENOIDS	Act as antioxidants that neutralize free radicals, enhance immunity High intake is associated with low cancer rates	Parsley, carrots, spinach, kale, winter squash, apricots, cantaloupe, sweet potatoes
FLAVONOIDS	Prevent the attachment of cancer-causing hormones to cells by blocking receptor site	Most fruits and vegetables, including parsley, carrots, citrus, broccoli, cabbage, cucumbers, squash, yams, eggplant, peppers, berries
CURCUMIN	Decreases inflammation Assists the liver in detoxifying carcinogens and hormones Arrests cell division in cancer cells	Turmeric
ELLAGIC ACID	Neutralizes carcinogens in the liver Antioxidant Inhibits cancer cell divisions	Red raspberries, walnut skin
ISOFLAVONES *(genistein and daidzen)*	Bind to the estrogen receptor so that harmful estrogens can't bind Block the formation of blood vessels to tumors	Soybeans, tofu, miso, lentils, dried beans, split peas, garbanzo beans, green beans, green peas, mung bean sprouts, red clover sprouts

PHYTOCHEMICAL SOURCES AND HEALTH VALUES

PHYTOCHEMICAL	EFFECT	FOOD SOURCES
ISOFLAVONES *(continued)*	Inhibit enzymes that might cause cancer Inhibit activation of breast cancer genes Lower cholesterol	
INDOLES	Decrease the estrogen that initiates breast cancer	Raw cabbage, broccoli, Brussels sprouts, kale, cauliflower, bok choy, kohlrabi, mustard, turnips
ISOTHIOCYANATES	Prevent DNA damage Block the production of tumors induced by environmental chemicals Act as antioxidants Assist liver detoxification	Mustard, horseradish, radishes, turnips, cabbage, broccoli, cauliflower, Brussels sprouts, kale, bok choy, watercress, garden sorrel
LIMONOIDS	Induce protective enzymes in liver and intestines that fight cancer	Citrus fruit rind, essential oils of lemon, orange, celery, lemongrass
LINOLENIC ACID	Regulates production of prostaglandins in cells	Flaxseeds and flaxseed oil
LYCOPENE	Protects from cell damage	Tomatoes, red grapefruit, guava
LUTEIN	Protects against cell damage	Spinach, kiwi, tomato, grapes
MONOTERPENES	Antioxidant properties Induce protective enzymes Inhibit cholesterol production in tumors Stimulate the destruction of breast cancer cells Inhibit growth of cancer cells	Cherries, lavender, parsley, yams, carrots, broccoli, cabbage, basil cucumbers, peppers, squash, eggplant, mint, tomatoes, grapefruit
PHENOLIC ACIDS	Block the effects of free radicals Inhibit the formation of nitrosamine, a carcinogen	Berries, broccoli, grapes, citrus, parsley, peppers, soy, squash, tomatoes, grains
PLANT STEROLS *(beta-sitosterol)*	Prevent cells from becoming cancerous and lower cholesterol levels in the body	Broccoli, cabbage, soy, peppers, whole grains
POLYPHENOLS	Act as antioxidants Reduce damaging effects of nitrosamines Kill human cancer cells	Broccoli, carrots, green tea, cucumbers, squash, mint, basil, citrus
PROTEASE INHIBITORS	Block the activity of enzymes involved in the growth of tumors	Beans and soy products

PHYTOCHEMICAL SOURCES AND HEALTH VALUES

PHYTOCHEMICAL	EFFECT	FOOD SOURCES
QUERCETIN	Slows down cell division in cancer cells Anti-inflammatory	Onions, apples, green cabbage
QUINONES	Neutralize carcinogens	Rosemary, pau d'arco tea
SULFORAPHANE	Increases the ability of the liver's detoxifying enzymes to remove carcinogens Antioxidant	Broccoli sprouts, broccoli, cauliflower, Brussels sprouts

⑦ Consume Approximately 40 Grams of Protein Daily

Choose primarily vegetarian rather than animal sources of protein. Fish, beef, veal, lamb, pork, and eggs, even if they are organic, often contain high concentrations of toxins, which are a contributing factor to many women's health conditions.

DID YOU KNOW...

Fish are the most contaminated of the animal protein sources. Dioxins, which are extremely carcinogenic, have been found in the bodies of fish at concentrations 159,000 times higher than the water they swim in. Similarly, a 10,000 times greater concentration of PCBs is found in fish tissues than in their surrounding waters.

VEGETARIAN SOURCES OF PROTEIN

SOY FOOD	PROTEIN CONTENT (GRAMS)	QUANTITY REQUIRED
Miso	5.9	½ cup
Tofu, silken	8.1	½ cup
Tofu, firm	15.6	½ cup
Soybeans, boiled	16.6	½ cup
Soybeans, dry-roasted	39.6	½ cup
Soy milk	5.6	1 cup
Tempeh	19.0	½ cup
Soy protein powder	58.1	1 oz
Kidney beans	15	1 cup, cooked
Lentils	16	1 cup, cooked
Split peas	17	1 cup, cooked
Chickpeas	14.5	1 cup, cooked
Almond butter	5	2 tbsp
Almonds	2.8	12
Sunflower seeds	6.5	1 oz
Pumpkin seeds	7	1 oz (142 seeds)
Sesame seed butter	2.6	1 tbsp

Protein should be sufficient but not excessive to prevent cancer and needs to be combined with quality oils for optimum health. The average adult requires approximately 30 to 50 grams per day. Adequate vegetarian protein would include 2 to 3 servings a day of either 1 cup of cooked legumes, ½ cup tofu, 1 cup of soy milk, 1 tbsp nut butter, or 2 tbsp of nuts or seeds. Protein-rich legumes include kidney beans, soybeans, chickpeas, split peas, and lentils.

8 Avoid Food-Borne Toxins

Foods high in PCBs, dioxin, brominated fire retardants (PBDEs), and heavy metals contribute to learning disabilities, hypothyroidism, estrogen dominance, low progesterone, hormone imbalance, immune dysregulation, cancer, endometriosis, uterine fibroids, osteoporosis, and heart disease.

Dietary mercury is primarily found in king mackerel, shark, swordfish, grouper, tuna, saltwater bass, bluefish, halibut, lobster, orange roughy, and marlin. Of several types of fish tested, farmed salmon was the most contaminated with PCBs and PBDEs. PCBs, dioxin, and PBDEs are not found in significant amounts in vegetables and fruit.

These foods should be avoided to prevent and reverse breast cysts and breast cancer, uterine fibroids and uterine cancer, endometriosis, thyroid imbalance, PMS, ovarian cysts and ovarian cancer, and Alzheimer's disease.

9 Eat Soy and Other Phytoestrogens Daily

As long as you are not allergic to it, each day eat either ½ cup of firm tofu or tempeh and drink 1 cup soy milk, or consume a combination of soy foods, aiming for 25 g of soy protein daily and at least 65 mg of isoflavones. Also use 2 to 4 tbsp ground flaxseed and 2 tbsp pumpkin seeds daily. Eat red clover and mung bean sprouts weekly.

Phytoestrogens are weak estrogens that bind to receptor sites for estrogen, displacing the body's strong estrogens and environmental estrogens. We need a constant supply of them throughout the day to prevent diseases linked to excess estrogen. Beans, especially when sprouted, contain protective phytoestrogens in smaller amounts. Soy contains higher levels.

Soy foods help to prevent breast cancer and heart disease. Short-term exposure to dietary isoflavones found in soy is especially beneficial for newborns and girls who have not yet reached puberty. This early exposure may decrease risk of breast cancer caused by carcinogens later in life. Introduce your children to moderate but not extreme amounts of soy products when they are young, with higher amounts before and through puberty.

DID YOU KNOW...

High-protein diets that encourage weight loss may promote cancer by causing excess acidity. Excess protein obstructs the transportation of oxygen, which favors formation of cancer cell colonies. During the breakdown of amino acids in high animal protein diets by intestinal bacteria, toxins produced in the colon are linked to increased colon cancer risk. High-protein diets also cause more calcium to be pulled from our bones, promoting osteoporosis and a deficiency of alkaline minerals.

DID YOU KNOW...

The foods highest in total amounts of PCBs, dioxin, PBDEs, aluminum, cadmium, and lead, in decreasing order, are shellfish, freshwater fish, pizza, butter, hamburger, saltwater fish, cold cuts, wieners, ice cream, canned fish, ground beef, French fries, veal, processed cheese, lamb, organ meat, beef steak, evaporated milk, cheddar cheese, poultry, yogurt, eggs, pork, and whole milk.

FOOD-BORNE TOXINS

FOOD	PCB *pg/g*	DIOXIN *pg/g*	PBDE *ppt*	ALUMINUM *ng/g*	CADMIUM *ng/g*	LEAD *ng/g*	TOTALS
DAIRY FOODS							
Whole milk	98.1	0.057	3.39	109.7	2.04	1.68	215
2% milk	45.3	0.049	0.11	74.12	1.92	1.74	123
1% milk	26.1	0.024	0.15	97.4	1.49	0.8	125
Skim milk	9.4	0.007	0.01	64.6	2.21	0.83	77
Evap. milk	68.9	0.061	0.02	1144	4.33	2.56	1219
Cream	148.1	0.157	20.81	266	1.73	0.6	438
Ice cream	131.5	0.135	18.35	2878	7.31	7.5	3077
Yogurt	42.3	0.024	8.47	272	2.08	1.85	707
Cheddar cheese	405.5	0.424	94.9	553	2.76	14.2	1070
Cottage cheese	38.6	0.047	0.5	513	2.76	2.84	558
Processed cheese	337.6	0.23	81.4	1428	5.08	9.73	1862
Butter	842.9	1.108	264.5	5689	15.13	14.1	6827
MEAT AND FISH							
Beef steak	139.2	0.107	46.2	1250	4.47	8.12	1448
Beef roast	334.2	0.11	25.3	528	8.82	8.09	905
Ground beef	296	0.463	120.8	1711	24.67	23.3	2176
Pork	96	0.017	40.8	279	4.94	3.38	424
Veal	67.5	0.075	205.7	1593	2.4	3.42	1872
Lamb	184.2	0.093	39.6	1319	4.06	16.2	1563
Cold cuts	219	0.089	217.4	5404	7.89	13.6	5861
Organ meat	145.4	0.229	19.2	1201	142.4	35.3	1544
Wieners	277.1	0.234	163.2	2826	12.1	9.47	3288
Eggs	363.4	0.067	79.6	206	6.17	0.51	656
Poultry	93.2	0.064	37.7	886	4.29	2.36	1024
Marine fish	4208	0.032	1165	846	3.38	12.8	6235
Freshwater fish	7210	0.599	1462	397	4.08	6.58	9080
Canned fish	1563	0.118	36.3	791	12.21	2.68	2405
Shell fish	245	0.076	58	9225	15.27	20.7	9564
Meat soup	8.7	0.009	5.5	152	3.29	4.01	174
OTHER FOODS							
Cooking fat	13.2	0.262	121.4	0	89	23.9	248
Margarine	19.9	0.092	4.4	0	49	23.5	97
Pizza	161.5	0.097	274.9	8167	26	13.1	8642
French fries	107.5	0.025	35.6	1712	64	5.19	1924
Hamburger	134.2	0.119	58.5	6446	21	5.24	6665

CALORIE, PROTEIN, ISOFLAVONE, AND FAT CONTENT OF SOY FOODS

SOY FOOD	CALORIES (KCAL)	PROTEIN (GRAMS)	ISOFLAVONES (MG)	FAT (GRAMS)
½ cup soybeans	149	14.3	70	7.7
½ cup tempeh	165	15.7	60	6.0
¼ cup soy nuts	202	15	60	10.9
½ cup tofu	94	10	38	5.9
¼ cup soy flour	81.7	12.8	25	0.3
½ cup soy milk	79	6.6	10	4.6
½ cup texturized soy protein	59	11	28	0.2

Soy Allergies

Soy is a relatively common food allergy. Reactions to soy include fatigue, bloating, and gas. If you notice these symptoms, avoid or limit your exposure to soy.

Thyroid Function

Soy needs to be eaten with seaweed. The phytoestrogens found in soy (genistein and daidzen) block an enzyme (thyroid peroxidase) that is responsible for attaching iodide ions to the amino acid tyrosine to form the thyroid hormones T4 and T3. Instead, the iodide ions attach to either genistein or daidzen, causing a deficit of thyroid hormones. When fed soy formula without the addition of iodine or seaweeds, infants are more likely to develop autoimmune thyroid disease later in life.

When iodide is added to the diet along with soy, this effect on the thyroid is diminished substantially or eliminated. We need to incorporate sea vegetables in our diets or take a kelp supplement regularly to offset the potential of soy and the raw brassicas for interfering with thyroid function. If soy formulas are given to infants, then the formula should also contain small amounts of iodine or seaweed, such as kombu. The thyroid effects of soy can be monitored by testing thyroid function through blood tests and by tracking body temperature.

Soy and the Menstrual Cycle

Breast cancer risk is, in part, linked to the total estrogen exposure and the cumulative number of menstrual cycles a woman experiences in her lifetime. Because of their higher consumption of soy foods, Japanese women have an average menstrual cycle length of 32 days as opposed to 28 to 29 days for North American women. Japanese women have fewer menstrual cycles over their life span than North American women, have lower levels of estradiol overall, and are less likely to be diagnosed with breast cancer.

Soy Summary

While soy is an extremely beneficial food in breast cancer prevention and treatment, it may not be suitable for everyone.

⑩ Avoid Sugar and Limit Sweeteners

Included in this category of restricted foods are sweeteners, such as honey, maple syrup, and rice syrup, soft drinks, juice-flavored drinks, powdered instant drinks, canned juices, candy, chocolate bars, granola bars, chocolate, donuts, and cookies. Limit sweets to a treat perhaps once weekly. Instead use fruit, stevia, frozen fruit desserts, and sugar-free natural fruit jams. Dilute your natural fruit juices with water.

When we consume sweets, a type of white blood cell called the phagocyte decreases its numbers within 30 minutes. This decline lasts for over 5 hours, with a 50% reduction in phagocytes approximately 2 hours after ingestion, leading to a poorly functioning immune system.

Sweets will also promote an overgrowth of yeast and parasites in the intestinal tract and increase the likelihood of dental caries. Sweets can elevate blood glucose, insulin, and IGF-1, predisposing us to obesity, polycystic ovary syndrome, insulin insensitivity, or metabolic syndrome, diabetes, breast cancer, and cardiovascular disease. Excess sugar creates acidity, making us more susceptible to osteoporosis.

⑪ Avoid Saturated Fats, Most Vegetable Oils, and Hydrogenated Oils

Instead, use unheated flaxseed oil, uncontaminated fish oil, and extra virgin olive oil. If you are in good health, consume 1 to 2 tbsp of flaxseed oil daily, along with at least 2 tbsp of ground flaxseeds. Also use fish oil capsules (2000 to 3000 mg daily), but be sure they are free of contaminants. Buy refrigerated flax oil and use it within 6 weeks. Consume small amounts of omega-6 oils in the form of raw unsalted nuts and seeds (1 to 2 tablespoons daily) or use borage or evening primrose oil (1000 mg daily).

Saturated fats, found in meat, butter, animal products, coconut oil, and peanut oil, increase cancer and heart disease risk, as do hydrogenated and partially hydrogenated fats, which are found in cookies, crackers, margarine, and processed foods.

However, two groups of fats are essential for life. These essential fatty acids maintain the integrity of the cell membrane, making it less vulnerable to carcinogenic substances. Essential fatty acids help transport oxygen from the air in the lungs to each cell membrane in the body, where the oxygen acts as a barrier to viruses, bacteria, parasites, and cancer. Essential fatty acids are found around the DNA, where they regulate chromosome stability, preventing damage from radiation and

chemical toxicity. They are required in cell membrane formation, are essential in the health of the immune system, and help to buffer excess acid in the body

Omega-3 fatty acids, found primarily in flaxseed oil, purslane, black currant seed oil, and cold water fish oils, decrease inflammation, pain, and arthritis; reduce PMS and symptoms of endometriosis; improve mental function and memory; help to prevent diabetes; decrease heart disease risk; and protect us from most cancers.

Omega-6 fatty acids found in vegetable oils and evening primrose oil will promote breast cancer if not balanced with at least twice as much omega-3 oil. Olive oil is neutral, and can be consumed liberally as long as it does not cause weight gain.

⑫ Limit Dairy Foods (Milk, Cheese, Butter)

Although dairy products are high in calcium, they are reservoirs of environmental toxins and are difficult to digest. Many people's immune systems are stressed by them. A small amount of low-fat yogurt (toxins are found in fat) and goat cheese is acceptable, as long as you are not allergic to it.

Cows are treated with hormones and antibiotics and are fed grains that may have been sprayed with pesticides. These toxins accumulate in the fat of the cow over its life span and are discharged into its milk. Homogenized milk also contains the enzyme xanthine oxidase, which damages epithelial cells of blood vessels, contributing to cardiovascular disease.

Our bodies can react to dairy products by producing both inflammation and excess mucus or dampness. Inflammation can cause inflammatory bowel disease, joint problems, heart disease, and Alzheimer's disease, as well as accelerated cancer growth. Dampness accumulates in particular areas and can be linked to certain conditions. In the eustachian tubes, it leads to chronic ear infections; in the sinuses, sinusitis. In the lungs, it contributes to asthma. And in the breasts, uterus, or ovaries, it may cause tumor formation.

⑬ Limit or Avoid Alcohol Use

Drink less than two to three alcoholic beverages weekly.

Alcohol use causes a woman to be more susceptible to breast cancer. A weekly intake of four to seven drinks or more will increase risk. In one study, the risk increase was 250% for women who drank two or more drinks daily. Women who have even one drink a day have an 11% higher risk of breast cancer.

DID YOU KNOW...

Several studies have shown a link between dairy consumption and cancer risk, including two Harvard University studies of milk from hormone-treated cows. The Physicians' Health Study and the Nurses' Health Study found that insulin-like growth factor 1 (IGF-1), a protein that is elevated in the milk of cows treated with bovine growth hormone, increases risk of both breast cancer and prostate cancer. North Americans, in particular, should avoid dairy products because of the presence of bovine growth hormone.

Alcohol may interfere with the liver's ability to detoxify both chemicals and excess estrogen in the body. Moderate consumption of alcohol increases blood glucose levels and the production of insulin and IGF-1, which increase risk of adult onset diabetes and promote the development and/or growth of breast cancer and uterine fibroids.

14 Avoid Known Food Sensitivities

Suspect a food sensitivity if you have strong cravings or are experiencing an addiction to a particular food. The most common food sensitivities are to dairy, wheat, yeast, sugar, chocolate, corn, soy, eggs, beef, pork, citrus, tomatoes, peanuts, other nuts, shellfish, strawberries, and gluten (found in wheat, rye, oats, barley, spelt, and kamut), as well as individualized foods. Many people also react to pesticides, food colorings, and food preservatives.

Foods sensitivities trigger IgE or IgG antibody reactions that result in a variety of symptoms. IgE reactions are immediate and severe and may cause rashes, difficulty breathing, fainting, or anaphylactic shock. IgG reactions are delayed and may appear an hour or several days after eating an offending food. They are, therefore, difficult to detect. See the Seasonal Cleansing and Rejuvenation Program section of this book for ways to test for food sensitivities.

15 Eat 'Super' Foods

As often as possible, eat the following 'super' foods to maintain health and prevent many women's ailments. Together, they also prevent inflammation, lower cholesterol, and aid in cancer prevention.

Be sure to include in your 'super food' diet plenty of pure water. Water is needed to allow the kidneys to excrete toxins on a regular basis and to keep the body alkaline. Drink 2 liters or quarts of pure water daily.

SUPER FOOD HEALTH EFFECTS

SUPER FOOD	GOOD HEALTH EFFECTS
FLAXSEED *2 tbsp freshly ground flaxseeds daily*	High fiber for increasing bowel movements and cleansing the colon Contain phytoestrogens to prevent breast cancer and alleviate menopausal hot flashes A complete protein
FLAXSEED OIL OR UNCONTAMINATED FISH OIL *2 tbsp daily uncooked (keep refrigerated)*	High in omega-3 essential fatty acids to help prevent cancer, arthritis, heart disease, depression, skin affections, and Alzheimer's disease Keeps your cell membranes strong
TURMERIC *2 tsp or more daily*	One of the best anti-inflammatories to alleviate arthritic symptoms Decreases the risk of most cancers and helps to prevent Alzheimer's disease Assists in liver detoxification
GARLIC *2 cloves daily*	Natural antibiotic and anti-parasitic Lowers cholesterol and blood pressure, preventing heart disease Helps to prevent many types of cancer Assists in liver detoxification
RAW NUTS AND SEEDS *2–4 tbsp daily*	High in zinc and magnesium, which are common mineral deficiencies linked to lowered immune function, anxiety, and heart disease Pumpkin seeds are anti-parasitic
SEAWEEDS *2 tbsp daily*	Good vegetarian sources of calcium and iron Nori, dulse, hiziki, arame, and kombu are highly alkaline, rich in minerals, and high in beta carotene Brown seaweeds, like kelp, help to pull radioactive particles out of the body so they can be excreted
ORGANIC SOY (NON-GMO) *25 grams daily*	Helps to lower cholesterol and blood pressure Helps to prevent breast and uterine cancers Eat with seaweeds as a source of iodine Avoid if allergic
RAW BRASSICAS *½ cup or more daily*	Cabbage, cauliflower, broccoli, kale assist the liver in detoxification pathways, improve estrogen metabolism, and help to prevent breast and uterine cancer when eaten raw Raw cabbage juice heals stomach and duodenal ulcers
SHIITAKE MUSHROOMS *3–4 times daily*	Enhance the immune system and help prevent cancer

SUPER FOOD HEALTH EFFECTS

SUPER FOOD	GOOD HEALTH EFFECTS
BLUEBERRIES, RASPBERRIES, STRAWBERRIES *½ cup or more daily*	High in antioxidants that help to prevent cancer and improve vision
COOKED TOMATOES *weekly*	High in lycopene, an antioxidant that helps prevent breast, lung and cervical cancer
EXTRA VIRGIN OLIVE OIL *1–2 tbsp daily*	Moves the bile through the liver and gallbladder, facilitating the removal of toxins
LEGUMES *½ cup or more daily*	Contain high amounts of potassium and magnesium Low glycemic index Contain phytic acid, which helps to prevent the growth of cancer
ROSEMARY AND CORIANDER *several times a week*	Rosemary facilitates liver detoxification of hormones and chemicals Coriander helps to remove toxic metals, such as mercury, cadmium and lead
ORGANIC GREEN TEA *2 or more cups daily*	Stimulates metabolism to assist in weight loss Helps to prevent cancer

16 Tune Your Diet to the Seasons

Using the guidelines in the Seasonal Cleansing and Rejuvenation Program section, choose foods that are appropriate for each season and that help with detoxification and rejuvenation of the organs associated with that season.

In this way, you will effectively cleanse and rebuild your body throughout the year and live more harmoniously with the cycles of nature. Developing seasonal rhythms for nutrition and for detoxification are effective ways of creating good health and lifelong well-being.

Meal Plans

If you were successful in adopting most of these Best Dietary Strategies for Optimum Health, here is what your daily diet might look like. Eat every 2 hours to normalize the adrenal glands and thyroid, to keep blood sugar and insulin levels stable, and to decrease cravings.

MEAL PLAN

ON RISING	• Green drink: either 1–3 tsp Greens+, Pure Synergy, Barley Green, spirulina or other green powder in water • Or: 1–3 oz of wheatgrass juice • Followed by two glasses filtered or spring water, with a little lemon or lime juice added, plus a pinch of cayenne pepper
BREAKFAST	• 1 cup whole grain cereal (use barley, oatmeal, buckwheat, quinoa, millet meal, amaranth, brown rice) with 2–3 tbsp freshly ground flaxseeds, 3 tbsp oat bran, 1 tsp psyllium, 1 tbsp wheat bran (if tolerated), small amount of stevia if desired, plus $\frac{1}{2}$–1 cup organic soy milk • Or: fruit by itself (in warmer weather)
SNACK	• 2 cups fresh vegetable juice, especially carrot, beet, and cabbage, with 1 tsp dulse or kelp powder and 2 tsp ground flaxseed • Or: 1–2 pieces fruit, especially, cherries, apple, pear, banana, orange, grapefruit, tangerine or berries • Or: raw vegetables • 2 glasses filtered or spring water or herbal tea (Yogi tea, green tea, licorice root, Essiac, red clover, pau d'arco, mint, dandelion, rosehip)
LUNCH	• 1–2 cups salad with cabbage, lettuce, spinach, onion, garlic (eaten at the beginning of the meal so their enzymes will aid digestion) • $\frac{3}{4}$ cup vegetables (raw or steamed, including $\frac{1}{2}$ cup brassicas) • $\frac{1}{2}$ cup mung bean, red clover, sunflower or broccoli sprouts (in salad or in bean and rice dish) • 1–2 tbsp flaxseed oil or fish oil, as salad dressing, and over beans and grain • $\frac{1}{2}$–1 cup beans, with onion, garlic, ginger, turmeric (hummus, bean dips, bean soup, or bean and grain dish) • $\frac{1}{2}$–1 cup grain, preferably whole grain rather than flour products (rice, millet, barley, quinoa, buckwheat) • 3–4 shiitake mushrooms (several times weekly)
SNACK	• 1–2 tbsp raw almonds, pumpkin seeds, walnuts and/or sunflower seeds • 2 cups vegetable juice (especially carrot, beet, cabbage, dulse powder with added watercress, parsley, cilantro, kale, mustard greens, garlic, ginger, sprouts, dandelion greens, or apple) • 2 glasses filtered or spring water or herbal tea, as above
DINNER	• Green drink (as before breakfast, taken $\frac{1}{2}$ hour before dinner) • 1 cup salad with fresh sprouts, onions and garlic, raw sunflower or pumpkin seeds, and grated organic citrus peel • $\frac{1}{2}$ cup firm organic tofu or tempeh (if not allergic) • $\frac{1}{2}$-1 cup whole grains (wild rice, quinoa, millet, rice, barley, and buckwheat — omit this if you want to lose weight) • $\frac{3}{4}$ cup vegetables, raw or lightly steamed • $\frac{1}{2}$ cup red clover, sunflower, mung bean, or broccoli sprouts • 2 tbsp sea vegetables (hiziki, arame, wakame, nori, dulse, kelp) • 1–2 tbsp flaxseed oil and 1 tablespoon olive oil as part of salad dressing or over grain or vegetables
SNACK	• 2 glasses filtered or spring water or organic green tea or Yogi tea (with cinnamon and ginger)

Age-Appropriate Supplements

*I*deally, *we would satisfy our nutritional needs by eating nutrient-rich, non-toxic food, but our soil has been depleted of essential nutrients and contaminated with agricultural and industrial chemicals, making our food potentially toxic. Nutritional supplements address this deficiency and can counteract the effects of many environmental toxins.*

DID YOU KNOW...

Vitamin, mineral, amino acid, essential fatty acid, and digestive enzyme supplements are now a necessary component of good health.

During the course of our life, our nutrient needs will change somewhat. The following nutrient amounts are selected to prevent many age-specific ailments of women and are discussed more fully under the health conditions later in the book.

Start with a good multivitamin and mineral supplement and work with a nutritionally oriented health-care practitioner to choose from the selection below.

Choose vitamin and mineral supplements that are derived from food rather than synthetic sources whenever possible.

DAILY RECOMMENDED SUPPLEMENTS

SUPPLEMENT	0–2 YEARS	3–10 YEARS	11–18 YEARS	19–29 YEARS	30–50 YEARS	>50 YEARS
Vitamin A		2,000 IU	5,000 IU	15,000 IU	15,000 IU	15,000 IU
Beta carotene		5,000 IU	10,000 IU	25,000 IU	25,000 IU	25,000 IU
Vitamin B-1		5 mg	10 mg	20 mg	30 mg	30 mg
Vitamin B-2		2 mg	5 mg	10 mg	15 mg	15 mg
Vitamin B-3		25 mg	50 mg	100 mg	300 mg	300 mg
Vitamin B-5		25 mg	100 mg	200 mg	500 mg	1000 mg
Vitamin B-6		25 mg	50 mg	100 mg	100 mg	100 mg
Vitamin B-12		100 mcg	250 mcg	500 mcg	800 mcg	1,000 mcg
Folic acid		250 mcg	500 mcg	1 mg	2 mg	3 mg
Biotin		50 mcg	100 mcg	200 mcg	300 mcg	300 mcg
Vitamin C		500 mg	1,500 mg	2,000 mg	3,000 mg	3,000 mg
Vitamin D		300 IU	500 IU	600 IU	600 IU	800 IU

DAILY RECOMMENDED SUPPLEMENTS

SUPPLEMENT	0–2 YEARS	3–10 YEARS	11–18 YEARS	19–29 YEARS	30–50 YEARS	>50 YEARS
Vitamin E		50 IU	200 IU	400 IU	600 IU	800 IU
Vitamin K-1		20 mcg	50 mcg	100 mcg	100 mcg	150 mcg
Calcium		400 mg	800 mg	1,000 mg	1,000 mg	1,500 mg
Magnesium		200 mg	400 mg	500 mg	500 mg	750 mg
Iron (only use if low)	10 mg	10 mg	18 mg	0–60 mg	0–60 mg	0–40 mg
Zinc		15 mg	30 mg	50 mg	50 mg	50 mg
Manganese		5 mg	10 mg	20 mg	20 mg	20 mg
Copper		1 mg	1–2 mg	2–4 mg	2–4 mg	2–4 mg
Potassium (use diet)		1 gm	2 gm	2–3 gm	2–3 gm	3 gm
Iodine (from kelp)		50 mcg	100 mcg	200 mcg	200 mcg	200 mcg
Selenium		50 mcg	100 mcg	200 mcg	200 mcg	200 mcg
Chromium		100 mcg	200 mcg	300 mcg	600 mcg	800 mcg
Vanadium			100 mcg	300 mcg	300 mcg	300 mcg
Boron			1 mg	3 mg	3 mg	3 mg
Molybdenum		50 mcg	100 mcg	200 mcg	300 mcg	300 mcg
Silicon (orthosilicic acid)		10 mg	20 mg	20 mg	50 mg	50 mg
Strontium					300 mg	600 mg
HCl + Digestive enzymes					use before meals	use before meals
N-acetyl cysteine				1,000 mg	1,500 mg	1,500 mg
Indole-3-carbinol or DIM				300 mg	300 mg	300 mg
Bromelain					600 mg	600 mg
Curcumin				1,000 mg	1,500 mg	1,500 mg
Shou wu					2,400 mg	3,600 mg
Coenzyme Q10				60 mg	100 mg	100 mg
Alpha lipoic acid				100 mg	200 mg	200 mg
Glucosamine sulphate					1,000 mg	1500 mg
Ipriflavone						600 mg
Ginkgo biloba						240 mg
Hawthorne berry						750 mg
Probiotic with L. acidophilus and B. bifidus				2 capsules	2 capsules	4 capsules
Inulin				20 gm	20 gm	20 gm
Pure fish or algae oil	500 mg	500 mg	1,000 mg	2,000 mg	3,000 mg	3,000 mg
Flaxseed oil	½ tsp	1 tsp	1 tbsp	1 tbsp	2 tbsp	2 tbsp
Psyllium seed powder			1 tsp	3 tsp	3 tsp	4 tsp
Ground flaxseed		1 tsp	1 tbsp	2 tbsp	2 tbsp	3 tbsp

Living with Nature's Rhythms

We are all part of the great rhythms of the universe. The solar seasons, the lunar phases, our daily waking and sleeping, our menstrual cycle and hormone levels, our breathing patterns and heartbeat, our developmental progression through conception, birth, infancy, childhood, adolescence, adulthood, middle age, old age, and death — these natural rhythms are encoded in our cells and in our genes. We are born into these rhythms and we die by these rhythms. This is the ceaseless river of existence.

When we align ourselves with nature's rhythms, our bodies are best prepared to be healthy. Natural medicine borrows from ancient knowledge (Native American, Chinese, Ayurveda, Yoga) to develop preventive strategies that maintain balanced rhythms in the body and mind, as well as treatment strategies for the conditions and diseases that beset us when we fall out of step with natural cycles.

In this section of the book, we will look at circadian, ultradian, lunar, hormonal, and developmental rhythms in our lives. Later, we devote a section to a program for maintaining health based on the rhythm of the seasons.

Daily and Monthly Health Cycles

The circadian, ultradian, and lunar rhythms of nature, governed by the light of the sun, the reflecting moon, and the earth's magnetic field, program the ebb and flow of our hormones through their daily, monthly, and seasonal fluctuations. Our menstrual cycle, fertility, and life cycle from conception to crone are precisely orchestrated by these hormones. We'll look first at these daily and monthly cycles before becoming familiar with our hormones and the role they play in escorting us from infancy to old age.

Circadian Rhythms

Our biological clocks have been working in precision since mammals appeared on the planet 200 million years ago, set by daily, monthly and seasonal light/dark cycles. Our circadian clocks are located in the suprachiasmatic nucleus of the hypothalamus in our brain.

Circadian rhythms are based on the natural alternation from day to night and night to day. Light stimuli reach the retina of the eye and travel to the hypothalamus. Chemical messages from the suprachiasmatic nucleus signal the pineal gland, located in the center of the brain, to produce the hormone melatonin in the dark early hours of the morning, whether we are sleeping or awake.

Melatonin directs the cooperative, coordinated synchronization of numerous biochemical and physiological systems in the rest of the body, helping to regulate rhythms of blood pressure, sleep and wakefulness, the immune system, physical movement, and the timing of other hormonal secretions.

Bring Back the Night Sky

Our ancestors from the genus *Homo* coordinated their 5 million years of activity around the light of the sun and moon. However, humans all over the planet are now exposed to unnatural light at night that disturbs our biological clocks. Traffic lights, neon signs,

streetlights, Christmas lights, television and computer screens, automobile headlights, and security lights interfere with the ancient dialog we have with darkness, the moon, the stars and the rising and setting sun. Light pollution has altered the night sky.

In recent years, international efforts have begun to decrease light pollution, pioneered primarily by astronomers, many of them members of the International Dark Sky Association with headquarters in Tucson, Arizona. Anti-light pollution legislation has been passed in the Czech Republic, parts of Australia, several U.S. states, Lombardy in Italy, and Calgary in Canada.

In Ontario, the Torrance Barrens, a 4800-acre conservation reserve in the Muskoka region, and Manitoulin Island are both designated Dark Sky Reserves.

Chinese medicine stresses the importance of balancing yin and yang, darkness and light. On a cosmic level, the night sky, the moon, and women's bodies are yin in nature, connected through a deep sympathetic resonance. When we light up the night sky in our cities, we stress our yin aspects, creating subtle imbalances in women's bodies. To enable healing of women's disorders, we need to bring back the night sky.

DID YOU KNOW...

If we are exposed to light between 1:00 and 3:00 a.m., our melatonin levels decrease and our biorhythms are thrown off balance. Saliva testing done on many breast cancer patients demonstrates a nightly melatonin deficiency.

SIGNS AND SYMPTOMS OF BIORHYTHMIC IMBALANCE

Our body and mind give us cues that we are losing healthy circadian and ultradian balance. Listen to these cues on a daily basis and consider ways to change your lifestyle to re-establish biorhythmic harmony. Otherwise, more serious health conditions may force you to rest.

- Excessive sighing and yawning, fatigue
- Wandering mind, with an inability to concentrate
- Excessive fantasizing
- Procrastination
- Muscle tension and fatigue
- Hunger pains or thirst, emotional eating
- Addictive cravings — sugar, coffee, cigarettes, alcohol
- Physical restlessness, with a need to stretch and move about
- Sense of feeling depressed or vulnerable
- Lapses in memory
- Mistakes in writing or speaking
- Irritability and impatience
- Headaches

Ultradian Rhythms

A basic 'rest-activity' cycle is programmed into our physiology, whereby we are naturally active for 90 to 120 minutes at a time, but then require a 20-minute break to balance the glandular, immune, and nervous systems. When we are stressed and expected to perform beyond our capacity for prolonged periods of time, these rhythms are disrupted.

The 'lowest' time of day for many people is between 3:00 and 4:00 p.m. At this time the circadian and ultradian cycles overlap in their low phases, causing a drop in energy and function. There is also a decrease in the adrenal hormone, cortisol, during this period.

When we override and disrupt our ultradian cycles by chronically ignoring the need to rest during an intense period of activity, we set the stage for development of illness. Hormonal imbalances, such as hypothyroidism, progesterone deficiency, adrenal burnout, and excess testosterone or prolactin, frequently occur after periods of stress. These imbalances may lead to a variety of illnesses, including uterine fibroids, breast cancer, chronic fatigue syndrome, PMS, polycystic ovary syndrome, severe menopausal symptoms, and immune system dysregulation.

BIORHYTHM TESTS

The pattern of daily melatonin and cortisol secretions are good markers of biorhythm balance. Ask your health-care practitioner to measure these levels for you in your saliva and blood.

Melatonin
Levels are highest between 1:00 a.m. and 3:00 a.m. and are low during the day. Nighttime levels can be checked with saliva testing.

Cortisol
Levels should peak in the early hours of the morning and be lowest at midnight. By measuring the levels of this hormone in blood at 8:00 a.m. and 6:00 p.m. on the same day, we can gauge how unbalanced our circadian and ultradian rhythms may be. The evening cortisol level should be about half of the morning level.

HEALTH TIPS CHECKLIST

Balancing Your Circadian and Ultradian Rhythms

To balance your biorhythms, adopt some of these personal and political strategies. Check them off ☑ as you incorporate them into your lifestyle.

- ☐ Ask your doctor to check saliva or blood levels of cortisol several times a day (including a.m. and p.m. levels) and salivary melatonin between 1:00 a.m. and 3:00 a.m.
- ☐ Keep lights out at night. Keep your bedroom dark except during the three days beginning with the full moon.
- ☐ Program at least two rest periods of 20 minutes into your day. These may include quiet reflection, a short nap, journaling, knitting, a walk outdoors, prayer, breathing exercises, mantra and mindfulness meditation, or visualization. Schedule one of these 20-minute breaks between 3:00 p.m. and 4:00 p.m. when the circadian and ultradian cycles and adrenal glands overlap in their low phases.
- ☐ Eat at consistent meal times; have regular healthy snacks between meals.
- ☐ Spend time outside in natural light each day, without glasses or sunglasses.
- ☐ Establish a regular time to go to bed at night and to get up in the morning.
- ☐ Limit your late nights out to two or less per week.
- ☐ Use only as much artificial light as you need, both indoors and outdoors.
- ☐ Enjoy the night sky by walking in moonlight and stargazing.
- ☐ Install shielded outdoor lights that direct light downward and not outward or upward.
- ☐ Illuminate billboards and signs from the top, with light directing downward.
- ☐ Do not let the light from your fixtures spill into your neighbor's yard or window.
- ☐ Use outdoor LPS (low pressure sodium) fixtures because they are the most energy efficient and produce the least heat.
- ☐ Use light timer controls or motion sensors on outdoor lighting.
- ☐ Use opaque blinds to prevent light from shining in your window at night.
- ☐ Educate businesses and homeowners in your area about light pollution and link up with the International Dark Sky Association (www.darksky.org).
- ☐ Encourage your city council to pass legislation banning light pollution.

LIGHT POLLUTION

A 2001 study estimated that one in four people on the planet live under the glow of a sky that is brighter than on nights when the moon is full. About two-thirds of the global population lives under skies polluted by artificial light.

SHABD KRIYA YOGA MEDITATION TO BALANCE BODY RHYTHMS

Resetting Body Rhythms

Meditation can help to reset circadian and ultradian rhythms. Practice this exercise (known as Shabd Kriya) before going to bed to encourage a deep sleep and to regenerate the nerves. The rhythm of the breath helps to re-set your body rhythms. Try this routine nightly for the greatest benefit.

1. Sit in a comfortable position with your spine straight and your chin pulled back slightly. Place your hands in your lap, with the palms up and your right hand over the left.

2. Touch the pads of the thumbs together and point them forward.

3. Focus your eyes on the tip of your nose with the eyelids half closed.

4. Inhale in four equal parts, mentally repeating the mantra sounds SA TA NA MA, one syllable for each inhale. (Rhymes with "ahh"). These sounds mean "birth, life, death, rebirth."

5. Hold the breath, repeating the mantra mentally four more times for a total of 16 beats.

6. Exhale in two equal parts, mentally repeating the mantra WAHAY GURU. This means "experience of ecstatic wisdom." Continue for 15 minutes.

Breathing Rhythms

Ordinarily we breathe predominantly through one nostril at a time for a 90- to 120-minute period, and then breathe through both nostrils for approximately 20 minutes. This is followed by predominance of the other nostril for another 90 to 120 minutes. This cycle occurs throughout the day and night.

Other physiological and psychological processes influenced by ultradian rhythms, including the desire to eat and sleep, dreaming and wakefulness, immune system activity and hormonal secretions, stress reactions and mood changes, mental concentration and cell replication — are governed by the same 90- to 120-minute periods as the breath cycle. As the breath cycle comes into balance through practicing breathing exercises, other ultradian rhythms normalize as well.

Balanced Breathing and Breast Cancer

Western society chronically neglects the body's need for a 20-minute break every 2 hours or so. We replace these times of potential integration with 'addictions', such as coffee, cigarettes, alcohol, sugar, and recreational drugs, which compound the

BREATHING BALANCE

Left Nostril

When the left nostril is dominant, the right hemisphere of the brain exhibits more activity. The right hemisphere is linked to creative thought, intuition, non-linear thinking, a sense of timelessness, and appreciation of art, music, and poetry. With left nostril dominance the parasympathetic nervous system is activated, causing us to feel more relaxed. Blood pressure will often decrease with left nostril breathing. Hot flashes in menopausal women may dissipate.

Right Nostril

When the right nostril is dominant, the left hemisphere of the brain shows more activity. The left hemisphere is related to linear thinking, assertiveness and aggressiveness, concentrated study, athletic activity, mathematical problem solving, and logic. With right nostril dominance the sympathetic nervous system is activated, causing us to feel more alert and charged, ready for action. Right nostril breathing will often elevate blood pressure slightly and prepare us for intense physical activity, study, or assertive exchanges.

Balance

The 20-minute period when both nostrils are dominant is a time of integration between the hemispheres. This is often the time when we want to daydream, fantasize, reflect, have a break from what we were doing, move around, or process emotional material. It is the time of reconciliation between mind and body, when we are more open to receive and pay attention to the messages from the body. It is the time when we are primed to receive intuitive impulses, inner guidance, and connect to our spiritual selves. During this 20-minute break, we are more apt to acknowledge emotions we have suppressed.

problem. These addictions further alienate us from the messages our bodies send us, from our emotional truths, and from our spiritual identities.

When the pineal gland is not functioning properly, there will be increased cell division and multiplication and a greater likelihood of cancer. The complete process of cell division typically takes between $1\frac{1}{2}$ to 2 hours, with a 20-minute critical period of time when molecules called 'cyclins' accumulate in the cell to determine if and when it will divide. We know that cell division is linked with the breath cycle through ultradian rhythms, so that normalizing the breath cycle can help to normalize cell division.

When we develop and practice a slow, meditative breath, nightly melatonin levels increase as the pineal gland responds with renewed vigor. We can help to prevent breast, ovarian and uterine cancers by keeping our melatonin levels high through an evening meditation practice.

CASE STUDY: *BREATH OF LIFE*

Helen is an attractive, well-dressed art gallery owner, the mother of one child, who came to us to help relieve her anxiety. She felt that "life was decided by outside factors" and that "she couldn't live up to what was expected of her." Her mother died suddenly in a car accident when Helen was 9. Helen was also recovering from breast cancer, after being treated with a lumpectomy, intravenous vitamin C, ozone therapy, and chelation therapy to remove excess mercury, iron, and aluminum.

When prompted, Helen said she often dreamed of having another child, but in her dream she fears she is not able to care for her child and leaves the child unattended. We spoke about ways that she could take care of her inner life and nourish the abandoned child within her. We discussed her capacity to say "no" to requests and the need for her to make more time for herself. For her anxiety, I asked her to repeat the affirmation, "I can only do what I am capable of at the present time. I honor my need to relax. It is in God's hands." This helped her immensely.

Testing revealed that she had low levels of zinc, selenium, and molybdenum, a common finding, especially in people with a cancer history. She also was deficient in hydrochloric acid, as revealed through a gastro-test, so her minerals weren't being absorbed. She collected saliva at 2:00 a.m. and testing revealed her melatonin level to be 8.4, when it should be over 15.

We taught her how to do alternate nostril breathing and asked her to practice it nightly before bed. Three months later, we tested saliva again at 2:00 a.m. and melatonin levels were now 16. She remarked that she no longer felt anxious. By this time, she was also practicing yoga and rebounding (jumping on a small trampoline) daily and felt amazingly well.

Menstrual Cycle

The moon rotates on its axis once every $29\frac{1}{2}$ days and circles the earth at the same rate, taking $29\frac{1}{2}$ days for one revolution around the earth. This is known as a lunar cycle. As it orbits the earth, we see the moon in several phases, when varying amounts of sunlight are reflected from its surface. The new moon (no visible moon) occurs when the moon sits between the sun and the earth with its reflecting surface facing the sun but not the earth. The full moon occurs when the moon's entire reflecting surface is lit by the sun and the moon is suspended on the side of the earth furthest from the sun. The dark phase of the moon is the time in between. Our menstrual cycle follows this lunar rhythm.

Our female bodies resonate with the waxing and waning of the moon an average of 500 times over the 37 or so years during which we menstruate, as the female bodies of primates have been doing for the last 30 million years. Many of us ovulate and bleed

in rhythm with the full moon or the new moon starting between the age of 8 and 13, finishing between the age of 45 and 55.

The menstrual cycle and its hormonal dancers are carefully choreographed by the reflecting moon each month to whet our sexual appetite, moisten the vagina so it welcomes intercourse, mature and release a ripened egg from an ovarian follicle, and prepare the uterus for implantation of an embryo. During its monthly sonata, the fluctuating light of the sun (yang) reflected off the moon (yin) affects first the hypothalamus, then the pineal and pituitary glands, and finally the ovaries, adrenals, and thyroid glands. Each of these glands plays a role in our menstrual cycle.

Irregular Periods

Although at one time the majority of women's menstrual cycles were synchronized with the lunar cycle, this is no longer the case. A study of more than 800 women between the ages of 16 and 25 in Scandinavia found that only 30% of women menstruated around the new moon. A double-blind study of 305 Brooklyn College graduates between 19 and 35 years old found that almost two-thirds of them began their periods during the light half of the lunar cycle (the time from the first quarter, through the full moon, to the last quarter).

DID YOU KNOW...

Among the Nazca boobie bird populations on the Galapagos Islands, lower nighttime melatonin levels occur during the full moon. Moonlight suppresses melatonin in these seabirds, as it would likely do with us if we slept outdoors. A study on women showed that melatonin levels peaked before and during menstruation and were lowest during ovulation. This would make sense if the women in this study were ovulating around the full moon, when light at night suppresses melatonin.

HEALTH TIPS CHECKLIST

☙ Normalizing Your Menstrual Cycle

To establish a rhythm between your fertility cycle and the lunar phases, here are several strategies you can try.

☐ Use Light Therapy: If your menstrual cycle is irregular, you might try normalizing it with light treatments that mimic moonlight. Scientists have shown that light stimulation in a timed fashion can influence the time of ovulation and regulate the menstrual cycle. Turn a soft light on in your bedroom at night for 3 or 4 days starting on day 14 if your cycles are irregular. If you live under a dark sky, let the moonlight in at night to regulate your cycle.

☐ Observe the quality of your emotions during the lunar phases: Notice the times of the month when you feel expansive and when you feel more inward. Walk in the moonlight or in the darkness of the new moon, alone or with a partner, a few evenings a month. Become conscious of how the expanding and contracting lunar cycle affects you. Honor and support your hormonal shifts each month, the polarities of yin and yang, as you view them mirrored in the night sky.

☐ Develop your relationship with the moon: The earth and moon are held together in a gravitational embrace as they circle the sun, and the tonalities of this dance are experienced within us. The light of the sun, reflected by the moon, is an ancient archetypal rhythm that we have internalized, and it rules our sexuality and fertility. Whether you menstruate with the new moon or the full moon or fall somewhere in between, you can develop a relationship with the earth's lovely partner.

Balancing the Four Phases of the Menstrual Cycle

Many women experience irregular menstrual cycles, beginning at different times each month and lasting different durations. Our menstrual rhythms were more regular when we were more consistently exposed to moonlight and the lunar phases. Like the lunar cycle, the menstrual cycle can be divided into four phases. The following chart describes the physiology and psychology of the menstrual phases, while presenting the lifestyle, diet, and supplements that will help to balance each of the phases. These will be further explained in the chapter on Hormone Balance and the section on Women's Conditions.

PHYSIOLOGY AND PSYCHOLOGY	SUPPORTIVE AND BALANCING STRATEGIES
PHASE ONE: MENSTRUATION (DAY 1–5)	
• Melatonin peaks just before and during menstruation • Estrogen and progesterone decline just before menstruation • Uterine lining is shed and we bleed for about 5 days • In Chinese medicine, the movement of blood relies on the liver qi and liver blood • During the new moon (yin, feminine), the sun (yang, masculine) is not reflected by the moon; this is the perfect time for a woman to be alone, nourishing her yin nature • Release negative thought patterns, emotions, desires, addictions • Enhance creativity, intuition, spirituality	• On day 1, the first day of menstrual bleeding, take 3 pellets of the homeopathic remedy Hypophysinum 200K, to balance the pituitary gland • Use the Chinese herbs Xiao Yao Wan and/or acupuncture or moxibustion (Liv-3, CV-6, GB-34, Sp-8, St-29, Sp-10, Sp-6, L-7, K-6, Sp-4, P-6) to move the blood if there is too little; stop using if there is too much bleeding • Take dietary sources of iron, such as seaweed, pumpkin seeds, oatmeal, beets, and molasses • Get together with other women "on their moon" to reflect, nourish yourself, empower the feminine • Sleep in a dark room during your menstrual flow to mimic the new moon

PHYSIOLOGY AND PSYCHOLOGY	SUPPORTIVE AND BALANCING STRATEGIES
PHASE TWO: PROLIFERATIVE, FOLLICULAR, OR PREOVULATORY PHASE (DAY 6–13)	
• Hypothalamus releases Follicle-Stimulating Hormone Releasing Factor (FSH-RF) into the blood to activate the pituitary • On day 6, the pituitary gland secretes FSH, which stimulates growth of a dominant follicle containing a mature egg in the ovary; other follicles recede • In this phase the blood and yin are empty • This is a good time to begin new projects, act in the world • Cells from the maturing ovarian follicle secrete increasing amounts of estrogen • Increase in left brain activity, such as verbal fluency, and a decline in right brain activity, such as drawing or map reading as estrogen rises • Emotions and behavior may be directed toward the outer world • Estrogen stimulates the endometrium (uterine lining) to thicken and grow, like the waxing moon • As estrogen levels rise, FSH levels drop and the hypothalamus releases Luteinizing Hormone Releasing Factor (LH-RF), causing the pituitary to secrete LH • LH surge triggers the mature follicle to burst open 9 hours later, releasing an egg. (Birth control pills block this surge, inhibiting the release of the egg.) • Testosterone is highest on day 13, enhancing sexual energy • Estrogen makes the cervical mucus thinner and more alkaline to promote transport and survival of sperm • Intercourse 8 days before ovulation up to ovulation may result in pregnancy • Sperm survive up to 120 hours (5 days) before ovulation, occasionally 7 days • You are most fertile 48 hours before ovulation	• On day 7, take 3 pellets of the homeopathic remedy Folliculinum 200K to regulate estrogen • Nourish the blood, yin, liver, and kidneys with herbs (tang kuei, ligusticum, schizandra, rehmannia, shou wu) and/or acupuncture or moxibustion (CV-4, CV-6, St-36, Bl-20, K-3) • Support estrogen if it is low (infertility or peri-menopause) with estrogenic herbs (fennel root, ginseng, alfalfa, ground flaxseed, licorice root, red clover, tang kuei) • Use 2 tbsp flaxseed oil as well as 2 tbsp of ground flaxseed daily • Use American ginseng, nettle, damiana, and/or saw palmetto to increase libido (and testosterone) if low • Have sex during the 2 days before ovulation if you are trying to conceive • Avoid unprotected intercourse during days 6–19 of a 26–32 day menstrual cycle if you do not wish to become pregnant • Decrease or eliminate foods that contain harmful estrogen or the estrogenic chemicals PCBs, dioxin, phthalates, bisphenol-A, and brominated fire retardants, as these promote estrogen dominance and are linked with endometriosis, menstrual pain, uterine fibroids, and breast and ovarian cysts. These include freshwater fish, pizza, butter, hamburger, saltwater fish, cold cuts, wieners, ice cream, canned fish, shellfish, ground beef, French fries, veal, processed cheese, lamb, organ meat, beef steak, evaporated milk, cheddar cheese, poultry, yogurt, eggs, pork, and whole milk

PHYSIOLOGY AND PSYCHOLOGY	SUPPORTIVE AND BALANCING STRATEGIES
PHASE THREE: OVULATION (MIDCYCLE, DAY 14, LASTING 36 HOURS)	
<ul><li>LH surge triggers ovulation 9 hours later (the release of an egg)</li><li>Follicle ruptures and releases an egg</li><li>Ovaries are at their most radiant, like the full moon</li><li>Vaginal secretions give off sexually attracting odors (pheromones)</li><li>Mental-emotional activity may be at its peak, with intense emotions</li><li>As the cervix is open and receptive, we may be most receptive to new ideas</li><li>Egg is coaxed into the fallopian tube by its fingerlike extensions</li><li>Inside the fallopian tube, tiny hairs direct the egg to the uterus</li><li>Body temperature rises right after ovulation by about 0.4°F</li><li>Cervical mucus is thinnest, very elastic, can stretch into a long thread</li><li>Egg stays alive for about 24 hours once it is released from the ovary</li><li>If sperm are present as the egg reaches the uterus, fertilization can occur</li><li>36% of women conceive if intercourse occurs on the day of ovulation</li><li>Cervical mucus dries into a fern-like pattern when placed on a slide, caused by estrogen</li></ul>	<ul><li>Use 3 pellets of homeopathic Ovarinum 200K to regulate the ovary on day 14.</li><li>Honor your fertility, your femininity, your womanhood, your connection to the moon (and the sun's light reflected by the moon; yang reflected by yin)</li><li>Integrate your inner masculine and inner feminine; have sex if you want to conceive; or schedule your wedding on a full moon</li><li>Give birth to your self — consider a special meditation or fast, paying attention to your dreams</li><li>Nourish kidney essence with the herbs Ho Shou Wu and schizandra</li><li>Expose yourself to a soft light at night, or actual moonlight, for 3 or 4 days starting on day 14 if your cycles are irregular or if you want to synchronize them with the lunar cycle</li></ul>

PHYSIOLOGY AND PSYCHOLOGY	SUPPORTIVE AND BALANCING STRATEGIES
PHASE FOUR: SECRETORY, LUTEAL, OR POSTOVULATORY PHASE (DAY 15–28)	
<ul><li>Ruptured follicle fills with blood; then clotted blood is replaced by yellow, fatty cells to form the corpus luteum, or "yellow body"</li><li>Corpus luteum produces mostly progesterone and some estrogen; progesterone is needed to maintain a pregnancy. (The morning after pill blocks progesterone.)</li></ul>	<ul><li>Use 3 pellets of homeopathic Luteininum 200K on day 21 to balance progesterone and estrogen</li><li>Support progesterone production with chastetree berry, wild yam, saw palmetto, tang kuei, soy, ground flaxseed, and adrenal support</li><li>Support kidney yang if deficient; move liver qi if stagnant</li></ul>

PHASE FOUR: SECRETORY, LUTEAL, OR POSTOVULATORY PHASE (DAY 15–28) *cont'd*

- Yang energy rises from the kidney and the liver qi rises
- Progesterone and estrogen thicken the endometrial lining (causing swelling) and increase its blood supply, preparing it for implantation of an embryo
- Elevated estrogen and aldosterone cause salt and water retention
- Progesterone decreases salt retention
- Serotonin levels may drop, contributing to depression
- You may feel more reflective, assessing what you want to change in your life; listen to your dreams and intuition; acknowledge and express your feelings
- Progesterone keeps the body temperature higher after ovulation
- Pregnancy is unlikely after the rise in temperature
- Cervical mucus thickens, with no fern-like pattern, as this is inhibited by progesterone
- We are more prone to vaginal yeast infections during this time
- Cortisol and thyroid hormones may decrease during this phase, contributing to premenstrual anxiety, depression, irritability, food cravings
- Breast swelling may begin 10 days before menstruation, probably due to either high estrogen or prolactin, and/or deficient progesterone
- We are more prone to headaches, fatigue, and joint pain
- If implantation does not occur, the corpus luteum degenerates on day 25 and is replaced by scar tissue
- Without the corpus luteum, progesterone and estrogen levels drop and the uterine lining thins, like the waning moon
- Towards the end of the luteal phase melatonin peaks and the endometrium produces prolactin, which may further increase breast swelling
- Secretory or luteal phase is almost always 14 days; variations in menstrual cycle length are usually due to changes in the follicular phase

- Use potassium foods to decrease salt and water retention (carrot juice, avocado, papaya, cantaloupe, mango, banana, kiwi, figs, pineapple, azuki beans, lentils, pinto beans, tofu, squash, potato)
- Use dandelion greens, tea, or tincture to support the liver and act as a diuretic
- Decrease your stress (say "no" more often); support the adrenal glands with vitamin B complex, extra B-6 and B-5, vitamins C and E, magnesium, adrenal glandular tissue and/or herbs (licorice root, Siberian ginseng, ho shou wu, rhodiola, ashwaganda, borage, and oats)
- Support the thyroid with kelp, zinc, selenium, L-tyrosine, guggul
- Take 2 tbsp flaxseed oil and 3000 mg fish oil daily
- Avoid sugar; use chromium to decrease sweet cravings; eat small meals frequently
- Stop twice daily and do pranayama for 20 minutes
- Use oral Lactobacillus acidophilus to protect from vaginal infections, or insert a capsule vaginally at night
- To decrease breast swelling, use 3 pellets of homeopathic Folliculinum 15CH on days 7, 14, and 21 of the menstrual cycle to decrease estrogen dominance
- If you have PMS, test saliva between days 20 and 23 of a 28-day cycle (when progesterone is highest) for progesterone, estradiol, estrone, and estriol; determine whether you have a progesterone deficiency or estrogen excess; consider a sauna detox program to eliminate chemicals that may be interfering with progesterone or causing estrogen dominance
- If temperature does not rise after ovulation, you may have progesterone deficiency
- Check salivary cortisol 4 times during the day to determine adrenal deficiency
- Track your basal body temperature daily to determine a possible underactive thyroid (if your underarm temperature is consistently lower that 36.6°C or 97.8°F, this may be the case); low temperature may also be due to iron deficiency, low progesterone, adrenal fatigue or all of the above

Sacred Sex

The Kundalini yoga tradition teaches that women have 11 moon centers — erogenous zones of the body that are activated at different phases of the lunar cycle and influence our emotions and way of viewing the world. Our psyche is focused on one of the moon centers for 2½ days and then moves on to the next. The order of the moon centers is different for each woman — it's up to us and our sexual partner to discover which one predominates on a particular day.

The fluctuations in sexual desire during the menstrual cycle interweave with the rhythm of our moon centers to determine how we express ourselves sexually. When we are attentive to the pattern of our moon centers and menstrual cycle, we gain more awareness of ourselves as sexual and fertile beings. During foreplay, have some fun by inviting your sexual partner to discover your most active moon center.

Guidelines for Sacred Sex

Our sexuality, like our spirituality, is part of our wholeness. When treated with respect and consciousness, sex becomes a vehicle to merge physically and spiritually with another person. Sexual energy can also be channeled into spiritual devotion, healing, exercise, or creative expression — music, dance, writing, or fine art. Though it takes discipline and creativity, we can decide how we are going to use our sexual energy rather than being pulled by it into addictive, abusive, or unsatisfying behavior patterns and relationships.

MOON CENTERS: LOCATIONS AND QUALITIES

Hairline:	steady, stable, clear, realistic
Cheeks:	unpredictable
Ear lobes:	intelligent, principled
Lips:	verbal, interactive, communicative
Back of the neck:	sensitive, romantic
Breasts:	compassionate, giving
Belly button	insecure, exposed, vulnerable
Inner thighs:	affirming
Eyebrows:	imaginative, visionary
Vagina:	deep
Clitoris:	extroverted, socially communicative

If you are in a committed relationship and want to enhance and spiritualize your sexual experience, here are some yogic guidelines.

Take the time to make it special. For a woman's sexual energy to reach a peak, a sensual exchange should begin 72 hours before intercourse. This may involve romantic dinners, long walks in nature, foot massage, conversation, enjoyment of the arts, meditation, yoga, hand-holding, and stimulation of your moon centers. Encourage your partner to set aside one weekend a month for this kind of intimacy, and choose a time during your menstrual cycle when your libido is highest. Make it a consciously creative rather than a haphazard or predictable act.

Create a sacred setting. Set the stage for sex by cleaning your bedroom, preparing it with flowers, candlelight, fresh fruit, decorative pillows, a book of love poetry, massage oil, music that facilitates intimacy, and any other special touches that appeal to the heart and senses.

Massage one another. Communicate your love and desire through whole body touch. Ideally, this dual massage can take close to an hour and will create relaxation, expansiveness in your aura and readiness for intercourse. (If you are in a same-sex relationship, massage one another according to the first sequence below). This type of massage follows the flow of sexual energy, beginning at the pituitary gland and moving down through the chakras.

- Ask your partner to massage and kiss you slowly, patiently, methodically, and creatively in the following areas to stimulate your erogenous zones — first your breasts and nipples, then neck and lips, then your hairline, eyebrows, cheeks and ears, especially the earlobes. Once the breasts, nipples, and earlobes have been stimulated, you will be more receptive and relaxed in the genital area. Then proceed to your inner thighs, calves, belly, lower back, clitoris, and vagina.
- Meanwhile you can massage and stimulate your partner's erogenous zones — head and scalp, hairline, face, and earlobes. From here proceed to the buttocks, the inside of the thighs, testicles, penis, navel, chest, nipples, and any other areas along the way that bring pleasure.
- Merge with the divine in one another. During intercourse, breathe consciously, look into each other's eyes, and see the divine in one another. Be attentive to sensations in your spine and forehead. Your unified sexual energy can rise through pathways in the spine to culminate in sacred sexual ecstasy, where time stands still and all boundaries disappear.
- Relax afterwards. Take the time after intercourse to caress one another, relax, and bask in your intimacy.

Hormone Balance

*H*ormones are chemical messengers that move through the bloodstream, affecting cells of the body that have receptors for them. Different hormones are produced by different glands. Hormones work together to maintain a constant environment inside the body, despite outside changes.

Hormonal secretions can be rhythmic, tied to the solar and lunar cycles, instantaneous, or active over very long periods of time, such as the action of growth hormone throughout childhood. Hormones act by binding to particular receptors in or on the cells of their target tissues. Receptors usually have a strong affinity for one particular hormone. The hormone then affects the cell nucleus to create a specific protein, which usually acts as an enzyme with a characteristic action. The action causes a shift in the body's metabolism.

We need a steady production of hormones, since they persist for only a few minutes to a few hours, and then are utilized by their target cells or are metabolized in the liver. Like musicians in an orchestra, hormones are dependent upon one another, constantly adjusting their expression to produce the music that vibrates in and directs the body. Any imbalance in one hormone is likely to make the whole symphony sound out of tune.

Functions of the Endocrine System

The endocrine system comprises a network of interacting glands and organs that secrete hormones. Each hormone has a specific contributing function in keeping the body healthy. Some hormones serve to activate other hormones. In yoga physiology, the major glands are associated with specific chakras. Good health depends on the flow of energy at these points. Yoga exercises can be used to help balance the chakras, glands, and hormones.

FUNCTIONS OF THE ENDOCRINE SYSTEM

GLAND AND HORMONES	LOCATION AND CHAKRA	GENERAL FUNCTION
HYPOTHALAMUS CRF, GnRh, TRH, PIF, GRF, Somatostatin	Behind the eyes in the brain Associated with the 6th and 7th chakras (third eye and crown)	Controls the secretions of the pituitary gland, body temperature, hunger, thirst and sexual drive Stimulates the pineal gland to secrete melatonin, which orchestrates body rhythms
PINEAL GLAND Melatonin	In the center of the brain Associated with the 7th chakra (crown)	Regulates circadian and ultradian rhythms Often called the body's biological clock
PITUITARY GLAND ACTH, TSH, Prolactin, Growth Hormone, FSH, LH, Vasopressin, Oxytoxin	Behind the eyes in the brain Associated with the 6th chakra (third eye)	Controls bone growth and regulates the other glands Often called the master gland
THYROID GLAND T4, T3, Calcitonin	In the front of the throat Associated with the 5th chakra (throat)	Maintains an optimal metabolic rate in tissues, controlling the rate of fuel use in the body, its sensitivity to heat and cold Supports immune function Protects us from bone loss during pregnancy
PARATHYROID GLANDS PTH	Behind the thyroid Associated with the 5th chakra (throat)	Helps to regulate the amount of calcium in the blood Stimulates bone building
THYMUS Thymosin	Behind the upper sternum Associated with the 4th chakra (heart)	Coordinates white blood cells (especially T cells) and the immune system Destroys viruses, fungi, some bacteria, and cancer cells Shrinks with age
LIVER IGF-1	Under the right rib cage Associated with the 3rd chakra (navel)	Regulates growth and blood sugar metabolism Detoxifies body systems
PANCREAS Insulin, Glucagon	Under the left rib cage Associated with the 3rd chakra (navel)	Controls blood sugar levels Helps to digest food (non-hormonal function)

FUNCTIONS OF THE ENDOCRINE SYSTEM

GLAND AND HORMONES	LOCATION AND CHAKRA	GENERAL FUNCTION
OVARIES Estrogen, Progesterone	In the lower abdomen on either side of the groin Associated with the 2nd chakra (sex organs)	Control sexual development, maturation and release of eggs, fertility *Estrogen:* Causes multiplication of breast cells Thickens uterine and lining Maintains vaginal thickness and lubrication Encourages formation of collagen in skin Inhibits breakdown of bone, increasing density *Progestorone:* Prepares uterus for implantation Maintains development of the placenta Develops milk-secreting cells during pregnancy Causes maturation of breast cells during pregnancy Helps prevent breast cysts and cancer Increases libido
ADRENAL GLANDS Cortisol, Aldosterone, DHEA, Testosterone, Adrenaline, Noradrenaline	On top of kidneys Associated with the 1st and 2nd chakras	Control salt and water balance in the body Help us adapt to stress Generate fight-or-flight reaction in response to life-threatening situations or unexpected emotional stress Decrease allergies Regulate sleep and mood Increase resistance to viruses, bacteria, fungi, allergies, cancer Stimulate bone formation Prevent osteoporosis, arthritis, lupus, autoimmune disease Help to maintain normal sex hormone levels Increase libido, sexual arousal

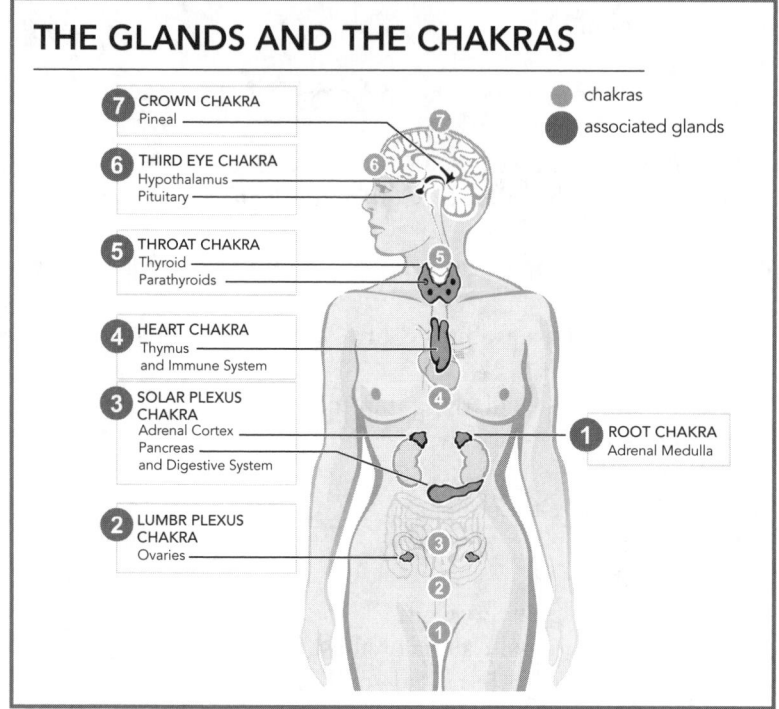

THE GLANDS AND THE CHAKRAS

- 7 CROWN CHAKRA
  Pineal
- 6 THIRD EYE CHAKRA
  Hypothalamus
  Pituitary
- 5 THROAT CHAKRA
  Thyroid
  Parathyroids
- 4 HEART CHAKRA
  Thymus
  and Immune System
- 3 SOLAR PLEXUS CHAKRA
  Adrenal Cortex
  Pancreas
  and Digestive System
- 2 LUMBR PLEXUS CHAKRA
  Ovaries
- 1 ROOT CHAKRA
  Adrenal Medulla

chakras

associated glands

Causes of Hormone Imbalances

Subtle imbalances in hormones can cause a variety of women's health conditions and symptoms. We need to know which hormones are abnormally high or low because several hormonal imbalances can contribute to the same conditions or symptoms. Ask your health-care practitioner to evaluate your hormone levels. See the Resource Directory at the back of the book for labs that do extensive hormone testing.

Many women's ailments are linked to specific hormonal imbalances, which can be triggered by any one or a combination of the following:

- Stress and overexertion
- Not enough time for relaxation and play
- Improper breathing
- Improper diet — excess saturated or hydrogenated fat, sugar, refined carbohydrates, meat, dairy, toxins in fish
- Nutritional deficiencies — such as vitamins B-5, B-6 and C, zinc, selenium, magnesium, tyrosine, tryptophan, essential fatty acids
- Food sensitivities
- Environmental allergies
- Infectious organisms and/or imbalance in intestinal flora
- Intestinal toxins, such as yeast toxins
- Impaired liver function or liver stagnation
- Elevated blood sugar

- Excess alcohol
- Smoking
- Exposure to strong electromagnetic fields or dirty power
- Radiation exposure
- Environmental chemicals, including PCBs, dioxin, pesticides, phthalates, bisphenol A, PVC, fire retardants, parabens in cosmetics
- Exposure to hormone-disrupting chemicals or hormonal excess in utero
- Pharmaceutical drugs, birth control pill, hormone replacement therapy
- Heavy metals, particularly cadmium, mercury, and lead
- Lack of exercise or excessive exercise
- Light at night
- Lack of exposure to sunlight
- Shift work
- Insomnia
- Obesity or being underweight
- History of emotional trauma or abuse
- Negative thought patterns and emotions
- Imbalances in the chakras
- Organ disharmonies, blood deficiency, or yin and yang imbalances

Estrogen Imbalance

Estrogen is the hormone that makes us female, so an estrogen imbalance is usually at the core of many women's health conditions.

Estrogen Production

The ovaries begin to produce estrogen during puberty — typically, when a girl is anywhere between 10 and 14 years of age. The pituitary hormone, FSH, signals the ovaries to produce estrogen from puberty onward. During a single menstrual cycle, the ovaries

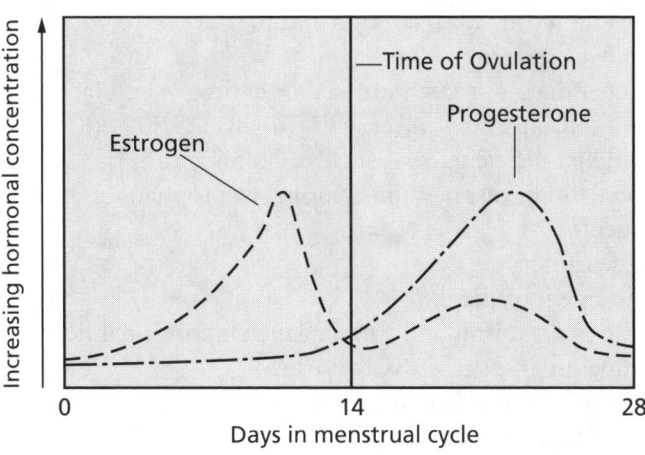

produce increasing amounts of estrogen from the first day of the period leading up to the day of ovulation in an effort to prepare the uterus for a possible pregnancy. Estrogen levels peak just before ovulation. After ovulation, estrogen levels drop for a few days and then increase less dramatically between days 18 to 23, followed by a gentle decline until the end of the menstrual cycle.

Kinds of Estrogen

The body produces three main types of estrogen: estrone (E1), estradiol (E2), and estriol (E3). These are categorized as either 'strong' estrogens (estrone and estradiol) or 'weak' (estriol). Of the three forms of estrogen, higher levels of estradiol and estrone are linked with increased breast, uterine, and ovarian cancer risk. Estriol is associated with decreased risk, except when given at very high concentrations.

Strong Estrogens

More than 50% of the body's estrogen is a form of estrone, produced in the ovaries and fat cells. In turn, estrone is made into a storage form called estrone sulphate. Estradiol, produced in the ovaries, is the strongest of the three estrogens, being 12 times more active than estrone and 1,000 times more potent in its effects on breast and uterine tissue than estriol.

The ovaries shut down production of estradiol and estrone during menopause. After menopause, the adrenal glands produce the hormones testosterone and androstenedione in higher amounts, which can be converted into estradiol and estrone in fat cells (and in breast, skin, bone, and other tissues) through the action of the enzyme, aromatase. If we block the aromatase enzyme, we can decrease the production of estradiol and estrone after menopause.

Weak Estrogens

Estriol, a short-acting weak estrogen, is produced by the placenta during pregnancy and synthesized from a breakdown product of estradiol and estrone in the liver. Estriol matures breast cells during pregnancy, making them less vulnerable to damage from radiation and chemicals. All estrogens compete for the same receptor sites, so estriol exerts its protective effect when it binds to cell receptors, preventing the attachment and action of estradiol, estrone, and xenoestrogens from the environment.

The types of food we eat can facilitate or block the conversion of estradiol and estrone to estriol. Improving liver function with specific nutrients, such as indole-3-carbinol (or DIM), curcumin, vitamin B complex, and NAC, assists this conversion. The use of iodine compounds or sea vegetables may increase estriol levels in pre- and post-menopausal women.

DID YOU KNOW...

The more menstrual periods a woman has in her lifetime (early onset of menstruation and late menopause), the greater amount of estrogen she will be exposed to in her lifetime and the more likely her chances are of developing breast cancer. Women with ovarian failure who produce little or no estrogen or whose ovaries have been removed reduce their breast cancer risk by 70% to 90%. Men also have very little breast cancer because their estrogen levels are low.

DID YOU KNOW...

Women who excrete more estriol in their urine may have a lower risk of breast cancer. Estriol may protect the breasts, ovaries, and uterus from the growth enhancing and tumor-producing effects of estradiol and estrone.

ESTROGEN SOURCES

Estrogen comes into our bodies from five possible sources:

Ovaries, Placenta, Adrenal Glands

Estradiol and estrone are made by the ovaries and can be converted to estriol in the liver. Estrogen is also made by the placenta during pregnancy (estriol) and the fat cells after menopause (estrone).

Foods and Herbs

We get estrogen from a class of foods and herbs called phytoestrogens. Certain plants, such as soy, flaxseeds, legumes, mung bean and clover sprouts, pumpkin seeds, wild indigo, licorice root, mandrake, bloodroot, thyme, yucca, hops, verbena, turmeric, yellow dock, and sheep sorrel, contain components that act like weak estrogens. Phytoestrogens protect us from conditions related to estrogen dominance by displacing strong estrogens from their receptor sites.

Animal Products

Meat, poultry, dairy products, and fish may naturally contain estrogen. Animals may also have been fed or injected with estrogen to increase fat or milk production. Fish and mammals may also have accumulated environmental chemicals (xenoestrogens) in their fat from environmental sources or pesticide residues over their lifespan. A high meat and dairy based diet tends to promote breast, uterine, and ovarian ailments. Although fish oils are protective, contaminants present in many sources of fish may cause hormone disruption and cancer.

Environmental Chemicals

Some xenoestrogens bind to estrogen receptors and mimic estrogen in our bodies, causing estrogen excess. Because we have inefficient mechanisms for breaking them down, they tend to persist in our bodies for life and are passed on to the next generation in utero and through breast milk. They have a cumulative and synergistic effect. These chemicals are present in some pesticides, plastics, petrochemicals, detergents, cosmetics, solvents, chlorinated water, fire retardants, lice shampoos, and other sources.

Synthetic Estrogens

We are exposed to these when we take the birth control pill, fertility drugs, and/or hormone replacement therapy during menopause. Their effects also promote cancer.

Estrogen Dominance

Many women's ailments, including breast cysts and cancer, uterine fibroids and cancer, ovarian cysts and cancer, endometriosis, polycystic ovary syndrome, and hypothyroidism are caused or promoted by excess estradiol, estrone, environmental estrogens, and synthetic estrogens with a relative deficiency of progesterone. This is known as estrogen dominance. Estrogen often acts in tandem with other hormones, primarily insulin, IGF-1, and high or low cortisol, in promoting these conditions. Often low melatonin and low thyroid function accompany estrogen dominance.

Estrogen Receptors

Estrogen is not active until it binds to a receptor. Estrogen fits into its receptor sites much as a key might fit into a lock. The greater the number of estrogen receptors we have in our breast, uterine, and ovarian cells, the more vulnerable we are to increased cell division caused by estrogen. Melatonin from the pineal gland and butyrate, produced by *Bifidobacterium bifidus* in the large intestine, decrease the production of estrogen receptors.

Sex Hormone Binding Globulin (SHBG)

Some of the body's circulating estrogen hooks onto SHGB, a carrier molecule that shuttles estrogen (and some testosterone) through the bloodstream to its target organs. When estrogen is bound to SHGB, it is inactive. If we increase SHBG levels, we can tie up a little more estrogen so that there is less 'free' estrogen available. Adequate thyroid hormones help protect us from estrogen excess by increasing the liver's production of SHBG.

The hormones insulin, IGF-1, and testosterone decrease the amount of SHGB when their levels are too high, freeing up estrogen. High levels of cortisol, the stress hormone, can increase the production of all three of these hormones further, so we need to keep it (and our stress) under control. If the thyroid is underactive with fewer circulating thyroid hormones, there will be less SHBG.

Estrogen Metabolites

Estrogen is broken down by enzymes in the liver, where it is bound to glucuronic acid through a process called glucuronidation. The glucuronide complex passes from the liver into the bile, then into the intestines and out through the stool.

During the breakdown of estradiol and estrone in the liver, several products or metabolites are formed. Among these metabolites, those called C2 (good) estrogens are harmless. However, C16 (bad) and especially the C4 (ugly) estrogen metabolites can be harmful and carcinogenic. The C4 estrogen accumulates in breast cells and can attach to DNA to cause mutations, specifically damaging the p53 tumor suppressor gene, whose job is to stop cancer cells from dividing.

The C4 estrogen pathway is activated by pesticides and other environmental estrogens, dioxin, car exhaust, paint fumes, alcohol, caffeine, pharmaceutical drugs, sugar, a high-fat diet, fried or rancid fats, and inadequate protein.

Fortunately, once made, the C4 estrogens can be inactivated in the liver. The brassica plant family (cabbage, broccoli, Brussels sprouts, kale) contains a chemical called indole-3-carbinol that decreases production of the C4 and C16 metabolites. The indoles are destroyed through cooking, so these foods should be consumed raw or lightly steamed.

DID YOU KNOW...

Pesticides, the use of hormone replacement therapy, and a high body mass index can all increase the number of estrogen receptors in breast, uterine and ovarian cells, contributing to the growth of benign and malignant tumors. Part of the dramatic rise in breast cancer rates over the last five decades is not so much due to female hormones but to the environmental chemicals that mimic female hormones and our body's inability to break them down and eliminate them.

DID YOU KNOW...

Breast cancer patients have significantly lower ratios of the C2 estrogen metabolite to C16 metabolite, in contrast to women without breast cancer, who have higher ratios. Studies haven't been done yet on the C2 and C4 ratio in women, but it may prove to be more significant than the C2:C16 ratio in assessing risk.

ESTROGEN QUOTIENT

Research has demonstrated that a mathematical formula, called the estrogen quotient, is a valuable index for predicting breast and endometrial cancer. To determine your estrogen quotient, ask your health-care practitioner to measure your levels of estriol, estrone, and estradiol.

$$\text{Estrogen quotient} = \frac{\text{Estriol}}{\text{Estrone} + \text{Estradiol}}$$

When the estrogen quotient is 0.5 to 0.8, there may be an increased cancer risk, whereas a quotient above 1.2 offers protection.

The functional ability of the liver and efficiency of bowel elimination influence these estrogen ratios; accordingly, improving liver and bowel function will increase both the amount of C-2 hydroxyestrone and estriol, thus decreasing risk.

CASE STUDY: *REDUCING ESTROGEN DOMINANCE*

Kim, age 34, came to see us complaining of constant breast tenderness with cystic breasts that were more tender one week before her period. She also experienced fatigue, mood swings, depression, insomnia, poor digestion, constipation, frequent abdominal pain, and a skin rash around her eyes. Her menstrual periods occurred every 23 days. Her periods had begun early, at age 11.

We used saliva testing initially to determine if her progesterone was low, but surprisingly it was normal. However, her estradiol was high at 10.5 (normal is 0.2–5.0); her estrone was very high at 29.4 (normal is 1.0 to 4.5), and her estriol was normal at 9.2 (normal is <10). Her estrogen quotient was 0.23, putting her in the risk zone for breast cancer. One of her aunts had died from breast cancer. Her C2:C16 hydroxyestrone ratio was 6.78, which was acceptable.

Further testing revealed that her TSH levels were elevated at 12.13 (normal is 0.35 to 4.5) indicating an underactive thyroid. Her melatonin levels were also low. Her high estrogen levels were likely suppressing thyroid function, which, in turn, contributed to her depression, mood swings, constipation, insomnia, and fatigue. The root cause of her problem was estrogen dominance, which had been present since early puberty.

We prescribed 2 tbsp ground flaxseeds daily, 600 mg curcumin, 3 tsp psyllium seed powder, 1 tbsp bentonite, 100 drops of Rosemarinus, 1000 mg NAC, 4 drops of liquid iodine, 50 mg zinc, an herbal formula to cleanse the liver, an herbal formula for the lymphatic system, and a Chinese herbal formula to relax the liver called Bupleurum & Tang Kuei. Her medical doctor prescribed dessicated thyroid for her.

Three months later, her estradiol was 1.2, estrone was 1.3, estriol was 2.5, and the estrogen quotient was 1. Although not perfect, this was much better. Her mood swings and depression were greatly improved, the breast tenderness was gone, cysts were reduced, the skin rash was negligible, and digestion and bowel movements were normal.

HEALTH TIPS CHECKLIST

◆ Balancing Estrogens

To establish estrogen balance, adopt the following clinical nutrition strategies for diet and supplements. Check them off ☑ as you go.

☐ To evaluate your balance of estrogens and risk of breast and uterine cancer, check your ratio of C2 estrogen to C16 estrogen and the estrogen quotient yearly through a saliva or urine test. This can be used as a routine annual test to assess women at risk for estrogen driven cancers, followed by work at prevention with diet changes and nutritional supplementation.

☐ To prevent a lowering of SHBG (which would make more estrogen available), improve thyroid function, and consume a low-fat vegetarian diet and phytoestrogens, chiefly flaxseed, soy, and red clover sprouts. Keep insulin, IGF-1, testosterone, and cortisol in check.

☐ To reduce the number of estrogen receptors, increase melatonin by balancing circadian and ultradian rhythms, supplement with *Bifidobacterium bifidus*, and decrease exposure to xenoestrogens. Eat organic food. Maintain an ideal weight and avoid hormone replacement therapy.

☐ To increase glucuronidation by 75%, supplement with ellagic acid, found in red raspberries (especially Meeker raspberries). This reaction is also assisted by high fiber, probiotics, vitamin B-6, fish oil, and calcium-D-glucarate, naturally present in oranges and apples.

☐ To assist your liver in making more C2 estrogen metabolites and fewer C4 and C16 metabolites, eat brassicas (cabbage, broccoli, Brussels sprouts, and kale) regularly. Take at least 300 mg of indole-3-carbinol as a supplement or 150 mg of DIM to achieve a similar effect. Other dietary and nutritional substances that help with the conversion of estrogen to the 'good' C2 metabolite are a low-fat diet, ground flaxseeds, fiber, fish oil, vitamin B complex, D-limonene, magnesium, zinc, N-acetyl cysteine, rosemary, schizandra, milk thistle, curcumin (from turmeric), soy, and red clover.

☐ To raise your estrogen quotient favorably, supplement with curcumin, ground flax, DIM, methionine, cysteine, liver herbs, and fiber. Estriol levels can be increased naturally with the inclusion of sea vegetables (for iodine), flaxseeds, soy products, and other phytoestrogens in your diet.

Hormonal Imbalances in Women

An imbalance of estrogens is not the only hormone disruption that can cause illness. Common hormonal imbalances in women and the conditions and symptoms that are associated with them are listed in the following chart.

HORMONAL IMBALANCES IN WOMEN

HORMONE IMBALANCE	WOMEN'S HEALTH CONDITIONS AND SYMPTOMS
ESTROGENS Elevated estrogen (estrogen dominance)	**Conditions:** early puberty; uterine fibroids, uterine cancer; ovarian cysts, ovarian cancer; breast cysts, breast fibroadenoma, breast cancer; PMS; endometriosis; hypothyroidism; autoimmune diseases; increased risk of gallbladder disease **Symptoms:** blood clots; impaired blood sugar; water retention; depression, anxiety; headaches
ESTROGENS Estrogen deficiency	**Conditions:** infertility; amenorrhea; osteoporosis; menopausal hot flashes; vaginal dryness. **Symptoms:** decreased sexual arousal; poor memory; depression; elevated cholesterol, high LDL, low HDL, elevated blood pressure; poor sleep; aging skin with wrinkles
ESTROGENS Disturbed estrogen quotient	**Conditions:** breast cancer; uterine cancer
ESTROGENS Disturbed ratio of C2 to C4 and/or C16 hydroxyestrones	**Conditions:** breast cancer; uterine cancer
PROGESTERONE Progesterone deficiency	**Conditions:** infertility; PMS; prolonged or heavy menstrual bleeding; breast tenderness, breast cysts, breast fibroadenomas, breast cancer; uterine fibroids and uterine cancer; ovarian cysts; polycystic ovary syndrome; lowered libido; hypothyroidism; adrenal fatigue; miscarriage; increased cardiovascular disease **Symptoms:** fatigue; insomnia; anxiety; coronary artery spasm
ACTH Low ACTH	**Symptoms:** low energy and motivation; poor memory
CORTISOL High cortisol	**Conditions:** PMS; polycystic ovary syndrome; hypothyroidism. **Symptoms:** muscle weakness, muscle wasting; thinning skin; elevated glucose; insulin resistance and a tendency for easy weight gain and diabetes; fat deposition in chest, abdomen, and head; peptic ulcer; slow wound healing; lowered immune function; increased infections; constriction of blood vessels with elevated blood pressure
CORTISOL Low cortisol	**Conditions:** PMS; menopausal hot flashes; nausea in pregnancy; hypothyroidism; lupus; chronic fatigue syndrome; fibromyalgia; low libido; allergies and asthma **Symptoms:** inability to handle stress; crave stimulants — sugar, chocolate, caffeine, cigarettes; mental confusion; poor concentration; low blood pressure; dizziness; rapid heartbeat with exertion; fatigue; joint pain; increased inflammation anywhere; increased skin pigmentation; hypoglycemia; aching calves, flat feet; weak ankles and knees; increased white blood cell production; inflammation and autoimmune disease susceptibility

HORMONAL IMBALANCES IN WOMEN

HORMONE IMBALANCE	WOMEN'S HEALTH CONDITIONS AND SYMPTOMS
ALDOSTERONE High aldosterone	**Conditions:** PMS (water and salt retention); high blood pressure **Symptoms:** increased potassium loss in urine; slow irregular heartbeat; muscle cramps; fatigue; constipation; insomnia
ALDOSTERONE Low aldosterone	**Symptoms:** low blood pressure; dizziness; fatigue; frequent urination; excess perspiration; salt craving; muscle twitches; cardiac arrhythmia.
DHEA High DHEA	**Conditions:** converted to estrogen in breast cancer cells; may increase tumor growth in estrogen-driven cancers
DHEA Low DHEA	**Conditions:** heart disease; fibromyalgia; lupus; osteoporosis. **Symptoms:** fatigue; poor memory; decreased libido; anxiety; nervousness; decreased dreaming; elevated blood pressure; high cholesterol; atherosclerosis, increased infections; poor recovery after stress
TESTOSTERONE High testosterone	**Conditions:** PMS; amenorrhea; polycystic ovary syndrome; miscarriage; increased breast cancer risk **Symptoms:** easily angered; increased facial hair; increased muscle mass
TESTOSTERONE Low testosterone	**Symptoms:** low energy; little drive; poor memory; depression; no sexual orgasms; low libido; elevated blood pressure during or after menopause; loss of muscle mass
INSULIN Elevated insulin	**Conditions:** precocious puberty; amenorrhea; dysmenorrhea; polycystic ovary syndrome; diabetes; hypothyroidism; cardiovascular disease; breast cancer; uterine cancer; ovarian cancer **Symptoms:** high cholesterol, atherosclerosis; elevated testosterone; elevated estrogen
INSULIN Insulin resistance or insensitivity (metabolic syndrome)	**Conditions:** irregular periods; polycystic ovarian syndrome; preeclampsia in pregnancy; cardiovascular disease; adult onset diabetes **Symptoms:** high blood pressure; high cholesterol; elevated LDL, low HDL
INSULIN Low insulin	**Condition:** type 1 diabetes. **Symptoms:** low endurance.
INSULIN-LIKE GROWTH FACTOR (IGF-1) Elevated IGF-1	**Conditions:** precocious puberty; breast cancer; lung cancer; polycystic ovary syndrome; uterine fibroids; uterine cancer; ovarian cysts; ovarian cancer **Symptoms:** causes increased growth of tissue; promotes growth and invasiveness of malignant cells; decreases production of SHBG, which results in more available estrogen; stimulates increased estrogen production in the ovaries

HORMONAL IMBALANCES IN WOMEN

HORMONE IMBALANCE	WOMEN'S HEALTH CONDITIONS AND SYMPTOMS
GROWTH HORMONE Elevated growth hormone	**Conditions:** precocious puberty and early breast development; breast cancer; polycystic ovary syndrome; uterine fibroids; uterine cancer; ovarian cysts; ovarian cancer **Symptoms:** increases estradiol long term; elevates IGF-1; promotes cell multiplication
GROWTH HORMONE Decreased growth hormone	**Conditions:** amenorrhea; osteoporosis **Symptoms:** exhaustion; poor recovery from exertion; high LDL, low HDL, high blood pressure
THYROID HORMONES Underactive thyroid gland	**Conditions:** amenorrhea; PMS; heavy periods; menopausal hot flashes; endometriosis; polycystic ovary syndrome; infertility; miscarriage; breast cysts; breast cancer; fibromyalgia; osteoarthritis; cardiovascular disease **Symptoms:** low energy, especially in the morning; poor memory, slow thinking; anxiety and depression, worse in the morning, better when physically active; elevated cholesterol, high or low blood pressure; slow pulse (<70 bpm); numbness in hands and feet; carpal tunnel syndrome; dry skin, decreased perspiration; weight gain with puffy face and eyelids; hair falling out; husky voice; intolerance to cold; slow digestion, gas, constipation
THYROID HORMONES Overactive thyroid gland	**Conditions:** menopausal hot flashes **Symptoms:** nervousness, restlessness, irritability, insomnia; palpitations, rapid pulse; bulging eyes; enlarged thyroid; diarrhea, increased hunger; infrequent or scanty periods; weight loss, muscle weakness, tremors; increased perspiration; hair loss; heat intolerance; high blood pressure
PTH Decreased PTH	**Symptoms:** causes low levels of calcium in the blood, muscle spasms
PTH Elevated PTH	**Symptoms:** causes high levels of calcium in the blood, possibly calcium-containing kidney stones.
PROLACTIN Elevated prolactin	**Conditions:** amenorrhea; PMS; polycystic ovary syndrome; infertility; breast cancer; osteoporosis **Symptoms:** increases cell division in breast cells, causing increased breast density; can inhibit estrogen, causing amenorrhea or osteoporosis; may cause breast-milk secretion in non-breastfeeding women
MELATONIN Low melatonin	**Conditions:** precocious puberty; uterine fibroids; uterine cancer; breast cancer **Symptoms:** low energy in the morning; disturbed body rhythms; insomnia; morning anxiety and agitation; increases effects of estrogen dominance

HORMONE BALANCING STRATEGIES

ESTROGEN

Excessive Strong Estrogens (estrone and estradiol) due to:

- Lack of exercise
- High intake of meat
- High-fat diet
- Obesity
- Constipation
- Early puberty, late menopause
- Birth control pill, hormone replacement therapy
- Light at night

Increase Estriol (Weak Protective Estrogen) by:

1. Eating brassica family foods (cabbage, broccoli, kale, etc.)
2. Using indole-3-carbinol or DIM
3. Eating sea vegetables
4. Supplementing with iodine

Decrease Estradiol and Estrone by:

1. Increasing daily exercise
2. Eating vegetarian, low-fat diet, no dairy
3. Improving liver detoxification and bowel elimination (2 to 3 bowel movements/day)
4. Stalling puberty

Increased C4 and C16 Estrogens linked to:

- Xenoestrogens, pesticides, especially lindane
- Dioxin, car exhaust, paint fumes
- Phenols, formaldehyde
- Mercury, lead, arsenic, thallium, tin
- Pharmaceutical drugs
- Intestinal toxins and harmful bacteria
- Sugar, a high-fat diet, fried or rancid fats
- Inadequate protein

Make More C2 Estrogen, Less C4 and C16; Inactivate C4 Estrogen by:

1. Promoting formation of C2 estrogens with brassicas (cabbage, broccoli, brussel sprouts etc.) indole-3-carbinol or DIM, rosemary, schizandra, St. John's wort
2. Assisting Phase 2 methylation with methionine, SAM, MSM, choline, betaine, vitamins B6, B12, B2, folic acid, magnesium
3. Assisting Phase 2 glutathione conjugation with milk thistle, curcumin, ellagic acid, alpha lipoic acid, cysteine, NAC, goat whey, soy nuts, broccoli sprouts (sulforaphane), green tea, limonene and perillyl alcohol (essential oils of lemon, celery, sweet orange, palmarosa, lavender), zinc, selenium
4. Improving diet: low-fat diet, EPA (fish oil), ground flaxseeds, increased fiber, wheat bran, psyllium, probiotics, soy, red clover, phytoestrogens
5. Assisting glucuronidation with ellagic acid (red raspberries), vitamin B-6, psyllium, wheat bran, legumes, high fiber, calcium-D-glucarate (oranges, apples), fish oil, probiotics
6. Normalizing progesterone

HORMONE BALANCING STRATEGIES

ESTROGEN

Increased Production of Strong Estrogens (Estrone and Estradiol) due to: ● Aromatase enzyme	**Inhibit Aromatase by:** 1. Using chrysin (strong) >1500 mg/day 2. Eating ground flaxseed (moderate) 3. Eating genistein (soy) (weak) 4. Supplementing with zinc 5. Taking melatonin
Decreased SHBG (Sex Hormone Binding Globulin) due to: ● High cortisol ● High insulin ● High IGF-1 ● High testosterone ● Low thyroid	**Increase SHBG by:** 1. Adding more fiber, ground flaxseeds, soy, red clover sprouts to diet 2. Eating a low-fat vegetarian diet 3. Improving thyroid function 4. Normalizing cortisol, insulin, IGF-1, testosterone
Increased Number of Estrogen Receptors due to: ● Pesticides ● Xenoestrogens ● Hormone replacement therapy ● High Body Mass Index	**Decrease Number of Estrogen Receptors by:** 1. Taking melatonin and progesterone (decreases receptors in endometrium) 2. Supplementing with *Bifidobacterium bifidus* to increase butyrate
Xenoestrogens Attach to Estrogen Receptors from: Pesticides, PCBs, dioxin, PVC, phthalates, bisphenol A, brominated fire retardants, nonylphenyl ethoxylates, cadmium, mercury, lead	**Block Estrogen Receptors by:** 1. Increasing phytoestrogens: flax, soy, red clover, mung bean sprouts, pumpkin seeds 2. Using indole-3-carbinol, DIM 3. Supplementing with quercetin

PROGESTERONE

Decreased Progesterone due to: ● Phthalates ● PCBs ● Herbicides ● Hexachlorobenzene ● High cortisol levels ● High insulin levels ● Excess refined sugars and carbohydrates	**Increase Progesterone by:** 1. Supplementing with vitamins B-6, vitamin E, selenium, zinc, boron, chaste tree berry, stoneseed 2. Eating soy, ground flaxseed 3. Improving liver, bowel and adrenal function 4. Ensuring adequate melatonin levels 5. Normalizing cortisol levels 6. Normalizing insulin, avoid sugar 7. Normalizing thyroid (use zinc, tyrosine, seaweeds, selenium, guggul to increase T3) 8. Using progesterone cream (as a last resort)

HORMONE BALANCING STRATEGIES

PROLACTIN

High Prolactin due to:
- Estrogen dominance
- Underactive thyroid (high TRH)
- Hypoglycemia
- Stress
- Surgery
- Excess exercise
- Pregnancy
- Suckling
- Sexual intercourse
- Medications: phenothiazines, butyrophenones
- Sleep (it's secreted at night)

Decrease Prolactin by:
1. Normalizing low progesterone
2. Normalizing low thyroid
3. Normalizing blood sugar: eat small meals frequently
4. Reducing stress/use relaxation
5. Improving detoxification and elimination of estrogen
6. Using L-tyrosine to increase dopamine
7. Increasing melatonin by sleeping in a dark room and meditating before bedtime

TESTOSTERONE

Elevated Testosterone due to:
- High insulin levels
- Chronic stress, high cortisol
- Excess sugar and refined carbohydrates
- Polycystic ovary syndrome

Decrease Testosterone by:
1. Using flaxseed
2. Using chrysin
3. Eating seaweed or supplementing with iodine
4. Practicing relaxation or meditation daily
5. Avoiding sugar and refined carbohydrates
6. Exercising 1 hour a day or more

Deficient Testosterone due to:
- Aging
- Lack of exercise
- Stress; adrenal fatigue

Increase Testosterone by:
1. Supplementing with saw palmetto, American ginseng, nettle, damiana, sarsaparilla, zinc
2. Using fish oil plus evening primrose or borage oil
3. Restoring adrenal glands (see Cortisol)
4. Using testosterone cream (as a last resort)

Hormone Balancing Strategies

With the help of your health-care practitioner, use these guidelines to help balance your hormones.

HORMONE BALANCING STRATEGIES

THYROID HORMONES

Low Thyroid Function due to:

- Ionizing radiation: X-rays, nuclear power and weapons
- Lead, cadmium, mercury
- PCBs, pesticides, phthalates, dioxin, brominated fire retardants
- Prescription drugs: tamoxifen, steroids, etc.
- Excess estrogen levels
- Low progesterone levels
- High or low cortisol levels
- Impaired liver detoxification
- Low hydrochloric acid and mineral deficiencies
- Food sensitivities
- Intestinal toxins

Normalize Thyroid Hormone Production by:

1. Normalizing progesterone
2. Improving detoxification and elimination of estrogen
3. Detoxifying metals and chemicals (work to reduce environmental production)
4. Testing hydrochloric acid levels and increasing if necessary
5. Testing for and avoiding food sensitivities
6. Detoxifying bowel and using probiotics
7. Reducing or avoiding goitrogenic foods: raw brassicas, soy, millet, peanuts, pine nuts
8. Normalizing cortisol
9. Using tyrosine, iodine, or kelp
10. Using bladderwrack and ashwagandha
11. Using desiccated thyroid
12. Using T3, T4 hormones as last resort

Improve RT3:T3 Ratio; Increase Conversion of T4 to T3 by:

1. Detoxifying: mercury, cadmium, lead, chemicals
2. Using tyrosine, cysteine, iodine
3. Supplementing with zinc, selenium, copper, vitamin B-12
4. Using guggul
5. Eating flaxseed oil, fish oil, small amount of evening primrose or borage oil

Hyperthyroid Condition due to:

- Excess iodine
- Chronic stress/cortisol imbalance
- Radiation exposure
- Excess liver yang, with yin deficiency

Normalize Thyroid Hormones by:

1. Decreasing stress
2. Practicing daily relaxation/meditation
3. Using Chinese herbs to relax the liver
4. Supplementing with motherwort, skullcap, bugleweed, lemon balm, magnesium, vitamin B complex
5. Avoiding radiation

HORMONE BALANCING STRATEGIES

INSULIN

High Insulin Levels and Insulin Resistance due to:

- Excess sugar, soft drinks, alcohol, refined carbohydrates
- Animal fats
- Excess omega-6 fatty acids
- Obesity
- High blood sugar
- Chronic stress; high cortisol
- Lack of exercise

Normalize Insulin by:

1. Eating protein with each meal
2. Eating low glycemic carbohydrates
3. Avoiding sugar
4. Increasing fiber in diet
4. Increasing daily exercise
5. Practicing relaxation, meditation, yoga
6. Maintaining ideal weight
7. Supplementing with chromium, magnesium, zinc, vanadium, niacin, vitamin B complex, alpha lipoic acid
8. Using flax or fish oil, Gymnema sylvestre, cinnamon, bitter melon
9. Using 5-HTP to reduce sugar cravings

INSULIN-LIKE GROWTH FACTOR-1 (IGF-1)

Increased IGF-1 due to:

- Moderate alcohol consumption
- High insulin levels
- High growth hormone levels
- Drinking milk from growth hormone fed cows (USA)
- Bovine colostrum intake
- Low levels of binding protein IGFBP-3

Decrease IGF-1 by:

1. Eating a vegan diet
2. Supplementing with chromium, alpha lipoic acid, omega-3 oils
3. Taking tamoxifen (in estrogen receptor positive breast cancer, it lowers IGF-1, although it has side effects)

CORTISOL

High or Low Cortisol Levels due to Stress, Overexertion, Childhood Abuse result in:

- High blood glucose
- High insulin, increased IGF-1
- Fat deposition in torso/more estrogen in breasts
- Depressed T-killer cells
- Low progesterone
- Increased testosterone
- Decreased efficiency of thyroid hormone
- Decreased melatonin production

Normalize Cortisol by:

1. Practicing meditation and relaxation
2. Counseling
3. Finding supportive people or group
4. Supplementing with vitamin B complex, vitamin C, magnesium, zinc, MSM
5. Using Relora to lower cortisol and relax
6. Using Ho Shou Wu, Siberian ginseng, licorice root, borage, oats, schizandra, rhodiola, ashwagandha, suma to support adrenals and increase cortisol

HORMONE BALANCING STRATEGIES

MELATONIN

Decreased Melatonin due to:	Increase Melatonin by:
• Shift work	1. Eating foods high in tryptophan
• Light at night	2. Supplementing with vitamins B-3 and B-6, calcium, magnesium, zinc
• Insomnia	
• Chronic exposure to strong electromagnetic fields, above 2 mG	3. Meditating or praying before bedtime
	4. Sleeping in dark room
• Alcohol, caffeine, nicotine, drugs	5. Getting 20 minutes in natural light in a.m.
• Cortisol imbalance	6. Exercising daily
	7. Normalizing cortisol

GROWTH HORMONE

Increased Growth Hormone due to:	Decrease Growth Hormone by:
• Stress	1. Reducing stress/using relaxation
• Hypoglycemia	2. Normalizing blood sugar and eating small meals frequently
• Strenuous exercise	
• Increased estrogen	3. Decreasing estrogen
• Dairy containing bovine growth hormone	4. Avoiding dairy or beef products containing bovine growth hormone
• Colostrum products	
• During sleep it naturally rises	

DID YOU KNOW...

The changing hormone levels that occur with aging predispose us to earlier sleep onset, earlier morning awakening, easy awakening through the night, and a more shallow sleep.

Hormones and Aging

As we age, our hormonal balance shifts. For example, both thyroid hormones and cortisol may circulate for longer periods in the bloodstream because they are metabolized more slowly in the liver. This will cause both the thyroid and adrenal glands to produce less of these hormones. Other hormones, such as estrogen and progesterone, decline as we age due to the aging of the ovaries.

Melatonin, TSH, testosterone, prolactin, and growth hormone levels all decrease with aging. The decline of melatonin makes us more susceptible to disturbances of circadian rhythms and to cancer.

The nasal breathing cycle loses its rhythmicity with aging, also coinciding with the drop in melatonin. The mean levels of ACTH and cortisol increase as we age. Aging can also cause changes in the sensitivity of target cells to hormones, caused by a loss of receptors for that specific hormone. All of this underscores the need for more frequent testing of hormones as we age and affirms the importance establishing hormone balancing practices in our daily lives.

In the next chapter, we outline testing procedures and strategies to follow at each stage of a woman's life to promote health at every age.

DID YOU KNOW...

Prana is the universal life force that permeates and moves through all living things, coordinating thought processes as well as biochemical and physiological functions.

MEDITATION FOR NERVOUS SYSTEM BALANCE

● *Balancing the Hormone and Nervous Systems*

To help balance your hormones, try this meditation, which will strengthen your nervous system so that you can cope with stress more easily, balance the pituitary gland so your hormones are better regulated, and enhance intuition through its effect on the 6th chakra.

1. Sit cross-legged or in a chair with your hands resting on your knees. Touch the tips of your index fingers and thumbs together (gyan mudra). Have your eyes almost closed.
2. Inhale in 10 equal parts or sniffs. With each part of the inhale, move the hands mechanically (in small jerks) one-tenth of the way toward the forehead. The palms face up and all the fingers are straight during the inhale.
3. On the 10th inhale rest your palms on your forehead, covering the eyes and third eyepoint, with the fingers pointing up.
4. As you exhale through the nose, join the fingertips of your two hands and let the hands come down in front of the centerline of the body in a slow smooth motion.
5. Separate the hands at the level of the navel point and return them to the original position on your knees, in gyan mudra.
6. On each short inhale, mentally vibrate the mantra "Wha" (which means experience of ecstasy) and on the exhale mentally vibrate "Guru" (which means wisdom). Continue for 3 to 11 minutes.

YOGA FOR BALANCING THE GLANDS AND LYMPH

Here is a set of four yoga exercises for balancing the glands and the lymphatic system.

◉ Pituitary Gland Balance

This exercise stimulates the pituitary gland to create balance between the parasympathetic and sympathetic nervous system.

1. Sit cross-legged with the arms extended straight out to the sides parallel to the ground, your palms facing up.
2. Begin moving your middle finger up and down rapidly.
3. Using a strong breath, inhale through the nose as your raise the finger and exhale through the nose as you lower it.
4. Continue for 3 to 7 minutes.

◉ Lymphatic Circulation

This exercise improves spinal flexibility and makes the body more resilient to stress and shock. It improves lymphatic circulation in the chest, underarm and breast area.

1. Remaining cross-legged, stretch your arms out in front, parallel to the ground. Place your left hand over your right, interlacing the fingers with the palms facing down.
2. Begin to swing your arms rapidly from side to side, moving the head and neck in the same direction as the arms. Keep your elbows straight.
3. Inhale through the nose as you swing to the left, exhale through the nose as you swing to the right.
4. Continue moving with a powerful breath for 3 to 5 minutes.

◉ Parathyroid Glands

This exercise balances the parathyroid glands, stimulates weight loss, and moves the lymph.

1. Still sitting, extend the arms straight out in front, parallel to the ground. Make fists of your hands with the thumbs tucked inside touching the fleshy mound below the little finger.
2. Keeping the arms and hands straight, bring the left arm up as the right arm goes down.
3. Continue alternating moving the arms up and down forcefully, coordinating the movement with powerful breathing for 3 to 8 minutes.

◉ Prana and Apana Balance

This exercise balances prana and apana, corrects the energy of the navel, and increases the prana flowing through the breast area. It also improves the flexibility of the pelvis.

1. Sit with the soles of your feet pressed together. Pull the feet in toward the groin, keeping your knees as close to the floor as possible.
2. Interlace your fingers and place your hands in your lap.
3. Inhale and raise your hands above your head while simultaneously drawing your knees up towards the center of the body.
4. Exhale and lower the knees and arms down to the original position.
5. Continue rhythmically, coordinating the movement with powerful breathing for 3 to 8 minutes.

Women's Health through the Ages

O*ur health exists on a continuum and, like history, is dependent on what has gone before. If we want to have good health for our whole life, and if we want to protect the health of our children, we can start early — before we conceive the next generation.*

What follows is a guide to good health practices, tests, and supplements for each stage of a woman's life, beyond the basic four steps to good health. For all ages, follow the Best Dietary Strategies for Optimum Health described in the Food as Medicine section.

These practices are elaborated further in subsequent sections of the book. Here, we provide a preview of that information — or a quick review once you have read ahead.

Before Conceiving the Next Generation

We begin the cycle of life at conception, ensuring the good health of our children and ourselves at this most important and exciting stage of life.

Health Practices
- Ask your health-care practitioner to check your blood levels for pesticides, PCBs, and brominated fire retardants. Check to see what toxins are in your neighborhood by submitting your postal code to www.pollutionwatch.org in Canada or www.scorecard.org in the United States.
- With your partner, finish a 100-hour sauna detoxification at least 3 months before conception to remove chemicals that could harm your fetus in utero and through breast milk. For instructions, see the Seasonal Cleaning and Rejuvenation Program section.
- Filter your water, and store it in glass, not plastic.
- Make your home a safer place to raise children:
  - Replace carpet with hardwood flooring and eliminate lead paint.
  - Create a dust-free play area for your infant to decrease exposure to brominated fire retardants.

- Do not use green pressure-treated wood on outside decks or play sets because of its high arsenic content.
- Remove products containing foam from your home. Eliminate plastic as much as possible. Avoid polyvinyl chloride (PVC) in windows, flooring, blinds, and furniture.
- If you are building a new house, find out what materials are being used and insist that they be non-toxic and sustainable.
- See the Pregnancy chapter in the Women's Conditions section of this book for other guidelines.

SPIRITUAL PRACTICE AND RITUALS

At the time of conception, not only your physical health but also your emotional well-being and spiritual state may influence the future life of your child. Do not have sexual intercourse when you are angry or when you have unresolved issues with your partner. Nurture spiritual intimacy as well as sexual intimacy by praying, meditating, or reading sacred scriptures or poetry together before intercourse. Sex provides an opportunity for spiritual as well as physical union. Honor and receive one another as an embodiment of the divine. For more guidelines, see the sacred sex discussion in the Hormone Balance chapter.

During Pregnancy

Health Practices

- Spend time outside in areas where the air is fresh. Exercise and stretch daily.
- Practice prenatal yoga. Meditate regularly throughout pregnancy. See the Sa Ta Na Ma meditation in the Pregnancy chapter of the Women's Conditions section.
- Create a calm, uplifting environment for yourself during pregnancy. Remove yourself from negative people and environments.
- Take turns with your partner in gently massaging your abdomen and the growing fetus inside with cold-pressed almond oil throughout your pregnancy, sending loving thoughts and speaking warm words to your child. Almond-oil massage will also prevent stretch marks.
- Take *Lactobacillus acidophilus* capsules or powder during the last month of pregnancy. If the birth is caesarian, give your child *Lactobacillus acidophilus* powder immediately after birth, followed by *Bifidobacterium bifidus* for the next few days or weeks to inoculate the bowel with healthy flora. If you or your child need antibiotics during pregnancy, delivery, or after the birth, supplement with these probiotics at the same time.

- Avoid chemical toxins — paint, perfumes, nail polish, most cosmetics, strong cleaning products, new furniture, new cars, and new homes. Avoid radiation by not having X-rays if possible. Fly as little as possible.
- Plan as natural a childbirth as possible.

SPIRITUAL PRACTICE AND RITUALS

Women can be supported during pregnancy with ritual ceremonies, such as the traditional 'shower,' where the pregnant woman is welcomed to the community of mothers with gifts and games, or the yogic tradition of celebrating the 120th day of pregnancy by welcoming the incoming soul. For this ceremony, family, friends, and community members are invited to a celebration that can include prayer, chanting, food, dancing, and gift-giving for the mother-to-be. If you are pregnant, design an uplifting ceremony to celebrate the new soul.

Continue to surround yourself with uplifting environments through the later months of pregnancy. Decrease stress, negativity, anger, and worry.

Affirming Your Child's Developmental Stage

Our children, while in the womb, need to feel loved and secure. You and your partner can talk to your child during pregnancy, affirming your love, with these positive sentiments:

You are wanted and loved.

We'll take care of you.

You are strong, healthy, and whole.

You are perfect just as you are.

You belong here with us.

We are receptive to your feelings and needs.

You are coming here for a reason.

DID YOU KNOW...

Some children are able to recall an event that occurred while they were in the womb, and can describe the emotional state their mothers experienced at the time.

Infancy

Health Practices

- Breastfeed for at least 9 months, preferably for a year.
- To prevent lifelong allergies and autoimmune disease, be careful about how and when you introduce foods to your child:
- Start with vegetables and fruits only at 6 months.
- Add cooked millet meal, oatmeal, barley, and quinoa at 9 months.
- Add tofu and legumes at 12 months.
- Add small amounts of organic chicken (if you are not vegetarian) at 18 months.

- Add nut butters, small amounts of wheat, citrus, and organic eggs at 21 months.
- Continue supplementation with *Lactobacillus acidophilus* and *Bifidobacterium bifidus* to promote healthy intestinal flora and prevent eczema and allergies.
- Give your infant $\frac{1}{2}$ tsp flaxseed oil or omega-3 algae oil (or very pure fish oil) starting at 6 months to support brain development.
- Minimize the amount of fruit juice you give to your child. Make sure it is organic and dilute it with 2 parts water to 1 part juice. Avoid sugar so your child grows up without sweet cravings and with strong teeth.
- To help with teeth and bone development, use the homeopathic tissue salts Calc phos, Silicea, and Calc fluor, all in a 6X potency, 2 tablets of each daily.
- Feed your infant moderate amounts of diluted organic soy milk after 12 months of age to prevent breast cancer later in life.
- Avoid dairy and minimize wheat. Eat a variety of foods and rotate them.
- Do not give your child a plastic soother, which may contain estrogenic chemicals. Provide drinks in sturdy glass cups. Do not buy plastic or foam toys — choose wood and cloth instead.
- Massage your infant with cold pressed almond oil daily during infancy.

SPIRITUAL PRACTICE AND RITUALS

Your newborn child's security and biological rhythms will be strengthened by repetitive actions and rituals. These can include:

- Creating a quiet time on waking when you sit in meditation or prayer with your child, if just for a few minutes.
- Blessing your food before eating.
- Going outside on daily walks in a park, forest, field, or lakeside.
- Taking an evening bath.
- Telling an evening bedtime story and saying a prayer.

If possible, try to spend the first 40 days after birth in quiet seclusion with your partner and infant to establish secure bonding and to protect your infant from overstimulation and negativity. At this time, the child's aura is wide open and will be receptive to all vibrations, good and bad. Create a serene nest in your home to welcome your child gently to this incarnation. Try to restrict the number of visitors and do not take your infant into busy or loud public places during this 40-day period.

Affirming Your Child's Developmental Stage

The messages we need to give our children during the first two years are:

Birth to 6 months

It's okay for you to be here, to be fed, touched, and taken care of.

Your needs will be taken care of.

I like to hold you, be near you, and touch you.

You have a right to be here.

6 to 18 months

It's all right for you to explore and experiment.

You can do things and be supported at the same time.

You can be curious and manipulate your surroundings.

It's okay for you to initiate activities and actions.

You can gain approval while doing what you want.

18 to 24 months

I'm glad that you are growing up.

You can think for yourself.

It's all right for you to let others know when you are angry.

It's okay for you to say no and to separate from me.

You can express what you need and I will listen.

Early Childhood (Ages 2–10)

Health Practices

- Ask your health-care practitioner to test your child annually for zinc deficiency.
- Give your children at least three fruits each day, a salad, and 1 to 2 cups of steamed vegetables. Serve cooked whole grains like oatmeal, brown rice, basmati rice, wild rice, barley, buckwheat, quinoa, amaranth, and millet, rather than bread, pasta, and boxed cereal.
- Supplement with calcium, a multivitamin, and vitamin C.
- Use dulse powder and sea salt in your cooking to supply needed trace minerals.
- Make sure your daughters exercise at least 1 hour a day.
- Prevent your daughters from becoming overweight to delay puberty and prevent diabetes.

DID YOU KNOW...

Medical opinion is divided over the benefits and risks of vaccinations. Talk to a healthcare practitioner about the pros and cons of vaccination for infectious diseases. Discuss how to minimize the harmful effects of vaccination, especially the mercury and aluminum present in vaccinations to prevent autism.

SPIRITUAL PRACTICES AND RITUALS

Try to establish daily and seasonal practices and rituals in your children's lives that will sustain them into adulthood. These might include:

- Taking a morning shower followed by some yoga stretches and prayer.
- Blessing your food together before meals with a prayer or mantra.
- Giving thanks at the end of the day for what has occurred or use a specific prayer. Bless the people in your lives and others who are suffering.
- Doing a short breathing exercise or meditation before bed.
- Introducing them to the scriptures of your religious tradition or all traditions and reading passages with them once a week.
- Celebrating the solstices, equinoxes, and religious holidays according to your tradition.

- Restrict computer and television time. One study found that regular time spent working on a computer disturbed the balance between the hypothalamus, pituitary, and adrenal glands in 6-year-old children.
- Begin weekly saunas for $\frac{1}{2}$ hour at a time.
- Avoid food and drinks packaged in plastic. Send sandwiches to daycare or school wrapped in waxed paper and a brown paper bag, a stainless steel sandwich box, or a hot lunch in a stainless steel thermos. Send filtered water in a small stainless steel thermos or arrange for filtered water to be dispensed from glass at school.
- Avoid plastic or vinyl boots, raincoats, umbrellas, and toys.
- Store-bought pajamas often contain brominated fire retardants. Wash them several times before allowing your children to wear them.
- Teach your children how to use a skin brush before showering to move the lymph.
- Keep fingernails cut short and encourage frequent handwashing to prevent parasite infection. Keep pets outside of bedrooms. Do a parasite cleanse once a year. See the Seasonal Cleansing and Rejuvenation section for guidelines.

Affirming Your Child's Developmental Stage

Before the age of 7, children learn by imitation and example. They are eager to participate in whatever activities we will do with them. Try to provide them with a wide range of hands-on experiences, which might include creative activities or play with painting, clay modeling, music, dance, sports, martial arts, and yoga.

Involve them with simple tasks at home, such as setting the table and washing dishes. Read to your children and encourage them to read on their own. At this age, they need stories about courage in overcoming obstacles and noble sacrifice.

Engage them in activities with you that benefit others or the earth — food drives for the needy, environmental clean-ups, tree planting on Earth Day, planting the garden or tending a community garden.

The messages you can give your child during this period are:

You don't have to act scared, sick, sad, or angry to be taken care of or to get what you need.

You can have your own view of the world, to be who you are, and to test your power.

You can be powerful and still have needs.

It's okay for you to act and find out the consequences of your behavior.

You can explore who you are and find out what you are about.

You can do things your way and make mistakes.

You can disagree and think differently from others.

You can trust your feelings and intuition to guide you.

Adolescence (Ages 11–18)

Health Practices

- Continue to test for zinc deficiency annually. Also use the oxidata test at least once a year to determine free radical activity and the need for antioxidants.
- Avoid the birth control pill, if possible, using barrier methods of birth control or abstinence. Avoid sexual intercourse during the fertile time of the menstrual cycle.
- Encourage regular consumption of organic tofu and organic soy milk (unless there is a soy allergy) to prevent breast cancer and heart disease.
- Add 1 to 2 tbsp of ground flaxseed and 1 tbsp oat bran to breakfast cereals. Take very pure fish oil or algae oil daily.
- Eat turmeric, onions, garlic, ginger, raw brassicas, and seaweed daily.
- Supplement with extra calcium (with magnesium and vitamin D), vitamin C, and a multivitamin daily.
- Avoid cosmetics that contain lead, parabens, phthalates, and sodium laurel sulphate. Dr. Hauschka, Weleda, and Aubrey are companies that produce safe cosmetics. See www.thinkbeforeyoupink.org and www.nottoopretty.com for more information on contaminants in cosmetics.
- Do sauna therapy for at least 1 hour weekly to eliminate toxins.
- Practice skin brushing before showering once a day to move the lymph.
- Try yoga and meditation to learn to handle stress.

DID YOU KNOW...

You should begin monthly breast self-exams at age 17 and annual PAP and chlamydia tests if sexually active.

SPIRITUAL PRACTICES AND RITUALS

If we honor the onset of menstruation with an empowering rite of passage, we can positively shape young women's relationships between the cycles of nature and their bodies, fertility, creativity, and femininity. Collaborate with other women in your life in designing a meaningful ritual to acknowledge menstruation as a vital rite of passage. Here are some suggestions:

- Schedule the event on the evening of a full moon and celebrate the link between the phases of the menstrual cycle and the phases of the moon.
- Invite the women gathered to share positive stories about their relationship with their menstrual cycle, fertility, or the moon.
- Serve tea made from nettle, tang kuei, and red raspberry, which are tonics for the uterus and blood.
- Read stories, myths, or poems about the moon and coming of age.
- Link the fertility of women to the fertility of the earth. Honor the earth's role in providing nourishment for building blood and bringing forth new life. Observe the similarity between the ovaries ripening and releasing an egg to a young woman's emerging ability to express her power, creativity, and radiance.

Similarly, breast development can be celebrated by teaching your daughter simple breast self-massage (see the Fibrocystic Breast Disease chapter in the Women's Conditions section) and giving her massage oil containing essential oils of lavender, palmarosa, lemon, rosemary, and juniper in a base of extra virgin olive oil or almond oil. Your daughter can invite her friends over to make their own massage oil if you provide them with the ingredients.

Affirming Your Child's Developmental Stage

At this stage of their development, girls need some of the following affirmations from you:

You can take responsibility for your own needs, feelings, and behavior.

We can disagree and still respect and love one another.

You can have sexual feelings and determine how they are expressed or met responsibly.

You can act in a mature way and still ask for what you need, or ask for help.

You have a place and a voice among adults.

My love is with you wherever you are.

You are welcome to come home again.

Young Adulthood (Ages 19–29 years)

Health Practices

- Ask your health-care practitioner to conduct the following tests annually:
  - blood pressure
  - free radical activity (oxidata test)
  - zinc taste test
  - red blood cell elements
  - essential fatty acids
  - fasting glucose, insulin, and IGF-1
  - salivary levels of estradiol, estrone, estriol, and progesterone between days 20 and 23 of your menstrual cycle; cortisol 4x on a single day to determine subtle endocrine imbalances that can be adjusted naturally; melatonin between 1:00 a.m. and 3:00 a.m.; C2/C16 hydroxyestrone ratio in urine
  - pelvic exam and PAP test
  - chlamydia if you are sexually active
  - clinical breast exam
- On your own, conduct the following tests:
  - breast self-exam monthly
  - skin exam monthly to detect changes and early lesions
  - pH of your urine and saliva weekly
- Eat $\frac{1}{2}$ cup organic tofu and drink 1 cup of organic soy milk daily. Add 2–4 tbsp ground flaxseed and 2 tbsp oat bran to breakfast cereal. Use 2 tsp turmeric, 2 cloves garlic, raw brassicas, and seaweeds daily.

DID YOU KNOW...

Approximately 20% of North American women over age 18 have high blood pressure, but about one-third of them don't know it.

SPIRITUAL PRACTICES AND RITUALS

This is a time to come to terms with your spiritual identity and to become part of a larger community where you feel a sense of belonging and trust. You may want to explore different ways of expressing your spiritual identity:

- Being alone in nature
- Creating art — painting, sculpture, music, poetry
- Worshipping in a church, synagogue, mosque, or temple
- Charitable service
- Practicing yoga, meditation, tai chi, or qi qong
- Reciting and studying scripture

Commit to an ongoing relationship with your soul by engaging in daily spiritual practice. This will carry you through life's hardships and prepare you for death.

- Avoid cosmetics and health-care products that contain lead, parabens, phthalates, and sodium laurel sulphate.
- Do aerobic exercise at least 40 minutes a day or 4 hours a week as well as yoga or stretching at least 3 times weekly.
- Practice a breathing exercise or meditation for at least 11 minutes daily to relax, balance hormones, and decrease liver stagnation.
- Conduct an annual bowel, kidney, liver, and gallbladder cleansing. For instructions, see the Seasonal Cleansing and Rejuvenation Program section.
- Do a 100-hour sauna detoxification program once every 5 years and then an hour a week as maintenance. For instructions, see the Seasonal Cleansing and Rejuvenation Program section.
- Practice skin brushing before showering once a day to move the lymph. For instructions, see the Seasonal Cleansing and Rejuvenation Program section.

Affirming Your Developmental Stage

The following affirmations may help in this phase of your life:

> *I define my values and beliefs for myself — and I commit to them.*
>
> *I am true to myself even while honoring the opinions and uniqueness of others.*
>
> *I am lovable at every age, and have the capacity to love others.*
>
> *My needs are important and deserve to be met.*
>
> *I have the right to learn and study what is meaningful to me.*
>
> *I can decide whom I want to associate with, and can say no to social obligations.*
>
> *I have a definite place in the world, an important role to play.*
>
> *I have the right to use and develop my skills and talents in doing something that makes me happy.*
>
> *I have the right to change my mind.*

Maturity (30–50 years)

Health Practices

- Ask your health-care practitioner to conduct the following tests annually:
  - blood pressure
  - free radical activity (oxidata test)
  - zinc taste test
  - red blood cell elements
  - essential fatty acids
  - fasting glucose, insulin, and IGF-1

- salivary levels of estradiol, estrone, estriol, and progesterone between days 20 and 23 of your menstrual cycle; cortisol 4x on a single day to determine subtle endocrine imbalances that can be adjusted naturally; melatonin between 1:00 a.m. and 3:00 a.m.; C2/C16 hydroxyestrone ratio in urine
- pelvic exam and PAP test
- chlamydia if you are sexually active
- clinical breast exam and thermogram
- ultrasound, fine needle aspiration, mammography, and biopsy to come to a definitive diagnosis if you find a suspicious breast lump
- traditional Chinese medicine pulse and tongue test for imbalances
- darkfield microscopy and biological terrain assessment
- dental exam (twice a year) to check for periodontal disease
- baseline for thyroid hormones and function by age 35 — basal body temperature, TSH, free T3, free T4, reverse T3, antimicrosomal antibodies, antithyroglobulin antibodies, possibly TRH stimulation test
- starting at age 35, bone resorption with the urine test that measures deoxypyridinoline, indicating bone loss
- baseline bone mineral density scan at age 50 and every 2 to 4 years thereafter. Start earlier if you have been a smoker or if you reached menopause before age 45
- baseline at age 30, and then retest every 1 to 5 years for levels of cholesterol, LDL, HDL, triglycerides, lipoprotein-a, homo-cysteine, C-reactive protein, fibrinogen, fasting insulin, and fasting glucose to detect early cardiovascular disease and diabetes
- colonoscopy at age 50 to rule out colon cancer
- occult blood in the stool starting at age 50

- On your own, conduct the following tests:
  - breast self-exam monthly
  - skin exam monthly to detect changes and early lesions
  - pH of your urine and saliva weekly
- Eat 1/2 cup organic tofu plus 1 cup of soy milk daily to prevent breast cancer. Use 2 to 4 tbsp ground flaxseed, 2 tbsp oat bran, 3 tsp psyllium seed powder as fiber daily. Eat 2 tsp turmeric, 2 cloves garlic, 2 tbsp seaweed, 1 onion, 3 tsp cinnamon daily.
- Avoid cosmetics and health-care products that contain lead, parabens, phthalates, and sodium laurel sulphate.
- Practice skin brushing before showering once a day to move the lymph. For instructions, see the Seasonal Cleansing and Rejuvenation section.
- Do a 100-hour sauna detoxification program once every 5 years and then 2 hours a week as maintenance. For instructions, see the Seasonal Cleansing and Rejuvenation section.

DID YOU KNOW...

Although breast cancer is the leading cause of death in North American women between 35 and 50, you can reduce your risk of the disease by up to 60% when you exercise 4 hours weekly.

SPIRITUAL PRACTICE AND RITUALS

Despite the demands of your career and family, make time each day to listen to your intuition, to quiet your mind with yoga or meditation, to do a breathing exercise before bed, and to pray. If you have trouble doing this on your own, join an existing class or gather a group of women together who can support each other spiritually.

Be sensitive to the ways in which your psyche shifts throughout your menstrual cycle, and nurture yourself with some quiet time while you are having your period.

If you have a family, develop meaningful rituals that coincide with the cycles of nature — schedule family hikes or vacations during the solstice periods and discuss how each of you can use the transformational energy during these times for growth.

- Conduct an annual bowel, kidney, liver, and gallbladder cleanse. For instructions, see the Seasonal Cleansing and Rejuvenation Program section.
- Walk an hour a day and practice stretching 3 times weekly (tai chi, yoga, pilates).
- Practice a breathing exercise or meditation for at least 11 minutes daily to relax, balance hormones and decrease liver stagnation.

Affirming Your Developmental Stage

This is the life stage during which many of us are most productive, and during which we often struggle with juggling family, career, spiritual growth and taking care of our physical and emotional health. Some affirmations to remember during this phase are:

I can be successful with my career while being sensitive to my family's needs.

I have a right to put my own needs before the needs of others sometimes.

I deserve to enjoy myself and experience fulfillment in my life today.

I care for my physical body while I work and care for my family.

I have a right to sexual fulfillment and exploration within my relationship.

I listen to my inner guidance and follow through with its directives.

I make time to explore and develop my spirituality, despite other obligations.

I deserve the best possible life for myself and can change my circumstances for the better.

Elder (over 50 years)

Health Practices

- Ask your health-care practitioner to conduct the following tests annually:
  - blood pressure
  - electrocardiogram at age 50, then every 3 to 5 years to monitor heart health
  - eye exam every 1–4 years
  - oxidata test (free radical activity)
  - zinc taste test
  - red blood cell elements
  - essential fatty acids
  - fasting glucose, insulin, and IGF-1
  - salivary levels of estradiol, estrone, estriol, and progesterone between days 20 and 23 of your menstrual cycle; cortisol 4x on a single day to determine subtle endocrine imbalances that can be adjusted naturally; melatonin between 1:00 a.m. and 3:00 a.m.; C2/C16 hydroxyestrone ratio in urine
  - pelvic exam and PAP test
  - clinical breast exam and thermogram.
  - ultrasound, fine needle aspiration, mammography, and biopsy to come to a definitive diagnosis if you find a suspicious lump
  - traditional Chinese medicine pulse and tongue test for imbalances
  - darkfield microscopy and biological terrain assessment
  - dental exam (twice a year) for periodontal disease
  - basal body temperature and thyroid hormones — TSH, free T3, free T4, reverse T3, antimicrosomal antibodies, antithyroglobulin antibodies, possibly TRH stimulation test
  - bone resorption with the urine test that measures deoxypyridinoline, indicating bone loss
  - bone mineral density scan every 2 to 4 years after age 50
  - cholesterol, LDL, HDL, triglycerides, lipoprotein-a, homocysteine, C-reactive protein, fibrinogen, fasting insulin, and fasting glucose to detect early cardiovascular disease and diabetes
  - occult blood in the stool at age 50 to rule out colon cancer and then every 5–10 years thereafter, more frequently if polyps are discovered
  - presence of *Helicobacter pylori* in the stomach
  - vitamin B-12 and hydrochloric acid deficiency

- On your own, conduct the following tests:
  - breast self-exam monthly
  - skin exam monthly to detect changes and early lesions
  - pH of your urine and saliva weekly

DID YOU KNOW...

Currently, one in two women over 50 will suffer a vertebrae fracture because of decreased bone density. Women typically lose 30% of their skeletal structure between age 45 and 75.

- Eat ½ cup organic tofu plus 1 cup of organic soy milk daily to prevent cancer.
- Use 2 to 4 tbsp ground flaxseed, 2 to 4 tbsp oat bran, and 3 tsp psyllium seed powder daily to improve elimination and normalize cholesterol and blood sugar.
- Use 3 tsp turmeric, 2 cloves garlic, 2 tbsp seaweed, 1 onion, 3 tsp cinnamon daily to prevent Alzheimer's disease, heart disease, diabetes, and cancer.
- Take digestive enzymes before meals along with apple cider vinegar or herbal bitters before meals to stimulate hydrochloric acid production.
- Use 2 to 4 tbsp flaxseed oil and 3000 mg fish oil daily to prevent heart disease, arthritis, cancer, and memory loss.

SPIRITUAL PRACTICES AND RITUALS

When menstruation ceases, we enter another stage of our lives. We can honor our age, wisdom, and power with an affirming ritual that celebrates our maturity. Traditionally, the elder or crone was revered as one who understood the cycle of creation. Sacred medicines were administered by women elders to community members.

If we have nurtured them, our intuition, insight, and power to speak our minds are at their peak during this phase. We can inspire and guide others, perhaps even change the course of history (herstory) with our wisdom and experience.

To honor this passage, create a ritual using the following suggestions as a guide:

- Choose a symbolic way to represent the passage — you could go on a canoe trip, climb a mountain, or do a long solo hike before your ceremony. If you are holding a gathering, you could pass through a gate, walk through a door, or stand before the moon.
- Choose a sacred object that will represent your initiation into your elder phase — a necklace or ring, a special hat or scarf — and have someone place it on you.
- Celebrate with music, chanting, food, drink, and socializing.
- Schedule the rite on the new moon or full moon.
- Invite other women to speak one by one in a circle about the strength, wisdom, and power you have to share. Pass around a candle, stone, talking stick, or other sacred object as each person speaks.
- Create a photo album that illustrates your life story. Add reminiscences and reflections.
- Write out and read to others your own realizations about the purpose of the next phase of your life.

During this stage in our lives, we can focus most fully on our spiritual development, with diminishing demands from work and family. Become more committed to your spiritual practice, spending more time in yoga, meditation, and prayer. We need these as we age to maintain our flexibility, youthfulness and hormone balance. Find the spiritual teachers you need to stay inspired. You may want to volunteer your time to help others or for an environmental cause — do what brings you meaning and serves the greater whole.

- Brush twice daily and floss teeth once daily to prevent periodontal disease and heart disease. Avoid root canals. Use methacrylate or porcelain fillings.
- Practice skin brushing before showering once a day to move the lymph. For instructions, see the Seasonal Cleansing and Rejuvenation section.
- Walk an hour a day and adopt a weight-resistance program to maintain bone density. Practice stretching three times weekly (tai chi, yoga, pilates).
- Practice a breathing exercise or meditation for at least 11 minutes daily to relax, balance hormones, and decrease liver stagnation.
- Do a 100-hour sauna detoxification program once every 5 years and then 3 hours a week as maintenance to prevent diseases caused by toxicity. For instructions, see the Seasonal Cleansing and Rejuvenation section.
- Conduct an annual bowel, kidney, liver, and gallbladder cleansing. For instructions, see the Seasonal Cleansing and Rejuvenation section.
- Use the homeopathic flu prevention protocol annually from October to May. See the Seasonal Cleansing and Rejuvenation section for instructions.

Affirming Your Developmental Stage

During this stage of your life you have accumulated power and wisdom that can be shared. Keep the following affirmations in mind as you pass on these gifts:

I bless and release my children as they leave home.

I create space for my unfolding self.

I open to receive guidance for how I am to live my remaining years.

I acknowledge my years of experience, wisdom and power and choose how best to share these.

I make my spiritual development a priority.

I give back to my family, community and the earth in ways that are meaningful to me.

I make peace with my past, and heal old wounds and misunderstandings.

I prepare myself for death, and to relinquish this earthly body and all attachments.

DID YOU KNOW...

You can eliminate over 80% of your lifetime body burden of environmental chemicals with 100 hours of sauna detoxification.

LOOKING AHEAD ...

When we maintain well-balanced biorhythms, we ensure our good health through the stages of our lives. However, environmental toxins, outside of our immediate control, can disrupt these natural rhythms and cause ill health and disease. In the next section, we examine how we have been exposed to these toxins and how we can restore not only our own health but also the health of our Mother Earth.

The Earth is our first mother. Her soil, water, air, and energy nourish our bodies and shape our health from the moment of conception onward. However, we have violated the earth by contaminating the soil, squandering fresh water, polluting the air, and dissipating her energy. The consequences of our carelessness now threaten our well-being. As the earth becomes progressively polluted, so do our individual bodies.

To heal ourselves, we need to heal the earth. Ecological medicine is needed to cleanse and renew both our bodies and our planet. We can give nutrients back to the soil, decrease pesticide use, protect our water resources, use clean power, and practice conservation. This is urgent. We must direct our energies toward protecting the sanctity and integrity of the earth. We invite all women to join wholeheartedly in this endeavor to heal the earth and to heal ourselves.

This section of the book provides a guide to identifying health risks in your environment and strategies to minimize these risks. You can become an active participant in renewing the earth's four elements — soil, water, air, and energy (fire) — and in creating a healthy body ecology. Together, we can make a difference.

Our Soil

Not unlike our bodies, soil is a living biological entity composed of a community of organisms, organic matter, and minerals. A healthy soil provides a high mineral and nutritional reservoir to nurture the vitality of the plants and, in turn, the animals, including humans, that are sustained by it. Plants require at least 24 minerals for optimum growth that move up the food chain, directly or indirectly to us. However, many of us are chronically deficient in these minerals because we have mismanaged our soil.

Mismanagement of the earth's soil has caused demineralization, contamination, and loss of fertility of millions of acres of land because of erosion, compaction, and acidification, as well as contamination by heavy metals and pesticides. When we use pesticides and chemical fertilizers, when we produce acid rain, and when we release untreated waste from industrial plants and sewage plants into the environment, we contaminate soil and water with chemicals and toxic metals that eventually end up in our drinking water and in the food on our plates. We then store these chemicals and metals in our breasts, uterus, thyroid gland, kidneys, adrenal glands, brain, blood vessels, bones, fat, and elsewhere — where they cause disease.

To establish good health, we need to honor the cycle of life, restore mineral balance to the soil and our food, and eliminate from the environment and our bodies harmful chemicals and heavy metals.

Mineral Deficiencies

Many women are deficient in calcium, magnesium, potassium, zinc, selenium, chromium, iron, molybdenum, and iodine. Deficiency can be due to inadequate dietary supply or to poor absorption by the stomach and small intestine. Because a balanced and rich supply of minerals is so essential to human health, we need to audit our own mineral bank balance annually to assess deficiencies, excesses, and the presence of toxic metals.

BODY MINERAL CONTENT

While 96% of our body weight is derived from four elements — oxygen (65%), carbon (18.5%), hydrogen (9.5%), and nitrogen (3.2%) — the remaining 4% of our makeup is derived from minerals that are present in the form of salts and trace elements. These salts include calcium (1.5%), phosphorus (1.0%), potassium (0.35%), sulfur (0.25%), sodium (0.15%), magnesium (0.05%), chlorine, iodine, and iron. Trace minerals comprise less than 0.5% of our body weight, but they are essential cofactors in enzyme reactions in the body and decrease our accumulation of toxic metals. The primary trace elements are chromium, cobalt, copper, fluorine, manganese, molybdenum, selenium, tin, vanadium, and zinc.

Several tests are needed for a complete overview of mineral status, summarized in the following charts. Consult with your health-care practitioner for more information about these tests, for referrals to testing labs, and for interpretation of the results. Your health-care provider will help you to identify and correct mineral deficiencies and detoxify heavy metals.

Iodine Level Test

You can test your iodine level at home without resorting to a lab. Follow these instructions:

- Purchase 2% Lugol's solution or tincture of iodine at a drug store.
- Apply a 3-inch patch on your inner thigh, belly, or inner upper arm.
- If the stain disappears within 24 hours, you are iodine deficient.
- If you are iodine deficient, consult with your health-care provider. Iodine deficiency can seriously affect the health of your thyroid gland, which governs your metabolic rate.

Toxic Metals

In many areas around the world, the soil is contaminated with toxic metals, such as lead, cadmium, mercury, aluminum, arsenic, uranium, copper, chromium, and excess zinc. The most common source of these toxic metals is untreated wastewater from industrial plants. We also come into contact with toxic metals in everything from food containers to household furnishings, paint, cookware, cigarette smoke, dental fillings, cosmetics, hair dyes, lipstick, pressure-treated wood, jewelry, and household plumbing. In North America, information on the release of toxic metals and industrial pollutants is available through www.cec.org. Find out which industries are contaminating your area by entering your postal code or zip code into the websites www.pollutionwatch.org (Canada) or www.scorecard.org (U.S.A.).

DID YOU KNOW...

When we deplete the minerals in the soil, we destroy its fertility. As the earth loses its fertility so do we — deficiencies of zinc, selenium, iodine, magnesium, and boron, along with pesticide exposure, can contribute to infertility in women and to falling sperm counts in men.

DID YOU KNOW...

Some minerals, notably copper, iron, manganese, selenium, zinc, chromium, vanadium, molybdenum, nickel and cobalt, are needed by the body in small amounts, but in excess become toxic. Other minerals, such as cadmium, lead, mercury, aluminum, arsenic, bismuth and uranium, are not needed in the body and are toxic to varying degrees in any amount.

MINERAL DEFICIENCY TESTS

METHOD	ACCURATE FOR:	NOT ACCURATE FOR:
HAIR MINERAL ANALYSIS (from a reliable laboratory)	Antimony, mercury, cadmium, lead, arsenic, copper, manganese, excess cobalt, molybdenum, somewhat accurate for zinc, chromium, selenium, vanadium	Calcium, magnesium, sodium, potassium, boron, iodine, iron
24-HOUR URINE TOXIC METAL TEST	Aluminum, antimony, arsenic, beryllium, bismuth, lead, cadmium, mercury, nickel, platinum, thallium, thorium, tin, tungsten, uranium	Other minerals
URINE TEST	Iodine, potassium and sodium ratio (all 24-hour urine tests), calcium (Sulkowitch test)	Other minerals
WHOLE BLOOD TEST	Potassium, zinc, iron (test total iron binding capacity, ferritin, hemoglobin, % transferrin saturation)	Calcium, magnesium, selenium
PACKED RED BLOOD CELL ELEMENTS ANALYSIS	Potassium, zinc, magnesium, selenium, chromium, copper	Unknown
URIC ACID LEVEL	Uric acid is decreased with molybdenum deficiency	Other minerals
WHITE BLOOD CELL LEVELS	Magnesium, zinc, copper	Unknown
ZINC TASTE TEST	Zinc deficiency	Other minerals
SKIN TEST	Iodine	Other minerals

DID YOU KNOW...

Coal-fired power plants generate a large amount of airborne mercury. In lakes and rivers, bacteria convert mercury into methyl mercury, which accumulates in fish, making them dangerous to eat.

Toxic metals give up a negative particle (electron) to form a positively charged ion, known as a cation. Cations attach to negatively charged cell membranes, gaining entry to our cells to bind with receptor sites, where they displace essential minerals and inactivate vitamins, disrupting enzymes, energy production, and cellular function.

Toxic metals concentrate in the hair and the excretory tissue, allowing us to assess levels through hair analysis, urine tests, and stool samples. Toxic metals are excreted through the kidneys and the gastrointestinal tract. We can also sweat them out through the skin.

Cilantro Chelation Pesto

Fresh cilantro (Chinese parsley) draws mercury, lead, and aluminum from the body. This delicious pesto can be eaten daily during a metal detox or after the removal of dental fillings — or any time at all! Use daily for at least 3 weeks as an annual detox for mercury, lead, and aluminum. Cilantro is also available in tablet or capsule form. The recommended dosage is 100 mg taken 4 times daily for 4 weeks or more.

2 cups	packed fresh cilantro (Chinese parsley)
$\frac{2}{3}$ cup	extra virgin olive oil
4	cloves garlic
$\frac{1}{3}$ cup	Brazil nuts (for selenium)
$\frac{1}{3}$ cup	sunflower seeds (for cysteine)
$\frac{1}{3}$ cup	pumpkin seeds (for zinc, magnesium)
2 tsp	dulse powder (for minerals)
4 tbsp	lemon juice (for vitamin C)
	Liquid amino acids (optional)

DIRECTIONS

Process the cilantro and oil in a blender until the cilantro is chopped. Add the garlic, nuts and seeds, dulse, and lemon juice. Then mix until the ingredients are finely blended into a paste. Add amino acids (to taste) if you wish and blend again. Serve as a vegetable dip or with baked potatoes, pasta, toast, or rice. Since this pesto freezes well, purchase cilantro in season and freeze in dark glass jars.

Chelation Therapy

Chelation is the process by which chemicals are tightly bound to minerals. The chelating agent grabs on to a metal ion (chelation means "claw"), pulling it from its binding site, and carrying it out of the body through the urine or stools. Chelation therapy is used by specially trained medical doctors, naturopathic doctors, and osteopaths to eliminate heavy metals and to reverse cardiovascular disease. Dimercaptosuccinic acid (DMSA), dimercaptopropane sulfonate (DMPS), and ethylene diamine tetraacetic acid (EDTA) are man-made chelating agents that can be used orally or intravenously.

Toxic Metal Effects

The following chart summarizes sources of some toxic metals, their effects in the body, symptoms of toxicity, and specific agents that help to eliminate them. For more information on detoxification, see the Seasonal Cleansing and Rejuvenation Program section and consult a health-care practitioner experienced in metal detoxification.

DID YOU KNOW...

In women, metal toxicity can be a causative factor in infertility, miscarriage, hormonal imbalances, hypothyroidism, breast cancer, and uterine fibroids. Infectious organisms, such as the bacteria chlamydia, *Candida albicans*, the herpes simplex virus, and cytomegalovirus, may be resistant to antibiotics or drug/herbal treatments when there are localized deposits of mercury and/or lead present.

TOXIC METAL EFFECTS

ALUMINUM

SOURCES: aluminum foil, antacids, aluminum cookware, auto exhaust, pottery, canned food, nasal spray, drinking water, toothpaste, antiperspirants, pesticides, cigarettes, dental amalgams, bleached flour, dairy, processed cheese, non-dairy creamers, infant milk formulas, processed food, fruit juices, soft drinks, cosmetics, table salt, coffee whitener, bauxite deodorant crystal, the herb equisetum (horsetail), drinking water, soil.

EFFECTS AND SYMPTOMS: binds to phosphate in the GI tract to help prevent absorption; binds to phosphate groups on DNA and RNA; accumulates in bone, liver, kidney and brain; interferes with bone mineralization; disrupts protein formation in cell nucleus; may cause fatigue; fatty degeneration in liver and kidney; accumulates in neurons; link with Alzheimer's disease, neuron plaques, and Parkinson's disease, learning disabilities, hyperactivity.

ELIMINATION AGENTS: vitamin C, alpha-ketoglutaric acid, pyridoxal 5-phosphate, phosphatidylcholine, cilantro, adequate iron and calcium, silicon as orthosilicic acid (BioSil from Jarrow), vitamin E, oral glycine, beta carotene, NAC, omega-3 and omega-6 oils, oral or intravenous EDTA.

ANTIMONY

SOURCES: tobacco, cigarette smoke, gunpowder, meats, vegetables, seafood, flame retardants in textiles, dyes, metal work factories, paints, glass, ceramics, solder, batteries, bearing metals, semiconductors, rubber processing, mining, smelting, hazardous waste sites, some de-worming or anti-protozoic drugs.

EFFECTS AND SYMPTOMS: accumulates in adrenals, thyroid, kidney, liver, spleen, bone; inhibits enzyme function; may cause conjunctivitis, muscle weakness, nausea, low back pain, headache, changes in lung function, chronic bronchitis, emphysema, pleural adhesions, high blood pressure, angina, metallic taste in mouth, gastrointestinal disorders, anorexia, fatigue, hemolytic anemia, blood in urine, kidney failure.

ELIMINATION AGENTS: magnesium, selenium, vitamin C, vitamin E, zinc, NAC, reduced glutathione, alpha lipoic acid, DMSA or DMPS.

ARSENIC

SOURCES: pressure-treated wood, seafood (shellfish, fish), air, drinking water, metal refining/smelting; galvanizing, etching, plating processes; insecticides, rat poison, pesticides, fungicides; wallpaper and plaster; wine and beer; paint pigment; auto exhaust; soil; colored chalk; chemical and glass manufacturing.

EFFECTS AND SYMPTOMS: deposits in liver, kidney, skin, spleen; accumulates in cell mitochondria and interferes with energy production; disables alpha lipoic acid; interferes with normal DNA repair; damages genetic material in white blood cells; combines with hemoglobin to cause red blood cell destruction, anemia; heart failure; jaundice, neuropathy, skin irritation, eczema; gingivitis; bronchitis; garlic-like breath; fatigue, nausea, diarrhea, hair loss, loss of skin pigment in spots, white-streaked nails; Raynaud's syndrome, blue fingers, basal cell carcinoma; lung cancer; muscle pain, weight loss, low blood pressure, chest pain.

ELIMINATION AGENTS: L-methionine, magnesium, B complex, vitamin C, vitamin E mixed tocopherols, selenomethionine, iodine, zinc, alpha lipoic acid, reduced glutathione, oral or intravenous DMSA or DMPS (is best).

BISMUTH

SOURCES: drinking water, fruits, vegetables, pharmaceuticals, antacids, anti-diarrhea and ulcer medications, cosmetics, lipstick, automatic sprinklers, solders, pigments, paints, semiconductors, electronic components, batteries, metal mining and refining.

TOXIC METAL EFFECTS

BISMUTH (cont'd)

EFFECTS AND SYMPTOMS: inactivates enzymes, interferes with methylation and the liver's ability to metabolize estrogen; found in liver, kidneys, soft tissues, bones. Affects nervous system and mucous membranes; too much causes kidney toxicity; confusion, lowered appetite, weight loss, weakness, joint pain, skin rash, tremors, diarrhea, dark stains on gums.

ELIMINATION AGENTS: methionine as SAM, alpha lipoic acid, vitamin C, vitamin E, zinc, selenium, reduced glutathione, NAC.

CADMIUM

SOURCES: refined foods — flour, rice, white sugar; soft water, pottery, organ meats, batteries, cigarette smoke, mining and smelting, drinking water, seafood (shellfish, crab, shrimp), liver and kidney meats, electroplating, silver polish, fertilizers, soft drinks, dairy, PVC plastic, dental fillings, paint pigments, insecticides, fungicides, commercial fertilizers, motor oil, car exhaust.

EFFECTS AND SYMPTOMS: damages genetic material, inducing cancer; collects in the cell mitochondria and strongly decreases energy production; interferes with synthesis of vitamin D; decreases cytochrome P450 liver detox enzymes; displaces zinc, copper, and iron; stored in liver, kidneys, placenta, lungs, brain, bones; higher amounts are found in uterine fibroid tissue; has an estrogenic effect; settles in the arteries, linked to high and low blood pressure; learning disabilities; increased salivation, fatigue, weight loss, muscle weakness, kidney damage, microcytic anemia, emphysema, protein in urine, nausea, vomiting, diarrhea.

ELIMINATION AGENTS: zinc, iron, selenium, L-methionine, NAC, vitamin D, calcium, magnesium, adequate copper, oral DMSA or DMPS, or intravenous EDTA (is best) or DMPS, cilantro.

COPPER

SOURCES: copper cookware, drinking water, IUDs, pesticides, plumbing pipes, seafood, swimming pools, vitamin supplements, wine and beer, birth control pills.

EFFECTS AND SYMPTOMS: iron deficiency, high blood pressure, heart attack, schizophrenia, stuttering, autism, hyperactivity, PMS, depression, insomnia, senility, hypoglycemia; may accelerate Parkinson's disease.

ELIMINATION AGENTS: vitamin C, zinc, selenium, oral and intravenous DMPS, EDTA.

LEAD

SOURCES: calcium from bonemeal, soil, brass key rings, canned pet food, pottery, pewter, cigarette smoke, drinking water, lead bullets, fish, mascara, lipstick, hair dye, cosmetics, newsprint, dairy, organ meats, pencils, pesticides, fuel additives, PVC containers, stained glass, old paint, wine and beer, car batteries, cable coverings, plumbing pipes and drains, toothpaste, pencils, X-ray shielding.

EFFECTS AND SYMPTOMS: damages DNA, causes chromosome breaks; lead is absorbed when there is a deficiency of calcium, iron, or zinc; competes with calcium in the body; 95% is stored in bone; also stored in aorta, kidney, brain, adrenals, thyroid, liver; found in red blood cells and urine; poisons and damages cell mitochondria; causes cell death; strongly interferes with cellular detoxification; inhibits enzymes that form hemoglobin; can shorten life span of red blood cells by 50%, causing microcytic anemia; disrupts liver detoxification; accumulates in the kidneys, damaging function; inhibits release of neurotransmitters; causes learning disabilities; lower IQ; blocks kidney excretion of uric acid (gout); acts as a xenoestrogen; stimulates cell division in breast cancer cells; loss of appetite, tremor, constipation, joint pain, headache, insomnia, metallic taste, muscle ache; interferes with thyroid function.

ELIMINATION AGENTS: vitamin C, vitamin B-1, adequate calcium, iron, zinc, selenium, bran, vitamin E mixed tocopherols, beta carotene, cilantro, reduced glutathione, oral DMSA or intravenous DMSA (is best), DMPS or EDTA.

TOXIC METAL EFFECTS

MANGANESE

SOURCES: Infant formulas, metal industries.

EFFECTS AND SYMPTOMS: May cause lower dopamine levels, learning disabilities, iron deficiency anemia, weakness, irritability, impotence.

ELIMINATION AGENTS: Vitamin C, zinc, selenium, alpha lipoic acid, vitamin E mixed tocopherols, EDTA.

MERCURY

SOURCES: Coal-fired power plants; pesticides; all fish; dental amalgams; vaccinations; cosmetics; drinking and well water; fertilizers; floor wax; laxatives; latex paints; wood preservatives; batteries; fabric softeners; cinnabar (jewelry); auto exhaust, fungicides; air conditioner filters; industrial waste; thermometers; thermostats; mercury can be absorbed through skin, inhaled or ingested.

EFFECTS AND SYMPTOMS: Inactivates monoamine oxidase enzymes (in the mitochondria), causing cell death; accumulates in brain, liver, adrenal glands and kidneys; depletes zinc from brain; causes mitochondrial damage and decreases detoxification ability of liver and kidneys; methyl mercury from fish can cause nerve, birth, and genetic defects, tremor, loss of coordination, decreased vision/hearing/touch, learning disabilities, poor concentration, loss of teeth, hair loss, vertigo, insomnia, fatigue, headache, numbness of lips, toes, fingers, excess salivation, hypertension, skin rash, decreased immunity, autoimmune disease, kidney disease; damages cell membranes; increases free radical damage; interferes with protein synthesis; can contribute to Alzheimer's and Parkinson's disease; is estrogenic and may be a contributing cause in breast cancer, infertility, thyroid disease, and hormone imbalance.

ELIMINATION AGENTS: Selenomethionine, vitamin E mixed tocopherols, vitamin C, zinc, cilantro, chlorella, rosemary, alpha lipoic acid, manganese, zinc, copper, NAC, reduced glutathione, wheat bran, oral or intravenous DMSA, or intravenous or oral DMPS (is best), EDTA suppositories.

NICKEL

SOURCES: Cocoa, nuts, hydrogenated oils, water, tobacco, soil, sewage sludge, dental crowns and bridges, stainless steel manufacturing, electroplating, oil combustion, industrial waste, car exhaust, car batteries, tires, brakes; baking powder; cigarette smoke; coal powered generators; cooking ware and utensils; drinking water; fertilizers; batteries; household plumbing; processed foods; jewelry; handling coins.

EFFECTS AND SYMPTOMS: Accumulates in kidney, liver, skin, brain; skin rash — increased skin sensitivity in allergic patients, eczema; stomach ache; chronic bronchitis, reduced lung function, cancer of the lung and nasal sinuses; kidney damage, immune deficiency, neurotoxin, developmental toxin; stimulates the growth of breast cancer cells.

ELIMINATION AGENTS: Vitamin C, zinc, selenium, iron, riboflavin, alpha lipoic acid, vitamin E mixed tocopherols.

Pesticides

Pesticides are ubiquitous, accepted toxins used agriculturally, as well as in homes, lawns, schools, public buildings, airplanes, stores, parks, along power lines and roadsides. Herbicides, insecticides, and pesticides make their way through the food chain to our bodies, often with damaging effects. They silently, insidiously, and progressively affect us all, especially children, the unborn fetus, the chemically sensitive, those who are immune deficient, people with asthma, and the elderly. Breastfed infants are at the top of the food chain, receiving the highest dosage. Pesticides can have a powerful detrimental synergistic effect when several are used and when they are combined with toxic metals.

Food Contamination

Many foods have several pesticide residues on them. To minimize our exposure to pesticides, we can buy organically grown food, particularly those foods that are most contaminated with pesticide residues. To find out more about what pesticides and herbicides are in your foods and which foods are safest, see the website www.foodnews.org or www.ewg.org.

DID YOU KNOW...

Lipstick commonly contains lead, as well as bismuth, which can be toxic if used over time. You can test your lipstick for lead by putting some on your hand and scratching it with a gold ring. If the lipstick color changes to black, it contains lead.

DID YOU KNOW...

The average North American peach has 31 pesticide residues, while a strawberry may have 40. Commercial baby foods have high pesticide levels.

CASE STUDY: *A CLEAN BABY*

Jennifer was in her mid-twenties when she came to see us suffering from endometriosis, which we treated with Chinese herbs and dietary changes. After her pain and menstrual discomfort were alleviated, she asked how she could prepare for pregnancy. We love this question: so few women ask it, even though humanity's future depends on how we prepare for having a child. We told her about the potential effects on the fetus of the chemicals present in women's bodies and breast milk, explaining how she could eliminate them through 100 hours of sauna detoxification. She agreed to do the sauna cleanse before conceiving. (Most couples can't wait, ignore this advice, and become pregnant as soon as they are able.)

We ran a blood test to assess the levels of 22 different chlorinated pesticides so we could do a comparison after she had completed the sauna therapy. Eleven pesticides were detected in significantly high amounts. Jennifer became more conscientious about buying organic fruits and vegetables, eliminated dairy and fish, and ate little animal protein — only occasional organic chicken and eggs. She followed our instructions for a sauna cleanse, spending an hour a day in an infra-red sauna during 3 months, which reduced her pesticide levels by 86%.

We lost touch with her, but just over a year later, met her at a health show when she stopped by, carrying an infant boy. We dropped what we were doing, jumped up, and cheered, "A clean baby!"

ADVERSE HEALTH EFFECTS OF PESTICIDES

HEALTH EFFECTS	EXAMPLES OF HEALTH EFFECTS
CARCINOGENIC EFFECTS	• At least 40 pesticides are known to cause cancers, such as childhood leukemia, brain tumors, Wilms' tumor, non-Hodgkin's lymphoma (linked to the common lawn pesticide 2,4-D), sarcomas, and cancers of the prostate, breast, ovary, thyroid, liver, stomach, testes, bladder, kidney and other organs. • Pesticides known to be linked with breast and/or ovarian cancer include atrazine, cyanazine, 1,3-dichloropropene, dichlorvos, endosulfan, ethalfluralin, ethylene oxide, estridiazole, methoxychlor, oryzalin, prometon, propazine, simazine, terbuthylazine, terbutryn, tribenuron methyl and lindane. • Pesticides linked to thyroid cancer include maneb, zineb, mancozeb, and hexachlorobenzene. • Children with brain cancer are twice as likely to have been exposed to pesticides at home than are healthy children.
REPRODUCTIVE AND DEVELOPMENTAL EFFECTS	• More than 40 pesticides including methyl bromide and metam sodium are known to cause birth defects. • American communities with atrazine residues in their drinking water showed a two to three fold increase in all birth defects. • Children of pesticide applicators and residents of agricultural areas are most at risk of birth defects if they were conceived in the spring, when pesticide use is highest. • Occupational exposure to pesticides contributes to miscarriages and birth defects involving the musculoskeletal system.
HORMONE DISRUPTION EFFECTS	• Many pesticides mimic or block estrogen, while others block male hormones or thyroid hormones. • Effects of hormone disruptors include altered circulating hormone levels (lowered progesterone, lowered thyroid hormones, higher estrogen), nipple development in males, decrease in penis size, increase in incidence of undescended testes, poor sperm quality contributing to infertility, early puberty in girls, breast and ovarian cysts and cancer, changes in sexual behavior, increased premenstrual symptoms in women. • Pesticides that act as hormone disruptors include 2,4,5-T, 2,4-D, alachlor, aldicarb, amitrole, benomyl, beta-HCH, carbaryl, cypermethrin, DBCP, dicofol, esfenvalerate, ethylparathion, fenvalerate, h-epoxide, kelthane, kepone, malathion, mancozeb, maneb, methomyl, metiram, metribuzin, mirex, nitrofen, oxychlordane, permethrin, synthetic pyrethroids, transnonachlor, tributyltin oxide, trifluralin, vinclozolin, zineb, and ziram.
IMMUNE DYSFUNCTION	• Pesticides damage immune organs, suppress the immune system, and increase the susceptibility to infectious disease.

ADVERSE HEALTH EFFECTS OF PESTICIDES

HEALTH EFFECTS	EXAMPLES OF HEALTH EFFECTS
RESPIRATORY DISEASE	• Asthma has been linked with captafol, sulfur, pyrethrins, pyrethroids, tetrachloroisophthalonitrile, organophosphates, and N-methyl carbamate insecticides. • Lung ailments associated with pesticide exposure include chest tightness, chronic cough and phlegm, chronic bronchitis, Wegener's granulomatosis, and pulmonary fibrosis.
NEUROLOGICAL AILMENTS	• Symptoms of memory loss, nerve conduction delays, vertigo, reduced vibration sensitivity, anxiety, irritability, and depression may be related to pesticide exposure. • The fumigants methyl bromide, sulfuryl fluoride, and dichloropropene may cause personality changes and shortened attention span. • Organophosphate exposure can cause changes in visual and spatial processing, disturbed neurotransmitter function, muscle weakness, loss of reflexes, and sensory impairment. Organophosphates include chlorpyrifos, used in flea dips and insect sprays, and malathion, used to deter mosquitoes. • Seizures and tics may be related to exposure to lindane (used for hair lice), endosulfan, and dieldrin. • Learning disabilities in children may be related to low-level pesticide exposure during the development of the nervous system in utero, and during growth spurts. • Areas of the brain commonly affected by pesticides include the limbic system, basal ganglia, hippocampus, and cerebellum. Several of these centers affect our emotions. • Parkinson's disease may be associated with paraquat, dieldrin, and the manganese-based fungicides maneb and mancozeb.

LEVELS OF FOOD CONTAMINATION

MOST CONTAMINATED FOODS		LEAST CONTAMINATED FOODS	
FRUITS	VEGETABLES	FRUITS	VEGETABLES
1. Peaches	1. Spinach	1. Avocado	1. Cauliflower
2. Apples	2. Bell peppers	2. Pineapple	2. Brussels sprouts
3. Strawberries	3. Celery	3. Plantains	3. Asparagus
4. Nectarines	4. Potatoes	4. Mangoes	4. Radishes
5. Pears	5. Hot peppers	5. Watermelon	5. Broccoli
6. Cherries	6. Green beans	6. Plums	6. Onions
7. Red raspberries	7. Head/leaf lettuce	7. Kiwi	7. Okra
8. Imported grapes	8. Cucumbers	8. Papaya	8. Cabbage
9. Blueberries	9. Carrots	9. Grapefruit	9. Eggplant

Chemical Contamination

A host of other environmental toxins come to rest in our bodies from plastics, cosmetics, cleansers, fire retardants, industrial products, and their chemical byproducts. Many of these products have been designed for convenience with no thought of their long-term effects on human health and the environment. They enter our bodies through the food we eat, the water we drink, the air we breathe, and the products we use on our skin.

We need to become familiar with them, avoid using products that contain them, and discourage their use. Safe alternatives are available.

The Precautionary Principle

In January 1998, an international group of physicians, scientists, politicians, lawyers, and environmental advocates met at Wingspread in Racine, Wisconsin, to define the Precautionary Principle:

The release and use of toxic substances, the exploitation of resources, and physical alterations of the environment have had substantial unintended consequences affecting human health and the environment. Some of these concerns are high rates of learning deficiencies, asthma, cancer, birth defects, and species extinction, along with global climate change, stratospheric ozone depletion, and worldwide contamination with toxic substances and nuclear materials.

We believe existing environmental regulations and other decisions, particularly those based on risk assessment, have failed to protect adequately human health and the environment — the larger system of which humans are but a part.

We believe there is compelling evidence that damage to humans and the worldwide environment is of such magnitude and seriousness, that new principles for conducting human activities are necessary.

While we realize that human activities may involve hazards, people must proceed more carefully than has been the case in recent history. Corporations, government entities, organizations, communities, scientists, and other individuals must adopt a precautionary approach to all human endeavors.

Therefore, it is necessary to implement the Precautionary Principle:

"When an activity raises threat of harm to human health or the environment, precautionary measures should be taken even if some cause and effect relationships are not fully established scientifically. In this context the proponent of an activity, rather than the public, should bear the burden of proof."

DID YOU KNOW...

In 2004, the World Wildlife Fund tested the level of industrial toxins in the blood of 47 Europeans, most of whom were members of the European Parliament. Out of 101 chemicals tested, a total of 76 were found, with a median number of 41 chemicals present in each individual tested.

DID YOU KNOW...

In a 2003 study led by the Mount Sinai School of Medicine in New York in collaboration with the Environmental Working Group and Commonweal, researchers at two laboratories found an average of 91 industrial chemicals, pollutants, and toxic metals in the blood and urine of nine volunteers, with a total of 167 chemicals found in the group. Of these 167 chemicals, 76 cause cancer, 94 are toxic to the nervous system, and 79 cause birth defects or abnormal development. It is likely that each of us has a similar inventory of chemicals and metals in our blood.

Since being adopted by the United Nations, this principle has been cited in several legal decisions and legislative acts. In September 2001, the European Parliament banned several brominated fire retardants, invoking the Precautionary Principle. In 2002, the Supreme Court of Canada upheld the pesticide ban bylaw instituted by the small town of Hudson, Quebec. In July 2003, the California senate passed a bill to ban the manufacture, distribution, and sale of materials coated with brominated fire retardants by January 1, 2008. In January 2003, the European Parliament banned two phthalates, the reproductive toxins DBP and DEHP, from being used in cosmetics, such as perfumes, deodorants, hair sprays, and nail polish. In October 2004, the European Union nations banned the phthalates DEHP, DBP, and BBP from all toys and child-care articles, as well as the phthalates DINP, DIDP and DNOP in toys for children less than 3 years of age that could be placed in their mouths.

COMMON ENVIRONMENTAL CONTAMINANTS

PCBs (Polychlorinated Biphenyls)

ACTION: lowers immunity; disrupts thyroid and ovarian hormones; may cause breast cancer; related to low birth rate; poor growth; hyperactivity; impaired learning and memory.

SOURCE: old paints, varnishes, inks, microscope oil, hydraulic fluids, electrical transformers, PCBs concentrate in fish; fish consumption increases our levels.

ALTERNATIVES: although production of PCBs has stopped, they still persist in the environment. Avoid fish, meat, and dairy, or choose low-fat sources to minimize exposure.

PVC (Polyvinyl Chloride)

ACTION: disrupts hormones.

SOURCE: cars, children's toys, food containers, credit cards, blinds, raincoats, furniture, building supplies, water pipes, window frames, flooring, exterior siding for homes, wallpaper, blow-up furniture, shower curtains, sterile gloves, medical infusion bags, yoga mats.

ALTERNATIVES: wood, metal or natural rubber; polyethylene, polypropylene or corn or plant-based products as plastic alternatives; use glass for food containers; use polyethylene for gloves and infusion bags; use natural rubber, hemp or cotton yoga mats.

BISPHENOL-A

ACTION: disrupts thyroid function; lowers progesterone levels; increases breast cancer risk.

SOURCE: present in epoxy resins and polycarbonate plastics, including Nalgene water bottles; used to seal cracks in water pipes; present in composite plastic tooth fillings and in dental bonding agents; used to line metal can food containers.

ALTERNATIVES: avoid canned food and plastic water or juice containers. Store food and water in glass. Use porcelain or methacrylate fillings in your teeth and a bonding agent that does not contain bisphenol-A.

COMMON ENVIRONMENTAL CONTAMINANTS

PHTHALATES (DEHP, DINP, DIDP, DBP, DnOP, DnHP)

ACTION: toxic to the thyroid (decreases T4); liver and kidney toxicity; harms reproductive tract; causes harm to developing fetus; mimics the hormone estrogen; causes earlier puberty and breast development in girls.

SOURCE: added to plastics to make them soft and flexible; found in building products, children's toys, balls, children's polymer clay, food packaging; medical devices — tubing, blood bags; infants' teething rings and pacifiers; vinyl upholstery; tablecloths; raincoats; adhesives; glue, latex adhesives; food containers; garden hoses; shoes and shoe soles; car undercoating; wires and cables; carpet backing; pool liners; solvents for dyes; vinyl tiles; artificial leather; food conveyor belts; traffic cones; canvas tarps; notebook binders; cosmetics, nail polish; dishwasher baskets; flea collars.

ALTERNATIVES: avoid the use of plastic or use only polyethylene or polypropylene plastics or sustainable bioplastic made from corn and other plants. Do not use teething rings and pacifiers with your infants. Purchase or make toys from fabric, wood and metal. Use furniture made from wood and natural cloth fibers. Use cotton tablecloths, rubber garden hoses, wood-floor coverings. Find cosmetics that are phthalate-free.

DIOXIN

ACTION: blocks testosterone in men; interferes with thyroid function; may contribute to endometriosis and reproductive abnormalities; birth defects; promotes cancer; damage to thymus gland and immune system, urinary tract, liver and bile ducts; can cause severe acne.

SOURCE: released into the air after the incineration of PVC, from hospital incinerators; from magnesium and nickel smelting and steel production; manufacturing of pesticides and herbicides; most human exposure (95%) to dioxin occurs through consumption of beef, fish and dairy; accidental building fires and burning of household waste are a source of dioxin release; dioxin is created during the bleaching of pulp and paper and may be present in tampons; formed during wastewater and drinking water treatment.

ALTERNATIVES: use medical supplies, tubing and infusion bags that are PVC-free; do not use PVC in building materials; ban PVC worldwide; do not use chlorine in the bleaching of pulp and paper — use a hydrogen peroxide process instead; use municipal reverse osmosis or ozonation to purify drinking water; eat organic, avoid pesticide use; avoid or minimize consumption of fish, meat and dairy; use alternative to tampons. Trim fat from meat and remove the skin from poultry and fish. If using dairy products, choose low fat.

FURANS

ACTION: carcinogen; toxic to developing fetus; toxic to liver; infertility; suppresses immune system; hormone disruptor; high exposure may cause severe acne.

SOURCE: byproducts of plastic production; manufacturing of iron and steel; industrial bleaching and incineration; produced from burning of diesel fuel, fuel used for agricultural purposes, and home heating; produced during generation of electrical power.

ALTERNATIVES: ban PVC; use industrial processes that do not produce dioxins and furans — stop incineration; implement regulations to eliminate dioxin and furan release from pulp mills; increase consumption of vegetables, fruits and grains; decrease fish, meat and dairy; avoid burning garbage that may contain wood preservative or plastics; avoid cigarette smoke.

COMMON ENVIRONMENTAL CONTAMINANTS

INDUSTRIAL SOLVENTS

ACTION: carcinogenic; toxic to the nervous system; headache, drowsiness; nausea; poor coordination; memory loss; confusion; leukemia, anemia, lymphoma, lung cancer, bladder cancer.

SOURCE: includes ethyl benzene, xylene and toluene. Used in small amounts in gasoline, and in industrial solvents.

ALTERNATIVES: Develop chemical processes that do not require toxic industrial solvents.

NONYLPHENOL ETHOXYLATES

ACTION: disrupts hormones.

SOURCE: industrial soaps and detergents; natural and synthetic textile processing; plastic manufacturing; pulp and paper making; petroleum refineries; pesticides; oil extraction; added to plastic to make it soft. Found in water bottles, juice containers, food packaging.

ALTERNATIVES: ban nonylphenol ethoxylates and use alternative processes; use glass water bottles and juice containers.

BROMINATED FIRE RETARDANTS (PBDEs)

ACTION: interferes with thyroid hormones; carcinogen; causes behavior and memory problems; damages central nervous system.

SOURCE: present as a fire retardant in plastic appliances, computers, TVs; present in upholstery foam; mattresses and futons; children's pajamas; carpets and drapes; added to hard styrene plastics.

ALTERNATIVES: lobby to ban PBDEs. Avoid foam; use wooden blinds or cloth drapes without PBDEs; use wool or cotton carpets; avoid using plastic.

PARABENS (Methyl, Propyl, Butyl, and Ethyl Paraben)

ACTION: hormone disruptor, mimicks estrogen and linked to breast cancer.

SOURCE: used as a preservative in cosmetics, shampoo, and toothpaste (read labels).

ALTERNATIVES: cosmetic companies that do not use parabens include Aubrey, Weleda, Dr. Hauschka, AnneMarie Borlind Natural Beauty, Logona, Organic Essentials Skincare, and Sante Kosmetics.

HEALTH TIPS CHECKLIST

Decreasing Exposure to Toxic Chemicals

To decrease your exposure to toxic environmental chemicals, follow these guidelines. Check off ☑ each practice once you have established it as part of your lifestyle.

☐ Minimize your use of plastic. Take bins, cloth bags, or cardboard boxes to do your grocery shopping and avoid using plastic bags. Store your food in glass. Drink out of glass rather than plastic bottles. Avoid canned food with plastic liners. Purchase wooden, metal, or fabric toys for your children.

☐ Use building materials, blinds, flooring, and furniture made from wood, metal, or natural fabric. Avoid using PVC in siding, window frames, blinds, or furniture. Choose to paint rather than wallpaper your walls. Use eco-friendly paint.

☐ Avoid using synthetic carpets but instead use wool or cotton throw rugs. Avoid using foam or vinyl furniture products.

☐ Clean your home with baking soda and vinegar rather than using harsh chemicals or chlorine.

☐ Do not use cosmetics and hair dyes with phthalates, parabens, and synthetic colors labeled FD&C or D&C, followed by a color and a number. Many of these are carcinogens. Hair dyes may also contain toxic metals, such as lead. Avoid cosmetics with synthetic fragrances, which include most perfumes. Use essential oils instead.

☐ Visit the websites www.thinkbeforeyoupink.org, www.nottoopretty.org and www.bcaction.com and take action to urge cosmetic manufacturers to make safe products for women.

☐ Do a 100-hour sauna detoxification program before you conceive your children to avoid exposing the fetus to any toxins your body has accumulated. For instructions, see the Seasonal Cleansing and Rejuvenation section.

◕ *Becoming Politically Active*

To ensure our good health and the health of our children, we must protect the earth's soil and our food. Check off ☑ the following practices as you incorporate them into your lifestyle.

☐ Support organic farmers by buying organic food or growing your own. Discourage the use of pesticides and chemical fertilizers.

☐ Become informed about pesticides used locally in parks, schools, and hospitals and push to have them banned. Look at the website www.scorecard.org in the United States or www.pollutionwatch.org in Canada to see what toxins are being released into the environment near you. Lobby industry and government to decrease them.

☐ Compost manure from livestock operations and prevent nitrogen and phosphorus fertilizers from running off into watersheds.

☐ Compost your kitchen scraps, grass clippings, and garden waste. If you garden, add compost and organic matter to your soil regularly. Encourage your community to establish a municipal composting program.

☐ Reduce soil exposure to wind and water in your area by planting cover crops, hedges, or trees.

☐ Reduce our planetary reliance on livestock grazing (and consequent soil erosion, loss of topsoil and desert formation) by shifting to a primarily vegetarian diet.

☐ Buy goods that can be recycled indefinitely, burned, or decomposed without toxic residue, and do not buy goods that will one day end up in a waste disposal site.

Our Water

*M**any seemingly improbable factors have graced us with life. The unseen hands of the evolving universe have placed the earth just the precise distance from the sun for water to exist at this time in all three phases — gas, liquid, and solid. Venus is too warm and Mars is too cold to allow this possibility. All of life on Earth owes its existence to the presence of water, which appeared as the planet cooled almost 4 billion years ago and will disappear as the sun expands into a red giant and scorches the Earth in another few billion years.*

Water is the medium in which all chemical reactions occur in our bodies. Many chemical reactions, including digestion, involve hydrolysis and are dependent upon water. Water acts as a cooling agent for the cells so they are not overheated during exercise. It helps to lubricate our joints. If we are deprived of water, we'll die within 60 to 80 hours.

Water Pollution

Unfortunately, we are contaminating this life-giving, precious, finite natural resource. Bacteria from human sewage or animal waste contaminates the drinking water in China, India, and most developing countries, as well as water supplies in some developed countries, as was the case with E. coli contamination of the municipal water supply in Walkerton, Ontario, in 2000 that killed seven and sickened 2,300 individuals. Each year, 50 to 100 million tons of contaminants pour into the Great Lakes from the surrounding watershed, with 25 million tons of this being pesticides. The Great Lakes comprise 27% of the earth's global lake waters.

The rivers and lakes are the earth's umbilical cord that brings us water and minerals; the oceans are our collective amniotic fluid. If the rivers and oceans are contaminated, so will the water be that makes up 70% of our physical structure.

Water Quality

To assess the burden of contaminants in your water, seek out laboratories that can test for bacteria, toxic metals, and chemical contaminants, such as pesticides and plastic residues.

They can also test for pH, redox potential, and resistivity. The pH tests measures acidity or alkalinity; redox potential tests the potential for free radical activity and cellular damage; and resistivity reflects mineral status. Health-care practitioners who use biological terrain assessment procedures may be able to check these variables in your drinking water and advise you as to how to change them. The optimal values for drinking water are:

- pH: 6.5 to 6.8 (slightly acidic)
- rH2 (redox potential): 25 to 28 atmospheres of hydrogen at the cathode per centimeter squared
- r (resistivity): greater than 6000 ohms (thus low in minerals).

CASE STUDY: WELL CONTAMINATION

Marie was diagnosed with breast cancer shortly after a very stressful year and came in to see us with her 25-year-old daughter, Angela, wanting to do everything she could for them to stay well. Angela's chief complaints were fatigue and anxiety.

We tested both of them for toxic metals using hair analysis. Both women showed high levels of arsenic, while Marie also demonstrated high mercury levels, likely from her dental fillings. Angela's arsenic levels were particularly high, more than 10 times acceptable levels. We sent a sample of their well water for testing, which confirmed that there were high amounts of arsenic in their drinking water. Further testing also revealed the presence of 4-bromofluorobenzene, D4-1,2-dichloroethane, D8-toluene, D14-terphenyl, D5-nitrobenzene, 2-fluorobiphenyl, 2,4,6-tribromophenol, decachlorobiphenyl (a PCB) and 2,4,5,6-tetrachloro-m-xylene. Many of these chemicals are carcinogens, mimic the hormone estrogen, and, along with her stress, may have contributed to Marie's breast cancer. Marie lives in a country home with no farms adjacent to her property but within 10 miles of a waste disposal site. Toxins from that site may have leached into the water table, making their way to her well through groundwater.

For the time being, Marie and Angela take several 2-gallon glass jugs to a local water depot and have them filled with reverse osmosis water each week. Although not the most convenient solution, it is the safest one until they determine what, if anything, can be done to purify their well water.

To treat her toxic overload, we sent Marie to a biological dentist to have her mercury fillings changed to methacrylate, which was accomplished over a 2-month period. Both Marie and Angela have followed a detoxification program for mercury and arsenic, with urine tests now verifying that these have been reduced to insignificant levels.

Water Filters

There are several kinds of filters that can be purchased for home use to remove most water contaminants. The best system is a reverse osmosis system with built-in activated charcoal, if you can afford it. Otherwise, go with the activated carbon block filter without silver.

HEALTH TIPS CHECKLIST

◕ Ensuring Water Quality

To preserve water quality on the Earth and in our bodies, consider the following lifestyle changes. Check them off ☑ once you have established them in your daily life.

☐ Use a reverse osmosis filter with activated charcoal in your home or on your kitchen tap to remove chlorine and other contaminants. If your water source is a well, test for contaminants regularly.

☐ Use safe water pipes. Alkylphenols and phthalates, both hormone-disrupting chemicals, are commonly used in water pipes, and these chemicals may leach into the drinking water. Safe pipes to use are polyethylene and polypropylene.

☐ Maintain the rainforest and plant trees. The rainforests, in particular, but all forests, in general, pump water from the soil into the air, where the moisture can collect in clouds and eventually bring rain. Plant a tree in your neighborhood annually.

☐ Use conscious positive thoughts, prayer, mantra, or music to energize the water in your environment (rivers, lakes, wells, springs), as well as your drinking water.

Water Deficiency

Though water contamination is a serious problem, global freshwater shortages loom ahead of us. The human demand for water tripled between 1950 and 1990 and is predicted to double again by 2035. Many of the world's great freshwater holding tanks or aquifers are drying up because we have extracted the water from them faster than they are refilling. It is estimated that by 2050, the human population will be 9.4 billion — and a billion of us will suffer from a water scarcity.

Dehydration

Even when we have adequate supplies of water, many of us don't drink enough and suffer from chronic dehydration without knowing it. Many health ailments are related to chronic dehydration and can be cured by drinking $2\frac{1}{2}$ to 3 quarts or liters of water daily.

DID YOU KNOW...

When we are water deficient, our filtration of toxins through the kidneys suffers, and we have fewer stools. Headaches, fatigue, joint pain, inability to concentrate, and digestive disturbances increase. Waste accumulates in our body cells.

WATER FILTER RATINGS		
TYPE OF FILTER	**HOW IT WORKS**	**WHAT IT REMOVES**
SCREEN FILTERS	A fine membrane removes bacteria from water.	Bacteria
ACTIVATED CARBON FILTERS	Adsorb contaminants, but bacteria can proliferate in poorly functioning carbon filters. Do a good job at removing organic chemicals but do not remove toxic minerals, such as aluminum, cadmium, and copper. Some of these filters contain silver to discourage bacterial growth, but too much silver can be toxic to our kidneys. Avoid carbon filters with silver. Use a filter with a rated capacity for 2000 gallons and with a carbon block rather than powdered activated charcoal.	Pesticides, radon, volatile organic chemicals
REVERSE OSMOSIS FILTERS	Contain a membrane that removes contaminants and some minerals. Work slowly, producing only a few gallons of water a day, discarding about 90% of incoming water. Usually they are combined with an activated carbon filter in one unit. Can cost several hundred dollars and need to be well maintained.	Bacteria, organic matter, inorganic matter, pesticides, PCBs, lead, aluminum, nitrates, radium, uranium, fluoride
DISTILLATION	Water is boiled, turned to steam, and collected as water again after passing through a series of baffles. Some chemicals have lower boiling points than water and will collect in the distilled end product, unless removed by carbon. Some organisms are heat resistant and will not be killed by distillation. Minerals are removed from the water, and, over time, mineral deficiencies may occur in the person who drinks it. The distillation process is slow and the water tastes flat.	Some chemicals, most but not all organisms, minerals, fluoride
ULTRAVIOLET TREATMENT	Ultraviolet rays change the molecular structure of bacteria and destroy their DNA. Some parasites and viruses are not affected, however.	Bacteria

HEALTH TIPS CHECKLIST

☚ Conserving Water

To conserve water, consider the following lifestyle changes. Check them off ☑ once you have established them in your daily life.

☐ Flush toilets are a major contributor to depleting our global freshwater reserves. Flush less often. Put bricks or a water filled glass jar in your toilet tank to decrease the volume of water required to fill the tank. Purchase a low-flush toilet or ideally a composting toilet if you are building a new home.

☐ Repair all leaks and drips immediately. A dripping tap can waste 2 gallons or 8 liters of water daily.

☐ Turn the water off while you are using soap or shampoo and reduce your showers to less than 5 minutes, preferably 3 minutes.

☐ Give your grass lawn a facelift and plant groundcover that does not need watering.

☐ If you live in a rural environment with clean air, collect rainwater and use it for watering plants and gardens or washing hair.

☐ Eat less meat or become a vegetarian — it takes 100 times more water to produce a pound of meat as it does to grow a pound of wheat.

Acid/Alkaline pH Balance

What Is pH?

The term pH refers to the concentration of hydrogen ions in a solution, which controls the speed of chemical reactions and the electrical conductivity in that solution. The pH scale is logarithmic and ranges from 1 (very acidic, high hydrogen ion concentration) to 14 (very alkaline, low hydrogen ion concentration), with a pH of 7 being neutral.

An acid is defined as any substance that when dissolved in water dissociates to give up corrosive hydrogen ions. Vinegar, being acid, has a pH of 3, while baking soda, being alkaline, has a pH of 8.3. Water, with a neutral pH of 7, contains an equal concentration of hydrogen ions (acids) and hydroxyl ions (alkaline bases).

pH is one of the most important regulators of biological systems and homeostasis, strongly influencing the ease or difficulty with which chemical reactions occur. In an acid environment, reactions occur more quickly with less resistance and more heat (a faster flow of electricity), while an alkaline environment slows down chemical processes because of increased electrical resistance. Microorganisms and all plant and animal species prefer a precise pH range in both their external and internal environments for optimal vitality.

HEALTH EFFECTS OF DEHYDRATION

HEALTH CONDITION	EFFECTS OF CHRONIC DEHYDRATION
PEPTIC OR DUODENAL ULCER, GASTRITIS, HEARTBURN	Insufficient water to sustain a healthy mucus lining in the stomach allows acid penetration and damage.
ARTHRITIC PAIN	Decreased lubrication in joint cartilage causes increased friction and abrasion of the joint.
LOW BACK PAIN	Since 75% of the weight of the upper body is supported by the water volume stored in the 5th lumbar disc, decreased volume means less support.
ASTHMA AND ALLERGIES	With dehydration there is an increased production of histamine, a neurotransmitter that regulates both water balance and the contraction of the bronchi of the lungs. Elevated histamine will cause increased lung contraction to ensure that less water evaporates from the lungs during breathing.
HYPERTENSION	With dehydration there is a loss in blood volume so blood vessels close capillaries in less active areas. This results in increased tension in blood vessels.
ELEVATED CHOLESTEROL	When necessary, cholesterol protects our cells from dehydration by plugging up gaps in cell membranes so that the cell wall is impervious to the passage of water and water stays inside the cell.
ANGINA	With dehydration, histamine and other water regulating chemicals are increased. If they spill into the circulation in the heart, they can cause vasoconstriction and pain.
DEPRESSION	When the brain lacks enough water, it generates less electrical energy and brain function decreases, leading to depression.
CONSTIPATION	The large intestine will remove water from the stools in an effort to conserve it when there is dehydration. This leads to fewer, harder stools.
OBESITY	The brain creates the sensation of thirst and hunger simultaneously to satisfy its needs. We don't recognize thirst but confuse it with hunger. If we were to drink water routinely every half hour before eating, we would satisfy thirst and not overeat.

Acidification

Today on a planetary and personal level, we are imbalanced with a tendency toward an overly acidic external and internal environment.

Soil

Certain diseases manifest in an overly acid or overly alkaline pH range in the soil. Most food crops prefer a soil pH of 6.3 to 6.8 because the availability of plant nutrients is highest in this range.

Beneficial soil bacteria and earthworms prefer a pH range of 6.3 to 6.8, although fungi, molds, and anaerobic bacteria are more prolific in soil with a lower pH. Many important soil organisms die at a pH below 6.0.

At a pH below 5.5, important nutrients, such as nitrogen, phosphorus, potassium, sulfur, magnesium, and calcium, are insoluble and not available to be taken up by plant roots. Increased acidity leaches the alkaline, negatively-charged minerals (calcium, magnesium, potassium) from the soil and washes them away so they are unavailable to plants. Other positively charged minerals accumulate in excessive amounts in acid soil, resulting in increased absorption and toxicity to plants. These include zinc, aluminum, iron, cobalt, cadmium, manganese, mercury, and copper. Plants growing in overly acidic soil are more vulnerable to diseases, insects, droughts, and frosts.

Alkaline minerals that neutralize acidity include calcium, magnesium, sodium, and potassium. If the soil and rock in a geographical area contains an abundant amount of any of these, as does limestone (composed of compressed layers of shells from tropical sea creatures, rich in calcium carbonate), the acid can be neutralized. If, however, the geology of an area consists of granite, siliceous sand, or quartz, the soil and water will be much more vulnerable to the effects of acid rain.

Water

The water that is hospitable to most fish has a pH range between 6.5 and 9.0. A pH below this causes embryos to stop maturing, young fish to die, and a decline in fish species. Acidity increases the availability of toxic metals, such as aluminum, mercury, and cadmium, which may be naturally present in surrounding bedrock, clay particles, and soil. Eventually, lakes become 'dead', without fish, and contaminated with toxic metals. Crustaceans, such as clams and crayfish, suffer at a pH range lower than 6.5 when their shells, made of calcium compounds, begin to dissolve in only slightly acidic water, mimicking osteoporosis in women.

DID YOU KNOW...

Acid rain refers to the precipitation of rain, snow, or fog with a pH of 5.5 or less, caused by the presence of sulfur dioxide or nitrogen oxide in the air, generated from the burning of coal or oil for electricity; from copper, nickel and zinc smelters; from the exhaust fumes of cars; and, in much smaller amounts, from volcanic eruptions and organic decay. Acid rain not only upsets the pH balance in water bodies but also in our bodies.

Our Bodies

Like the soil and the water in the external environment, our internal environment needs to maintain optimal pH values for homeostasis and good health. With the exception of stomach acid and vaginal secretions, most fluids and tissues of the body function best within the same pH range as healthy soil and lakes — between 6.5 and 8.0.

Symptoms of Increased Acidity

We produce more acids than we excrete as we grow older, depositing them in our joints, blood vessel walls, and tissues. Symptoms associated with increased acidity include irritability, fatigue, colds, headaches, sore throats, flu, hair loss, dry hair, weak nails, inflammation of tendons and cartilage, stiff achy joints, and osteoporosis. When the extracellular fluid becomes acidic, we may be susceptible to excess mucus, chronic infections, fibromyalgia, arthritis, gallstones, kidney stones, cysts, and benign tumors. As acids accumulate, they can penetrate inside the cell and cause damage to the DNA, leading to cancer. Cancer cells themselves produce acids, compounding the problem.

Acid Production from Foods and Exercise

When carbohydrates, proteins, and fats are metabolized, they produce inorganic acids. The strongest acids — sulphuric acid, nitric acid, and phosphoric acid — are formed from the break down or oxidation of animal protein, while carbohydrates produce acetic and lactic acid. Diets high in animal protein are the worst for producing a buildup of acid waste that both encourages cancer growth and causes minerals to be lost from our bones.

When we exercise, our muscles also produce lactic acid. When lactic acid and carbon dioxide combine with water, carbonic acid is formed. Anyone who exercises vigorously needs to take extra care in monitoring pH levels and neutralizing acids.

Stress and anger also increase acid production.

Health Effects of pH Imbalance

The chart below summarizes optimal pH ranges for various body tissues, fluids, and secretions, as well as the meaning of abnormal pH values.

HEALTH EFFECTS OF pH IMBALANCE

TISSUE/FLUID IDEAL pH	MEANING OF ABNORMAL pH VALUES
BLOOD Venous 7.3 -7.35 Arterial 7.43	Increased acidity of the blood (below 7.3) indicates an over acid condition caused by excess animal protein or toxicity with impaired function of the liver, kidney, and lymphatic system, and/or shallow breathing (with increased retention of carbon dioxide, which is acid). Alkalinizing powder, a vegetarian diet, breathing exercises, stretching, and detoxification therapies may be helpful. Increased alkalinity of the blood (above 7.35) may indicate a more extreme overall acidity due to overconsumption of acid-forming foods (animal protein and grains) or excess acid production within the body (from fungal overgrowth, excess exercise, stress, aging, or from cancer cells). The kidneys compensate by sending more alkaline bicarbonate into the blood. When the blood pH is increased, calcium is being lost from the bones.
SALIVA 6.5 -7.0	Saliva pH reflects digestive strength and activity of the gastrointestinal tract. Lowered saliva pH can be due to inadequate neutralization, drainage, and detoxification of acids produced by the body or acids generated from food. This may be associated with heartburn, esophageal reflux, and hydrochloric acid deficiency in the stomach or impairment in the kidney's ability to eliminate acids. A more alkaline diet, the use of an alkaline powder, deep breathing exercises, and support for kidney detoxification would be helpful. Increased saliva pH is indicative of stress within the liver and pancreas, reduced digestive capacity, and insufficient elimination of acids. There will be increased fermentation and putrefaction of foods by intestinal flora. Management should include thorough chewing while eating; stress reduction and support for the adrenal glands; breathing exercises; a decrease in animal protein and grains; use of digestive enzymes and a probiotic; liver, kidney, and lymphatic drainage; and an increase in magnesium, potassium, and trace minerals.
URINE 6.0–6.5 on rising, after removal of acid waste through the night 6.5–7.2 in day	Overly acid urine pH indicates excess acids are being produced and held within the body, possibly as a result of excess acid-producing foods (animal protein and grains); incomplete digestion and the need for enzymes; shallow breathing; a deficiency of the alkaline minerals (calcium, magnesium, sodium and potassium); or poor kidney function with decreased acid elimination. Overly alkaline urine may be caused by bacterial infection, by the inability of the kidney to excrete excess acids; by an excessive intake of the alkaline minerals; hydrochloric acid deficiency of the stomach; or a diet deficient in grains and protein. Management includes improving liver and kidney function, increasing hydrochloric acid, cleansing the blood, and adjusting mineral balance and diet.
ESOPHAGUS 5.0–6.0	There may be heartburn if stomach acid rises into the esophagus, lowering the pH.
STOMACH JUICES 1.2–3.0 (due to presence of hydrochloric acid)	When stomach acid is deficient and the pH is higher, there will be poor absorption of protein and minerals. Increased presence of parasites and harmful bacteria occurs with hydrochloric acid deficiency.

HEALTH EFFECTS OF pH IMBALANCE

TISSUE/FLUID IDEAL pH	MEANING OF ABNORMAL pH VALUES
SMALL INTESTINE: Duodenum 6 Jejunum, ileum 7.45–7.6	Candida albicans and other harmful bacteria and parasites flourish, causing gas and putrefaction, when the small intestine pH is too acid or too alkaline. As a crafty opportunist, candida is genetically equipped to thrive in its harmful fungal phase in either an acidic or alkaline environment. Candida and fungal overgrowth cause additional acid production, which increases the solubility and absorption of toxic metals, such as cadmium, mercury,and aluminum, but may decrease the absorption of trace minerals.
PANCREATIC JUICE 7.1–8.2	After eating, the pancreas secretes sodium bicarbonate, which is alkaline, along with digestive enzymes. About 1500 ml of pancreatic juice is secreted daily, which helps to neutralize stomach acid and raise the pH in the small intestine.
BILE 7.6–8.6	Bile is secreted by the cells of the liver and is either stored in the gallbladder or released into the duodenum. Bile is composed of 97% water and 0.7% bile salts, which contain sodium and potassium. Along with pancreatic juice, bile neutralizes stomach acid to raise the pH in the small intestine. It also emulsifies fats to prepare them for digestion and absorption.
GALLBLADDER 7.0–7.8	The gallbladder concentrates bile so that its water content is 89% and it becomes less alkaline than liver bile. When the gallbladder is removed, there is a constant slow discharge of bile into the duodenum from the bile duct.
LARGE INTESTINE 6.5–6.8	Slightly acidic pH is maintained by *Bifidobacterium* and *Lactobacilli*, which discourage the overgrowth of unhealthy bacteria and fungus.
BONE 8.1	The high alkalinity of bone tissue provides an alkaline reserve that the body can draw upon when needed to buffer excess acidity and stabilize the pH of the blood.
VAGINAL FLUID 3.5–4.5	Lactobacilli species keep the vaginal pH in this range and help protect against fungal, bacterial, and viral vaginal infections. A higher vaginal pH is usually linked with bacterial (4.5–5.5) or Trichomonas (6.0–6.5) infection, while a lower pH (<4.5) may indicate candida or fungal infection. Several strains of lactobacilli (particularly *L. acidophilus* and *L. delbruecki*) inhibit the growth of both bacteria and fungus.
STOOL 6.3–7.2	Overly acid stool can be caused by diarrhea, bacterial overgrowth in the small intestine, or poor digestion of fat or carbohydrate. Overly alkaline pH of stool (>7.2) can be caused by excess protein consumption, deficiency of *Lactobacilli* and *Bifidobacterium*, slow transit time, constipation or inadequate dietary fiber.

HEALTH EFFECTS OF pH IMBALANCE

INTRACELLULAR pH 6.0–7.4 (depending on cell type)	Excess dietary protein, alcohol, coffee, and sugar acidify local tissues and favor bacterial and fungal overgrowth. Increased acidity causes a rapid rate of metabolism and faster utilization and subsequent deficiency of vitamins, minerals, and enzymes, with concurrent intracellular accumulation of toxic metals.
EXTRACELLULAR pH 7.35–7.4 (includes fluid outside of cells in body tissues; plasma; and lymph)	Cancer cells thrive when there is an overproduction of acid within the cells and in the extracellular environment and when there are more toxic metals and lowered oxygen levels. Cancer cells themselves produce more acids.

Adjusting pH

The body has several regulatory mechanisms that adjust pH to prevent excess acidity or alkalinity.

Buffer Systems: Buffers combine with an acid or a base (an alkaline substance) to neutralize them, including the bicarbonate buffer, the phosphate buffer, and the protein buffer, which is the most powerful buffering system in the body fluids.

Respiratory System: Our respiratory system is one to two times more powerful in buffering excess acid or base as is the combined effect of the three chemical buffering systems used by the body fluids. Carbon dioxide, an acid, is constantly being produced by different intracellular metabolic processes, as carbon in foods is eventually oxidized by oxygen to form carbon dioxide. We can also decrease our acidity when we eat less food (particularly animal protein) to produce less carbon dioxide, and increase the depth and/or rate of our breathing to eliminate carbon dioxide faster. Both of these strategies will help to raise the pH of the extracellular fluids.

Kidneys: The kidneys regulate pH by increasing or decreasing the concentration of bicarbonate (an alkaline substance) in the body fluids and dumping acidic hydrogen ions (formed from carbon dioxide) into the tubular fluid of the kidneys, which forms urine.

Bones: The body can balance pH by drawing calcium from the bones when the extracellular fluids are too acidic. Our bones contain calcium carbonate, the same calcium that is found in the limestone rock that buffers soil and water from the damaging effects of acid rain, and in the shells of crustaceans that begin to disintegrate when the pH of lake water is below 6.5.

HEALTH TIPS EXERCISE

Breath of Fire

This exercise will help to eliminate acids, improve your energy levels, increase oxygen, strengthen your nerves, detoxify your lungs, and increase overall alkalinity.

- Sit cross-legged or in a chair and raise your arms up to a 60-degree angle from the horizontal, forming a 'V' above your head. Curl your fingers into the palms, making a fist, but keep the thumbs pointing up straight and pull them back slightly. Close your eyes and look up between your eyebrows, holding your gaze steady there.
- Begin breath of fire. Inhale as the belly comes out; exhale as you bring it in, keeping up an even rhythm with the belly pumping in and out. The inhale should equal the exhale in strength and intensity.
- Once you have the rhythm, speed up your breathing so that you are doing 2 to 3 breaths per second. Continue for 1 to 3 minutes.
- After a while, gradually increase the time to 11 minutes daily.

HEALTH TIPS CHECKLIST

Decreasing Acidification

This regimen for decreasing acids and restoring pH balance in your body will reduce your risk of heart disease, cancer, arthritis, and osteoporosis. Check off ☑ each strategy as you go.

- ☐ Monitor the pH of your urine and saliva weekly.
- ☐ Maintain a primarily vegetarian diet, with 80% alkaline-forming foods and only 20% acid-forming foods. Limit protein to 35 to 40 grams daily. Plan your meals around a main vegetable dish, rather than grain or protein. Use fruits as snacks.
- ☐ Add seaweeds to your diet — nori sheets, dulse powder added to soups, seaweed salads.
- ☐ Practice breath of fire or deep breathing exercises for 11 minutes daily and be conscious of breathing slowly and deeply throughout the day.
- ☐ Use a powdered green supplement (for example, Greens+, Pure Synergy, Barley Green, chlorella, spirulina) 1 to 3 times daily between meals, or drink vegetable juices between meals.
- ☐ Drink 2 to 3 liters or quarts of water daily. Check the pH of your water — it should be 6.5–6.8.

Charting Your pH Balance

Urine and saliva pH can be measured easily with pH paper, available at drug stores and health food stores. Purchase litmus paper with a pH range of 4.5 to 7.5.

A pH reading that falls below 7 is acidic, while a pH reading above 7 is alkaline, and 7 is neutral.

Urine and Saliva Testing Directions

1. Test your saliva first thing in the morning when you get out of bed, before brushing your teeth, or eating. Lick and wet the end of a strip of litmus paper, compare the color to the pH chart, and write down the number on the chart below. The pH should be 6.6–6.8. The saliva pH is a reflection of the intracellular pH and should never be below 6. If it is, there is no alkaline mineral reserve and the body does not have the minerals necessary to process food properly.

2. Check the pH of the first and second urine of the day. The first urine reflects the acid load from the day before that your kidneys have processed through the night. It should be 6.5–6.8. The second urine should be 6.8, signifying that the acids from the day before are gone, the kidneys are no longer overwhelmed, and there are enough alkaline minerals present in the body to raise the pH.

3. Check your saliva pH 5 minutes after eating something at breakfast. This number should be higher than what it was when you woke up. Ideally, it should be 8.5 after breakfast. This signifies that the alkaline minerals have been utilized for digestion. The more it goes up, the more these minerals are available. Coffee depletes these minerals.

4. Check the pH of the urine between meals. It should be in the range of 7.0 to 8.5. After eating, the stomach secretes hydrochloric acid to digest the food and stimulates the pancreas to make sodium bicarbonate, which is alkaline. The urine pH 1 to 2 hours after eating should reflect the availability of sodium bicarbonate and register as alkaline. If the urine pH is less than 7.0 at these times, you have too much acid waste.

5. Do this testing at least once a month when you have not taken alkaline minerals for a couple of days to see that you are moving to a more alkaline state.

pH CHART

DATE	TIME OF DAY	URINE pH	TIME OF DAY	SALIVA pH
	1st urine 2nd urine between meals		on rising 5 min. after breakfast before lunch	
	1st urine 2nd urine between meals		on rising 5 min. after breakfast before lunch	
	1st urine 2nd urine between meals		on rising 5 min. after breakfast before lunch	
	1st urine 2nd urine between meals		on rising 5 min. after breakfast before lunch	
	1st urine 2nd urine between meals		on rising 5 min. after breakfast before lunch	
	1st urine 2nd urine between meals		on rising 5 min. after breakfast before lunch	
	1st urine 2nd urine between meals		on rising 5 min. after breakfast before lunch	

Our Air

Earth currently sustains a rich diversity of life because of the presence of water along with abundant atmospheric oxygen. For about a billion years, the Earth's atmosphere has consisted of high levels of oxygen and carbon dioxide, first manufactured by photosynthetic single-celled organisms known as cyanobacteria in the oceans and later by plant life on land. New plant growth continues to release oxygen, while carbon dioxide is absorbed by plants. This balance between oxygen and carbon dioxide ensures the quality of the air we breathe.

Air pollutants in our indoor and outdoor environments have compromised the quality of our air, contributing to an increase in respiratory illness and cancer. Once we recognize the source of these pollutants, we can take steps to restore clean air in our homes, workplaces, and communities.

Outdoor Air Pollutants

We are exposed to more than 188 air pollutants in industrialized areas in North America that contribute to cancer, neurological disorders, and respiratory problems, as well as affecting fetal development. Of these 188 air pollutants, 10 different air pollutants are responsible for 99% of estimated cancer risks, the 'leader' being vehicle diesel fuel emissions.

A typical gas-powered lawn mower in California pollutes as much in one year as 43 new cars, each driven more than 12,000 miles annually. Los Angeles and Phoenix have offered rebates to their citizens who turn in their gas mowers in exchange for electric ones.

10 MOST HAZARDOUS AIR POLLUTANTS

1. Diesel
More than 50 hazardous air pollutants are found in diesel emissions, accounting for almost 80% of the estimated lifetime cancer risk associated with outdoor air pollutant exposures.

2. Benzene
Produced primarily from gasoline motor vehicle exhaust, gas service stations, agricultural burning, and wildfires, benzene is also highly hazardous to our health.

3. Carbon tetrachloride
Used in dry cleaning in the past and to fumigate grain, carbon tetrachloride is released during chemical manufacturing and petroleum refining.

4. Chromium
This air-borne pollutant is released from chrome plating industries, oil combustion, sewer sludge incineration, cement production, and municipal waste incinerators.

5. Polycyclic Aromatic Hydrocarbons and their Derivatives
Released through car exhaust, smoke from woodstoves and fireplaces, fly-ash from coal-fired electric generating plants, petroleum refineries, and industrial machinery manufacturers, these compounds are produced by incomplete combustion of fossil fuels and vegetation.

6. 1,3 Butadiene
Most of these emissions come from incomplete combustion of gasoline and diesel fuels. Other sources include vehicle tires, petroleum refining, biomass burning, wood-burning stoves, agricultural burning, and forest fires.

7. Formaldehyde
Produced in atmospheres containing organic chemicals, ozone, and nitrogen oxides, formaldehyde is also released through vehicle exhaust, fuel combustion, stone, clay and glass production, and boilers, furnaces, and engines.

8. Coke Oven Emissions
Manufacturing plants that use coke (a product made from coal) to extract metal from ores like iron cause these emissions.

9. Acrolein
A byproduct of fires, burning fossil fuels, tobacco smoke, and cooking animal and vegetable fats, acrolein is also produced during the manufacturing of acrylic. It is used to kill aquatic plants in irrigation canals and to destroy microorganisms in water treatment plants.

10. Smog
Emissions from the burning of fossil fuels, which include sulfur dioxide and nitrogen oxide, combine with ozone, aerosol droplets, and solid particles in the air, interacting with water vapor to produce a noxious cloud of sulfuric, nitric, and nitrous acids that aggravates asthma.

HEALTH TIPS CHECKLIST

❧ *Restoring Air Quality Outdoors*

To preserve air quality on the earth and in our bodies, consider the following lifestyle changes. Check them off ☑ as you go.

- ☐ Determine the air pollutants in your area by accessing the website www.pollutionwatch.org in Canada or www.scorecard.org in the United States to see what risk these toxins pose to your health. Push for better monitoring of air and hefty fines for polluters.
- ☐ Use your car less or use a more fuel-efficient or hybrid car. Avoid diesel fuel.
- ☐ Replace your gas lawn mower with an electric or push mower or, better yet, replace your lawn.
- ☐ Support the use of solar and wind power.
- ☐ If you live in a polluted area, find a nearby piece of forest where you can walk and breathe in cleaner air at least once weekly.
- ☐ Plant as many trees as you possibly can.

Indoor Air Pollutants

Air pollutant levels are commonly higher in our homes, workplaces, and schools than outdoors. Since most of us spend over 90% of our lives indoors, we need to attend to the quality of our indoor air to ensure good health.

Tobacco Smoke

Tobacco smoke contains a mixture of over 4,000 chemicals, many of which are toxic or known carcinogens. Symptoms related to tobacco smoke exposure include nasal congestion, persistent cough, eye irritation, wheezing, bronchitis, recurrent ear infections, asthma, and other lung diseases. Long-term exposure can lead to emphysema, heart disease, and lung cancer. Tobacco smoke can affect the fetus adversely. Smoking related illnesses are the second leading cause of death in Canada.

Brominated Fire Retardants

Present in foam, furniture, televisions, computers, carpets, and drapery fabric, brominated fire retardants collect in household dust and may interfere with memory and thyroid function when we inhale them. Toddlers inhale them in high doses when crawling on carpeted floors.

Combustion Products

Combustion products may originate from gas furnaces, stoves, clothes dryers, and water heaters, as well as gas or kerosene space heaters and fireplaces. Pollutants from these include carbon monoxide, nitrogen dioxide, and sulfur dioxide.

Exposure to carbon monoxide may mimic flu symptoms, with fatigue, headache, dizziness, nausea, vomiting, rapid heartbeat, angina, and mental confusion. Nitrogen and sulfur dioxide exposure can cause irritation to the mucous membranes of the eyes, nose, throat, and respiratory tract, as well as aggravating asthma and causing bronchitis.

Animal Dander, Molds, Dust Mites

Sensitivities to these substances may cause cough, shortness of breath, tightness in the chest, asthma, nasal congestion, fatigue, eye irritation, and recurrent fever. Reactions will be intensified if the relative humidity in the home or work environment is above 50%.

Volatile Organic Compounds

Reactions to volatile organic compounds (pesticides, formaldehyde, solvents, cleansers) may include eye irritation, nose and throat discomfort, headaches, skin reactions, shortness of breath, nausea and vomiting, nosebleeds, bloodshot eyes, fatigue, and dizziness.

Lead and Mercury Vapors

Lead is a common household toxin, absorbed from old paint flakes and dust and from leaded ceramic glazes or glass. Indoor mercury exposure can result from exposure to latex paint containing phenylmercuric acetate (PMA), which was added to paint until it was banned in 1991.

Radon

After smoking, radon is the second leading cause of lung cancer. A naturally occurring radioactive gas emitted from some areas of the earth as the element radium (a product of uranium) decays, radon breaks down into radioactive and carcinogenic decay particles that can initiate the cancer process in lung tissue when it is inhaled.

Asbestos

Asbestos may still be found in heating systems, acoustic insulation, and floor and ceiling tiles in older homes. As asbestos disintegrates with age, microscopic fibers are released into the air, which can result in serious lung disease.

HEALTH TIPS CHECKLIST

🐾 *Decreasing Exposure to Indoor Pollutants*

Consider the following practices to decrease exposure to indoor air pollutants or to eliminate hazardous substances.

- ☐ Maintain a smoke-free indoor environment.
- ☐ Vent gas stoves to the outside and have them inspected once a year.
- ☐ Do not idle your car in an attached garage.
- ☐ Clean operating fireplace chimneys before each heating season.
- ☐ If you have a gas stove or furnace, install a carbon monoxide detector in your home.
- ☐ Use an electric rather than a gas stove.
- ☐ Keep the relative humidity of your environments below 45% and use a dehumidifier in your basement. Use exhaust fans in bathrooms and kitchens and vent clothes dryers to the outside.
- ☐ Disinfect your humidifier regularly with a 3% hydrogen peroxide solution and drops of essential oils of thyme, oregano and/or tea tree.
- ☐ Keep your basement dry.
- ☐ Remove carpeting or keep it to a minimum. Use hardwood floors.
- ☐ Keep pets out of bedrooms.
- ☐ Vacuum or wet mop (rather than sweep) floor areas regularly and vacuum furniture.
- ☐ Wash bedding and stuffed toys often in water at a temperature of above 130°F to kill dust mites.
- ☐ Use mattress protectors to deter dust mites. Use non-allergenic bedding and pillows, avoiding feathers, wool, and kapok.
- ☐ Avoid furniture and building materials made from particle-board; use solid wood instead.
- ☐ Use proper ventilation and a HEPA air filter when working with toxic agents or in an office with new carpeting, photocopying services, particle-board furnishings, and/or fresh paint. If you have respiratory symptoms, filter your bedroom air at night.
- ☐ If you live in an older home, remove leaded paint using protective masks and filters or cover it with non-toxic paint.
- ☐ To reduce the possibility of radon exposure, seal cracks and holes in foundation walls and floors.
- ☐ Use non-toxic cleaning agents, such as baking soda and vinegar.
- ☐ If you must use solvents, paint thinners, and/or paints, wear a mask and store your unused remains in a garage rather than in your home.
- ☐ If your work or hobbies involve the use of solvents, glues or chemicals, as in photography, woodworking, oil painting and certain crafts, ventilate your work area and consider using a HEPA air filter to thoroughly clean the air.

Our Energy (Fire)

Our sun, from which we derive most of our planetary heat, light, and energy, has existed for 5 billion years, and like many of us, is now considered to be in middle age. Without the sun, there would be no plant or animal life on Earth. We can take some comfort in knowing that the sun is not predicted to burn up its hydrogen fuel for another 5 billion years or so, but in the meantime our burning of fossil fuels to produce energy and provide transportation is warming up the planet, dangerously. At the same time, we are polluting our bodies with man-made energy — nuclear radiation, electromagnetic fields (EMFs), and 'dirty' power. Global warming and electromagnetic pollution threaten our survival. This is an urgent health crisis. We need to act together to find a viable solution.

Global Warming

DID YOU KNOW...

The average Canadian contributes more than 5 tonnes of greenhouse gas emissions to global warming each year, which comprises more than a quarter of Canada's total emissions. Almost 50% of this comes from automobile use; 29% from space heating and air conditioning; 11% from water heating; 7.5 % from appliances; and 2.5 % from lighting.

Greenhouse gases absorb and trap infrared radiation from the sun in the lower part of the Earth's atmosphere, preventing heat from escaping into outer space and resulting in an accelerated warming of the earth. They also cause depletion of the ozone layer, increasing our exposure to solar ultraviolet radiation.

Greenhouse gases include naturally occurring water vapor, carbon dioxide, methane, nitrous oxide, ozone, and man-made halogenated fluorocarbons, perfluorinated carbons, and hydrofluorocarbons. The predominant greenhouse gas is carbon dioxide, accounting for half of all human-generated global warming. Methane, released from landfills, wetlands and bogs, livestock, coal mining, and gas pipeline leaks, traps energy 20–30 times more efficiently than carbon dioxide. Methane may become the most harmful greenhouse gas in coming years.

Greenhouse Gases Sources

Human activity has increased production of greenhouse gases by about 30% since the industrial revolution began in the early 1800s, primarily due to the burning of fossil fuels (coal, oil, and gas) for energy and transportation. Deforestation also contributes to this problem (when trees are cut down less carbon dioxide is absorbed), as well as irrigation, animal grazing (which results in increased methane production), and cement manufacturing.

Oxygen Deficiency or Excess

Multicellular organisms appeared on earth 670 million years ago, only because the atmospheric oxygen rose from 1% to 21%, which it still averages today. In the last 20 years, there has been a very small decline in atmospheric oxygen (0.03%) caused by global warming. Vegetation may grow more quickly overall as global temperatures increase, so, thankfully, our generous reservoir of oxygen is not likely to be exhausted anytime soon. Significantly higher or lower levels of atmospheric oxygen would dramatically change our planet. At oxygen levels less than 15%, fires would not burn, and at levels above 25%, even wet organic matter would burn easily.

The Kyoto Accord

The Kyoto Accord is an international agreement adopted in December 1997 in Japan that set binding targets for developed countries to reduce greenhouse gas emissions an average of 5.2% below 1990 levels, in order to address global warming. Although the accord took effect on February 16, 2005, many countries have yet to make significant decreases in greenhouse gas emissions.

Yin Deficiency, Yang Excess

From a traditional Chinese medical perspective, human-driven excess heat, activity, and energy consumption is exhausting the yin, the feminine principle in our lives, burning it up and generating a yang excess. On the planet, yin deficiency/yang excess results in weather extremes, drought, shortage of water, depletion of forests, mineral deficiencies, species extinction, and the formation of deserts. In a woman, yin deficiency leads to symptoms of adrenal burnout, hyperthyroidism or hypothyroidism, chronic fatigue syndrome, organ exhaustion, frequent infections, autoimmune disease, anxiety, palpitations, insomnia, dryness of the skin, increased thirst, irregular periods and in a menopausal woman, hot flashes, and vaginal dryness. Our illnesses are entwined with massive planetary disharmony.

DID YOU KNOW...

In the United States, transportation alone accounts for more than 25% of energy consumption and a third of its greenhouse gas production, while the generation of electricity from coal- and oil-fired plants is responsible for 40% of emissions.

DID YOU KNOW...

Canada signed the Kyoto Agreement but The United States did not. The United States contains 5% the world's population but produces 25% of total annual emissions of greenhouse gases, while Canada, with one-tenth of the American population, produces 2%. Canada has committed to a 6% reduction in emissions by 2012. In the efforts to comply with the Kyoto Accord, Canadians are being encouraged to reduce emissions by 1 tonne per person.

HEALTH EFFECTS OF GLOBAL WARMING

CLIMATE & PLANETARY CHANGE	HEALTH EFFECTS
DIRECT EFFECTS	
Rise in global temperatures.	Increased deaths from heatstroke, heart attacks, respiratory distress, particularly in the elderly.
Increase in extreme temperature occurrences, both hot and cold.	Deaths, injuries, psychological distress, burden placed on public health systems.
Increased frequency of other extreme weather events, such as hurricanes, flooding, drought, ice storms, forest fires.	Deaths, drowning, injuries, psychological distress, loss of home and community, re-location, increased insect and rodent-borne diseases.
INDIRECT EFFECTS	
Increase in air pollution, smog and ground level ozone; prevalence of spores, pollen, and molds.	Increased asthma and allergies as well as other respiratory disorders and deaths. When temperatures rise above 32°C, more ozone is formed at ground level, increasing the sensitivity of people with asthma to allergens and spurring the development of asthma in children.
Regional positive or negative changes in agricultural productivity with longer growing seasons in some areas; decreased food production in tropical and subtropical countries; increased drought or flooding in others; increased pests or plant diseases.	Changes in availability of food; starvation and dehydration in some areas. Increased violence in the search for food and water. Malnutrition and impairment of children's growth and development. Increased infant mortality.
Increase or change in range and activity of mosquitoes, parasites, viruses, ticks, and other disease-causing insects.	Increase or change in distribution of malaria, Lyme disease, dengue fever, Leishmaniasis, flu epidemics, trypanosomiasis, schistosomiasis, West Nile virus.
Change in types and frequency of infectious organisms found in water and food.	Changed or increased incidence of diarrhea and other infectious diseases, such as cholera and E. coli infections.
Sea levels rise (45 to 88 cm by 2100) with flooding of coastal and island populations. More than half the world's population lives within 40 miles or 60 kilometers of the sea.	Rising sea levels will increase prevalence of malaria and cholera; disrupt food production; cause mass migrations of people; and stress public health resources.
Changes in economy, infrastructure, supply of resources, food and water.	Social and economic stress, political and civil strife, psychological distress.
Melting permafrost and ice flows in the Arctic, leading to a change in food supply for the Inuit.	Reduced capacity of the Inuit to live off the land, malnutrition.
Depletion of the ozone layer caused by greenhouse gases, resulting in increased exposure to solar ultraviolet radiation.	Immune deficiency disorders, with increased susceptibility to infection and risk of cancer. Sunburn, premature skin aging, skin cancer, malignant melanoma, cataracts, retinal damage.
Changes in fish populations because of rising temperatures and sea levels.	Potential loss of protein sources for fish-consuming populations.

HEALTH TIPS CHECKLIST

🍃 *Personal Solutions to Global Warming*

Make changes to your personal lifestyle to assist in solving global warming. Check them off ☑ as you go.

🍃 *Home Heating and Cooling*

☐ Consider the use of wind, solar, and geothermal power to replace power generated by fossil fuels.

☐ If you are building a new home in a northern climate, consider an earth berm around the north side of your home for insulation and large windows or a greenhouse on the south side for passive solar heat. Place windows in advantageous spots to reduce the need for indoor lighting.

☐ Consider living in a smaller dwelling to save electricity and to conserve materials.

☐ Insulate your walls, ceilings, floors, basements, doors, and water pipes.

☐ Install a storm door with a screen to prevent energy loss and improve ventilation.

☐ Replace old windows with argon-filled, double-glazed windows to reduce emissions of carbon dioxide.

☐ To control heat gain in the summer, install awnings on upper storey windows.

☐ Paint your house a light color if you live in a warm climate or a dark color if you live in a cold climate.

☐ Install a high-efficiency furnace or air conditioner to save up to 40% on heating and cooling costs.

☐ Plant shade deciduous trees. Low-growing evergreen shrubs planted near basement walls will help to keep warmth in during the winter and cool in during the summer.

☐ Use caulking and weather stripping to plug air leaks around doors and windows

☐ Request a home energy audit from your utility company to find out where your home is poorly insulated or is not energy efficient. Begin with the least expensive changes that have the greatest benefit.

☐ Do not overheat or overcool your house. In the winter set your thermostat at 68°F in the daytime, and 55°F at night, using warm blankets, a hot water bottle, or a duvet to warm the bed. In the summer, keep it at 78°F to provide the most comfort for the least cost.

☐ If you work away from home, get a timed thermostat that will automatically turn off the heating or cooling when you leave the house, and turn it on shortly before you return.

☐ Clean or replace air filters as needed, as more energy is required to draw air through dirty filters.

☐ Try to get by with ceiling fans and well-placed fans rather than air conditioning.

🍃 *Home Appliances*

☐ Turn down the temperature on your refrigerator (it accounts for 11% to 20% of home electricity consumption) to 37°F and your freezer to 3°F. Replace an old refrigerator with a new energy efficient model, which uses 50% less energy.

☐ Cool your food before placing it into the fridge.

☐ Chest freezers are more energy efficient than upright models. Do not place your freezer close to a heat source, such as a furnace, radiator, or dryer.

☐ Use cool or warm water for washing clothes, rather than hot water. A front-loading washing machine can cut hot water use by 60% to 70 % compared to a top-loading machine.

☐ Retire your clothes dryer and install a clothesline outside and/or in the basement.

☐ Use less hot water by installing low-flow showerheads

☐ Turn down the temperature on your water heater to 120°F (50°C) or invest in a solar water heater.

☐ Wrap your water heater in an insulating jacket.

☐ Wash dishes by hand and let them air dry or dry them manually.

☐ Use fewer electrical appliances — electric carving knives, mixers, and hairdryers, for example.

☐ Turn your computers, VCRs, DVD players, televisions, and radios off when not in use.

☐ Choose energy-efficient appliances — in Canada and the United States, look for the Energy Star label.

Lighting

☐ Buy energy efficient, full-spectrum, compact fluorescent bulbs for your most-used lights. The bulb must be full-spectrum and include near ultraviolet wavelengths for optimal health. These are available from garden shops.

☐ Turn your lights out when not in use; use indoor lighting as little as possible; choose bulbs with lower wattage.

☐ Use wreaths and bows for outdoor Christmas decorations, rather than lights, unless they are solar powered.

Transportation

☐ Walk, bike, carpool, or use public transit more often. This is the most important thing you can do to reduce greenhouse gases.

☐ Live without a car. If you do buy a car, choose a smaller car that is fuel efficient or a hybrid.

☐ Have your car serviced every 5000 miles or so to maintain fuel efficiency.

☐ Use good quality multigrade oil to reduce engine friction and increase fuel efficiency.

☐ Use properly filled radial tires to improve fuel economy by at least 4%.

☐ If your car has an air conditioner, be sure to have its coolant recovered and recycled when you have your car serviced.

☐ Investigate the possibility of using biodiesel fuel (made from recycled vegetable oils or soy oil) and ethanol whenever it becomes available in your area.

Reduce, Re-use, Recycle

☐ Reduce the waste you generate by buying minimally packaged goods, choosing reusable products rather than disposable ones, and recycle whenever possible.

☐ Help to establish recycling and composting programs in your town.

☐ Reduce the weekly garbage you set out for pickup by 50%.

☐ Call or write manufacturers who use plastic containers to switch to recyclable glass. Request that packaging be made from paper and corn rather than Styrofoam or plastic.

☐ Donate old clothing, furniture, appliances, and books to stores, charities, libraries, churches, or individuals who can resell them or use them for parts.

☐ Buy food (grains, nuts, beans), detergent, shampoo, and toilet paper in bulk to save on packaging.

☐ If you need to buy something new, choose good quality that will last to keep the energy used in manufacturing new goods to a minimum. Maintain and repair your possessions so they last as long as possible.

☐ Do not buy disposable products — whether they be diapers, cameras, paper plates, or plastic cutlery.

☐ Rent, borrow, or share items that you will not use often. These might include things as diverse as a lawn mower, rototiller, breadmaker, videocamera, or a canoe.

Cooking and Eating

☐ Keep lids on pots when cooking or boiling water to reduce energy use. When boiling water, use a kettle for greater efficiency, and boil only the amount you need.

☐ Use a toaster oven rather than a conventional oven when possible for heating smaller quantities of food.

☐ Eat more raw food, less cooked food to save on electricity and preserve enzymes.

☐ Buy locally grown seasonal fruits, vegetables, and food whenever possible to reduce the energy and emissions needed for transportation and refrigeration.

☐ Become a vegetarian so that fewer acres are needed globally to pasture livestock or feed them grain, and consequently fewer trees will be cut down and forests will be saved.

Electromagnetic Energy Disturbances

The effect of electromagnetism on our health has only begun to be understood in recent years. Electromagnetism holds the atoms together that make up our bodies and is necessary for all chemical reactions to occur, including biochemical reactions that regulate and restore our health.

Sources of electromagnetic energy include solar radiation, the rotation of the Earth, and bioelectronic energy in our bodies. Natural or man-made electromagnetic fields in our environment can be beneficial to our health, but, increasingly, we are disrupting these energy fields, exposing ourselves to grave health risks. Once we understand our ties to the magnetic field of the Earth and electromagnetic frequencies from the sun, we can be more careful about minimizing electromagnetic interference patterns that undermine our health.

ELECTROMAGNETIC FIELDS

When electrons flow through a conducting material, an electrical current is produced, which generates a magnetic field in the space that surrounds the conducting material. The rate and amount of current flow through the conducting material determines the strength of the magnetic field. Magnetic fields are infinite, not easily shielded, and pass through objects and walls, traveling at the speed of light. Much like sound waves that become larger as they move through space, magnetic fields weaken as they expand outward and mix with background fields, but in theory never end.

DID YOU KNOW...

In December 2004, Germany turned on the world's biggest solar park that, along with other solar parks and Germany's 16,000 windmills, currently produces 10% of the country's electricity. The Germans project that by 2020, at least 20% of the nation's electricity will come from renewable sources. In California in December 2004, Governor Arnold Schwarzenegger set a goal that one million buildings in the state will be powered by solar energy, including half of all new homes, by 2018.

Electromagnetic Radiation

Composed of massless particles called photons traveling or radiating in a wave-like pattern at the speed of light, electromagnetic radiation originated with the birth of the universe 13.7 billion years ago. While there is a wide spectrum of electromagnetic radiation, only a few wavelengths from space reach the surface of the Earth. We receive just the right amount of electromagnetic radiation from the stars, sun, and solar wind in the visible, infrared, and ultraviolet spectrum to promote life on Earth. We are also shielded from excess gamma rays, X-rays, and UV radiation through the filter created by the Earth's atmosphere and own magnetic field. If more of these forms of electromagnetic radiation reached us, they would destroy most organisms on the planet.

We have, however, created technology that has depleted the ozone layer in the atmosphere, allowing more ultraviolet radiation to reach the earth. Burning fossil fuels has contributed to this health risk. We have also created technology that emits gamma rays, X-rays, microwaves, and radio waves. Nuclear bomb testing and nuclear power generation have contributed to this health problem.

Core Magnetic Field

The pulsing blood of liquid iron and nickel that are on fire in the outer core of our spinning Earth create an electric current that has been turned on for 3 billion years. This electric current creates a magnetic field around the earth that also penetrates our bodies. Our hearts and brains are synchronized to the heartbeat of the Earth.

Biomagnetic Fields

The electrical activity that occurs in our bodies produces biomagnetic fields. All living cells and chemical processes rely on electromagnetic interactions between molecules, which are responsible for the making and breaking of chemical bonds, the release of energy from food, the production of cellular energy, and the transport of minerals, nutrients, hormones, neurotransmitters,

and neuropeptides across cell membranes. When our biomagnetic fields are strong, all of these functions work more efficiently. Electric and magnetic fields generated by body tissues and organs are also part of our rapid internal communication system, orchestrating harmony and organization within and between cells.

Heart

The heart produces the strongest electromagnetic activity of any tissue in the body. The moving blood is an excellent electrical conductor due to its high salt content, and magnifies magnetic energy because of the iron contained in red blood cells. Red blood cells transport electromagnetic energy from the heart to the rest of the body. The heart's magnetic field measures at 10^{-3} gauss, which is one millionth the strength of the Earth's magnetic field and about one-thousandth of the background magnetic field in a city environment.

Brain

Brain activity also produces an electromagnetic field, hundreds of times weaker than the heart's field.

Muscles

Each of our muscles produces a small magnetic pulse when it contracts, which it radiates into surrounding space.

Mictrotubules

In recent years, scientists have determined that the hollow, spaghetti-shaped microtubules present in all our cells act as miniature fiber optic cables capable of transmitting electromagnetic frequencies, not unlike the fiber optic cables that carry high speed information to us through the Internet. The water in and around the cell and within the microtubules 'records' the information or 'consciousness' contained in frequencies and photons. This information is then communicated through the microtubules nearly simultaneously to all parts of the body, causing shifts in neuropeptides, biochemistry, and cellular function.

In the future, healing with light frequencies, sound, homeopathy, intention, mantra, music, magnetic fields, and color will become more prevalent as we realize that magnetic fields, photons of light, phonons of sound, and consciousness act as the template for the ordering of matter.

DID YOU KNOW...

Health-care practitioners who use their hands to heal can emanate a biomagnetic field that is 1000 times stronger than the field generated by the heart.

DID YOU KNOW...

When shielded from the Earth's magnetic field in underground rooms, subjects developed irregular and chaotic biological rhythms with disturbances in sleep, body temperature, and urination. Normal rhythms were restored when they were exposed to a weak electromagnetic field of 10 Hz, which mimicked the earth's field.

Radiation Fallout

Global background radiation (gamma rays) has increased since the 1940s when the first man-made nuclear bombs exploded. Since then, we have been exposed to gamma rays released from nuclear reactor accidents; nuclear fallout from weapons testing; weapons containing depleted uranium (the dust from depleted uranium remains radioactive for 4,500 million years); and radioactive disposal sites. Flying at high altitudes — 'too close to the sun' — reduces the protection offered by the full atmosphere. We are also exposed to X-ray radiation during mammograms and other radiology procedures.

Health Effects of Excess Radiation Exposure

- Damage to cell membranes caused by the formation of free radicals
- Decrease in white blood cell count and depressed immunity
- Formation of irregularly shaped red blood cells, which may result in anemia, fatigue, short-term memory loss
- Damage to DNA
- Susceptibility to leukemia, hypothyroidism, thyroid cancer, lung cancer, breast cancer, bone cancer, Hodgkin's disease
- Birth defects and increased infant mortality
- Multiple chemical sensitivities
- Kidney damage
- Depression

Electromagnetic Pollution

Other human inventions besides nuclear arms and reactors generate extremely low-frequency electromagnetic fields (ELFS), radio waves, microwaves, X-rays, and gamma rays that contribute to electromagnetic pollution. This 'electrosmog' can undermine our health.

Long-term exposure to artificial electromagnetic fields (EMFs) in the extremely low frequency radio wave and microwave frequencies can have serious effects on our health. Sources of EMFs include microwaves used in ovens and cellular telephones, as well as 'dirty power'.

Electromagnetic Pollution Research Findings

- In women and men exposed occupationally to extremely low-frequency electromagnetic fields, there was an increased incidence of breast cancer: 60 Hz magnetic fields enhance breast cancer cell proliferation by blocking melatonin.
- In employees in the utility industry exposed to extremely low-frequency 50 Hz fields, there was higher risk of amyotrophic lateral sclerosis (ALS) and multiple sclerosis (MS).

DID YOU KNOW...

Women's breasts and thyroid tissue are very sensitive to radiation, which contributes significantly to breast cancer development and thyroid dysfunction. The effects of radiation are cumulative and may manifest as cancer any time within 40 years after exposure.

DID YOU KNOW...

The U.S. Atomic Energy Commission recommends that we consume 2–3 ounces or 60–80 grams (wet weight) of sea vegetables per week or 2 tablespoons daily to protect from radiation toxicity. This should be increased fourfold during or after direct exposure to radiation.

NUTRITION PROTECTION AGAINST RADIATION SICKNESS

The following foods and supplements can be used daily to protect against radiation toxicity. Increase intake during mammography, X-rays, or other radiation exposure, including airline travel.

Foods

- Sea vegetables, 2 tbsp, or 3 kelp tablets, daily to elevate iodine and sodium alginate. Sodium alginate binds to radioactive molecules and can increase excretion by 80%. Iodine protects the thyroid from radiation — we need 150 mcg to 1000 mcg daily (575 mg of Norwegian kelp contains 359 mcg of iodine).
- Turmeric, 2 or more tsp daily, or curcumin, 500–1000 mg, 3 times daily, to decrease the damaging effects of radiation.
- Yams, squash, carrots, Swiss chard, or spinach daily to provide beta carotene, or use a supplement containing Dunaliella algae, 25,000–50,000 IU daily.
- Cooked tomato sauce, ½ cup daily during exposure, to provide lycopene content.
- Whey (goat is best) or soy protein powder, 1 tbsp daily, to provide cysteine.
- Reishi, maitake, and shitake mushrooms to sustain immune health.
- Dietary fiber, 45 grams daily, to deter absorption of radiation and improve its excretion.
- Foods from the brassica family daily — kale, cabbage, broccoli, cauliflower — to protect the liver.
- Miso soup a few times a week to help excrete radioactive particles and deter cancer.
- Dried beans, lentils, or tofu daily in the diet to prevent the initiation of cancer.

Supplements

- Antioxidant supplements containing vitamin C, E, coenzyme Q10, zinc, selenium, grape seed extract, alpha lipoic acid, and NAC to discourage free radical damage and the development of cancer.
- Calcium and potassium supplements to aid in the excretion of radioactive particles, such as cesium-137.
- Flax oil (unheated), 2 tbsp, or uncontaminated fish oil, 2000 mg daily, to protect cell membranes.
- Vitamin B-3 (niacin), B-12, and B complex to help to repair DNA damage.
- Green tea daily to remove radioactive isotopes and protect from cancer.

- Female radio and telegraph operators exposed to extremely low-frequency (50Hz) fields and radio frequencies are more susceptible to breast cancer.
- In children exposed to extremely low-frequency electromagnetic fields emanating from the generation, transmission, and use of electricity, there was an increased incidence of childhood leukemia, as well as increased mortality rates for all cancers and leukemia in certain age groups living within 2 kilometers of an AM radio broadcasting tower of over 100 kW.

- Microwave exposure from cell phone use increases the risk of tumors in the head, including acoustic neuroma and uveal melanoma. While individuals were using a cell phone and for 15 to 20 minutes after the cell phones were turned off, there was a slowing down of brain waves as measured by an EEG.
- In rats exposed to 15 min of 900 MHz pulsed microwaves (cell phone frequencies), there was brain neuron damage and immediate changes in neurotransmitter receptors.
- In people living near television and radio broadcasting transmitters, there was an increased risk of hematopoietic and lymphatic tissue cancer. People who reside near cell phone towers experienced circulatory problems, sleep disturbances, irritability, depression, blurred vision, concentration difficulties, nausea, lack of appetite, headache, and vertigo.
- In individuals with heart problems, there was interference with the proper functioning of artificial pacemakers.
- In rats that were exposed to 910 MHz fields (in the frequency range of cell phones) for 2 hours a day for 30 days, there was DNA damage to bone marrow cells.

Microwave Ovens

Heat generated by microwaves begins with friction in the cells and molecules where water is present, leading to the rupture of cell membranes and the loss of the electrical potential between the inside and outside of the cell. Microwave cooking changes the nutrients in food, causing hemoglobin levels to drop, cholesterol to increase, white blood cell count to decrease, and susceptibility to bacterial infection to increase. Amino acids, the building blocks of protein, undergo changes in shape that the body may have difficulty utilizing.

Dirty Power

Regular 'clean' power or electricity enters our homes through power lines at a frequency of 60 Hz, whereas 'dirty' power occurs when this 60 Hz frequency is polluted with high frequency signals from radio waves that flow through both the wires and through the earth. More than 70% of electrical current returns to the utility power substation through the earth, rather than through wiring, because the wires are overloaded with high frequencies generated by modern electronic devices, such as computers, VCRs, fax machines, and televisions. Electricity returns to the substation by the path of least resistance, often flowing through soil and water. We may unwittingly become part of an electrical circuit when we stand on our lawn or wash dishes in our kitchen sink.

RADIO-WAVE SICKNESS SYMPTOMS

In humans, health problems related to 'dirty' power have been termed radio-wave sickness, characterized by a distinct set of symptoms.

Neurological

Headaches, dizziness, nausea, poor concentration, attention deficit disorder, memory loss, irritability, depression, anxiety, insomnia, fatigue, weakness, tremors, muscle spasm, numbness, tingling, altered reflexes, muscle and joint pain, leg/foot pain, flu-like symptoms, fever, epilepsy, stroke, paralysis, multiple sclerosis, ALS, Alzheimer's disease, Parkinson's disease

Cardiac

Palpitations, arrhythmias, chest pain or pressure, blood pressure irregularities, slow or fast heart rate, shortness of breath

Respiratory

Sinusitis, bronchitis, pneumonia, asthma

Dermatological

Skin rash, itching, burning, facial flushing

Eye Symptoms

Pain or burning in the eyes, pressure behind the eyes, deteriorating vision, floaters, cataracts

Other

Digestive problems; abdominal pain; enlarged thyroid; ovarian pain; dryness of the lips, tongue, mouth and eyes; excessive thirst; dehydration; nosebleeds; internal bleeding; hypoglycemia or diabetes; immune dysregulation; hair loss; teeth pain; poor sense of smell; ear ringing; chronic fatigue; fibromyalgia; cancer

Detecting Electromagnetic Pollution

Electric fields, magnetic fields, and radio/microwave fields can be measured by common gauss meters. Survey your home and workplace to find problem areas. Prolonged exposure to a magnetic field higher than 2 mG can be detrimental to health, as can chronic exposure to radiowaves or microwaves.

Dirty power is measured by plugging a specially designed meter into an electrical outlet. The instrument first filters out the clean 60 Hz wavelength (which may be harmful by itself) and then registers the high frequency fields above 10,000 Hz, which significantly add to the total electrical pollution. This instrument can be ordered from www.bio-ag.com in Canada or from www.stetzerelectric.com in the United States.

HEALTH TIPS CHECKLIST

🔹 *Decreasing Electromagnetic Pollution*

To decrease your exposure to electromagnetic pollution, consider the following guidelines.

- ☐ Purchase or rent a gauss meter as well as a meter to measure dirty power and assess the electromagnetic fields around your home.
- ☐ Pay attention to the location of hydro lines, cell phone towers and AM radio transmission towers. Keep a 'safe' distance from the source of electromagnetic fields. At a distance of 2.5 feet or 76 centimeters, the fields are 80% less powerful.
- ☐ Do not buy a house or live within 2 kilometers or 1.2 miles of a cell phone tower or AM radio transmission tower; 60 to 200 feet or 18 to 60 meters from distribution lines and 300 to 1,000 feet or 92 to 305 meters from transmission lines. Cell tower strobe lights emit 'dirty' power.
- ☐ Keep EMFs under 1 mG in the bedroom .Move televisions, clock radios, and lamps at least 2.5 feet or 0.75 meters from your bed or where you sit for long periods of time.
- ☐ Avoid using electric blankets, heating pads, and water beds.
- ☐ Do not use a microwave oven. Remove it from your home.
- ☐ Turn off all electrical devices when not in use including your computer.
- ☐ Use a wind-up watch rather than one with a quartz crystal or battery — these, too, emit electromagnetic energy.
- ☐ Use a regular phone, rather than a cordless phone or cell phone. Have your phone company install a radio frequency filter on your phone line to cut out these frequencies.
- ☐ Steel-belted radial tires can expose car passengers to fields as high as 50 mG, which is too much if you are spending hours a day in a car. Spend less time in a car.
- ☐ Do not use touch lamps or halogen lights.
- ☐ Hire an electrician to: a) inspect for and eliminate loose or poor connections; b) replace poorly made switches, fixtures and appliances; c) replace dimmer switches with regular On/Off switches; d) make sure the wire between the meter and your electrical box is wide enough so it doesn't bottleneck high frequencies.
- ☐ Have your utility company trim branches bumping or touching overhead wires; and ask them to replace split-volt connectors with crimp-on connectors if the split-volt connectors are on your line.
- ☐ Design your office so that your exposure to EMFs from computers, photocopiers, and printers is less than 2 mG (0.2 microteslas).
- ☐ Purchase high frequency filters and plug these into your electrical outlets to reduce dirty power. You will need about 20 of these for an average house.
- ☐ Use rubber gloves when washing dishes or stand on a non-conductive rubber or cloth mat.
- ☐ If you live off the grid and have alternative (solar or wind) power, install filters to clean up the wave form the inverter generates.

Balancing Our Bioelectronic System

To detect bioelectronic imbalance in your body, we can test for two markers: redox potential (assesses state of oxygen, free radical damage, antioxidant status) and resistivity (assesses electrical conductivity and movement of ions) — in each of the body fluids: blood, urine, and saliva.

Redox Potential

When an atom loses electrons and becomes positively charged, this process is called oxidation, and when an atom gains electrons and becomes negatively charged, this process is called reduction. The redox potential refers to the amount of electron activity or the back and forth movement of electrons between molecules. The redox potential is a measure of how quickly this back and forth oxidation-reduction process is occurring.

When atoms gain electrons (and are reduced), they are more stable and less likely to cause harm to the body. When they lose electrons and are oxidized, they become unstable or 'free'. Free radicals can contribute to a wide variety of health conditions.

Free Radicals and Antioxidants

Oxygen is vital for our cells to create and store energy necessary for proper cell function. Normally, an oxygen molecule has four pairs of electrons. Although oxygen is relatively stable in air, when it is absorbed into the body, it can become active and unstable, attaching to molecules that have lost electrons, such as environmental toxins. These molecules are positively charged and exist in the oxidized state.

DID YOU KNOW...

We generate free radicals when we are exposed to things like cigarette smoke, cooked fats, chemicals, and radiation. If we can supply the body with electron donors, known as antioxidants, we can mop up the reactive oxygen species to neutralize them so that the body's electrons and oxygen are preserved.

IMBALANCED REDOX POTENTIAL CAUSES AND SOLUTIONS

FLUID	REDOX POTENTIAL (rH2)
URINE Normal: 22–26	**Low rH2 (<22)** **Causes:** greater number of electron donors than electron acceptors; electrons excreted in the urine rather than being used to produce energy in cell mitochondria; associated with degenerative disease, including cancer, and premature aging; associated with a urinary tract infection. **Solutions:** treat urinary tract infection; improve cell metabolism with coenzyme Q10, L-carnitine, vitamin C, NAC, reduced glutathione; adjust antioxidants, perhaps lowering the amount given, as they aren't being utilized; balance pH with magnesium, potassium, adrenal support, and thyroid support.
	High rH2 (>26) **Causes:** mitochondria are impaired in their ability to produce energy because of interference from heavy metals, chemicals, drugs and/or pesticides. **Solutions:** improve oxidative phosphorylation with coenzyme Q10, L-carnitine, dimethylglycine, ferulic acid; improve cell metabolism with lipoic acid, vitamins B-2 and B-5; detoxify heavy metals and chemicals.

IMBALANCED REDOX POTENTIAL CAUSES AND SOLUTIONS

FLUID	REDOX POTENTIAL (rH2)
BLOOD Normal: 20–24	**Low rH2 (<20)** **Causes:** excess use of antioxidants, chelation, or ozone therapy; or a destructive health condition that causes rupture of the cell nucleus. **Solutions:** decrease antioxidant use; rule out degenerative disease leading to cell nucleus destruction.
	High rH2 (>24) **Causes:** not enough antioxidants to quench ongoing free radical activity, resulting in a decreased ability of the mitochondria to produce high–energy cellular fuel, which causes fatigue; deficit of intracellular oxygen, leading to increased susceptibility to fungal infections; exposure to toxic metals, pesticides, infectious agents, chemical residues, cooked and trans fats, radiation exposure, aging and chronic stress. **Solutions:** eliminate toxic metals and chemicals (use saunas, remove mercury amalgam fillings); eat organic vegetarian diet; eliminate infectious agents; support the immune system (zinc, selenium, vitamin C, astragalus, echinacea, goldenseal); support liver function (use NAC, curcumin, magnesium, milk thistle, dandelion); improve lymph congestion; increase antioxidants; improve cell metabolism with lipoic acid, B complex, and L-carnitine.
SALIVA Normal: 20–24	**Low rH2 (<20):** **Causes:** excess use of antioxidants (do not take antioxidants during the 48 hours before the test); metal plates and dental appliances; possibly tumors. **Solutions:** decrease use of antioxidants; remove metal plates and dental appliances prior to testing; investigate tumor as a possibility.
	High rH2 (>24): **Causes:** often associated with increased free radical activity in the liver, perhaps due to pesticide or chemical exposure, or toxic metals; overburdened lymphatic system or chronic emotional stress. **Solutions:** improve liver function with NAC, curcumin, milk thistle, dandelion; improve digestion with enzymes and probiotics; support lymphatic system with deep breathing, rebounding, daily exercise; improve cell metabolism; detox metals and chemicals.

When some oxygen electrons are donated in an effort to neutralize toxins or are used elsewhere as a normal part of cell metabolism, the remaining oxygen becomes positively charged and unstable, setting out to find other unpaired electrons. It 'robs' electrons from where they are being used, such as in cell membranes, the mitochondria, or the DNA, damaging tissue and leaving more unstable molecules behind. This results in the formation of a cascade of free radicals or reactive oxygen species, which generate more cellular and DNA damage, speed up the aging process, result in a deficiency of oxygen within our cells, and contribute to ailments, such as chronic fatigue syndrome, arthritis, and cancer.

Fruits and vegetables are rich in antioxidants. In supplement form, antioxidants include vitamin C, vitamin E, zinc, selenium, N-acetyl cysteine, coenzyme Q10, alpha lipoic acid, grape seed extract, and microhydrin.

Imbalanced Redox Potential

Redox potential can be measured in blood, urine, and saliva using such tests as Biolectronics of Vincent (B.E.V.), Bio-Electronic Terrain Analysis (BE-T-A), or Biological Terrain Assessment (BTA). Ask your health-care practitioner for more information on these tests and discuss the results based on this list of causes and solutions.

Resistivity

Resistivity is a measure of the electron conductivity in body fluids and the level of resistance to the flow of electrons. High resistivity means that there will be less movement of substances in and out of cells, biochemical reactions and cell metabolism will be slower, and toxicity will build up both in the extracellular fluid and inside our cells, contributing to degenerative disease.

Resistivity reflects our overall mineral status, determined by mineral intake, digestive capacity, mineral absorption (stomach, pancreas,

DID YOU KNOW...

An excess of positively charged atoms (oxidation) in our bodies contributes to rapid aging.

RESISTIVITY IMBALANCE CAUSES AND SOLUTIONS	
FLUID	**RESISTIVITY**
BLOOD Normal: 180–225	**Low (<180)** **Causes:** may indicate an elevation of minerals, caused by an excess of toxic metals; an inability of the kidneys to adequately filter properly; dehydration; or from excess mineral supplementation. **Solutions:** kidney drainage (can choose from Unda 2, 7, 45, Renelix, Ulmus campestre, Juniperus, berberis, goldenrod, *uva ursi*, marshmallow root, horsetail, yarrow, parsley, asparagus); cleanse the blood (protease, Mucokehl, red clover, echinacea, yellow dock, burdock); exercise daily to improve circulation; drink 2 liters or quarts of water daily; detoxify the lymph (rebounding, Chelidonium plex, Unda 233, 21, Itires, Lymphdiaral, phytolacca, cleavers, calendula, wild indigo, scrophularia nodosa)
	High (>225) **Causes:** may be caused by mineral deficiency/poor absorption of minerals. **Solutions:** increase minerals through foods or supplementation, especially magnesium, potassium, and trace minerals (including copper-silver-gold oligotherapy); improve digestion with proper chewing; assess hydrochloric acid production in the stomach and increase if necessary with gentian, wormwood, Unda 4, Silicea 6X, or HCl tablets with meals; increase intestinal absorption by removing food allergies (dairy, wheat etc.) and supplement with digestive enzymes and a probiotic (*Lactobacilli* and *Bifidobacterium*); normalize adrenal function to ensure conservation of sodium and potassium; make sure minerals aren't being lost through perspiration (saunas and exercise) or excess water consumption.

RESISTIVITY IMBALANCE CAUSES AND SOLUTIONS

FLUID	RESISTIVITY
SALIVA Normal: 160–200	**Low (<160)** **Causes:** excess minerals in the fluid surrounding the cells and in the lymphatic vessels (suspect heavy metal toxicity) blocking the transport of waste out of the cells and through the lymph; impeding the flow of nutrients into cells; resulting in increased cellular toxicity and cell degeneration, fluid congestion and stagnation, with possible edema. **Solutions:** Daily exercise; deep breathing; 2 liters or quarts of pure water daily; check for toxic metals; massage; saunas; dry brushing of the skin; detoxify the lymph; improve kidney, liver, and bowel function.
	High (>200) (higher than 300 suggests osteoporosis) **Causes:** low mineral concentration due to inadequate intake from foods or supplementation; poor absorption, possibly due to leaky gut syndrome; excess water consumption. **Solutions:** chew food thoroughly; ensure adequate hydrochloric acid in the stomach; use digestive enzymes to increase absorption; heal leaky gut with zinc, L-glutamine, vitamin A, and probiotics; increase mineral-rich foods (nuts, seeds, seaweeds, spinach, kale, Swiss chard); support adrenal function with B complex, vitamin C, herbs or glandular derivatives; supplement with magnesium, potassium and trace minerals; include copper-silver-gold oligotherapy.
URINE Normal: 25–60	**Low (<25)** **Causes:** overabundance of minerals being eliminated by the kidney through the urine, possibly due to dehydration. **Solutions:** consume 2 liters or quarts of water daily, decrease salt intake, cleanse the blood and lymph.
	High (>60) **Causes:** mineral deficiency in the body, which may result in enzyme deficiency, due to inadequate intake or poor absorption; reduced kidney function, with inability of the kidneys to concentrate waste products; adrenal exhaustion, as excessive sodium and potassium may be lost in the urine. **Solutions:** correct adrenal exhaustion; increase potassium, magnesium, and ionic trace minerals; use copper-silver-gold oligotherapy; improve digestion and absorption with HCl, enzymes and probiotics; increase mineral-rich foods; support kidney function.

and small intestine function), and kidney function. Although most minerals are conductors, the minerals with the highest conductivity and lowest resistivity are silver, copper, and gold. These can be taken in trace or homeopathic amounts to improve electron conductivity.

Resistivity Imbalance

Resistivity can also be assessed in blood, urine, and saliva using B.E.V., BE-T-A, or BTA tests. Again, ask your health-care practitioner for more information on these tests and discuss the results based on this list of causes and solutions.

Our Bodies

N
ot surprisingly, a polluted exterior environment creates a polluted interior environment in our bodies, affecting us primarily through the gastrointestinal tract from the esophagous to the stomach, through the small intestine and large intestine, to the colon and anus. In this case, the old saying, "We are what we eat," has an ironic twist. Contaminated food and water contaminate our digestive system, leading to almost every illness we know.

Body Ecology

Within our bodies, we have a digestive garden to tend that is approximately 250 square meters in size, an area larger than a tennis court. This is the turf that lines the intestinal tract. The lining of our gut, much like the soil of the Earth, is host to a community of organisms that feed on the organic by-products of our digestion. More than 400 different bacterial species comprise the intestinal microflora, weighing in at 3½ pounds (the weight of your liver) and totaling several trillion organisms, which is at least 10 to 100 times more than the number of cells in our bodies.

Because the composition of intestinal flora is one of the most important determinants of lifelong health, we would do well to become professional gardeners of our internal landscape.

Microflora Sources

As fetuses, we were all microbiologically sterile. On our ride through the birth canal, our mouths came in contact with the primary inhabitant of the vagina, *Lactobacillus,* and we were inoculated with our first bacterial species, which took up residence in our intestinal tract.

If we were breastfed, we acquired during the first days and weeks of our lives massive amounts of *Bifidobacterium,* which is responsible for the maturation of our immune system, contributing to lifelong immune fitness and a lowered susceptibility to allergies. (If we were Caesarian born, however, we were 'colon'-ized instead by

DID YOU KNOW...

Eating vegetables, fruits, and dietary fiber promotes the growth of protective *Bifidobacterium*, while a diet of meat with few fruits and vegetables promotes the growth of potentially harmful *Bacteroides*.

bacteria present on the skin and in the environment around us, making us more susceptible to allergies as infants and having a detrimental effect on our immune system.)

After about age 50, as though by some prearranged agreement, the protective *Bifidobacterium* decrease, and *Bacteroides* and *Clostridium perfringes* organisms increase to form about 80% of the flora. *Bacteroides* can transform non-carcinogens in the gastrointestinal tract into carcinogens, such as heterocyclic amines and nitrosamines, ushering us to our decline. At death, bacteria, along with fungi, help to decay our bodies, recycling the corpse to return minerals to the earth.

SPECIAL SUPPLEMENTATION WITH *LACTOBACILLI* AND *BIFIDOBACTERIUM*

If your child is born by Caesarian section, sprinkle ⅛ tsp of human derived *Lactobacillus acidophilus* into his or her mouth immediately after birth to inoculate the bowel with this protective organism.

If your child is being fed formula rather than breastmilk, supplement with ¼ tsp *Bifidobacterium* daily starting 2 days after birth and continue for six months.

After age 50, supplement with *Lactobacilli* and *Bifidobacterium* daily.

Bowel Flora Distribution

Most of the bowel flora is concentrated in the last part of the small intestine, the ileum, and the large intestine. The ileum has slower peristalsis, lower pH, and lower redox (oxidation-reduction) potentials that allow for increased microbial growth. In the ileum there are *Lactobacilli, Streptococci, Bacteroides, Eubacteria,* and *Bifidobacteria.*

The large intestine is the main site of bacterial proliferation, where they form one-third of the bulk of our stools. More than 99% of the bacteria present in the large intestine are anaerobic, meaning that they thrive in an area of low oxygen and use fermentation of our food as a source of energy. *Lactobacilli* are more predominant in the small intestine, while *Bifidobacteria* abound in the large intestine.

Gut Disease

While these natural microflora are necessary for good health, other bacteria, fungi, parasites, yeasts, and viruses present in the body can cause a variety of infections or produce antigens that cross-react with specific body tissues, causing the production of antibodies and an immune response against the involved tissue. This occurs in autoimmune diseases such as rheumatoid arthritis, lupus, diabetes, and autoimmune thyroid disease, as well as a variety of infections.

Bacterial infections commonly exist in the teeth, jawbone, tonsils, sinuses, and colon. Chronic infection may also predispose us to various cancers.

Good Flora, Bad Flora

While some bacteria are very beneficial to our health, others are harmful. Ridding ourselves of the harmful bacteria is essential. Still, bacteria may be beneficial or harmful, depending upon their level in the bowel. Maintaining their balance is, therefore, important for our health.

Bacteria, Fungi, and Yeast that May Benefit or Harm
- Eubacteria (mostly beneficial)
- Bacteroides (mostly beneficial)
- Veillonellae
- Enterobacteria
- E. coli
- Streptococcus
- Anaerobic gram-positive cocci
- Peptococcus
- Methanogens
- Clostridia paraputrefecium
- Candida albicans
- Candida glabrata
- Aspergillis niger

Harmful Parasites
In addition to harmful bacteria, fungi, and yeasts, there are more than 100 parasites that can enter the body and cause harm, including vitamin B-12, iron, vitamin A, and mineral deficiencies. The intestinal fluke has been linked to all cancers.
- Protozoa (amoeba, giardia)
- Roundworm
- Pinworm
- Hookworm
- Tapeworm
- Dog heartworm
- Whipworm
- Trichinella
- Anisakid worms
- Flukes
- Spirochetes
- Toxoplasmosis
- Trichomonas
- Entamoeba histolytica
- Cryptosporidium
- Strongyloides

DID YOU KNOW...

The stomach pathogen *Heliobacter pylori* may contribute to the development of stomach ulcers or cancer if it is present. This organism is present in 10% of adults under age 29 and 47% of those over age 60.

BENEFICIAL VS. HARMFUL BACTERIA AND FUNGI

BENEFICIAL BACTERIA	ACTIONS
Bifidobacteria **Lactobacilli** **Saccharomyces boulardii (fungus)**	• Inhibit the growth of harmful bacteria, yeast and external pathogens • Benefit immune function and help us to resist infection • Prevent DNA damage and mutations (*Lactobacilli*) • Possess anti-tumor properties ie. butyrate produced by *Bifidobacteria* • Prevent colon cancer (*Bifidobacteria*) • Break down environmental carcinogens • Bind toxic metals and carry them out in stools • Reduce liver toxicity • Reduce food intolerances/allergies; increase secretory immunoglobulin A • Reduce cholesterol and triglycerides • Break down hormones, including estrogen • Convert dietary flavonoids and phytoestrogens so the body can use them to protect us from cancer (*Clostridia p.*) • Stimulate metabolic rate and help with weight loss or gain • Conserve protein by recycling urea • Decrease gas and distension • Assist in the digestion and/or absorption of food and the minerals calcium, magnesium, iron, zinc and copper (*Bifidobacteria*, *Lactobacilli*, and *Bacteroides*) • Tighten the cell junctions of the intestinal lining to prevent leaky gut (*Bifidobacteria* and *Lactobacilli*) • Make nonessential amino acids • Assist in the synthesis of vitamin K, biotin, vitamin B12, folic acid, pantothenic acid, pyridoxine, thiamine, riboflavin, niacin, short chain fatty acids, digestive enzymes, and protein • Alleviate diarrhea
HARMFUL BACTERIA	ACTIONS
Pseudomonas aeruginosa **Yersinia enterocolitica** **Vibrionaceae** **Staphylococci** **Clostridium perfringens** **Clostridium difficile** **Sulphate reducers**	• Cause increased histamine production, resulting in allergic symptoms, asthma, hay fever, skin eruptions • Produce toxins that may be absorbed systemically to trigger inflammation anywhere or injure the intestine directly, causing irritable bowel syndrome, colitis or Crohn's disease • Toxins can contribute to arthritis, asthma, skin symptoms, arteriosclerosis, hypertension, liver disorders, autoimmune disease, lowered immunity, vaginal or urinary tract infections, brain or liver abscess, endocarditis, septicemia • Contribute to local or systemic infection

BENEFICIAL VS. HARMFUL BACTERIA AND FUNGI	
HARMFUL BACTERIA	**ACTIONS**
Proteus Salmonella Shigella Klebsiella Campylobacter Helicobacter pylori	• Cause diarrhea, constipation • Produce potential carcinogens (Bacteroides) • Produce toxic hydrogen sulfide • Cause intestinal putrefaction (produce ammonia, hydrogen sulfide, amines, phenols, indoles) • Accelerate the aging process

Dysbiosis

Dysbiosis refers to a chronic imbalance in our bowel flora. Dysbiosis is a primary cause of many of the health ailments that plague us today, just as the loss of the topsoil and desertification is a pressing global issue.

The composition of the intestinal flora can be disrupted by the use of antibiotics, the birth control pill, hormone replacement therapy, chemotherapy, radiation, as well as the consumption of chlorinated water and ingestion of dairy and meat obtained from animals that were fed antibiotics and/or hormones. Repeated antibiotic use and improper diet have done to the gut terrain what the overuse of pesticides and chemical fertilizers have done to our global soil.

Antibiotics

Antibiotics kill not only invading bacteria but also 90% to 99% of the healthy flora. Harmful organisms, such as *Staphylococci, enterococci, E. coli, Candida albicans,* and *Klebsiella,* may proliferate within the colon to fill the ecological vacuum created by antibiotic use.

White Blood Cell Inaction

Antibiotics turn off the action of our white blood cells against the offending bacteria, leaving toxins generated by bacteria destruction in the interstitial spaces. This toxic material may penetrate the cell membrane and cause damage to the mitochondria and cell nucleus, particularly if repeated antibiotics are used. This may explain the link between repeated antibiotic use and increased susceptibility to breast cancer.

DID YOU KNOW...

Individuals given antibiotics during the first 2 years of life will have increased allergies in their teenage years.

Candidiasis and Leaky Gut

An overgrowth of *Candida albicans* and other yeasts in the large intestine is a common outcome after antibiotic use because the protective *Lactobacilli* and *Bifidobacterium* population have been destroyed. When *Candida albicans* attaches to the epithelial cells of the intestinal lining, it produces elongated extensions called hyphae that penetrate the lining, creating tiny holes or a leaky gut. This generates an inflammatory response that may cause an assortment of symptoms seen in individuals with candidiasis — joint pain, muscle aches, low-grade fever, gas and bloating, food and environmental allergies and fatigue. Excessive intake of sugars, yeasted breads, refined carbohydrates, dairy, fermented foods, alcohol, foods containing fungus (such as cheese, peanuts, mushrooms, melon), and vinegar further promote candida overgrowth and increase symptoms.

Natural Medicine Alternatives

Instead of taking antibiotics, use garlic, grapefruit seed extract, olive leaf extract, echinacea, goldenseal, barberry, coptis, Oregon grape, usnea, *Uva ursi*, wild indigo, oil of oregano (short-term use only), or the Sanum homeopathic remedy Notakehl as an antibacterial. Simultaneously support the immune system with vitamin C, beta carotene, zinc, vitamin B-6, and astragalus.

If antibiotics must be used, a candida overgrowth can be prevented by taking a quality supplement containing *Lactobacilli* and *Bifidobacterium* at lunch time while antibiotic dosages are taken morning and evening. Continue the probiotic for 3 months. Also use grapefruit seed extract, garlic, caprylic acid, or olive leaf extract to deter candida.

Reversing Dysbiosis

Lactobacilli and Bifidobacteria

Beneficial *Lactobacilli* and *Bifidobacterium* bowel bacteria create short-chain fatty acids and enzymes that break food particles down and assist with our absorption of calcium, magnesium, and iron, just as soil fungus known as mycorrhizae feed minerals to the roots of plants. Supplementing our diet with these good bacteria helps to counteract dysbiosis and restore bowel flora balance.

Prebiotics (Inulin)

Prebiotics are soluble fiber food substances known to enhance the growth of specific beneficial gut microorganisms, such as *Bifidobacteria* and *Lactobacilli*, although our own digestive systems do not break them down. Prebiotics include long fruit sugar molecules known as fructo-oligosaccharides. These

INULIN CONTENT OF COMMON FOODS

PLANT SOURCE	INULIN CONTENT (GRAMS/100 GRAMS)	PLANT SOURCE	INULIN CONTENT (GRAMS/100 GRAMS)
Onion (one medium-sized)		**Globe artichoke** (leaf/heart)	4.4
Raw	4.3	**Banana**	0.5
Dried	18.3	**Wheat**	
Cooked	3.0	Bran	2.5
		Flour	2.4
Jerusalem artichoke (6 tubers)	18.0		
Chicory root	41.6	**Rye**	
		Cereal baked	0.7
Asparagus root/tuber			
Raw	2.5	**Barley**	
Boiled	1.7	Cereal raw	0.8
		Cooked	0.2
Leek (one large bulb)		**Dandelion greens**	
Raw	6.5	Raw	13.5
		Cooked	9.1
Garlic (6 large cloves)			
Raw	12.5		
Dried	28.2		

include galacto-oligosaccharides, found in breast milk; soy oligosaccharides, and inulin, a fructo-oligosaccharide found in asparagus, chicory, barley, garlic, and Jerusalem artichoke. Inulin consumption also results in a decrease in the production of beta-glucuronidase in the colon, which lowers circulating estrogen and helps to protect us from breast cancer.

Historically, daily intake of inulin is estimated to have been 25 to 32 grams, while today in Western Europe and North America, with diets deficient in soluble fiber, average consumption is 2 to12 grams per day. One way to restore a healthy balance of bowel flora is to eat inulin-rich foods, ideally eating 20 grams of inulin daily.

Probiotics

Probiotics are microorganisms taken orally or rectally to balance the intestinal flora when it is disturbed. Probiotics containing healthy bacteria may include some of the following species: *Lactobacillus acidophilus, Lactobacillus bifidus, Lactobacillus bulgarus, Lactobacillus lactis, Lactobacillus rhamnosus, Bifidobacterium bifidus, Bifidobacterium breve, Bifidobacterium longum,* and *Saccharomyces boulardi.* Since they do not permanently colonize the intestine, they should be taken regularly in sufficient quantities, and are best taken with meals.

DID YOU KNOW...

Prebiotics enhance the absorption of calcium from the colon in adults, helping to prevent osteoporosis.

DYSBIOSIS CONDITIONS

CONDITIONS	SYMPTOMS AND EFFECTS
UROGENITAL CONDITIONS	Chronic bladder infections, interstitial cystitis, chronic pelvic inflammation, endometriosis, chronic vaginal infections, chronic cervical dysplasia, infertility, repeated herpes outbreaks
INTESTINAL CONDITIONS	Gas and bloating, diarrhea and constipation, irritable bowel syndrome, colitis, Crohn's disease, diverticulitis, diaper rash in infants, abdominal pain, anal itching or rash, food intolerances/allergies, colon cancer
SKIN CONDITIONS	Acne, rosacea, psoriasis, eczema, vitiligo, fungal infections, nail fungus, boils, pruritus (itchy skin)
ORAL CONDITIONS	Repeated canker sores, gingivitis, thrush, periodontal disease, cold sores
NERVOUS SYSTEM CONDITIONS	Learning disabilities, hyperactivity, autism, poor concentration, poor memory, fuzzy thinking, tics, seizures
EAR, NOSE, AND THROAT CONDITIONS	Chronic ear infections, chronic sinusitis, chronic tonsillitis, post-nasal drip, hay fever and allergies, itchy ears or nose
LUNG CONDITIONS	Asthma, chronic bronchitis, emphysema
INTESTINAL CONDITIONS	Gas and bloating, diarrhea and constipation, irritable bowel syndrome, colitis, Crohn's disease, diverticulitis, diaper rash in infants, abdominal pain, anal itching or rash, food intolerances/allergies, colon cancer
MUSCULOSKELETAL CONDITIONS	Chronic fatigue syndrome, fibromyalgia, Lyme's disease, arthritis, myasthenia gravis
OTHER CONDITIONS	Any autoimmune disease, cardiovascular disease, diabetes, Reiter's syndrome, Sjögren's syndrome

REVERSING DYSBIOSIS WITH SHORT CHAIN FATTY ACIDS

SHORT CHAIN FATTY ACIDS	FUNCTIONS
ACETIC ACID (produced by *Bifidobacterium*)	Antimicrobial against yeast, mold and bacteria; provides energy for colon epithelial cells.
PROPRIONIC ACID	Provides energy for colon epithelial cells; helps to lower cholesterol.
LACTIC ACID	Inhibits growth of acid-sensitive bacteria; increases our tolerance to lactose (in milk).
BUTYRIC ACID	Provides 50% of the energy for colon epithelial cells; anti-cancer substance, controlling apoptosis (cell death), normalization of cancer cells, and cell turnover rate; strongly helps prevent colon cancer as well as breast cancer.

Gut Mucosal Barrier

The epithelial cells that line the intestine are paradoxically both the barrier that separates what is contained inside the intestinal tract from the rest of the body and the main gate for nutrient absorption into the blood.

When this mucous membrane is thinned and the intestinal villi are atrophied, the bacterial flora that reside in the mucous layer become deficient. The primary cause of an atrophied intestinal mucous membrane is ingestion of allergenic proteins, primarily dairy, meat, and eggs, and increased acidity. Wheat, gluten grains, corn, citrus, peanuts, sugar, tomatoes, and individualized food sensitivities may also disturb the mucous membrane.

Nutrients and Herbs for Gut Mucosal Repair

Specific nutrients and herbs can be used to help repair the gut mucosal barrier. Several supplement companies offer formulas for this purpose. A combination of an alkaline powder, L-glutamine, vitamin A, zinc, aloe, and slippery elm, taken for 3 months, can also help to heal the intestinal lining.

DID YOU KNOW...

If a woman is unable to breastfeed her child, then a concentration of 0.8 grams of oligosaccharides per 100 mL of formula can be used to stimulate the population of *Bifidobacterium* so that it approximates that of breastfed infants. Soy formula is much less allergenic to infants than cowbased formulas.

NUTRIENTS AND HERBS FOR GUT MUCOSAL REPAIR	
NUTRIENT	**FUNCTION**
ALKALINIZING POWDER ½ tsp 2x daily in warm water away from meals	Restores normal alkaline pH of the small intestine, which helps normalize the mucous membrane and villi, allows a healthy bacterial layer to develop and discourages candida, harmful bacteria, and parasites.
L-GLUTAMINE 5 g daily	Prevents mucosal damage and atrophy, decreases gut permeability in upper GI tract, repairs gut mucosal cells, decreases risk of infection.
ARGININE 5 g daily	Improves immunity, normalizes intestinal permeability, improves intestinal recovery after radiation treatment, helpful with ulcerative colitis, inhibits tumor growth, decreases infection risk.
GLUTARATE 500 mg daily	Supplies energy to cells of the lower GI tract, decreases gut permeability.
VITAMIN A 20,000–50,000 IU	Helps to restore mucous membrane and villi, alleviate diarrhea, decreases gut permeability.
ZINC 30–50 mg daily	Helps to restore mucous membrane and villi, alleviate diarrhea, decreases gut permeability.
FOLIC ACID 3–10 mg daily	Regenerates new cells in the small and large intestine.

NUTRIENTS AND HERBS FOR GUT MUCOSAL REPAIR

NUTRIENT	FUNCTION
FLAXSEED OIL OR FISH OIL 2000–4000 mg daily	Decreases inflammation.
BROMELAIN 200–600 mg daily	Decreases inflammation.
CURCUMIN 500–1500 mg daily	Decreases inflammation.
QUERCETIN 500–1500 mg daily	Decreases inflammation.
N-ACETYL GLUCOSAMINE (NAG) 500–1000 mg daily	Establishes normal intestinal mucous production.
DEGLYCYRRIZED LICORICE (DGL) 500 mg daily	Establishes normal intestinal mucous production, soothes and coats the intestinal lining.
ALOE LEAF CONCENTRATE 150–450 mg daily	Decreases inflammation, promotes tissue repair.
SPOTTED CRANESBILL 150–450 mg daily	Astringent, decreases inflammation, stops bleeding.
CABBAGE 150–300 mg daily	Heals ulcerated tissue due to high glutamine content.
GOLDENSEAL 100–300 mg daily	Astringent, has antibiotic properties, heals mucous membranes.
SLIPPERY ELM 150–450 mg daily	Decreases inflammation, heals intestinal lining.
MARSHMALLOW ROOT 150–450 mg daily	Decreases inflammation, soothes intestinal lining.
UVA URSI 150–450 mg daily	Decreases inflammation, soothes intestinal lining; eliminates harmful bacteria.
FICUS CARICA (GEMMOTHERAPY) 50 drops 3x daily	Helps restore an atrophied intestinal mucous membrane lining.

Eliminating Unhealthy Organisms

Most of us, at one time or another, have harmful bacteria, fungi, viruses or parasites as cohabitants of our intestines (or elsewhere in the body). These organisms need to be eliminated while we simultaneously restore and nourish beneficial intestinal flora, detoxify the colon, adopt a healthy diet, normalize pH, decrease stress, eliminate heavy metals and toxins, and heal the gut lining. The following chart is a quick guide to combating infectious organisms with natural therapies. Some natural medicine suppliers blend formulas for this purpose. If you use a formula, be sure that it contains most of the following substances: goldenseal, garlic, grapefruit seed extract, wormwood, cloves, black walnut, thyme oil, and oregano oil.

DID YOU KNOW...

An increasing number of bacterial species resistant to drugs has resulted in uncontrolled epidemics in institutional settings and pose a frightening public health risk as we run out of antibiotic alternatives.

ELIMINATING UNHEALTHY ORGANISMS

ORGANISM	FOODS	SUPPLEMENTS	HOMEOPATHIC REMEDIES
CANDIDA ALBICANS Other yeast and fungi	Eat: garlic, pau d'arco tea Avoid: all sugars, alcohol, yeast in baked goods, dairy, vinegar, pistachios, peanuts, mushrooms, high glycemic carbohydrate, fermented foods, limit fruit to one daily between meals or avoid fruit	Allicin (from garlic), undecyclenic acid, berberine (from goldenseal, coptis, barberry, bloodroot), burdock, caprylic acid, grapefruit seed extract, phellodendron, Artemesia capillaris Essential oils of: cinnamon bark, tea tree, oregano, thuja, thyme, sage, palmarosa, myrrh	Candida albicans 8x to 500x or a single remedy based on symptoms. Sanum remedies: Fortakehl Pefrakehl Exmykehl Albicansan Pleo San Cand D5 Nigersan, Mucokehl Sankombi Complex remedies: Unda #3 Dr. Reckeweg BIO 82
BACTERIA	Eat: garlic, ginger, cranberry juice, lemon	Allicin (from garlic) berberine (from goldenseal, coptis, barberry), sanguinarine (from bloodroot), grapefruit seed extract, coptis, phellodendron, pulsatilla Gemmotherapy: Ficus carica Juglans regia Essential oils of: cinnamon bark, tea tree, oregano, pine, lemon, juniper, thyme, lavender, myrrh	Sanum remedy: Notakehl Polysan formulas (Spenglersans) Dr. Reckeweg BIO 87

ELIMINATING UNHEALTHY ORGANISMS

ORGANISM	FOODS	SUPPLEMENTS	HOMEOPATHIC REMEDIES
PROTOZOA (amoeba, giardia)	Drink: cranberry juice	Allicin (garlic), berberine (goldenseal, coptis, barberry), grapefruit seed extract, phellodendron, pulsatilla, Artemesia capillaris Essential oils of: cinnamon bark, tea tree, oregano, thyme	Amoeba — Meeba Liquid Giardia — Guardi Aqua Liquid (both from Kroeger Herb Products)
FLUKES (in liver, blood, lung, or lymph)		Goldenrod, goldenseal, cloves, black walnut, milkweed	Single remedy: Chelidonium Triema Liva Liquid Triema Blud Liquid Triema Loongae Liquid (lung) Triema Lymf Liquid
ROUNDWORM, HEARTWORM, HOOKWORM, STRONGYLOIDES, WHIPWORM, PINWORM, TRICHINELLA, TAPEWORM, CRYPTOSPORIDIUM	Eat: ground pumpkin seeds, garlic, horseradish, pomegranate juice (4 glasses daily), papaya seeds, onions, carrot tops, radishes, kelp, raw cabbage, apple cider vinegar, ground almonds, calmyrna figs, cranberry juice, and sauerkraut	Black walnut, cloves, wormwood allicin (garlic), male fern, betel nut, rue, tansy Gemmotherapy: Juglans regia Essential oils of: cinnamon, thyme, tea tree, wormseed, boldo, hyssop, clove, anise, fennel	Single remedies: Cina 4CH, 3 pellets, 3 times daily) Calc carb, Chelidonium Nat mur Nat phos Sabadilla Silicea Spigelia Sulphur Terebinthum Complex remedies: Unda 17 and 39 Dr. Reckeweg R56
VIRUSES	Eat: shiitake mushrooms	Echinacea, garlic, goldenseal, coptis, lomatium, St. John's wort, phyllanthus, marigold, coenzyme Q10 Gemmotherapies: Acer campestre Platanus Essential oils of: cinnamon, basil, camphor, melissa, myrrh, oregano, palmarosa, sage, tea tree, thyme, thuja	Sanum remedy: Quentakehl Complex remedy: Dr. Reckeweg BIO 88

Changing Our Earth Attitudes

The current degradation of our soil, water, and air reflects the prevailing belief that humans have the right to dominate and subjugate the natural world. Our attitudes need to change from ownership of the Earth to stewardship. The following chart compares our outdated attitudes toward the earth to emerging attitudes that will promote planetary, personal, and interspecies healing so we can live on the Earth in a sustainable way.

CHANGING OUR EARTH ATTITUDES

OWNERSHIP	STEWARDSHIP
• Man is meant to inherit the Earth and have dominion over it. • The welfare and survival of humans takes precedence over the welfare and survival of all other species. • Any individual or corporation can 'own' a piece of the Earth or its resources.	• The Earth has a finite supply of resources. • The Earth exists to support all of its changing, interdependent, evolving life forms. • No one 'owns' the Earth or its resources. We are privileged to care for the earth and use its resources.
EXPLOITATION	**SUSTAINABILITY**
• The Earth has an infinite supply of resources ready to be exploited. The Earth exists to support economic development. • Contaminating soil, water, and air with toxic metals and pesticides is acceptable while growing food and manufacturing goods for human consumption. • Using carbon-based energy, despite its contribution to global warming, and nuclear energy, despite its dangers, is acceptable. • Toxic waste sites that contaminate surrounding soil, water, and air are acceptable.	• The Earth has a finite supply of resources to be sustained. The Earth exists to nurture our health and well-being. • Using raw materials that are natural, non-toxic, recyclable, renewable, and biodegradable is preferable, as is eating food that is organically grown and not genetically modified. • Using renewable energy, including wind, solar, and geothermal power, to minimize global warming is responsible. • Sustainability involves reducing, re-using and recycling raw materials to avoid waste.
POPULATION GROWTH	**POPULATION CONTROL**
• Our world can accommodate an increase in population from its current 6 billion to a projected 10 billion within the next 50 years.	• Population growth must be curbed to decrease illness, suffering, death by starvation, and widespread depletion of natural resources.

Looking Ahead

Despite the impact of environmental toxins on our body ecology, there are remedies to detoxify, cleanse, rejuvenate, and restore balance to our bodies. In the next section, we present a season-by-season program for preventing illness.

Seasonal Cleansing and Rejuvenation Program

Traditional Chinese medicine stresses the need to cleanse the body and rejuvenate the spirit throughout the 'five' seasons of the year — fall, winter, spring, summer, and late summer (August 21 to September 20). In this healing tradition, the health of our organs is tied to the rhythm of the seasons and the five phases or elements of life — metal, water, wood, fire, and earth. In this section, we bring together the information from the previous sections, Living with Nature's Rhythms and Restoring Harmony with the Earth's Elements, to create a program you can follow season by season, year by year to establish good health and maintain well-being.

The program we present here for cleansing and rejuvenation follows the traditional Chinese medicine model but also includes modern diagnostic tests for women that fit into the seasonal theme. After a year, you will have achieved a full assessment and cleansing of your body's systems. Working together with your natural health-care practitioner and medical doctor, you can use this seasonal program as a guide to optimize your health year after year.

We recommended that you consult your health-care practitioner at least every 3 months to diagnose any imbalance at its beginning stage so that your whole body is kept finely tuned. This program gives you the opportunity to live in greater alignment with the rhythms of nature while caring for your own well-being.

Fall Program

September 23–December 20
Caring for Your Lungs, Large Intestine, Skin, and the Metal Element

On the fall equinox, occurring September 22 or 23, day and night are equal in length everywhere on the planet. The sun rises precisely in the east, arcs through the sky for 12 hours, and sets exactly in the west, disappearing for another 12 hours. This begins a 6-month period when yin and darkness expand, peaking at the winter solstice, and then contracting until they equalize once again at the spring equinox.

Fall is a time to relish the abundance of food at the end of the growing season; to reflect with gratitude on all we have been given in our lives; to seek balance and harmony in our inner and outer worlds; to release physical and emotional baggage; and to cleanse and prepare for a period of deep introspection. It is a time of letting go, particularly of old grief and attachments.

Organs

In our bodies, the organs associated with the fall period are the lungs and large intestine, which govern the skin. Fall is associated with the metal element, so this season is fitting for assessing toxic metal overload and mineral balance.

Lungs

Our lives begin with a cry that expands the lungs after we are born. Likewise, the circulation of chi or prana throughout the body begins with the lungs. When we inhale, oxygen diffuses across a single cell membrane lining the alveoli to the capillaries, the small blood vessels in the lungs. The oxygen combines with hemoglobin in the red blood cells and becomes their precious cargo, delivered via the bloodstream to every cell in our body. Each cell breathes by taking in oxygen and releasing carbon dioxide. When we exhale, the lungs release carbon dioxide, toxic gases, and the end products of cell metabolism back to the air.

DID YOU KNOW...

If waste products are not removed efficiently (we should have a bowel movement about 18 hours after each meal), they can build up along the lining of the large intestine, become reabsorbed as poisons, cause bacterial imbalance and dysbiosis, and prevent the absorption of minerals.

Large Intestine

After the small intestine has completed its digestion of food, the large intestine receives what remains, absorbing water and the minerals calcium, magnesium, iron, zinc, and copper with the help of the bowel bacteria.

Skin

Our skin shields us from microorganisms, helps us adapt to heat and cold through sweating or shivering, keeps water inside the body, and pushes waste to the outside. A precursor to vitamin D is carried to our skin through the blood. When it is exposed to ultraviolet light from the sun, it is converted to a substance that becomes vitamin D.

If we have a lung weakness with asthma, we may be more prone to eczema. Dysbiosis and toxicity in the large intestine may manifest as acne, boils, redness, psoriasis, or eczema. A deficiency of hydrochloric acid in the stomach may cause broken blood vessels and redness in the cheeks and nose. A pale face may indicate anemia or a deficiency in the lungs, while a red face can signify hypertension. Dry skin can alert us to a deficiency of essential fatty acids, found in flaxseed oil, fish oil, and evening primrose oil, or a hypothyroid condition.

DID YOU KNOW...

Our skin reflects what is going on inside of us, both physically and emotionally. When we are stressed or angry, we may be more susceptible to hives and eczema. Before our menstrual periods, we may experience acne.

SCREENING TESTS

☞ For Your Lungs, Large Intestine, and Skin

Work with your health-care practitioners to complete some of the following tests each fall. There is no need to do them all at once. Check off those that you complete each year. See the Resource Section at the back of the book for testing laboratories.

- ☐ Mineral testing: hair analysis, urine analysis, RBC minerals, zinc tally, iodine skin test
- ☐ Urinary indican for bowel toxicity
- ☐ Blood test for pesticides, PCBs, and brominated fire retardants
- ☐ Chest X-ray
- ☐ Occult blood in the stool
- ☐ Colonoscopy
- ☐ Eosinophils in blood (screens for parasites)
- ☐ Comprehensive digestive stool analysis with parasitology
- ☐ Comprehensive parasitology profile
- ☐ Candida albicans assay
- ☐ Urinary D-arabinitol (detects early invasive candidiasis)
- ☐ Skin resistance testing for yeast and parasites
- ☐ Red blood cell fatty acids
- ☐ Skin exam

Fall Program

Restoring Depleted Minerals
(September 21 ongoing)

To ensure your diet includes sufficient minerals, eat mineral rich foods daily from the following food groups. Aim for 8 servings of fruits and vegetables each day. Check them off as you add them to your weekly diet. See the Food as Medicine section for more information.

- Sea vegetables: dulse, nori, kelp, and kombu
- Nuts and seeds: Brazil nuts, pumpkin seeds, sunflower seeds, sesame seeds, almonds, pecans, walnuts, tahini, almond butter
- Grains: oatmeal, wheat germ, amaranth, wild rice, brown rice, pearl barley, millet
- Sprouts: mung bean, red clover, broccoli, sunflower seed
- Vegetables: Swiss chard, kale, parsley, spinach, broccoli, avocado, fresh vegetable juices
- Fruits: bananas, figs, apples, kiwi
- Beans and legumes: aduki beans, mung beans, black-eyed peas, lentils, tofu
- Greens: powdered organic green supplements, such as Greens+, barley green, spirulina, wheat grass, chlorella, or Pure Synergy

Eliminating Toxic Metals
(September 21–December 21)

After analyzing your hair and urine for toxic metals, choose from this list of herbal, homeopathic, and nutritional therapies to help with their elimination. A detoxification regimen releases metals from where they have been stored in the body, so there may be an initial increase of metals in hair, urine, or stool before levels decline. Sixty percent of individuals are clear in about 9 months, although many individuals may require a metal detoxification regimen for 2 years, as metals (particularly lead) are released sequentially from deeper tissue levels.

For best results, combine these therapies with the bowel cleanse, sauna detoxification, and clay bath programs that follow in this chapter.

Herbal Remedies
Ideally, the following herbs should be taken as a blended tea or in tincture form: juniper, bladderwrack, nettle, astragalus, red clover, burdock root, milk thistle, dandelion, barberry, marshmallow root.

Mineral Supplements
Take a good multi-mineral supplement that includes calcium, magnesium, zinc, selenium, copper, iron, chromium, and manganese to help displace toxic metals from their binding sites, as well as prevent their absorption. Magnesium needs to be

---

HOMEOPATHIC DRAINAGE FORMULAS

Choose one of the following three options:

1. Heel detox kit containing: Lyphosol (detoxifies lymph), Nux vomica-Hommacord (detoxifies liver), Berberis-Homaccord (detoxifies kidney). Use 10 drops of each formula, 3x daily, by putting 30 drops of each preparation in 1.5 liters or quarts of spring water and drink throughout the day. Continue for at least 6 weeks.

2. Pekana remedies including: apo-Hepat spag. drops (detoxifies liver), Renelix spag. drops (detoxifies kidney), Itires spag. drops (stimulates lymphatic system), Toxex spag. drops (stimulates excretion of metals), Dalektro N drops (homeopathic minerals that stimulate enzymes). Use 15-20 drops of each formula, 3x daily, by putting 45 drops of each in 1.5 liters or quarts of spring water and drink throughout the day. Continue for at least 6 weeks. Do not use with metal spoons or cups.

3. Unda remedies: Unda 2 (drains kidneys), Unda 20 (drains liver), Unda 48 (drains cellular toxins), Chelidonium plex (drains lymph, liver, kidney and gallbladder). For Unda 2, 20, and 48, use 5-10 drops of each directly on the tongue simultaneously, 3x daily. For Chelidonium plex, use 15 drops, 3x daily directly on the tongue or in a little water. Continue all four remedies for a minimum of 6 weeks.

---

supplied in generous amounts (600 mg). Minerals should be taken at least 3 hours away from chelating agents. Do not use copper and iron if you have cancer.

Alkalinizing Powder
Use a blend of 40% potassium bicarbonate, 26% calcium carbonate, 14% magnesium carbonate, and 20% sodium bicarbonate in $\frac{1}{2}$ tsp warm water twice daily, away from meals, to help prevent absorption of toxic metals.

Probiotics
Lactobacillus and *Bifidobacterium* are bowel flora that help to escort toxic metals out through the bowel. Take with meals twice daily.

Special Foods
Kelp tablets, chlorella tablets, cilantro, charcoal tablets, garlic, miso, wheatgrass, parsley, and soy protein or whey protein (goat source may be preferable to cow) are agents for supporting effective detoxification.

Dental Care
Remove and replace silver/mercury amalgam dental fillings. If you have any root canals, ask your health-care practitioner how they may be affecting your health. Have a cavatat ultrasound done if possible and affordable. Otherwise, ask your dentist to do a panoramic X-ray, looking for areas of infection.

HEALTHY RECIPE

Fiber Drink

This drink will not only cleanse the bowel but also reduce constipation. Activated charcoal tablets can also be taken along with the fiber drink to remove toxins.

3 oz	apple juice, preferably organic (contains apple pectin)
10 oz	room temperature or lukewarm filtered or spring water (chlorine-free)
1 tbsp	freshly ground flaxseeds (fiber source, bowel lubricant)
½ tsp	slippery elm powder (soothes intestinal lining, anti-cancer)
2 tsp	psyllium seed powder (fiber bulking agent)
1 tsp	wheat bran, if tolerated (fiber that removes methylmercury)
1 tsp	chicory root extract powder (contains inulin, a prebiotic)
1 tbsp	liquid bentonite clay (attracts heavy metals, absorbs toxins)
½ tsp	probiotic formula containing *Lactobacilli acidophilus* and *Bifidobacterium longum*
½ tsp	cinnamon (discourages unhealthy bowel flora, normalizes blood sugar and insulin)

DIRECTIONS

Shake this well in a glass mason jar and drink immediately, chewing each mouthful several times before swallowing. Follow with 2 glasses of water.

SERVING

Drink this 4 times daily (for example, at 7:00 a.m., 11:00 a.m., 3:00 p.m., 8:00 p.m.) for 1 week.

Bowel Cleansing Diet
(September 21–28)

This regimen will remove most, if not all offending food allergens, allow the colon to heal, facilitate the excretion of metals and old fecal matter, and prepare the colon for the yeast and parasite cleanse and sauna therapy. Fiber drinks, alkaline soup, vegetable juice, green products, and water will be your only food for the week.

Fresh Vegetable Juice

Vegetable juices supply us with a rich source of vitamins, minerals, and phytonutrients to help with cleansing and rejuvenation. Juice 5 pounds of organic carrots, 4 stalks organic celery, 3 small beets, and a few leaves of either kale or Swiss chard, along with 2 apples, a thumb size piece of fresh ginger root, and 2 cloves of garlic. Drink 4 glasses of this throughout each day.

Filtered Water

Drink 2.5 to 3 liters or gallons of filtered water daily. Fill a
2-gallon glass jug with chlorine-free water and drink it, plus a
little more, throughout the day.

HEALTHY RECIPE

Metal Clearing Alkaline Broth Soup

2	sweet potatoes (high in beta carotene, alkaline)
2	onions (liver support, antibacterial)
4	carrots (high in potassium and beta carotene, alkaline)
3	celery stalks (alkaline, high in sodium)
1	bunch parsley (kidney cleanser)
6	stalks asparagus (kidney cleanser)
2 cups	organic spinach (rich in minerals)
2 cups	cilantro (pulls out heavy metals)
3	cloves garlic (liver support, antibacterial)
2 gallons	filtered water
2 tbsp	turmeric (liver support, anti-inflammatory)
1 tbsp	dulse powder (rich in minerals, alkaline, restores thyroid)
1 tsp	cayenne (increases circulation)
	Brown rice miso (or freshly ground flaxseeds if intolerant)

DIRECTIONS

Chop vegetables. Fill large soup pot with water and add chopped vegetables. Add
turmeric powder, dulse powder, and cayenne. Bring to a boil. Simmer for 2 hours. Pour
through a strainer into another pot. Compost the vegetables and keep the broth, or
blend the vegetables separately and freeze them to add to another soup at a later date.
Mix 2 tsp miso in a cup with 2 tbsp of the soup broth and stir until it dissolves — then
add this amount to each bowl of soup before serving. The miso should not be boiled.
If you do not tolerate miso or if you have a problem with candidiasis, substitute freshly
ground flaxseeds for the miso. The soup broth will keep for 4 days; freeze any extra in
half full glass jars.

SERVING

Drink 2–3 cups of warm broth three times daily, at 8:00 a.m., noon, and 5:00 p.m. for 1 week.
Continue to have this soup several times a week, with the vegetables included, for
another month to help with metal detoxification.

CHLORELLA TABLETS OR GREEN POWDER

Chlorella is a microscopic freshwater algae that has survived on Earth for more than 2.5 billion years. It contains 60% protein, all of the essential amino acids, various vitamins (including B-12), and minerals. Chlorella boasts the highest amount of chlorophyll known in any plant. It cleanses the intestines, neutralizes acids, reduces harmful bacteria in the bowel pockets, and clears mucus. If chlorella is not available or too costly, choose instead Greens+, Pure Synergy, spirulina, or barley green.

Dose: Use 3–10 chlorella tablets or 1–3 tsp of a green powdered supplement mixed in water three times daily at 10:00 a.m., 4:00 p.m., and 6:00 p.m. If you have not used green supplements in the past, start with the lower amount.

Bowel Cleansing Enemas
(September 21–28)
During this week of bowel cleansing, use 2–3 enemas daily — a coffee enema in the morning and a bentonite enema in the afternoon or evening.

Bentonite Enemas
Bentonite is a form of volcanic ash that has a negative charge that can attract, absorb, and carry away 200 hundred times its own weight in toxins. Bentonite enemas remove mucus and fecal matter attached to the colon wall. Use 2 tbsp of bentonite per quart or liter of water.

Coffee Enemas
In addition to cleansing the bowel, a coffee enema helps to detoxify the liver. The caffeine acts as an herbal stimulant that speeds up the emptying time of the bowel, removes toxins accumulated in the bile ducts of the liver, and causes an increased flow of bile. A toxic liver will dump many of its toxins into the bile and eliminate them in a few minutes.

Coffee Enema Preparation
1. Add 2–3 tbsp of organic, freshly ground, lightly roasted coffee beans to 5 cups of distilled or filtered water. There must be no chlorine in your water. If you are sensitive to coffee, use the lesser amount. Store ground coffee beans in the freezer to prevent rancidity if you are not using them all right away.
2. Make the coffee fresh for each enema. Use an enamel, glass, or stainless steel pot.
3. Let it boil for 3 minutes, then simmer for 20 minutes. Strain and allow it to cool to the body's temperature (98.6°F), or until it feels comfortable to the touch.
4. Do not use a coffee enema if you have gallstones. If you become dizzy, nauseous, or light-headed, stop the enema process.

DIRECTIONS FOR GIVING YOURSELF AN ENEMA

1. Pour the enema liquid (about 4 cups) into an enema bag connected to plastic or rubber tubing. Clamp the tube as you pour in the liquid. Hang the enema bag $1\frac{1}{2}$ to 2 feet above the body. Change the height as needed to control the speed of intake into the colon. Place a large towel or mat on the floor of the washroom or in a room close by.

2. A fountain syringe is the best enema applicator. Lubricate the nozzle with sesame, almond, flaxseed, or olive oil.

3. Lie on the mat or towel on your right side, with both legs drawn into the abdomen. Alternatively, you can start the enema in a knee-to-chest position with your chest on the floor and your buttocks in the air. This position allows the force of gravity to aid the flow of water into the colon. You can also lie on your back with a pillow beneath your buttocks.

4. Breathe deeply while you begin the enema. Slowly insert the nozzle several inches into the rectum using a rotating motion. If the tube is inserted too rapidly or forcefully it can cause kinking inside of the colon, which may cause discomfort. Release the clamp and let the mixture flow in slowly.

5. If the solution comes into the colon too fast, lower the enema bag; if it comes in too slowly, raise the bag a little higher. If you experience cramping, then the solution is coming in too quickly. Stop the flow by pinching the enema tube and then lowering the bag. Wait until the cramps have stopped before allowing the solution to flow again. It may take several minutes for the enema solution to enter the body. If it does not seem to flow freely, the enema tube may be twisted or kinked. Slowly pull it part of the way out and then insert it again until it has gone in several inches.

6. When all the enema solution has emptied from the enema bag, lift the tube into the air to allow gravity to push all the solution through the end of the tube. Then remove the applicator from the rectum. (If you don't lift the tube, you'll end up with some solution on the floor.)

7. Retain the fluid for 10 to 12 minutes. If you cannot hold all the fluid in the colon with one enema, repeat it two or more times in sequence, emptying the bowel in between.

8. While retaining the fluid, massage your abdomen with your fingers. Begin with a circular motion on the lower left side of the abdomen, moving straight upwards toward the ribs, then across the abdomen just beneath the ribs from left to right, and then down the right side of the abdomen. If there are tender spots, massage until the tenderness is gone.

9. While the solution is in the colon, change positions every few minutes: 3 minutes right side, 3 minutes stomach, 3 minutes on your back, 3 minutes left side. This helps the enema solution reach all parts of the colon.

10. When the bile duct empties, you will hear or feel squirting beneath the right rib cage. This is a sign that you have succeeded in releasing toxins from the liver.

11. Sterilize the enema syringe after each use by boiling it or thoroughly cleansing it with soap and water and soaking it for 5 minutes in a solution of 2 cups water and 4 drops of tea tree oil or grapefruit seed extract.

Cleansing Yeast and Parasites
(October 1–December 15)

After you have done the bowel cleanse for a week, begin a yeast and parasite cleanse and continue for 10 weeks. Our intestines commonly house excessive amounts of yeast (candida), other fungi, harmful bacteria, and/or parasites, although these organisms can reside virtually anywhere in the body.

- Continue the fiber drink from week one, taking it twice daily.
- Take 2 capsules of oil of oregano twice daily.
- Add an antifungal, antiparasitic formula that contains black walnut, wormwood, cloves, grapefruit seed extract, and goldenseal. Use this twice daily and continue for 10 weeks. Since parasite eggs commonly hatch around the full moon, continue for two full moons.
- Eat 2 cloves of raw garlic daily for 10 weeks. Use garlic capsules if this is not possible.
- Eat $1/2$ cup raw or soaked pumpkin seeds daily.
- Drink 1 glass of diluted unsweetened cranberry juice daily.
- Drink 2 cups of taheebo (pau d'arco) tea daily.
- Use cinnamon and ginger, adding them to foods or using in tea form.
- Avoid all sugars, alcohol, yeast in baked goods, dairy, vinegar, pistachios, peanuts, mushrooms, high glycemic carbohydrates, and fermented foods. Limit fruit to one daily between meals or avoid fruit.
- Eat raw and steamed vegetables, legumes, cooked whole grains, vegetable and grain soups, bean and rice combinations, tofu, other nuts and seeds (excluding peanuts and pistachios).

Skin Brushing and Hot/Cold Showers
(September–December Ongoing)

Skin brushing maximizes your cleansing by stimulating the lymphatic system to expel toxins through the skin. Make this a daily lifestyle practice.

Instructions:

1. Do this in the morning when you rise and before you go to bed at night.
2. Use a long handled, natural bristle brush, with a brush pad about the size of your hand, or a loofah mitt.
3. Start with the soles of your feet. Brush in a circular motion as you move up your body, feet to legs, hands to arms, back to abdomen, and chest to neck.
4. Follow the morning dry brush massage with an alternating hot-cold shower (hot for 3 minutes, cold for 30 seconds), repeating the hot-cold pattern three times, or just have a cold shower.

Sauna Detoxification

(September 29 Ongoing)

Although all saunas are beneficial, far infrared are the most effective kind because their rays penetrate 4–5 cm beneath the skin and cause proteins, collagen, fats, and water molecules to vibrate slightly, which speeds up the metabolic exchanges between cells and elevates temperature. Toxins are more easily released when chemical bonds are broken. The body reacts to infrared rays by dilating blood vessels and circulation is improved significantly. With better circulation, oxygen is carried more efficiently to the mitochondria for energy production, and carbon dioxide and cellular toxins are carried away more quickly, relieving our bodies of their chemical burden.

DIRECTIONS FOR A SAUNA DETOXIFICATION PROGRAM

Duration

Designate 80–100 hours for sauna detoxification in the shortest time period you can comfortably manage. After you complete your detox program, continue using the sauna an hour a week or more as maintenance.

Sauna Selection

Choose a sauna with a vent or window to allow old air out and new air in; avoid the use of plywood, glues, and finishes; choose poplar over cedar to avoid sensitivities to the fumes (terpenes) from cedar; install a full spectrum light bulb in your sauna.

Caution

If you are taking any kind of medication, the sauna may cause it to be metabolized more quickly, so your dosage may need to be adjusted over time. Ask your doctor to check liver enzymes and kidney function before beginning sauna therapy, and request a complete physical exam.

Also consult with your health-care provider before going into the sauna if you have lymphedema; heart, kidney or liver disease; a seizure disorder; anemia; you are pregnant or breastfeeding; or you are recovering from surgery.

Before the Sauna

1. *Supplements:* Over time, you will sweat out vitamins and minerals during the sauna program. These need to be stocked before and replenished after the program.
2. *Oils:* The following oils should be taken daily before and during the sauna cleanse. If your sweat becomes oily during the sauna, reduce your oil intake.
   - Evening primrose oil, 1000 mg
   - Flaxseed oil, 2 tbsp
   - Uncontaminated fish oil, 3000 mg
   - Extra-virgin olive oil, 1 tbsp
   - Lecithin, 2 tsp

3. *Water:* Aim to drink 1–2 liters (4–8 cups) of water before your sauna.

4. *Meals:* Wait 1 hour after eating before going into the sauna or 2 hours after a large meal. Avoid alcohol and drugs during sauna detoxification

5. *Exercise:* To stimulate the circulation of blood and lymph, use aerobic exercise for 20–30 minutes in the form of rebounding, running, or using a treadmill.

6. *Dry skin brush:* After the aerobic exercise, use a dry skin brush on the legs, arms, and trunk, starting at the feet using small circular movements and moving up the body toward the heart.

7. *Record-keeping:* Record blood pressure, pulse rate, temperature, number of breaths per minute, and your weight before entering the sauna.

8. *Fluids:* Take into the sauna 1 liter or quart of water containing any one of the following three homeopathic drainage protocols or a herbal tea with alkaline salts.

Homeopathic Protocols

- 15 drops each of Lyphosot (detoxifies lymph), Nux vomica-Hommacord (detoxifies liver), Berberis-Homaccord (detoxifies kidney) from Heel; or

- 15 drops each of apo-Hepat spag. drops (detoxifies liver), Renelix spag. drops (detoxifies kidney), Itires spag. drops (stimulates lymphatic system), Toxex spag. drops (stimulates excretion of metals), Dalektro N drops (homeopathic minerals that stimulate enzymes) from Pekana, ordered through Biomed; or

- 5 drops each of Unda 2 (assists kidneys in removing toxins from the circulatory system), Unda 15 (speeds up the breakdown of toxins, stimulates immunity), Unda 7 (assists in the breakdown and elimination of toxins through the kidney), Unda 48 (drains cellular toxins). Add 8 drops of Chelidonium plex (drains lymph, liver, kidney, and gallbladder) ordered through Seroyal. Use this protocol for your first 5 weeks of sauna detox. From week 6 to 11, use Unda 2, Unda 15, Unda 48, Unda 12 (helps to eliminate toxins through the skin), and Chelidonium plex. From week 12 to 17, use Unda 2, Unda 14 (increases enzyme activity, unblocks chronic disease states), Unda 48, and Unda 233 (improves venous and lymphatic circulation).

During the Sauna

1. *Start:* Soon after the aerobic exercise and dry brush, start your sauna, accompanied by a partner.

2. *Temperature:* Maintain the temperature in an infrared sauna between 48.8°C (100°F) and 54.4°C (130°F); in an electric sauna from 54.4°C (130°F) to 75°C (160°F).

3. *Duration:* Start with 10–20 minutes initially to see how your body adjusts to it.

4. *Sweating:* Place one clean dry towel over the seat of the sauna to absorb perspiration and toxins, one behind you or over your shoulders, and another on the floor under your feet. Wipe off your sweat with a small hand towel, so that new perspiration comes more quickly to the skin. Wipe in movements directed toward your heart (rather than away), starting with your feet and moving up the body, to stimulate lymph flow. You might use several hand towels in sequence. Before leaving the sauna, wipe all the sweat off so that it is not reabsorbed when you enter cooler air. Use a fourth towel to wipe off after your shower. Use fresh towels each time you have a sauna.

5. *Breathing:* Practice slow, long deep breathing while in the sauna to assist liver detoxification and improve lymphatic circulation.

6. *Fainting and Sleeping:* Because some people experience unpleasant symptoms as chemical toxins are released, your partner is there to help you in the event that you faint or fall asleep. If you feel too warm, leave the sauna and have a cool shower before returning. Salt or potassium deficiency could occur if you fall asleep. Symptoms include extreme tiredness or weakness, headache, muscle cramps, clammy skin, nausea, dizziness, vomiting, and fainting. Should any of these symptoms occur, take sea salt in water, potassium gluconate tablets, or alkalinizing powder. Miso soup with a banana may also be on hand.

7. *Heart Rate and Respiration:* Check your pulse rate every 15 minutes while in the sauna to ensure that it is not irregular or too fast or slow. A normal pulse is 60-80 beats per minute. If your blood pressure, pulse rate, or number of breaths per minute increase by 10 or more, you've had enough. Drink more water and take extra minerals. When you return another day, start at a lower temperature for a shorter duration. If you weigh less after a sauna, drink enough water to make up for the loss. If your oral temperature rises over 100°F (38°C), stop your sauna. Stop your sauna if you experience nausea, headache, weakness, irregular or fast heart rate, shortness of breath, dizziness, confusion, muscle spasms, or cramps. Cool down with slightly warm water, followed by cooler water.

8. *Heat Stroke:* If suddenly your body stops sweating and your skin becomes hot and dry, this may be a sign of heat stroke. Cool off with a lukewarm or cool shower and take a glass of water with 1 tsp alkaline powder plus 1/2 tsp sea salt. Take another 200 mg of magnesium citrate as well as 200 mg calcium citrate. Drink the herbal tea, which is rich in minerals, to replace what is lost through sweating while in the sauna. Muscle cramps or irregular heart rhythm are a sign of magnesium deficiency.

9. *Sittings:* Aim for 1–6 sittings of 15-20 minutes each, for 5 consecutive days, then off for 2, though each person may be different in terms of the length of time they are able to spend in the sauna. Take cool showers between sauna sittings to activate your circulation. Some of you may be able to do three sessions, each 1 hour long, every day for 3 weeks (or two sessions of 1 1/2 hours each).

After the Sauna

1. *Clean up:* Clean the sauna by spraying 3% hydrogen peroxide onto the wood and wiping with a clean cloth after each visit.

2. *Extra Supplements:* In addition to the supplements listed in the Vitamin and Mineral Supplement Schedule, take curcumin (1000 mg) and Indole-3-carbinol or DIM (300 mg) to assist the liver in detoxifying chemicals, as well as NAC (500 mg), coenzyme Q10 (100 mg), and alpha lipoic acid (300 mg) to assist the liver and protect the mitochondria from toxic overload.

3. *Homeopathic Remedies:* Take two more doses of one of the three sets of remedies listed in the preparation instructions in a little water later in the day.

4. *Rest:* Ensure you have sufficient rest while on the program, 8 hours of sleep daily. The program works best when done at the same time daily.

HERBAL TEA

During your sauna, drink 2 cups of herbal tea containing an equal mixture of burdock, cleavers, milk thistle, dandelion, red clover, yarrow, peppermint, and Chinese licorice. If you do not sweat easily, add lemon juice and a pinch of cayenne to this tea. Add 1 tsp alkaline powder, mixed in a little water or in the tea.

VITAMIN AND MINERAL SUPPLEMENT SCHEDULE

NUTRIENT	BEGINNING THERAPY	ENDING THERAPY
Niacin	50-100 mg	2000-4000 mg
Vitamin A	5,000-10,000 IU	50,000 IU
Vitamin D	400 IU	2,000 IU
Vitamin C	1,000 mg	6,000 mg
Vitamin E	800 IU	2,400 IU
Vitamin B complex	100 mg	300 mg
Calcium	500-1,000 mg	2,500-3,000 mg
Magnesium	250-500 mg	1250-1500 mg
Iron	18-36 mg	90-108 mg
Zinc	50 mg	75-90 mg
Manganese	4–8 mg	20-24 mg
Copper	2–4 mg	10-12 mg
Potassium	45-90 mg	225-270 mg
Iodine	400 mcg	1200 mcg
Selenium	200 mcg	400 mcg
Chromium	200 mcg	600 mcg
Vanadium	200 mcg	400 mcg
Boron	3 mg	6 mg
Molybdenum	400 mcg	800 mcg
Silicon	15 mcg	40 mcg

Clay Baths
(October–December Weekly)

Use bentonite clay baths once weekly to eliminate chemical and metal toxins through the skin. Heavy metals such as mercury, arsenic, aluminum, cadmium, lead, and chemicals including those from cigarette smoking, can be decreased substantially in 5–10 weeks. A good source for the clay is www.magneticclay.com.

NIACIN SUPPLEMENTATION DURING SAUNA THERAPY

Niacin increases peripheral circulation and mobilizes chemicals from fatty tissue. Initially, a dose of 50–100 mg of niacin is recommended daily until you have a flushing reaction within several hours. When this flushing reaction is no longer evident at this dosage, it should be increased incrementally in 100 mg units to between 2000 and 4000 mg daily. At 1000 mg, most patients increase the niacin in 500 mg increments rather than 100 mg units. Any dose above 2000 mg must be monitored with liver function tests. Sauna therapy is complete (that is, you have dumped most of your chemical toxins) when there is no more flushing after 2,000 – 4,000 mg of niacin.

Enhancing Immunity
(October ongoing)

Homeopathic Flu Prevention Program
Fall is the time to begin a homeopathic flu prevention program that you can continue until May so that you are protected from viral respiratory conditions through the winter. This is a safe and effective alternative to the traditional flu shot, which may contain toxic mercury and aluminum.

1. Take 3 pellets of Influenzinum 9CH on the first and third Saturday of the month (or pick another day) beginning in October. This must be purchased each year because it is a homeopathic remedy made from the previous year's flu strains.
2. Take 3 pellets of Thymuline 9CH on the second and fourth Saturday.
3. Take Influenzinum 9CH on the 1st of every month and Thymuline 9CH on the 15th of every month from November until May.
4. If you experience flu symptoms despite having taken these remedies, use either Occilococcinum 200K or Dolicoccil 1000 right away. Take 3 pellets or a single dose tube mornings and evenings for 2 days.

Breathing Exercises
Along with the immune formula, practice a breathing exercise, known as Sitali Kriya for at least 11 minutes daily, to assist with lung detoxification. By slowing down and deepening our breath, we maximize our lung capacity. This practice helps us to take in more oxygen, release more waste, keep us alkaline, balance the glandular system, and move the lymphatic fluid through the lymphatic vessels to detoxify us further.

Sitali Kriya Exercise

1. Sit cross-legged or in a chair with your hands resting on your knees. Round your lips and, if you can, curl your tongue into a 'U' as though you were going to sip through a straw. If you are unable to do this (because you lack the gene for it), round your lips and place the tip of the tongue against the lower lip.

2. Inhale very slowly through the curled tongue, exhale slowly through your nose. Focus your gaze between your eyebrows, with eyes closed as you continue the breathing pattern.

Stop-Smoking Program

If you are a smoker, make this your time to quit. Lung cancer is the second most frequently diagnosed cancer in women (breast cancer is first), and only 17% of women diagnosed survive 5 years or more. Since 1971, the incidence and death rates for lung cancer have increased fivefold. More women in North America now die of lung cancer than any other type of cancer — it is responsible for 25% of all cancer deaths in women.

Besides the remedies listed here, practice breathing exercises and find a practitioner skilled in using acupuncture as part of a stop-smoking protocol.

Homeopathic Stop-Smoking Drainage Remedies

- Unda 5 and Unda 19 (from Seroyal) helps to detoxify the lungs and free up blocked emotions. Use 5 drops of each 3 times daily directly on your tongue.
- Dr. Reckeweg R77 helps with symptoms of nicotine withdrawal. Use 15 drops 3 times daily in a little water.
- Corylus avellana, made from the hazelnut tree bud, increases circulation to the lungs, improves the function of the alveoli, and helps to remove tar from the lungs. Use 50 drops, 3 times daily.

Herbal Stop-Smoking Remedies

Buy these herbs separately and mix them together in equal parts or find a blend that contains them. Take 50 drops of the mixture 3 to 5 times daily.

- *Lobelia inflata* tincture decreases the craving for nicotine and helps expel lung toxins.
- *Avena sativa* (oats) tincture strengthens the adrenal glands and helps you adapt to stress.
- *Eleutherococcus* (Siberian ginseng) helps you to adapt to stress.
- *Passiflora* is tranquilizing and relaxing.

HEALTHY HERBAL FORMULA

Herbal Immune Power Formula

Immune boosting herbs taken from October until March can tonify your lungs and immune system, preventing chest infections and related asthma. Look for the following herbs as a mixture in tincture form, buy them separately and mix them up together, or order the formula from www.healthybreastprogram.on.ca. Many of our patients come in each fall to pick up their bottle of this year after year. Use 50 drops twice daily from October until March.

40	parts astragalus
20	parts codonopsis
10	parts ganoderma
10	parts St. John's wort flowers
5	parts pau d'arco
5	parts ligustrum

CONTRAINDICATIONS

St. John's wort is contraindicated during chemotherapy and if you are taking an SSRI antidepressant. Omit it from the formula if this is the case.

Nutritional Support for Stop-Smoking Program

- Vitamin C: 2000 mg, 3 times daily with meals
- Magnesium citrate: 150 mg, 3 times daily with meals
- Vitamin B complex: 50 mg, 3 times daily with meals
- Zinc picolinate: 50 mg, daily between meals
- Vitamin A: 25,000 IU, 2 times daily for 1 month
- Adrenal glandular tissue (such as TAD+ from Seroyal) — take one with breakfast and lunch

Fall Foods

Ideal foods for maintaining your health in the fall tend to be foods that are grown in or harvested during the season.

Fiber: Fiber increases the frequency of bowel movements and decreases toxicity. The highest fiber foods are legumes such as kidney beans, chickpeas, black beans, lentils, mung beans, azuki beans; rice bran, wheat bran, oat bran, ground flaxseed and psyllium. Fruits, vegetables, and whole grains also contain fiber. High-fiber diets will reduce your risk of colon cancer significantly. Colon cancer is the third leading cause of cancer deaths in women in Canada and the United States, after lung and breast cancer.

Sour foods: These stimulate the process of contraction, withdrawing and going inward, and include sourdough bread, sauerkraut, olives, pickles, leeks, adzuki beans, apple cider vinegar, lemons, limes, grapefruit, and green apples.

Moistening foods: The lungs and colon are weakened by excess dryness, which occurs when we use indoor heating. This may cause a dry cough, dry skin, or nosebleeds. Foods to moisten dryness include tofu, tempeh, spinach, barley, millet, pear, seaweeds, almonds, sesame seeds, ground flaxseed, flaxseed oil, and extra-virgin olive oil.

Pungent foods: Mucus and phlegm in the lungs and large intestine are cleared with pungent foods, including cayenne, chili peppers, garlic, turnip, horseradish, cabbage, radish, and daikon radish.

Foods high in beta carotene: Beta carotene protects the mucus membranes of the body, strengthens immunity, and guards against cancer. Foods high in beta carotene include carrots, sweet potatoes, squash, pumpkin, seaweeds, chlorella, algae, kale, parsley, cilantro, broccoli, spinach, beet greens, and turnip.

Foods to avoid: Foods that aggravate the lungs and colon should be minimized or avoided. These include dairy, meat, wheat, sugar, saturated fats, and heated oils.

PROTECTING THE AIR

For your home, investigate using air filters, install a dust filter on forced-air furnaces, replace carpets with hardwood flooring, and decrease your use of plastics. Drive your automobile less. Find out who the chemical and heavy metal polluters are in your city and take action with friends and neighbors to demand cleaner standards in industry, supported by government legislation.

Winter Program

December 21–March 20
Caring for Your Kidneys, Adrenal Glands,
Bladder, Bones, and the Water Element

O*n the winter solstice, occurring December 21 in the northern hemisphere, the sun rises the latest and sets the earliest, giving us the shortest day and the longest night of the year. This is a time for us to go deeply within, to bring light to the dark places, the shadow side of ourselves, just as on this day the sun casts the longest shadows. As we reflect upon the passing of another year, we can release the parts of ourselves that are incongruent with our authentic nature and go through a little death. We can make amends with family and friends as we celebrate the holiday season, acknowledging the light that binds us.*

Winter is the most yin season, a time for storing and conserving energy — to slow down, rejuvenate, rest, nourish our inner life, restore our foundation, and deepen our roots — within ourselves, within our family, and within our spiritual community and faith.

Organs

In our bodies, the organs, glands, and tissues associated with the winter period are the kidneys, adrenal glands, bladder, and bones.

Kidneys

In traditional Chinese medicine, the kidneys are thought of as the root of the body's energy. The element associated with the kidneys is water. Water-soluble toxins, waste, trace amounts of amino acids, hormones, and minerals are eliminated through the body's great filter, the kidneys. They contain about one million tiny filtration units called nephrons, which collectively cleanse 180 liters of blood in 24 hours.

DID YOU KNOW...

Besides removing uric acid, urea, and ammonia, the kidneys also regulate acid/alkaline balance; maintain the balance of electrolytes, such as calcium, magnesium, chloride, sodium, and potassium; and manage water distribution in the body.

Adrenal Glands

Your adrenal glands sit like miniature caps on top of your kidneys and help you respond appropriately to stress. Despite their small size, they make about a dozen hormones that circulate through the blood and influence many aspects of women's health. Adrenal hormones include cortisol, aldosterone, DHEA, testosterone, androstenedione, pregnenolone, epinephrine, norepinephrine, and dopamine.

Bladder

Your bladder is the muscular holding tank for urine released by the kidneys — and a storehouse for emotions. When we are 'pissed off,' we are more likely to experience a bladder infection, which can sometimes be cleared when we express held-in anger. Fear or anxiety may manifest as a strong urge to urinate, bedwetting, or incontinence.

DID YOU KNOW...

Childbirth, being overweight, and aging may cause weakness in the sphincter muscle that holds the urethra closed, resulting in loss of bladder control when jumping, running, laughing, coughing, or sneezing. This can be improved with exercises that strengthen the pelvic floor muscles.

SCREENING TESTS

For Your Kidneys, Bladder, and Bones

Work with your health-care practitioners to complete some of the following tests each winter. There is no need to do them all at once. Check off those that you complete each year. See the Resources Section at the back of the book for testing laboratories.

- ☐ pH monitoring of urine and saliva at home
- ☐ Urinalysis using a dipstick
- ☐ Blood test to assess blood, protein, or white blood cells
- ☐ Biological terrain assessment — pH, redox potential, and resistivity of saliva, urine, and blood
- ☐ Darkfield microscopy or live blood analysis
- ☐ Pulse and tongue diagnosis according to TCM
- ☐ Electrodermal testing
- ☐ Koenigsburg test for adrenal insufficiency
- ☐ Ragland postural blood pressure test
- ☐ Pupillary response to light to test for adrenal insufficiency
- ☐ Salivary cortisol and DHEA measured at 7 a.m., 11 a.m., 3 p.m. and 7 p.m.
- ☐ Urine test for bone resorption
- ☐ Bone mineral density scan using dual energy bone densitometry (DEXA)
- ☐ Dental exam

Bones

Like the rock that supports soil and plant life, our bones are our structural foundation, relying on our kidneys, small intestine, bowel flora, thyroid and parathyroid glands, mineral availability and absorption, body pH, hormone balance, and weight bearing exercise for their strength. Our bones are designed to support us for the duration of our lives, yet one out of two American women will suffer an osteoporosis-related bone fracture after the age of 50.

Winter Program

Kidney Cleanse
(December 21 to March 20)

Nutrition and Supplement Program
- Drink 2½ liters or quarts of pure filtered water daily.
- Use ½ tsp alkaline powder in warm water twice daily while monitoring urine and saliva pH with litmus paper.
- Take magnesium citrate (300 mg) and vitamin B-6 (100 mg) daily to help prevent and dissolve kidney stones.
- Use homeopathic Silicea 6X tissue salt, 3 pellets, 2–3 times daily for kidney drainage.

Homeopathic Kidney Cleanse Program
Follow one of these four protocols:
1. December 21 to January 13: Unda 258, 5 drops 3x daily to clear kidneys of stones.
   January 20 to February 12: Unda 258 and Unda 45, 5 drops of each 3x daily.
   February 19 to March 1: Unda 7; 5 drops 3x daily.
2. December 21 to March 20: Use 15 drops, 3x daily, each of Renelix, Dalektro N, and Toxex (Pekana). Take these simultaneously in a little water 15 minutes or more away from meals.
3. December 21 to January 21: *Juniperus* (gemmotherapy), 30 drops 3x daily, with *Ulmus campestre* (gemmotherapy), 50 drops 3x daily, mixed together in a little water.
   January 22 to March 20: *Ulmus campestre* (gemmotherapy), 50 drops 3x daily.
4. December 21 to February 1: Herbal tincture containing 25% gravel root (*Eupatorium purpureum*), 25% hydrangea, 15% dandelion (*Taraxicum officianalis*), 15% nettle (*Urtica dioica*), 10% corn silk (*Zea mays*), and 10% goldenrod (*Solidago Canadensis*). Leave the goldenrod out if you know you are allergic to it. Take 40 drops 3x daily.

DID YOU KNOW...

Your kidney yin nourishes your tissues and organs and builds the blood. It can be depleted by chronic disease, stress, overexertion, extensive breastfeeding, or chronic blood loss.

DID YOU KNOW...

Your kidney yang is the body's furnace, supplying heart and energy to all the organs.

Tonifying Kidney Essence

Work with a Chinese medicine practitioner to evaluate the strength of your kidneys through pulse and tongue diagnosis and a careful history.

- Fortify your kidneys each winter by using Ho Shou Wu and schizandra berry, in tea, tablet or tincture from December 21 until March 21. (Do not use schizandra in pregnancy.)
- For more support, add 50 drops of the gemmotherapy *Ribes nigrum* in the morning to tonify kidney yang and the adrenal glands and 50 drops of the gemmotherapy Sequoia in the evening to tonify kidney yin. Avoid Sequoia if you have an estrogen-related cancer.

Supporting Adrenal Glands
(December 21–March 20)

With your health-care practitioner, determine whether your adrenal glands are underactive, overactive, or just fine using one or more of the tests listed above. If they are underactive, use the nutritional supplements and make the lifestyle changes recommended.

Lifestyle Support

- Spend at least 20 minutes daily doing a breathing exercise. Practice Breath of Fire for 3 minutes each morning and long deep breathing through the left nostril only (block your right nostril with your right thumb) before bed.
- Exercise 40 minutes daily to elevate cortisol slightly.
- Eat regular meals and healthy snacks between meals to stabilize cortisol levels.
- Avoid sugar, chocolate, caffeine, and high-glycemic carbohydrates that cause a spike and then a drop in cortisol.
- Replace coffee with green tea, yogi tea, or a roasted chicory or barley coffee substitute.
- Take a 20-minute break between 3:00 and 5:00 p.m. when cortisol levels are lower.
- Go to bed before 10:00 p.m.
- Consume ½ to 1 tsp of salt daily, especially if you crave it, but if you have high blood pressure, check with your physician first.
- Reduce or eliminate time spent being with people or doing things that drain your energy.
- Spend at least half an hour each day doing something you really enjoy.
- Laugh daily.

HEALTHY RECIPE

Yogi Tea

Yogi tea is a warming, yang tonic for the kidneys, especially during the winter months. It helps to prevent colds and flu, prevents inflammation, and regulates insulin.

40 oz	water
12	whole cloves
16	whole green cardamom pods, cracked open
16	whole black peppercorns
2	cinnamon sticks
8	slices fresh ginger root
2	black tea bags (Jasmine)
2 cups	organic soy milk

DIRECTIONS

Bring the water to a boil. Add the cloves, cardamom, peppercorns, cinnamon sticks, and ginger. Boil for 45 minutes or longer. When it reaches a rich reddish brown color, turn off the heat. Drop in the black tea bags for 1 minute and then remove them. Add organic soy milk to individual servings as desired. Sweeten with honey or maple syrup. Tea can be stored in the refrigerator for several days.

ADRENAL NUTRITIONAL SUPPLEMENTS

SUPPLEMENT	DAILY DOSAGE
Vitamin C (with bioflavonoids)	500 mg vitamin C and 250 mg bioflavonoids, slowly increasing to 4000 mg vitamin C and 2000 mg bioflavonoids. Spread the dosage out through the day.
Vitamin E (mixed tocopherols)	400–800 IU
Vitamin B-5 (pantothenic acid)	1500 mg (3 doses of 500 mg)
Vitamin B-3 (niacin)	25–50 mg
Vitamin B-6 (pyridoxyl -5-phosphate)	50–100 mg
Vitamin B complex	50–100 mg
Magnesium citrate	400 mg taken before bed
Dessicated adrenal cortical extracts from bovine source	300–1,000 mg daily
Shou wu, licorice root, Siberian ginseng, ashwaganda, borage, and oat, particularly if you are vegetarian and object to taking the adrenal extract.	as recommended by your health-care practitioner

Bladder Exercises (Kegels)

Kegels exercises strengthen the muscles of the pelvic floor and help to prevent urinary incontinence (leakage) and uterine prolapse in women after childbirth or as we age. The pelvic muscles help to support the urethra so that it doesn't give out when we cough, sneeze, jump or do anything that increases intra-abdominal pressure. When practiced consistently, they help 75% of women with incontinence.

Directions:

1. Squeeze the muscle that would stop the flow of urine (known as the pubococcygeous muscle) and hold it in a contracted state as you count to 3.
2. Relax the muscle as you count to 5. Repeat this 4 more times.
3. Do this sequence 3 times daily. It's easy to do while you are sitting on the toilet.
4. After several days, increase the squeezing time to 7 seconds, and then to 10 seconds. Repeat the sequence 5 times, and practice it 3 times daily.
5. It is important that you do not contract your abdominal, thigh, or buttock muscles at the same time — just focus on the vaginal area. This is also an interesting exercise to practice during lovemaking.

Bone-Building Program

Nourish your bones no matter what your age with the following nutrients and exercise. See the chapter on Osteoporosis in the Women's Conditions section for a more complete bone-building regimen.

BONE BUILDING PROGRAM	
BONE BUILDING NUTRIENTS	DAILY DOSAGE
Microcrystalline hydroxyapatite or calcium citrate-malate	250 mg, 4 times daily
Magnesium citrate	125 mg, 4 times daily
Strontium	600 mg
Vitamin D	600 IU
Boron	3 mg
Vitamin C	1000 mg twice daily
Vitamin K1	100 mcg
Orthosilicic acid	5-10 drops

Weight-Bearing Exercises

The remodeling of your bones is stimulated by electrical charges generated within the bone matrix itself when you exercise. Walk briskly, dance, use a treadmill, play sports, skip — find an exercise you can do each season, especially in the winter, to activate the remodeling process. Exercise at least 40 minutes each day.

Dental Care

As your teeth are connected to meridian pathways that affect every part of your body, make an effort to schedule dental exams at least twice a year. Floss your teeth daily to decrease inflammation and infection in the gums. Use 100 mg water or fat-soluble coenzyme Q10 and 2000 mg vitamin C daily to strengthen your gums and heart. Use a toothpaste that does not contain fluoride, parabens, isopropyl alcohol, or sodium laurel sulphate.

Winter Foods

Use the following foods to support your kidneys, bladder, adrenal glands, and bones during the winter months.

Liquid foods: drink warming herbal teas with ginger, nettle, fennel seeds, licorice root, and cinnamon in the winter, and use an abundance of vegetable and bean soups to promote kidney cleansing.

Salty foods: a little salt is beneficial to the kidneys and adrenal glands, while too much can cause tightness in the kidneys and bladder. Use miso, seaweeds, sea salt, millet, and barley.

Bitter foods: a small quantity of bitter foods nourishes the heart, which may also be stressed in winter. Use lettuce, watercress, endive, escarole, turnip, celery, asparagus, alfalfa, rye, oats, quinoa, and amaranth.

Warming foods: ginger, cinnamon, garlic, black pepper, cloves, fennel, cayenne, roasted root vegetables (yams, potatoes, beets, carrots), flaxseed oil. Minimize your intake of cold foods, such as salad greens, raw vegetables and fruit, cold drinks, and ice cream.

Kidney yang tonics (warming): walnuts, black beans, quinoa, onions, leeks, garlic, chicken, lamb (seldom), trout, wild salmon (use seldom because of contaminants), cloves.

DID YOU KNOW...

Parathyroid hormone levels are highest in the winter, when this hormone is needed to help the kidneys activate vitamin D to increase calcium absorption in the intestine and accelerate bone growth. Vitamin D levels are normally lower in winter due to lack of sunlight.

Kidney yin tonics (blood building): mung beans, mung bean sprouts, string beans, black beans, aduki beans, kidney beans, black soybean, lentils, tofu, wild rice, millet, barley, sweet rice, wheat berries, potato, parsley, asparagus, seaweeds, spirulina, chlorella, red raspberries, blackberries, blueberries, watermelon, rosehip tea, and red raspberry tea.

Adrenal tonics (energy enhancing): oatmeal, Siberian ginseng, licorice root tea, sea salt.

Bladder cleansers: aduki beans, lima beans, celery, carrots, winter squash, potatoes, asparagus, diluted lemon juice, cranberry juice.

Bone builders: sesame seeds, tahini, hummus, almonds, kale, broccoli, carob, amaranth, figs, dandelion greens, spinach, collards, black-eyed peas, soybeans.

RENEWING THE WATER ELEMENT

We can protect our kidneys by preserving the water quality in our homes, in our communities, and on the Earth. Take steps to ensure that the water that will become 70% of your physical body is pure.

Spring Program

March 21–June 20
Caring for Your Liver, Gallbladder, Tendons, Joints, and the Wood Element

O*n the spring equinox, occurring March 20 or 21, day and night are equal in length, and for the next 6 months we experience an abundance of sunlight and an expansion of yang energy, which peaks at the summer solstice, retreating to equalize with yin and darkness at the fall equinox.*

Spring is a time of new beginnings, fertility, conceiving ideas, and laying the groundwork for things to come. It is a time to restore health, to build new relationships, to express our emotional truths, to expand on current projects and to plant seeds that may one day come to fruition. As winter's ice breaks up and currents flow, the waters of spring nourish new growth.

Organs

In our bodies, the organs associated with spring are the liver and gallbladder, which govern the muscles, joints, tendons, and ligaments.

Liver

The emotion of anger strongly affects the liver, causing stagnation of energy and blood when we hold anger in or excessive internal heat if we express anger too much. The health of the liver is reflected in our eyes and nails. Blurred vision, bloodshot eyes, yellow sclera, ridged, soft or brittle nails each communicate the liver's condition. The flavor associated with the liver is sour — a little sour food improves liver function while too much can damage.

As the kidneys are associated with water, the liver is linked with the wood element. As in the cycle of the seasons when water nourishes the growth of trees, the kidneys are said to be the mother of the liver. If the liver is overactive, it will deplete the kidneys; if the kidneys are deficient, the liver will lack support.

The liver blood nourishes the tendons, muscles, and joints. When the liver is deficient, there may be pain, weakness, and stiffness.

DID YOU KNOW...

The liver stores the blood when the body is at rest, and many menstrual symptoms are related to the inability of the liver qi to move the blood properly, often because of underlying anger, depression, or frustration.

DID YOU KNOW...

The function of bile (which is mostly water with bile salts and lecithin) is to make fats more water-soluble so that they can be digested and absorbed by the small intestine.

Gallbladder

Your liver makes about 500 ml of bile a day, which is pumped through canals in the liver to one large tube called the common bile duct. The common bile duct drains into the duodenum, the first part of the small intestine. In between meals, the gallbladder, an expandable sac connected to the common bile duct, stores bile until we need it for digesting fatty foods. When we eat protein and fat, the gallbladder contracts and empties its contents into the duodenum.

SCREENING TESTS

For Your Liver, Gallbladder, Female Hormones, Thyroid, Breasts, Uterus, Ovaries, Cervix, Eyes

Work with your health-care practitioners to complete some of the following tests each spring. There is no need to do them all at once. Check off those that you complete each year. See the Resources Section at the back of the book for testing laboratories.

- ☐ Liver and gallbladder palpation
- ☐ Liver detoxification profile
- ☐ Liver function tests:
    - ☐ Bilirubin
    - ☐ Liver enzymes: AST, ALT, alkaline phosphatase, gamma-glutamyltransferase, liver dehydrogenase
- ☐ Abdominal ultrasound
- ☐ Pulse and tongue diagnosis according to TCM
- ☐ Breast self-exam
- ☐ Clinical breast exam
- ☐ Breast infra red thermography
- ☐ Breast mammography
- ☐ Basal body temperature test for thyroid function
- ☐ Thyroid function tests:
    - ☐ TSH (normal is 0.35-4.5, although above 2.5 is suspicious)
    - ☐ Free T4 (norm is 9-23 pmol/L)
    - ☐ Free T3 (norm is 3.5-6.5)
    - ☐ Reverse T3 (norm is 0.12–0.54)
    - ☐ Anti-thyroid peroxidase antibodies (norm is < 1:100)
    - ☐ Anti-thyroglobulin antibodies (norm is < 1:80)
- ☐ Saliva, urine, and/or blood tests for progesterone, estradiol, estrone, estriol
- ☐ C2/C16 hydroxyestrone, SHBG, testosterone, melatonin
- ☐ Pelvic ultrasound
- ☐ PAP smear to assess the cervix and pelvic exam
- ☐ Sexually transmitted disease screening
- ☐ Eye exam

Spring Program

Supporting Liver Detoxification
(March 21–April 14)

The liver uses a two-step detoxification sequence known simply as Phase 1 and Phase 2 to protect us from outside chemicals as well as internally generated endotoxins. Each of these steps uses different types of enzymes that require specific nutritional support. After Phase 1 detoxification, toxins can be 60 times more harmful than they were when they entered the body. We need our Phase 2 enzymes to neutralize them quickly.

If Phase 2 enzymes can't keep up with the pace of the Phase 1 enzymes, dangerous toxins will enter the bloodstream, potentially causing free radical damage, inflammation, damage to the DNA, and cancer. If Phase 2 liver detoxification is not efficient, we will store more environmental chemicals in our fat cells. This is one of the root causes of women's diseases — including uterine fibroids, endometriosis, breast cysts, breast cancer, infertility, hypothyroidism, ovarian cysts, and cancer. It is incredibly important that we support our Phase 2 detoxification system to prevent free radical damage and the storage of these toxins elsewhere in the body.

DID YOU KNOW...

An excellent Chinese herb for nourishing the liver blood is *Shou Wu*.

LIVER SUPPLEMENTS	
LIVER SUPPORT SUPPLEMENTS	DAILY DOSAGE
N-acetyl cysteine	500 mg, 3 times daily
Curcumin	500 mg, 3 times daily
Vitamin B complex	100 mg
Choline	250 mg, 3 times daily
L-methionine	100 mg, 3 times daily
Multimineral	200 mcg selenium 50 mg zinc 300 mg magnesium
Indole-3-carbinol or DIM	150 mg, twice daily
Calcium D glucarate	500 mg, 3 times daily
Alpha lipoic acid	150 mg, twice daily
Probiotic Lactobacillus and Bifidobacterium	2 capsules

Nutritional Support for Phase 2 Enzymes

For these 3 weeks, eat raw brassicas (broccoli, cauliflower, cabbage, Brussels sprouts, kale, kohlrabi), soy, whey powder, onions, garlic, sunflower seeds, green tea, peppers, citrus, legumes, oatmeal, turmeric, tofu or miso, beets, organic apples, pears, seaweed and salads daily, along with whole grains, legumes, and extra-virgin olive oil. Avoid meat, dairy, eggs, wheat, peanuts, and other nuts and oils (except flaxseed oil, fish oil, and olive oil). Have 2–4 tbsp freshly ground flaxseeds, 2 tbsp flaxseed oil, and 1 tbsp psyllium seed powder daily. Juice a combination of carrot, beet, apple, kale and ginger, drinking 1–2 liters or quarts daily. Drink chamomile tea and green tea.

Homeopathic Support for Liver Detoxification

Choose one of the following protocols to assist with liver detoxification and drainage:
1. Unda 1, Unda 20, Unda 243, and Unda 258, 5 drops of each 3x daily for 3 weeks.
2. Hepar compositum (Heel), 10 drops 3x daily for 3 weeks.
3. Gemmotherapies Juniperus and Rosemarinus, 50 drops of each 3x daily for 3 weeks
4. Herbal tincture containing milk thistle, dandelion, schizandra, globe artichoke, chelidonium, bupleurum and barberry, 50 drops 3x daily. (You can order this as the Liver Loving Formula from www.healthybreastprogram.on.ca)

Liver Flush

(April 15–24)

A liver flush stimulates the liver to eliminate toxins and cholesterol, increases bile flow, and moves liver blood. Prepare yourself physically and psychologically with relaxation and breathing exercises daily, a vegetarian diet, and consciously release negative thought patterns, old resentments, and anger. If you have cancer, chronic disease or a serious health problem, do the liver flush under the supervision of someone experienced with detoxification regimens.

Liver Flush Formula

1. Mix together freshly squeezed grapefruit juice to make 1 cup of liquid. Water it down to taste with filtered water if desired.
2. Add 1–2 cloves of fresh garlic plus 2 tsp of fresh ginger juice or grated ginger.
3. Mix in 1 tbsp of high-quality extra-virgin olive oil from a metal or opaque glass container and blend the mixture together. This stimulates bile flow.
4. Add a pinch of cayenne, 2 tsp turmeric powder, and 1 tbsp organic soy protein powder (omit this if you have a soy allergy). Mix it up. These assist liver detoxification pathways.

HEALTHY RECIPE

Cleansing Tea

Follow the liver flush with 2 cups of a cleansing tea.

1	part fennel
¼	part burdock
1	part fenugreek
¼	part licorice root
1	part flax
	Pure water
1	part peppermint

DIRECTIONS

Use 1 oz or 28.5 g of the herbs to 20 oz or 570 ml of water. Mix the herbs, except for peppermint. Add water. Simmer the herbs for 20 minutes, then add peppermint. Let it steep for 10 more minutes. Drink 2 cups each morning after the liver flush. Continue this regimen for 10 days.

5. Drink in the morning, waiting 1 hour before eating. Keep your diet simple the rest of the day, eating mainly fresh fruits and vegetables or mung beans and rice cooked with vegetables.

Castor Oil Packs

(April 15–May 15)

Castor oil packs can be used anywhere on the body to break up scar tissue and adhesions, soften masses, and draw out toxins from as deep as 4 inches. A castor oil pack improves elimination through the bowel, kidneys, and bladder, stimulates peristalsis, and protects the mucous lining of these organs. It improves absorption and assimilation in the digestive organs, balances acid secretions in the stomach, and stimulates the liver, pancreas and gallbladder.

Directions

1. Use undyed cotton cloth or wool flannel and drizzle it with cold-pressed castor oil. (Palma Christi brand is best; it contains no solvents). Squeeze the cloth to distribute the oil evenly. The cloth can be used several times before it is washed. Store it in a covered glass container between treatments.
2. Place the cloth on the upper right quadrant of the abdomen, over the liver area, or if you have ovarian cysts, uterine fibroids, or breast cysts, you can place a pack over these areas as well, or simply rub in castor oil. Cover the cloth with a layer of plastic to prevent the oil from getting messy.

3. Place a dry towel over the plastic and a hot water bottle or heating pad on the towel. If you are using a hot water bottle, cover it with a dry towel to hold the heat. The heat should be as warm as can be tolerated.
4. Leave this on the abdomen for 1 to 1½ hours.
5. Use daily or every other day for 4 weeks.

Cleansing the Gallbladder
(May 16–June 6)

Gallbladder Flush Program
After spending several weeks preparing the liver and gallbladder, you are ready for the gallbladder flush to eliminate any remaining sludge or small stones. This flush will also help to relieve you of allergies, bursitis, shoulder and upper back pain. It is best if you have also done a parasite cleanse (Fall) and a kidney cleanse (Winter) before you tackle this gallbladder cleanse. Do not do this flush if you are pregnant, if you have liver disease, if the gallbladder is nonfunctional, if you have large stones, or if you are very overweight.

Directions
1. For the 5 days before the gallbladder flush, drink 6 cups of organic apple juice daily, eat 5 fruits daily, and take 2 tbsp of olive oil daily. Avoid all other fatty foods, nuts, and oils. You may also eat vegetables, grains, and legumes. Drink 2 liters or quarts of water daily.
2. Two days before the flush, take 200 mg of magnesium citrate 3 times daily and Dioscorea (wild yam) tincture 30 drops 3 times daily. These prevent spasms in the bile duct.
3. On the day of the flush, take either 1 tbsp of disodium phosphate or Epsom salts in ½ cup warm water after lunch. These open up the valves of the bile duct, allowing stones to pass through. Repeat this 2 hours later. For dinner, have 2 cups of freshly squeezed grapefruit juice. Before bed, drink ½ cup extra-virgin olive oil with ½ cup of lemon or grapefruit juice. Drink this standing up.
4. Go immediately to bed and lie on your right side, with your right knee pulled up into your chest. The sooner you lie down the more stones will come out. If any cramping occurs, take 30 drops of Dioscorea tincture.
5. The next morning take 1 tbsp disodium phosphate or Epsom salts in ¾ cup warm water between 6:00 and 7:00 a.m. Repeat 2 hours later. In another 2 hours, you can eat, beginning with fruit juice, and then vegetables and grains. Later in the day, expect loose stools and look for small pea-green or tan

stones floating in the toilet. You may feel a little unwell for 1 or 2 days afterward.

6. Repeat the flush in 2 weeks if needed.

Homeopathic Gallbladder Flush Program

Follow one of these two regimens as you do the gallbladder flush:

1. Unda 74, Unda 226 and Unda 258, 5 drops of each 3x daily for 3 weeks.
2. Chelidonium plex (Unda), 8 drops 3x daily for 3 weeks.

Joint Support

(March 21–June 20)

If you have joint stiffness, pain, or arthritis, support your joints with this 3-month program each spring to decrease inflammation and toxicity in the joint space.

Nutritional Joint Support

Foods to avoid: meat, dairy, sugar and sweeteners, alcohol, peanuts, oranges, tomatoes, potatoes, eggplant, pepper, wheat, saturated (animal) fat, most vegetable oils.

Foods to eat: all other fruits and vegetables, legumes (lentils, chickpeas, azuki beans, mung beans), tofu, rice, millet, barley, quinoa, amaranth, spelt, kamut, other nuts and seeds, flaxseed oil, olive oil.

DID YOU KNOW...

Several microorganisms, including *Endolimax nana*, *Yersinia enterocolitica*, *Blastocytishominis*, *Clostridium*, *Salmonella*, and *Staphylococcus*, when present in the intestines can cause symptoms of arthritis.

JOINT SUPPORT SUPPLEMENTS	
JOINT SUPPORT SUPPLEMENTS	DAILY DOSAGE
Pinus Montana (gemmotherapy)	50 drops, 3 times daily
Betula pubescence (gemmotherapy)	50 drops, 3 times daily
Glucosamine sulphate	500 mg, 3 times daily
Pure fish oil	1000 mg, 3 times daily
Curcumin	500 mg, 3 times daily
Boswellia	500mg, 3 times daily
Oil of oregano	5 drops, twice daily
Probiotic *Lactobacillus* and *Bifidobacterium*	2 capsules, twice daily
Alkaline powder	1/2 tsp in warm water, twice daily away from meals
Herbal tincture: devil's claw, black cohosh, burdock, juniper (equal parts)	40 drops, 3 times daily

Breast Self-Massage

Our breast health is strongly influenced by the liver's ability to circulate energy, detoxify chemicals, and manage hormones, particularly estrogen. Liver stagnation and impaired detoxification pathways may result in breast swelling or cysts. Our breasts also need to move daily to allow circulation of lymphatic fluid, which helps to cleanse toxins from the breast area. Breast massage supports this process.

See the chapter on Fibrocystic Breast Disease in the Women's Conditions section for breast self-massage instructions, as well as yoga exercises and nutrients for breast health. Practice breast self-massage three times a week.

Spring Foods

Foods that support the liver: cabbage, sauerkraut, cauliflower, Brussels sprouts, broccoli, broccoli sprouts, other sprouts, kale, dandelion, salad greens, beets, red peppers, carrots, onions, garlic, soy, sunflower seeds, pumpkin seeds, sesame seeds, almonds, spirulina, whole grains, flaxseed oil, fish oil, olive oil, apples, other juicy fruits, lemon juice, grapefruit juice, turmeric powder.

Foods that remove liver stagnation: onions, leeks, garlic, mustard greens, turmeric, basil, bay leaf, cardamom, cumin, fennel, dill, ginger, black pepper, horseradish, rosemary, mint, cabbage, broccoli, cauliflower, Brussels sprouts, beets, strawberry, peach, cherry, raw vegetables and fruit, apple cider vinegar with honey.

Foods to avoid: Avoid the foods that cause liver stagnation — red meat, cream, cheese, eggs, butter, rich nuts, lard, margarine, most oils (except fish, flaxseed and olive oil), alcohol.

Sour foods that improve the liver: apple cider vinegar, lemon, lime, grapefruit.

Bitter foods that cleanse the liver: rye, romaine lettuce, asparagus, amaranth, quinoa, citrus peel.

Foods that cool liver heat: mung beans, mung bean sprouts, celery, seaweeds, kelp, lettuce, cucumber, tofu, watercress, millet, plum, chlorella, spirulina, daikon radish, rhubarb.

Foods that build liver yin and blood: mung beans, mung bean sprouts, cucumber, tofu, millet, flaxseed oil, spirulina, chlorella, dark grapes, raspberries, blackberries.

CARING FOR THE WOOD ELEMENT

Each spring, honor the wood element by planting a tree. Participate in the renewal of the Earth's forests by organizing a tree planting campaign or joining an existing one. Be inspired by Wangari Maathai — the Tree Woman of Kenya. Since 1977, she has worked to save Africa's natural environment by planting trees to combat deforestation caused by mining, logging, agriculture, and the burning of wood for fuel. Maathai's Green Belt Movement, with more than 80,000 members (primarily women), has established more than 1000 tree nurseries and planted 30 million trees across Africa.

Summer Program

June 21–September 20
Caring for Your Heart, Small Intestine,
Blood Vessels, and the Fire Element

O*n the summer solstice, occurring June 21 in the northern hemisphere, the sun rises the earliest and sets the latest, giving us the longest day and the shortest night of the year. On this day, the sun is at its most northern position relative to the earth.*

Summer is a time of joy, celebration, expansiveness, connectedness, reaching outward as we thrive on the sun's light and the increase in yang energy. Take advantage of this with outdoor exercise, sun bathing, socializing, visits to the beach, hikes in nature, outdoor festivals, and travel. As gardens mature and fresh produce is readily available, our palates prefer watery foods (fresh ripe fruit and leafy green salads) to balance the excess yang of summer.

Organs

The organs and tissues associated with summer are the heart, small intestine, gums, tongue, blood vessels, and blood. The element that rules them is fire. When the fire element is deficient or blocked, there may be poor assimilation, emotional coldness, poor circulation, and a pale face. When fire is excessive or imbalanced, there may be excess heat, chronic inflammation, difficulty with speech, gum disease, intestinal problems, atherosclerosis, hypertension, heart disease, and a red face.

Heart

Our heart beats on average 100,000 times a day, and 3 billion times in a 70-year lifespan. This untiring muscle rhythmically thrusts the blood, carrying electromagnetic energy through the blood vessels. The center of compassion, our heart stores the spirit, reflected in the brightness of the eyes, and is associated with insight, love, faith, and creativity. An imbalance in the heart may cause insomnia, overexcitability, vivid dreams, seizures, excess or lack of emotion. The emotion associated with the heart is joy

DID YOU KNOW...

The heart generates a magnetic field of 10^{-3} gauss, which is one millionth the strength of the earth's magnetic field.

(or absence of joy), the taste is bitterness, the sound is laughter, and the odor is burning. Most disorders of the heart are associated with deficiency — either deficient heart qi, deficient heart yang, deficient heart blood, or deficient heart yin. The heart communicates with the tongue. Stuttering, slurred speech or a deviated tongue may signify a heart imbalance or the possibility of a stroke.

Western medicine now acknowledges a connection between periodontal disease, chronic inflammation, atherosclerosis and heart disease. Chinese physicians had figured this out centuries ago, viewing each of them as being related to a fire imbalance.

Gums

Chronic inflammation and infection in the gums predisposes us to heart disease. The oral bacteria *Bacteroides gingivalis*, when present in weak gums, can be transported through the blood to the heart, where it causes heart valve infections. Several bacteria present in the mouth can damage blood vessel walls, contributing to atherosclerosis, and there is a direct correlation between the degree of periodontal disease and likelihood of a heart attack.

Blood Vessels

Our 100,000 kilometers or 60,000 miles of blood vessels are susceptible to oxidative damage by free radicals. Some of these include heavy metals (particularly cadmium, lead, and mercury), toxic fats, chemicals, radiation, and cigarette smoke. To keep the heart and blood vessels healthy, we require regular exercise and a primarily vegetarian diet low in sweets and refined carbohydrates and high in fruits and vegetables, fiber, flaxseed oil and fish oil, nuts and seeds.

Small Intestine

After drawing out nutrients and delivering them to the blood to nourish the rest of the body, the small intestine separates 'the clean from the unclean' and drives the unclean waste into the large intestine with its muscular movements. Its job is one of assimilation and sorting, recognizing what the body needs to keep and what can be converted to waste. Prone to inflammation and atrophy from stress, acidity, imbalanced flora, food allergies, or infectious organisms, our enormous carpet of intestinal villi will benefit from an annual healing regimen, which in turn improves our absorption of nutrients.

A common problem with the small intestine is the presence of a leaky gut, where inflammation creates increased permeability of the intestinal lining, allowing large molecules from incompletely digested food to enter the bloodstream. This results in increased white blood cell activity and triggers allergy symptoms.

DID YOU KNOW...

One of the most harmful substances to the heart and blood vessels is elevated insulin, which stimulates the liver to produce more damaging LDL cholesterol and slows down its breakdown. Stress causes harm to the heart and blood vessels, while joy and laughter help us heal.

SCREENING TESTS

🍂 For Your Heart, Small Intestine, Blood Vessels, and Gums

Work with your health-care practitioners to complete some of the following tests each summer. There is no need to do them all at once. Check off those that you complete each year. See the Resources Section at the back of the book for testing laboratories. Also see the chapter on Heart Disease and Stroke in the Women's Conditions section if your values for the cardiovascular tests are less than ideal.

- ☐ Blood pressure (normal is 120/80 mm/Hg)
- ☐ Stress test
- ☐ Electrocardiogram (ECG)
- ☐ Tongue and pulse diagnosis according to TCM
- ☐ Darkfield microscopy
- ☐ Biological terrain assessment
- ☐ Hair analysis or 6 hr. provoked urine test for toxic metals

🍂 If you are over 45, consider the following tests annually:

- ☐ Total cholesterol: normal is <= 190 mg dL; <5.0 mmol/L; when it is 5-6 mmol/L, heart attack risk doubles
- ☐ HDL cholesterol: normal is 35-110 mg/dL; 1.30-1.55 mmol/L; higher is more beneficial; increased heart disease risk when < 46 mg/dL; <1.2 mmol/L
- ☐ LDL cholesterol: normal is: <= 115 mg/dL; < 3.0 mmol/L; higher values increase risk
- ☐ Triglycerides: ideal is 35-150 mg/dL; < 1.7 mmol/L; increased heart disease risk when 150–400 mg/dL; >1.7mmol/L; considered high when > 401–1000 mg/dL; considered very high when >1000 mg/dL
- ☐ Lipoprotein-(a): ideal is <= 20 mg/dL; <= 200 mg/L; moderate risk is 20-40 mg/dL (200–400 mg/L); high risk is > 40 mg/dL (above 400 mg/L)
- ☐ Total cholesterol/HDL ratio: ideal is < 3.9
- ☐ Ratio of LDL to HDL: ideal is <0.5

🍂 Markers of Chronic Inflammation

- ☐ Ferritin: normal is 6-159 ng/mL
- ☐ Fibrinogen: normal is 150-400 mg/dL; lower values are better
- ☐ C-reactive protein: low risk is < 1 mg/dL; average risk is 1–3 mg/dL; high risk is over 3 mg/dL

🍂 Markers of Oxidative Stress (Excess Free Radical Activity/Antioxidant Deficiency)

- ☐ Coenzyme Q10: normal is 0.80-1.50 mg/L
- ☐ Vitamin E: normal is 12.0-50.0 mg/L
- ☐ Lipid peroxides: normal is <= 1.0 nmol/mL
- ☐ Homocysteine: ideal is <= 8 nmol/mL; borderline high 8–12 nmol/L; high > 12 nmol/L
- ☐ Oxidata test: normal is +1

☞ Other Markers for Heart Disease Risk

- ☐ Red blood cell magnesium (normal is 40-70 ppm packed cells)
- ☐ Fasting insulin (normal is 2.0-12.0 uIU/mL or <100 pmol/L)
- ☐ Red blood cell fatty acids

☞ Assessing Gum Disease

- ☐ Periodontal exam
- ☐ TOPAS gum toxicity test

☞ Testing for the Small Intestine

- ☐ Food sensitivity testing
- ☐ Intestinal permeability testing

Summer Program

Regular Exercise Routine

(June 21 ongoing)

Exercising at least 40 minutes a day is one of the most important things we can do for the heart and circulatory system. Use the summer months to establish an exercise program — whether it be walking, cycling, going to the gym, playing sports, rebounding, or swimming. Find something that you can continue year after year. Exercise outdoors in the morning to expose yourself to sunlight.

Normalizing pH of Urine and Saliva

(June 21 ongoing)

Most of the small intestine needs an alkaline pH to properly absorb nutrients. The intestinal villi will atrophy when continuously exposed to animal proteins, especially during the first year of life before we could properly digest them. To heal the atrophy of the intestinal lining, we can use an alkaline powder, $\frac{1}{2}$ tsp in warm water twice daily, away from meals, and avoid animal protein and known allergens for one or more months. For more information on pH balance, see the Food as Medicine section and Restoring Harmony with the Earth's Elements sections.

Eliminating Allergies

(June 21–August 21)

If you can afford blood tests for food sensitivity testing, get it done and rotate your foods as much as possible over a 5-day period so you aren't consuming the same foods day after day. Electrodermal testing for food sensitivities is another option.

To allow your intestinal lining time to recover, you can also simply avoid the common food allergens for 3 months — wheat, dairy, pork, beef, eggs, corn, citrus, peanuts, chocolate, soy, sugar, tomatoes, yeast, and mushrooms.

Gum Care
(June 21 ongoing)
Our teeth and gums are common sites for infection to develop. This contributes to chronic inflammation, cardiovascular disease and/or cancer.
- Schedule dental checkups and a periodontal exam twice a year
- Floss your teeth daily
- Use a Q-tip or your finger to rub oil of oregano along the gum line once daily
- Mix 2 drops of tea tree oil into your toothpaste. Rub it onto your gums and wait 5 minutes before brushing your teeth
- Take coenzyme Q10, 100-200 mg daily (this is also fabulous for your heart)
- Take vitamin C, 2000-4000 mg daily

Arterial Cleansing and Inflammation Reduction
(June 21–July 21)

Artery Cleansing Diet
For one or more months of the year, cleanse your arteries of residual fat and cholesterol with this diet plan.

1. *On waking:* Squeeze $\frac{1}{2}$ of a lemon into a glass of water with a pinch of cayenne, $\frac{1}{2}$ tsp honey or maple syrup, and 1 tsp psyllium seed powder. Drink this, followed by another glass of water.
2. *Breakfast:* Eat fruit salad with 1 tbsp freshly ground flaxseed. Take uncontaminated pure fish oil (1000 mg), 3 tablets of an arterial cleansing multivitamin formula, and vitamin C (1000 mg).
3. *Mid-morning:* To dissolve plaque, take Wobenzyme (5 tablets) or Nattokinase (60-100 mg). As an anti-inflammatory, take curcumin (500 mg).
4. *Lunch:* Eat a large salad with romaine lettuce, spinach, cucumber, radish, onion, mung bean sprouts, sunflower sprouts (if available), 2 cloves chopped garlic, chopped celery, avocado, 1 tbsp freshly ground flaxseed, firm tofu cubes sautéed in ginger and turmeric, fresh walnut pieces, lemon and olive oil dressing. Take uncontaminated fish oil (1000 mg), HH from Inno-Vite (3 tablets), and vitamin C (1000 mg).

HEALTHY RECIPE

Mung Beans and Rice

Yields 4–6 servings.

1 cup	mung beans
1 cup	basmati rice
9 cups	water
4–6 cups	chopped vegetables (carrots, celery, zucchini, broccoli, etc.)
2 tbsp	extra virgin olive oil
3	onions, chopped
1/3 cup	minced ginger root
6	cloves garlic, minced
3 tsp	tumeric powder
1/2 tsp	pepper
1 tsp	(heaping) garam masala
1 tsp	sweet basil
2	bay leaves
5	pods of cardamom seeds

DIRECTIONS

Soak beans overnight. Rinse thoroughly. Bring water to a boil, add beans and bay leaves. Boil over a medium heat. When the beans have split, add rice. Prepare vegetables. Add vegetables to the cooking rice and beans. Heat a little water with olive oil, and sauté onions, garlic, and ginger over a medium-high heat. Add tumeric, pepper, garam masala, and cardamom seeds. When nicely done, combine onions with cooking mung beans and rice. You will need to stir the dish often to prevent scorching. Add basil. Continue to cook until completely well done over a medium-low heat, stirring often. The consistency should be rich, thick and soup-like, with ingredients barely discernible.

5. *Mid-afternoon*: Take Wobenzyme (5 tablets) or Nattokinase (60-100 mg) and curcumin (500 mg).
6. *Dinner*: Eat mung beans and rice. Take uncontaminated fish oil (1000 mg), HH from Inno-Vite (3 tablets), vitamin C (1000 mg), and vitamin E (400 IU).
7. B*efore bed*: Take Wobenzyme (5 tablets) or Nattokinase (60–100 mg) and curcumin (500 mg).

Tonifying the Heart
(June 21–July 21)
This program for strengthening the heart muscle is particularly important if you are over 50 or you have an increased risk of heart disease.

- Crataegus as a gemmotherapy or herbal tincture, 25-50 drops, 3x daily
- Homeopathic Unda 8, Unda 25, and Unda 33, 5 drops of each, 3x daily, for 3 weeks
- Coenzyme Q10, 100-200 mg daily
- Foods high in magnesium and potassium (see Summer Foods)
- Exercise 1 hour a day

Renewing the Intestinal Lining
(July 21–August 21)
Once you have eliminated harmful bacterial flora, avoided food allergies, and normalized the pH of the small intestine, you can use nutrients to heal the intestinal lining.

Directions:
For a month of intestinal healing use the following supplements. Do not follow this program during pregnancy.
- Probiotic *Lactobacillus acidophilus* and *Bifidobacterium bifidus,* 2 capsules, twice daily
- Barberry (*Berberis vulgaris*) tincture, 10-30 drops, 3 times daily, 15 minutes before meals
- Homeopathic Unda 3, Unda 50, and Unda 39, 5 drops of each, 3x daily
- Gemmotherapies *Ficus carica* and *Juglans regia,* 50 drops of each, 3x daily, 15 minutes or more away from food
- L-glutamine, 1000 mg, 3 times daily between meals
- Zinc picolinate, 50 mg daily between meals
- Slippery elm capsules or powder, 150 mg, 3 times daily
- Vitamin A, 30,000 IU daily
- Folic acid, 1 mg, 3 times daily

Summer Foods
Foods that remove residues of fat and cholesterol from the arteries:
Mung beans (the best food), mung bean sprouts, sunflower sprouts, soybeans, tofu, natto (fermented soy), tempeh, lentils, other legumes and peas, rye, oats, amaranth, buckwheat, radish, horseradish, hot peppers, garlic, onion, leek, scallion, cabbage, spinach, mint, dandelion greens, kale, broccoli, parsley, asparagus, bell pepper, rosehip, tomato, citrus, celery, seaweeds, chlorella, cucumber, almonds, hazelnuts, flaxseed, pumpkin seed, poppy

DID YOU KNOW...
In inflammatory bowel disease, unfriendly organisms (such as *Bacteroides Vulgatus* in colitis or harmful strains of *E. coli* in Crohn's) or the substances they secrete can invade or irritate the mucous membrane of the intestine to create lesions and inflammation. Friendly bacteria can promote healing.

seed, walnut, sardine, wild salmon (occasionally), raw honey, bee pollen, cayenne, peppermint, ginger, psyllium.

Bitter foods to cleanse and cool the heart (use less in summer, more in fall/winter): romaine lettuce, alfalfa sprouts, rye, quinoa, asparagus, celery, radish, scallions, apple cider vinegar.

Foods high in magnesium: tofu, soybeans, buckwheat, rye, figs, black-eyed peas, Swiss chard, almonds, cashews, filberts, brown rice, Brazil nuts, pecans, kelp, walnuts, pumpkin seeds, banana, beet greens, avocado, baked potato, oat bran.

Foods high in potassium: juices (prune, carrot, tomato, grapefruit, orange, grape, pineapple, and apple, although fruit juices should be in small quantities so that glucose and insulin are not elevated), dried figs, papaya, prunes, cantaloupe, banana, mango, apricot, kiwi, pear, apple, avocado, potato, squash, sweet potato, carrot, adzuki beans, white beans, lima beans, tofu, soybeans, black turtle beans, pinto beans, lentils, kidney beans, navy beans, mung beans, chick peas, rye, carob, pearl barley.

Foods for summer: apples, watermelon, salads, sprouts, fruit, cucumber, lemons, limes. Hot spicy food in summer brings excess body heat to the surface to be released — these include cayenne, hot peppers, fresh ginger, horseradish, black pepper.

Foods to avoid: Avoid heavy foods in summer — meat, eggs, nuts, seeds, grains, fatty food.

For intestinal healing, avoid common food allergies: wheat, dairy, eggs, pork, beef, citrus, tomato, peanuts, sugar, mushrooms, yeast.

HONORING THE FIRE ELEMENT

Just as the fire element is imbalanced in so many of us, with heart disease being the primary cause of death and intestinal dysbiosis being ever so common, so we have upset the fire element on the planet. Global warming, increased forest fires, desertification, and freshwater shortages are all signs of fire out of control. The best prevention strategy for global warming is also the best strategy for preventing heart disease — use your car less and walk more.

Late Summer

August 21–September 20

Caring for Your Stomach, Spleen, Pancreas, Muscles, and the Earth Element

L ate summer, between the heat of summer and the coolness of fall, is correlated with the earth element in traditional Chinese medicine, which governs the central part of the body — the stomach, spleen, and pancreas. This is a time to take in nourishment of all kinds that will sustain us physically, emotionally, and spiritually through the rest of the year — great food, a family vacation, good music, and other enriching experiences.

Organs

The organs associated with late summer are the stomach, spleen, and pancreas, which function to transform and transport food into nutrients we can utilize. The stomach and spleen also govern the muscles. Excessive dampness from weather, living in damp environments, or from mucus forming foods, such as dairy, wheat, sweets, excess meat and fats, or an excess of raw foods, can harm the spleen, while too many sweets damage the stomach, pancreas, and spleen. All of our digestive secretions work better when we are relaxed.

Stomach

Our stomach helps us to absorb protein and minerals using specialized glands that secrete mucus, hydrochloric acid, intrinsic factor, and pepsin. Hydrochloric acid not only kills bacteria and parasites before they pass further, it also lowers the stomach pH enough so that the enzyme pepsin can begin protein digestion and stimulates bile flow in the liver. Intrinsic factor allows us to utilize vitamin B-12.

These abilities decrease with age in many of us. As we approach 60 years of age, more than half of us are deficient in hydrochloric acid, which means we will also be protein and mineral deficient. We also become more prone to the bacteria *Helicobacter pylori,* present in 10% of adults under age 29 and 47% of those over 60. It can cause the development of stomach ulcers or cancer.

DID YOU KNOW...

Low hydrochloric acid may predispose us to *H. pylori* infection, and a deficiency of antioxidant vitamins C, E, and A and zinc may encourage its spread. Fortunately, a simple blood or saliva test measuring antibodies can alert us to its presence.

Spleen

Although the spleen is not normally considered a digestive organ, in traditional Chinese medicine it is thought to transform nutrients from digestion into blood and energy. When the spleen is weak, our bodies are unable to use the nourishment from food, and we may be fatigued and pale as a result. The upward-moving spleen energy is also responsible for holding the organs in place, and a prolapsed uterus, hemorrhoids, hernia and varicose veins are all signs of spleen deficiency. Another function of the spleen is to keep the blood in the vessels, so excess bleeding — whether nosebleeds, rectal bleeding, or excess uterine bleeding — may be signs of a spleen weakness. The spleen also functions as a component of our immune system, full of white blood cells, and is a powerful filter of blood poisons.

Pancreas

The pancreas serves a twofold function as a digestive organ (secreting enzymes and bicarbonate) as well as an endocrine gland with insulin-secreting cells that help to lower blood sugar.

Digestion

The digestive aspect of the pancreas is stressed when we eat too much food or when we eat primarily cooked food. For some people, though, a raw food diet is too cooling and will weaken digestion and increase internal dampness and phlegm, particularly when consumed in cooler weather. Cooking food in a slow cooker or steaming vegetables will conserve enzymes and make food more digestible. Signs of pancreatic enzyme deficiency include abdominal bloating, gas, indigestion, undigested food in stools, food allergies, and nutrient deficiencies.

Blood Sugar

Insulin helps transfer glucose into our body's cells to be used for energy production. Too much sweet food causes excess insulin secretion, followed by a sharp drop in blood sugar, when we may experience symptoms of hypoglycemia — fatigue, irritability, dizziness, weakness, mood swings, and shakiness. Over time a diet high in sweets and high glycemic carbohydrates causes obesity, which can lead to insulin resistance (decreased ability of insulin to move glucose into fat and muscle and to shut off glucose release from the liver) and diabetes. Signs of insulin resistance (also called metabolic syndrome) are obesity (particularly around the abdomen), high blood pressure, elevated insulin, high triglycerides, low HDL, increased inflammation, increased atherosclerosis, and susceptibility to heart disease and stroke.

DID YOU KNOW...

Calorie restriction is one accepted practice to encourage longevity. When enzymes are conserved by cutting down calories, they can be used for detoxification, healing, and repair, promoting a long and healthy life.

DID YOU KNOW...

Sugar is one of the most damaging substances to human health. Now added to so many foods, it sets us up for dental cavities, diabetes, obesity, PMS, mood swings, depression, candida and parasitic overgrowth, osteoporosis, and cancer.

SCREENING TESTS

✎ For Your Stomach, Spleen, Pancreas, and Muscles

Work with your health-care practitioners to complete some of the following tests each late summer. There is no need to do them all at once. Check off those that you complete each year. See the Resources Section at the back of the book for testing laboratories. If you hold weight around the abdomen (as opposed to your hips) and have high blood pressure, ask your doctor to check you for insulin insensitivity or metabolic syndrome.

- ☐ Gastro-test or string test to measure hydrochloric acid levels
- ☐ Blood or saliva test for antibodies to *H. pylori*
- ☐ Comprehensive digestive stool analysis
- ☐ Fasting insulin: normal is < 100 pmol/L
- ☐ Fasting glucose: normal is 3.6-6.0 mmol/L; elevated is 6.1–6.9 mmol/L; possible diabetes if >6.9
- ☐ Metabolic syndrome profile measures insulin, glucose, HDL, triglycerides, arachidonic acid, eicosapentaenoic acid, ADMA
- ☐ Glucose tolerance test (to detect hypoglycemia)

Late Summer Program

Stimulating Hydrochloric Acid Production

Ask your health-care practitioner to test your hydrochloric acid levels. If it is low, try one or more of the following remedies for 6 weeks and retest. If there is no improvement, use an alternate approach.

- Relax while you eat, smell your food before eating to stimulate appetite, chew slowly, and don't drink with your meals.
- Drink 1 tbsp apple cider vinegar in a little water 15 minutes before lunch and dinner.
- Take 15 drops of wormwood tincture (*Artemesia absinthum*) orally 15 minutes before lunch and dinner.
- Use homeopathic Unda 4, 5 drops, 3x times daily, 15 minutes before meals
- Take 1 capsule of betaine HCl and pepsin with each meal for one day. If no burning is experienced, use 2 capsules with each meal the following day. Increase the dosage each day until you are taking 6 capsules with a large meal or until you experience burning in the stomach. If you experience burning, use one less capsule at the following meal. Maintain this dosage as long as

no burning is experienced. Once you feel burning, reduce the dosage until your stomach produces HCl on its own, which may take up to 12 months.

Eliminating *Helicobacter pylori*

Check for *Helicobacter pylori* if you are over 50, if you have low hydrochloric acid levels, or if you have had an ulcer, burning in the stomach, or gastritis. Fingerprick test kits that give results in 10 minutes are available. If *H. pylori* is present, use the following protocol and retest in 2 months:

- Manuka honey, 4 tbsp daily
- Oil of oregano, 3 capsules, twice daily
- *Ficus carica* (Fig tree bud) gemmotherapy, 50 drops, 3 times daily
- Bismuth subcitrate, 240 mg, twice daily before meals (order from a compounding pharmacist)
- Probiotic *Lactobacillus acidophilus* and *Bifidobacterium bifidus*, 2 capsules, twice daily, taken away from the oil of oregano

Balancing Blood Sugar

(August 21–September 21)

For this month balance blood sugar with the following:
- Cut all refined sugar from your diet by avoiding sugar, sweets, soft drinks, and high-glycemic carbohydrates. For more information on low glycemic foods, see the Food as Medicine section.
- Use chromium picolinate, 200 mcg, 3 times daily
- Use fish oil, 3000 mg daily
- Use homeopathic Unda 3, Unda 34, and Unda 20 to regulate blood sugar, 5 drops of each, 3x times daily for 3 weeks.
- Use the oligotherapy Gammadyn Zi-Ni-Co (zinc-nickel-cobalt) to regulate the pituitary, adrenals and pancreas, 1 tablet every other day.

Boosting Digestive Enzymes

(August 21–September)

Raw food preserves enzymes and can give the pancreas a rest. If you tolerate raw food well, try a totally raw food diet for 1 to 4 weeks. You can also take high protease digestive enzymes between meals to decrease toxins in the blood and to continue your arterial cleansing program.

Late Summer Foods

Foods that heal the stomach lining: raw cabbage, raw potato, carrot juice, slippery elm.

Foods to strengthen the stomach: millet, kale, cabbage, celery, garbanzo beans, parsnip, shiitake mushrooms.

Foods to strengthen the spleen: warming foods strengthen, while an excess of cold foods weaken. Tonifying foods are rice, oats, spelt, winter squash, carrot, rutabaga, parsnip, turnip, garbanzo beans, black beans, peas, sweet potato, yam, pumpkin. Also pungent vegetables and spices — leek, garlic, onion, black pepper, ginger, cinnamon, fennel, nutmeg. Small amounts of sweeteners strengthen the spleen (while large amounts weaken) — use rice syrup, barley malt, molasses, cherry, date.

Foods to assist the pancreas: cinnamon, garlic, fenugreek, burdock root, walnuts.

Foods to avoid: sugar, tropical fruit juices, food additives, high glycemic carbohydrates, dairy, excess meat, fatty foods.

HONORING THE EARTH ELEMENT

Our body is only as healthy as the food we put into our mouths, which reflects the quality of the soil. Buy organic food as much as possible, compost your food scraps to return minerals to the earth, and help your community reduce pesticide use. Nurture a vegetable garden or participate in a community garden. Take whatever small steps you can to protect the mineral and bacterial balance, pH, and plant life of the soil in your community so that it can continue to nourish future generations and other species.

Looking Ahead

Despite our best efforts to establish and maintain good health, we do sometimes experience illness. The next section addresses specific women's conditions from early puberty to menopause, offering complementary natural and conventional strategies for preventing and treating these conditions, based on the four principles of good health — improve nutrition, restore balance, detoxify and rejuvenate, and integrate body, mind, and spirit.

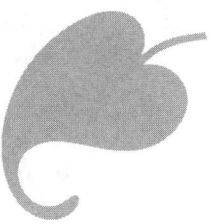

Women's Conditions

Precocious (Early) Puberty

Have you noticed that girls seem to be developing breasts at an earlier age? A few generations ago, it was common for girls to begin to menstruate at 15 or 16 years of age, but now both menstruation and breast development begin earlier. Medical texts currently state that the average age of sexual maturation for girls is 11, when breast budding occurs, followed by menstruation at age 13. Puberty is considered to be early when breasts develop before age 8 and regular menstruation occurs before age 10.

Categories

- True precocious puberty: primarily caused by tumors in the hypothalamus, ovary, or brain.
- Precocious pseudopuberty: due to other subtle causes that are never identified. Most cases (75%) fall into this category.

Causes

Environmental

- Overabundance of chemicals acting as environmental estrogens (pesticides, plastics, polyvinyl chloride, cosmetics, solvents, fire retardants).
- Environmental chemicals (dioxin, PCBs, fire retardants) interfering with thyroid function, even in utero. When thyroid function is low, there is more circulating estrogen.
- Bovine growth hormone in dairy products, which causes puberty to occur earlier (by elevating levels of growth hormone and IGF-1, which stimulate estrogen and breast development).

Dietary

- Diets high in the wrong kinds of fats – animal fat, dairy fat, trans fats, heated fats. Too much omega-6 oil (found in most vegetable oils) and too little omega-3 oil (found in flaxseed and fish).
- Increased consumption of foods high in estrogen – beef, pork, chicken, dairy, eggs.
- Insufficient dietary fiber, causing less estrogen to be eliminated and higher insulin levels. High insulin causes more fat to be stored, which causes elevated estrogen.
- Diets high in sugar and refined carbohydrates, which cause weight gain and elevated estrogen.

Lifestyle

- Obesity in girls. When there are higher fat levels, the body produces more estrogen and insulin.
- Light at night, which suppresses melatonin, allowing estrogen to be more dominant.
- Lack of exercise, which keeps insulin, IGF-1, and estrogen elevated.

TESTS TO MONITOR PRECOCIOUS PUBERTY

Since precocious puberty sets the stage for so many women's ailments, we should be on the lookout for subtle hormonal imbalances, catch them early, and correct them. Some hormones to check annually in girls with early puberty include:

- Fasting insulin (blood)
- Testosterone (blood or saliva)
- Prolactin (blood)
- Basal body temperature
- Thyroid panel, which includes TSH, free T3, free T4, reverse T3, anti-microsomal antibodies, anti-thyroglobulin antibodies (blood)
- Estradiol, estrone, and estriol and the ratio between them (saliva)
- C2/C16 hydroxyestrone ratio (urine)
- Progesterone (saliva)
- Morning and evening cortisol (saliva or blood)
- IGF-1, growth hormone (blood)

Prevention and Treatment

Environmental

- Recognize the environmental estrogens in plastics, pesticides, polyvinyl chloride, cosmetics, solvents, fire retardants, PCBs, and dioxin. Participate in campaigns that seek to ban these. Avoid buying products that contain them.
- Before you conceive your children, complete a 100-hour sauna detoxification program so that you will not pass your body burden of chemicals on to your children. See the Seasonal Cleansing and Rejuvenation Program section for guidelines.
- When your children are age 5, take them into the sauna with you for 15 minutes at a time several days a week. Continue this regularly as they grow older, extending the time.

Dietary

- Avoid fish, red meat, butter, cheese, and milk, even if they are organic, to prevent the accumulation of xenoestrogens in your children's fat cells.
- Do not feed your children sugar, soda/pop, or excess fruit juice. Encourage them to drink filtered water and organic soy milk, almond milk, or rice milk. Decrease all sweets.

DID YOU KNOW ...

Many of the conditions in this book can be prevented if we address the combined factors that are causing earlier onset of puberty in our daughters. That is where we must begin.

Precocious (Early) Puberty

- Use extra-virgin olive oil to cook with and add unheated flaxseed oil to food after it's cooked. Avoid butter, margarine, animal fat, hydrogenated oils, and trans fats.
- Use 2 tbsp freshly ground flaxseed, 2 tsp turmeric, and soy daily to decrease the effects of chemical estrogens.

Lifestyle

- Make exercise a priority for you and your children, at least 4 hours a week. Restrict television and computer games.
- Make sure your children sleep with the lights out, with no street lights shining through the window (moonlight is fine).
- Teach them at a young age how to handle stress – through play, music, breathing exercises, or short meditations.
- Make sure they have an outlet to express their feelings.
- Don't rush your daughter through childhood.

Conventional Medicine

Drug Therapy

Medroxy progesterone and cytoprene are used to stop or reverse sexual development. LHRH agonists block the development of secondary sexual characteristics and slow down skeletal maturation so that a normal height is achieved.

CASE STUDY: *ARRESTING PUBERTY*

Lilian brought her 6-year-old daughter Michelle in to see us because she had early breast development. We talked about possible early exposure to hormone-disrupting chemicals that might have triggered her sexual development (particularly phthalates), and suggested weekly saunas, organic food, and avoidance of plastic. Because Michelle was about 20 pounds overweight, we recommended she participate in martial arts classes four times a week. We replaced her favorite beef burgers with veggie burgers and decreased her estrogen exposure by cutting out milk and cheese.

We asked her to take 3 tsp of psyllium seed powder mixed in water daily to remove excess estrogen and 1 tbsp of ground flaxseed with her breakfast cereal. To keep her insulin levels low, she cut out all sugar and artificial sweeteners, eating instead four pieces of fruit daily. We also asked her to avoid high-glycemic carbohydrates, eating instead bean soups, tofu stirfries, and bean wraps.

Though it was difficult at first, Michelle began to lose weight, feel more energetic, and her self-esteem improved. She became quite proficient in martial arts. When Michelle began to menstruate at age 10, we discussed the link between early puberty and breast cancer (early puberty doubles lifetime risk) and recommended a primarily vegetarian diet with soy milk and ground flaxseeds daily and a long-term exercise program.

Premenstrual Syndrome

If you are like most women (80%), you recognize that your period is coming by characteristic emotional and physical changes. Premenstrual syndrome (PMS) refers to a group of more than 150 different symptoms that occur cyclically after ovulation, up to 2 weeks before our monthly menstrual period, and improve shortly after menstruation starts. About 30% of women consider these symptoms to be problematic, while 5% to 10% of us consider them to be debilitating. PMS affects women most during their thirties and forties.

Categories

For convenience and ease of treatment, PMS symptoms have been divided into four categories, known as PMS-A (for anxiety), PMS-C (for cravings), PMS-D (for depression), and PMS-H (for hyperhydration, or water retention). Although somewhat arbitrary, these categories reflect specific hormonal, neurotransmitter, circadian, and ultradian rhythm imbalances. They respond to different treatment strategies. Many women with PMS, for instance, have low serotonin levels (a neurotransmitter that keeps us happy) after ovulation. Women generally do not fit snugly into one category but exhibit a variety of symptoms.

PMS SYMPTOMS, IMBALANCES, AND TREATMENTS		
PMS-A (ANXIETY) *(affects 65-75 % of PMS sufferers)*		
SYMPTOMS	IMBALANCES	TREATMENTS
Anxiety	Too much estrogen relative to progesterone in the latter half of the menstrual cycle (luteal phase)	Liver and bowel detoxification
Tension, feeling 'on the edge'		Thyroid support
Irritability, anger	Low serotonin	Adrenal support
Fault-finding with one's partner	Drop in TSH and cortisol (thyroid and adrenal function) during luteal phase	Chaste tree berry
Mood swings		St. John's wort
Insomnia		5-HTP
Depression	High norepinephrine/cortisol ratio	Vitamin B-6
Suicidal thoughts		Calcium
Low self-esteem	Increased testosterone	Flaxseed oil
Sensitive to rejection or criticism		Relaxation
Feeling overwhelmed		

MENSTRUAL CONDITIONS

PMS-C (CRAVINGS) *(affects 33 % of PMS sufferers)*

SYMPTOMS	IMBALANCES	TREATMENTS
- Craving (sweets, chocolate, carbohydrates) - Increased appetite - Headaches - Fatigue - Fainting spells, dizziness - Heart palpitations	- Drop in cortisol causes sugar cravings - Imbalance in body's regulation of insulin and cortisol - Low serotonin may cause carbohydrate cravings — carbohydrate ingestion can temporarily raise serotonin levels - Deficiency in PGE1 (a beneficial prostaglandin) can cause low blood sugar with sweet and food cravings	- Adrenal support - Magnesium - Chromium - 5-HTP - Vitamin B-6 - St. John's wort - Flaxseed oil - Fish oil

PMS-D (DEPRESSION) *(affects 25-35 % of PMS sufferers)*

SYMPTOMS	IMBALANCES	TREATMENTS
- Depression - Forgetfulness - Confusion - Lethargy, sluggishness, tires easily - Withdrawal, disinterest in usual activities - Insomnia	- Drop in thyroid hormones during the luteal phase may trigger symptoms - Low serotonin levels may cause low melatonin	- Thyroid support - 5-HTP - St. John's wort - Vitamin B-6 - Calcium - Magnesium - Flaxseed oil

PMS-H (HYPERHYDRATION OR WATER RETENTION)
(affects over 50 % of PMS sufferers)

SYMPTOMS	IMBALANCES	TREATMENTS
- Breast swelling and tenderness - Abdominal bloating - Weight gain of over 3 pounds (1.5 kg) - Swelling of the face, hands, fingers, and ankles	- Increased estrogen relative to progesterone (estrogen causes salt and water retention) - Increased aldosterone, an adrenal hormone elevated during stress, which causes water retention - Excess sugar intake causes elevated insulin to rise quickly, which triggers sodium and water retention - Elevated prolactin, which may be higher when the thyroid is underactive, when dopamine (a neurotransmitter) levels are lower, or there is excess estrogen	- Magnesium - Calcium - Chromium - Vitamin B-6 - Vitamin E - Dandelion (an herbal diuretic) - Thyroid support - Liver and bowel detoxification - Decreased salt - Relaxation

> 🦋 PMS symptoms not listed in the previous categories include diarrhea, constipation, vaginal itching, uterine cramping, changes in libido, backache, acne, incoordination, clumsiness, increased joint pain, night sweats, hives, cold sores, insomnia, nausea, and vomiting.

Causes

Beside hormonal imbalances, emotional and dietary factors can contribute to PMS symptoms.

Emotional Factors

- In Chinese medicine, emotional strain is considered to be the major contributor to PMS. Women who have been sexually or physically abused are more likely to experience PMS symptoms than women without an abusive past.

DID YOU KNOW …

One study showed a 78% improvement in PMS symptoms of anxiety, breast tenderness, headaches, insomnia, and digestive upsets using acupuncture versus a 6% improvement in a control group. Acupuncture points used for liver qi stagnation include Liv-3, GB-34, GB-41, Sp-6, TW-6, and P-6. They are best done the week before and the week after ovulation.

TCM FOR PREMENSTRUAL SYNDROME

In traditional Chinese medicine, PMS is considered to be primarily a result of liver qi stagnation, although other patterns of rising phlegm-fire, liver blood deficiency, liver and kidney yin deficiency, and spleen and kidney yang deficiency may also play a role. The liver in TCM is responsible for the smooth flow of energy everywhere in the body, and adjusts the rise and fall of hormones. Stress, overwork, and emotional repression disturb liver function.

Treatment: A liver cleansing diet, deep breathing, meditation, relaxation, and exercise benefit the liver and release stuck qi. Specific Chinese herbal formulas are used to move the liver energy, the most common one being *Xiao Yao Wan*. In our experience, this herbal formula is the single most effective treatment for PMS.

Dietary Factors

- Deficiencies of calcium, magnesium, zinc, vitamin B-6, vitamin E, and essential fatty acids, such as flaxseed oil and fish oil, may contribute to PMS.
- Caffeine causes a further imbalance in the regulation of cortisol and blood sugar, inhibiting the liver's ability to manage serotonin, estrogen, and progesterone and causing more breast tenderness and swelling in some women.
- Alcohol consumption in the premenstrual phase aggravates symptoms by interfering with the liver's detoxification ability and by causing imbalances in blood sugar levels.
- Animal fats found in meat and dairy products increase production of harmful inflammatory prostaglandins (PGE2 and PGF2) that aggravate PMS symptoms.

DID YOU KNOW …

One study found that women with PMS consume 62% more refined carbohydrates, 275% more refined sugar, 79% more dairy products, 78% more salt, 53% less iron, 77% less manganese, and 52% less zinc than women with no PMS symptoms.

Prevention and Treatment

Improve Nutrition

In addition to following the Women's Health Diet Plan (Section 2), use the following dietary strategies and nutritional supplements to further balance your estrogen to progesterone ratio, your insulin, and your cortisol:

DIETARY THERAPY FOR PMS	
FOODS TO AVOID	FOODS TO EAT
Sugar (avoid or reduce)	4 fruits daily plus 4 servings vegetables
White flour products and baked goods (avoid or reduce)	Whole grains: barley, rice, amaranth, quinoa, millet, buckwheat
Coffee and caffeine (avoid or reduce)	Herbal teas
Foods that contain PCBs, dioxin, and brominated fire retardants — these include fish, dairy, beef, pork, lamb, eggs (see chart in Women's Health Diet)	Tofu, beans, nuts, and seeds as protein sources Use occasional organic chicken if desired (1-2 times weekly)
Peanuts increase arachidonic acid production, which aggravates PMS	Other nuts and seeds in moderation – sunflower, pumpkin, almond
Fruits and vegetables sprayed with pesticides (which disrupt hormones and are estrogenic)	Organic fruits and vegetables
Animal-derived (saturated) fats and most vegetable oils	Extra-virgin olive oil (1 tbsp), unheated flaxseed oil (2 tbsp daily), and pure fish oil (1-2 tsp)
Excessive amounts of raw brassicas (cabbage, cauliflower, broccoli) if you suspect a thyroid problem	2 tbsp of seaweed daily to support thyroid function (nori, dulse, hiziki). Use cooked brassicas liberally
Excess salt if you have water retention	2 tsp of turmeric, 2 tbsp freshly ground flaxseeds, and 1 tbsp psyllium daily to improve estrogen metabolism and elimination
Alcohol (or have minimally)	2 liters or quarts of pure water daily

NUTRIENT THERAPY FOR PMS

NUTRIENT	ACTION	DOSAGE
CALCIUM	• Reduces symptoms of mood swings, depression, swelling, bloating, and cramping	400 mg, 3 times daily
MAGNESIUM	• Reduces water retention, weight gain, swollen limbs, and abdominal bloating • Assists vitamin B-6 and essential fatty acid metabolism	200 mg, 3 times daily
CHROMIUM PICOLINATE	• Stabilizes blood sugar • Decreases sweet cravings	200 mcg, twice daily
ZINC PICOLINATE	• Helps to lower prolactin levels • Assists liver detoxification	30-50 mg, daily
VITAMIN B-6 (pyridoxil-5-phosphate)	• Reduces depression, anxiety, irritability, mood swings, and water retention • Improves the liver's ability to metabolize estrogen, increases progesterone, and increases the synthesis of the neurotransmitters serotonin and dopamine	100 mg, daily
VITAMIN B COMPLEX	• Assists in liver detoxification • Helps us adapt to stress • Calms nerves	50 mg, daily
VITAMIN E	• Reduces the release of arachidonic acid • Decreases levels of the inflammatory prostaglandin PGE2, while simultaneously increasing production of the beneficial prostaglandin PGE1, which helps to relieve premenstrual breast swelling and tenderness	400-800 IU, daily
MULTIVITAMIN (with 200 mcg selenium)	• Provides needed vitamins and trace minerals	1 tablet, daily
NAC (N-acetylcysteine)	• Assists liver detoxification and estrogen metabolism	500 mg, twice daily
CURCUMIN	• Acts as a powerful anti-inflammatory that decreases production of the harmful PGE2 prostaglandin • Assists in liver detoxification and metabolism of estrogen.	500 mg, 3 times daily or 2 tsp turmeric in food
TCM FORMULAS: *Xiao Yao Wan* or *Bupleurum & Tang Kuei* or *Woman's Balance* or *Relaxed Wanderer*	• Alleviate liver stagnation • Harmonize the emotions	Use as directed on bottle or by health-care practitioner. These brands have been tested to be free of heavy metals.

NUTRIENT THERAPY FOR PMS		
NUTRIENT	ACTION	DOSAGE
FLAXSEED OIL AND/OR PURE FISH OIL (use uncontaminated oil)	• Promote the formation of PGE2 and decrease inflammation • Fish oil is also effective in controlling PMS food cravings	2 tbsp flax/ 3000 mg fish oil, daily
ROSEMARINUS (gemmotherapy)	• Helps the liver to metabolize estrogen	50 drops, 3 times daily
CHASTE TREE BERRY (tincture or capsule)	• Helps to increase progesterone and decrease prolactin levels (by binding to dopamine receptors), balancing premenstrual hormones • Helps to decrease breast swelling, irritability, anger, headache, and bloating	1 ml, twice daily; or 200 mg, daily for at least 3 months
ST. JOHN'S WORT	• Increases serotonin levels • Avoid St. John's wort if you are taking an SSRI anti-depressant	300 mg, 1-3 times daily
5-HTP	• In combination with vitamin B-6, it may improve premenstrual tension, mood swings, and irritability by increasing serotonin levels	100-200 mg, 3 times daily
THYROID SUPPORT Kelp, L-tyrosine, selenium, T100 (AOR)	• Increases thyroid hormones to alleviate depression	As directed by a health-care practitioner
ADRENAL SUPPORT Vitamin B-5, vitamin C, dessicated adrenals, Siberian ginseng	• Normalizes cortisol and aldosterone levels to decrease sugar cravings and water retention	As directed by a health-care practitioner

DID YOU KNOW ...

If your temperature is consistently below 97.8°F or 36.6°C, suspect an underactive thyroid. If it does not rise after ovulation, suspect estrogen excess with progesterone and/or thyroid and adrenal insufficiency.

Restore Balance

- Spend at least 20 minutes outside in the early part of the day (without sunglasses) to increase serotonin and nightly melatonin levels. If this is not possible, expose yourself to a bright full spectrum light for an hour in the morning.
- Sleep in a dark room to increase melatonin production at night. This may decrease estrogen's activity and help regulate other hormones, including cortisol and prolactin. Keep regular hours, going to bed before 11 p.m.
- Exercise 40 minutes a day to decrease estrogen levels and to increase endorphin levels, which elevate mood. Aerobic exercise is more effective than resistance training.

- Establish a regular meditation practice that includes long deep breathing to normalize ultradian rhythms, decrease stress, relax the liver, and balance hormones. Practice a pranayam for 20 minutes before bed.
- Assess your specific hormonal and neurotransmitter imbalances during days 20 to 23 of your menstrual cycle with saliva, urine, and blood tests if necessary.
- Evaluate fatty acid status by testing red blood cell fatty acids. This will show dietary deficiencies or excesses of all of the fatty acids so that you can be more selective in determining which oils you might increase or decrease in your diet or with supplementation.

DID YOU KNOW ...

One study has shown that chaste tree is as effective as Prozac for PMS. Another study found a 51% improvement in PMS symptoms after 2 months of treatment with 300 mg of St. John's wort standardized to 900 mcg of hypericin.

HOMEOPATHIC REMEDIES FOR PMS

To balance your menstrual cycle:

Use homeopathic remedies to balance your menstrual cycle, starting on Day 1 of your period. Continue for 3 months or cycles. When using hormonal organotherapy remedies in homeopathy, the potencies below 9CH stimulate; 12CH or 200K regulate; and 15CH and higher suppress a particular hormone.

DAY	MEDICINE	DOSE
Day 1	Hypophysinum (pituitary) 200K	3 pellets taken once
Day 7	Folliculinum (estrogen) 200K	3 pellets taken once
Day 14	Ovarinum (ovary) 200K	3 pellets taken once
Day 21	Luteinum (progesterone) 200K	3 pellets taken once

- If progesterone is low you can use Luteinum 4CH between days 20-25 (replaces Luteinum 200K on day 21).
- If thyroid function is low, use Thyroidinum 4CH, 3 pellets once daily from day 14 to 28.
- If thyroid function is imbalanced, consider Unda 10, Unda 1000 and Unda 273, 5 drops of each 3x daily from day 21-27.
- If there is confirmed estrogen dominance and consistent breast tenderness, use Folliculinum 15CH on days 7, 14, and 21 for 3-6 months to suppress estrogen.

To detoxify:

- Homeopathic Unda 10, 21, and 48 to balance hormones and decrease cellular toxins at 5 drops of each 3x daily for 3 weeks of 1 month. The next month use Unda 1, Unda 20, and Unda 243 to help the liver manage hormones, at a dosage of 5 drops, 3x daily, for 3 weeks. Alternate these two protocols for several months until symptoms are resolved.
- Cimicifuga plex (Unda) to balance hormones and alleviate PMS symptoms, taking 15 drops once daily from days 14 to 28 of your cycle. Use this along with Chelidonium plex (Unda), 8 drops 3x daily to assist the liver in managing hormones.

DID YOU KNOW ...

One study found higher red blood cell and hair levels of lead, arsenic, and mercury in women with PMS compared to symptom-free women. To eliminate your body burden of chemicals and heavy metals, use ongoing sauna detoxification.

DID YOU KNOW ...

You can use your PMS symptoms as a barometer for how well you are taking care of yourself and how well your needs are being met. Acknowledge underlying anger or frustration wherever it exists and open communication lines to let those feelings out.

- Test red blood cell minerals to determine mineral deficiencies and toxic metals. Supplement with those that are deficient; eliminate toxic metals.

Detoxify and Rejuvenate

- To increase bowel detoxification and to eliminate estrogen excess: use 1 tbsp psyllium, 1 tbsp wheat bran (if tolerated), and 2 tbsp of ground flaxseed daily. Aim for three bowel movements daily.
- To normalize bowel flora and to help break down and eliminate estrogen: use *Lactobacillus acidophilus* and *Bifidobacterium bifidum* (10 billion daily) in powder or capsule form.
- To detoxify your liver: use herbs (milk thistle, dandelion, bupleurum, schizandra, chelidonium, globe artichoke, barberry, turmeric), specific nutrients (choline, methionine, curcumin, indole-3-carbinol, NAC, vitamin B complex, magnesium), castor oil packs, and the liver flush. See Seasonal Cleansing and Rejuvenation section for guidelines.

Integrate Body, Mind, and Spirit

- Ask yourself where in your life your energy is stuck – in your relationship, in your work, in addictive eating habits – and take steps to move that energy. Work with a therapist if need be to move forward in your life or to develop more nurturing self-care habits.
- If you have been abused in the past, take care to create a safe, supportive environment around yourself.
- Practice yoga or meditation one or more times weekly to aid in relaxation and hormone balance.
- Plan some fun activities with friends during your premenstrual time – and do things that will make you laugh (to increase endorphins).
- Schedule a massage once a month during the 2 weeks before your period.

Conventional Medicine

Progesterone Cream

Progesterone cream is commonly prescribed for PMS by both medical and naturopathic doctors only after a progesterone deficiency has been demonstrated through saliva or blood tests and then monitored every few months to see that levels are within normal limits and not too high.

- **Use:** If you have a verified progesterone deficiency, your doctor may prescribe oral Prometrium (micronized natural progesterone) or a cream that contains approximately 400 mg of natural progesterone per ounce. Use ¼ tsp of the cream twice

HERBAL FORMULA FOR PMS

This herbal combination for PMS will decrease breast swelling and water retention, normalize moods, alleviate depression, help you adapt to stress, tone the uterus, and decrease menstrual pain. Mix the tinctures separately in the recommended ratios.

25% St. John's wort (*Hypericum perfoliatum*)

25% Chaste tree berry (*Vitex agnus-casti*)

15% Bupleurum

15% *Tang kuei* (*Angelica sinensis*)

10% Siberian ginseng (*Eleutherococcus senticosis*)

10% Dandelion (*Taraxicum officinalis*)

Dose: Use 1 tsp, 3 times daily, either through your whole menstrual cycle or from ovulation to the onset of your period.

daily, starting 10 days before your period is due. However, if your PMS symptoms begin at ovulation, start using the cream on day 8.

- **Dose:** Precise dosing is determined by testing serum or salivary progesterone and estradiol, and assessing the ratio of estrogen to progesterone. When estrogen is lower, decreased concentration of progesterone is effective (from 0.5% to 3%). Dosage can be adjusted until symptoms are relieved. Be precise with your dosing and rub the cream into fatty areas of the skin, such as the upper arms, breasts, buttocks, and inner thigh.
- **Quality:** Be sure that your cream has actual progesterone in it (3%) and is not simply a wild yam or soy-based cream. A pharmaceutical step is needed to convert wild yam or soy into actual progesterone; otherwise, it will be ineffective.

Selective Serotonin Reuptake Inhibitors (SSRIs)

The antidepressants Prozac (fluoxetine) and sertraline are effective when taken for the 2 weeks preceding the menstrual period because they prolong serotonin activity. In one study, Prozac reduced PMS symptoms by 65% when 10 to 20 mg was used for 3 months, either during the luteal phase only or continuously. However, side effects included headaches, weight loss, and inability to have orgasms. Sertraline was effective in a dosage of 50 to 150 mg taken for the 14 days before menstruation. However, most of the time PMS can be treated very well with natural therapies without resorting to pharmaceuticals.

Birth Control Pills

The pill decreases estrogen, progesterone, and testosterone, providing temporary relief of symptoms that return once the pill is discontinued.

TOP 5 STRATEGIES

1. Supplement with calcium-magnesium
2. Take vitamin B-6 (100 mg).
3. Use the Chinese herbal formula *Xiao Yao Wan* or *Bupleurum & Tang Kuei.*
4. Exercise 40 minutes a day.
5. Establish a regular meditation practice.

CASE STUDY: *ABUSE AND STRESS*

Gwen was 32 when she came to our office. She was in psychotherapy because she had wicked irritability for 6 days before her period, so much so that she avoided contact with her friends for fear she would alienate them. She had difficulty maintaining a long-term relationship and seemed to attract men who were either physically abusive or irresponsible. Yet she wanted to have a child. While making an effort to record her dreams, Gwen was disturbed by a sequence in which she was sexually abused by her brother, who was 5 years older. After months of deliberation, she spoke with an older sister whom she trusted, and asked if this could be so. Her sister confirmed what Gwen's unconscious had kept hidden for 25 years.

We counseled Gwen to create a safe, nurturing, non-confrontational environment around her, particularly before her periods. After carefully considering all of her symptoms, we recommended the homeopathic remedy Sepia, which she believed helped her process her anger and pain more easily over several months, and gave her the courage to confront her brother.

Gwen worked as a social worker in a group home for pregnant teenagers, a stressful job. Her premenstrual anxiety, irritability, and mood swings were heightened as her stress level escalated. We suggested that Gwen take time during the 2 weeks before her periods to come to three yoga classes a week, and we gave her a breathing exercise to practice before bed. We also scheduled monthly massages one week before her period was due. As Gwen learned to relax and express her feelings about her abuse in a safe environment, she shifted some of her beliefs about men. She is now dating a man who seems kind and responsible.

Amenorrhea

While it is normal for periods to be absent before puberty, during pregnancy, while breastfeeding, and after menopause, if they cease at other times, the cause must be determined with medical testing. If you have missed one period or more, first make sure you are not pregnant before testing for amenorrhea. Using the guidelines that follow, you can determine whether your missed periods are due to a hormonal imbalance, blood deficiency, or other cause.

Categories

- Primary amenorrhea: when menstruation fails to occur by age 16.
- Secondary amenorrhea: when menstruation has previously occurred but has been absent for at least 3 months in a woman with a history of regular cycles or 6 months in a woman with a history of irregular periods.

Causes

If the cause of primary amenorrhea is genetic or structural, it cannot be addressed with natural medicine. If it is due to other causes, natural medicine may be of benefit.

- In 30% of cases, primary amenorrhea is caused by a genetic abnormality that results in a defect in the ovaries and/or uterus.
- Hormonal imbalances in the interactions between the hypothalamus, pituitary, ovaries, adrenal glands, and thyroid glands are usually a factor.

DID YOU KNOW …

If a 16-year-old has not yet had her period, she should be checked medically with a physical and pelvic exam and blood tests to determine the cause.

DID YOU KNOW …

One study of the impact of environmental exposure to chemicals showed that high levels of dioxin can cause amenorrhea.

TESTS FOR AMENORRHEA

Some of the tests that will determine the cause of primary or secondary amenorrhea include:

- Medical history, physical exam, breast exam, and pelvic exam
- Pregnancy test
- Pelvic ultrasound to rule out polycystic ovaries
- Blood tests for cholesterol
- Blood tests for FSH, LH, prolactin, estradiol, progesterone, testosterone, androstenedione, DHEA-sulphate, cortisol, insulin, IGF-1, growth hormone, and thyroid function
- Genetic testing if necessary for primary amenorrhea

TCM FOR AMENORRHEA

Two of the main causes of amenorrhea in traditional Chinese medicine are yin deficiency with dried blood or stagnation of energy and blood.

Yin deficiency with dried blood

This deficiency condition is related to liver and kidney qi exhaustion, insufficient blood in the uterus, and deficiency in the penetrating and conception meridians, which are the energetic pathways that nourish the uterus. Symptoms include emaciation, dry skin, fatigue, dizziness, palpitations, flushed cheeks, dry mouth, and night sweats.

Treatment: Commonly used acupuncture points include Bl-18, Bl-23, Bl-17, CV-4, Sp-6, K-6. Classical formulas for this condition include *Tang Kuei Four Combination* or *Tang Kuei and Salvia Formula*.

Stagnation of energy and blood

Stagnant blood is an excessive condition related to liver qi stagnation that causes the blood to coagulate and obstruct the penetrating and conception meridians. Symptoms include abdominal bloating and pain, chest congestion, pain in the sides beneath the rib cage, and scaly skin. This is a more common pattern in women whose menstrual cycles abruptly stop.

Treatment: Commonly used acupuncture points include CV-3, Sp-8, LI-4, Sp-6, Liv-3, Sp-10. Formulas for this condition include *Stasis-Transforming Formula* or *Cinnamon & Poria Formula* or *Cinnamon & Hoelen Formula*.

- Other causes include malnutrition, anorexia nervosa, strenuous exercise, radiation or chemotherapy exposure, infectious disease (such as mumps or tuberculosis), pituitary tumors, autoimmune disease, or structural defects.
- It is also possible for a teen to be pregnant just before the onset of her first period.

Causes of Secondary Amenorrhea

Some causes of secondary amenorrhea (excluding pregnancy, breastfeeding, and menopause) include toxin or radiation exposure; autoimmune disease; anemia; anorexia; obesity; strenuous exercise; nutritional deficiencies; excess stress; psychological factors; failure of the hypothalamus to release hormones that stimulate the pituitary; adrenal tumor; underactive thyroid; pituitary tumor or dysfunction; elevated prolactin from the pituitary; and polycystic ovaries or other ovarian dysfunction.

Prevention and Treatment

Be sure to determine the cause of missed periods before treating with natural therapies, for several reasons:

- If your amenorrhea is due to low estrogen levels or low body mass index (BMI), you may have decreased bone mineral density (as estrogen inhibits bone breakdown) and an increased risk of osteoporosis. Adolescence is a critical period for enhancing optimal lifelong bone mineralization. A gain in body weight is the best way to restore bone density if you are underweight.
- If you are producing estrogen but your ovarian follicles do not fully mature and ovulation does not occur (as in polycystic ovaries), your uterine lining may thicken and you may be at increased risk of uterine cancer. This is accompanied by low progesterone.
- If you are not pregnant and there is a hormonal imbalance rather than a more serious pathology causing you to miss your periods, then the strategies below may help.

Improve Nutrition

In addition to following the Women's Health Diet Plan (Section 2), use the following dietary strategies and nutritional supplements. Work with a health-care practitioner in choosing some or all of the supplements below, depending on the cause of your amenorrhea.

Diet

- Ensure that you are ingesting 40 grams of protein daily and at least 1500 calories daily, of which 20% is derived from healthy fats, such as nuts and seeds, extra-virgin olive oil, flaxseed oil, and fish oil. If you are underweight, too little fat may result in low cholesterol and subsequent low estrogen production.
- About 55% to 65% of your calories should be derived from complex carbohydrates, such as brown rice, wild rice, millet, oatmeal, amaranth, quinoa, barley, spelt, kamut, and buckwheat.

DID YOU KNOW ...

Excessive exercise can both disturb the function of the hypothalamus and cause elevated prolactin, which can suppress menstruation. It will also exhaust your kidney energy, which sustains your blood.

NUTRIENT THERAPY FOR AMENORRHEA		
NUTRIENT	ACTION	DOSAGE
CALCIUM	• Necessary for bone health	400 mg, 3 times daily
MAGNESIUM	• Assists liver function, vitamin B-6, and essential fatty acid metabolism	200 mg, 3 times daily
VITAMIN D	• Necessary for healthy bone formation	800 IU, daily
ZINC PICOLINATE	• Helps to lower prolactin levels and assist liver detoxification	30-50 mg, daily

NUTRIENT THERAPY FOR AMENORRHEA		
NUTRIENT	ACTION	DOSAGE
VITAMIN B-6 (pyridoxil-5-phosphate)	• Necessary for progesterone production	100 mg, daily
FOLIC ACID	• Necessary for formation and maturation of red blood cells	1-2 mg, daily
VITAMIN B-12	• Necessary for formation and maturation of red blood cells	100-500 mcg, daily
VITAMIN B COMPLEX	• Assists in liver detoxification • Helps us adapt to stress • Calms nerves	50 mg, daily
VITAMIN C	• Antioxidant • Aids in the absorption of iron	1,000-2,000 mg, daily
VITAMIN E	• Protects against free radical damage • Anti-inflammatory	400-800 IU, daily
MULTIVITAMIN (with 200 mcg selenium)	• Provides needed vitamins and trace minerals	one, daily
IRON	• Use only if anemic • Makes up hemoglobin, which transports oxygen in the blood	18 mg, daily
BORON	• Increases estrogen production	3 mg, daily
SELENIUM	• Antioxidant • Needed for proper thyroid function • Aids in detoxification	200 mcg, daily
FLAXSEED OIL	• Decreases inflammation	2 tbsp, daily
PURE FISH OIL/EVENING PRIMROSE OIL (in 2:1 ratio)	• Decreases inflammation • Protects cell membranes	2,000 mg:1,000 mg, daily
OLIGOTHERAPY: ZINC-COPPER	• Balances hormones	1 dose held under the tongue for 2 minutes, every other day for 6 weeks
HOMEOPATHIC UNDA 1, UNDA 10, UNDA 16	• Regulate the glands	5 drops of each, 3x daily for 3 weeks of the month

NUTRIENT THERAPY FOR AMENORRHEA		
NUTRIENT	ACTION	DOSAGE
GEMMOTHERAPY: SEQUOIA AND ROSEMARINUS	• Sequoia (redwood shoots) elevates estrogen • Rosemarinus balances estrogen metabolism and assists liver detoxification	30-50 drops of each, 3x daily
HOMEOPATHIC HYPOTHALAMINUM 200K	• Regulates the hypothalamus	3 pellets on new moon and full moon
CHINESE HERBAL FORMULA: *Tang Kuei* 25%, *Shou Wu* 25%, chaste tree berry 25%, bupleurum 15%, nettle 10%	• Nourishes the blood and removes liver stagnation • Chaste tree berry increases LH and progesterone, normalizing the luteal phase of the menstrual cycle when taken for at least 3 months • Inhibits prolactin release by binding dopamine receptors	50 drops tincture, 3 times daily
NATURAL HORMONE THERAPY (if needed)	• Restores hormone balance	As directed by health-care practitioner

Restore Balance

• Sleep in a dark room throughout the month, except on the night of the full moon and for 2 days afterward. Expose yourself to low level light on those 3 nights to mimic moonlight. This may help to regulate the hypothalamus and hormones.

• Establish regularity in your sleep schedule (to bed before 11:00 p.m.) and establish regular eating patterns. This will help to normalize ultradian rhythms and hormones.

• Maintain a steady healthy weight. Rapid weight gain or loss, or being underweight or overweight, can prevent the hypothalamus from releasing hormones that regulate the menstrual cycle.

• Balance thyroid function. If your basal body temperature is low (below 97.8°F or 36.6°C) when taken under your arm before rising, then your thyroid may be underactive. If your thyroid is underactive, you may also have elevated prolactin, which suppresses menstruation. See the Hypothyroid chapter in this section for treatment.

• Starting the day before the new moon and continuing for 2 days following, use herbs that promote menstruation, known as emmenagogues. These include black cohosh, blue cohosh, fennel seed, parsley root, and rosemary leaf. Mix any three of these in tincture form and use 30 drops, 3 times daily.

HOMEOPATHIC REMEDIES FOR AMENORRHEA

Try the following homeopathic remedies on the allocated days to help balance hormones. Continue for 3 months.

DAY	MEDICINE	DOSE
New moon	Hypophysinum (pituitary) 200K	3 pellets taken once
7 days later	Folliculinum (estrogen) 200K	3 pellets taken once
Full moon	Ovarinum (ovary) 200K	3 pellets taken once
7 days later	Luteinum (progesterone) 200K	3 pellets taken once

DID YOU KNOW ...

High stress will create imbalance in the hypothalamus and can elevate cortisol and prolactin. If you are a perfectionist or a high achiever, stop pushing yourself, take on less, and examine your need to achieve. Use meditation, relaxation, massage, and yoga to unwind. Identify your stressors and eliminate some of them.

Detoxify and Rejuvenate

- Remove heavy metals and chemicals. One study showed that there was greater lead accumulation in bone when women stopped menstruating. Check your toxic metal levels annually and eliminate them to assist with optimal glandular and neurotransmitter function. See the Seasonal Cleansing and Rejuvenation Program section for guidelines.

Integrate Body, Mind, and Spirit

- Address eating disorders. If you have an eating disorder, such as anorexia or bulimia, work with a health-care team to help address your emotions and beliefs and regulate diet, eating patterns, and exercise.
- Examine emotions you have about being a woman, about your sexuality, about growing up. Is there a part of you that wants to stay a child, and if so, why? Is there a part of you that believes being a woman is inferior to being a man? Is there a part of you that wants to remain dependent on a parent or other provider?
- Use bodywork. Explore massage, rolfing, cranial sacral therapy, Reiki, or other body-centered therapies to bring awareness to emotions connected to your body image, sexuality, creativity, intimacy, maturation, independence, perfectionism, ovarian function, and second chakra issues.
- Consider NeuroModulation Technique (NMT) to release thought patterns and emotional patterns interfering with optimal hormone function and to balance hormones.
- Use affirmations. Choose from the following affirmations any that seem appropriate for you (or develop your own) and repeat them daily to reprogram your thought patterns:

HERBAL FORMULA FOR AMENORRHEA

25% *Tang kuei (Angelica sinensis)*

25% *Shou wu (Polygonum multiflorum)*

25% Chaste tree berry (*Vitex agnus-casti*)

15% Bupleurum (*Bupleurum scorzoneraefolium*)

10% Nettle (*Urtica dioica*)

Dose: Mix the herbs together in the above ratios. Take 50 drops ($\frac{1}{2}$ tsp) of the mixture, 3 times daily for at least 3 months to nourish the blood, normalize estrogen and progesterone, and move liver qi.

It is safe for me to grow up.
I accept my imperfections.
I feel myself maturing into an independent and capable
*   woman.*
As a woman I honor my creativity, fertility, and power.
I am growing more comfortable with my sexuality each day.
I listen to and honor my sexual needs and boundaries.
I release the past and move into my full expression as
*   a woman.*

Conventional Medicine

Hormone Replacement Therapy

If blood or saliva tests have confirmed that you have a hormonal imbalance and the above methods have not brought on your period after 3 months, you may need hormone replacement therapy. The therapy differs according to the kind of hormonal balance.

- If both estrogen and progesterone are low, the following protocol, recommended by naturopath Tori Hudson may be useful:
  - Estriol 1mg/estradiol 0.125 mg/estrone 0.125; 1 capsule two times daily, days 1 to 25 or continuous (starting on the new moon).
  - Add oral micronized progesterone, 100 mg twice daily, days 16 to 25 each month (starting 2 days after the full moon). Check blood levels of estradiol and progesterone after 3 months to adjust dosage if necessary.
- If your estrogen levels are normal but you are not ovulating and progesterone is low (as with polycystic ovaries), along with 200 mg or 40 drops of chaste tree berry daily, use 400 mg/day of oral natural progesterone for 10 days (starting 2 days after the full moon) or $\frac{1}{4}$ tsp of natural progesterone

DID YOU KNOW ...

Amenorrhea can be a response to your fears and beliefs around these issues as your hypo-thalamus responds directly to your thoughts and feelings. If you have been sexually abused, work with a therapist to create a feeling of safety around sexuality.

TOP 5 STRATEGIES

1. Take the herbal formula for amenorrhea.

2. Follow the Women's Health Diet Plan.

3. Maintain a healthy steady weight.

4. Examine emotions you have about being a woman.

5. Use homeopathic Unda 1, Unda 10, and Unda 16 to regulate the glands.

cream twice daily from days 16 to 25. Use saliva and/or blood tests to regulate dosage.

- If the ovaries are not working, conventional medicine may use synthetic hormone replacement therapy, such as conjugated estrogens (Premarin) and medroxyprogesterone acetate (Provera). These may be in the form of tablets or cream. Increasingly, natural progesterone (Prometrium) and Estradiol in the form of patches or gel are being used, although Premarin is sometimes still prescribed orally.

- If prolactin is high, drugs such as bromocriptine, capergoline, and quinagolide are used to decrease it. If polycystic ovary syndrome is present, sometimes progestin is used to slough off the endometrium, or antiestrogens, such as clomiphene or tamoxifen, are given to induce ovulation and restore fertility.

- If there are increased androgens (for example, testosterone), this may be due to pituitary adenomas, an increase in androgen precursors (like DHEA and DHEA-S), or a reduction in testosterone binding globulin. Reversal occurs with bromocriptine. If androgen excess is due to polycystic ovaries, then correction of the underlying insulin resistance is imperative. Metformin 500 mg per day both helps to improve insulin resistance and also enhances weight loss, which is often a significant problem.

CASE STUDY: *MENSTRUAL CYCLE RESUMES*

Sophia came to us for help because she had not had her period for the previous 2 years, though all her blood tests were normal. She was a beautiful 26-year-old who went to strenuous dance classes four times a week. She had always taken care of her mother, managing her finances, buying groceries, and cleaning the house, even as a teenager. Sophia acknowledged that she had grown up too soon and resented her early responsibilities. From age 16 to 22, Sophia had been bulimic and still wrestled with food, experiencing severe food reactions. She controlled her diet very carefully.

We determined from pulse and tongue diagnosis that Sophia had a blood and yin deficiency. We prescribed Tang Kuei and Salvia. We also asked Sophia to limit her dancing to two classes weekly and to take two yoga classes a week. We analyzed her diet and increased her consumption of nuts, seeds, flaxseed oil, and fish oil. We recommended a good multivitamin and mineral formula, as well as 1000 mg of Bone Up, a calcium magnesium formula. Because Sophia had been a vegetarian for several years, we also recommended 1000 mcg of vitamin B-12 a day, with 1 mg folic acid.

Within two months of seeing us, Sophia met a young man, with whom she developed a loving and trusting relationship. They developed a satisfying sexual relationship. After 3 more months of taking her supplements and being in this relationship, Sophia's menstrual cycle returned and became regular.

Dysmenorrhea (Menstrual Pain)

If you have menstrual pain, join the majority — over half of the menstruating women on the planet do, too. Pain is most often experienced just before or during the first 2 days of the menstrual period and eases as the flow continues. The pain can be in the pelvic region, lower back, or may radiate down the thighs. For some women, the pain is debilitating and forces them to take time off work or school. Nausea, vomiting, fatigue, headache, increased urination, and diarrhea may occur along with the pain.

Many women rely on drugs, such as Advil, Anaprox, and Ponstan, to treat pain and stay functional. However, natural medicine alternatives are equally effective for prevention and treatment.

Categories

- **Primary Dysmenorrhea:** The pain is monthly and associated with menstruation, but there is no physical abnormality or observable pelvic disorder. It usually manifests within 6 to 12 months of the onset of menstruation, is most intense in women 20 to 24 years old, and may decrease after childbirth. Smoking and being overweight make the cramping worse.
- **Secondary Dysmenorrhea:** The cyclical monthly pain is associated with an underlying condition, such as uterine fibroids, endometriosis, pelvic inflammatory disease, adhesions, ovarian cysts, polyps, narrowing of the cervical opening, or congenital malformation.

Causes of Primary Dysmenorrhea

- Fats found in red meat, dairy fat (cheese, butter, milk, yogurt), and shellfish. These fats promote the formation of arachidonic acid and eicosanoids, including the prostaglandins PGF2-alpha and PGE2, which cause uterine contractions and pain. Women with dysmenorrhea produce 8 to 13 more PGF2-alpha than women who are pain-free.
- Excess sugar and refined carbohydrates causing high insulin levels. High insulin levels activate an enzyme called delta 5 desaturase, which converts healthy fats found in evening primrose, borage seed oil, and vegetable oil into arachidonic acid. If sugar and insulin are kept low, this enzyme is not activated. Arachidonic acid produces the family of eicosanoids (PGE2 and its relatives) that trigger inflammation and pain.

DID YOU KNOW ...

Primary dysmenorrhea is classified as either spasmodic or congestive in nature. The pain of spasmodic dysmenorrhea is sharp and vise-like, caused by constriction and tightening of the uterine muscle, while the pain of congestive dysmenorrhea is more often a dull ache in the pelvis and lower back, frequently accompanied by bloating, breast tenderness, and headache.

DID YOU KNOW ...

Fats found in flaxseed oil, fish oil, evening primrose oil, and borage oil can form beneficial eicosanoids that will help to offset pain-producing inflammatory eicosanoids.

Dysmenorrhea (Menstrual Pain)

DID YOU KNOW ...

Traditional Chinese medicine considers menstrual pain to be related to anger, frustration, resentment, and hatred, the emotions we have trouble transforming. These emotions lead to liver qi stagnation and liver blood stagnation, which causes blood stagnation in the uterus, resulting in pain.

- Stress and emotional factors. Cramps may reflect an underlying conflict with being female. The uterus is an organ that has been perpetually wounded in women all over the world – it stores the collective memories of rape, incest, and abortion.
- Exposure to cold and dampness. According to traditional Chinese medicine, a cause of spasmodic dysmenorrhea is exposure to cold and dampness, especially during puberty.
- Overwork or chronic illness. When the blood has insufficient energy to move properly, there is stagnation and pain.
- Pelvic or lumbar misalignment. Misalignment of the third lumbar vertebrae, which is in the lower spine at about the level of your belly button, can contribute to painful periods.
- Poor circulation and low oxygen supply to the uterus. Lack of exercise and poor breathing will decrease the blood and oxygen supply to the uterus.
- Displacement of the uterus. If the uterus is displaced forwards, backwards, or to the side, it may be more likely to spasm.
- Liver and bowel toxicity. Liver and bowel toxicity and an overabundance of harmful organisms (dysbiosis) will increase the biological, chemical, and heavy metal burden in the uterus that contribute to inflammation. Inflammation creates congestion, which causes swelling and pain.

CHINESE MEDICAL SYMPTOMOLOGY FOR DYSMENORRHEA

QUALITY OF PAIN	WHAT IT MEANS
Pain before your period	Liver qi stagnation
Pain during your period	Liver blood stagnation
Pain before and during your period	Condition of excess or fullness
Pain after the period	Condition of deficiency or emptiness
Pain relieved by heat	Internal cold or blood stasis from cold or stagnation of qi and blood
Pain aggravated by heat	Heat present in the blood
Pain better after passing clots	Stagnation of blood
Pain with swollen abdomen	Stagnation of qi
Burning pain	Heat in the blood
Cramping pain	Cold in the uterus
Stabbing or pulling pain	Stagnation of blood
Bearing down pain before the period	Stagnation of blood
Bearing down pain after the period	Kidney deficiency
Pain on the sides of the lower abdomen	Liver is involved
Pain in the lower back and sacrum	Kidney deficiency

Prevention and Treatment

Improve Nutrition
In addition to following the Women's Health Diet Plan (Section 2), use the following and nutritional supplements.

Restore Balance
- Exercise 40 minutes a day to improve circulation and move qi and blood.
- See a bodyworker to manipulate and massage your lower back.
- Rest with a hot water bottle over your lower abdomen while you have cramps.

DID YOU KNOW ...

A study of 100 women with painful periods who were between the ages of 18 to 21 found that 50 mg of vitamin E, 3 times daily, improved dysmenorrhea symptoms after 2 months.

NUTRIENT THERAPY FOR DYSMENORRHEA		
NUTRIENT	ACTION	DOSAGE
VITAMIN B3 (NIACIN)	• Decreases pain • Improves circulation	100 mg, hourly during cramps
VITAMIN B6	• Improves liver detoxification • Needed to make beneficial prostaglandins	100 mg, daily
VITAMIN C (with bioflavonoids)	• Decreases menstrual cramps when combined with vitamin B-3	1,000 mg, twice daily
VITAMIN E (mixed tocopherols)	• Decreases inflammation	400 IU, daily
CALCIUM	• Helps to decrease both PMS and menstrual pain and cramping	800-1,200 mg, daily
MAGNESIUM	• Decreases muscle spasm and pain	500-800 mg, daily
ZINC	• Improves liver detoxification • Helps to make beneficial prostaglandins	30-50 mg, daily
CURCUMIN	• Decreases the formation of inflammatory prostaglandins • Helps liver detoxification	500 mg, 3 times daily
BROMELAIN	• Decreases pain and inflammation	300 mg, twice daily
ROSEMARINUS (gemmotherapy)	• Improves liver function and metabolism of estrogen	30-50 drops, 3 times daily
HERBAL TINCTURE: Crampbark (30%), black cohosh (30%), pasqueflower (20%), dandelion (20%)	• Antispasmodic and relaxant, decreases pain	30-50 drops, 3 times daily, 3 days before and during menses as needed

Dysmenorrhea (Menstrual Pain)

NUTRIENT THERAPY FOR DYSMENORRHEA		
NUTRIENT	ACTION	DOSAGE
FLAXSEED OIL	• Decreases inflammation	2 tbsp, daily
PURE FISH OIL	• Decreases inflammation	1,000 mg, 3 times daily
PROBIOTICS: *Lactobacillus* and *Bifidobacterium*	• Normalize the bowel flora and decreases bowel toxicity	2 capsules, daily
PSYLLIUM SEED POWDER	• Increases bowel movements, decreases bowel toxicity	1 tbsp with 2 glasses water
ACUPUNCTURE AND CHINESE HERBAL FORMULAS: *Hsiao Yao Wan* or *Bupleurum & Tang Kuei Formula*	• Treatment is often geared to moving liver qi stagnation and blood	Acupuncture points: Liv-3, CV-6, GB-34, Sp-8, St-29, Sp-10, Sp-6, Lu-7, K-6, Sp-4, and P-6. Take herbs as directed by a health-care practitioner.

HOMEOPATHIC REMEDIES FOR DYSMENORRHEA

- **Decrease uterine congestion and prevent pain with:** Unda 10, Unda 245 and Unda 74 through the month, 5 drops of each, 3x daily

- **During menstrual pain, choose one of the following:** Unda 219 for spastic dysmenorrhea, 5 drops hourly or as needed for pain

- Upelva (from Pekana), 20 drops, 4x daily

- Cimicifuga plex (Unda), 15 drops, 3x daily

Detoxify and Rejuvenate

- Cleanse the bowel with increased dietary fiber, using psyllium, and ground flaxseeds.
- If *Candida albicans* or parasites are suspected, do a 10-week cleanse. For instructions, see the Seasonal Cleansing and Rejuvenation Program section (Fall).
- Detoxify the liver. For instructions, see the Seasonal Cleansing and Rejuvenation Program section (Spring).
- Use nightly castor oil packs over the uterus the week before your period is due.

HERBAL FORMULA FOR MENSTRUAL PAIN

This formula will both decrease spasm and relieve uterine congestion, preventing pain.

30% Cramp bark (*Viburnum opulus*)

30% Black cohosh (*Cimicifuga racemosa*)

20% Pasque flower (*Pulsatilla anemone*)

20% Dandelion (*Taraxicum officinalis*)

Dose: Use 30 drops in a little water, 3 times daily for 3 days before your period, and use 30-50 drops every 1-2 hours as needed for menstrual pain.

Integrate Body, Mind, and Spirit

- Listen to your body. If your uterus is speaking to you through pain, ask why. What is it objecting to? Are you being abused because you are a woman? Have you abused your uterus? Is it expressing a conflict you have yet to articulate in words? Come to terms with your role as a woman and define that role for yourself, rather than accepting others and society's expectations.
- Use affirmations to reprogram your psyche around what it means to be a woman. Choose one or more of the following or develop your own script:

> *I respond on my own terms as a woman.*
> *I release my anger and am ready to move forward.*
> *I can say "no" to what doesn't feel right to me, and still be respected.*
> *I deserve equality in my family, relationship and work.*
> *I readily release the pain of the past from my uterus. It is time to let go.*

- Practice slow, long, deep breathing for 11 minutes before bedtime.
- Practice yoga several times a week to stretch, strengthen, and relax the abdominal, pelvic, and back muscles, and to align the lumbar vertebrae.
- Book a massage, perhaps a uterine massage, the week before your period to relieve pelvic congestion.

DID YOU KNOW ...

When 100 mg of vitamin B-3 (niacin) was given every 2 to 3 hours to 80 women while they were experiencing menstrual cramps, there was a 90% improvement, which was further enhanced with 300 mg/day of vitamin C and 60 mg/day of rutin.

Conventional Medicince

NSAIDs

Conventional medicine recommends non-steroidal anti-inflammatory drugs to be taken before the onset of the period, such as Advil, Nuprin, Anaprox, and Ponstan, to block the formation of series 2 prostaglandins. Although these work, they do not address the cause of the pain.

Birth Control Pills

Birth control pills suppress ovulation and the hormonal changes of the menstrual cycle. They can significantly decrease menstrual pain, but they are carcinogens, and if used at all, should only be used for a short time.

TOP 5 STRATEGIES

1. Use the Chinese herbal formulas *Xiao Yao Wan* or *Bupleurum & Tang Kuei*.
2. Exercise 40 minutes daily.
3. Take vitamins B-3, B-6, C, and E.
4. Supplement with a calcium/magnesium formula.
5. Detoxify your liver and bowel.

CASE STUDY: *PLEASANT SURPRISE*

Clara originally came to see us for recurrent bladder infections. She was an ambitious architect, a perfectionistic who enjoyed social gatherings and fine wines. She had two young children.

Once her bladder problems cleared up with a diet and supplements that decreased candida, she requested help with her menstrual pain. She had taken Anaprox each month for years to deal with the pain rather than treat the cause.

We told Clara about the role of animal protein and dairy in creating inflammation, explaining the link between inflammation and menstrual pain. We had her cut down on these foods, switch to soy milk, and forego summer barbecues. We prescribed 3000 mg fish oil, 1500 mg curcumin, and the Chinese herbal formula Bupleurum & Tang Kuei after detecting a wiry pulse and redness around the sides of her tongue, both signs of liver stagnation. We suggested 11 minutes of long deep breathing before bed and had her focus the breath in the pelvic area to induce relaxation. After 2 months on this program, Clara was pleasantly surprised by the disappearance of menstrual pain.

Irregular Periods

While a menstrual cycle of 28 to 30 days is optimal, cycles are considered normal if a period occurs every 21 to 35 days and lasts from 4 to 7 days. Be concerned if you cycle is longer, shorter, or sporadic. If your menstrual cycle is irregular, you should try to synchronize it with the lunar cycle to create a natural rhythm.

Causes

- Irregular sleep hours and disconnection to the lunar cycle (night shifts).
- Seasonal changes in light and dark.
- Thoughts and emotions, particularly around issues of family or blood relatives.
- Stress and travel.
- Chemical toxicity that causes a progesterone deficiency, as from DDT or DDE.
- Hormonal imbalance between the hypothalamus, pituitary, ovaries, pancreas, adrenals, and thyroid.
- Imbalance between the organs that regulate qi and blood, especially the liver, kidney and spleen.

DID YOU KNOW ...

Women with cycles longer than 40 days are twice as likely to develop type 2 diabetes as women with regular cycles. An extra long cycle may indicate an underlying problem called insulin resistance that is associated with polycystic ovary syndrome (PCOS). If PCOS is the cause, you should also be tested for diabetes.

TCM HERBAL FORMULAS FOR IRREGULAR PERIODS

CAUSE	ACTION	HERBAL FORMULA
Liver qi stagnation	Creates heat (so the liver is unable to store the blood). The period will be too early and there will be an excess of bright red blood, accompanied by irritability, breast tenderness, and menstrual pain.	*Xiao Yao Wan* or *Bupleurum & Tang Kuei*
Kidney yin deficiency	Disrupts the penetrating and conception meridians. There will be low back pain, dizziness, and pale blood. If the cycle is long and the menstrual blood is dark and clotted, it also indicates stagnation of blood.	*Zhi Yin Ba Wei Wan* or *Gu Yin Jian* (patent formulas) or *True Yin Formula* or *Jing Qi Formula*
Spleen deficiency	Disables the production of blood. There may be fatigue, loose stools, gas, and bloating.	*Wen Wei Yin* (patent formula) or *Ginseng & Astragalus Formula*
Cold condition	Causes the period to be too late, with too little blood, and thin watery blood. The individual will be pale and sensitive to cold, with a pale tongue and slow pulse.	*Women's Precious Formula* or *Tang Kuei & Salvia*

TCM FOR IRREGULAR PERIODS

In traditional Chinese medicine, the generation, circulation, and control of blood (which is yin) depend on its regulation by qi or energy (which is yang). Qi and blood, like yin and yang, exist in a cyclic interdependent relationship — qi is the commander of blood, while blood is the mother of qi.

Chinese medical theory outlines the regulation of blood as follows: the heart controls the blood; the liver stores and regulates the blood; the spleen keeps the blood in the vessels; the kidney stores the essence from which the blood is made; the lungs control the circulation of qi that commands the blood. The spleen and stomach are also a source of qi and blood. Any disturbance in these organs can potentially disturb the menstrual cycle.

Commonly used acupuncture points for irregular periods include CV-4, Sp-6 (always), and a selection based on symptoms from Sp-10, Liv-2, St-36, Sp-4, Liv-3, GV-4, and P-6.

Prevention and Treatment

Improve Nutrition

In addition to following the Women's Health Diet Plan (Section 2), supplement with the following nutrients.

NUTRIENT THERAPY FOR IRREGULAR PERIODS		
NUTRIENT	ACTION	DOSAGE
CALCIUM CITRATE	• Prevents bone loss and mood swings that may accompany regular periods	400 mg, 3 times daily
MAGNESIUM CITRATE	• Assists vitamin B-6 and essential fatty acid metabolism	200 mg, 3 times daily
CHROMIUM PICOLINATE	• Decreases insulin resistance • Helpful for polycystic ovary syndrome	200 mcg, twice daily
ZINC PICOLINATE	• Needed for liver detoxification • Needed for insulin metabolism • Prevents heavy metal toxicity	30-50 mg, daily
VITAMIN B-6	• Improves liver detoxification • Needed to make progesterone	100 mg, daily
VITAMIN B COMPLEX	• Needed for liver detoxification • Necessary for production of adrenal hormones • Helps regulate insulin metabolism	50 mg, daily

NUTRIENT THERAPY FOR IRREGULAR PERIODS

NUTRIENT	ACTION	DOSAGE
VITAMIN E	• Protects cell membranes and essential fatty acids from damage from heavy metals and pollutants	400-800 IU, daily
MULTIVITAMIN (with 200 mcg selenium)	• Ensures adequate vitamins and minerals	once daily
NAC (N-ACETYL CYSTEINE)	• Improves liver detoxification	500 mg, twice daily
CURCUMIN	• Improves liver detoxification • Cools liver heat • Anti-inflammatory	500 mg, 3 times daily
CHINESE HERBAL FORMULAS: *Xiao Yao Wan* or *Bupleurum & Tang Kuei*	• Regulate the menstrual cycle by decreasing liver qi stagnation	Use as directed on bottle or by health-care practitioner
ROSEMARINUS (gemmotherapy)	• Liver drainage and hormone balance	50 drops, 3 times daily
FLAXSEED OIL AND/OR PURE FISH OIL	• Important for hormone balance, strengthen cell memebranes, anti-inflammatory	2 tbsp flax/ 2000, mg fish oil, daily
EVENING PRIMROSE OIL	• Helps balance female hormones	1,000 mg, daily
PROBIOTICS: *Lactobacillus* and *Bifidobacterium*	• Assist in heavy metal and chemical clearance • Helps to metabolize estrogen	2 capsules, daily
PSYLLIUM SEED POWDER	• Helps to detoxify the bowel • Clears heavy metals, chemicals and excess hormones	1 tbsp with 2 glasses water
THYROID SUPPORT (if needed)	• When the thyroid is balanced, estrogen dominance may decrease	Kelp, L-tyrosine, selenium, T100 (AOR)
ADRENAL SUPPORT (if needed)	• When cortisol is normalized, thyroid hormones and progesterone normalize	Vitamin B-5, vitamin C, dessicated adrenal, Siberian ginseng

Restore Balance

Lifestyle

- Exercise 40 minutes daily or 4 hours weekly to circulate liver qi and blood.
- Maintain a healthy weight to keep your glands and hormones balanced.
- Sleep in a dark room most of the month. From day 14 to 17 of your cycle, sleep with a 100-watt lightbulb on, with a shade that directs light toward the ceiling to mimic moonlight.

HOMEOPATHIC REMEDIES FOR IRREGULAR PERIODS

The following homeopathic remedies on the allocated days will help to balance your menstrual cycle. Continue for 3 to 6 months.

DAY	MEDICINE	DOSE
Day 1 (first day of your period)	Hypophysinum (pituitary) 200K	3 pellets taken once
Day 7	Folliculinum (estrogen) 200K	3 pellets taken once
Day 14	Ovarinum (ovary) 200K	3 pellets taken once
Day 21	Luteinum (progesterone) 200K	3 pellets taken once

Herbal Regimen

- Use estrogenic herbs (fennel root, ginseng, alfalfa, ground flaxseed, licorice root, red clover, tang kuei) during the first 2 weeks of your menstrual cycle.
- Then use progesterone-enhancing herbs (chaste tree berry, wild yam, saw palmetto, tang kuei, yarrow, lady's mantle) for the next 2 weeks of your cycle.

Other Conditions

- Treat anemia. If menstrual cycles are too close together and heavy, check for iron deficiency anemia. Use ferrous sulphate, Floravit, or a combination of yellow dock, tang kuei, and nettle tincture to increase iron, in combination with 2000 mg vitamin C. Also use Ferrum phos 6X tissue salt, 4 pellets twice daily.
- Evaluate and balance thyroid function. See the Thyroid chapter in this section for guidelines.
- Evaluate the adrenals and support them if necessary. See the Hormone Balance chapter in Living with Nature's Rhythms section for guidelines.

Hormone Therapy

- Consider use of natural progesterone. If saliva testing between days 20 and 23 indicates low progesterone, first try the Restore Balance strategies for 3 to 6 months and retest. If it is still low, consider using natural 3% progesterone cream, 1 tsp twice daily, from day 18 to 28 of your cycle. Retest saliva in 1 month while on the cream and adjust dosage as required.

Detoxify and Rejuvenate

- Detoxify the bowel, kidneys, liver and do a sauna detox. See Seasonal Cleansing and Rejuvenation Program section.
- Use homeopathic drainage therapy: Unda 10, Unda 21, and Unda 48 to balance hormones and decrease cellular toxins, 5 drops of each, 3x daily, for 3 weeks of one month. The next month use Unda 1, Unda 20, and Unda 243 to help the liver manage hormones, at a dosage of 5 drops 3x daily for 3 weeks. Alternate these two protocols for several months until the cycle has normalized.

Integrate Body, Mind, and Spirit

- Acknowledge unexpressed anger, particularly toward family members, and express it.
- Communicate your sexual needs to your partner and experiment with ways to give and receive pleasure.
- Decrease stress. Use prayer, relaxation, entertainment, play, or therapy to relax.
- Practice meditation or pranayam for 20 minutes before bed.

Conventional Medicine

Drug Therapy

To regulate women's cycles, conventional medicine uses the birth control pill or medroxyprogesterone acetate for 1 to 14 days each month. Although effective, these do not deal with the underlying cause of the imbalance.

DID YOU KNOW ...

A study of Southeast Asian women found that women with higher DDT and DDE levels had lower progesterone levels and a shorter luteal phase, causing the period to be too early. It is likely that many other chemicals do the same, although PCBs were found not to interfere with cycle length.

TOP 5 STRATEGIES

1. From day 14 to 17 of your cycle, sleep with a 100-watt lightbulb on to mimic moonlight.
2. Treat with acupuncture and selected Chinese herbal formulas.
3. Use homeopathic drainage (Unda 10, Unda 21, and Unda 48, alternating with Unda 1, Unda 20, and Unda 243).
4. Detoxify the bowel, kidneys, and liver.
5. Take a single homeopathic remedy prescribed by an experienced homeopath.

Menorrhagia (Heavy Periods)

If you have menorrhagia, or excessive menstrual flow, often combined with prolonged bleeding (and a total loss of blood of more than 80 ml or 5 tbsp), ask your doctor to check you for iron deficiency anemia and hypothyroidism. Menorrhagia occurs in 10% to 15 % of women and is common as we approach menopause. If you have this condition, you will need to change pads or tampons every hour or two, may have large clots, and will often be anemic.

DID YOU KNOW ...

Twenty percent of teenage girls with very heavy bleeding have a blood clotting disorder called von Willebrand's disease.

Categories

- Primary menorrhagia: caused by a disturbance in prostaglandin production or factors that are not readily identifiable.
- Secondary menorrhagia: related to a clinically identifiable cause.

Causes of Secondary Menorrhagia

- Iron deficiency anemia.
- Uterine fibroids or polyps, uterine or cervical infection, uterine cancer, pelvic inflammatory disease, cervical polyps, cervical cancer, tubal ligation, or an IUD.
- Endometrial hyperplasia (abnormal thickening of the uterine lining).
- Atopic pregnancy and miscarriage.
- Underactive thyroid.

TESTS FOR SECONDARY MENORRHAGIA

To determine what the cause of heavy menstrual bleeding may be, you may need one or more of the following tests. If all of these tests are normal, you have primary menorrhagia.

- Basal body temperature charting and thyroid function tests
- Complete blood count to rule out anemia
- Pregnancy test
- Pelvic exam and ultrasound to identify uterine fibroids or polyps, ovarian tumors and to measure endometrial thickness
- Endometrial biopsy or a dilation and curettage (D&C)
- Testing for sexually transmitted diseases
- Pap smear
- Testing for blood clotting factors, prothrombin time

Causes of Primary Menorrhagia

- Increased arachidonic acid in the endometrium results in the overproduction of the family 2 series of eicosanoids, which causes endometrial thickening, dilation of blood vessels, and excess bleeding. Red meat, dairy, shellfish and peanuts promote this, while fish oil and flaxseed oil generate the beneficial family 3 series of eicosanoids.
- A hormonal imbalance that prevents ovulation. This could be triggered by stress, infection, brain neurotransmitter imbalance, being underweight, heavy exercise, chemical toxicity, imbalanced body rhythms, working night shifts, smoking, and age. If ovulation does not occur, the corpus luteum does not form, which results in excess bleeding.
- Vitamin A deficiency.
- Food sensitivities.
- Excess toxicity. The body may be trying to eliminate toxins through the blood.
- Overexertion. A long period of overexertion weakens the kidney and liver yin. When the kidney yin is deficient, it fails to build the blood, exhausting the yin further.
- Chronic illness. Chronic illness and excessive worry weaken the spleen, whose job it is to keep the blood in their vessels.

DID YOU KNOW ...

A bleeding uterus is a sign of possible emotional stress, expressing unconscious grief, crying tears of blood. In Chinese medicine, any emotion can lead to stagnation of qi, which develops into excess heat. Heat makes the blood reckless, causing it to burst out of the blood vessels.

DID YOU KNOW ...

Heavy menstrual bleeding should not be treated until the cause is determined.

TESTS FOR PRIMARY MENORRHAGIA

These causes may be identified through the following tests:

- Red blood cell fatty acid analysis
- Hormone level testing of FSH, LH, estradiol, estrone, progesterone
- Serum vitamin A levels
- Food sensitivity testing if other symptoms warrant it
- TCM pulse and tongue diagnosis

Prevention and Treatment

Improve Nutrition

In addition to following the Women's Health Diet Plan (Section 2), supplement with the following foods and nutrients:

Diet

- Eat 2 to 3 cups of green leafy vegetables a day for their iron and vitamin K content, which helps in blood clotting.
- Eat 1 tbsp molasses daily if iron is low.
- Add 2 tsp of turmeric to your cooking daily to decrease PGE2.

Menorrhagia (Heavy Periods)

NUTRIENT THERAPY FOR MENORRHAGIA		
NUTRIENT	ACTION	DOSAGE
VITAMIN K (as phytonadione)	• Increases blood clotting ability	5-10 mg, daily
VITAMIN A	• Helps to stop bleeding	25,000 mg, twice daily
IRON (ferrous sulfate)	• Use only if serum ferritin is low • Replaces iron stores and decrease bleeding	30-100 mg, daily
VITAMIN C (take with iron)	• Improves iron absorption • Decreases capillary fragility	1000 mg, twice daily
BIOFLAVONOIDS	• Decrease capillary fragility	1000 mg, twice daily
VITAMIN E (mixed tocopherols)	• Decreases capillary fragility • Increases PGE1 prostaglandins	400 IU, daily
FLAXSEED OIL	• Encourages formation of beneficial prostaglandins	2 tbsp, daily
PURE FISH OIL	• Encourages formation of beneficial prostaglandins	1000 mg, twice daily
EVENING PRIMROSE OIL	• Encourages formation of beneficial prostaglandins	1000 mg, daily
CURCUMIN	• Decreases inflammation	500 mg, 3 times daily
OLIGOTHERAPY: ZINC-COPPER (Zn-Cu)	• Balances hormones	1 dose held under the tongue for 2 minutes, every other day
ROSEMARINUS (gemmotherapy)	• Improves liver detoxification and estrogen metabolism	50 drops, twice daily
RUBUS IDAEUS (gemmotherapy)	• Astringent drainage remedy for uterus • Helps to stop bleeding	50 drops, 3 times daily
HERBAL FORMULA: Yellow dock 20%, *Tang Kuei* 20%, nettle 20%, chaste tree 40%	• Increases iron stores and progesterone	1 tsp, twice daily throughout the month
HERBAL FORMULA: Shepherd's purse 40%, red root 30%, yarrow 30%	• Stops bleeding	20-40 drops every 2 hours while bleeding

Restore Balance

- Assess thyroid function and treat hypothyroidism. See the Hypothyroidism chapter in this section for guidelines.
- Assess adrenal function and support adrenals. See the Hormone Balance chapter in the Living with Nature's Rhythms for guidelines.
- Consider using progesterone cream. Saliva testing during days 20 to 23 of your cycle can tell you whether your progesterone is low. If it is, use ¼–½ tsp of 3% natural progesterone cream from days 12 to 26 of your cycle.
- Exercise 40 minutes a day to improve circulation and hormone balance.
- Consult an acupuncturist and use Chinese herbs to correct four major energetic imbalances. Each of these is treated differently.
  - Heat in the blood from stagnant liver qi
  - Kidney and liver yin deficiency heat
  - Qi deficiency from spleen weakness
  - Stagnation of blood

Detoxify and Rejuvenate

- If you smoke, get on a program to stop. See the Seasonal Cleansing and Rejuvenation Program section for stop-smoking programs.
- Follow the liver, bowel, and sauna detoxification program outlined in the Seasonal Cleansing and Rejuvenation section.
- Avoid tampons. Use pads instead to allow blood to flow naturally and to avoid contact with dioxin, bleach, and other chemicals in tampons.
- For hormone balance and drainage of the uterus: use Unda 10, Unda 21, Unda 48, and Unda 245, 5 drops of each, 3 times daily, for 3 weeks of the month.

DID YOU KNOW ...

If heavy, prolonged bleeding is due to lack of ovulation (as in women approaching menopause) and low progesterone, then natural progesterone can be used to substitute for what the body is not making. This can help to control bleeding.

HERBAL IRON TONIC AND MENSTRUAL REGULATOR

20%	Yellow dock (*Rumex crispus*)
20%	*Tang Kuei*
20%	Nettle (*Urtica dioica*)
40%	Chaste tree berry (*Vitex agnus-casti*)

Dose: Take 1 tsp twice daily to restore iron. Do not use chaste tree berry during pregnancy.

Integrate Body, Mind, and Spirit

- Acknowledge your emotions. Bring to your awareness any event for which your uterus may be grieving. Have your children left home? Have you feelings to process after an abortion? Have you lost a family member? Are you grieving the child you never had? Are you still hurting after sexual abuse? Are you mourning lost creativity? Use reiki, body-centered psychotherapy, dreamwork, or another modality to process feelings.

Herbal Formula for Heavy Bleeding

40%   Shepherd's purse (*Capsella bursa-pastoris*)

30%   Red root (*Ceanothus americanus*)

30%   Yarrow (*Achillea millefolium*)

Dose: Use 20-40 drops every 2 hours to stop heavy bleeding. Do not use during pregnancy.

Yunnan Pai Yao Formula

The Chinese herbal product *Yunnan Pai Yao*, commonly known as the "stop bleeding pill," contains raw pseudoginseng root and other ingredients that work very well for uterine bleeding, but should be used with Herbal Iron Tonic and Menstrual Regulator formula, the Herbal Formula for Heavy Bleeding formula, or an appropriate Chinese herbal formula that addresses your specific imbalance. It is available in Chinese herbal pharmacies.

Conventional Medicine

Hormone Therapy

- If bleeding is uncontrolled despite the above measures, your medical doctor may prescribe one of the following therapies:
  - Natural estradiol, conjugated estrogen, and intramuscular progestins.
  - Oral estrogens for 20-25 days, followed by progestin or natural progesterone for 10 days.
  - Oral contraceptives, until bleeding is controlled.

Surgery

- Surgical options for uncontrolled bleeding include a D&C, which will stop bleeding temporarily; endometrial ablation; and hysterectomy. A hysterectomy should only be considered if other treatments have failed and bleeding is debilitating.

TOP 5 STRATEGIES

1. Supplement with fish oil.
2. Take vitamin A.
3. Use the Herbal Formula for Heavy Bleeding.
4. Use Chinese herbal formulas and acupuncture to correct energetic imbalance.
5. Follow the Women's Health Diet Plan.

CASE STUDY: *INTEGRATIVE SUCCESS*

Georgina's life read like a tragedy – she was sexually abused as a child, her father committed suicide, her mother was an alcoholic, and she was now a single mother barely scraping by. At 44, she began to experience heavy, prolonged menstrual bleeding for 3 weeks of every month. Her condition proved to be especially difficult to treat.

Saliva testing revealed high estradiol and estrone and low progesterone. From a Chinese medicine perspective, she had a spleen deficiency combined with liver heat and a kidney yin deficiency. Her thyroid results were normal but anemia was a constant concern because of the severe blood loss.

We first prescribed Chinese herbs to strengthen the spleen and remove liver heat. After 2 months, the bleeding had decreased somewhat, but was still debilitating. We then had her use 3% progesterone cream, 1/2 tsp twice daily, starting on day 10 of her cycle. This decreased the bleeding to 10 days a month but it remained very heavy. We added an herbal combination of shepherd's purse and yarrow, as well as the Chinese "stop bleeding pill" Yunnan Pai Yao. Still her bleeding continued.

We talked about her emotions. Georgina was still strongly affected by her childhood traumas. Her uterus seemed to be expressing all of these emotions. She was adamant about not having a hysterectomy, but she agreed to an endometrial ablation, where the inner lining of the uterus is removed. Although her bleeding stopped after this surgery, it resumed 6 months later.

At this time we had her continue all of her previous supplements, but added in NAC, curcumin, indole-3-carbinol, ground flaxseed, psyllium seed powder, and herbs to detoxify the liver and decrease estrogen. Her bleeding abated and remained under control until she became menopausal 3 years later.

This is an example of how integrative medicine was needed to help Georgina. Her case is unusual — bleeding in most women is brought under control in a few months with natural therapies.

Menopause

Menopause naturally occurs when our ovaries no longer respond to stimulation from the pituitary gland to secrete estrogen and progesterone. The menses usually become irregular and stop between the ages of 45 and 55, with the average age being 52. Menopause can last from 6 to 13 years, during which our psyche is programmed to change, just as our bodies go through hormonal shifts. The menopausal sparks our bodies give off are designed to ignite a transformative process. While not a menstrual disorder in itself, menopause symptoms can be discomfiting.

DID YOU KNOW ...

We are officially menopausal when the menstrual periods have been absent for a full year, when estrogen and progesterone levels are low, and when follicle-stimulating hormone (FSH) and luteinizing hormone (LH) are high.

Transformation and Balance

Yang

During menopause, the yang rises. Our hidden power, our inner fire, comes to the surface. This fire may give us the energy we need to begin a new career, remodel our bodies with a fitness and dietary regime, leave or invigorate a stale relationship, develop an abandoned talent, travel the world, give back to our community or to the Earth. Whatever it is you have been putting off, whatever part of yourself remains underdeveloped, whatever your dreams whisper to you at night, now is your time to really listen and follow through. Your psyche will direct you; trust where it leads.

Yin

The menopausal fire (yang) will wear us out unless we support its complement, the yin, which is reflected in the blood and body fluids and rooted in the kidneys. To do this you will need to:

- Support the parasympathetic nervous system with minerals, herbs, and breathing exercises.
- Regenerate the kidney yin with foods, herbs, and/or acupuncture.
- Take time to relax and nourish your inner life.
- Restore your inner feminine, your receptive nature.

SYMPTOMS

You may have virtually no symptoms, other than cessation of menstrual periods as you pass through menopause, or you may experience any one or more of the following symptoms. Although we will focus on treatments for hot flashes, insomnia, anxiety, depression, and vaginal dryness, these strategies apply to most of the other symptoms.

- Hot flashes
- Anxiety and depression
- Vaginal dryness
- Sweating
- Irregular periods
- Sore breasts
- Sleep disturbances
- Nervousness
- Fatigue
- Dizziness
- Joint pain
- Headache
- Fast heartbeat
- Decreased libido
- Bladder incontinence

Hot Flashes

Hot flashes are episodes of flushing lasting a few seconds to a few minutes, with increased heart rate, palpitations, skin blood flow, and skin temperature, accompanied by a sensation of heat and sometimes dizziness. Nearly 60% of us will experience hot flashes before any menstrual changes occur. Hot flashes typically last from 1 to 5 years.

Causes

- An imbalance in the hypothalamus, the part of the brain that regulates temperature. Hot flashes coincide with ultradian surges in LH (a hormone from the pituitary), which is secreted in bursts every 30 to 60 minutes or longer. Each hot flash begins as an LH level spike.
- Neurotransmitters, such as endorphins, serotonin, and GABA (gamma aminobutyric acid), modulate the hypothalamic release of a hormone that causes LH to be released. A disturbance in their actions on the hypothalamus may also cause the LH rise. The disturbance is magnified by stress.
- Specific prostaglandins (molecules composed of fatty acids that affect hormones), known as PGE2 and PGF2a, stimulate the hypothalamus. These prostaglandins are increased by a diet containing red meat, dairy fat, peanuts, sugar, and shellfish, and they are inhibited by bromelain, fish oil, antioxidants, and curcumin from turmeric.
- A drop in estrogen levels activates the sympathetic nervous system to release higher amounts of the stimulating brain neurotransmitter norepinephrine, which results in dilation of blood vessels, flushing, and sweating.

DID YOU KNOW …

Hot flashes affect 75% of North American women, but less than 10% of women in Japan, Hong Kong, Pakistan, and Mexico. Perimenopausal women with hot flashes are 4.4 times more likely to be depressed than perimenopausal women who do not experience hot flashes. Clearly, we have something to learn from attitudes, lifestyles, and diets of other cultures.

DID YOU KNOW …

Menopausal women who do not experience hot flashes can withstand changes in core body temperature of 0.4°C (up or down) without sweating or shivering. This temperature range is termed a "thermoneutral zone." Women with hot flashes react to core body fluctuations with sweating and shivering and lack a thermoneutral zone.

RISK FACTORS THAT AGGRAVATE HOT FLASHES

- Drop in estrogen levels
- Physical inactivity
- Exhaustion
- Stress/overwork
- Inability to relax
- Hot drinks
- Spicy foods
- Alcohol
- Food containing histamine (cheese, red wine)
- Chocolate
- Caffeine
- Smoking
- Red meat, dairy fat, peanuts, shellfish
- Hot weather or very cold weather
- Maternal history of hot flashes
- Menopause before age 52
- Onset of menstrual period before age 12
- History of irregular periods
- High levels of thyroid stimulating hormone during menopause (low thyroid function)
- Pharmaceuticals: Tamoxifen, aromatase inhibitors used after a breast cancer diagnosis

TCM FOR HOT FLASHES

In traditional Chinese medicine, menopausal symptoms are thought to arise from five main patterns of disharmony. Women are treated individually with herbs and acupuncture depending on the pattern of symptoms they exhibit.

Kidney yin deficiency: with delayed, scanty or absent menstruation, hair loss, vaginal dryness; decreased vaginal secretions; dizziness; ringing in the ears; tinnitus; hot flashes; night sweats; excess heat in the chest, palms and soles of the feet; insomnia; dry itchy skin; and weakness of the lower back and knees. The tongue is red with a scanty coat and the pulse is thready and rapid.

Liver qi stagnation: with irritability, nervousness, swelling just beneath the ribs, constipation, palpitation, insomnia, mood swings, and fatigue. The tongue is red with a thin yellow coat and the pulse is wiry.

Blood deficiency: with dizziness, hot flashes, increased perspiration, insomnia, dry skin, pale complexion, mood swings, and muscle pain. The tongue is pale with a thin coat and the pulse is thready.

Uprising deficiency heat: with severe night sweats and hot flashes, heat in the bones, irritability, dizziness, nervousness, and weight loss. The tongue is red with a thin coat and the pulse is thready and rapid.

Kidney yang deficiency: with heavy menstrual bleeding, bleeding between periods or absent periods, soreness and weakness of lower back and knees, swelling of the face and extremities, cold extremities, loose stool, excess urination, and bladder incontinence. The tongue is pale with a thin coating and there is a deep, thready, weak pulse. (There are no hot flashes but this may be a menopausal pattern.)

DID YOU KNOW ...

An overly acidic body terrain can cause hot flashes. Symptoms can be addressed with an alkaline, primarily vegetarian, diet. Relaxation and deep breathing exercises decrease acidity, activate the parasympathetic nervous system, and reduce hot flashes.

Prevention and Treatment

Improve Nutrition

In addition to following the Women's Health Diet Plan (Section 2), use the following foods and nutrients:

Diet

- Eat 20 grams of organic soy protein a day from tofu, soy milk, and soy protein powders. This is equivalent to $\frac{1}{2}$ cup tofu plus 1 cup soymilk, which together contain 58 mg of isoflavones.
- Use 2 tbsp of seaweed daily to support thyroid function.
- Eat foods that build the kidney yin, which include mung beans, mung bean sprouts, string beans, black beans, aduki beans, kidney beans, black soybeans, lentils, tofu, wild rice, millet, barley, potato, parsley, asparagus, seaweeds, spirulina, chlorella, red raspberries, blackberries, blueberries, and watermelon.

NUTRIENT THERAPY FOR HOT FLASHES		
NUTRIENT	ACTION	DOSAGE
BLACK COHOSH (Remifemin)	• Decreases hot flashes • Activates the parasympathetic nervous system	40 mg, twice daily or 2 ml, twice daily
CHINES HERBAL FORMULAS: *Chih Pai Pa Wei Wan* or *Rehmannia and Scrophularia*	• Most commonly indicated Chinese herbal formula for hot flashes • Increases kidney yin while reducing excess heat (yang)	As directed by health-care practitioner
HESPERIDIN	• Relieves hot flashes	900 mg, daily
HESPERIDIN METHYL CHALCONE	• Decreases hot flashes • Strengthens blood vessel walls • Decreases pain and weakness in the legs • Eliminates leg cramps	300 mg, daily
VITAMIN C	• May decrease harmful prostaglandins that increase hot flashes	600 mg, twice daily
GAMMA ORYZANOL (ferulic acid)	• Reduces hot flashes	300 mg, daily
VITAMIN E MIXED TOCOPHEROLS	• Reduces hot flashes, fatigue, palpitations, dizziness, anxiety and mood swings • Decreases vaginal dryness	400-800 IU, daily
CALCIUM-MAGNESIUM VITAMIN D	• Balance the interaction between the sympathetic and parasympathetic nervous system • Maintain bone density • Improve relaxation and sleep	1,000-1,500 mg calcium; half magnesium
VITAMIN B COMPLEX	• Helps liver detoxification • B-6 (100 mg) increases serotonin production, supports adrenals, relieves depression	50-100 mg, daily
CURCUMIN	• Decreases inflammation and harmful prostaglandins	500 mg, three times daily
BROMELAIN	• Supports protein digestion • Decreases inflammation • May reduce the production of the harmful prostaglandins PGE2 and PGF1a that disturb the balance of the hypothalamus	300 mg, twice daily, between meals
SEQUOIA (gemmotherapy)	• Supports the yin • Decreases hot flashes	50-100 drops, 1-3 times daily, especially before bed

Menopause (Hot Flashes)

NUTRIENT THERAPY FOR HOT FLASHES		
NUTRIENT	ACTION	DOSAGE
UNCONTAMINATED FISH OIL	• Balances prostaglandins	1000 mg, 2-3 times daily
ALKALINE POWDER	• To bring urine pH between 6.8-7.2	½ tsp, twice daily
ADRENAL SUPPORT	• Adrenaline glands and fat cells take over estrogen production after menopause	Work with health-care practitioner
THYROID SUPPORT	• Thyroid gland is often unstable during menopause and thyroid hormones may need to be balanced	Work with health-care practitioner

DID YOU KNOW ...

Exercise increases the concentration of endorphins, which reduce hot flashes, and can decrease circulating amounts of FSH and LH. When we exercise, our adrenal glands convert the male hormone adrostenedione into estrogen.

Restore Balance

- Exercise at least 40 minutes a day. Regular exercise balances neurotransmitters, which regulate the hypothalamus and control thermoregulation.
- Practice slow, long, deep breathing through the left nostril only (by blocking your right nostril with your right thumb) for 20 minutes twice daily to activate the parasympathetic nervous system (decreasing norepinephrine), to alkalinize the body, and to balance the hypothalamus and glands.
- Sleep in a dark room (except during the full moon) to increase melatonin levels so that you sleep more soundly and your body's rhythms can be harmonized.
- Correct pH imbalance. Monitor the pH of your urine and saliva and adopt a primarily alkaline diet to activate the parasympathetic nervous system. See the Women's Health Diet Plan. Use ½ tsp twice daily of an alkaline powder in a little warm water, away from meals.
- Calm the nervous system. If you are on edge or have trouble sleeping, support your nervous system with homeopathic Unda 9 (5 drops, 3x daily) or Passiflora plex (8 drops, 3x daily), and/or the gemmotherapy *Tilia tomentosa* (50 drops, 3x daily), or the herbs passionflower, valerian, skullcap, and hops.
- Regulate the hypothalamus and activate the parasympathetic nervous system. Use 3 pellets twice monthly of Hypothala-minum 200K to regulate the hypothalamus, which, when imbalanced, may cause hot flashes.
- Use the oligotherapy trace element combination zinc-copper (Zn-Cu) as a catalyst to restore balance to the hypothalamus, thyroid, pituitary and adrenal glands. Take one pellet or one tsp of liquid (holding it in your mouth for 2 minutes) 2–3 times a week in the morning before breakfast for several weeks. Then stop for a few weeks and resume again.

CHINESE HERBAL FORMULAS FOR HOT FLASHES

When Chinese herbal formulas are matched specifically to your pattern of imbalance, they work extremely well and are usually needed for only a few months. The brands listed below are manufactured in the U.S. and are not contaminated with heavy metals.

For Kidney yin deficiency: *Zhi Bai Di Huang Wan* or *Anemarrhena Phellodendron & Rehmannia Formula* or *Rehmannia and Scrophularia*

For Liver qi stagnation: *Chai Hu Jia Long Mu Tang* or *Bupleurum & Dragon Bone Combination* or *Calm Dragon Formula* or *Ease Plus* or *Bupleurum D* or *Jia Wei Xiao Yao San* or *Bupleurum & Peony Formula*

For Blood deficiency: *Si Wu Tang* or *Tangkuei Four Combination* or *Tang-kuei 18* or *Gui Pi Tang* or *Ginseng & Longan Combination*

For Uprising deficiency heat: *Er Xian Tang* or *Curculigo & Epimedium combination* or *Three Immortals* or *Two Immortals* or *Temper Fire*

For Kidney yang deficiency: *You Gui Wan* or *Eucommia & Rehmannia Formula* or *Rehmannia Eight Formula* or *Rehmannia 8* or *Li Zhong Tang* or *Ginseng & Ginger Combination*

- Support your adrenal glands. Test cortisol and DHEA in saliva or blood and, if these hormones are low, modify your lifestyle to include more relaxation and breathing exercises. Use vitamin B complex, vitamin B-5, and extra vitamin C, as well as adrenal glandular extracts and/or herbal support, such as *Ho Shou Wu*, schizandra, Siberian ginseng, licorice root, ashwagandha, oat, borage and the gemmotherapies *Ribes nigrum* and/or *Sequoia*.
- Support your thyroid gland. See the Hypothyroidism chapter in this section for testing, symptoms, and treatment strategies.

Herbal Therapies for Hot Flashes
Black cohosh (Cimicifuga racemosa)

- Black cohosh has been used in Europe in more than 1.5 million women and has very few side effects. The recommended daily dose ranges from 40–80 mg (standardized to 2.5% triterpenes). At least 4-12 weeks of treatment may be required before its benefits are apparent. The most commonly used tablet form of black cohosh is Remifemin.
- *Dose:* Tincture is taken in doses of 2 ml twice daily.

DID YOU KNOW ...

One study demonstrated that 6 to 14 acupuncture treatments, scheduled twice weekly, reduced hot flashes by over 50% in women who had been experiencing hot flashes for over a year. The average daily number of hot flashes experienced by the women was 14 on the first visit, and by the last visit this had reduced to 1.41 during the day and 0.86 at night.

Menopause (Hot Flashes)

DID YOU KNOW ...

Over 11 clinical trials on black cohosh in a proprietary formula called Remifemin show that it is as equally effective as estrogen in decreasing menopausal hot flashes, sweating, heart palpitations, sleep disturbances, mood swings, tension, nervousness, mental fatigue, memory loss, low libido, urinary incontinence, vaginal dryness and joint pain. It is safe to take if you have had breast cancer.

DID YOU KNOW ...

Schizandra is an effective tonic for the kidneys, adrenals, and liver. It is also an excellent herb to stop excess sweating, as it restores the kidney essence. It is a calming herb, known also to improve memory and vision and to promote sleep. Take in tincture form, 1 ml, three times a day.

Chaste Tree Berry (Vitex agnus-casti)

- Chaste tree berry can help to remedy a progesterone deficiency when used long term. As the transition into menopause begins with a drop in progesterone, this herb will ease related symptoms, such as mood swings, breast swelling, disinterest in sex, and irregular periods.
- *Dose:* Tincture form, 1 ml taken 3x daily. Chaste tree berry should not be used during pregnancy.

Astragalus

- Astragalus tonifies the blood, and is helpful for women who are experiencing heavy menstrual bleeding in the perimenopausal years. It improves energy and stamina and stops excess perspiration. It supports the immune system and is a very safe herb to use long term.
- *Dose:* Tincture form, 1 ml taken 3 times daily.

Valerian

- Valerian restores the nervous system by alleviating depression and anxiety and promotes sleep. It smooths out the irritability that often accompanies menopause, and modulates two yin neurotransmitters that, when imbalanced, may contribute to hot flashes – serotonin and GABA. It also tonifies the kidney yin.
- *Dose:* Tincture form, 1 ml, twice daily.

Motherwort

- Motherwort releases tension caused by emotional and mental stress, relaxes the heart and reduces anxiety, irritability, palpitations and insomnia. It increases blood flow through the coronary arteries and helps to lower blood pressure. It is contraindicated during pregnancy.
- *Dose:* Tincture form, up to 3 ml, daily.

St. John's Wort

- St. John's wort is an herbal antidepressant and increases the activity of both serotonin and GABA, the relaxing (yin) neurotransmitters, in the brain. It helps to relieve menstrual pain, muscle tension, headaches and promotes sound sleep.
- Dose: Tablet form, 300 mg, 3 times daily; tincture form, 1 ml, 3 times daily. Do not use St. John's wort when you are out in the sun – it may cause an easy sunburn — if you are currently taking an SSRI anti-depressant, or during chemotherapy.

HOMEOPATHIC REMEDIES FOR HOT FLASHES

Combination Therapies

Try one of the following combinations that have been developed to address hot flashes.

- Sepia plex (Unda): 5 drops taken 3x daily or as needed with a hot flash
- Klimakt-Heel (Heel): 1 tablet dissolved under the tongue 3x daily
- Dr. Reckeweg R10: 10-15 drops taken 3-6x daily
- Klifem (Pekana): 15 drops 3x daily

Single Therapies

Hot flashes can completely resolve using a single homeopathic remedy that is prescribed after evaluating your physical and emotional health on all levels. Select them based on your indications.

- **Sepia:** tends to be chilly during the day and when going to bed, but hot at night. Hot flashes at night with drenching sweats followed by chilliness. Fatigue and irritability during the day. Bladder leakage from coughing, laughing or sneezing. Craving for vinegar and sour things. Involuntary crying, particularly before her period.

- **Lachesis mutus:** always feels hot but has cold extremities. Intense hot flashes around the head and neck. Intolerance to scarves, turtlenecks or anything around the neck or waist. Hot flashes at night or upon waking. Hot flashes before menstrual period. Purplish color to the face. May be passionate, intense, suspicious, jealous.

- **Pulsatilla:** hot flashes when anxious or upset. Needs fresh air, open windows, feels better outdoors. Aggravated by heat. Hot flashes may be worse before bed or between 2-4 p.m. Headaches occur at the end of the menstrual period. Craves creamy foods, generally not thirsty.

- **Belladonna:** flushed face, sudden intense hot flash, with throbbing. Dry throat and mouth, with either great thirst for cold water or aversion to drinking. Menstrual flow is hot, breasts may be swollen and hot before her period. Palpitations in the heart from the least exertion. Feet may be icy cold.

- **Ferrum metallicum:** pale face alternating with easy flushing from emotions or exertion; coldness of the extremities. General weakness and tendency to anemia. Tendency to obesity. Irritable, gets excited and argues easily. Hot flashes may be worse at midnight. Involuntary urination.

- **Sanguinaria:** intense heat and redness of the face with throbbing sensations all over the body. Red, burning cheeks. Hot flashes associated with headache, rushing of blood to the head, or humming in the ears. Very thirsty.

- **Glonoine:** hot flashes with sensation that head will burst, flushed and sweaty face, pulsating carotid artery in neck. May feel pounding in the heart with high blood pressure. Feels pulsation throughout the body, throbbing in the head. Irritable. Dizzy on standing.

- **Calcarea carbonica:** feels hot and sweaty with the least activity, but the skin may feel cold and clammy to the touch. Sweating on the head, scalp and back of the neck, mostly at night. Tendency to be pale with easy weight gain and a lack of stamina – gets out of breath easily. Underactive thyroid. Periods may be too early, heavy and long. Feet are cold at night, wears socks to bed.

- **Sulfur:** always feels warm, excessive sweat with a strong odor. Uncovers feet at night due to excess heat. Tendency to skin symptoms and eczema, which may be worse after a shower.

DID YOU KNOW ...

Hot flashes enable your body to discharge toxins (previously shed during monthly bleeding) through perspiration. This may protect you from diseases related to toxicity, heavy metals, and chemicals (such as Alzheimer's and Parkinson's diseases) later in life. Use your hot flashes to detoxify.

Detoxify and Rejuvenate

- Detoxify the liver. See the Seasonal Cleansing and Rejuvenation section for guidelines.
- Cleanse the bowel by consuming 45 grams of fiber, using a probiotic, and taking 1 tbsp. of psyllium seed powder daily. Make sure you have two to three bowel movements daily.
- Use homeopathic drainage: Unda 10, Unda 16, and Unda 1000 for the menopausal transition period to balance hormones, 5 drops of each, taken 3x daily, for 3 weeks of each month.

Integrate Body, Mind, and Spirit

- Acknowledge your feelings. If you experience anger, use it to reclaim part of your sleeping self, to push you out of submissiveness to a boss, a husband, or a family member, or to begin a new course of study, career or project. Identify the source of your anger and what it would take to resolve it, rather than suppressing or medicating it.
- Release the past. To move forward to this next phase of your life, you need to let go of old resentment, guilt, or regret, and make peace with your past. In doing so, you create more space for your future.
- Revitalize your sexual self. Your sexual needs may increase or decrease as you near menopause, and some women find that their sexual preference changes at this time. Find ways to rediscover your sexual nature and to give and receive pleasure. See the information on Vaginal Dryness in this chapter, if this is an issue for you.

MENOPAUSAL BALANCE AND HOT FLASH FORMULA

This formula addresses menopausal symptoms of hot flashes, excess perspiration, adrenal fatigue, kidney yin and yang deficiency, bladder weakness, depression, anxiety, palpitations, breast swelling and insomnia. Purchase the herbs separately in tincture form and mix them up in the appropriate ratios.

- **40%** Black cohosh
- **20%** Chaste tree berry
- **20%** Schizandra
- **10%** Astragalus
- **10%** St. John's wort
- **5%** Valerian
- **5%** Motherwort

Dose: 1 tsp 3 times daily, taken between meals.

Conventional Medicine

Hormone Replacement Therapy

Natural Progesterone Cream

- Using natural progesterone cream for treating hot flashes has received mixed reviews. One study of 102 postmenopausal women applying ½ tsp progesterone cream (containing 20 mg progesterone) or placebo daily for 1 year found a significant improvement in hot flashes in the treated group. However, eight women treated with the progesterone cream experienced some vaginal bleeding, and one woman experienced thickening of the uterine endometrial lining. Another 3-month study of 80 postmenopausal women compared the use of 32 mg progesterone cream daily with a placebo cream and found no change in hot flashes, mood, sexual feelings, or bone density from use of the cream. For these reasons, we recommend the Restore Balance therapies above first for treating hot flashes.

Conjugated Estrogens

- Conjugated estrogens with or without progestin (synthetic progesterone) alleviate hot flashes but may increase risk of heart attacks, stroke, deep vein thrombosis, pulmonary embolism, gallbladder disease, breast cancer, vaginal bleeding, and weight gain. Other adverse effects of HRT include headache, nausea, water retention, phlebitis, breast tenderness, and irritability.

Medications

In addition to SSRI antidepressants (such as venlafaxine) and antihypertensive medications (such as clonidine), Gabapentin is prescribed for hot flashes.

Gabapentin

- This anti-seizure medication resembles the neurotransmitter GABA. It has no estrogenic defect, no effect on the liver, and is excreted solely through the kidneys. It may be a particularly useful therapy for women with a history of breast cancer if natural health treatments are unsuccessful.

DID YOU KNOW ...

In several clinical trials, Gabapentin was found to reduce hot flash frequency by about 44%, severity by 53%, and duration by 74% after 4 weeks when 300 mg was taken 3 times daily.

TOP 5 STRATEGIES

1. Chinese herbal formula to balance the underlying condition, most often a kidney yin deficiency. Use Chih Pai Pa Wei Wan or Rehmannia and Scrophularia formula.
2. Black cohosh, alone or in the Menopause Balance and Hot Flash Formula.
3. Practice slow, long, deep breathing through the left nostril for 20 minutes twice daily.
4. Exercise 40 minutes a day.
5. Follow the Women's Health Diet Plan.

CASE STUDY: *HOT FLASH RELIEF*

Gloria was feeling exhausted from having drenching hot flashes every 2 hours through the night and several times during the day. Vaginal dryness made intercourse painful. She was increasingly short-tempered with the Grade 8 students she taught and had difficulty concentrating on her lesson plans. She noticed her memory was going, and it bothered her. There was a gnawing feeling of dissatisfaction inside her, which she found difficult to articulate.

We explained to Gloria the link between hot flashes and kidney yin deficiency and stressed the need for relaxation, as well as exercise. She began to do left nostril breathing nightly before bed and made a point of walking for 40 minutes every morning before going in to work. She also cut out coffee. We also discussed the connection between certain prostaglandins, foods, and hot flashes, and had her decrease meat and dairy, replacing them with beans and tofu. She began to use ground flaxseeds, seaweeds, turmeric, and flaxseed oil regularly in her diet. We also encouraged her to drink 2 liters of water a day. She found her irritability improved with this.

We recommended the Chinese herbal formula Rehmannia and Scrophularia, 3 pills taken 3 times daily, along with vitamin E, 800 IU daily. Within a month, Gloria's hot flashes had gone, her sleep was much improved, and she had less vaginal dryness.

Insomnia, Anxiety, and Depression

The sleeplessness induced by hot flashes and yin deficiency may intensify anxiety and depression for some women. As the forces of yin and yang play tug of war during menopause, hormones fluctuate, neurotransmitters adjust, our sleep changes, and some of us swing through moods of depression, anxiety, panic, and irritability. There may be some unfinished business tucked away in our psyche bubbling to the surface for us to resolve. Stress may be the common denominator causing both hot flashes and mood changes.

The causes of insomnia, anxiety, depression, panic, and irritability are, for the most part, the same as the causes of hot flashes described previously. Women with depression are more symptomatic during times of hormonal transition – puberty, pregnancy, after childbirth, and during the menopausal years. The thyroid and adrenal glands are called upon to adjust to fluctuating hormone levels and need support.

Prevention and Treatment

Improve Nutrition
In addition to following the Women's Health Diet Plan (Section 2), try these nutritional strategies:

> **DID YOU KNOW ...**
>
> Research shows that women who experience hot flashes in the perimenopausal years are more prone to anxiety and depression than postmenopausal women.
>
> **DID YOU KNOW ...**
>
> One study found that women who for 2 months took a morning formula containing panax ginseng, black cohosh, soy and green tea extracts, as well as an evening formula containing black cohosh, soy, kava, hops and valerian, had a reduction in hot flashes, anxiety, and depression by 50%, 56%, and 32%, respectively.

NUTRIENT SUPPLEMENTS

- **To alleviate depression:** use vitamin B complex (50 mg), B-6 (100 mg), B-12 (500 mcg) folic acid (2 mg).

- **To help with sleep and anxiety:** use calcium citrate (1200 mg) and magnesium citrate (600 mg), in divided doses including before bed.

- **For anxiety, depression, and insomnia:** use 5-HTP (100 mg) twice daily with food.

- **For insomnia, irritability, and forgetfulness:** use the Chinese herbs schizandra and zizyphis, mixed in equal parts, 40 drops, twice daily, or 2 cups tea daily.

- **For general symptoms:** use 2 tbsp unheated flaxseed oil; uncontaminated fish oil (3000 mg); black cohosh (Remifemin 40 mg) twice daily; St. John's wort (300 mg) 3 times daily; and Menopausal Balance and Hot Flash Formula.

Restore Balance

- To decrease anxiety and increase serotonin and endorphins: exercise at least 3 times a week for a total of 4 or more hours
- To balance the hypothalamus and glands: meditate for 20 minutes before bed.
- To decrease anxiety and balance hormones: use homeopathic Unda 9, Unda 10, and Unda 16, 5 drops of each, 3 times daily, for 3 weeks of each month.
- To decrease anxiety: use *Tilia tomentosa* gemmotherapy, 40 drops, 3 times daily.
- Expose yourself to sunlight or bright full spectrum light 1 hour each morning.
- Laugh each day for 10 minutes – you'll be happier for it.
- Consult with Chinese medicine and homeopathic medicine practitioners for balancing herbs, acupuncture, and constitutional remedies.
- Restore adrenal and thyroid function and balance. See the Hormone Balance chapter in the Living with Nature's Rhythms section and the Hypothyroidism chapter in this section.

Detoxify and Rejuvenate

- Cleanse the liver with milk thistle, dandelion, and turmeric. See the Seasonal Cleansing and Rejuvenation Program section for guidelines.
- Cleanse the bowel with 1 tbsp psyllium seed powder daily and 2 capsules of *Lactobacillus acidophilus* and *Bifidobacterium bifidus*. See the Seasonal Cleansing and Rejuvenation section for guidelines.

HERBAL FORMULA FOR INSOMNIA, ANXIETY, AND DEPRESSION

30% St. John's wort (*Hypericum perfoliatum*)

20% Siberian ginseng (*Eleutherococcus senticosus*)

20% Motherwort (*Leonurus cardiaca*)

20% Schizandra (*Schisandrae chinensis*)

10% Valerian (*Valerian officinalis*)

Dose: Mix together the above tinctures and use 30-50 drops, 3 times daily. Do not use during pregnancy.

Integrate Body, Mind, and Spirit

- Plan wonderful things for the years ahead – courses to take, friends to visit, places to travel, hobbies to pursue.
- Envision your ideal future each day.
- Support or volunteer for a cause or organization to add meaning to your life.
- Become spiritually connected to develop serenity – prayer, service, worship.

Conventional Medicine

Hormone Replacement Therapy

The value of HRT for treating anxiety and depression of menopause has received mixed reviews. A study of 152 postmenopausal women over 12 months found that although estradiol (HRT) relieved their hot flashes, it had no effect on anxiety and depression, while other studies have found estradiol to be effective.

Drug Therapy

Use pharmaceuticals as needed if the above natural regimen is not sufficient.

TOP 5 STRATEGIES

1. Use vitamin B complex, B-6, B-12, folic acid, fish oil, and calcium-magnesium.
2. Use 5-HTP.
3. Exercise 40 minutes daily, preferably outdoors in natural light.
4. Use the Herbal Formula for Insomnia, Anxiety, and Depression.
5. Meditate for 20 minutes before bed.

Vaginal Dryness (During Menopause)

Two-thirds of women over 75 experience vaginal dryness and pain with sexual intercourse. Nevertheless, sex is good for us because it stimulates mucus secretion, keeping the vagina moist. The logical solution is to remain sexually active before and after menopause! Sex can be comfortable at any age.

As estrogen levels decline during menopause, the cell layers that line our vaginas become thinner and more sensitive to irritation. Our vaginas before menopause have a pH of 4.0, whereas after menopause the pH is about 6.0, making the environment less acidic. *Lactobacilli*, the friendly acid-producing guardian bacteria that normally inhabit the vagina, decrease in number after menopause, and we become more vulnerable to vaginal infections. The mucus-producing glands of the vagina atrophy and we have less lubrication. Sex, for some women, is painful.

Prevention and Treatment

Improve Nutrition

In addition to following the Women's Health Diet Plan (Section 2), try these dietary and supplement strategies.

Diet

- Eat 2 tbsp of freshly ground flaxseeds daily for their friendly phytoestrogens.
- Drink red raspberry leaf tea twice daily.

NUTRIENT SUPPLEMENTS

- **To nourish vaginal tissues:** mix equal parts of *Tang Kuei*, black cohosh, nettle and saw palmetto tinctures, and use 30 drops orally, 3 times daily, for 3–6 months.

- **To heal dry irritated tissues:** use vitamin E mixed tocopherols (800 IU), vitamin A (25,000 IU), zinc picolinate (50 mg) orally.

- **To raise levels of essential fatty acids:** use flaxseed oil (2 tbsp), clean fish oil (3000 mg), and evening primrose oil (1000 mg) .

- **To nourish and lubricate:** apply almond oil with vitamin E vaginally before bed.

- **To heal irritated vaginal tissues:** apply calendula cream morning and evening.

- **To increase *Lactobacilli*:** apply candigen cream (Genestra) vaginally.

- Take *Lactobacillus acidophilus* (oral capsules or powdered) once daily.

Restore Balance

- Practice Kegels exercises to improve muscle tone and blood circulation to the vagina and bladder. These are fun to practice with music that has a great beat. See the Seasonal Cleansing and Rejuvenation Program section for guidelines.
- *Rubus idaeus* (red raspberry shoot) gemmotherapy, 50 drops twice daily.
- Homeopathic Vagininum 4CH, 10 drops or 3 pellets 2x a day, 3 weeks on, 1 week off.
- Wear cotton or silk underwear; avoid nylon.
- Avoid soaps, douches, and bubblebaths.
- In TCM, vaginal dryness is due to kidney yin deficiency with accompanying heat. Use *Zhi Bai Di Huang Wan Jia Jian* or *Rehmannia & Scrophularia* or *Temper Fire* or *Anemarrhena, Phellodendron & Rehmannia*.

HOMEOPATHIC REMEDIES FOR VAGINAL DRYNESS

Several homeopathic remedies may help with vaginal dryness, but are best prescribed by a homeopath based on your totality of symptoms. Match your indications with the remedy.

- **Nat mur:** involuntary urination when walking, coughing, or laughing; sadness and weepiness, but worse with consolation; craving for salt; vagina is dry, may be raw, red, inflamed; may be history of cold sores.

- **Sepia:** uterine prolapse and sensation as if it would fall out; feel chilly; hot flashes; irritable and indifferent to those she loves; morning nausea; craves vinegar; vaginal itching; aversion to sex; vaginal pain during intercourse.

- **Lycopodium:** burning in vagina with discharge; craves sweet; gassy from beans and bread; prefers warm food and drinks; low self-confidence; usually thin and dry physique.

- **Platina:** vaginal itching, tingling, hypersensitive to touch; may be proud and arrogant; contempt for others; high sex drive; nausea; gassy; feels better when walking.

- **Arsenicum album:** burning, scorching vaginal pain; worse with exertion; thirsty, drinks many frequent sips; restlessness, anxiety, fear of being alone and of death.

- **Graphites**: aversion to sex; pale profuse white vaginal discharge; dryness and cracking of skin with fissures, eczema and sticky discharges; indecisive; cries when hearing music.

- **Sulphur:** vaginal burning and itching, worse after bathing; feels hot, sticks feet out of covers at night; selfish and untidy; craves spicy and sweet foods; history of eczema.

Integrate Body, Mind, and Spirit

- Keep your sex life alive with romance, spontaneity, cuddling, and experimentation.
- Vaginal lubrication responds to your thoughts and emotions, so indulge!
- Use an affirmation, such as *I nourish my sexual and sensual nature,* and then live it.

Conventional Medicine

Estriol Cream

Estriol is a safe, weak estrogen that is protective against breast cancer. It significantly improves vaginal dryness, makes sex enjoyable, and decreases bladder and vaginal infections. Your doctor can prescribe it and a compounding pharmacist can make it. Use at a dose of 0.5mg/g of cream. Insert 1 g nightly for 2 weeks, then twice weekly for 8 months.

Conjugated Estrogens

Conjugated estrogen (Premarin) and estradiol (Estrace) are available in vaginal creams or in a tablet called Vagifem. Estring is a silicone-based ring impregnated with estrogen that fits in the vagina like a diaphragm and must be replaced every 3 months. While these products work, they can cause side effects of vaginal discharge and may stimulate overgrowth of the uterine lining.

TOP 5 STRATEGIES

1. Use vitamin E.
2. Keep your sex life alive.
3. Practice Kegels exercises.
4. Use estriol cream.
5. Use Chinese herbs.

Conscious Conception

Our collective future depends on how well we prepare for conception physically, environmentally, nutritionally, emotionally, and spiritually. Here are three steps to follow in preparing for conception so that you and your partner can have a healthy child.

Prevention and Preparation

Improve Nutrition
In additional to following the Women's Health Diet Plan (Section 2), use the following foods and supplements to boost your nutrition so you can strengthen yourself and nourish the fetus:

Diet
- Be sure to eat 8 servings of fruits and vegetables daily for adequate vitamins, minerals, and antioxidants.
- Eat almonds, sunflower seeds, and pumpkin seeds regularly for minerals.
- Eat organic food for a year before conceiving.
- Use only extra-virgin olive oil and unheated flaxseed oil in your food.

Nutrient Supplements
- Use a multivitamin and mineral formula daily, along with extra folic acid (800 mcg), calcium (800 mg), and magnesium (400 mg), ideally for a year before conceiving.
- Use uncontaminated fish oil (3000 mg) or marine algae oil daily.

Detoxify and Rejuvenate
Do not conceive until you are free of toxic metals and chemicals. Take the time to cleanse your body to avoid any risk to the fetus.

Toxic Metals
- Check your body burden of toxic metals with a 6-hour provoked urine test and spend at least 4 months doing a metal cleanse before retesting. See the Seasonal Cleansing and Rejuvenation Program section for guidelines.
- Remove sources of metal toxicity from your environment — for example, pressure-treated wood.
- Remove any mercury amalgam fillings in your teeth and detoxify for mercury.

DID YOU KNOW ...

You can stay metal free by taking on a daily basis vitamin C (2000 mg), vitamin E mixed tocopherols (400 IU), zinc (50 mg), selenium (200 mcg), alpha lipoic acid (200 mg), NAC (500 mg), a multivitamin, and regular coriander, as well as eating an alkaline diet.

DID YOU KNOW ...

Brominated fire retardants, often found in household dust, cross the placenta in utero and are present in the same concentration in the fetal placenta as they are in the mother.

Toxic Chemicals

- Check your body burden of toxic chemicals by testing blood for levels of organochlorine pesticides, brominated fire retardants, and PCBs. Do a 100-hour sauna detox before conception and then retest. See the Seasonal Cleansing and Rejuvenation Program section for guidelines.
- Remove carpets and foam from your home before conception. Use furnishings that will not trap dust.
- Do not use pesticides around your home, and encourage your neighbors and community to do the same.
- Avoid chemical hair dyes and cosmetics containing lead, phthalates, and parabens,
- Refrain from smoking, drinking alcohol, using recreational drugs, and drinking coffee for 3 months before trying to conceive.
- Reduce your levels of dioxins, PCBs, PBDEs, pesticides, phthalates, and bisphenol-A by:
  - Avoiding or minimizing fish, beef, pork, dairy fat, ideally for 3 years, before conceiving
  - Not eating food stored in Styrofoam or plastic – store food in glass
  - Avoiding canned food (most cans are lined with bisphenol-A)
  - Not using aluminum cookware – use stainless steel or glass

Integrate Body, Mind, and Spirit

- Exercise 40 minutes daily for 3 months before conceiving.
- Develop a meditation practice and/or a daily time for prayer with your partner, even if it's only for 5 minutes.
- Surround yourself with people who are uplifting, well-meaning, and positive, and remove yourself from negative people and environments.
- If you live a fast-paced, stressful life, slow down and reduce stress.
- Develop a regular yoga practice to build a flexible, relaxed body, and mental calmness.
- Develop a feeling of receptivity toward having a child, rather than pushing to make it happen.
- Talk with your partner about how you will raise a child – sort out differences. Will you expose your child to a particular religious tradition, will your child be vegetarian, will your child, if a boy, be circumcised, will your child be immunized? And so on.
- Resolve areas of conflict in your relationship before conceiving.
- Address issues from your family of origin so your child enters a harmonious extended family environment.

Infertility

If you have been having difficulty conceiving, natural therapies may be of help. For pregnancy to occur, three obvious steps must follow one another: 1) a sperm must be available; 2) an egg must be available; and 3) the sperm has to meet the egg at a time and place conducive to fertilization. Though this sounds simple, there can be many glitches in the process.

Common Causes

- Ovulation problems (eggs not being released from the ovarian follicles, as in amenorrhea and polycystic ovary syndrome)
- Blocked fallopian tubes
- Cervical mucus problems
- Sperm problems

Tests for Infertility

The first thing for an infertile couple to figure out is where the problem lies.

Women

Tests to determine cause of infertility include medical history and physical examination, as well as a protocol of questions that leads to further tests.

Protocol

1. Is there a hormonal imbalance?
- Underactive thyroid. Start with the basal body temperature test, and if your temperature is consistently below 36.6°C or 97.8°F, follow through with thyroid function blood tests. You may need the more involved TRH stimulation test to confirm subtle hypothyroidism.
- Low estrogen (check in blood or saliva)
- Low progesterone (check in blood or saliva)
- High prolactin (check in blood)

2. Is ovulation occurring?
- Basal body temperature chart to look for a temperature rise at ovulation. See Birth Control chapter in this section for guidelines.
- Ultrasound monitoring of the ovaries at ovulation time
- Levels of luteinizing hormone, which stimulates ovulation
- Progesterone levels between day 20 to 23 of menstrual cycle
- Uterine biopsy

DID YOU KNOW ...

Infertility is defined as the inability to conceive a child after having regular unprotected intercourse for a full year. In North America, about one in every five or six heterosexual couples is infertile.

DID YOU KNOW ...

In women, 15% to 20% of the time infertility is due to a problem with ovulation, 15% to 40% of the time there is a blockage in the fallopian tubes, and 5% of the time there is a problem with cervical mucus.

DID YOU KNOW...

A hysterosalpingogram (who can say it?) is an X-ray of the uterus and fallopian tubes that is taken after your period. It may show a defect from birth of the uterus or fallopian tubes, uterine fibroids, or adhesions in the uterus, fallopian tubes, or pelvis. A laparoscopy may be performed using a small viewing tube inserted through an abdominal incision to view the uterus, fallopian tubes, and ovaries.

3. **Are your fallopian tubes blocked? Is your uterus normal? Check for:**
   - Infection (pelvic inflammatory disease)
   - Congenital abnormality
   - Previous ectopic pregnancy may rupture tubes
   - Previously ruptured appendix
   - History of other lower abdominal surgery may block tubes 67% to 93% of the time
   - Endometriosis, implants, adhesions, scarring
   - Tubal ligation
   - Uterine fibroids

4. **Is your cervical mucus friendly to sperm? Check for:**
   - Cervical mucus is inhospitable to sperm when examined around the time of ovulation, after intercourse
   - Cervical mucus is overly thick
   - No sperm are present in mucus
   - Mucus contains antibodies to sperm, causing them to clump together

5. **Are there any emotional factors that may be causing subtle hormonal imbalances?**

Men
To rule out a problem with the male, a semen analysis is done to look for:
   - Infection (for example, chlamydia) in the genitourinary tract
   - Sperm count (lowered by smoking, alcohol, marijuana, environmental pollutants)
   - Sperm motility
   - Number of abnormal sperm

STOP SMOKING

Cigarette smoking makes it three times more difficult to conceive. See the Seasonal Cleansing and Rejuvenation Program section for stop smoking guidelines.

Smoking can:
   - Damage the cervical mucus and the tiny hairs known as cilia that coax the egg down the fallopian tube
   - Decrease the number and viability of eggs
   - Cause an earlier menopause, fewer fertile years
   - Increase risk of ectopic pregnancy
   - Increase risk of miscarriage
   - Increase possibility of fallopian tube infection

- Antibodies to sperm
- Intact sperm cell membranes
- Ability of sperm to bind to an egg and penetrate inside

Prevention and Treatment

Address Causes

- If you are infertile because you are not ovulating, follow the guidelines in the Amenorrhea or Polycystic Ovary chapters in this section to get your body back on track.
- If you are having trouble conceiving because of endometriosis, follow the suggestions in the Endometriosis chapter in this section.
- If your fallopian tubes are blocked, use castor oil packs nightly over them. See the Seasonal Cleansing and Rejuvenation Program section for guidelines. Use the remedies to break up scar tissue listed in the Endometriosis chapter in this section.
- If you have an allergic reaction to your partner's semen, your body may be too acidic. Check your pH, and if overly acidic, use alkaline powder and an alkaline diet. See the Food as Medicine and Seasonal Cleansing and Rejuvenation Program sections for guidelines.
- If you have been on the birth control pill and your cycles are irregular, use the supplements listed in the Birth Control chapter of this section to regulate them.

Improve Nutrition

In addition to following the Women's Health Diet Plan (Section 2), use the following supplements, along with a good multivitamin or prenatal vitamin and magnesium formula (1000 mg) to enhance fertility:

- Nutritional deficiencies of folic acid, iron, zinc, vitamin B6, and iodine can cause infertility.

DID YOU KNOW ...

A massage therapy called the Wurn Technique (SM) is designed to break down scar tissue and adhesions by stretching tightened areas for a sustained period until tension is released, creating elongation of tissues and improved movement.

DID YOU KNOW ...

Together with Chinese herbs, acupuncture can be very effective in helping a woman conceive. In one study of 106 non-ovulating infertile women, 41 conceived after a series of acupuncture treatments.

HERBAL REGIMEN TO BALANCE MENSTRUAL CYCLE

- From the end of the menstrual period to ovulation: use false unicorn root (*Chamaelirium luteum*), tang kuei (*Angelica sinensis*), and red clover (*Trifolium pratense*).

- From ovulation until the period begins: use chaste tree berry (*Vitex agnus casti*) and tang kuei (*Angelica sinensis*).

Infertility

NUTRIENT THERAPY FOR INFERTILITY		
NUTRIENT	**ACTION**	**DOSE**
UNCONTAMINATED FISH OIL	Needed for glandular balance	3000 mg, daily
VITAMIN B-6	Normalizes progesterone	100 mg, daily
VITAMIN B-12	Prevents anemia Needed for thyroid	6 mg, daily
FOLIC ACID	Improves fertility Prevents birth defects	800 mcg, daily
VITAMIN C	Improves ovarian function Needed for smokers	1,000-3,000 mg, daily
VITAMIN E MIXED TOCOPHEROLS	Can prevent miscarriage	400 IU, daily
IRON	Prevents anemia	18 mg, daily
MAGNESIUM	Relaxant prevents spasm of fallopian tube	400 mg, daily
SELENIUM	Needed for healthy thyroid function	200 mcg, daily
ZINC	Protects against heavy metal toxicity	30 mg, daily
KELP (IODINE)	Needed by the ovaries and thyroid	1,500 mg, daily
PABA	Increases pregnancies in 75% of infertile women	100 mg, 4 times daily
L-ARGININE	Improves fertilization rates	800-1,600 mg, daily

DID YOU KNOW ...

Continued exposure to electromagnetic fields higher than 16 mG increases miscarriage risk. Check your environment with a gauss meter. Decrease mobile phone use before conceiving and during pregnancy.

Restore Balance

- Sleep in a dark room at night. Walk outside in the sunlight (without sunglasses) for at least 20 minutes a day to increase melatonin and balance body rhythms.
- Balance the vaginal flora with 2 capsules of *Lactobacillus acidophilus* taken orally.
- Support the adrenal glands with the gemmotherapy *Ribes nigrum,* 40 drops, 3 times daily.
- Switch from coffee to nettle, red raspberry, and red clover tea, which enhances fertility. Caffeine adversely affects fertility.
- Reduce exposure to air and water pollutants, pesticides, household and industrial chemicals, solvents, pesticides,

radiation, and heavy metals, including lead, mercury, arsenic, and cadmium, which increase free radical formation that damages our precious eggs.

- Use meditation to relax. Stress can cause the fallopian tubes to contract.
- Take extra folic acid and vitamin B-6. These nutrients balance elevated levels of homocysteine, which can cause miscarriage.

HOMEOPATHIC REMEDIES FOR INFERTILITY

- To improve drainage of reproductive organs: Use Unda 10, Unda 21, Unda 243, and Unda 48, taking 5 drops of each, 3x daily, for 3 weeks of the month. These will help to clear toxins.
- To regulate hormones: Use Unda 10, Unda 16, and Unda 1000, 5 drops each, 3x daily during the following month.

Alternate these two regimens from one month to the next. They are fine to take in pregnancy.

Detoxify and Rejuvenate

- Eliminate heavy metals. This can improve conception in previously infertile women.
- Eliminate chemicals. Complete a 100-hour sauna detox program before conceiving. Women with higher levels of the pesticide DDT or its metabolites, DDE and DDD, are less likely to conceive. See the Seasonal Cleansing and Rejuvenation Program section for guidelines.
- Use the gemmotherapies *Rubus idaeus* and Rosemarinus, 50 drops of each, 3 times daily, while trying to conceive. Stop the Rosemarinus once you are pregnant.

DID YOU KNOW ...

Dental personnel exposed to mercury vapor have rates of infertility, stillbirths, and miscarriages 3.5 times the average.

Integrate Body, Mind, and Spirit

- Acknowledge your feelings around having a child. It is normal to have reservations or feel ambivalent. Are you afraid of the birthing process? Are you feeling uncomfortable about the changes that will occur in your body during pregnancy — or in your independence afterward? Are you insecure in your relationship and worry that it may not last? Are you holding on to grief or loss from the past? Talk about your feelings openly with your partner.
- Allowing rather than pushing. Conception is an act of receiving and openness, not an act of pushing or forcing. Pregnancy and giving birth bring with them remarkable shifts in consciousness for women. One of the great lessons learned is to trust your body and the flow of life.

HERBAL REMEDIES

Herbs that tone the uterus, preparing it for implantation of a fertilized egg:

- Tang kuei (*Angelica sinensis*)
- Blue cohosh (*Caulophyllum thalictroides*)
- Crampbark (*Viburnum opulus*)
- False unicorn (*Chamalerium luteum*)
- Squaw vine (*Mitchella repens*)
- Red raspberry (*Rubus idaeus*)

Other nourishing herbs:

- Red clover (*Trifolium pratense*): nourishes blood; detoxifies; contains calcium, magnesium, protein, vitamin B complex, and vitamin C
- Nettle (*Urtica dioica*): blood tonic rich in trace minerals, balances hormones

Herbal Formula for Enhancing Fertility

- 25% chaste tree berry (*Vitex agnus casti*)
- 25% tang kuei (*Angelica sinensis*)
- 25% red clover (*Trifolium pratense*)
- 25% red raspberry (*Rubus idaeus*)

Dose: Mix the herbal tinctures together in equal parts and take 30 drops, 3 times daily. Do not use chaste tree berry or tang kuei during pregnancy.

DID YOU KNOW ...

If natural methods have not worked to help you conceive, then conventional medicine may assist you: 80% of cases of infertility are treated with drugs or surgery. Multiple births occur in 10% to 20% of cases of fertility drug use.

- Meditate for 20 minutes, twice daily, to relax.
- Use affirmations:

> *I am a creative, sensual, fertile, sexual being who can nourish others while taking care of my own needs.*
> *I am receptive to a soul incarnating through me, if it be Thy will.*
> *The creative energy of the universe gives birth through me, and I accept.*

Conventional Medicine

Fertility Drugs

- Fertility drugs, such as Clomid, can be used, followed by intercourse or injection of sperm.
- Bromocriptine is a drug used for women with elevated prolactin levels.

Surgery

- Surgery on the ovaries, fallopian tubes, or uterus may be necessary to remove scar tissue.

In Vitro Fertilization

- In vitro fertilization may be necessary for some couples if the fallopian tubes are blocked. Fertility drugs are given to stimulate the ovaries to produce multiple eggs. The mature eggs are suctioned from the ovary and carefully placed in a laboratory culture dish with male sperm for fertilization, and then placed in an incubator. About two days later, three to five embryos are transferred to the woman's uterus. If pregnancy does not occur, the process may be repeated the following month.

TOP 5 STRATEGIES

1. Use acupuncture and Chinese herbs.
2. Use vitamin B-6, B-12, C, E, folic acid, PABA.
3. Eliminate heavy metals and chemicals.
4. Use the Herbal Formula for Enhancing Fertility.
5. Meditate for 20 minutes, twice daily.

Birth Control

As sexually active women, we have a responsibility to ourselves, future offspring, and the planet to take charge of our fertility, with or without our partner's cooperation, so that pregnancy, if it occurs, is either a conscious choice or a desirable accident. Do not leave your risk of becoming pregnant to your partner or to chance – this is your body. The consequences of pregnancy will affect you for the rest of your life, whether you have a child or not. Carefully consider the available methods of birth control, weighing such factors as long-term health risks, convenience, effectiveness, comfort, and environmental impact. Barrier methods are the only methods that will protect you from sexually transmitted diseases and decrease your risk of cervical dysplasia.

PROS AND CONS OF BIRTH CONTROL METHODS

METHOD	ADVANTAGES	DISADVANTAGES	PRECAUTIONS
ABSTINENCE	100% effective	No intercourse	
WITHDRAWAL	77%-84% effective Maintains relationship with lunar cycle	Requires discipline and control May decrease sexual fulfillment	Male is in control Woman is victim should pregnancy occur
SYMPTO-THERMO METHOD Relies on charting your menstrual cycle, cervical mucus, morning body temperature, position, texture, and openness of the cervix	90% effective Develops awareness of one's body rhythms Keeps relationship with the lunar cycle Enhances normal body rhythms Freedom from drugs, chemicals, and their side effects No cost No yeast infections	Does not protect against sexually transmitted diseases Need discipline for it to work Passion of the moment may override the method Needs to be combined with barrier methods on fertile days Requires cooperation of sexual partner	Menstrual cycle needs to be regular (cycle can shift with stress, travel, illness, diet, exercise, season)
CONDOM Spermicide is added to the condom material, usually latex, which is pulled over the penis as a barrier	88%-98% effective Easy to use Inexpensive Prevents sexually transmitted diseases Reduces risk of cervical dysplasia by protecting from virus transfer Maintains relationship with lunar cycle	3% failure rate when used properly 14% failure rate when used improperly Best results when used with spermicide Condoms may break Reliance on male partner May decrease spontaneity and sensation	May irritate vagina in some women who have a latex allergy, although other kinds are available

PROS AND CONS OF BIRTH CONTROL METHODS

METHOD	ADVANTAGES	DISADVANTAGES	PRECAUTIONS
DIAPHRAGM WITH SPERMICIDE Barrier that holds spermicide against the cervix to prevent sperm entry	82%-94% effective Can insert up to 6 hours before intercourse Noninvasive Inexpensive Easier to fit and put in than cervical caps Maintains relationship with lunar cycle	6% failure rate when used properly 20% failure rate when used improperly Must be initially fitted by health professional Must leave in for 8 hours after intercourse Need to reapply spermicide to have intercourse a second time Increases urinary tract infections Does not prevent STDs May be uncomfortable Need to insert	Higher failure rate if you have sex more than 3 times weekly
CERVICAL CAP Barrier designed to hold spermicide against the cervix to prevent sperm entry	82%-94% effective Can insert 30 minutes to 48 hours before intercourse Inexpensive Good for women who have frequent sex, as it can be left in for 48 hours Maintains relationship with lunar cycle	May cause vaginal odor and discharge if left in too long May cause trauma to cervix May be difficult to insert and fit properly Risk of toxic shock if cap left in longer than 48 hours	To heal trauma to cervix, use zinc (50 mg), vitamin A (25,000 IU), folic acid (2 gm)
REALITY FEMALE CONDOM Barrier method consisting of a thin polyurethane device that is inserted vaginally and also covers the labia	95% effective Protects against STDs Protects labia Can be inserted up to 8 hours before intercourse Does not need to be removed immediately after intercourse Decreases risk of cervical dysplasia Stronger than latex Feels more natural than a male condom 70% prefer female condom to male condom Woman is in charge of her fertility – more safety and security	Can only use it once Need to practice inserting it several times to become comfortable with it	Must be sure penis enters condom and does not slide between condom and skin

REPRODUCTION

PROS AND CONS OF BIRTH CONTROL METHODS

METHOD	ADVANTAGES	DISADVANTAGES	PRECAUTIONS
IUD Device inserted into the uterus to prevent implantation	97%-99% effective Inexpensive Reversible Lasts 10 years Need no planning	Increased risk of pelvic infection and ectopic pregnancy May cause increased cramping and bleeding Must be inserted by MD If pregnancy occurs, miscarriage can occur in half the cases	Support liver qi with *Xiao Yao Wan*
TUBAL LIGATION Fallopian tubes are cut, tied, or blocked so the egg doesn't make it to the uterus	98% effective Continuous protection	Permanent, though tubes can be surgically reconnected Invasive surgery may cause increased cramps, irregular periods, heavier bleeding Lowers progesterone levels afterward May result in earlier menopause	May disturb liver qi — support liver qi with *Xiao Yao Wan* Use chaste tree berry to increase progesterone, decrease PMS
MALE VASECTOMY Tubes that carry sperm from the testes (vas deferens) are cut	More than 99% effective Continuous protection Less invasive than tubal ligation	Difficult to reverse Invasive surgery May cause bleeding or inflammation Tubes can occasionally reopen spontaneously	A man is not immediately sterile after a vasectomy, only after 15-20 ejaculations, because of sperm stored in the seminal vesicles
BIRTH CONTROL PILL Combination of synthetic estrogen and progestin Used by more than 90 million women worldwide Acts as a carcinogen	99% effective Continuous protection Reversible Decreases risk of ovarian and uterine cancer Decreases anemia Decreases menstrual cramps	Blocks relationship to lunar cycle Needs to be taken daily Increased blood clots, heart attack, stroke, depression, mood swings, nausea, migraines, yeast and chlamydia infections Increased breast and liver cancer risk Increased cervical dysplasia Deficiencies of vitamin B-6, B-1, B-2, B-3, B-12, folic acid	Use high potency B complex, folic acid, zinc, vitamin E, fish oil, flaxseed oil, curcumin, bromelain, Rosemarinus to decrease side effects

PROS AND CONS OF BIRTH CONTROL METHODS			
METHOD	ADVANTAGES	DISADVANTAGES	PRECAUTIONS
NORPLANT IMPLANT CAPSULES Low-dose synthetic progesterone in capsules inserted under the skin of the upper arm while under anesthetic	> 99% effective Don't need to plan protection	Blocks relationship to lunar cycle Cause irregular menses Capsules are removed and replaced every 5 years Difficult to remove in some women	Same as Depo-provera below
DEPO-PROVERA Injection that contains synthetic progesterone that suppresses ovulation and creates thicker cervical mucus that impedes sperm Used by more than 30 million women worldwide	More than 99% effective Continuous protection for up to 5 years Mostly reversible — fertility returns in 70% within 12 months Don't need a daily pill Lowers risk of endometrial cancer	Blocks relationship to lunar cycle Injections by MD required 4 times yearly Stimulates appetite, weight gain, irregular bleeding, depression, irritability, headache May cause diabetes Increases breast cancer risk Suppresses menstruation entirely after 1 year of use, and it can take a year for fertility to resume Bone mineral density decreases after one injection May cause anaphylaxis	Increase exercise to build bone density and use calcium (1200 mg), magnesium (600 mg), boron (3 mg), vitamin D (800 IU), ipriflavone (600 mg) daily To decrease insulin and blood sugar, prevent weight gain and diabetes, use chromium (600 mg), fish oil (3000 mg), flaxseed oil (2 tbsp), alpha lipoic acid (200 mg), niacin (500 mg) daily Avoid sugar, red meat, dairy, alcohol and refined carbohydrates

Natural Birth Control

If young women were taught natural birth control routinely by their mothers or in school and encouraged to practice it, perhaps we would see a shift in the collective consciousness in women and in our relationship to the Earth, as well as a decrease in breast cancer, cervical dysplasia, diabetes, depression, heart disease, stroke and liver cancer in women worldwide. This technique is empowering, increases awareness of one's body, develops a cooperative relationship with one's sexual partner, and enhances our connection to the natural world. We are not dependent on a pharmaceutical company for sexual freedom.

DID YOU KNOW ...

If you do not wish to become pregnant, avoid intercourse on days 5 to 19, or for 7 days before ovulation and 24 hours after ovulation.

Birth Control

- Natural birth control involves ongoing awareness of one's own fertility cycle by charting the onset of menses, changes in cervical mucus leading up to ovulation, morning body temperature, noticing the rise in temperature that occurs just after ovulation, and the condition of the cervix. The observation of changes in vaginal discharge is the most accurate way to predict ovulation.
- This method is useful both in determining when the best time is to conceive and in knowing when it is essential to use barrier methods of birth control.

CHARTING OVULATION

You must determine when ovulation occurs by charting cervical mucus and temperature for the sympto-therm method of birth control to work. If you chart your menstrual cycle for 6 months before relying on this natural birth control method, you will know the shortest and longest number of days within which your cycle occurs. Follow these procedures to determine when you are ovulating during your menstrual cycle.

- When menstruation stops, there is very little cervical mucus. Your cervix feels dry and there is no discharge on your underwear. You are usually not fertile.

- Cervical mucus is apparent about 6 days before ovulation. As estrogen levels rise, the cervical mucus becomes thinner and more alkaline in order to promote transport and survival of sperm. This signals the beginning of your fertile time.

- The cervix becomes softer, more moist, its opening widens, and it rises (is further away) as ovulation approaches. Before and after this time, the cervix is firm, dry, positioned lower in the vagina, easier to reach and its opening feels closed. These changes can be felt by inserting one or two fingers vaginally and feeling the cervix. Be sure to wash your hands thoroughly first.

- An egg is released from a follicle during ovulation, which usually occurs 14 days before your period begins. The luteal, post-ovulation phase of your cycle is usually stable, while the follicular, pre-ovulation phase, can vary in length. It may be affected by stress, travel, illness, and diet.

- Your basal body temperature, taken under your arm, rectally, or orally first thing in the morning before you get out of bed rises 0.6–0.8°F just after ovulation has occurred. This is caused by rising progesterone levels.

- Your fertile time is usually over at the end of the third day in a row of elevated temperature.

- Around ovulation, the cervical mucus is thinnest, very elastic, and will stretch into a long thread — like a raw egg white. The last day of this type of mucus is called your "peak day" of mucus discharge. Ovulation occurs either 2 days before or after this peak day 95% of the time.

- An egg survives for 24 hours and can be fertilized within 24 hours after ovulation.

Sympto-Thermo Method

- Most women's cycles occur every 26 to 32 days, so you can potentially become pregnant between days 5 to 19 of your cycle, although you are unlikely to become pregnant on days 5 to 8.
- You are fertile 7 days before ovulation and 1 day after ovulation for a total of 8 days. Do not have unprotected intercourse during these 8 days.
- You are most fertile 48 hours before ovulation and within 24 hours after ovulation.
- Use male or female condoms if you have intercourse on your fertile days.
- Male or female condoms used in addition to this method will prevent sexually transmitted diseases and decrease risk of HIV and cervical dysplasia.

Oral Contraceptives

Risks

- Affect mood and neurotransmitter levels
- Can increase depression, decrease libido
- May cause hair loss, fatigue, bloating, breast tenderness, breakthrough bleeding
- May elevate blood pressure
- Can elevate liver enzymes
- May lead to weight gain
- Interferes with absorption of vitamin B-1, B-2, B-3, B-6, B-12, C, E, folic acid, zinc, selenium
- Takes an average of 9 months to conceive after stopping the pill
- Affects carbohydrate metabolism
- Increases risk of type 2 diabetes by 60%
- Increases risk of heart disease (5-fold higher risk), stroke (2.75-fold higher risk), pulmonary embolism (10-fold higher), deep venous thrombosis due to increased blood clotting (4-fold higher, breast cancer (if begun before age 20 and used for 5 or more years), cervical cancer (2.5-fold higher), cervical dysplasia, liver cancer (5-fold higher), thyroid cancer (0.5-fold higher), gallbladder disease in young women, inflammatory bowel disease (2-fold higher risk)

Abortion

When birth control methods fail (or when couples ignore them), when women are raped, do not desire a child, or are unable to have a child, some women choose abortion. Children deserve to be wanted, loved, and welcomed into the world, and women deserve the right to choose to proceed with a pregnancy or not, after weighing many factors. If you have chosen to go ahead with an

BIRTH CONTROL PILL HERBAL FORMULAS AND HOMEOPATHIC REMEDIES

If you have come off the pill and your cycles are irregular, consider the following treatments to restore balance.

SUPPLEMENT	DOSE
Xiao Yao Wan or *Bupleurum & Tang Kuei* to regulate liver qi	As directed on bottle for 3 months
Sepia 6 CH to balance hormones	3 pellets, once daily, for 6 weeks or more
Rosemarinus (gemmotherapy) for the liver	50 drops, 3 times daily
Homeopathic Unda 10, Unda 21, and Unda 74 to balance hormones and improve liver drainage	5 drops each, 3 times daily, for 3 weeks of the month for 3 months
Combined homeopathic remedies during your menstrual cycle to balance hormones:	
Day 1: Hypophysinum (pituitary) 200K	3 pellets taken once
Day 7: Folliculinum (estrogen) 200K	3 pellets taken once
Day 14: Ovarinum (ovary) 200K	3 pellets taken once
Day 21: Luteinum (progesterone) 200K	3 pellets taken once

HEALING HERBS, NUTRIENTS, AND REMEDIES

- Zinc: 50 mg once daily, starting 3 days before the abortion procedure and continuing for 1 week afterward to promote healing.
- Vitamin A: 25,000 IU starting 3 days before and continuing for 1 week afterward to promote healing.
- Uncontaminated fish oil: 1000 mg twice daily after the procedure to decrease cramping.
- Calcium and magnesium in a 2:1 ratio: Use 1000 mg daily in divided doses starting 3 days before and continuing for several days afterward to decrease cramping.
- Homeopathic Ignatia 1M: Take 3 pellets of this remedy once daily for a week after the abortion to help release grief.
- Homeopathic Arnica 200CH: 3 pellets before the procedure and 3 pellets every 3 hours after the procedure to decrease bleeding and bruising.
- Homeopathic Bellis perennis 30CH: 3 pellets, 3x daily, for 3 days after the procedure to decrease soreness of the uterus.
- Goldenseal tincture: 20 drops 3 times daily beginning the day before the procedure and continuing for 5 days afterward to prevent infection and reduce bleeding
- Crampbark, pasque flower, and motherwort tincture: Mix these three together in equal parts and use 30 drops every 2-3 hours after the procedure, then 3 times daily for the next 3 days to decrease cramps and promote healing.

BIRTH CONTROL PILL SUPPLEMENTS

If you choose to use the birth control pill despite these risks, take the following supplements to reduce potentially harmful side effects.

SUPPLEMENT	DOSE
Vitamin B-6 (pyridoxine)	100-200 mg, daily
Folic acid	1-2 mg, daily
Vitamin B-12	200-1000 mcg, daily
Vitamin B-1 (thiamine)	30 mg, daily
Vitamin B-2 (riboflavin)	10 mg, daily
Vitamin B-3 (niacin)	15 mg, daily
Vitamin C	1,000 mg, twice daily
Vitamin E mixed tocopherols	400 IU, daily
Zinc	30-50 mg, daily
Selenium	200 mcg, daily
Uncontaminated fish oil	1,000 mg, 3 times daily
Unheated flaxseed oil	2 tbsp, daily
Rosemarinus (gemmotherapy)	50 drops, twice daily
Milk thistle and dandelion tincture	30 drops, 3 times daily
Curcumin	500 mg, 3 times daily
Bromelain	300 mg, twice daily
Freshly ground flaxseed	2-4 tbsp, daily

abortion, or if you have had one in the past, there are some natural remedies and practices that might ease your process.

Integrate Body, Mind, and Spirit

- Communicate to the fetus your feelings about an unwanted pregnancy and your need to end the pregnancy.
- Release any guilt or fear of punishment you experience, and honor your right to choose.
- Find a doctor or clinic that respects women's right to choose and women's dignity.
- Talk to a supportive counselor about your feelings.
- Let yourself feel all your emotions, write them down to work through them.
- If possible, take your partner or a friend with you for support.

DID YOU KNOW ...

Women need to allow time to process all of their feelings after an abortion and release them, especially guilt. Some women fail to do this, and many years later, their bodies create a symptom, usually in the reproductive organs, to remind them of this unfinished emotional work.

Pregnancy

Pregnancy brings us the sacred task of shaping the physical, emotional, and spiritual life of another human being, thus steering the direction of humanity. The spiritual, hormonal, and physical changes that occur during pregnancy allow us to shape-shift internally as well. If we have time for reflection and integration and feel emotionally supported through our pregnancies, our consciousness can mature and transform. If we feel stressed, unsupported, or misunderstood, this opportunity for transformation may be missed. As we transform through pregnancy and childbirth, humanity transforms. The fetus absorbs our thoughts, feelings, and consciousness while in utero.

Fetal Risks

Not only is the fetus reactive to our thoughts and emotions; it is also very sensitive to toxin exposure because of its small body mass and developing organs, with effects that can persist for life.

Prevention and Treatment

Improve Nutrition

In addition to following the Women's Health Diet Plan (Section 2), adhere to these dietary and nutrient supplement guidelines:

Diet

- Eat organic legumes, organic tofu, nuts and seeds as your primary protein sources – about 50 g daily during the first trimester, increasing to 60 to 80 g during the last trimester.
- Consume nuts and seeds as snacks, especially almonds, sunflower seeds, and pumpkin seeds to keep blood sugar stable and supply you with important minerals. (Avoid peanuts).
- Eat 3 tbsp of flaxseed oil daily.
- Avoid sugar, fried foods, and junk food.

Restore Balance

- Get 8 hours of sleep each night; nap if necessary during the day. Don't push yourself.
- Walk an hour a day and practice prenatal yoga, stretching, and deep breathing 3 times a week or more to prepare your body for childbirth.
- Drink a mineral-rich tea of nettle, oatgrass, raspberry leaf, equisetum, and alfalfa.

FETAL RISKS	
SUBSTANCES TO AVOID	**EFFECTS ON FETUS OR LATER IN LIFE**
Alcohol	Can cause fetal alcohol syndrome, birth defects, hyperactivity, poor concentration, lower IQ, heart murmur, facial deformity
Smoking and Second-hand Smoke	Lower birth weight, increase miscarriage, increased risk of sudden infant death syndrome (SIDS), increase risk of ectopic pregnancy, respiratory problems, asthma
Caffeine (coffee, coke, chocolate, black tea, caffeinated medications)	Miscarriage, birth defects, lower birth weight, smaller head circumference, hyperactivity in children
PCBs, dioxin, phthalates, bisphenol-A, brominated fire retardants, pesticides	Immune deficiency, ear infections, reproductive abnormalities, thyroid problems, low progesterone, endometriosis, breast cancer
Solvents, paints, furniture stripper, varathane, oven cleaners, dry cleaning chemicals, paint thinners, nail polish remover	Increased miscarriages Children may become chemically sensitive
Chemical dyes, formaldehyde, PVC, benzene, oil paint	Premature birth Increase stillbirths
Cosmetics	Hairdressers, aestheticians, beauticians who have daily contact with cosmetics have increased miscarriages and greater genetic abnormalities in offspring
Heavy metals (lead, mercury, cadmium, arsenic)	Neurological problems, learning disabilities, thyroid imbalance
Pharmaceutical drugs	Some can cause birth defects, lower IQ, nutritional deficiencies
Recreational drugs	Marijuana used with alcohol may cause more miscarriages
Electromagnetic fields >16mG	Increase risk of miscarriage
X-rays, radiation exposure	DNA damage, birth defects, cancer susceptibility, leukemia

- Support your adrenals and thyroid gland. These are commonly stressed through pregnancy, so have your health-care provider conduct tests to check your hormone levels. See the Hormone Balance chapter in the Living with Nature's Rhythms section for ways to support these glands.

NUTRIENT THERAPY FOR HEALTHY PREGNANCY

NUTRIENT/DOSE	ACTION	FOOD SOURCES
FOLIC ACID 800 mcg	Deficiency causes low birth weight and pregnancy mask (brown discoloration of face) Prevents birth defects	Brewer's yeast, black-eyed peas, lentils, lima beans, orange juice, kidney beans, romaine lettuce, leeks, leafy greens, nuts, whole grains, watercress, parsley
VITAMIN B-3 (NIACIN) 100 mg	Promotes higher birth weight and longer length babies	Chicken, brown rice, sunflower seeds, almonds, soy, eggs, wheat germ, garlic, dandelion, parsley
VITAMIN B-2 (RIBOFLAVIN) 20 mg	Commonly low in pregnancy Activates vitamin B-6 Needed for utilization of folic acid	Yogurt, broccoli, almonds, brewer's yeast, wild rice, soy, watercress, parsley, dulse, kelp, rose hip tea
VITAMIN B-1 (THIAMINE) 30 mg	Commonly low in pregnancy Higher birth weight with supplementation	Green peas, organic bell peppers, sunflower seeds, brewer's yeast, soy, navy beans, kidney beans, rolled oats, seaweed, brown rice, red clover tea, raspberry leaf tea
VITAMIN B-6 (PYRIDOXINE) 100 mg	Often low in pregnancy Relieves nausea and vomiting May prevent toxemia of pregnancy Prevents leg cramps	Bran, watermelon, banana, avocado, chicken, turkey, tomato juice, sunflower seeds, soy, sweet potato, potato, broccoli
VITAMIN B-12 500 mcg	Needed for proper homocysteine metabolism Protects against miscarriage Prevents neural tube defects Prevents anemia	Animal protein, spirulina, chlorella, fermented soy, seaweeds
VITAMIN A Not more than 6,000 IU daily	Decreases toxemia of pregnancy Birth defects are increased when over 10,000 IU are consumed as a supplement during pregnancy Best to take as beta carotene to avoid too high a dose	Dunaliella algae, carrot juice, spirulina, chlorella, dandelion leaf, sweet potato, mango, spinach, pumpkin, squash, cantaloupe
VITAMIN C 1,000 mg	Helps to form collagen Prevents leg cramps during pregnancy Prevents toxemia of pregnancy	Orange juice, peppers, guava, grapefruit juice, watermelon, cantaloupe, kiwi, Brussels sprouts, cauliflower, broccoli, cabbage, parsley, rose hip tea
VITAMIN D 800 IU	Helps with absorption of calcium and is needed for bone and teeth formation, but is toxic in high doses	Sunshine, uncontaminated fish oil, cashews, egg yolks, sprouted seeds

NUTRIENT THERAPY FOR HEALTHY PREGNANCY

NUTRIENT/DOSE	ACTION	FOOD SOURCES
VITAMIN E 400 IU	Commonly deficient in pregnancy; when low, there is increased risk of miscarriage, premature, and low birth-weight babies, toxemia of pregnancy	Brown rice, parsley, wheat germ, sunflower seeds, almonds, pecans, hazelnuts, sweet potato, tempeh, flaxseed oil, tofu, cooked spinach
CALCIUM (microcrystalline hydroxyapatite, citrate-malate, or citrate) 1,000 mg	Low dietary calcium is associated with toxemia of pregnancy, loss of bone density, insomnia, leg cramps, nervousness, increased pain during childbirth If the fetus doesn't get enough calcium, the result may be poor bone structure, bowed legs, crooked teeth	Almonds, sesame seeds, collards, kale, dandelion greens, tofu, molasses, parsley, broccoli, Swiss chard, watercress, raspberry leaf tea, nettle tea
IRON (Floravit or Floradix, ferrous fumarate, or ferrous gluconate) 30 mg	Prevents anemia Supplement only if serum ferritin is low Take separate from vitamin E Do not use ferrous sulphate or ferrous chloride	Almonds, sunflower seeds, walnuts, dried apricots, prunes, raisins, liver, tofu, Swiss chard, cooked spinach, beet greens, pumpkin seeds, seaweeds, blackstrap molasses
MAGNESIUM (magnesium aspartate or magnesium citrate) 500 mg	Deficiency is associated with toxemia of pregnancy, premature births, low birth weight	Soy, buckwheat, rye, figs, black-eyed peas, Swiss chard, almonds, cashews, brown rice, kidney beans, filberts, lima beans, Brazil nuts, pecans, kelp, walnuts, banana
ZINC 30 mg	Needed for fetal growth and immune system strength Deficiency is associated with miscarriage, premature delivery, fetal distress, neural tube defects, low birth weight, toxemia of pregnancy	Wheat germ, turkey, Swiss chard, lima beans, potato, oats, pumpkin seeds, soy, ginger, wild rice, lentils
BIOFLAVONOIDS 200 mg	Prevents miscarriage	Citrus fruit, apricots, tomatoes, currants, strawberries, onions, apples, cabbage
FISH OIL OR FLAXSEED OIL (3,000 mg) **EVENING PRIMROSE OR BORAGE OIL** (1,000 mg)	Use uncontaminated fish oil and/or flaxseed oil in at least a 2:1 combination with evening primrose or borage oil to nourish the developing fetal brain	Avoid fish during pregnancy Ground flaxseeds
COENZYME Q10 100 mg	Increases cellular energy Prevents early miscarriage	Organic beef (occasional), spinach, grains, beans

NUTRIENT THERAPY FOR HEALTHY PREGNANCY

NUTRIENT/DOSE	ACTION	FOOD SOURCES
PHOSPHATIDYL-CHOLINE (LECITHIN) 1 tsp	May improve spatial memory of children Improves brain development in utero	Wheat germ, soy, eggs
LACTOBACILLUS ACIDOPHILUS Taken orally and inserted vaginally	During a vaginal birth, this bacteria inoculates the infant's intestines with healthy flora. Oral intake will increase vaginal flora, but it can also be used in a douche, or inserted vaginally as capsules or cream during the last trimester Helps to prevent thrush	Organic low-fat yogurt with live culture (use sparingly)

DID YOU KNOW ...

You can tonify the uterine muscles and increase the blood supply to the fetus with gemmotherapy Rubus idaeus (red raspberry shoots), 50 drops 3 times daily. Alternatively, you can drink raspberry leaf tea. Continue after delivery to prevent postpartum bleeding.

Detoxify and Rejuvenate

- Use dandelion tincture, 30 drops, 3 times daily, as a gentle liver and kidney cleanser.
- Squeeze half a lemon in a cup of water in the morning and eat grated beets in salad to cleanse the liver.
- Drink 2 to 3 liters or quarts of water daily stored in glass, not plastic, to keep flushing your kidneys.
- Use homeopathic Unda 2, Unda 20, Unda 243, and Unda 74 to support drainage of the liver, kidneys, and venous system.
- Use the tissue salt Ferrum phos 6X to increase iron absorption, 3 pellets, twice daily. You can also use Calc phos 6X and Calc fluor 6X for healthy bone growth.

Integrate Body, Mind, and Spirit

- Spend time with positive, supportive people and in uplifting environments.
- Homeopathic remedies carefully prescribed during pregnancy can have major long-term benefits to both you and your child. Miasmatic remedies, used to decrease susceptibilities to certain

HERBAL FORMULA FOR CHILDBIRTH PREPARATION

40% Blue cohosh (*Caulophyllum thalictroides*) — tones uterus

20% Squaw vine (*Mitchella repens*) — tones uterus

20% False unicorn root (*Helonias dioica*) — softens the cervix

20% Cramp bark (*Viburnum opulus*) — antispasmodic

Dose: Mix the above herbs in tincture form and take ½ tsp twice daily. Starting at 36 weeks of pregnancy (not sooner), use this herbal formula to prepare the uterus and cervix for childbirth.

illnesses, may be prescribed during pregnancy to benefit the fetus. Your emotional state and dreams will help guide a homeopath in choosing a remedy.

- Meditate throughout your pregnancy.

PREGNANCY MEDITATION: KIRTAN KRIYA

This meditation will balance you and your child mentally, emotionally and spiritually. If you have any trouble doing it, contact a kundalini yoga teacher in your area.

This mantra connects us to the cycle of creation. From the infinite comes life, which leads to transformation, change and death; and from death comes rebirth and a connection to the infinite.

Instructions

1. Sit with a straight spine, with your eyes closed. Focus your gaze between the eyebrows. You will be saying the following mantra:

- SAA: means infinity, cosmos, beginning
- TAA: life, existence
- NAA: death, change, transformation
- MAA: rebirth

One repetition takes 3 to 4 seconds.

2. Rest your hands on your knees and:

- on the sound SAA, touch the index finger and thumb together with firm pressure
- on the sound TAA, touch the middle finger and thumb together
- on the sound NAA, touch the ring finger and thumb together
- on the sound MAA, touch the baby finger and thumb together
Repeat the cycle continuously.

- You will chant this in three levels – first out loud (centered in the world), then in a strong whisper (the language of longing to merge), then silently (the language of infinity)
- Begin by repeating the mantra out loud, moving the fingers as described above, for 5 minutes. Then whisper for 5 minutes. Vibrate the mantra silently for 10 minutes. Then whisper for another 5 minutes, and finish with 5 minutes out loud. Follow with one minute of silent prayer, for a total of 31 minutes.

TOP 5 STRATEGIES

1. Take a prenatal multivitamin along with clean fish oil.
2. Walk an hour a day, practice prenatal yoga, and deep breathing
3. Eat organic food
4. Use *Rubus idaeus* (red raspberry) as a gemmotherapy or tea
5. Meditate throughout your pregnancy to stay calm

REPRODUCTION

Morning Sickness

Nausea and vomiting are common in the first trimester of
pregnancy and may be related to low blood sugar, adrenal fatigue,
the effects of increased thyroid hormone (T4) on smooth muscle
relaxation in the stomach, nutritional deficiencies (especially
vitamin B-6), or emotional factors. If you are nauseous during
pregnancy, examine any unsettling emotions, such as fear,
resistance, anxiety, or stress.

Prevention and Treatment

Improve Nutrition

In addition to following the Women's Health Diet Plan (Section 2),
try these dietary and supplement strategies:

Diet
- Eat every 2 hours throughout the day.
- Eat plenty of protein, such as almonds, bean dips, nut butter, or
  soy milk.
- Have a snack before bed (rice cake with almond butter) and
  crackers or toast first thing in the morning.
- Chew dry crackers to relieve nausea.
- Eat bland foods – rice, pasta, soup broth.
- Avoid greasy or fried foods.

Nutrient Supplements
- Drink gingerroot tea (simmer six $\frac{1}{4}$-inch slices of ginger root in
  4 cups water for 30 minutes) sweetened with honey or take
  ginger root capsules, 250 mg, 4 times daily.
- Use 20 drops of wild yam tincture, 2 to 3 times daily.

Restore Balance
- Use the Chinese herbal formula *Citrus & Pinellia* to treat
  nausea.
- Use acupuncture or acupressure. Point P6, located 3 finger
  widths above the wrist crease on the under side of the arm
  between the two tendons, relieves nausea when stimulated. You
  can massage this point with your thumb, buy sea bands with
  small magnets that are worn over the area, or go for
  acupuncture treatments.

HOMEOPATHIC REMEDIES FOR MORNING SICKNESS

The most commonly used remedies for morning sickness are Sepia and Colchicum. Consult with your health-care practitioner for the remedy that best matches your indications.

- **Colchicum:** can't stand even the smell of food, especially fish; can faint from odors; craves food but doesn't want it once she smells it; stomach feels cold; thirsty for carbonated drinks or alcohol.

- **Sepia:** nausea with smell or sight of food; worse in morning; nausea worse when lying on side; bitter taste in mouth; craving for sour foods; vomiting after eating; vomiting of bile; exhaustion; backache; irritability; constipation; feels better with vigorous exercise or dancing; aversion to having sex.

- **Magnesia carbonicum:** constant nausea; startles when touched; sour taste in mouth, sour belching; craves fruit, vinegar, vegetables, meat.

- **Ipecac:** persistent nausea and vomiting; nausea from looking at moving objects; irritable; no coating on tongue; excess saliva.

- **Asarum:** nausea during first month of pregnancy, worse after eating; no appetite; vomiting; wants alcohol; no coat on tongue; feels faint.

- **Aletris farinosa:** persistent nausea with fatigue, fainting and dizziness; anemia, tired all the time; disgust for food; vomiting.

- **Anacardium:** nausea worse before and after eating, relieved by eating; bloated after eating; nervous person; stomach feels empty; sensation of a plug in the throat or rectum.

- **Carbolic acid:** nausea with irritability and headache; desires stimulants and tobacco; no appetite; constant belching; vomiting; abdominal bloating; flatulence.

- **Cimicifuga:** nausea and vomiting caused by pressure on spine; pointed, trembling tongue; depression; feels like she's in a cloud; stiff neck and back.

- **Gossypium:** nausea and vomiting before breakfast; no appetite; feels faint, can't get out of bed; swollen labia; nervous chills, backache.

- **Lobelia:** extreme nausea and vomiting; excess saliva; feels faint and weak in the stomach; light complexion; feels worse from afternoon until midnight; white coat on tongue.

- **Mercurius sol:** poor memory; hair loss; tremors; sweet or metallic taste in mouth; increased saliva; bad breath; wants cold drinks.

- **Nat phos:** nausea with a sour taste in the mouth and sour vomit; increased acidity; hunger after vomiting.

- **Nux vomica:** nausea in the morning and after eating; feels a weight and pain in the stomach feels worse after eating; vomiting with increased retching; stomach sensitive to pressure; loves fats; constipation with frequent but ineffective urge for stool.

- **Pulsatilla:** not thirsty and aversion to warm food and fats; taste of food remains a long time; vomiting of food eaten earlier; sad, cries easily; changeable; feels better walking outside.

- **Tabacum:** continuous nausea, worse smelling tobacco smoke; vomiting worse from movement; increased spitting; nausea feel better uncovering the abdomen; sinking feeling in pit of stomach; feels hopeless, forgetful; dizziness on opening eyes.

Detoxify and Rejuvenate

- Detoxify the liver and gallbladder with foods: apple cider vinegar, olive oil, cabbage, beets, kale, lemon, grapefruit. See the Seasonal Cleansing and Rejuvenation section for guidelines.
- Use homeopathic Chelidonium plex (Unda), 8 drops, 3x daily, as a liver/gallbladder cleanse.
- Use the tissue salts Nat phos 6X and Nat sulph 6X, 3 pellets of each, 3x daily.

Integrate Body, Mind, and Spirit

- Acknowledge your feelings around being pregnant, your worries, and trust in the process, visualizing everything going smoothly.
- Nausea may be linked to not being ready to accept the pregnancy. Give yourself time to breathe deeply, relax, go for walks, get some fresh air every day and come to terms with the experience.
- Using NeuroModulation technique, nausea may be relieved by treating it as an allergy to the fetus

---

HERBAL FORMULA FOR NAUSEA

- **25%** Black horehound (*Ballota nigra*)
- **25%** Meadowsweet (Filipendula)
- **25%** Chamomile (Matricaria)
- **25%** Anise (Pimpinella)

Dose: Mix these tinctures together in equal parts and take 5-8 drops as needed.

TOP 5 STRATEGIES

1. Take vitamin K-3 (5 mg) with vitamin C (25 mg).
2. Take vitamin B-6 (50 mg).
3. Use ginger-root capsules (250 mg), 4 times daily.
4. Use adrenal glandular formulam (150 mg), twice daily.
5. Take Herbal Formula for Nausea as needed.

Muscle Cramps

Muscle cramps in the sides, legs, and feet, common toward the end of pregnancy, are due to either lack of calcium, deficiency of sodium, poor circulation, lactic acid buildup, or a vitamin B-6 deficiency.

Prevention and Treatment

Improve Nutrition

Supplement the Women's Health Diet Plan (Section 2) with the following nutrients:

- Calcium and magnesium in a 2:1 ratio: 1000 mg: 500 mg.
- Calcium: 500 mg, at bedtime
- Vitamin B-6: 50 mg, daily
- Vitamin E: 400 IU, daily
- Vitamin C: 500 mg, daily

Restore Balance

- Normalize pH. Check the pH of urine and saliva and use the alkaline powder if you are too acidic. Use $\frac{1}{2}$ tsp in warm water twice daily. Increase your vegetable and fruit intake.
- Increase your water intake (2 to 3 liters or quarts daily) to help eliminate lactic acid.
- Use the tissue salt Mag phos 6X, 3 pellets, 3 times daily, to decrease muscle cramps.
- Exercise daily, with walking, swimming, yoga, or stretching.
- Have a massage once a month to improve tissue circulation and decrease tension.
- Sit with the leg stretched forward and pull your toes and ball of the foot toward your knee (flex your foot) when a leg cramp is occurring.
- Apply a hot water bottle or heated bean bag to the area to relieve the cramp.

DID YOU KNOW ...

You can prevent muscle cramps by stretching the calf muscles with lunges. Place one foot forward, bending the knee and leaning forward, keeping your back leg straight with the heel flat on the floor. You can place your hands against a wall for balance. If you do this before bed, you will be less likely to cramp during the night.

TOP 5 STRATEGIES

1. Take calcium and magnesium — 1,000 mg : 500 mg.
2. Normalize pH by using alkaline powder (½ tsp), twice daily.
3. Take vitamiin B-6 (50 mg).
4. Drink 2 liters or quarts of water daily.
5. Exercise daily.

Varicose Veins and Hemorrhoids

Varicose veins and hemorrhoids in pregnancy are due to softening of the muscular walls of the veins caused by increased progesterone, combined with the added pressure on the venous system because of an increase in blood volume and body weight. Constipation will make them worse.

Prevention and Treatment

Improve Nutrition

In additional to following the Women's Health Diet Plan (Section 2), try these dietary and supplement strategies:

Diet

- Increase dietary fiber (ground flaxseed, psyllium, bran, beans, beets, carrots).
- Eat foods that contain bioflavonoids, which increase the elasticity of the veins: berries, purple skinned fruits and vegetables, garlic, onions, leeks, okra, buckwheat, oranges, lemon, grapefruit, peppers, whole grains.
- Eat oatmeal, which is high in silicon, to maintain the elasticity of veins.
- Use 2 tbsp of flaxseed oil and 1 tbsp freshly ground flaxseed daily.

Nutrient Supplements

- Vitamin E mixed tocopherols: 400 IU, daily.
- Vitamin C: 2000 mg with 1000 mg bioflavonoids, daily, to build up connective tissue and increase elasticity.

HERBAL REMEDIES FOR HEMORRHOIDS

- Use a grated potato with slippery elm powder poultice. Make a patty the size of a quarter and apply on a hemorrhoid for 20 minutes. It will feel better after several treatments.

- Soak cotton gauze in witch hazel and apply topically to the hemorrhoid, or use a spray bottle to apply diluted witch hazel to your legs. Witch hazel is astringent and tightens tissues, reducing swelling.

Restore Balance

- Lie down once or twice during the day for 15 minutes and elevate your feet. Prop them up on a chair or against a wall.
- When you shower, alternate hot and cold water (start with hot, finish with cold) to improve blood circulation.
- Walk briskly for 40 minutes a day to improve circulation.
- If you do a lot of standing, wear support stockings. Raise your legs up high for 10 minutes before putting them on.
- Avoid crossing your legs, wearing high-heeled shoes, or sitting for long periods of time.

DID YOU KNOW ...

After your 26th week of pregnancy, you should avoid lying on your back for too long. Your uterus will press on a large vein called the vena cava, which will restrict blood flow to your legs. Try resting on your left side for better movement of blood.

HOMEOPATHIC REMEDIES FOR VARICOSE VEINS AND HEMORRHOIDS

Single Remedies

- For varicose veins in pregnancy: arnica, carbo veg, causticum, ferrum metallicum, fluoric acid, graphites, hamamelis, lycopodium, nux vomica, phosphorus, and pulsatilla.

- For hemorrhoids: aesculus, ammonium muriaticum, antimonium crudum, capsicum, collinsonia, hydrastis, lachesis, lycopodium, natrum muriaticum, nux vomica, sepia, sulphur, and zincum metallicum.

Combination Remedies

- For hemorrhoids: Paeonia plex (Unda), 8 drops, 3x daily; or Unda 8, Unda 36, and Unda 74, 5 drops, 3x daily.

- For varicose veins: Hamamelis plex (Unda), 8 drops, 3x daily, and Unda 233.

TOP 5 STRATEGIES

1. Increase dietary fiber to 45 g daily.
2. Lie down twice daily and elevate your feet.
3. Use vitamin C with bioflavonoids.
4. Use Paeonia plex (for hemorrhoids) and Hamamelis plex (for varicose veins).
5. Walk briskly for 40 minutes a day.

Heartburn

Increased progesterone in pregnancy relaxes smooth muscles, including the stomach and cardiac sphincter (at the top of the stomach), and slows down peristalsis (muscular contractions) of the small intestine and stomach so that food remains longer in the stomach and ferments. As the uterus enlarges during pregnancy, it displaces the stomach upwards, and food and stomach acid can back up through the cardiac sphincter into the esophagus, causing acidic burning, heat, and pain.

Prevention and Treatment

Improve Nutrition

- Slowly chew raw almonds to relieve heartburn.
- Eat pineapple or papaya after meals for their digestive enzymes.
- Drink fennel seed, anise and/or mint tea an hour after eating.
- Take a liquid calcium magnesium mixture an hour after meals.
- Avoid greasy and spicy foods and other known foods that cause you heartburn.
- Avoid coffee and cigarettes because they irritate the stomach.
- Try food combining – eat carbohydrates separately from protein and fruit by itself.

HERBAL REMEDY FOR HEARTBURN

- Take 2 slippery elm capsules up to 3 times daily with warm water or tea to soothe mucous membranes and absorb acid. Or mix 1 tsp slippery elm with honey and water.

Restore Balance

- Use homeopathic remedies for heartburn in pregnancy: apis, capsicum, oxalic acid, zinc, Nat mur, and conium.
- Eat slowly and spend more time chewing your food.
- Eat smaller meals more frequently.
- Drink between meals, not with meals.
- Take $\frac{1}{2}$ tsp of alkaline powder in a little warm water, away from meals, twice daily.
- Don't lie down immediately after eating.

TOP 5 STRATEGIES

1. Eat smaller meals.
2. Use alkaline powder.
3. Take slippery elm.
4. Combine foods.
5. Chew almonds.

Hypertension

High blood pressure during pregnancy can be chronic, with consistent readings above 130/90, or due to the pregnancy itself (gestational hypertension), with a steady rise in blood pressure after 28 weeks. In both cases, blood flow is reduced to the placenta, and less oxygen is available to the fetus.

Prevention and Treatment

Improve Nutrition
- Eat ½ cup of grated beets daily to cleanse the liver.
- Eat several cloves of garlic a day, along with onions, parsley, cucumber, and celery.
- Increase foods high in potassium – potato skins, banana, carrot juice, prune juice, kiwi, avocado, azuki beans, grapefruit juice, cantaloupe, papaya, figs, squash, broccoli.
- Use uncontaminated fish oil (3000 mg) and flaxseed oil (2 tbsp).
- Use calcium (1200 mg) with magnesium (600 mg).
- Drink nettle and raspberry leaf tea regularly.
- Drink 2 to 3 liters or quarts of water daily to flush the kidneys.

Restore Balance
- Use homeopathic remedies for hypertension: aurum metallicum, calcarea carbonica, crataegus, glonoine, lachesis, natrum muriaticum, and veratrum.
- Walk an hour a day.
- Block your right nostril and breathe slowly and deeply through your left nostril for 11 minutes twice daily to activate the parasympathetic nervous system.
- Check the pH of your urine and saliva with litmus paper and normalize it with an alkaline diet and powder. See the Seasonal Cleansing and Rejuvenation Program section for guidelines.

Detoxify and Rejuvenate
- To support the circulatory system: Use homeopathic Unda 8, Unda 74, and Unda 233, 5 drops of each, 3x daily.
- To lower blood pressure: Mix together tinctures of motherwort, skullcap, tilia and crataegus in equal parts and take ½ tsp, 3 times daily.

Integrate Body, Mind, and Spirit
- Take time to address causes of stress and tension: acknowledge what's bothering you, and slow down your activities.
- Visualize your blood vessels relaxing and expanding several times throughout the day.

DID YOU KNOW …

Gestational hypertension may indicate or progress to pre-eclampsia, so women with this condition need to be followed carefully. If you are pregnant with high blood pressure, follow the guidelines below as well as the suggestions for preventing and treating pre-eclampsia.

DID YOU KNOW …

Hypertension in pregnancy can be caused by insufficient return of increased blood volume to your heart because your venous system is sluggish.

TOP 5 STRATEGIES

1. Walk an hour a day.
2. Eat several cloves of garlic a day.
3. Breathe slowly and deeply through your left nostril for 11 minutes, twice daily.
4. Use a tincture of motherwort, skullcap, tilia, and crataegus.
5. Increase foods high in potassium.

DID YOU KNOW ...

If you have had pre-eclampsia, you are more at risk of hypertension and heart disease later in life.

Pre-eclampsia

Pre-eclampsia (toxemia of pregnancy) is a serious condition that can occur after the 20th week (5 months) of pregnancy in 5% of pregnant women. The condition can also occur 2 to 4 days after delivery. If not managed properly, pre-eclampsia can progress to eclampsia, with spots before the eyes, headache, liver damage, breakdown of red blood cells, low platelets, convulsions, or death of the mother or child. Women with pre-eclampsia need to be monitored every 2 days, and if the condition worsens, a caesarean section is performed. Blood pressure may remain high for 6 to 8 weeks after delivery, but then returns to normal.

Symptoms of Pre-eclampsia

- Vasospasm
- Swelling
- Sudden weight gain
- High blood pressure (above 140/90)
- Protein in the urine

Causes

While the precise cause of pre-eclampsia is not known, the following factors play a role in its development:

- Insulin resistance
- Being overweight
- Lack of exercise
- Excess sugar, sweeteners, white flower and high-glycemic foods
- Increased free radical production
- Decreased antioxidants (low vitamins C and E, selenium, lycopene, beta carotene)
- Increased homocysteine (low folic acid, vitamins B-6 and B12)
- Increased triglycerides and LDL cholesterol
- Increased blood clotting and spasm of arteries
- Dysfunction with/damage to the endothelium (blood vessel lining)
- Poor blood flow to the placenta and all organs – constriction of blood vessels, formation of small clots, reduced circulating blood volume
- Nutritional deficiencies of calcium, magnesium, omega-3 fatty acids, arginine, protein
- Increased acidity and deficiency of alkaline minerals
- Emotional stress and dominance of sympathetic nervous system

Risk Factors for Pre-eclampsia

- Black skinned
- Previous history or family history of pre-eclampsia
- Being overweight (body mass index >32.3)

- Being older than 35 or younger than 18
- Being pregnant with more than one fetus
- First pregnancy
- Having had a small baby in the previous pregnancy
- High blood pressure before or during pregnancy
- Diabetes or strong family history of diabetes
- Disorders with increased blood clotting
- Premature detachment of the placenta from the uterus

Prevention and Treatment

Improve Nutrition
In addition to following the Women's Health Diet Plan (Section 2), try these dietary and supplement strategies:
- Avoid sugar, sweeteners, soft drinks, white flour, baked goods, high-glycemic foods.
- Avoid saturated fats (from red meat), trans fats, and excess omega-6 oils (most vegetable oils).
- Eat 60 to 80 grams of protein daily from nuts (except peanuts), seeds, beans, tofu and organic chicken and eggs if you are not vegetarian.
- Eat complex carbohydrates including whole grains, beans, vegetables.
- Eat foods high in magnesium – soybeans, tofu, buckwheat, figs, black-eyed peas, almonds, Swiss chard, brown rice, kidney beans, filberts, lima beans, Brazil nuts, banana, beet greens, avocado.
- Eat 8 servings of fruits and vegetables to increase antioxidant intake.
- Eat 2 tsp of turmeric daily to decrease inflammation.
- Drink 2 to 3 liters or quarts of water.
- Do not avoid salt – use a little sea-salt daily.
- Use flaxseed oil (2 tbsp) and extra-virgin olive oil (1-2 tbsp) daily.

Restore Balance
- Use homeopathic remedies that address toxemia: apis, arsenicum album, colchicum, gelsemium, helonias, kalium carbonicum, natrum muriaticum, mercurius corrosives, and sepia.
- Maintain a low-stress environment, with plenty of rest.
- Practice 11 minutes of left nostril breathing (block your right nostril with your thumb) twice daily to increase parasympathetic activity, decrease blood pressure.
- Check pH of urine and saliva and balance with alkaline foods and alkaline powder if needed. See the Seasonal Cleansing and Rejuvenation Program section for guidelines.

Pregnancy (Pre-eclampsia)

NUTRIENT THERAPY FOR PRE-ECLAMPSIA		
PURPOSE	**NUTRIENT**	**DAILY DOSE**
To decrease homocysteine levels	Folic acid Vitamin B-6 Vitamin B-12	2 mg 100 mg 800 mcg
To decrease free radicals	Vitamin C Vitamin E mixed tocopherols	1000 mg 400 IU
To decrease inflammatory eicosanoids and improve placental blood flow through vasodilation	Uncontaminated fish oil	3000 mg
To decrease blood pressure and activate the parasympathetic nervous system	Calcium Magnesium	1200 mg 600 mg
To decrease oxidative stress	Selenium	200 mcg
To regulate blood sugar	Chromium and Alpha lipoic acid	400 mcg 200 mg
To protect the endothelium of blood vessels and decrease blood viscosity	L-arginine	3000 mg
To ensure adequate nutrition	Multivitamin and mineral formula	

TOP 5 STRATEGIES

1. Use folic acid (2 mg), vitamin B-6 (100 mg), vitamin B-12 (800 mcg).

2. Increase exercise to lower insulin.

3. Maintain a low stress environment, with plenty of rest.

4. Use pure fish oil (3000 mg) daily.

5. Avoid sugar, sweeteners, soft drinks, white flour, baked goods, high-glycemic foods.

Detoxify and Rejuvenate

- To assist liver and kidney detoxification: use dandelion leaf tea or tincture.
- To improve liver drainage and protect the arteries: use homeopathic Unda 33, Unda 25, Unda 243, and Unda 20, 5 drops of each, 3x daily.

Integrate Body, Mind, and Spirit

- Associate with people from whom you feel support; remove yourself from environments where you feel criticized or stressed. Create a tranquil environment in your home or spend time in places where you feel peaceful.
- Accept the fact that you will soon be having a baby. Trust the process.
- Talk to the baby inside you and provide assurance that all will be well.
- Breathe deeply and relax.

Conventional Medicine

- Conventional medicine treats pre-eclampsia with magnesium sulphate, bed rest, and caesarean section, if necessary.

Miscarriage

If you have miscarried in the past, there is much you can do to prevent it from happening again. A miscarriage, though traumatic, is nature's way of ensuring quality control. Not all fetuses are destined to become human beings. As many as 60% of all pregnancies miscarry too early for women to realize it, and about 15% of all known pregnancies miscarry. If you do miscarry, wait at least 3 months before trying to conceive again.

If you miscarry two or more times, consult with your medical doctor to determine the cause. Work with both a conventional doctor and a natural medicine practitioner if you experience bleeding during pregnancy.

Causes

- **Hormonal factors (25% to 50 %)**
  - Hyperandrogenism (high male hormones, as in polycystic ovary syndrome)
  - Low progesterone
  - Elevated LH (luteinizing hormone)
  - Thyroid disease or elevated anti-thyroid antibodies
  - DES exposure in utero

- **Chromosomal abnormalities (10% to 70%)**
  - Occur in 26% of eggs and 10% of sperm
  - More common with older age of either parent

- **Reproductive tract abnormalities (6%-12%)**
  - Abnormal placenta
  - Abnormal uterus
  - Incompetent cervix (false unicorn root helps this)
  - Adhesions in the uterus
  - DES exposure in utero

- **Infections (1%)**
  - Mycoplasma, syphilis, toxoplasmosis, urecoplasma
  - Chlamydia, herpes

- **Systemic factors**
  - Cardiovascular disease
  - Kidney disease
  - Diabetes
  - Lupus
  - Blood clotting disorders (possibly with high homocysteine)
  - Immunological factors
  - Kidney energy deficiency (Chinese medicine)

DID YOU KNOW ...

Studies have shown that 60% of the time, miscarriages occurring in the first trimester have chromosomal abnormalities, and that 90% of defective fetuses are spontaneously aborted during early pregnancy.

DID YOU KNOW ...

Abnormal sperm occur more frequently in men exposed to chemicals, pesticides, and cigarette smoke during the two-month period before conception. One study showed that 48% of sperm were abnormal in unsuccessful pregnancies, while only 4% were abnormal in men who produced healthy children.

Pregnancy (Miscarriage)

DID YOU KNOW ...

In traditional Chinese medicine, a miscarriage may stem from the inability of the kidney energy to hold the fetus in the uterus. The kidney energy can be supported with shou wu (Polygonatum multiflorum), 30 drops of tincture, 3 times daily. The combination of the Chinese herbs *Cuscuta chinensis, Dipsaci Root (Xu duan), Loranthus (Sang Ji Sheng)*, and *Eucommia (Du Zhong)* calm the fetus and may help to prevent miscarriage.

- Environmental factors
  - Caffeine – coffee, black tea, chocolate, caffeinated medications (equivalent to more than 6 cups of coffee daily)
  - Alcohol, marijuana, cocaine, recreational drugs
  - Smoking
  - Anesthetics
  - Radiation exposure
  - Chemical exposure – dry cleaning fluids, paint thinners, paint strippers, rubber, plastic, cosmetics, wood preservatives, contaminated fish consumption
  - Heavy metals – especially cadmium
  - Electromagnetic fields stronger than 16 mG

- Nutritional deficiencies
  - Vitamin E, zinc, bioflavonoids, folic acid, vitamin B-6, vitamin B-12, coenzyme Q10

Prevention and Treatment

Improve Nutrition

- To prevent miscarriage: zinc (50 mg), folic acid (1 mg,) vitamin B-12 (400 mcg), and vitamin B-6 (100 mg), daily.
- To prevent miscarriage during the crisis period: vitamin E (400-2000 IU), daily.
- To prevent miscarriage when homocysteine levels are elevated: bioflavonoids, (200 mg), taken 3 times daily.

Restore Balance

- Rest in bed and call your physician if you begin to bleed during pregnancy.
- Use basal body temperature charting and saliva testing to see whether progesterone is low. If it is, use progesterone cream.
- Use temperature charting and blood tests (including thyroid antibodies) to check thyroid function and treat any imbalance.

HOMEOPATHIC REMEDIES FOR MISCARRIAGE

- To balance hormones and assist removal of intracellular and extracellular toxins: Unda 10, Unda 21, Unda 48, and Unda 245 for 3 months after a miscarriage before attempting a new pregnancy.
- If the thyroid is imbalanced: Unda 273, Unda 16 and Unda 1000. Use 5 drops of each, mixed in a little water, taken 3x daily, 15 minutes or more away from meals.

HERBAL REMEDIES

Formula to prevent chronic miscarriage:

- False unicorn root (Helonias dioica)
- Black haw root bark (Viburnum prunifolium)
- Crampbark (Viburnum opulus)
- Raspberry leaf (Rubus idaeus)
- Squaw vine (Mitchella repens)

Dose: Blend and take 20 drops daily starting 3 weeks before the habitual miscarriage, increasing the dosage to 50 drops during the last week.

Formula for threatened miscarriage with cramps and bleeding:

15%	Wild yam root (Dioscorea villosa)
10%	Raspberry leaf (Rubus idaeus)
30%	False unicorn root (Helonias dioica)
15%	Crampbark (Viburnum opulus)
30%	Shepherd's purse (Capsella)

Dose: Use one dropper-full of tincture every 30 minutes until all signs of miscarriage clear.

Detoxify and Rejuvenate

- Test for and detoxify heavy metals. See the Seasonal Cleansing and Rejuvenation Program section for guidelines.
- Test for chemicals and do the sauna detox program together before attempting to conceive again. See the Seasonal Cleansing and Rejuvenation Program section for guidelines.
- Avoid coffee, black tea, chocolate, and caffeinated medications.
- Stop smoking and avoid second-hand smoke. See the Seasonal Cleansing and Rejuvenation Program section for stop-smoking programs.
- Avoid alcohol, marijuana, recreational drugs, and pharmaceuticals.
- Avoid cosmetics during pregnancy that contain parabens, phthalates, or solvents.

Integrate Body, Mind, and Spirit

- Express your feelings. If you have miscarried, you may feel grief, guilt or are afraid to try again. Talk openly about your feelings with a friend, your partner or a therapist, or write them down in a journal.
- The homeopathic remedy Ignatia may help you release your grief if you have recently miscarried, while Nat mur may help if the miscarriage was in the past.

TOP 5 STRATEGIES

1. Take vitamin E (400 IU) to prevent miscarriage — up to 2000 IU a day if bleeding.

2. Take bioflavonoids (200 mg) 3 times daily.

3. Use Herbal Formula for Threatened Miscarriage.

4. Rest in bed if you bleed during pregnancy.

5. Call your physician or midwife.

YOGA FOR PREGNANCY

1. Stand up with your arms next to your ears and your palms together. Inhale while bending the upper body slightly back. Exhale, and bend forward the same amount. Continue for 1 to 3 minutes.
   This strengthens the lower back and adds flexibility to your spine.

2. Sit on your heels. Inhale while raising your body up in a kneeling position. Exhale, and sit back down on your heels. Rest your hands on your hips. Continue for 1 minute.
   This strengthens your thighs and relaxes the pelvis.

3. Sit up and stretch both legs out in front of you. Support your upper body with your hands on the floor. Inhale while raising your right leg up. Exhale, and lower the leg down to the floor. Continue for 1 to 3 minutes. Repeat with your left leg.
   This tones the abdominal muscles.

4. Bring the soles of the feet together. Interlace your fingers and place your hands over your toes. For 1 minute, rock side to side on your buttocks. Then bounce the knees up and down. Continue for 1 to 3 minutes.
   This relaxes and helps to open up the pelvic area.

5. Sit cross-legged. Inhale and push your chest forward as you straighten your spine. Exhale and push the lower spine down and back. Continue alternating this movement for 1 to 3 minutes.
   This keeps your spine flexible.

6. Squat with both feet flat on the floor. Interlace your hands with your elbows resting on your knees. Begin slow, long, deep breathing. Relax in this position for 1 to 3 minutes.
   This position prepares you for childbirth.

7. Sit cross-legged. Slowly roll your head in large circles. Continue for 1 to 3 minutes.
   This relaxes tension in your neck.

8. Relax on your side, keeping your lower leg slightly bent. Support your head with a pillow. Inhale and raise your leg up. Exhale, and lower the leg down. Continue for 1 to 3 minutes on each side.
   This tones the muscles of your thighs.

9. Totally relax on your side.

Labor and Delivery

If you are preparing to give birth, think about how you want the birth to go, and write out a birth plan to review with your doctor, birth attendant or midwife. The more carefully you consider the kind of birth you want, the more likely it will occur, and possibly provide you with one of the most rewarding experiences of your life. We don't get to give birth that often, and it is a huge event, so take charge of the parts of it you can.

Birth Plan

By answering the following questions, you can begin to plan a healthy labor and delivery experience. Use the extra space between questions to record your answers.

- Where will you have the birth — at home or in hospital?

- If the birth will be in hospital, at what point will you leave home to get there?

- Who will be at the birth with you?

- What will you have on hand during the birth – food, drinks, teas, music, heating pads, sitz bath, nightie, birthing stool?

- What kind of lighting will you have? Dim lights are preferable.

- Will you have a visual object to concentrate on during labor — a photograph, mandala, statue, religious symbol, candle or flowers?

- Do you prefer monitoring of the fetal heartbeat with a fetal stethoscope or a fetal heart monitor?

- How will you deal with the pain of labor – breathing exercises, visualization, meditation, movement, music, heated bean bags, massage, warm water, herbs, homeopathic remedies… or an epidural?

- What position are you most likely to prefer when giving birth — sitting, lying, in water pool, squatting with pillow support, on all fours?

- Will you photograph or videotape the birth? Who will do this?

- Will you have an episiotomy or use warm compresses, perineal massage, breathing, and careful pushing?

- How will your partner participate in the birth process — cutting the cord, holding the baby immediately after birth, bringing your child to you?

- Will you hold and nurse the baby immediately after birth or will the medical staff take the baby away for testing?

- Will you ask that the umbilical cord be drained before it is cut?

- Will you allow silver nitrate drops in the baby's eyes after birth?

- Will the baby be with you after birth or in a hospital nursery?

- Who will help you get started with breastfeeding?

Prevention and Treatment

Select a few of the following herbal and homeopathic remedies to have on hand and designate someone else in the birth room to administer them.

HERBS COMMONLY USED IN LABOR	
HERB/DOSAGE	**ACTIONS**
BLUE COHOSH *(Caulophyllum thalictroides)* ½ tsp hourly for a day until labor is progressing; if you are overdue, use it with Gossypium (cotton root bark) to relax and soften the cervix	When used before birth, makes delivery easier Stimulates uterine contractions, starts labor Tones the uterus; works best together with black cohosh
LOBELIA *(Lobelia inflata)* Use small doses frequently; 3-5 drops every 10-15 minutes for an hour	Softens the cervix; relaxes muscles Regulates blood pressure Relieves chills Revives birthing mother if she nears collapse
BLACK COHOSH *(Cimicifuga racemosa)* Use with blue cohosh, ½ tsp hourly until labor is progressing	Relieves back labor, uterine cramping, muscle pain
SQUAW VINE (PARTRIDGEBERRY) *(Mitchella repens)* 1-2 ml tincture up to 3 times daily in the final 2-3 weeks of pregnancy or 1 ml hourly until contractions are established for labor	Eases labor when used a few weeks before due date Establishes and maintains productive contractions during birth

HERBS COMMONLY USED IN LABOR

HERB/DOSAGE	ACTIONS
PASSIONFLOWER *(Passiflora incarnata)* 60 drops or 3 ml or 1 tsp every half hour as needed for relaxation	Helps to induce sleep if labor begins in the evening Promotes rest between contractions Relieves anxiety and panic during labor
SKULLCAP *(Scutellaria lateriflorae)* 40 drops or 2 ml every half hour as needed	Relieves pain Decreases tension and promotes rest Restores the nerves
YELLOW JASMINE *(Gelsemium)* 10-15 drops only every half hour when there is a tight cervix	For fear during labor Helps to open and relax the cervix, especially when there is underlying fear of pain, being a parent, or pushing the baby out
MISTLETOE *(Viscum album)* 60 drops or 3 ml and repeat every hour or two	Use during labor when contractions stall or become interrupted or irregular Use to decrease blood pressure along with motherwort *(Leonurus cardiaca)* and crampbark *(Viburnum opulus)*
SHEPHERD'S PURSE *(Capsella bursa-pastoris)* 30 drops to constrict the blood vessels, repeat 15 minutes later	Used for hemorrhage and excessive bleeding Constricts blood vessels and tissues Lowers blood pressure, contracts the uterus
YARROW *(Achillea millefolium)* 30 drops to constrict the blood vessels, repeat 15 minutes later	For post partum hemorrhage, can be mixed with Shepherd's purse (capsella) or Lady's mantle Use the drug Pitocin if herbs don't work or use Pitocin first
MOTHERWORT *(Leonurus cardiaca)* 50–100 drops every 2 hours	Not to be used until labor Eases early labor pains that begin prematurely Alleviates restlessness, anxiety, tension and insomnia Helps the uterus to contract after childbirth
VERVAIN *(Verbena officinalis)* 30 drops every 3 hours after labor begins	Promotes labor; relieves pain Generates strength, relieves depression, lifts spirit Reduces inflammation and swelling Promotes milk production Can help support and connect everyone in the birth room
TANG KUEI *(Angelica sinensis)* 1 tsp every 15 minutes for an hour until the placenta comes down	Use for a retained placenta

HOMEOPATHIC REMEDIES COMMONLY USED IN LABOR

REMEDY	ACTIONS
ACONITE 200CH 3 pellets every ½ hour as needed	For panic and extreme fear of death For trauma, shock and bleeding For exhaustion during labor
ARNICA 200CH 3 pellets hourly through labor, and once daily after the birth for a week	Decreases pain and bleeding, facilitates healing Helps combat fatigue, swelling and shock Can be dissolved in water and given to newborns if they have been bruised or hurt during birth
CAULOPHYLLUM 30CH 3 pellets every ½ hour until labor resumes	Can be use daily during the last 2-3 weeks of pregnancy to prepare for labor For stalled labor, when contractions are slow, too far apart and weak Use when irregular contractions are accompanied by weakness or exhaustion
CHINA 30CH 3 pellets daily	Use if there is weakness after loss of blood
KALI CARBONICUM 30CH 3 pellets every ½ hour until pain diminishes	For low back pain during labor that extends to the buttocks and thighs, or after-birth uterine pain For uterine pains when hard pressure feels good against the back
GELSEMIUM 200CH 3 pellets every ½ hour as needed	Use if you feel sleepy, exhausted, and can't keep your eyes open during labor For nervous trembling during or after labor, chattering teeth, fear of what may happen before or after labor begins
PULSATILLA 200CH 3 pellets every ½ hour as needed	To turn the baby if it is breech; to speed up the birth if it is overdue Use when labor is accompanied by shortness of breath, the need for air, or a feeling of suffocation Use when the mother is emotional, teary
VISCUM ALBUM 30CH 3 pellets every ½ hour	Helps move the baby out of the uterus and down the birth canal when labor is not progressing
SEPIA 30CH 3 pellets every ½ hour	For exhaustion and irritability during labor with a need to move around and exercise
CHAMOMILLA 200CH 3 pellets every ½ hour as needed	Use when labor is slow and non-productive, there is extreme irritability and intolerance to pain, with outbursts of anger and the inability to relax Use when the mother is frantic, unreasonable, can't stand to be touched Use when the mother feels hot and nothing pleases her

Postpartum Depression

Postpartum depression is a common occurrence after childbirth. What we need most after giving birth is support — someone to help cook, clean, do laundry, provide companionship and reassurance, and allow us time to bond with our child and partner — and rest. If it is possible for you, have a trusted friend or relative live with you for the first 40 days after birth or hire someone for this role. Stressors and family discord may promote postpartum depression. Giving birth and having a newborn naturally awakens in us experiences from our own early life, which we must process and integrate. If the environment around us is nurturing and supportive, this is more easily done, and deep healing can occur.

Categories

- **Postpartum Maternity Blues:** This is a depression that lasts only 24 to 48 hours after delivery. It is caused by hormonal shifts — estrogen increases after delivery, while progesterone levels drop, affecting neurotransmitter levels. It takes about 10 days for hormones to level out.
- **Postpartum Depression:** 10% to 20% of women experience mild to moderate depression that can last 6 to 8 weeks after giving birth, although it may persist for a year in some women. Symptoms include depression, feelings of loss, irritability, resentment, anger, changes in maternal feelings, insomnia, weepiness, feeling inadequate as a mother, fatigue, eating disorders, feeling out of control.
- **Postpartum Psychosis:** This is a rare reaction that occurs in one in a thousand births and is more common after a first pregnancy. Symptoms include severe mood disturbance, confused thoughts, bizarre behavior, insomnia, hallucinations, and delusions. These women usually need conventional medical intervention with medication.

Risk Factors

- History of depression or previous postpartum depression
- History of moderate to severe PMS
- Family predisposition
- Disappointing or traumatic experience during labor
- Infant death
- Sleep deprivation
- Difficult relationship with close family members
- Marital stress
- Early childhood loss of a parent or sibling
- History of physical or sexual abuse
- Lifestyle stress

DID YOU KNOW ...

Postpartum maternity blues occurs in 50% to 80% of women and is characterized by bouts of tearfulness, irritability, anxiety, and lack of confidence in handling the baby, accompanied by poor sleep.

Postpartum Depression

- Unfinished business with one's mother
- Lack of emotional support after birth
- Unplanned or unwanted pregnancy and birth
- Unexpressed anger that you believe you have no right to feel
- Thyroid imbalance
- Low progesterone

Prevention and Treatment

Improve Nutrition

In addition to following the Women's Health Diet Plan (Section 2), use these nutritional supplements for postpartum depression:

- Uncontaminated fish oil (3000 mg daily), containing at least 600 mg DHA, throughout pregnancy and while breast-feeding.
- Folic acid, 2 mg daily.
- Vitamin B-12, 1 mg daily, for proper neurological function.
- Vitamin B complex, 100 mg daily.
- Calcium, 1000 mg, and magnesium, 500 mg, daily.
- Use blood tests to assess iron deficiency and supplement with 30 mg daily if needed.

Restore Balance

- Use the gemmotherapy Rosemarinus, 50 drops, 3 times daily to lift your spirit.
- Use St. John's wort, with 0.3% hypericin, 300 mg, 3 to 4 times daily. Do not take St. John's wort with an SSRI antidepressant.
- Use light treatment: 90 minutes of exposure to bright light (6,000 lux) from a light box or sunlight, best in the morning.
- Begin a daily walking program. Get out for 1 hour a day in the morning sun.
- Schedule a massage once a week.
- Participate in a postnatal yoga class once weekly.
- Short-term use of bio-identical estrogen or progesterone may help some women.

HOMEOPATHIC REMEDIES FOR POSTPARTUM DEPRESSION

- Single Remedies: agnus castus, anacardium, aurum metallicum, cimicifuga, conium, ignatia, kali bromatum, lachesis, lilium tiglium, natrum muriaticum, platina, psorinum, pulsatilla, sepia, sulphur, tuberculinum and veratrum. Work with a homeopath who can choose the most appropriate remedy for you.

- Combination Remedies: Unda 10, Unda 9, Unda 16 and Unda 273, 5 drops of each, 3x daily, to regulate the glands and support the nervous system.

Detoxify and Rejuvenate

- Check copper levels using hair analysis and if excessive, treat with zinc supplements, 50 mg daily.

Integrate Body, Mind, and Spirit

- Address the unexpressed feelings you have towards your mother or father, your partner, your new baby, or events from the past. This is your time to bring them forth and to heal. If a therapist is not available, journal all your feelings, or draw them.
- Use the months immediately after birth to come to terms with your past and to heal old wounds. Use prayer, spiritual readings, meditation, or ritual to release trauma.

HERBAL FORMULA FOR POSTPARTUM DEPRESSION

25% Licorice root

25% St. John's wort

25% Skullcap

25% Rosemary

Dose: Mix the tinctures together and take 40 drops, 3 times daily. Do not use St. John's wort if you are taking an SSRI antidepressant. Avoid licorice root if you have high blood pressure.

Conventional Medicine

Drug Therapy

- Selective serotonin reuptake inhibitors (SSRIs) are recommended for postpartum depression. Paroxetine (Paxil) 20-50 mg /day, sertraline (Zoloft) 50-150 mg/ daily or fluoxetine (Prozac) 10-40 mg/day are most commonly used, although fluoxetine is best avoided in breastfeeding women.
- Other drugs that may be recommended include cyclic antidepressants (amitriptyline, clomipramine, doxepin, imipramine, nortriptyline, bupropion) or monoamine oxidase inhibitors (isocarboxazid, phenelzine, tranylcypromine).

TOP 5 STRATEGIES

1. Take uncontaminated fish oil containing at least 600 mg DHA.
2. Take 5-HTP, (100 mg), twice daily.
3. Take vitamin B complex, B-12, B-6, folic acid.
4. Use Herbal Formula for Postpartum Depression.
5. Walk an hour a day outside.

CASE STUDY: *DEPRESSION PREVENTION*

Johanna, a young mother with one child, came to see us midway through her second pregnancy. After her first baby, she had terrible postpartum depression that lasted 6 months and wanted to prevent it this time around. She was married to a man her parents disapproved of because he was a rock musician. Her relationship with her mother was difficult at the best of times, and though a part of her wanted her mother to be at the birth and help care for her and the new baby, another part of her felt that her mother's presence would feel like an invasion in her home. She did not want her mother to see the discord that existed between herself and her husband, revolving around his many late nights out playing music and his financial instability.

We talked about Johanna's birth plan and possible arrangements for care after the birth. Johanna agreed to ask her sister to come and stay with her after the birth to help with cooking and laundry for a month, so some of her stress was lifted and she could bond with the baby. She spoke with her mother and requested that she allow them to have their intimate family time alone during the birth, but that she would be happy to spend time with her 6 weeks after the baby was born. When her mother protested, Johanna stood her ground, and her mother accepted this decision.

We gave Johanna fish oil, a quality prenatal vitamin formula, extra vitamin B-6, B-12, and folic acid, calcium-magnesium, and 5-HTP for the rest of her pregnancy. When her daughter was born, we had her take an herbal formula containing St. John's wort, licorice root, rosemary, and skullcap, and suggested she walk in the early part of each day for an hour. This regimen worked — Johanna experienced no depression.

Breast-feeding

Breast milk is our children's first food. There is nothing as important to the health of future generations as protecting the quality of that food. The beneficial nutrients in breast milk help our children to cope better with some of its toxic additives. No formula has the same composition as breast milk, and nursing provides intimate contact and bonding between mother and child, for which there is no substitute. The composition of breast milk changes according to the age of the infant and length of time breast-feeding, meeting the changing nutritional needs of our children. Breast milk contains nutrients that prevent infection, stimulate immunity, and improve the function and development of the intestinal mucosa, preventing lifelong allergies and asthma.

While toxins in breast milk are a serious concern, we must all work to eliminate toxins in the environment and in our bodies before conceiving our children, rather than discourage breastfeeding.

Benefits of Breast-feeding

If you breast-feed:
- You will bleed less after birth, with decreased risk of hemorrhage.
- Your uterus will return to its normal size faster.
- You will return to your non-pregnant weight more easily.
- Your bones will remineralize more quickly.
- You will be less likely to have hip fractures postmenopausally.
- You will be less likely to get pregnant while breastfeeding.
- Your children will be healthier over their lifetime.

Risks of Breast-feeding

- At least 60% of the fat in breast milk is drawn from fat reserves from our bodies, in which environmental chemicals and toxic metals are stored.
- The average level of brominated fire retardants in the milk of 20 first-time mothers from the United States is 75 times the average found in European women.
- Young women from Seveso in northern Italy, who were exposed to high levels of dioxin from a spill in 1978, had levels in breast milk 25 years later that were twice as high as women's milk from neighboring villages.
- Mothers whose milk is more contaminated have children with greater cognitive and psychomotor problems, but fewer problems than appear in formula-fed children.
- We pass on at least 25% of our lifetime body burden of environmental toxins through breast milk to each nursing infant
- A baby can receive up to 5 times its lifetime limit of allowable levels of toxins, such as PCBs, dioxin, and PBDEs, within the first 6 months of breast-feeding.

DID YOU KNOW ...

If you breast-feed, you will be less at risk of breast cancer and ovarian cancer later in life.

DID YOU KNOW ...

More than 350 toxic substances are present in human breast milk. Some of these include perfumes, suntan oil, pesticides, DDT, heavy metals, PCBs, dioxin, furans, brominated fire retardants, phthalates, bisphenol-A, dry cleaning fluid, and rocket fuel.

FORMULA-FED VS. BREAST-FED BABIES

FORMULA-FED BABIES HAVE:	BREAST-FED BABIES HAVE:
80% increase in diarrhea and gastrointestinal upset	Lower rates of infection and gastrointestinal illness when breast-fed for at least 13 weeks
70% more middle ear infections	Fewer allergies
Twice as many respiratory infections	The longer the period of breast-feeding, the better cognitive development and academic performance
Increased allergies and asthma	
Increased eczema	Higher IQs from first grade through high school
Increased childhood diseases	Leaner bodies, possibly resulting in less obesity later in life
Lower cognitive development	
Higher risk of cardiovascular disease as adults	
52% higher risk of diabetes later in life when fed cow based formulas	

DID YOU KNOW ...

To decrease the possibility of causing allergic disease or asthma in your child, you can supplement with uncontaminated fish oil (3000 mg) or marine algae oil and curcumin (1500 mg) or turmeric (2 tsp) daily. DHA is needed for your child's brain development.

DID YOU KNOW ...

You can decrease the amount of toxins you pass on to your infant through breast milk by expressing extra milk at the end of each feeding and throwing it away. The 'hindmilk' (milk at the end of the feed) is richer in fat, which carries environmental toxins.

Prevention and Treatment

Improve Nutrition

- Eat organic food while breast-feeding.
- Avoid wheat, dairy, eggs, and any foods to which you may be allergic.
- If your child is colicky, avoid spicy food, onions, garlic, cabbage, broccoli, cauliflower, Brussel's sprouts, fruit juice, sugar.
- To decrease the toxic effects of pesticides, eat tofu or soy products with turmeric.
- Avoid contaminated fish and reduce or eliminate animal protein while breast-feeding to decrease body burden of PCBs, dioxin, and brominated fire retardants.
- Drink 2 to 3 liters or quarts of filtered water daily, but do not store it in plastic or drink from plastic bottles (use glass). Eighty-eight percent of breast milk is water — you want it to be pure.

Restore Balance

- Avoid environments where high concentrations of toxins are present. Go to a full serve gas station rather than filling up your car yourself. Avoid paint and newly renovated buildings. Get rid of your carpets before conception to decrease dust and PBDEs.
- Do not use cosmetics or nail polish during breastfeeding that contain phthalates or parabens.
- Do not dye your hair.
- Don't introduce food to your child until after 6 months, and then begin with pureed fruits and vegetables for several months. This will help to decrease lifelong allergies.

TOP 5 STRATEGIES

1. Eat organic vegetarian food.
2. Drink 3 liters or quarts of filtered water daily.
3. Avoid or remove environmental toxins.
4. Express and discard some hindmilk after each feed.
5. Use clean fish oil and curcumin daily.

Insufficient Milk Supply

After childbirth it can take 24 hours or more for milk to come in. Be patient. It is usually quite easy to increase milk supply unless previous breast surgery or trauma has disturbed the milk-producing glands or ducts.

Causes

- Stress
- Dehydration
- Exhaustion
- Poor nutrition
- Emotional factors

Prevention and Treatment

Improve Nutrition
- Do not substitute nursing with bottle-feeding.
- Drink 2 to 3 liters or quarts of filtered water daily (from glass, not plastic).

Restore Balance
- Slow down, get more rest, relax quietly while breast-feeding.
- Massage your breasts while in the shower.
- Nurse on demand, usually about every 2 hours.

HERBAL REMEDIES FOR INSUFFICIENT MILK SUPPLY

- Mix together tea or tinctures of blessed thistle, red raspberry, nettle, alfalfa, hops, and red clover. Drink tea several times daily or take 40 drops of tincture, 3 times daily.
- Simmer 4 tsp of fennel seeds in 1 quart or liter of water for 20 minutes. Drink 3 cups of warmed tea daily.
- Soak ½ cup pearl barley in 3 cups of cold water overnight. Alternatively, boil barley in water for 25 minutes. Strain out the barley. Drink warmed barley water several times daily, or make a barley and vegetable soup.

Plugged Duct (Mastitis)

An inflammation of the breast with local redness and heat can be caused either by a plugged milk duct or from a breast infection. If you have breast soreness or a lump with a fever or flu-like symptoms (feeling achy, tired, and run-down,) it is most likely an infection. If there is no fever, it is probably a plugged duct.

Prevention and Treatment

Restore Balance

- Use echinacea tincture (30 drops) and bee propolis tincture (10 drops), 4 times daily.
- Use phytolacca tincture (2 drops), once daily (not more).
- Breast-feed more often, or express milk from the affected breast more frequently.
- Increase your fluid intake.

HOMEOPATHIC REMEDIES FOR MASTITIS

- **Phytolacca:** Most commonly used remedy for mastitis; breast is hard and very sensitive; can have stitching or stinging pain while nursing that radiates from the nipple to the underarm or shoulder; feels chilly and/or achy; nipples may be cracked.
- **Bryonia:** For heat and painful swelling that feels worse with movement; better with pressure; fever.
- **Silicea:** May be a fissure in the nipple or breast; hard lumps in breast; feels sharp pains while nursing; child may refuse to nurse.
- **Belladonna:** For throbbing pain that comes on quickly; breast is red, hot and swollen, hard, feel heavy; red streaks from the nipple radiate outward; high fever.
- **Hepar sulf:** Breast is very sensitive; wants it covered and kept warm.

Detoxify and Rejuvenate

- Apply cold compresses between feedings to reduce swelling and pain.
- Use a paste of bentonite clay mixed with hot water or castor oil and apply it to the affected breast.

Integrate Body, Mind, and Spirit

- Take better care of yourself. Rest more and express what's bothering you.

TOP 5 STRATEGIES

1. Massage breasts in a warm shower.
2. Breast-feed or express milk more often.
3. Use echinacea and bee propolis, 4 times daily.
4. Use an appropriate homeopathic remedy or phytolacca.
5. Increase fluid intake.

CASE STUDY: *PAIN RESOLVED*

Elinor, a first time mother at 42, complained of redness, soreness, and a hard swelling in her breast twice during the last 4 months she was nursing her daughter, Brianna. Both times we gave her the homeopathic remedy Phytolacca 30CH, 3 pellets every 15 minutes, and in less than an hour the pain resolved. She needed no other treatment.

Thrush (Yeast Infection of the Breast)

Extremely sore nipples with burning, itching and/or shooting pain in the breasts is likely caused by a yeast infection or candida overgrowth. Your nipples may be a deep pink color, sometimes with tiny blisters, tenderness and discomfort, worse immediately after nursing. Your baby may also have signs of yeast overgrowth, with raised white patches in his or her mouth, or a diaper rash with raised red pustules or red scalded-looking buttocks.

Prevention and Treatment

Restore Balance
For you
- Avoid foods that increase the growth of candida – sugar, all sweeteners, yeasted baked goods, vinegar, peanuts, pistachios, mushrooms, alcohol, fermented foods.
- Use a probiotic with *Lactobacillus* and *Bifidobacterium*, 2 capsules, twice daily.
- Use an oral yeast killer – grapefruit seed extract, capryllic acid, or garlic, taken 3 times daily.
- Bathe your nipples in a solution of 1 tbsp vinegar to 1 cup water.

DID YOU KNOW ...

Before nursing, you can apply tea tree oil to your nipples (if it burns, dilute it in almond oil), and between feedings, you can apply diluted liquid grapefruit seed extract (2 drops per ¼ cup water). Be sure to rinse your nipples before nursing.

- Use either homeopathic Pefrakehl 5X drops (Sanum) to discourage candida, 10 drops once daily orally, and 3-5 drops rubbed into the nipples, or Pefrakehl 3X ointment topically.

For your baby

- Put 5 drops of liquid grapefruit seed extract (Citricidal or Nutribiotic) with 8 oz of water in a spray bottle. Spray genital area and buttocks after every diaper change.
- For oral thrush, use live culture yogurt. Place a little on your finger and coat your baby's mouth after each nursing, washing your hands well before and after.
- Give ¼ tsp *Lactobacillus acidophilus* orally in a little water twice daily.
- Use straight lemon juice in your baby's mouth.
- Mix 1 tsp baking soda in 1 cup water and, using a fresh cotton swab each time, wipe your baby's mouth after each nursing — the inside of the cheeks, gums and tongue.
- Use homeopathic Pefrakehl 5X (Sanum), 5 drops orally after each nursing, and rub drops or cream onto buttocks or genital area.

BATH FORMULA FOR THRUSH

Bathe baby's bottom 4 times daily for 15 minutes with one of these remedies:

- 2 tbsp white vinegar in 1 quart water
- 1 tbsp boric acid in 1 quart water
- 2 tbsp baking soda in 1 quart water
- 15 drops grapefruit seed extract in 1 quart water

TOP 5 STRATEGIES

1. Use oral and topical grapefruit seed extract.
2. Use oral *Lactobacillus* and *Bifidobacterium*.
3. Use topical Pefrakehl 5x drops (Sanum).
4. Avoid foods that increase Candida growth.
5. Bathe affected area in a solution of 1 tbsp vinegar to 1 cup water.

Cervical Dysplasia and Cervical Cancer

Cervical dysplasia is a precancerous condition of the cervix, detected by PAP tests when a woman has an annual physical exam. If left untreated, cervical dysplasia can progress to cervical cancer, which in some developing countries (India and Brazil, for example) is the leading cause of death among women (80% of all cervical cancers occur in low-income countries). Every sexually active young woman or woman over age 18 should have a yearly PAP test to ensure her cervix is healthy. Developing countries lack the resources to do this. There are no symptoms with cervical dysplasia until it has progressed to late-stage cancer, and then symptoms include vaginal bleeding, dark vaginal discharge, bleeding after intercourse, back pain, loss of appetite, and weight loss. Natural therapies work best in treating mild cervical dysplasia and can be used in conjunction with conventional medicine to prevent recurrence.

Stages of Cervical Cancer

- Cervical dysplasia most commonly affects women in their 20s.
- Carcinoma in situ (early cancer) affects women in their 30s.
- Invasive cervical cancer affects women older than 40.

PAP Test Results
- Normal
- Mild cervical dysplasia (early changes that are not yet cancerous)
- Severe dysplasia (late changes that are not yet cancerous)
- Carcinoma in situ (cancer confined to the outer layer of the cervix)
- Invasive cancer
- If results are not normal, a repeat test is scheduled in 3 months

Risk Factors
- Early age at first intercourse (younger than 16)
- Multiple sexual partners or sexually active with a man who has multiple sexual partners
- Giving birth before age 22
- Low socioeconomic status
- Black women are more prone
- Compromised immune system
- Nutritional deficiencies of folic acid, vitamin A, vitamin C, selenium, zinc
- Oral contraceptive use
- Herpes simplex virus (HSV) or human immunodeficiency virus (HIV)

DID YOU KNOW ...

Cervical dysplasia most often takes 10 to 15 years to progress to cervical cancer when left untreated. PAP smears save women's lives by detecting abnormal cells early enough to initiate treatment to reverse or eradicate abnormal cells. Cervical dysplasia is completely curable when detected early.

DID YOU KNOW ...

Smoking increases risk of cervical dysplasia and cancer up to four times. Carcinogens in cigarette smoke concentrate in cervical mucus at levels 10 to 20 times higher than in blood. Smoking depletes vitamin C.

343

DID YOU KNOW ...

Approximately 90% of cervical dysplasias are linked with the sexually transmitted human papilloma virus (HPV), although most women with the virus never get dysplasia. Approximately 70% of us have been exposed to the virus within our lifetimes, so other factors are at play.

DID YOU KNOW ...

By eating foods high in indole-3-carbinol and beta carotene, such as coleslaw, sauerkraut, carrots, beets, cabbage, and kale juice regularly. They can help to reverse cervical dysplasia.

Prevention and Treatment

Improve Nutrition

In addition to following the Women's Health Diet Plan (Section 2), try these dietary and nutrient therapies.

Diet

- Eat two salads and an orange vegetable daily (squash, sweet potato, carrot).
- Eat foods high in folic acid — brewer's yeast, black-eyed peas, lentils, lima beans, freshly squeezed orange juice, kidney beans, romaine lettuce, dandelion greens, and leeks.
- Eat cooked tomato sauce a few times a week for its protective lycopene, an antioxidant, along with olive oil, to improve its absorption.
- Eat 3 Brazil nuts daily for selenium.
- Eat 2 tsp turmeric daily to assist liver detoxification and decrease inflammation.
- Use 2 tbsp flaxseed oil daily.
- Drink several cups of organic green tea daily or use a green tea extract.

NUTRIENT THERAPY FOR CERVICAL DYSPLASIA		
NUTRIENT	**ACTION**	**DAILY DOSE**
Folic acid	Reverses mild dysplasia	10 mg, for 3 months
Vitamin C	Improves immunity	2,000-4,000 mg
Beta carotene	Heals tissues and strengthens immune system	200,000 IU
Vitamin B-6	Supports immune system	100-200 mg
Vitamin B-12	Supports immune system	800 mcg
Vitamin E mixed tocopherols	Promotes tissue healing	400-800 IU
Selenium	Activates immunity	200 mcg
Zinc	Heals tissues Builds immune strength	30-50 mg
Indole-3-carbinol	Helps reverse dysplasia	300 mg
NAC	Supports detoxification pathways and immune system	1,500 mg
Uncontaminated fish oil	Decreases inflammation	3,000 mg

Restore Balance

- Use homeopathic remedies as indicated: Conium, Kreosotum, Thuja, Hydrastis, Carbo animalis and Carcinosin. Work with a homeopath.
- Use barrier contraceptives, such as the male or female condom to decrease exposure to HPV.
- Normalize acid-alkaline balance after checking pH of urine and saliva. See the Seasonal Cleansing and Rejuvenation Program section for guidelines.

TCM FOR CERVICAL DYSPLASIA

In traditional Chinese medicine, cervical conditions can be linked with:

- Liver qi stagnation (often from unexpressed anger)
- Stagnation of blood (with frustration, tension, resentment, depression)
- Damp heat in the pelvic region (known as the lower warmer)

- **Remedies:** Two formulas that address these conditions are the patent formula *Ping Xiao Dan* and *Bupleurum and Peony*. *Xiao Yao Wan* or *Bupleurum & Tang Kuei* will address liver qi stagnation.

Detoxify and Rejuvenate

- Stop smoking. See the Seasonal Cleansing and Rejuvenation Program section for stop-smoking guidelines.
- Stop taking oral contraceptives. Use the sympto-thermo method along with barrier methods of birth control. See the Birth Control chapter in this section for guidelines.
- Support liver detoxification using NAC (500 mg), indole-3-carbinol (300 mg), curcumin (1500 mg) daily, plus milk thistle and dandelion.
- Support bowel and vaginal flora with *Lactobacillus acidophilus* and *Bifidobacterium bifidus*, 2 capsules daily, orally.
- Use homeopathic drainage herapy: Unda 10, Unda 21, Unda 48, and Unda 245, 5 drops of each, 3x daily, for 3 weeks of the month for several months.

Integrate Body, Mind, and Spirit

- If you feel lingering, unexpressed anger or guilt about your sexual experiences, currently or in the past, acknowledge those feelings. Express them by writing, drawing or working with a therapist or bodyworker.
- Communicate honestly with your sexual partner. Visualize your cervix as a sacred, beautiful opening to your femininity and creativity. Understand that you now have the power to say "yes" or "no" to anyone or anything as it approaches that opening.

DID YOU KNOW ...

Inserting a vitamin A suppository every other night into the vagina can help treat cervical dysplasia. On alternate nights, insert 2 capsules of herbal Vagistatin pushed up to the cervix, to help eliminate the HPV virus. Continue 1 to 3 months.

- Develop a healthy spiritual life to decrease alienation and despair and to build faith.
- Repeat a suitable affirmation several times daily.

> *I respect myself as a sexual being; I respect my sexuality.*
> *I open myself to nurturing, sacred sexual experiences.*
> *I can say "no" to sex I do not want.*

HERBAL FORMULA FOR CERVICAL DYSPLASIA

- Goldenseal (*Hydrastis canadensis*)
- Marigold (*Calendula officinalis*)
- Lomatium (*Lomatium dissectum*)
- Astragalus (*Astragalus membranaceus*)
- Thuja (*Thuja occidentalis*)

Dose: Mix together tinctures in equal parts and take ½ tsp, 3 times daily orally, for 3 weeks at a time, followed by a 1-week break. Use a probiotic containing *Lactobacillus acidophilus* and *Bifidobacterium bifidus* at a different time of day.

Conventional Medicine

LEEP Treatment

- This procedure uses electrosurgery to remove the affected tissue. It is the most common treatment.

Cryotherapy

- When there are small mild lesions, liquid nitrogen is used to freeze a half-centimeter layer of cervical tissue. This then breaks down and is discharged over the next 2 weeks.

Laser Conization

- This procedure uses laser light to destroy the affected layer of tissue.

Hysterectomy

- In advanced cases of cancer, hysterectomy is performed and radiation may be recommended.

TOP 5 STRATEGIES

1. Take folic acid (10 mg), daily.
2. Take Indole-3-Carbinol (300 mg), daily.
3. Take vitamin C (3000 mg), daily.
4. Take zinc (50 mg) and selenium (200 mg), daily.
5. Use the Herbal Formula for Cervical Dysplasia.

Uterine Fibroids

Fibroids are the most common benign tumor in women's reproductive tracts. Uterine fibroids (also known as leiomyomas or myomas) are typically slow-growing, non-cancerous growths occurring on the inside or outside walls of the uterus, composed of connective tissue and muscle. They most often feel round and firm, but can be soft or rock hard, are often found in groups, and vary in size from being microscopic to larger than a grapefruit. They are usually not tender on palpation. If you have a uterine fibroid, it is possible to shrink it with natural therapies.

Diagnosis

- Uterine fibroids are diagnosed during a pelvic exam and confirmed by ultrasound.
- The ultrasound will help to determine the contours of the uterus, the size of the fibroid, whether the ureters are compressed causing enlargement of the kidneys, and whether the fibroid is affecting the bowel.
- After initial diagnosis, a follow-up pelvic exam or ultrasound should be carried out in 4 to 6 months to determine the rate of growth of the fibroid.
- An annual pelvic exam thereafter is sufficient to monitor a fibroid.

Symptoms

- Increased menstrual symptoms – pain, heavy bleeding, irregular periods, mid-cycle bleeding
- Anemia due to increased blood loss
- Abdominal bloating, pressure or heaviness
- Enlarged abdomen
- Back pain
- Excessive vaginal discharge
- Pain or bleeding with intercourse
- Irritation to the bladder and increased urinary frequency
- Compression of the ureter, resulting in kidney enlargement
- Obstruction to the bowel
- Occasionally infertility
- Miscarriage, premature delivery, or increased blood loss during childbirth

DID YOU KNOW ...

Women are most affected by uterine fibroids between the ages of 40 and 44. They occur in nearly 70% of white women and more than 80% of black women by age 50, although 50% to 80% of women have no symptoms. If fibroids do not shrink at menopause or are fast growing, they may be malignant.

DID YOU KNOW ...

A uterine fibroid needs to be differentiated from an ovarian tumor, an abscess in the fallopian tube or ovary, endometriosis, adhesions in the pelvis, a rare pelvic kidney, a congenital anomaly, and a diverticulum from the colon. Surgical laparoscopy may be required for the final diagnosis.

Causes

Dietary Factors

- Excess animal protein
- Lack of green vegetables and fruit
- Excess saturated fat (cheese, butter, milk, dairy, meat, lard)
- Insufficient dietary fiber
- Excess acid-forming foods (animal protein and grain) and deficiency of alkaline-forming foods (fruits and vegetables)
- Pesticides and heavy metals in food

Bowel and Liver Toxicity

- When there are less than two or three bowel movements daily
- When there is dysbiosis and an imbalance in the bowel flora
- Due to alcohol consumption (beer in particular)
- Due to chemical and toxic overload

Hormone Imbalances and Insufficiency

- Oral contraceptive use and hormone replacement therapy are implicated in development of uterine fibroids.
- Fibroid growth is related to increased numbers of estrogen receptors in fibroid tissue combined with higher body levels of estrogens or exposure to xenoestrogens.
- Women with uterine fibroids may have a progesterone deficiency.
- Hypothyroidism is often present in women with fibroids.
- IGF-1, a growth hormone produced by the liver, is found in higher amounts in uterine fibroid cells than in healthy uterine tissue and works with estrogen to stimulate fibroid growth.
- Melatonin deficiency (caused by exposure to light at night or shift work) may predispose a woman to increased fibroid growth, as melatonin decreases numbers of estrogen receptors.

Other Factors

- Low physical activity along with obesity is a risk factor in developing uterine fibroids
- Uterine fibroids, particularly in the model used in traditional Chinese medicine, are related to blood and energy stagnation in the pelvis
- Fibroids may be related to toxins entering the lymph and blood circulation from an infected root canal

Prevention and Treatment

Improve Nutrition

In addition to following the Women's Health Diet Plan (Section 2), try these dietary strategies:

- Avoid chocolate, alcohol and coffee – these interfere with the liver's ability to transform estrogen into safe metabolites.
- If you have heavy periods, consume food sources of iron, such as seaweeds, pumpkin seeds, and molasses daily.
- Avoid peanuts because they increase the body's inflammatory response.
- Use olive oil for cooking (in a little water) and use flaxseed oil and pure fish oil on your food after it is cooked. Avoid butter, margarine, and all other oils.
- Use 2 tsp or more of turmeric daily.
- Use 2 tbsp of ground flaxseed daily.

Restore Balance

- Assess adrenal function and balance. See the Hormone Balance chapter in the Living with Nature's Rhythms section for guidelines.
- Assess melatonin levels through saliva samples taken between 1-3 a.m. If it is low, normalize levels. See the Hormone Balance chapter in the Living with Nature's Rhythms section for guidelines.
- Assess thyroid function using the basal body temperature test and blood tests. If thyroid function is low, correct it. See the Hypothyroidism chapter in this section.
- Decrease IGF-1 levels by avoiding sugar and high glycemic carbohydrates and adopting a primarily vegan diet.
- Maintain a healthy weight, with a body mass index of less than 23, to keep estrogen production low in your fat cells.

DID YOU KNOW ...

A study of 79 women scheduled for hysterectomies found that 23% had hypothyroidism as determined by a TRH/TSH stimulation test, whereas only 3.7% of women in a control group had disturbed thyroid function. An underactive thyroid results in more available estrogen, which causes fibroid growth.

DID YOU KNOW ...

Overweight is correlated with uterine fibroids. Women with a body mass greater than 25 are more susceptible to uterine fibroids.

ESTROGEN BALANCING REGIMEN

- Assess levels of estradiol, estrone, estriol, and progesterone in saliva on day 20 to 23 of your menstrual cycle.
- Normalize levels. See the Hormone Balance chapter in the Living with Nature's Rhythms section for guidelines.
- If progesterone is low, use ¼–½ tsp twice daily of 3% progesterone from day 14 to 28, applying the cream to your inner arms, chest, inner thighs, and/or buttocks.
- Recheck salivary progesterone levels between day 20 to 23 of your cycle while using the cream, 2 months after you begin to ensure that levels are in the optimal range.
- Avoid the birth control pill and hormone replacement therapy.
- Exercise 40 minutes daily to improve circulation to the liver and uterus, and to improve metabolism of estrogen. Consider rebounding, cycling, belly dancing, jogging.

HOMEOPATHIC REMEDIES TO DOWNSIZE FIBROIDS

- **Calcarea iodatum 6CH:** for small fibroids with much yellow or bloody vaginal discharge; increased sexual desire; difficult menstruation with absent, heavy, frequent or irregular periods; pain in the ovaries or uterus; there may be thyroid enlargement or enlarged tonsils. Use 3 pellets, 3x daily.

- **Fraximus americana 6CH:** for a swollen uterus or uterine prolapse, a heaviness in the lower abdomen, painful menstrual cramps, watery brown vaginal discharge. Use 3 pellets, 3x daily.

- **Silicea 6CH:** for heavy periods, bleeding between periods, fatigue, body feels very cold. Use 3 pellets 3x daily.

- **Thlaspi bursa 6CH:** for heavy, continuous uterine bleeding, frequent periods, bloody and dark vaginal discharge before and after the period, pain in the uterus on rising. Use 3 pellets, 3x daily.

- **Gossypium 6CH:** for swelling and itching of the labia, nausea and vomiting in the morning, watery menstrual flow, intermittent ovarian pain. Use 3 pellets, 3x daily.

- **Ustilago maydis 6CH:** for fibroids occurring around menopause; depression; heavy menstrual bleeding, with dark, clotted, stringy blood; burning in the ovaries. Use 3 pellets, 3x daily.

- **Calcarea carbonica 6CH:** for women who are overweight, pale, flabby, with easy perspiration and cold, damp extremities. Menstruation may be too early.

DID YOU KNOW ...

You can use bodywork, such as myofascial release and deep tissue massage to the pelvis, once weekly to improve circulation and lymphatic drainage.

DID YOU KNOW ...

Treatment of uterine fibroids by traditional Chinese medicine using acupuncture and herbs is very effective in reducing fibroids. In a study of 37 women undergoing 6 months of treatment, 22 reported improvement with either decreased rate of growth, reduced size, or complete cure.

HYDROTHERAPY TO REDUCE FIBROIDS

Use daily or weekly sitz baths with alternating hot and cold immersions. You will need two large wash tubs.

1. Put a towel on the bottom and around the back of the tubs where you will be leaning.
2. Fill the hot tub with enough water at a temperature of 106-110°F (41-43°C) to rise ½ inch above your navel.
3. Fill the cold tub with water at 55-75°F (12-24°C).
4. Cover your upper body with a sheet or blanket.
5. Alternate sitting in the hot tub for 2-5 minutes, followed by the cold immersion for 20-60 seconds. (If you are unable to do the cold immersion, use cold wet towels over the abdomen instead.)
6. Repeat this sequence 2-3 times, always beginning with hot and finishing with the cold immersion. Rest for at least ½ hour afterward, staying well covered.

TCM FOR UTERINE FIBROIDS

Diagnostic Patterns
- Blood stagnation, with accompanying cold
- Qi stagnation or blood dryness
- Spleen deficiency
- Dysfunction of the penetrating meridian or conception vessel meridian
- Deficiency of the yang motility meridian
- Excess of the yin motility meridian

DID YOU KNOW ...

A study of 110 premenopausal women with uterine fibroids less than 10 centimeters in diameter showed that after 12 or more weeks of using an extract daily containing 1.5 grams of *Gui Zhi Fu Ling Tang* formula, excess uterine bleeding and pain was improved in 90% of women and shrinkage of fibroids occurred in more than 60%.

CHINESE HERBAL FORMULAS TO RESOLVE FIBROIDS

Gui Zhi Fu Ling Tang Formula
This formula is taken as a tea to move the blood, move qi, dispel stagnant blood, and reduce abdominal masses.

To prepare the mixture:
Mix 9 grams each of:
- *Ramulus Cinnamomi cassiae* – cinnamon twig (*Gui Zhi*)
- *Sclerotium Poriae cocos* – hoelen (*Fu Ling*)
- *Semen persica* – peach kernel (*Tao Ren*)
- *Radix Paeonia rubra* – red peony root (*Chi Shao*)
- *Cortex Moutan radicis* – tree peony root (*Dan Pi*)

To make the tea:
Use a glass or enamel pot. Place the herbs in the pot and add clean cold water, filling to 1 inch above the level of the herbs. Soak plants for 1 hour. Place the pot over heat and bring to a boil, and then simmer, covered, for 1 hour. Strain the liquid into a glass container. Add water again to the same level and simmer again for 30 minutes. Strain into the same glass container.

- **Dose:** This should provide you with 2 cups of liquid. Drink 1 cup, warmed, twice daily. You may also buy enough of the herbs for 6 days, boil them in the same way, and keep 12 cups of the tea in the fridge, taking 1 cup warmed twice daily. Rest on the seventh day. Continue the tea for several months.

Other Formulas
- *Cinnamon & Poria Formula*: 3 tablets twice daily. It is contraindicated during pregnancy and breast-feeding.
- *Cinnamon & Rehmannia*
- *Chih-ko & Curcuma*

351

DID YOU KNOW ...

Using the gemmotherapies Rosemarinus (made from the young shoots of rosemary), 50 drops, 3x daily, will decongest the liver, and *Rubus idaeus* (from raspberry bush shoots) 50 drops, 3 times daily, will work as a drainage remedy for the uterus.

Detoxify and Rejuvenate

- Test for and detoxify heavy metals and schedule a 100-hour sauna detox to eliminate xenoestrogens. See the Seasonal Cleansing and Rejuvenation section for guidelines.
- Do a liver cleanse and the liver flush. See the Seasonal Cleansing and Rejuvenation Program section for guidelines.
- Apply castor oil packs over the uterus, entire abdomen, and liver 5 nights a week for 2 months. See the Seasonal Cleansing and Rejuvenation Program section for guidelines.
- Use bentonite clay, prepared as a paste and applied topically to the pelvis over the fibroid area daily for 3 weeks at a time, and not during the week of menstruation, to draw out toxic metals and chemicals. See the Seasonal Cleansing and Rejuvenation section for guidelines.
- Restore normal bowel flora by taking a probiotic containing *Lactobacillus acidophilus* and *Bifidobacterium.* Use 2 capsules daily with meals.
- Ensure three bowel movements daily: use 1 tbsp each of psyllium seed powder and wheat bran daily to decrease circulating estrogen levels. Eat 45 grams fiber daily.

LIVER SUPPLEMENTS TO HELP METABOLIZE ESTROGEN

LIVER SUPPLEMENTS	DOSAGE
Vitamin B complex	50-100 mg, daily
Vitamin B-6	100 mg, daily in total
NAC	500 mg, 3 times daily
Curcumin	500 mg, 3 times daily
Indole-3-carbinol and DIM mixture	300 mg, daily
Alpha lipoic acid	100 mg, twice daily
Magnesium citrate	300 mg, daily
Choline	250 mg, twice daily
Inositol	150 mg, twice daily
L-methionine	100 mg, twice daily

HOMEOPATHIC REMEDIES FOR FIBROIDS

- **Homeopathic drainage remedies to shrink fibroids:**
  Unda 1, Unda 20, Unda 258, 5 drops of each, 3x daily, taken directly in the mouth or in a little water for 3 weeks to assist liver and kidney detoxification. Wait one week, and then use Unda 243, Unda 10, Unda 48 and Unda 245, 5 drops 3x daily, for 3-6 months.

- **Homeopathic tissue salts to help dissolve fibroids:** Calc fluor 6X, 3 pellets 3x daily.

- Eliminate plastic containers, pesticides, polyvinyl chloride (PVC), brominated fire retardants, cosmetics containing phthalates and parabens, and toxic metals from your environment and do what you can in your community to restrict these.

Integrate Body, Mind, and Spirit

- Work with a psychotherapist and/or bodyworker to release the emotional and cellular memories that are obstructing the flow of energy in the uterus.
- Give birth to your creative self, whether it be through dance, music, art, pottery, writing, or any other creative activity.
- Address and resolve conflicts, anger or grief you may experience about having or not having children.
- Communicate with your partner about your sexual needs and engage your spontaneous, sensual and playful self more in your relationship and in life.
- Commit to a regular meditation practice under the guidance of a teacher.
- Repeat appropriate affirmations:

    I give birth to and allow space for my creative self this day and every day.

    I awaken to my full and glorious sexuality, and move with it.

    My uterus is fertile, fully prepared, and ready to nourish a child, as am I.

    I relinquish the need for a child, and give birth to my new self.

    I release my children into the world, and make time for me.

UTERINE FIBROID DISSOLVING FORMULA

This formula will help to relieve liver congestion and assist estrogen metabolism, circulate blood and energy to the uterus, increase progesterone, help stop excess bleeding, dissolve fibroids, relieve pain, and remove lymph congestion. It can also be used to diminish ovarian cysts and to relieve symptoms of endometriosis.

20%	Wild yam root (*Dioscorea villosa*)
20%	Lady's mantle (*Alchemilla vulgaris*)
20%	Chaste tree berry (*Vitex agnus casti*)
10%	Marigold (*Calendula officinalis*)
10%	Burdock (*Arctium lappa*)
10%	Red root (*Ceanothus americanus*)
10%	Cleavers (*Galium aparine*)

Dose: Mix the herbs together in tincture form in the above proportions and use 50 drops, 3 times daily, for at least 6 months. Contraindicated during pregnancy.

DID YOU KNOW ...

While a myomectomy may help a woman conceive, it is not curative – 15% to 30% of women who undergo one will eventually have another fibroid.

Conventional Medicine

Surgical Treatment

- Surgical options for women with uterine fibroids include myomectomy (removal of the fibroid from the uterus) or hysterectomy (total removal of the uterus). These are reserved for women who either have rapidly growing abdominal masses that may be uterine cancer; excessive and prolonged uterine bleeding unresponsive to other treatments; persistent or intolerable abdominal pain or pressure; urinary or bowel complaints; infertility; or repeated miscarriages.
- Myomectomy is more commonly done for women wanting to conceive, while hysterectomy is performed on women who have finished bearing children.

Drug Treatment

- Drugs that suppress ovarian hormones, such as gonadotropin-releasing hormone antagonists
- Drugs that oppose progesterone
- Progesterone alone
- Selective estrogen receptor modulators (SERMS), such as Tamoxifen or Raloxifene

YOGA FOR UTERINE FIBROIDS

Practice yoga exercises to circulate blood and energy in the pelvis. Here are three Kundalini yoga exercises:

1. Sit on your heels with your palms flat on your thighs. Close your eyes, focusing your gaze between the eyebrows. Bring your attention to the pelvis and uterus. Inhale deeply through your nose. Hold your breath and using your abdominal muscles, begin to pump the navel in and out as vigorously as possible. When you can no longer hold the breath, exhale through your nose. Hold the breath out and pump the navel again, in and out, for as long as possible. Then inhale and begin the sequence again, all the while directing the energy of the breath to the pelvic region. Continue for 2 to 3 minutes.

2. Sit cross-legged with your hands on your knees. Close your eyes, focusing your gaze between the eyebrows. Bring your attention to the pelvis and uterus. Keeping your head steady and facing forward, rotate your waist from right to left, inhaling as you come round the front and exhaling as you go round the back, as though you are drawing a circle with the waist around the centre line of the body. Push your chest forward as you come round the front (without leaning forward); press the lower spine down and back as you go around the back. After 1½ minutes, reverse the direction and continue another 1½ minutes.

3. Lie on your back. Bend your knees, bringing your heels close to your buttocks, shoulder width apart. Grab your ankles if you can; otherwise keep your arms at your sides. Inhale and lift your pelvis up as high as possible; exhale and lower it down. Imagine you are inhaling through the vagina into the uterus as you raise the pelvis, exhaling out through the vagina as you lower it. The breath is dissolving the fibroid, breaking it up as you exhale. Continue for 26 repetitions.

One of these drugs is usually used for 3 to 6 months; however, they (except for progesterone) may induce unpleasant side effects, such as hot flashes, vaginal dryness, and bone loss, and do not prevent the tumors from returning after the treatment is completed.

TOP 5 STRATEGIES

1. Follow the Women's Health Diet Plan, eating primarily vegetarian and avoiding dairy.
2. Correct hormonal imbalances – decrease estrogen dominance and IGF-1, increase progesterone and melatonin, normalize thyroid function.
3. Detoxify the liver and bowel.
4. Exercise 40 minutes each day.
5. Use Chinese or Western herbal formulas for 6 months.

CASE STUDY: *FIBROID SHRINKS*

Dierdre, a physiotherapist, was scheduled for a hysterectomy in 3 months because her fibroid was pressing on her bladder and interfering with her ability to urinate. She had heavy periods with large clots, and had been experiencing menstrual discomfort and back pain for 7 years, since her daughter was born. She had pain during intercourse, and sometimes her uterus felt as though it was on fire. She frequently dreamed of her mother, who was dead. She also confided that she was dissatisfied with her sex life, and did not find her partner attractive since he had gained weight. Her bowel movements were every 2 or 3 days, and though she was a vegetarian, she consumed cheese and yogurt daily.

We prescribed several nutritional supplements to help Dierdre's liver break down estrogen — curcumin, indole-3-carbinol, NAC — and had her use 3 tsp of psyllium a day and 2 tbsp of ground flaxseed to increase dietary fiber. We advised her to cut out all dairy and use more tofu and legumes. We prescribed the Chinese herbal formula Cinnamon and Poria, as well as chaste tree berry and the gemmotherapy Rubus idaeus. We added fish oil to her diet and suggested she take a good probiotic formula. We had her discontinue her coffee and wine intake.

Upon testing, we found that Dierdre had low progesterone and her adrenal glands were underactive, though her thyroid blood tests were normal. We prescribed 3% progesterone cream and an herbal formula for her adrenal glands. We also had Dierdre place castor oil packs over her lower abdomen and liver three times a week and exercise 4 hours a week.

Dierdre returned in 6 weeks to report that sex was no longer painful, that she was having three bowel movements a day, and that she had no more trouble with urination. The fibroid was undoubtedly still there, but had shrunk. Dierdre's improvement continued over the next year and she was able to avoid a hysterectomy.

Pelvic Inflammatory Disease (PID)

If you have pelvic inflammatory disease, you will need a combination of conventional and natural medicines. Pelvic inflammatory disease is a serious infection of the pelvic organs involving the uterine lining (endometritis), the fallopian tubes (salpingitis), the lining of the abdomen and pelvis (pelvic peritonitis), or an abscess in the ovary or fallopian tubes. It is caused by infection from a group of organisms, predominantly Neisseria gonorrhoeae *(the gonorrhea bacteria) and* Chlamydia trachomatis. *Other organisms that may be involved include* Mycoplasma *species,* Haemophilus influenzae, Streptococcus *species, and* Ureaplasma urealyticum. *Possible complications of PID include ectopic pregnancy, infertility, and chronic pelvic pain.*

DID YOU KNOW ...

More than one million American women are diagnosed with pelvic inflammatory disease annually and it requires hospitalization one-quarter of the time. Because of its seriousness, antibiotics are required. Natural therapies are used to support conventional treatments.

Symptoms

- Mild pelvic pain
- Tenderness of the cervix and ovaries
- Fever, chills
- Irregular vaginal bleeding or discharge
- Nausea, vomiting,
- Urinary discomfort and frequency,
- Lower abdominal pain, which is worse with pressure

Risk Factors

- Multiple sexual partners or a new sexual partner
- A non-monogamous sexual partner
- Not using barrier methods of contraception
- Being age 14 to 24
- History of a sexually transmitted disease
- Surgery to the uterus or cervix (followed by infection)
- Surgical abortion
- Caesarean section
- Bowel surgery
- May occur after endometrial biopsy
- Vaginal douching strongly increases risk of PID
- IUD insertion, increased risk for 20 days afterward, lower risk for 8 years thereafter
- Never being pregnant
- Cigarette, alcohol, or drug use
- Pelvic pain occurring during or within 1 week of menstruation

Prevention and Treatment

Improve Nutrition

In addition to following the Women's Health Diet (Section 2), consider these dietary and supplement strategies:

Diet

- Avoid foods that increase internal heat or disturb liver qi – meat, alcohol, hot sauce, spicy food, fried and fatty foods, coffee.
- Eat foods that clear heat and dampness, such as mung beans, daikon radish, carrots, carrot juice, lemon in water.
- Use 2 tbsp unheated flaxseed oil on your food daily to decrease inflammation.
- Eat a vegetarian diet with no dairy (dairy increases inflammation) and 8 servings of vegetables and fruits a day.

Nutrient Supplements

- To improve immune function: vitamin C (2000 mg); vitamin E mixed tocopherols (400 IU); vitamin A (50,000 IU); vitamin B complex (50 mg); zinc (50 mg); selenium (200 mcg) – all taken daily.
- To decrease inflammation: curcumin (1500 mg) and uncontaminated fish oil (3000 mg) – daily.

DID YOU KNOW ...

Your sexual partner must be treated to prevent re-infection. Always use barrier methods of birth control with new or non-monogamous sexual partners. Use of condoms greatly decreases risk of pain and infertility associated with PID.

TCM FOR PELVIC INFLAMMATORY DISEASE

- Chinese medicine is effective in treating chronic pelvic inflammatory disease. One study demonstrated reduction of pain and improvement in immune markers after 12 acupuncture treatments (3 per week), during which the following points were used for the first 6 treatments: GV-4, GV-14, GV-20, Bl-28, Bl-31, Bl-43, K-3. Points used during the next 6 treatments included: Liv-2, Sp-6, LI-4, LI-11, CV-3, St-30, St-36, TW-5, P-6. Sp-9 and K-5 were also occasionally used.

- In another study, 42 women with chronic PID were treated with a Chinese herbal formula. As a control group, 37 patients received the oral antibiotics gentamycin and metronidazole along with vitamin C. Of the 42 cases treated by Chinese medicine, 26 were completely cured, 9 had significant results, 4 had some results, and 3 had no results, giving a total effective rate of 92.8%. Of the 37 cases treated by Western medicine, 12 were completely cured, 8 had significant results, 6 had some results, and 11 had no results, giving a total effective rate of 70.3%.

Restore Balance

- Rest in bed while undergoing antibiotic treatment.
- Use alternating hot and cold sitz baths to improve circulation. See the Uterine Fibroids chapter in this section for guidelines.
- Use ice packs over the uterus while putting your feet in a bucket of hot water to reduce acute inflammation and pain.
- While using antibiotics to clear the infection, take a probiotic formula containing *Lactobacillus acidophilus* and *Bifidobacterium*.
- Do not practice vaginal douching.
- Stop smoking. See the Seasonal Cleansing and Rejuvenation Program section for guidelines.

HOMEOPATHIC REMEDIES FOR PID

- In acute PID with fever, along with antibiotics: use Unda 2, Unda 15, and Unda 37, 5 drops of each, 3x daily for kidney drainage and clearance of toxins
- To stimulate an immune response: use Echinacea compositum drop, 10 drops, 3x daily.
- To help clear residual bacterial infection: use Notakehl, 10 drops, 1-2x daily.
- To decrease inflammation, use Nymeel, 10 drops 3 or more times daily.
- After antibiotic treatment, to assist with cellular and uterine drainage: use Unda 245, Unda 48 and Unda 21, 5 drops of each, 3x daily, for 3 weeks.
- To dissolve scar tissue, reduce adhesions, and improve fertility: Thiosinaminum 6CH.

DID YOU KNOW ...

Other remedies and nutrients that assist in softening or breaking down scar tissue (from mild to strongly acting) include the gemmotherapies *Oleo europa* and *Viscum album*, as well as grape seed, vitamin E, the tissue salt Silicea 6X, and castor oil packs.

Detoxify and Rejuvenate

- Cleanse the bowel with 1 tbsp psyllium seed powder and 2 tbsp freshly ground flaxseed daily.
- Use castor oil packs over the pelvis (see Spring) 3 times weekly for 3 months after acute PID to prevent adhesions and scar tissue.

Integrate Body, Mind, and Spirit

- Chronic pelvic pain and inflammation may occur after sexual abuse. If you have been abused, work with a therapist who can help you release cellular trauma and emotional pain.

Conventional Medicine

- Acute pelvic inflammatory disease is conventionally treated with aggressive antibiotic therapy, and occasionally with a hysterectomy.

HERBAL FORMULA FOR CHRONIC PID

20% Goldenseal (*Hydrastis canadensis*)

20% Yarrow (*Achillea millefolium*)

20% Echinacea (*Echinacea augustifolium*)

20% Marigold (*Calendula officinalis*)

20% Pasque flower (*Pulsatilla anemone*)

Dose: Mix together in equal parts to strengthen immunity. Take 40 drops of the combination 3 times daily, 3 weeks on, 1 week off. Use in conjunction with *Lactobacillus acidophilus* and *Bifidobacterium bifidus*, taken at a different time.

TOP 5 STRATEGIES

1. Use antibiotic therapy.
2. Use acupuncture and Chinese herbal treatments.
3. Use homeopathic Notakehl (10 drops), twice daily.
4. Take *Lacto bacillus acidophilus* and *Bifidobacterium*.
5. Use the Herbal Formula for Chronic PID.

Endometriosis

If you are suffering from endometriosis, take heart – we have seen it respond well to natural medicine. Endometriosis occurs when the tissue that forms the lining of the uterus (endometrial tissue) implants in areas of the pelvis outside the uterus, and can sometimes be found in other parts of the body, such as the lungs, nose, or brain. Usually, wayward endometrial tissue attaches to the uterus, fallopian tubes, vagina, cervix, ovaries, bladder, and bowel. When the uterine endometrial lining is shed at the end of a menstrual period, the cells in the rogue tissue also bleed (or sometimes they run on their own monthly rhythm) into surrounding tissue, forming blood blisters that become cysts. This creates local inflammation and pain, and the cysts form scars or adhesions. Scars or adhesions on the ovaries or fallopian tubes can prevent pregnancy. The symptoms of endometriosis include pain before, during, and between the menstrual periods, irregular menstrual cycles, painful intercourse and infertility, although half of the patients with endometriosis have no symptoms. Although a pelvic exam and ultrasound may show endometriosis, a laparoscopy (when a surgeon inserts a small telescope through a pelvic incision to look for lesions) is the definitive diagnostic technique to reveal its extent, and biopsy confirms the diagnosis.

DID YOU KNOW ...

About 10% of menstruating women have endometriosis. The incidence is close to 50% in women who have been unable to conceive.

Theoretical Causes

- Retrograde bleeding: menstrual blood flowing backward pushes small bits of endometrial tissue through the fallopian tubes into the pelvic cavity.
- In women with altered immune function, the endometrial tissue survives and responds to the hormone estrogen (in healthy women it does not survive).
- Some women are born with endometrial tissue in the wrong place and a glitch in the immune system allows the tissue to become active.
- Higher levels of immunoglobulins IgM and IgG in women with endometriosis cause destruction of the body's own tissue. Their antibodies are attacking their ovaries and endometrial cells.
- Exposure to environmental chemicals that mimic estrogen, such as dioxin, has caused endometriosis in rhesus monkeys.
- Increased free radical production (oxidative stress) promotes the growth of endometrial tissue.
- Stagnation of qi and blood (according to Chinese medicine).

Risk Factors

- Having a mother or sister with endometriosis
- Menstrual cycles that are shorter than 25 days
- Menstrual periods that are longer than 7 days
- Estrogen dominance

- Hormone replacement therapy
- Environmental estrogens – dioxin and PCBs (ingested in fish, meat, dairy, exposure from hospital incinerators)
- Increased body fat
- Diet high in animal fat (causes high arachidonic acid, which increases pain)
- Lack of exercise from an early age
- Use of IUD
- Being a redhead
- Higher stress levels and poor adaptation to stress
- Childhood sexual abuse
- Alcohol use
- Prenatal exposure to high estrogen levels
- Poor liver function
- Bowel toxicity and constipation
- Dysbiosis – imbalance in bowel flora

Protective Factors

- Regular exercise
- Smoking – it lowers estrogen levels (but please don't smoke)
- Vegetarian diet that restricts dairy and sugar
- Avoidance of animal fat to reduce arachidonic acid (which causes inflammation and pain)
- High intake of antioxidants reduces adhesions
- Optimal liver function
- Increased dietary fiber
- Balanced bowel flora
- Optimal bowel function – three bowel movements daily (reduces estrogen)

Prevention and Treatment

Improve Nutrition

In addition to following the Women's Health Diet Plan (Section 2), consider these dietary and nutrient therapies:

FOODS TO AVOID

- Red meat, pork, poultry, all dairy, shellfish and peanuts to lower arachidonic acid levels and decrease inflammation and pain
- Caffeine, coffee, chocolate – caffeine makes symptoms worse
- Alcohol
- Fish – they contain very high levels of PCBs and dioxin
- Sugar – it increases conversion of fats to arachidonic acid

---

Diet

- Use 2 tsp or more of turmeric daily to inactivate environmental estrogens, cleanse your liver and decrease inflammation.
- Use 2 tbsp ground flaxseed daily to displace strong estrogens and cleanse the bowel.
- Add 2 tbsp unheated flaxseed oil to your food to decrease inflammation.
- Use 45 mg fiber daily: 2 tbsp wheat bran (if not allergic), 1 tbsp psyllium, 2 tbsp freshly ground flaxseed, and 1 cup beans daily to improve elimination of estrogen.

NUTRIENT THERAPY FOR ENDOMETRIOSIS		
NUTRIENT	**ACTION**	**DAILY DOSAGE**
Vitamin C	Enhances immunity	6,000 mg in divided doses
Beta carotene	Immune strength	50,000 – 100,000 IU
Vitamin B complex (with 100 mg B-6)	Improves estrogen metabolism	100 mg
Vitamin B-3 (niacin)	Improves circulation Relieves pain	100 mg can be taken every 3 hours
Vitamin E	Decreases inflammation Enhances immunity	400-1200 IU
Calcium-magnesium	Relaxes muscles Decreases cramping	1,200 mg calcium/ 600 mg magnesium
Selenium	Healthy immune function	200 mcg
Zinc	Improves immunity Lowers estrogen production in endometrial cells (by inhibiting aromatase enzyme)	50 mg
Kelp tablets (iodine)	Iodine can decrease strong estrogens and improve thyroid function	1,000 mg
Alpha lipoic acid	Antioxidant, decreases free radicals	200 mg
Curcumin	Decreases inflammation	1,500 mg
Melatonin	Decreases number of estrogen receptors	3 mg before bed
Uncontaminated fish oil	Increase anti-inflammatory prostaglandins Decrease inflammatory prostaglandins (PGE2, PGF2-alpha) Decrease endometrial growth Decrease pain	3,000 mg

NUTRIENT THERAPY FOR ENDOMETRIOSIS

NUTRIENT	ACTION	DAILY DOSAGE
Trace minerals manganese, copper and zinc (in a multimineral formula) plus the Ayurvedic herb amla (Indian gooseberry).	Increase superoxide dismutase, which eliminates free radicals that promote adhesion formation	manganese: 10 mg copper: 3 mg zinc: 50 mg amla: 2 berries
Herbal formula: chaste tree berry, black cohosh, black haw, crampbark, tang kuei, pulsatilla, ginger	Decreases the pain of endometriosis	As recommended by health-care practitioner
Herbal formula: shepherd's purse, red root and yarrow	Stops bleeding	As recommended by health-care practitioner
Herbal formula: astragalus, echinacea, and ganoderma (reishi mushroom)	Improves immune surveillance	As recommended by health-care practitioner

Restore Balance

- Use the oligotherapy Zinc-Copper (Zn-Cu), 3 times weekly, to regulate the glands.
- Exercise 40 minutes a day to improve circulation, increase endorphins, decrease circulating estrogen, and decrease pain.
- Apply ½ tsp natural progesterone cream (3%) on the skin twice daily from day 10 to 28 of your menstrual cycle to decrease the effects of estrogen.

HOMEOPATHIC REMEDIES FOR ENDOMETRIOSIS

- **To improve drainage:** Unda 245, Unda 10, and Unda 16, 5 drops of each, 3x daily, for 3 weeks of the month, alternating with Unda 20, Unda 48, and Unda 74 the next month.

- **To reduce pain:** Cimicifuga plex (Unda), 8 drops 3x daily, or Upelva drops (Pekana), 20 drops, 3x daily.

- **To reduce scar tissue:** Thiosinaminum 6CH, *Oleo europa* (gemmotherapy), grape seed, vitamin E, Silicea 6X, *Viscum album* (gemmotherapy), and castor oil packs.

- **To increase progesterone:** Luteinum 4CH on day 21 (3 pellets).

- **To decrease estrogen activity:** Folliculininum 15CH (3 pellets) on day 7, 14, and 21 of your menstrual cycle. This potency suppresses hormone activity.

TCM FOR ENDOMETRIOSIS

Treatment with acupuncture and Chinese herbs is very effective for women with endometriosis and improvement can occur within 6 months. A practitioner of Chinese medicine will be able to diagnose your pattern of disharmony and treat with appropriate herbal formulas and acupuncture.

Common Patterns of Disharmony

- Qi congestion and blood stagnation: use *Channel Flow*.
- Accumulation of cold causing blood stagnation: use *Cinnamon & Poria*
- Heat congestion with blood stagnation: use *Unlocking Formula*
- Qi and blood deficiency with blood stagnation: use *Tang Kuei & Salvia*

Detoxify and Rejuvenate

- Begin a 100-hour sauna detoxification program to remove your body burden of chemicals. See the Seasonal Cleansing and Rejuvenation Program section for guidelines.
- Cleanse your liver with indole-3-carbinol/DIM (300 mg), NAC (1500 mg), curcumin (1500 mg), alpha lipoic acid (200 mg), choline (1000 mg), milk thistle, and dandelion in tincture.
- To improve detoxification of estrogen use gemmotherapy: Rosemarinus, 50 drops, 3 times daily for 1 month, alternating with Juniperus, 40 drops, 3 times daily the next month.
- Assess whether there is a problem with candida or parasites in the gut and treat appropriately. See the Seasonal Cleansing and Rejuvenation Program section for guidelines
- Use a probiotic containing *Lactobacillus acidophilus* and *Bifidobacterium bifidus*, 2 capsules once daily to improve bowel flora and elimination of estrogen.
- Use castor oil packs before bed several times a week to improve pelvic circulation, soften adhesions and reduce pain. See the Seasonal Cleansing and Rejuvenation Program section for guidelines.
- Stop using products that contain dioxin – tampons, bleached toilet paper – and do not buy PVC (polyvinyl chloride).
- Eliminate environmental estrogens from your home – store food in glass, not plastic; drink water out of glass, not plastic. Avoid food cans lined with plastic. Avoid cosmetics, shampoo and toothpaste containing parabens.

Integrate Body, Mind, and Spirit

- Balance and nourish your emotional needs and inner life despite the demands of school, work, marriage and your external life.
- Ask for the emotional support you need.
- Release any pain you feel about being a woman and discover where you belong.
- Practice a meditation or breathing exercise for 20 minutes twice daily to relax and balance the glands. Meditate before bed to increase melatonin.
- Use affirmations to change the way you think and feel about being a woman. Consider the following, or create your own.

> *I love being a woman and I know where I belong.*
> *I am rested, relaxed and feel at ease; the battle is over.*
> *I listen to and make time for my feminine as well as my masculine side.*
> *I protect and defend my femininity and recognize when it is threatened.*
> *I honor my emotional needs and inner life despite external demands.*

DID YOU KNOW ...

Gonadotropin-releasing hormone analogs are the most popular treatment and conventional drugs include Leuprolide acetate, goserilin acetate, and nafarelin acetate.

HERBAL FORMULA FOR ENDOMETRIOSIS

15%	Chaste tree berry (*Vitex agnus casti*)
15%	Cramp bark (*Viburnum opulus*)
15%	Tang kuei (*Angelica sinsensis*)
15%	Shepherd's purse (*Capsella bursa-pastoris*)
10%	Yarrow (*Achillea millefolium*)
10%	Bupleurum (*Bupleurum scorzoneraefolium*)
10%	Astragalus (*Astragalus membranaceus*)
5%	Ganoderma (reishi mushroom)
5%	Ginger (*Zingiberis officinalis*)

Dose: Use 40-100 drops, 3 times daily, to alleviate pain, decrease bleeding, move stagnant qi and blood, and strengthen immunity. Do not use during pregnancy.

Conventional Medicine

Drug Therapy

- For mild to moderate pain, conventional medicine recommends nonsteroidal anti-inflammatory drugs, such as ibuprofen, naproxen and mefenamic acid, which relieve pain in about 80% of women with the disorder.
- Drug treatments for endometriosis are geared toward manipulating hormone levels, either through oral contraceptive use, progestins, or gonadotropin-releasing hormone (GnRH) analogs, which cause a decline in FSH and LH and inhibit ovulation and menstruation, putting women in a menopausal state.
- Oral contraceptives are usually recommended to be taken continuously, so there is no menstrual bleeding, and this prevents implanted endometrial tissue from enlarging, bleeding, and causing pain. They must be continued long term to be effective.

Surgery

- Surgery can bring long-lasting pain relief to some women.
- Adhesions are removed, so pregnancy becomes possible. Surgical techniques include laser surgery, electrocautery (burning), knife excision, and scraping.

TOP 5 STRATEGIES

1. Follow the Women's Health Diet Plan.
2. Use nutritional supplements – fish oil, vitamin E, vitamin B complex, zinc, kelp, curcumin, and alpha lipoic acid.
3. Exercise 40 minutes a day.
4. Detoxify the liver and bowel and use saunas.
5. Use Chinese herbs and acupuncture.

Uterine Prolapse

When the uterus loses its normal structural support, it can drop down into the vagina, occasionally protruding out beyond the vulva. If left untreated, friction, injury, or infection can lead to ulceration. A prolapsed uterus can occur after childbirth (from pushing too soon), with heavy lifting after childbirth, after surgery, with chronic coughing, prolonged constipation, or obesity. It will be more evident when you are tired. There will be a feeling of pressure, heaviness, or a falling out sensation that may be accompanied by urinary incontinence, pain, or irregular uterine bleeding. In Chinese medicine, a weakness in the spleen and/or kidney, combined with the above factors, causes uterine prolapse.

Prevention and Treatment Strategies

Restore Balance

- Have sex! It tones the uterus.
- If you are overweight, reduce calories and begin an exercise program to lose weight. See the dietary guidelines in the Polycystic Ovary Syndrome chapter in this section.
- Avoid heavy lifting, particularly after childbirth.
- Rest more.
- Avoid standing for long periods of time.
- If you have been coughing, treat the cough with natural therapies.
- Address constipation with increased fiber, fluids, and exercise.
- Practice Kegels exercises daily. Try doing 10 repetitions every hour.
- Western herbs for uterine prolapse include false unicorn root (*Helonias* or *Chamelirium luteum*) and black cohosh. Mix together and take 30 drops twice daily. Do not use in pregnancy.

TCM FOR UTERINE PROLAPSE

In traditional Chinese medicine, one of the jobs of the spleen it is to hold the organs up. Any prolapse signifies spleen deficiency. Acupuncture points commonly used to address this are GV-20, CV-6, GB-28, St-36, Sp-6, CV-12, Bl-20. An excellent formula is *Bu Zhong Yi Chi Wan*, affectionately known as the "push up pill." This is also available as *Ginseng & Astragalus Formula*.

Detoxify and Rejuvenate

- Cleanse the liver and bowel to decrease uterine congestion. See the Seasonal Cleansing and Rejuvenation Program section for guidelines.
- Homeopathic remedies to improve uterine drainage and blood circulation: Unda 246, Unda 74, and Unda 233, 5 drops of each, 3x daily, for 3 weeks.

Integrate Body, Mind and Soul

- If you are feeling unsupported and 'dragged down' by your responsibilities, ask for help and schedule activities that will lift your spirits.

SHOULDER STAND FOR UTERINE PROLAPSE

Practice shoulder stand for 1 to 3 minutes at the end of the day to allow gravity to reverse organ prolapse.

1. From a lying position, roll backward and lift your legs up in the air, supporting yourself on your upper arms and elbows with your palms placed flat on either side of your spine.

2. Hold the position with slow long deep breathing.

3. You can also shimmy up next to a wall and lift your legs and lower back up against the wall for balance.

HOMEOPATHIC REMEDIES FOR UTERINE PROLAPSE

- **Sepia:** feeling as if the uterus and vagina will fall out through the vulva; a bearing down sensation, worse in the afternoon; worse after childbirth; has to cross her legs or press against the vulva to prevent protrusion; irritable; indifferent to those she loves; sad; liver spots; feels cold easily; no interest in sex. The most commonly used remedy is Sepia.

- **Calcarea carbonica:** easy perspiration in general and around the external genitalia; tends to be overweight; catches colds easily and is sensitive to cold; dislikes fats, craves eggs; ailments from working too hard; uterine prolapse from reaching up or lifting.

- **Lilium tiglium:** bearing down sensation with an urgency to have a bowel movement, as though all the internal organs would fall out; better from rest and from crossing legs; uterus swollen, needs to be supported from the outside; anxious and depressed; afraid she may have an incurable disease; hurried and keeps busy.

- **Pulsatilla:** feels better walking slowly in fresh air; dislikes fatty food; cries easily and wants sympathy; downward pressure of uterus; prolapse during menses; nausea; pain in back; not usually thirsty.

- **Platina:** arrogant and has contempt for others; menstruation is early with dark clots; spasms and bearing down pain in uterus; increased libido.

- **Helonias:** weakness and dragging down weight in pelvis; great fatigue; backache; kidneys swollen, burning and aching; sadness; needs to occupy her mind to feel better.

- **Podophyllum:** uterine prolapse after childbirth, from heavy lifting, or during bowel movement; hemorrhoids during pregnancy; tenderness in the liver region, which feels better from rubbing.

- **Rhus tox:** swelling and itching of vulva; stiffness in joints; uterine prolapse after childbirth or from lifting.

- **Aurum metallicum:** uterine prolapse from straining, from reaching up, during menses and from lifting; uterus enlarged; depression; high blood pressure; feels worthless.

Conventional Medicine

HRT

- Estrogen and progesterone replacement therapy after menopause to improve the muscle tone of the uterus, though they may have serious side effects.

Surgery

- To shorten or reconnect pelvic muscles and ligaments that have been stretched or torn.

Pessary

- A device inserted into the vagina to support the uterus.

Hysterectomy

- Removal of the uterus, as a last resort.

TOP 5 STRATEGIES

1. Take *Ginseng & Astragalus Formula*.
2. Choose the appropriate homeopathic remedy.
3. Practice Kegels exercises.
4. Practice the shoulder stand.
5. Detoxify the liver and bowel.

CASE STUDY: *LEILA*

Leila was a yoga teacher in her 50s, with no children, who came to our clinic concerned with uterine prolapse and hypothyroidism. On the first visit we prescribed the Chinese herbal formula Ginseng & Astragalus, *along with nutritional supplements for her thyroid. By the third visit two months later, she remarked that she no longer experienced any discomfort or prolapse of the uterus.*

Uterine (Endometrial) Cancer

Uterine cancer begins in the endometrium or lining of the uterus. A third of the time, vaginal bleeding after menopause is due to uterine cancer, so immediately visit your doctor if you have this symptom. Tests that confirm the diagnosis are a PAP test (which will miss uterine cancer a third of the time) and an endometrial biopsy. Uterine cancer, left untreated, can spread to the cervix, fallopian tubes, ovaries, pelvis, lungs, bones, liver, and kidneys. About two thirds of women diagnosed and treated conventionally for uterine cancer are still alive 5 years later, so early diagnosis is critical to prevent further spread of the disease.

DID YOU KNOW ...

Uterine cancer is the fourth most common cancer among women, usually occurring in postmenopausal women between 50 and 60 years old, and is the most common cancer in the reproductive organs. It is primarily caused by increased exposure to estrogen.

Risk Factors

- Estrogen dominance
- Late menopause (after age 52)
- History of menstrual problems (excess bleeding, spotting, missed periods)
- Never having children
- History of infertility
- Hormone replacement therapy with or without progestins
- Tamoxifen (increases risk six-fold)
- Obesity
- High blood pressure
- Diabetes
- Inactivity
- Poor liver function, causing excess estrogen
- Chronic constipation, resulting in higher estrogen levels

Prevention and Treatment

Improve Nutrition

- In addition to following the Women's Health Diet Plan (2), these dietary and supplement strategies have proven to be effective:

Diet

- Eat foods that benefit the liver, such as beets, garlic, onion, leeks, carrots, lemon.
- Use at least 2 tbsp of seaweed daily (dulse, nori, hiziki etc.)
- Eat coleslaw, sauerkraut, or raw cabbage juice for its indole-3-carbinol, and other raw brassicas, such as broccoli, Brussels sprouts, cauliflower and bok choy.
- Eat foods high in beta carotene – carrots, yam or squash daily.

DID YOU KNOW ...

High tofu consumers reduce their risk of uterine cancer by 50%. Use tofu, tempeh, and legumes as your protein sources with a small amount of nuts and seeds.

NUTRIENT THERAPY FOR UTERINE CANCER

NUTRIENT	ACTION	DAILY DOSAGE
Beta carotene (from dunaliella, chlorella or spirulina)	Enhance immune system	50,000 IU
Vitamin C	Stimulates immune system Antioxidant	6,000 mg in divided doses
Vitamin B complex	Helps liver detoxification and metabolism of estrogen	50 mg
Vitamin B-6	Enhances immunity Lowers estrogen levels	100 mg
Vitamin E mixed tocopherols	Enhances immune system Antioxidant	400 IU
Zinc picolinate	Enhances immune system Helps liver detoxification	50 mg
Selenium	Improves thyroid function and immune system	200 mcg
Indole-3-carbinol	Converts harmful estrogens into protective ones	300 mg
Curcumin	Anti-cancer action, liver cleanser, and anti-inflammatory	1,500 mg
N-acetyl cysteine	Increases glutathione, which improves detoxification and immune function	1,500 mg
R-alpha lipoic acid	Powerful antioxidant	200 mg
Coenzyme Q10	Increases cellular oxygen Antioxidant	100-300 mg
Uncontaminated fish oil	Inhibits cancer Anti-inflammatory	3,000 mg
Melatonin	Helps to inactivate cancer cells	3-20 mg before bed
Herbal formula: astragalus, codonopsis, ganoderma, ligustrum, and schizandra	Improves immune function	As directed
Medicinal mushroom combination: shiitake, maitake, coriolus, reishi. Available as Host Defence or RM10 or use Maitake-D-fraction	Improves immune function	As directed
Herbal formula: Essiac in tea or tincture form, or combination of red clover, burdock root, cleavers, dandelion, and echinacea	Lymphatic cleanser	As directed

- Eat 2 or more tsp of turmeric daily.
- Eat 2 shiitake mushrooms daily, stopping for a few days after a month, then resuming.
- Eat 2 tbsp freshly ground flaxseeds daily as well as 2 tbsp flaxseed oil.
- Avoid alcohol, sugar, coffee – drink organic green tea instead several times daily.
- Eat 2 cloves garlic and one onion daily

Restore Balance

- Exercise at least 40 minutes a day to improve estrogen metabolism and circulation.
- Use rebounding (jumping on a small trampoline) 5 to 20 minutes a day to activate your lymphatic system and help with detoxification
- Many homeopathic remedies exist that address some of the symptoms of uterine cancer — work with both conventional medicine and homeopathy if you choose this option. Seek an experienced homeopath who can select a remedy for you.
- Monitor the pH of your urine and saliva and adopt an alkaline diet. Use ½ tsp alkaline powder in warm water, away from meals, twice daily.
- Look for a practitioner who uses darkfield microscopy and biological terrain assessment to monitor your progress toward health.
- Assess thyroid function and treat if necessary. See Hypothyroidism chapter in this section.
- Assess adrenal function and treat if necessary.
- Chinese medicine can treat the underlying disharmonies that made you susceptible to uterine cancer. Consult with a practitioner of TCM as you proceed through conventional medical treatment. Some of the imbalances associated with uterine cancer include:
  1) deficiency cold in the penetrating and conception vessel meridians; 2) deficiency of the yang motility meridian; 3) excess in the yin motility meridian and; 4) blood stagnation.

DETOX REGIMEN

See the Seasonal Cleansing and Rejuvenation Program section for guidelines.

- Do a bowel cleanse, liver cleanse and flush, and sauna detoxification.
- Check for and detoxify heavy metals.
- If you have silver mercury amalgam fillings, replace them with porcelain or methacrylate. If you have root canals, consider having root-canal teeth removed.
- Use a high quality probiotic formula, containing Lactobacillus acidophilus and Bifidobacterium bifidus, to balance bowel flora, decrease estrogen.

Detoxify and Rejuvenate

- Homeopathic remedies to cleanse the liver and balance hormones: Unda 1, Unda 20, and Unda 258, 5 drops of each, 3x daily, for 3 weeks of the month; the next month use Unda 10, Unda 14, Unda 21, and Unda 48, 5 drops of each, 3x daily.
- Homeopathic remedies to gently cleanse the liver, kidneys and lymph: Chelidonium plex (Unda), 8 drops, 3x daily.
- Gemmotherapy to detoxify the liver: Rosemarinus, 50 drops, 3x daily; alternating monthly with Juniperus, 40 drops, 3x daily.
- Oligotherapy to activate the immune system: copper-silver-gold (Cu-Au-Ag) every other day to release cellular toxins; on alternate days use Se (selenium). Continue for 6 weeks, then stop for a few weeks and resume again.

Integrate Body, Mind, and Spirit

- If there are any issues around intimacy, your relationship, sexuality or creativity that you feel conflicted about, discuss them with your partner, a friend or therapist, release them and move forward.
- Establish a daily practice of at least 20 minutes of relaxation, prayer, meditation, or visualization. A good time to do this is before bed.
- Any cancer confronts us with the possibility of death, and can push us more quickly to grow spiritually if we allow it. Use a cancer diagnosis to pursue inner work, meaning, things that bring you joy, creative pursuits, prayer, meditation, dreams, and aspirations you have been ignoring.

Conventional Medicine

Surgery

- If cancer is diagnosed, a hysterectomy to remove the uterus and all cancerous tissue should be performed, followed by recommended drug therapies and/or radiation if necessary.

Drug Therapy

- Discontinue hormone replacement therapy or tamoxifen.
- Sodium benzylidene ascorbate prolongs survival in women with uterine cancer.

TOP 5 STRATEGIES

1. Hysterectomy followed by recommended drug therapy and/or radiation.

2. Follow the Women's Health Diet Plan.

3. Use the nutritional supplements indole-3-carbinol, selenium, zinc, curcumin, NAC, R-alpha lipoic acid, coenzyme Q10.

4. Detoxify the liver and bowel and begin a sauna detox program.

5. Use a medicinal mushroom combination.

Ovarian Cysts

Ovarian cysts may form when ovulation fails to occur (the egg is not released from the follicle), leaving the developing follicle to grow beyond its normal time. Cysts may also form after ovulation if the corpus luteum persists. Ovarian cysts usually cause no symptoms, though you may experience a vague feeling of heaviness or pressure in the lower abdomen. Infrequently, they pose a problem when they rupture, bleed, or become twisted. A pelvic exam and ultrasound will confirm the presence of a cyst.

Causes

- Estrogen dominance with a progesterone deficiency
- Other hormonal imbalances, such as low adrenal function, an underactive thyroid, or low melatonin
- Accumulation of xenoestrogens, along with liver and bowel toxicity
- Emotional factors relating to sexuality, reproduction, and creativity. The ovaries are a common place for women to store tension, anger or jealousy.

Prevention and Treatment

Improve Nutrition

In addition to following the Women's Health Diet Plan (Section 2), try these dietary and supplement strategies.

- Avoid chocolate, alcohol and coffee — these interfere with the liver's ability to transform estrogen into safe metabolites.
- Use olive oil for cooking (in a little water) and use flaxseed oil and pure fish oil on your food after it is cooked. Avoid butter, margarine, and all other oils.
- Use 2 tsp or more of turmeric daily.
- Use 2 tbsp of ground flaxseed daily.

Nutrient Supplements

- Use antioxidants to promote tissue repair in your ovaries and to encourage small cysts to disappear faster: natural mixed carotenes (50,000 IU), vitamin C (2000 mg), natural vitamin E mixed tocopherols (400 IU), and selenium (200 mcg).
- Use uncontaminated fish oil (3000 mg) daily.
- Improve the liver's ability to metabolize estrogen with the following supplements:
  - Vitamin B complex: 50-100 mg, daily
  - Extra vitamin B-6: 100 mg, daily in total

- NAC: 500 mg, 3 times daily
- Curcumin: 500 mg, 3 times daily
- Indole-3-carbinol and DIM mixture: 300 mg, daily
- Alpha lipoic acid: 100 mg, twice daily
- Magnesium citrate: 300 mg, daily
- Choline: 250 mg, twice daily
- Inositol: 150 mg, twice daily
- L-methionine: 100 mg, twice daily

Restore Balance

- Assess hormone levels: adrenal function, melatonin levels, thyroid function, IGF-1 levels, and estradiol, estrone, estriol, and progesterone in saliva on day 20 to 23 of your menstrual cycle.
- If progesterone is low, use chaste tree berry tincture 30 drops, twice daily, for several months.
- Decrease IGF-1 levels by avoiding sugar and high-glycemic carbohydrates and adopting a primarily vegan diet.
- Maintain a healthy weight and a body mass index of less than 23 to keep estrogen production low in your fat cells.
- Use acupuncture and the Chinese herbal formula *Cinnamon & Poria.*

DID YOU KNOW ...

If chaste tree berry is inadequate in elevating progesterone after several months, use progesterone cream, ¼–½ tsp twice daily of 3% progesterone from day 14 to 28, applying the cream to your inner arms, chest, inner thighs, or buttocks. Recheck salivary progesterone levels between day 20 and 23 of your cycle, months after you begin to ensure that levels are in the optimal range.

HOMEOPATHIC REMEDIES FOR OVARIAN CYSTS

Left-sided Ovarian Cysts	*Right-sided Ovarian Cysts*
Apis	Apis
Colocynthis	Fluoric acidum
Kali bic	Iodum
Lachesis	Lycopodium
Podophyllum	Podophyllum
Thuja	

- Exercise 40 minutes daily to improve circulation to pelvis and to improve metabolism of estrogen. Consider rebounding, cycling, belly dancing, jogging.
- Use bodywork, such as myofascial release and deep tissue massage to the pelvis, once weekly to improve circulation and lymphatic drainage.
- Use sitz baths three or more times weekly to increase circulation to the pelvis. See the Uterine Fibroids chapter in this section for guidelines.

Detoxify and Rejuvenate

- Homeopathic drainage remedies to shrink cysts: Unda 1, Unda 20, Unda 258, 5 drops of each, 3x daily, taken directly in the mouth or in a little water for 3 weeks to assist liver and kidney detoxification. Wait 1 week, and then use Unda 243, Unda 10, Unda 48 and Unda 245, 5 drops 3x daily for 3 to 6 months
- Gemmotherapy to decongest the liver: Rosemarinus (made from the young shoots of rosemary), 50 drops, 3x daily.
- Eliminate plastic containers, pesticides, polyvinyl chloride (PVC), brominated fire retardants, cosmetics containing phthalates and parabens, and toxic metals from your environment and do what you can in your community to restrict these.

DETOX REGIMEN

See the Seasonal Cleansing and Rejuvenation section for guidelines.

- Schedule a 100-hour sauna detox to eliminate xenoestrogens.
- Do a liver cleanse and liver flush.
- Restore normal bowel flora by taking a probiotic containing *Lactobacillus acidophilus* and *Bifidobacterium*. Use 2 capsules daily with meals.
- Ensure three bowel movements daily: use 1 tbsp each of psyllium seed powder and wheat bran daily to decrease circulating estrogen levels. Eat 45 grams fiber daily.
- Apply castor oil packs over the lower abdomen and liver several times weekly.

Integrate Body, Mind, and Spirit

- Work with a psychotherapist or bodyworker to release the emotional and cellular memories that are obstructing the flow of energy in the ovaries.
- Give birth to your creative self, whether it be through dance, music, art, pottery, writing, or any other creative activity.
- Address and resolve conflicts, anger, and grief. Be aware of healing you may need to do around a history of sexual abuse, a past abortion, or a relationship conflict.
- Communicate with your partner about your sexual needs and engage your spontaneous, sensual and playful self more in your relationship and in life.
- Commit to a regular meditation practice.

Conventional Medicine

Oral Contraceptive

- Some medical doctors recommend oral contraceptives to hasten the regression of ovarian cycts.

Surgery

- Cysts larger than 6 cm (2.5 in) are removed surgically to rule out ovarian cancer.

Ultrasound Monitoring

- Otherwise, the size of ovarian cysts is monitored using transvaginal ultrasound to ensure that rapid growth does not occur, which might indicate ovarian cancer.

TOP 5 STRATEGIES

1. Use the antioxidants beta carotene, vitamins C and E, zinc, and selenium
2. Use castor oil packs over the pelvis and liver several times a week for 6 weeks
3. Take uncontaminated fish oil daily
4. Use chaste tree berry to elevate progesterone
5. Use a single homeopathic remedy that matches your symptoms

---

CASE STUDY: *RESOLVING OVARIAN CYSTS*

Sharon was 52 and not yet menopausal when she came to see us on January 18th with a left-sided ovarian cyst, determined by ultrasound to be 5 x 6 cm large. It was affecting her urination — she had to urinate frequently and was slightly incontinent at times. She was already using progesterone cream for a diagnosed progesterone deficiency and to control her PMS symptoms, which previously had been severe. She was a nurse who had for years worked shifts, and was beginning to have a few mild hot flashes.

We prescribed 3 mg of melatonin for her before bed because her melatonin was low due to shift-work. We gave her the homeopathic remedy Thuja 30CH, 3 pellets, once daily, and drainage remedies for the ovaries, glands, and kidneys, Unda 21, Unda 10, Unda 48, and Unda 45. We asked her to use 2 tsp of turmeric daily, as well as 2 tbsp of flaxseed oil. We prescribed a multivitamin and the Chinese herbal formula, Cinnamon & Poria. We asked her to limit her meat to only two times per week, replacing it with legumes and tofu; to replace milk with soy milk; and to drink 8 glasses of water a day. An ultrasound only a few weeks later on February 8th showed that the cyst had decreased in size considerably.

Polycystic Ovary Syndrome (PCOS)

Polycystic ovary syndrome (PCOS) is a complex disorder involving genetic, developmental, metabolic, dietary, emotional, and hormonal factors. Susceptibility to the disorder may begin during the second trimester in utero if a fetus is exposed to elevated testosterone levels. Although much about the condition is unknown, the primary defect involves insulin regulation, resulting in chronically high insulin and blood sugar levels.

There is a deficiency in a substance called D-chiro-inositol, which would ordinarily help glucose get inside cells, improve insulin sensitivity, and lower insulin production. High insulin prevents ovulation and stimulates the ovaries to produce more hormones called androgens, which include androstenedione and testosterone. If you have PCOS, you may experience low self-esteem or depression because of issues around weight, facial hair, or inability to conceive. Your condition can be improved or normalized with natural medicines.

DID YOU KNOW ...

Women with PCOS are strongly at risk of diabetes, high blood pressure, heart disease, and cancer, so it is important to make dietary and lifestyle changes early on to reduce these risks. It affects 5% to 10% of women and is a primary cause of infertility.

Symptoms

- Elevated fasting insulin levels
- Obesity, particularly around the waist (waist:hip ratio is >0.85)
- Elevated LH (luteinizing hormone), which causes the ovaries to produce more hormones called androgens
- Elevated androstenedione and testosterone (these are ovarian androgens)
- Increased facial hair (due to high testosterone)
- Thinning hair on the head (due to high testosterone)
- Acne (due to high testosterone)
- Ovulation does not occur, so periods are missed or are irregular
- Because ovulation does not occur, there is low progesterone
- Cysts on the ovaries
- Infertility
- Recurrent miscarriage (45% miscarry in first trimester)
- High prolactin in 25% of women
- Estrogen is constantly elevated, especially estrone
- Sex hormone binding globulin (SHBG) is decreased (inhibited by insulin), so there is more circulating estrogen and testosterone
- Increased levels of growth hormone
- Increased levels of IGF-1
- Increased susceptibility to breast cysts and cancer, uterine fibroids
- Elevated triglycerides (undesirable fats in the blood)

- High LDL, or 'bad' cholesterol; low HDL, or 'good' cholesterol
- Elevated cortisol, which contributes to insulin resistance and decreases progesterone
- Increased susceptibility to hypothyroidism (autoimmune Hashimoto's thyroiditis)

Risk Factors for PCOS
- Increased testosterone exposure in utero
- Low birth weight
- Early puberty

Tests for PCOS

If you have irregular periods, with cycles longer than 45 days, ask your doctor to do some or all of the following blood tests:
- Free testosterone
- DHEAS
- 17-hydroxyprogesterone
- LH/FSH ratio
- Prolactin
- TSH, free T4, free T3, anti-microsomal antibodies, anti-thyroglobulin antibodies
- Fasting insulin, glucose tolerance test
- HDL, LDL, triglycerides, cholesterol, homocysteine, C-reactive protein, fibrinogen

Prevention and Treatment

Improve Nutrition
In addition to following the Women's Health Diet Plan (Section 2), these dietary and supplement strategies have proven to be effective for PCOS:

Diet
- Eat less, but more frequently, to help decrease insulin resistance. Combine small amounts of vegetarian protein (almonds) with meals.
- Avoid high-glycemic carbohydrates, such as white rice, corn, millet, and white flour, and use low glycemic carbohydrates, such as pearl barley and legumes.
- Avoid red meat and dairy. These increase your risk of heart disease and cancer.
- Avoid all sugars and sweeteners other than stevia and whole fruit.
- Eat some low-glycemic soluble fiber with every meal to lower insulin. Choose from apples, cabbage, raw carrots, oatmeal,

DID YOU KNOW ...

Certain spices improve insulin activity, including cinnamon, cloves, nutmeg, bay leaves, and turmeric. Use these daily. Add turmeric to everything you can. Have ½ tsp cinnamon in some form with every meal or in Yogi Tea.

Polycystic Ovary Syndrome (PCOS)

NUTRIENT THERAPY FOR PCOS		
NUTRIENT	**ACTION**	**DAILY DOSAGE**
Uncontaminated fish oil	Keeps cell membranes flexible with more insulin receptors Improves glucose metabolism Promotes healthy prostaglandins Protects your heart, breasts and uterus	4,000 mg
Calcium/magnesium (2:1 ratio) with vitamin D	Maintains bone density Magnesium needed for insulin metabolism	1,000 mg calcium; 500 mg magnesium
Zinc picolinate	Decreases testosterone	50 mg taken between meals
Chromium picolinate or polynicotinate or use brewer's yeast tablets	Lowers insulin	600 mcg taken in divided doses with food
Biotin	Lowers blood sugar levels Improves insulin resistance	10 mg
Selenium	Enhances thyroid and liver function Prevents cancer	200 mcg
Vitamin C with bioflavonoids	Antioxidant	4,000 mg in divided doses
Vitamin B complex	Helps metabolize estrogen	100 mg
Vitamin B-6	Decreases testosterone	100 mg
Vitamin E mixed tocopherols	Antioxidant	400 IU
R-alpha lipoic acid	Antioxidant Regulates blood sugar	600 mg in divided doses
N-acetyl cysteine (NAC)	Lowers insulin levels	1,800 mg
Coenzyme Q10	Antioxidant Regulates blood sugar	200 mg
Cinnamon extract	Regulates blood sugar	300 mg in divided doses after meals
Saw palmetto extract (standardized to contain 95% liposterols)	Blocks the action of testosterone	320 mg

NUTRIENT THERAPY FOR PCOS		
NUTRIENT	**ACTION**	**DAILY DOSAGE**
Gymnema sylvestre	Helps regulate blood sugar levels	400 mg
Defatted fenugreek seed powder	Reduces cholesterol, triglycerides, and fasting blood sugar levels	50 mg, twice daily
Green tea extract (standardized to contain 80% total polyphenols and 55% epigallocatechin gallate)	Improves insulin sensitivity	400 mg

oatbran, sesame seeds, flaxseeds, psyllium seed powder, and beans (legumes).

- Drink Yogi tea after meals (with no sweetener) once or twice daily if you have missed your fiber in food form. See the Seasonal Cleansing and Rejuvenation Program section for the recipes.
- Drink several cups of organic green tea daily to lower testosterone and insulin.
- For breakfast have oatmeal or buckwheat, oatbran, sliced organic apple with skins, cinnamon (lots), and organic soy milk.

Restore Balance

- Let natural moonlight in through your windows around the full moon (when many women ovulate) or use a light at night for three nights starting with the day of the full moon, to mimic its effect.
- Assess progesterone levels, and if low, use 3% natural progesterone cream, ½ tsp twice daily, starting 2 weeks after your menstrual period begins and continuing until day 28. This will offset estrogen dominance.
- Assess adrenal function and use relaxation and meditation to lower cortisol.
- Assess thyroid function using the basal body temperature test, blood tests, and symptoms. If your thyroid function is low, see the remedies in the Hypothyroidism chapter of this section.

Detoxify and Rejuvenate

- Support your liver's ability to break down hormones and fats with the following nutrients: indole-3-carbinol or DIM (300 mg), N-acetyl cysteine (1500 mg), vitamin B complex (100 mg), choline (1000 mg), inositol (300 mg), methionine (300 mg), and magnesium (600 mg).
- Do a liver cleanse and liver flush. See the Seasonal Cleansing and Rejuvenation Program section for guidelines.

DID YOU KNOW ...

D-chiro-inositol, a form of niacin, has been found to normalize the menstrual cycles in 86% of women when a dosage of 1200 mg was given daily. It lowers insulin levels, decreases testosterone and triglycerides, and increases SHBG. Ask a compounding pharmacist about it.

DID YOU KNOW ...

By exercising 4 to 8 hours a week, you can increase muscle mass, decrease fat, and help to balance your hormones. Follow an exercise routine you enjoy that includes aerobic activity, such as brisk walking, cycling, rebounding, jogging or dancing for 1 to 2 hours daily, and strength training two to three times per week using free weights, weight machines, or exercise bands.

Polycystic Ovary Syndrome (PCOS)

HERBAL FORMULA FOR PCOS

20% Saw palmetto (*Serenoa serrulata*)
20% Licorice root (*Glycyrrhiza glabra*)
20% Chaste tree berry (*Vitex agnus casti*)
20% Gymnema leaf (*Gymnema sylvestre*)
20% Globe artichoke (*Cynara scolymus*)

Dose: Mix tinctures together and use 30-40 drops, 3 times daily, to lower blood sugar and insulin, decrease testosterone, increase progesterone, lower triglycerides and LDL, and assist liver detoxification.If you have hypertension, omit the licorice root. Do not use during pregnancy.

DID YOU KNOW ...

With PCOS, your eggs do not mature and are not released, leaving your ovaries in a state of perpetual pre-puberty. If there are ways you need to mature in your life, or if you have reservations about accepting yourself as a woman, examine and address those issues to move forward. Your masculine hormones are overactive, while your inner feminine hormones, represented by your eggs, never develop fully. Look at your life and see if there are ways that your inner masculine is thwarting the blossoming of the feminine.

- Homeopathic drainage remedies to help your liver manage hormones, balance your glands, and drain the ovaries: Unda 1, Unda 20 and Unda 243, 5 drops of each, 3x daily for 3 weeks of the month, alternating the next month with Unda 10, Unda 21, and Unda 48, 5 drops of each, 3x daily, for 3 weeks. Continue alternating monthly.
- Gemmotherapy to help the liver manage hormones: Rosemarinus, 50 drops, 3 times daily.
- Apply a castor oil pack over the pelvis 3 times weekly for an hour each time to improve lymphatic circulation and decrease congestion.
- Improve the elimination of hormones through the bowel with 1 tbsp psyllium, 2 tbsp ground flaxseed, and 1 tbsp wheat bran (if tolerated) daily.
- Use a probiotic containing *Lactobacillus acidophilus* and *Bifidobacterium bifidus*

Integrate Body, Mind, and Spirit

- Make time for relaxation. Stress increases cortisol and insulin levels, which are at the root of PCOS. Relax for at least 20 minutes twice daily, and slow your breathing down to less than four breaths a minute during these sessions.

Conventional Medicine

Drug Therapy

- **Meformin:** The most commonly prescribed conventional medication for PCOS is Metformin (Glucophage). It increases body cell sensitivity to insulin, so less needs to be secreted. By lowering insulin levels, Metformin lowers testosterone, androstenedione, and LH levels after 6 months of administration. It increases SHBG and enhances ovulation.

- **Oral contraceptives:** These artificially regulate the menstrual cycle and prevent excess hair growth in young women, but will cause insulin levels to be higher and increase long-term risk of heart disease and breast cancer.

- **Oral contraceptives plus spironolactone:** Spironolactone is a drug that inhibits the binding of testosterone to receptors in hair follicles and, consequently, decreases abnormal hair growth. However, side effects include excess urination, weight gain, breast tenderness, and dizziness. When oral contraceptives and spironolactone are stopped, PCOS symptoms return.

- **Ovulation induction:** Some drugs, such as Clomid, are used to induce ovulation in women who want to become pregnant. Though women may conceive, the underlying problem of insulin dysregulation remains. More than six cycles of Clomid increase the risk of ovarian cancer.

TOP 5 STRATEGIES

1. Follow the Women's Health Diet Plan, using low glycemic carbohydrates.
2. Exercise 8 hours a week.
3. Use the Herbal Formula for PCOS.
4. Use progesterone cream day 14 to 28 of your menses.
5. Use fish oil, chromium, NAC, CoQ10, alpha lipoic acid.

DID YOU KNOW ...

If natural therapies are ineffective in normalizing symptoms and hormones in women with PCOS, metformin can be used effectively. However, its side effects include gastrointestinal disturbance, fatigue, and vitamin B-12 deficiency (you may need a series of B-12 shots). With improved diet, exercise, and metformin, previously infertile women can become pregnant and reduce their risk of heart disease and diabetes. It is not known whether metformin is safe to take during pregnancy.

Vaginal Infections and Vaginitis

Vaginitis means inflammation of the vagina, with symptoms of burning, redness, swelling, or itching. Vaginitis can be caused by infectious organisms, such as bacteria, fungi (Candida albicans), or protozoa. The vagina can also be irritated by chemicals, spermicides, allergies to condoms or to your partner's semen, laundry soap, topical medications, douches, perfumes, tampons, and scented menstrual pads. Postmenopausal women may experience vaginal dryness and irritation caused by decreased estrogen. Before treating vaginitis, it is important to determine its cause. You will need to visit your doctor to confirm a diagnosis with a physical examination and microscopic exam of vaginal discharge. Bacterial infections that are not treated properly can spread to the uterus, urethra, and external labia, potentially causing pelvic inflammatory disease in some women. Once you have an accurate diagnosis, you can determine how to best treat it. Natural therapies are very effective in addressing vaginitis once the infectious organism is identified.

DID YOU KNOW ...

A serious concern in pregnant women, vaginal infections can cause early rupture of membranes, premature labor, infection of the uterus, and even death to the fetus.

DID YOU KNOW ...

Lactobacilli protect the vagina from fungal and bacterial infection, including *Staphylococcus aureus*, *Gardnerella vaginalis*, *Peptostreptococcus anaerobius*, and *Prevotella bivia.*

Causes

- More than 50 species of organisms comprise our vaginal flora, with *Lactobacilli* species making up 90% of the total flora. The ecological balance of these organisms is disturbed by drugs, antibiotics, the birth control pill, hormone replacement therapy, douches, spermicidal gels, and antibiotics.
- When antibiotics are used, the *Lactobacilli* population decreases and *Candida albicans* (which is unaffected by antibiotics) can attach to the vaginal wall, normally covered with *Lactobacilli*.
- Antibiotics rob us of this protection and do nothing to address the immune deficiency, dietary factors, or sexual practices that caused the initial infection.

Prevention and Treatment

Modify Lifestyle

- Wear loose cotton underwear, rather than synthetic. Avoid tight pants.
- Avoid wearing pantyhose — the synthetic fiber prevents proper air circulation and increases heat and humidity, which favors candida infection.
- Take bathing suits off soon after swimming — avoid lounging around in a wet bathing suit.
- Don't use towels or wash cloths that others have used.
- Wipe from front to back after a bowel movement.

VAGINITIS TYPES AND TREATMENTS		
TYPE OF VAGINITIS/CAUSE	**RISK FACTORS/ SYMPTOMS**	**TREATMENT**
Allergic vaginitis Allergic reaction to condom, semen, spermicide, chemicals	*Risk Factors:* chemical or known skin sensitivities to latex, perfumes, scents, bleach *Symptoms:* vaginal burning, redness, pain, itching	Vitamin E suppository or gelatin capsule inserted vaginally 1–2 times daily Vitamin E oil applied to vulva Douche of 10 drops of calendula tincture per cup of water
Hormonal vaginitis Decreased estrogen after menopause or other conditions of low estrogen — surgery, chemotherapy, radiation	*Symptoms:* vaginal dryness, burning, itching, pain or bleeding with intercourse	Lubricate with almond oil with added vitamin E Topical estriol cream vaginally Oral, injectable, or topical estrogen Vaginium 4CH, 3 pellets, daily
Bacterial vaginitis Overgrowth of normal or pathogenic bacteria (*Gardnerella, Bacteroides, Peptococcus, Mobiluncus*)	*Risk Factors:* diabetes, pregnancy, smoking, multiple sexual partners, contraceptives, oral sex, antibiotics, douching, lowered immunity, liver heat with spleen dampness *Symptoms:* burning, swelling, redness of vulva; thin, frothy, gray, odorous discharge (odor is stronger after intercourse); increased discharge; pain with urination; vaginal pH 5.0–5.5	*Lactobacillus acidophilus* capsules orally and vaginally as a cream or suppositories or douche On alternate days use vitamin E or vitamin A vaginal suppositories Insert carefully peeled garlic clove (don't nick) vaginally for 6 to 8 hours at night – thread it with a needle and cotton thread first so it can be easily removed Douche once daily with 20 drops goldenseal tincture and 10 drops calendula tincture in 1 cup of water Topical povidine iodine, 1 part iodine in 100 parts water and douche twice daily for 14 days Boric acid capsules (600 mg) placed high in the vagina twice daily for 14 days Oral metronidazole. Do not use if pregnant; avoid alcohol while using Ampicillin Opical clindamycin

VAGINITIS TYPES AND TREATMENTS

TYPE OF VAGINITIS/CAUSE	RISK FACTORS/ SYMPTOMS	TREATMENT
Candida vaginitis: 25–45% of vaginal infections caused by various species of Candida — 90% of the time it is *Candida albicans* Affects ages 15–50, rare after age 50 except for women on HRT	*Risk Factors:* stress, excess sugar, intestinal candidiasis, sexual activity, antibiotic use, pregnancy, diabetes, AIDS, Cushing's or Addison's disease, hypo- or hyperthyroidism, leukemia, lowered immunity, contraceptives, estrogen dominance, chemotherapy, radiation, liver heat with spleen dampness *Symptoms:* intense vulvar itching, pain with urination, pain with vaginal sex, redness, swelling, burning of vagina and vulva, worse before menses, watery to thick white or yellow odorless discharge like "cottage cheese," vaginal pH 4.0–4.5 (normal)	Diet low in sugar and refined carbohydrate, limit fruit to 1 daily No alcohol, yeast, fermented food, mushrooms, peanuts, vinegar, dairy Insert 2 *L. acidophilus* capsules at night, douche daily with yogurt or use Candigen cream Garlic capsules orally, 3 daily Douche with 5 drops grapefruit seed extract in 8 oz water every 12 hours for 3–9 days; treat partner with same mixture twice daily Douche with 2 tsp apple cider vinegar in 1 cup water once daily Povidine iodine (Betadine) or boric acid Exmykehl 3X suppositories, 1 inserted vaginally at night Topical Monistat, Femstat or Vagistat, antifungal creams, or suppositories
Trichomonas (protozoa): 25% of vaginal infections can occur at any age	*Risk Factors:* multiple sexual partners, black race, gonorrhea infection simultaneous with non-barrier birth control, elevated vaginal pH, liver heat with spleen dampness *Symptoms:* vulvar itching or burning pain with intercourse, painful urination, lower abdominal pain, vaginal redness, 'strawberry cervix', excess discharge that is thin, runny, yellow green or grey, with a rancid odor, frothy 25% of the time, vaginal pH of 6.0–6.5	*L. acidophilus* capsules orally and vaginally, or Candigen cream Peeled garlic clove inserted vaginally 2 times daily for 10 days Woman and partner, 3 garlic cloves daily, orally Povidine iodine (Betadine) or boric acid as described above Vagistatin capsules made from Chinese herbs, 2 inserted nightly until symptoms clear Metronidazole (Flagyl) orally for 7 days. Contraindicated in pregnancy; avoid alcohol while using.

- Avoid using bubble baths or artificially scented soaps. Use an acid soap for washing the vulva rather than an alkaline soap.
- Stay off the Pill – use a male or female condom with any new sexual partner, and the symptom-thermo method of birth control with a monogamous partner during your infertile days.
- If you have an infection, use condoms and have your partner treated for infection as well so you don't re-infect one another.
- Do not douche when not infected – it disturbs your healthy vaginal flora and makes you more susceptible to vaginal infections and cervical dysplasia.
- Don't use any chemical sprays or scents outside or inside the vagina.
- Avoid using scented tampons, pads, and toilet paper.

Improve Nutrition

In addition to following the Women's Health Diet Plan (Section 2), try these dietary strategies:

- Maintain a diet low in sugar and refined carbohydrates.
- Limit fruit to one or less daily.
- Avoid all alcohol, yeast, fermented food, mushrooms, peanuts, vinegar, and dairy.

Restore Balance

- Normalize pH of urine and saliva with an alkaline diet and use of an alkaline powder.
- For vaginal candida, use homeopathic Pefrakehl 5X drops, 5 drops, once daily before meals and 5 drops rubbed on to the vulva once daily.

DID YOU KNOW ...

To prevent vaginitis, try to avoid antibiotic use unless absolutely necessary. If you use antibiotics, take a probiotic containing *Lactobacillus acidophilus* and *Bifidobacterium bifidus* at a different time of day during antibiotic therapy and for a month afterward.

DID YOU KNOW ...

You may be more vulnerable to vaginal infection, particularly candida infection, if you have mercury toxicity. Use hair or urine testing annually to assess toxic metals and then follow a detox program to eliminate them. Replace silver mercury amalgam dental fillings with porcelain or methacrylate.

TCM FOR VAGINAL INFECTIONS

In traditional Chinese medicine, vaginitis is usually caused by pent-up emotions, causing liver stagnation and heat, combined with spleen weakness with inability to transport fluids. When body fluids stop flowing, dampness accumulates.

Treatment: Treatment is geared to eliminating excess heat and dampness through acupuncture, herbal formulas, and diet. Appropriate herbal formulas may include *Lung Tan Xie Gan Wan*, *Gentiana Drain Fire Formula*, *Quell Fire*, or *Phellostatin*. Work with a practitioner of TCM to determine your constitutional imbalance.

Detoxify and Rejuvenate

- If you are susceptible to candida vaginitis, it is very likely that you have a systemic problem. Cleanse the bowel with ground 2 tbsp flaxseed, 1 tbsp psyllium, a formula that kills candida (garlic, grapefruit seed extract, goldenseal or berberine, olive leaf extract, caprylic acid, oil of oregano, pau d'arco). Take quality

Lactobacillus acidophilus and *Bifidobacterium bifidus* capsules daily. Follow an anti-candida diet. Keep your immune system strong with dietary or supplemental intake of vitamin C (2000 mg), vitamin E mixed tocopherols (400 IU), beta carotene from Dunaliella (50,000 IU), Vitamin B-6 (100 mg), zinc (50 mg), and selenium (200 mcg).

- Once a year do a cleanse for *Candida albicans* and parasites, as well as a liver cleanse and liver flush, and a metal detoxification. See the Seasonal Cleansing and Rejuvenation Program section for guidelines.

Integrate Body, Mind, and Spirit

- Examine emotional causes to your vaginitis – are you angry at your sexual partner, or is your vagina reacting to infidelity? Do you have misgivings about your sexual behavior, or guilt? Were you sexually abused in the past, and is your vagina still reacting to that emotional imprint?
- Try journaling to your vagina and then write her response as she talks back to you. Or describe your symptoms and write them down using the words "I feel" or "I am" – for example, I feel hurt, I feel raw, I feel angry, I am sensitive, I am irritated.

TOP 5 STRATEGIES

1. Take 2 capsules of *Lactobacillus acidophilus* orally, daily.
2. Use condoms during intercourse.
3. Take boric acid capsules (600 mg) placed high in the vagina for 14 days.
4. Douche with goldenseal and calendula or grapefruit seed extract.
5. Eat a diet low in sugar and carbohydrates, no alcohol, yeast, fermented food, mushrooms, peanuts, vinegar, or dairy.

CASE STUDY: *RELEASING ANGER*

Victoria came to see us with severe vaginal and vulvar itching and pain that began after she had a passionate, sexual relationship with someone she deeply loved. Her partner then proceeded to date another woman and left Victoria in the lurch. She was feeling angry and hurt. On the first visit, we asked Victoria to "be" her vagina and vulva and speak about how she was feeling. She said "I feel raw, I am burning, I am angry, I am hurting" – a perfect account about how she was feeling emotionally. Her medical doctor had given her antibacterial creams that didn't seem to work. We gave her the homeopathic remedy Staphysagria, used to help someone move through their anger, along with some topical homeopathic antibacterial drops. Within 3 days her symptoms diminished and she was able to release some of her anger. We repeated the prescription 2 months later when her symptoms came back, and again they cleared within a couple of days.

Genital Herpes

If you have genital herpes, you are not alone – it is the most common sexually transmitted disease in the developed world. There are six different types of herpes virus that can infect humans, but only two of them are responsible for the painful, irritating, and embarrassing small ulcers that can occur on the skin or mucus membranes. It takes about 6 days after exposure for a lesion to manifest and the initial outbreak lasts 1 to 6 weeks. After the outbreak, the virus remains in an inactive state in the nerves that supply the infected area or in the spinal nerves. Though it may never be active again, the virus persists in the nerve, and genital herpes is technically considered incurable, though there is much you can do to prevent reactivation. If you have an outbreak of what you suspect may be genital herpes, see your medical doctor while the lesion is present to confirm or disprove the diagnosis. Chronic yeast infections may sometimes resemble herpes eruptions, and diagnosis is confirmed by taking a swab from the active sore. Since the virus is highly contagious and no obvious symptoms need be present to infect a sexual partner, male or female condoms provide the best protection.

Categories

- HSV-1 is the usual cause of cold sores on the lips and the cornea of the eye. It is responsible for 20% of genital herpes outbreaks. HSV-1 is spread by contact with secretions from or around the mouth,
- HSV-2 causes the other 80% of genital outbreaks. It is transmitted through direct contact with the sores, usually during sexual activity.

Symptoms

- Herpes lesions start with mild tingling or prickling, beginning about 2 to 5 days after initial infection, becoming a red papule that develops into a vesicle containing clear liquid, which progresses to a pustule.
- The pustule breaks open, leaving a burning ulceration, which scabs over. Genital herpes consists of many clusters of painful lesions around the genitals, anus, perineum, and surrounding area.
- The lesions may be painful during urination, accompanied by a fever, headache, light sensitivity, neck stiffness, nausea, body aches, and swelling of the inguinal (groin) lymph nodes.
- The first outbreak is usually the worst. Thankfully there are milder symptoms in future outbreaks, particularly if the infectious strain is HSV-1.
- The virus can be reactivated by physical or emotional stress, depression, anxiety, hostility, hormonal changes during the

DID YOU KNOW ...

About 75% of sexual partners of infected individuals will contract the virus if intercourse occurs during an outbreak, but about half of these individuals will never have symptoms. The virus can be spread through sexual activity when there are no apparent lesions.

Genital Herpes

menstrual cycle, overexposure to sunlight, a fever, immune deficiency, foods high in arginine, drugs, or unknown factors.
- Within the first year after infection, most women have 5-10 more outbreaks, many of which clear up within 10 days. Usually outbreaks become less frequent over time.

Prevention and Treatment

Modify Lifestyle
- Recognize early signs of an outbreak, such as tingling, prickling, and itching.
- Abstain from sexual contact during an outbreak.
- Use barrier methods of birth control with new sexual partners or with a previously infected sexual partner. Transmission of the virus is possible even without visible symptoms.
- Inform your sexual partner that you have previously been infected with herpes, so that condoms can be used. Herpes can be spread by oral-genital contact.
- The virus can be transferred from one body site to another, so when a lesion is present, either air dry after showering or pat yourself dry. Wash towels after single use.

Improve Nutrition
In addition to following the Women's Health Diet Plan (Section 2), use nutrient supplements during each phase of the infection:

To keep your immune system vital and help prevent outbreaks:
- Zinc picolinate: 50 mg
- Vitamin C with bioflavonoids: 3000 mg, daily, in divided doses
- Vitamin E mixed tocopherols: 400 IU, daily
- Beta carotene in food form, as from dunaliella algae: 50,000 IU, daily
- 2 garlic capsules, daily
- 3 St. John's wort oil capsules (Flora) as an antiviral, daily
- Lysine daily (this amino acid decreases recurrence rate): 1000 mg, daily

To prevent an outbreak when you experience tingling:
- 12 capsules of deodorized garlic when initial tingling occurs, followed by 3 capsules, 4 times daily for the next 3 days
- Lysine: 1000 mg, 3 times daily. Lysine is high in potatoes, brewer's yeast, beans, and eggs.
- Avoid foods high in arginine – chocolate, peanuts, almonds, cashews, sunflower seeds.
- Apply tea tree oil topically to the tingling area to prevent a lesion from occurring.

During an outbreak:

- Apply a concentrated extract (70:1) of Melissa officinalis (lemon balm) as cream (Herpalieve) to the affected area, 4 times daily, for 7 to 10 days for rapid healing and prevention of further outbreaks.
- Apply a licorice root extract containing glycyrrhetinic acid to inactivate the virus.
- Continue applying 3% bee propolis ointment, 4 times daily, for 10 days.
- Apply a 0.01 to 0.025% zinc sulfate solution, 3 times daily.
- Apply topical vitamin E with a Q-tip to the lesion to decrease pain and promote healing.

Integrate Body, Mind, and Spirit

- If you are troubled by your condition, talk to a counselor or your health-care practitioner to move through your emotions, clarifying the nature of the infection and releasing anger, shame, or guilt.
- As time passes and your outbreaks become infrequent — and as you manage your symptoms with effective natural therapies — your discomfort will diminish.

DID YOU KNOW...

Properly prescribed homeopathic remedies can work very well for genital herpes, preventing future outbreaks. Indicated remedies include arsenicum album, dulcamara, petroleum, rhus tox, natrum muriaticum, graphites, medorrhinum, sepia and thuja. Work with a skilled homeopath.

HERBAL FORMULA TO PREVENT GENITAL HERPES ACTIVATION

- Lemon balm (*Melissa officinalis*)
- Licorice root (*Glycyrrhiza glabra*)
- St. John's wort (*Hypericum perfoliatum*)

- **Dose:** Mix the tinctures together in equal parts and use 40 drops, twice daily. Do not use in pregnancy, if you have high blood pressure, or if you are taking an SSRI antidepressant. St. John's wort may make your skin more sensitive to the sun.

Conventional Medicine

- Conventional medicine recommends the antiviral medication Acyclovir (Zovirax), in pill or cream form, to treat herpes.
- Within 24 hours the virus is inactivated, but chronic use runs the risk of creating resistance to the medication.
- In clinical trials, it is not as effective as bee propolis or melissa.

TOP 5 STRATEGIES

1. Use bee propolis.
2. Take the Herbal Formula to Prevent Herpes Activation.
3. Use a carefully chosen homeopathic remedy.
4. Take oral zinc, vitamin C, vitamin E, beta carotene.
5. Take garlic capsules or eat fresh garlic.

Fibrocystic Breast Disease

Fibrocystic breast disease encompasses a wide variety of benign breast conditions associated with changes in breast physiology related to diet and hormonal fluctuations. If you notice soft, tender, moveable cysts in your breasts that are predominant 1 to 2 weeks before your period and diminish after your period, you may have this condition. The cysts are cyclic, vary in size, and are often painful, freely moveable and multiple, occurring in both breasts. If you have cystic breasts, you can change their consistency with dietary changes and supplementation. Develop the habit of performing breast self-exams each month, so that you recognize any changes that occur in your breasts, and draw a map of your breasts to document what you find. Since every palpable breast lump needs an accurate diagnosis to rule out breast cancer, ask your medical doctor to refer you for an ultrasound, fine needle aspiration, thermography, electrical resistance testing, or mammography (last resort). Be cautious about biopsies for fibrocystic disease – although sometimes they are necessary, a biopsied area may become cancerous years later.

DID YOU KNOW ...

Cystic breasts commonly affect up to 50% of pre-menopausal women between the ages of 20 and 50 years; 20% of women with this condition are able to feel swollen lymph nodes in the underarm area as well.

Causes

- Increased estrogen to progesterone ratio
- Underactive thyroid, which may cause elevated prolactin
- Iodine deficiency, which causes breast cells to be more sensitive to estrogen
- High estradiol and low testosterone
- Imbalance in the ratio between estrone and estriol (too much estrone, too little estriol)
- Nutritional deficiencies in vitamin E, vitamin B-6, iodine, coenzyme Q10, essential fatty acids
- Bowel toxicity
- Liver toxicity and stagnation of liver energy and blood
- Repressed emotions and stress
- Poor lymphatic circulation, possibly from a tight bra and lack of exercise
- Excess meat, dairy, the wrong dietary fats, and foods that create dampness
- Heavy metal toxicity (cadmium, lead, mercury)
- Accumulation of estrogenic chemicals in breast tissue (PCBs, dioxin, bisphenol-A, phthalates, PBDEs, parabens)
- Methylxanthine consumption in coffee, black tea, green tea, cola, chocolate, and caffeinated medications

Prevention and Treatment

Improve Nutrition

In addition to following the Women's Health Diet Plan (Section 2), these dietary and supplement therapies have proven to be effective:

Diet

- Eat onions and garlic daily. Onions contain quercetin, while garlic contains allicin – both of these protect the breasts and decrease cancer risk.
- Use turmeric, rosemary, dulse powder, and seaweeds daily.
- Eat red clover sprouts, mung bean sprouts, and broccoli sprouts regularly.
- Avoid methylxanthines, found in coffee, black tea, green tea, cola, chocolate, and caffeinated medications.

Nutrient Supplements

- Maintain healthy iodine levels using one of these three sources:
- Kelp tablets: 1500 mg, daily
- Aqueous molecular iodine: 0.07 to 0.09 mg per kg of body weight daily for 6 months (preferred type of iodine but may only be available by prescription)
- Lugol's Solution (sodium iodide): 5 to 10 drops daily, depending on body weight

NUTRIENT THERAPY FOR FIBROCYSTIC BREAST DISEASE		
NUTRIENT	**ACTION**	**DAILY DOSE**
Evening primrose oil and flaxseed or fish oil	May reduce breast pain	1,500 mg
	Promotes beneficial prostoglandins	3,000 mg
Vitamin B-6 along with a B complex	Improve estrogen metabolism	150 mg
Coenzyme Q10	Increases cellular oxygen	60–200 mg
Selenium	Helps prevent breast cancer	200 mcg
Indole-3-carbinol or DIM	Help metabolize estrogen	300 mg
N-acetyl cysteine	Helps liver deal with estrogen and toxins	1,500 mg

DID YOU KNOW ...

Herbal oils of phytolacca, calendula, and red clover, as well as essential oils of palmarosa, lavender, rosemary, juniper, lemon, sweet orange, and frankincense, are helpful in reducing cysts. Apply herbal and essential oils topically to the breast.

Restore Balance

- Exercise 40 to 60 minutes daily, moving your armpits and breasts to improve lymphatic circulation and estrogen metabolism. Rebounding (jumping on a small trampoline) is ideal.
- Assess thyroid function beginning with a basal body temperature chart, followed by blood tests if temperature is low. Treat hypothyroidism if indicated. See the Hypothyroidism chapter in this section for guidelines.
- Assess progesterone levels using saliva testing between day 20 and 23 of your menstrual cycle. If it is low, use chaste tree berry tincture, 50 drops, twice daily for 6 months. If there is no improvement, use 3% progesterone cream, 2 oz per month or 15 to 20 mg per day (¼ tsp twice daily) from day 14 to 27.

GEMMOTHERAPY FOR FIBROCYSTIC BREAST DISEASE

- **To cleanse the kidneys:** use Ulmus campestre (from elm tree bud), 50 drops, 3 times daily, for 2 months, along with 2 liters of water daily.
- **To improve liver drainage:** use Rosemarinus, 50 drops, 3 times daily.

- Determine whether you have too much of the strong estrogens (estradiol and estrone) and not enough of the weak protective estrogen (estriol) through saliva testing. See the Hormone Balance chapter in the Living with Nature's Rhythms section for guidelines.
- Use Folliculinum 15CH on days 7, 14 and 21 for 3-6 months to suppress estrogen.
- Use the Chinese herbal formula *Xiao Yao Wan* 8 pills, 3 times daily, or *Bupleurum & Tang Kuei*, 3 tablets, 2 to 3 times daily to move liver qi and liver blood.

Detoxify and Rejuvenate

- Follow the detoxification for heavy metals, bowel cleanse, kidney cleanse, and liver flush guidelines in the Seasonal Cleansing and Rejuvenation section.
- Use castor oil packs over the liver and breasts 3 or more times a week

---

HOMEOPATHIC REMEDIES FOR FIBROCYSTIC BREAST DISEASE

- **To improve lymphatic drainage**: use Chelidonium plex, Lymphosot, Lymphdiaral, or Itires, 8-15 drops, 3x daily.
- **To eliminate toxins:** use Unda 1, Unda 20 and Unda 258, 5 drops of each, 3x daily, for 3 weeks, followed by Unda 48, Unda 243, Unda 74, and Unda 258, 5 drops of each, 3x daily, for 3 weeks of the month, for 3 or more months.
- **To help reduce cysts:** use the tissue salt Calc fluor 6X, 4 pellets, once daily.

for 1-3 months to improve lymphatic circulation and reduce cysts.

- Avoid using antiperspirants and cosmetics containing aluminum, lead, phthalates, or parabens.
- Do not store food in plastic or drink from plastic bottles; avoid canned food with plastic; do not allow polyvinyl chloride (PVC) into your home.

Integrate Body, Mind, and Spirit

- Breast ailments can embody conflicts or imbalances in areas of mothering, nurturing, and nourishment, all issues associated with the heart chakra. Ask yourself if you take care of others at the expense of your own self-care, or if you have an unspoken conflict with your children or partner. Do you over-mother or overprotect your family and friends? Beneath an air of niceness, many of us stuff anger into our breasts.
- Begin a relaxation or meditation program, taking time out for 11 minutes twice daily to slow down your breathing and focus inward. This will relax the liver and help to balance hormones.

HEALTHY BREAST HERBAL FORMULA

20% Red Clover (*Trifolium pratense*)
20% Burdock root (*Arctium lappa*)
20% European mistletoe (*Viscum album*)
20% Cleavers (*Galium aparine*)
10% Calendula (*Calendula officinalis*)
5% Pike root (*Phytolacca decandra*)
5% Wild indigo (*Baptista tinctoria*)

Dose: 20-100 drops, 2-3 times daily, ½ hour before or 2 hours after a meal, for 3 months, once or twice a year.

HEALTHY BREAST OIL FORMULA

Use 20 ml each of:
- Phytolacca oil
- Calendula oil
- Dandelion oil
- Red clover Oil

Add 10 drops each of essential oils of:
- Palmarosa
- Lavander
- Rosemary
- Juniper
- Frankincense
- Lemon

Mix with 150 ml of carrier oil of:
- Extra-virgin olive oil

BREAST SELF-MASSAGE INSTRUCTIONS

Breast self-massage stimulates the flow of lymph to help remove toxins and congestion from our breasts. You might want to start in the shower by 'washing' your breasts with your hands until you are comfortable with massaging them. Massage in the Healthy Breast Oil Formula.

1. Place your hands on either side of your neck and gently move the skin back and down to your collarbone. Do this 15 times.

2. Place the palm of your hand under your underarm and gently pump your armpit. The movement is slightly up toward your shoulder and in toward your body. Do this 15 times.

3. With soft hands use the flat surface of three or four fingers to make small semi-circles around the outer part of your breasts working inward until you reach the areola. Do not press hard. Apply as much pressure as you would to stroke a young kitten.

4. With your hands cupped around your breast, gently pull your breast away from the chest wall and move your breast in a circular or up-and-down movement. This allows breast-generated lymph fluid to drain into the retro mammary space and out through the external lymph tubules in the axilla.

5. If you find a cyst or lump, do not try to massage it away. You may irritate it. About 80% of all breast lumps are benign, but it is important to bring any lump to your health-care professional's attention.

Conventional Medicine

Drug Therapy

- Diuretics, which increase fluid elimination but may cause more pain and lumpiness
- Painkillers
- Synthetic hormone therapy, such as the steroid danazol, which can be effective but may cause facial and body hair growth, deepening of the voice, weight gain, acne, and other side effects.

TOP 5 STRATEGIES

1. Use kelp, aqueous molecular iodine, or Lugol's Solution.
2. Practice yoga exercises for breast health.
3. Perform liver and bowel cleansing to improve metabolism and elimination of estrogen.
4. Take *Xiao Yao Wan* or *Bupleurum & Tang Kue*.
5. Apply Healthy Breast Formula and Healthy Breast Oil (topical).

KUNDALINI YOGA EXERCISES FOR HEALTHY BREASTS

Yoga exercises are effective for breast health because they improve lymphatic circulation, help liver detoxification, and help you relax. These exercises are taken from the teachings of Yogi Bhajan.

This set of five exercises can be practiced daily or several times weekly to improve lymphatic circulation to the breast area. Visualize your lymphatic and immune systems powerfully cleansing and protecting your breasts as you do them.

1. Sit in a chair or cross-legged on the floor and extend the arms out parallel to the ground with the elbows straight. Make the hands into fists with the middle finger extended. Begin circling the arms backward. The movement should be tight and powerful. Continue for 3 minutes and then increase the speed for 1 more minute.

2. Sit cross-legged and join the hands in Venus lock (interlaced) behind the head. Like a grinding wheel, roll the total spine around on the hips in a counter-clockwise rotation by working the abdomen. Roll down to the bottom and around in a deep circular movement. Continue for 3 minutes.

3. Sit cross-legged and place your thumbs on the pads at the base of your little fingers. Extend your arms out parallel to the ground with the palms facing down. Alternately begin to raise one arm up to 60 degrees while the other arm goes down 60 degrees. Continue the motion quickly and powerfully for 3 minutes. Inhale as the left arm comes up; exhale as the right arm comes up.

4. Still in a cross-legged position, with the arms out to the side and parallel to the ground. Curl your fingers into fists, with the thumbs pointing up. Twist from side to side. Inhale as you twist to the left, exhale as you twist to the right. Continue for 1 to 2 minutes.

5. Sit on your heels. Make the hands into fists with the thumbs inside. Powerfully pull one arm back while the other extends forward. As each arm is extended its full length, the fingers open up as if they were grabbing something. They close quickly and then pull very powerfully toward the body. Inhale as each arm comes forward; exhale as you pull it back. Imagine you are pulling your future toward you. Reach and grab it. Breathe powerfully in and out through your nose.

Fibroadenomas

Fibroadenomas are the third most frequent of all breast ailments after fibrocystic breast disease and breast cancer tumors. They are commonly seen in younger women. Unlike fibrocystic breast disease, the tumor is not cyclic, but is constantly present. It is not malignant, although its presence indicates the possibility of a higher risk for breast cancer later in life. The lump is firm, smooth, round, and moveable, like a marble under the skin. If a fibroadenoma breaks down on its own, it can develop into calcifications or microcalcifications. These may be associated with the development of breast cancer. A fine needle aspiration, mammogram, or biopsy is needed to differentiate a fibroadenoma from breast cancer.

Prevention and Treatment

- Follow the treatment strategies for fibrocystic breast disease.
- Use Chinese herbs and acupuncture to break down firm masses.

Conventional Medicine

- The primary conventional medical treatment for fibroadenomas is to do nothing other than monitor small tumors, or remove them surgically if they are large.
- Occasionally the drugs danazol sodium or tamoxifen are prescribed, but these have considerable side effects and do not result in a long-term cure.

TCM HERBS FOR FIBROADENOMAS

- Chinese medicine considers breast tumors to result from either liver qi stagnation and accumulation of phlegm or liver and kidney emptiness with accumulation of phlegm.
- Treatment: Formulas containing *Bombyx batryticatus*, *Pericarpum citri reticulatae viride*, *Sparganium*, *Taraxicum mongolium*, and *Curcuma zedoaria*. Combination formulas for benign breast tumors are Blue Citrus Tablets, *Chih-ko & Curcuma*, or the patent formulas *Ru Bi Xiao*, *Gua Luo Xiao Yao San*, *Xing Xiao Wan*, and *Nei Xiao Luo Li Wan*.

Breast Cancer

Among women worldwide, breast cancer is the most common cancer and the leading cause of cancer deaths. The Netherlands and the United States lead the world in the breast cancer epidemic, with Denmark, France, Australia, New Zealand, Belgium, Canada, and Sweden following close behind. Breast cancer is much less common in other parts of the world, indicating that dietary, environmental, and lifestyle factors play a large role in its occurrence. Countries with a low incidence include most of Africa, Haiti, Mongolia, Korea, China, India, Costa Rica, and Japan.

Breast cancer begins with changes in the DNA of the breast cell initiated by a variety of causative agents, including chemicals, radiation, free radicals, toxic metals, electromagnetic fields, chronic inflammation, genetic defects, drugs, viruses, bacteria, fungi, stress, and emotions. The best success in recovery from breast cancer is when a combination of conventional and naturopathic treatments is used. Consult with your health-care team about what therapies are most appropriate for you, and make your decisions after weighing all opinions and examining current research.

Categories

- There are approximately 30 types of breast cancer (and a series of grades or levels, indicating severity), that are divided into two categories: lobular and ductal.
- Most breast cancers are ductal; this category includes mucinous, papillary, and combination cancers.
- Breast cancers that are neither lobular nor ductal include Paget's disease and inflammatory carcinoma.

Symptoms

- A hard, irregular-shaped, non-tender lump that feels like it is attached to the underlying tissue, although any lump or change in your breast warrants investigation.
- Puckering of the skin near the lump site, bloody nipple discharge, and/or changes in nipple size and shape.

Breast Health Balance Sheet

This 'balance sheet' summarizes both the risk factors for breast cancer and the factors that protect us. Reduce the risk factors and increase the protective factors to help prevent breast cancer.

1. Make check marks beside the risk factors and protective factors that are true for you. The bracketed numbers to the right of some entries refer to how much that risk factor increases your likelihood of having breast cancer; that is, (+2) means your risk doubles, (+3.6) means it increases your risk more than three and a half times. If the number is beside a protective factor, it means that it decreases your risk by that amount.

DID YOU KNOW ...

Approximately one woman in nine in Canada and one in seven in the United States will develop breast cancer at some point in her life. In the 1920s, a woman's risk was one in 20. Breast cancer is a leading cause of death for women ages 35 to 50 living in North America.

DID YOU KNOW ...

You may want to select a team of practitioners to treat your cancer — an open-minded surgeon and oncologist, a naturopathic doctor experienced in treating breast cancer who also uses homeopathy as a modality, and someone trained in traditional Chinese medicine who can administer herbs and acupuncture.

2. Come back to the balance sheet at least once a year to see what progress you have made in adopting a breast health/cancer prevention program. If you feel overwhelmed on your first read through, put it aside and come back to it another day. Read *The Complete Natural Medicine Guide to Breast Cancer* by Sat Dharam Kaur for a more thorough explanation of these causes, and work with a naturopathic doctor to understand and correct some of the risk factors, especially the hormonal imbalances.

3. To calculate your 'body mass index' (see below), take your weight in kilograms or pounds and divide by the square of your height in meters or feet. To determine your waist-to-hip ratio, divide your waist measurement by your hip measurement.

BREAST HEALTH BALANCE SHEET

RISK FACTORS FOR BREAST CANCER	PROTECTIVE FACTORS FOR BREAST CANCER
HEREDITARY	
☐ Mother or sister with breast cancer (+2)	☐ No family history of cancer
☐ Relative with ovarian or endometrial cancer	☐ No family with ovarian or endometrial cancer
☐ Brother or father with prostate cancer (+4)	☐ No family with prostate cancer
☐ Light-skinned	☐ Dark-skinned
☐ Body mass index > 28	☐ Body mass index < 22.8
☐ Birth weight > 8.8 lb (+3.5)	☐ Birth weight < 6.7 lb
☐ Birth length > 51.5 cm	☐ Birth length < 50 cm
☐ Over 5' 6" tall	☐ Under 5' 6" tall
☐ Weight > 154 lb (+3.6)	☐ Appropriate weight; weight < 153 lb
☐ Waist to hip ratio >0.81 (+7)	☐ Waist to hip ratio < 0.73
REPRODUCTIVE	
☐ No children or children after 30	☐ Gave birth before age 20 or 30
☐ No children	☐ More than one child (-0.5 with 5 kids)
☐ No breast-feeding	☐ Breast-fed kids for at least 6 months (-2.5)

BREAST HEALTH BALANCE SHEET	
RISK FACTORS FOR BREAST CANCER	**PROTECTIVE FACTORS FOR BREAST CANCER**
LIFESTYLE AND HEALTH CARE	
☐ Aging	☐ Use antioxidants and anti-aging supplements
☐ High breast density (+1.8 - +6)	☐ Low breast density
☐ Lack of exercise	☐ Regular exercise (4 hours weekly) (-0.60)
☐ < 2 bowel movements per week (+4.5)	☐ 2 or more bowel movements daily
☐ Use prescription drugs: beta-blockers (Prozac, Paxil, Elavil); tricyclic antidepressants (Amoxapine, Clomipramine, Desipramine and Trimipramine, Haldol); steroids (Reserpine, hydralazine, Tagamet, metronidazole, vincristine, Nitrofurazone, Valium, Xanax, nitrogen mustard, procarbazine); cholesterol-lowering drugs; Claritin, Atarax, the diuretics Spironolactone and Furosemide, and the anti-cancer drugs (vincristine, acronycine, cytembena, and isophosphamide)	☐ Use herbal, nutritional, homeopathic, and naturopathic recommendations when possible instead of prescription drugs. Educate yourself on the side effects of medications before taking them.
☐ Dental problems: mercury fillings, root canals, chronic infection	☐ Replace mercury fillings with ceramic or methacrylate, remove root canal teeth, clear infection, investigate using Cavatat
☐ Imbalanced biological terrain	☐ Normalize biological terrain
☐ Chronic inflammation	☐ Vegetarian, no dairy fat in diet, use curcumin, bromelain and uncontaminated fish oil regularly
☐ Immune deficiency, allergies	☐ Follow immune-strengthening program
☐ Annual mammograms (from radiation exposure) (+.5)	☐ Monthly breast self exam; annual thermograms (-0.2)
☐ Cigarette smoking increases risk	☐ No smoking; avoid secondhand smoke
☐ Alcohol increases risk (> 3 drinks/week)	☐ Avoid alcohol or have minimally
☐ Use commercial hair dyes	☐ Use henna or natural hair dyes

BREAST HEALTH BALANCE SHEET

RISK FACTORS FOR BREAST CANCER	PROTECTIVE FACTORS FOR BREAST CANCER
LIFESTYLE AND HEALTH CARE	
☐ Have breast implants	☐ No breast implants; have them removed
☐ Wear a tight-fitting bra	☐ Go braless or use looser cotton bra
☐ Mineral and enzyme deficiency	☐ Eat organic, replace minerals and enzymes
☐ Parasitic infection	☐ Do parasite cleanse once or twice yearly
☐ Liver toxicity	☐ Do liver cleanse once or twice yearly
☐ Bowel toxicity	☐ Do bowel cleanse once yearly; replace flora
☐ Use of antibiotics	☐ Avoid antibiotics, deal with candidiasis
☐ Chemical toxins accumulate in fat tissue	☐ Use saunas regularly or sauna detox yearly
☐ Poor lymphatic circulation	☐ Use skin-brushing, rebounding, exercise
HORMONAL	
☐ Estrogen quotient is 0.5-0.8	☐ Estrogen quotient is 1.2-1.3 or higher
☐ Low ratio of C2 to C16 estrogen	☐ High ratio of C2 to C16 estrogen
☐ Low ratio of C2 to C4 estrogen	☐ High ratio of C2 to C4 estrogen
☐ Early onset of menstruation (<11) (+2)	☐ Late onset of menstruation (>14)
☐ Late menopause (>54)	☐ Early menopause (<45)
☐ Menstrual cycle <25 days (+2)	☐ Menstrual cycle 26-28 days
☐ Low progesterone (+5.4)	☐ Normal progesterone
☐ Fibrocystic breasts (+1.8)	☐ Healthy breast tissue
☐ Increased testosterone	☐ Normal testosterone
☐ Increased prolactin	☐ Normal prolactin

BREAST HEALTH BALANCE SHEET	
RISK FACTORS FOR BREAST CANCER	**PROTECTIVE FACTORS FOR BREAST CANCER**
HORMONAL	
☐ Increased growth hormone	☐ Avoid dairy with bovine growth hormone
☐ Increased insulin	☐ Normal insulin levels
☐ Women whose mothers had high estrogen levels during pregnancy	☐ Protect self/fetus from high estrogen in pregnancy
☐ Unbalanced thyroid; iodine deficiency	☐ Correct thyroid function; use seaweeds
☐ High blood levels of IGF-1 (+7)	☐ Normal blood levels of IGF-1
☐ Decreased melatonin levels	☐ High melatonin; meditation practice
☐ Sleep with light on at night: exposure to light at night decreases melatonin production, increases risk	☐ Sleep in a dark room; meditate shortly before bed
☐ Birth control pills used before age 20 or for more than 5 years before age 35 (+3)	☐ Natural fertility methods such as sympto-thermo method, condoms
☐ Use of Depo-Provera for birth control (+2)	☐ Use symptom-thermo method and condoms
☐ Use of fertility drugs in past	☐ Avoidance of fertility drugs
☐ Post-menopausal and >50 lb overweight	☐ Post-menopausal and not overweight
☐ Estrogen replacement therapy, especially when used for more than 5 years	☐ No estrogen replacement therapy, or have stopped for > 5 years
☐ Former use of the drug DES or your mother took it while pregnant (+0.4)	☐ No DES; avoid drugs in pregnancy
ENVIRONMENTAL	
☐ Exposure to radiation	☐ Seaweeds daily, miso and lentils 3x weekly
☐ Fly frequently	☐ Fly seldom
☐ Live within 50 miles of a nuclear reactor	☐ Live > 50 miles from a nuclear reactor

BREAST HEALTH BALANCE SHEET

RISK FACTORS FOR BREAST CANCER	PROTECTIVE FACTORS FOR BREAST CANCER
ENVIRONMENTAL	
☐ Continuous exposure to electricity and electromagnetic fields	☐ Live in the country with few electrical devices
☐ Work in the electrical trade (+0.7)	☐ Work away from excess electricity
☐ Install, repair telephones (+2.2)	☐ Do not work installing telephones
☐ Sleep within 2½ feet of electrical devices	☐ Sleep >3 feet away from electrical devices
☐ Sit < 2 feet from front, < 4 feet from sides of computer video display terminals	☐ Sit further from computer video display terminals and use them < 20 hours weekly
☐ Use an electric blanket	☐ Use cotton, wool, down blankets
☐ Have worked on a farm (+9)	☐ Never worked on a farm, or worked on organic farm
☐ Exposure to pesticides: food, lawn, farm, golf courses, public areas	☐ Eat organic, avoid pesticides
☐ Live in industrialized area	☐ Live away from industry & pesticide sprays
☐ Exposure to petrochemicals, gas stations	☐ Use car less
☐ Exposure to formaldehyde	☐ Choose products without formaldehyde
☐ Exposure to benzene	☐ Avoid benzene
☐ Exposure to organochlorines	☐ Recognize and avoid organochlorines
☐ Use of chemical or industrial cleansers	☐ Use of non-toxic cleansers
☐ Exposure to carcinogens	☐ Recognize and avoid known carcinogens
☐ Live near a hospital incinerator	☐ Live away from a hospital incinerator
☐ Live near a PVC recycling plant	☐ Live away from a PVC recycling plant
☐ Use plastics (exposure to bisphenol-A and phthalates)	☐ Avoid plastics, use glass, wax paper, cardboard, butcher paper

BREAST HEALTH BALANCE SHEET	
RISK FACTORS FOR BREAST CANCER	**PROTECTIVE FACTORS FOR BREAST CANCER**
ENVIRONMENTAL	
☐ Live near a chemical plant	☐ Live away from a chemical plan
☐ Live near a toxic waste site or dump	☐ Decrease waste; live away from a toxic waste site or dump
☐ Live near a sewage treatment plant	☐ Use a composting toilet, live away from a sewage treatment plant
☐ Use chlorine bleach	☐ Use non-chlorine bleach
☐ Drink chlorinated water	☐ Drink ozonated or filtered water
☐ Dry-clean clothing	☐ Avoid dry-cleaning; use natural detergents
DIETARY	
☐ High fat consumption: > 30% total calories	☐ Low-fat consumption: < 15% total calories
☐ Low fiber: < 10 grams daily	☐ High fiber: >45 grams daily (-0.30)
☐ Eat meat weekly	☐ Vegetarian (-0.30)
☐ Use dairy products	☐ Use soy milk, organic goat milk, or low-fat organic dairy
☐ Eat sweets, sugar products	☐ Have 2 or more fruits daily
☐ Use processed food	☐ Use whole, unrefined foods
☐ Use bread products regularly	☐ Use beans, whole grains
☐ Drink coffee	☐ Drink herbal teas, e.g., red clover, dandelion
☐ No soy products	☐ Organic soy products daily (unless allergic)
☐ No orange fruits and vegetables	☐ Use 2 foods high in vitamin A daily
☐ Use vegetable oils, animal fat, margarine and cooked oils; have low essential fatty acids	☐ Use extra-virgin olive oil, unheated flaxseed oil and uncontaminated fish oil

BREAST HEALTH BALANCE SHEET

RISK FACTORS FOR BREAST CANCER	PROTECTIVE FACTORS FOR BREAST CANCER
DIETARY	
☐ Minimal fruits and vegetables	☐ Use 6-9 servings of fruits and vegetables/day
☐ Eat mostly cooked food	☐ 50-85% raw food
☐ No brassicas (cauliflower, cabbage, broccoli)	☐ Raw brassicas daily
☐ High salt intake	☐ Low sodium/high potassium
☐ Overly acidic body	☐ Keep pH of urine and saliva at 6.6 -7.2
☐ Use of plastic food containers and wraps	☐ Use glass, ceramic containers
PSYCHOLOGICAL	
☐ Deny, bury, repress or hold on to anger	☐ Express anger constructively and let it go
☐ Ignore one's own needs; please others	☐ Define your needs; become assertive
☐ Feel alienation	☐ Find or create your community
☐ Death of a loved one or loss of a relationship within the previous one to five years	☐ Express your grief; find reasons for living, find something or someone to love
☐ Stress and the inability to relax	☐ Regular relaxation breaks
☐ Living a life following someone else's script rather than one's own	☐ Follow your deep desires and callings; create your path
SPIRITUAL	
☐ Hopelessness, despair	☐ Spiritual counseling, therapy, prayer, yoga
☐ Lack of a sense of purpose	☐ Develop a meaningful life, find your passion
☐ Lack of joy	☐ Laugh, play, have fun
☐ Loss of faith	☐ Create a relationship with your soul
☐ Foiled creative fire	☐ Express your creativity
☐ Ignore intuition	☐ Awaken and follow your intuition
☐ Lack of support	☐ Find at least one supportive person, support group or spiritual group

Prevention and Treatment

Improve Nutrition

You may choose to modify the Women's Health Diet Program with a specific dietary program for breast cancer prevention if you are at risk and supplement with specific nutritional therapies. Aim to increase your intake of the following organic foods over a two-week period. Check off your accomplishments.

DAILY FOOD (CHECK DAILY)	1	2	3	4	5	6	7	8	9	10	11	12	13	14
Vegetarian diet														
Raw food: 50% or more														
Broccoli sprouts (3x weekly)														
Mung bean sprouts (3x weekly)														
Red clover sprouts (3x weekly)														
Dandelion in season (3x weekly)														
Vegetable juice: 2 or more servings														
Cabbage: ⅓, juiced or raw														
Tomato products (2x weekly)														
Fruits: 2 or more														
Citrus Juice: organic (3 servings weekly)														
Vegetables: 4 or more servings														
Brassica family: 1 cup														
Onion: 1														

DAILY FOOD (CHECK DAILY)	1	2	3	4	5	6	7	8	9	10	11	12	13	14
Garlic: 2 cloves, raw is better														
Sea vegetables: 1/3 cup														
Shiitaki mushrooms (2x weekly)														
Flaxseed oil: 2 or more tbsp														
Olive oil for cooking, low heat														
Fiber: 45 g														
Whole grains: 1 cup														
Beans: 1-2 cups daily														
Flaxseeds: 2-4 tbsp, ground														
Pumpkin seeds: 2 tbsp, raw														
Wheat bran: 1 tbsp														
Protein: 40 g daily														
Tofu: 1/2 cup														
Soy milk: 1 cup														
Miso: 1 tbsp (3x weekly)														
Citrus peel: 1 tsp organic grated														
Turmeric: 1-2 tsp powder														

DAILY FOOD (CHECK DAILY)	1	2	3	4	5	6	7	8	9	10	11	12	13	14
Rosemary, Sage, Thyme, Ginger														
Water: 8 glasses filtered														
Alcoholic Drinks: < 2 /week														
Coffee: none														
Sugar: none														
Canned or Processed Food: none														
Dairy: none														

Restore Balance

- Homeopathic remedies for breast cancer: carcinosinum, scirrhinum, conium, phytolacca, bufo, hydrastis, sepia, thuja, lycopodium, sanguinaria, phosphorus, graphites, silicea, calendula, asterias. Work with a homeopath as well as a conventional medical doctor.
- Exercise 40 to 60 minutes daily, moving your armpits and breasts to improve lymphatic circulation and estrogen metabolism. Rebounding (jumping on a small trampoline) is ideal. Practice yoga exercises for breast health several times a week to improve lymphatic circulation. Practice Qigong exercises to improve energy flow and promote healing.
- Balance hormones. Test the following hormones in saliva and blood and normalize: TSH, free T3, free T4, antimicrosomal antibodies, antithyroglobulin antibodies, cortisol a.m. and p.m., insulin, prolactin, melatonin, IGF-1, estradiol, estrone, estriol, C2/C16 ratio, progesterone, testosterone. Check annually.
- Find a practitioner who uses Biological Terrain Assessment to check the redox potential, resistivity, and pH of blood, saliva, and urine. Balance these.
- Normalize blood viscosity. Test fibrinogen, plasma viscosity, and fibrin-D-dimers in blood annually and decrease blood viscosity with vitamin E, bromelain, fish oil, flaxseed oil, curcumin, and garlic.
- If you wear a bra, choose one that does not have an underwire, is loose-fitting, and when you take it off, there are no red marks on your skin. Wear bras less often.

DID YOU KNOW ...

Cancer thrives in an acid environment (low pH), so monitor pH of urine and saliva and keep it at around 6.8 to 7.2. See the Seasonal Cleansing and Rejuvenation Program section for guidelines.

DID YOU KNOW ...

Applying herbal and essential oils topically to the breast can be helpful. Mix herbal oils of phytolacca, calendula and red clover, and essential oils of palmarosa, lavender, rosemary, juniper, lemon, sweet orange, and frankincense.

Breast Cancer

NUTRIENT THERAPY FOR BREAST CANCER

NUTRIENT	On Rising	Before brkfst	With brkfst	Betwn meals	Before lunch	With lunch	Betwn meals	Before dinner	With dinner	Before bed
IP6 and inositol (mg)										4,000
Modified citrus pectin (g)										10
Ground flaxseed (tbsp)			2							2
Psyllium (tbsp)										1
Greens (tbsp)	1 tbs				1			1		
Vitamin B complex (mg)						50			50	
Vitamin C + bioflavonoids (mg)			2,000			2,000			2,000	
Alkaline powder	½ tsp									½ tsp
Vitamin E mixed tocopherals (IU)						400				
Cal Mag + Vitamin D (mg)						500			500	
Potassium (mg)						500				
Kelp (mg)						500			500	
Molybdenum (mcg)						300				
Chromium (mcg)						200			200	
Selenium (mcg)						200			200	
Zinc (mcg)				50						
Manganese (mcg)						5				
Green tea extract (cups)			3			4			3	
Oncolyn (tablets)		2							2	
Coenzyme Q10 (mg)			100			100			100	

NUTRIENT THERAPY FOR BREAST CANCER

NUTRIENT	On Rising	Before brkfst	With brkfst	Betwn meals	Before lunch	With lunch	Betwn meals	Before dinner	With dinner	Before bed
Alpha Lipoic Acid (mg)			100			100			100	
Grape Seed Extract (mg)			100			100				
Beta-Sitosterol (mg)			100			100			100	
Melatonin (if ER pos) (mg)										3-20
NAC (mg)			500			500			500	
Reduced glutathione (mg)			200			200			200	
Proteolytic enzymes (capsules)				5			5			
Bromelain (mg)				300			300			
Clean fish oil (mg)			1,500						1,500	
Flaxseed oil (tbsp)			1		1					
Probiotic + FOS + Bifidobacterium (capsules)			2						2	
Indole-3-carbinol or DIM (mg)			150						150	
Curcumin (mg)			500			500			500	
Ellagic Acid (mg)						40				
Quercetin (mg)				500			500			
Maitake D-fraction (drops)		30			30			30		
Liver formula: milk thistle, dandelion, bupleurum	½ - 1			½ - 1			½ - 1			
Kidney formula: Juniperus (drops)	50			50			50			

BREAST CONDITIONS

NUTRIENT THERAPY FOR BREAST CANCER

NUTRIENT	On Rising	Before brkfst	With brkfst	Betwn meals	Before lunch	With lunch	Betwn meals	Before dinner	With dinner	Before bed
Lymph formula: Healthy Breast Herbal Formula, Hoxsey Formula, or FlorEssence (tsp)	½ - 1			½ - 1			½ - 1			
Immune formula: astragalus, ganoderma, schizandra, ligustrum, codonopsis (tsp)	½ - 1			½ - 1			½ - 1			
Herbal formula: goldenseal, bloodroot, echinacea, juniper	½			½			½			
Sanum remedies: Mucokehl, Nigersan, Sanuvis, Citrokehl, Exmykehl	See doctor			See doctor			See doctor			
Unda remedies: 21, 48, 243 (drops)			5			5			5	
Garlic capsules			2			2			2	

DID YOU KNOW ...

Cleansing the bowel by increasing fiber to 45 grams a day and taking a probiotic containing *Lactobacillus acidophilus* and *Bifidobacterium bifidus* will help to eliminate excess estrogen. Psyllium and wheat bran are particularly effective in eliminating estrogen (1 tbsp each daily).

- Practice light breast self-massage several times weekly. See the Fibrocystic Breast Disease chapter in this section for guidelines.
- Begin a relaxation or meditation program, taking time out 11 minutes, twice daily, to slow down your breathing and focus inward. Meditate before bed to increase melatonin levels.

Detoxify and Rejuvenate

- Follow the detoxification for heavy metals and chemicals, bowel cleanse, kidney cleanse, parasite and yeast cleanse, sauna detoxification, and liver flush guidelines in the Seasonal Cleansing and Rejuvenation Program section.
- Use a gauss meter and stetzer meter to evaluate exposure to high electromagnetic fields (above 16 mG) or dirty power (readings above 300 mG).

- Use the oligotherapy copper-gold-silver (Cu-Au-Ag) twice weekly to stimulate the immune system.
- Use castor oil packs over the liver and breasts 3 or more times a week for 1 to 3 months to improve lymphatic circulation and reduce cysts.
- Avoid using antiperspirants and cosmetics containing aluminum, lead, phthalates, or parabens.
- Do not store food in plastic or drink from plastic bottles; avoid canned food with plastic; do not allow polyvinyl chloride (PVC) into your home.

GEMMOTHERAPY FOR BREAST CANCER

- **To cleanse the liver and kidneys:** use Juniperus, 50 drops, 3 times daily, for 6 weeks. Follow this with *Betula pubescence*, 50 drops, 3 times daily, for 3 months, and then Rosemarinus 50 drops, 3 times daily, for 3 more months.
- **To cleanse the kidneys:** use *Ulmus campestre*, 50 drops, 3 times daily, for 2 months, along with 2 liters of water daily.

Integrate Body, Mind, and Spirit

- Acknowledge your feelings, express them, get them 'off your chest.' Cancer sometimes occurs when we feel trapped in an emotional conflict.
- Breast cancer may appear when we have difficulty with a husband or partner that seemingly can't be resolved, or with a child. Perhaps we would like to leave a relationship but can't for financial reasons, or are afraid of what our relatives or friends may think.
- Develop your spiritual life in prayer or meditation; connect to a supportive spiritual community.
- Face the possibility of physical death and clear up unresolved issues. Identify what would give you the greatest joy and fulfillment and do it now – your immune system will follow.
- Do everything you can to get well while remembering that ultimately, we are not in charge. Surrender to a higher power.

DID YOU KNOW

To help prevent breast cancer, you should see a biological dentist who can replace silver mercury amalgam fillings with methacrylate or porcelain; assess toxicity levels in root canal teeth and remove them; and determine whether there is osteomyelitis (infection) in the jaw and clear it with surgery or other methods.

HERBAL FORMULAS FOR BREAST CANCER

- Detoxify the liver often using a combination of milk thistle, dandelion, globe artichoke, bupleurum, and chelidonium tinctures, 30 drops, 3 times daily, for 6 weeks or more.
- Activate the immune system with an herbal formula that includes astragalus, codonopsis, schizandra, ganoderma, pau d'arco, and St. John's wort.
- Use a combination of medicinal mushrooms that includes maitake, shiitake, reishi, agaricus blazei, and coriolus versicolor. These are available in a product called Host Defense.
- Detoxify the lymph using the Healthy Breast Herbal Formula. See the Fibrocystic Breast Disease chapter in this section for guidelines. Or substitute the Hoxsey Formula or FlorEssence.

HOMEOPATHIC REMEDIES FOR BREAST CANCER

- To improve lymphatic drainage: use Chelidonium plex, Lymphosot, Lymphdiaral, or Itires, 8-15 drops, 3x daily.
- To eliminate toxins: use Unda 1, Unda 20 and Unda 258, 5 drops of each, 3x daily, for 3 weeks, followed by Unda 48, Unda 243, Unda 74, and Unda 258, 5 drops of each, 3x daily, for 3 weeks of the month, for 3 or more months.
- To help reduce cysts: use the tissue salt Calc fluor 6X, 4 pellets, once daily.

DID YOU KNOW ...

Some women experience long-standing grief or guilt over the death of a loved one or pet, the loss of a relationship, or an abortion. These buried emotions are brought to the surface with a breast cancer diagnosis. Other women repress anger beneath a veneer of pleasantries and social rituals. Breast cancer brings with it the opportunity to transform grief and anger.

Conventional Medicine

Surgery

- Lumpectomy or mastectomy are used to remove diseased breast tissue and affected lymph nodes.
- Some women with estrogen receptor positive breast cancer also choose to have their ovaries removed surgically to decrease estrogen production.
- Other women choose to have both breasts removed to prevent a future recurrence in either breast.

Chemotherapy

- Drugs are used after surgery (or occasionally before surgery) to shrink the tumor and kill remaining cancer cells anywhere in the body.

Radiation

- Radiation is used usually after chemotherapy to destroy any cancer cells near the original cancer site.

Drug Therapy

- Tamoxifen attaches to estrogen receptors, preventing a woman's estrogen or environmental estrogens from stimulating cell growth.
- Aromatase inhibitors (anastrozole, letrosole and formestane) block the production of estrogen in fat cells and the ovaries by inhibiting the action of aromatase, an enzyme that converts testosterone and androstenedione into estrogen. These may cause hot flashes and osteoporosis in some women.
- Goserelin and similar drugs cause an artificial menopause and lower the pituitary gland's production of gonadotrophic hormones (LH and FSH) that stimulate the ovaries to produce estrogen and progesterone.
- Herceptin can kill breast cancer cells that have too many receptors for human epidermal growth factor (HER2), which occurs in up to 30% of breast cancers.

TOP 5 STRATEGIES

1. Follow the Breast Cancer Prevention Diet and the Women's Health Diet Plan.
2. Acknowledge and express your feelings; release buried or stuck emotions.
3. Develop purpose and meaning in your life.
4. Detoxify the liver, bowel, kidneys, and lymph and use an infrared sauna detox program.
5. Use coenzyme Q10, alpha lipoic acid, NAC, selenium, fish oil, curcumin, garlic, indole-3-carbinol.

DID YOU KNOW …

Tamoxifen is recommended for up to 5 years and can reduce mortality from breast cancer by up to 30%, recurrence by about 50%, and risk of cancer in the other breast by 40%. However, it increases risk of liver cancer and uterine cancer.

CASE STUDY: *WILLINGNESS TO HEAL*

Kerry had a lumpectomy for a highly aggressive breast cancer tumor. The pathology report came back with "unclear margins" — not all of the cancer had been removed — and a mastectomy was recommended. Kerry refused further conventional treatment and embarked on an odyssey through the natural medicine profession, steering herself to various practitioners as she was guided.

Her treatments thus far have included a macrobiotic diet for several years, numerous cleansing fasts, coffee enemas, removal of all mercury fillings in her mouth, continuous herbal and homeopathic formulas, topical bloodroot salves on the breast to remove the remaining cancer (done twice) over a period of several months, acupuncture, regular yoga classes, a new living arrangement with her husband that gave her more freedom, art therapy, biological terrain assessment every 3 months, a topical selenium paste, regular examination of her blood using dark-field microscopy, infrared saunas, Iscador treatment (a formula that uses mistletoe), NeuroModulation Technique, continuous emotional work, and body-centered therapy. In short, there's very little she hasn't tried in the alternative cancer realm.

Kerry has taken each of these treatments very seriously, and her compliance to all of them has been excellent and continuous. Through her journey, she has understood that cancer is a multifactorial disease and that all aspects of body, mind, and spirit need to be addressed for it to resolve.

Three years later, she feels better than ever, her tumor markers, which were once high, have dropped, and her white blood cell count, which was low for a long time, has jumped into the ideal range. We have no idea what to attribute her recovery to — only her dedication and faith in the natural healing process, her willingness to address everything that needs to be addressed, and grace.

Hypothyroidism

If you tend to feel cold, sluggish, and gain weight easily, your thyroid may be underactive. The thyroid, a small butterfly-shaped gland located beneath the voice box at the front of your throat, is critical in regulating metabolism. The job of thyroid hormones is to rev up the body's metabolic rate by increasing the number and activity of mitochondria, tiny 'furnaces' in every body cell that use oxygen to convert energy from food (glucose) into carbon dioxide, water, heat, and cellular energy. Thyroid hormones elevate body temperature, stimulate protein synthesis, increase the use of glucose and the breakdown of fats for energy production, and speed up the liver's excretion of cholesterol into bile. Thyroid hormones accelerate growth, particularly of nervous tissue, and affect moods, emotions, memory, and thinking processes. When the thyroid is unbalanced, we can suffer from a hypothyroid state (too little) or hyperthyroid state (too much). If thyroid hormones are deficient or unable to bind to their receptors, all of these processes slow down and a person will feel fatigued, cold, depressed, gain weight easily, may have high cholesterol, will have poor memory, and may have trouble thinking.

DID YOU KNOW ...

Thyroid imbalance is implicated in many women's disorders — PMS, amenorrhea, heavy menstrual bleeding, breast cancer, uterine fibroids, ovarian cysts, endometriosis, infertility, postpartum depression and miscarriage. An underactive thyroid often accompanies estrogen dominance, progesterone deficiency, and adrenal fatigue. If you suspect hypothyroidism, see your health-care practitioner for further tests and treatment.

Thyroid Hormones

- **TSH:** the thyroid gland is stimulated by a hormone from the pituitary gland called thyroid-stimulating hormone (TSH), which signals the gland to produce more or less thyroid hormones, depending on the need of the body.
- **TRH:** TSH is adjusted, in turn, by a hormone from the hypothalamus called thyrotropin-releasing hormone (TRH), which reads the cues from the blood and signals the pituitary to produce TSH.
- **T3 and T4:** The thyroid gland, when stimulated by TSH, makes two hormones, thyroxine (T4) and triiodothyronine (T3), from iodine and the amino acids tyrosine and phenylalanine (which is converted to tyrosine in the liver). Though 93% of what the gland produces is T4, T3 is the more biologically active hormone, and T4 is converted to T3 in the liver, kidneys, and body cells. This conversion is primarily dependent on the trace mineral selenium.

Tests for Thyroid Function

If only one of these tests is abnormal and your temperature is high or low, there is likely a thyroid imbalance. If none are abnormal, there may still be a thyroid problem – go with the temperature test and symptoms and work with someone experienced with natural therapies to adjust it.

THYROID IMBALANCE SYMPTOMS	
HYPOTHYROID STATE	**HYPERTHYROID STATE**
GENERAL SYMPTOMS	
a.m. underarm temperature lower than 97.8°F	a.m. underarm temperature higher than 98.2°F
Carpal tunnel syndrome, tendonitis, joint stiffness and swelling, muscle weakness, fibromyalgia, muscle and joint pain, increased rheumatoid arthritis	Fatigue and weakness
Puffy face, especially around the eyes, swelling of hands and feet, weight gain, difficulty losing weight	Weight loss, increased appetite
Slower speech, thick tongue, deep hoarse voice	Hyperactive state, racing thoughts, nervousness
Feels cold all the time, hard to stay warm	Feels warm most of the time, intolerant to heat
Frequent or chronic infections, particularly fungal or viral	Osteoporosis, increased calcium loss in urine
Low DHEA, DHEA-S and pregnenolone	High DHEA-S and pregnenolone sulfate
REPRODUCTIVE SYSTEM	
Low libido	Low or very high libido
PMS, prolonged heavy period, longer menstrual cycle	Irregular periods, usually more frequent, light menstrual flow
Failure to ovulate, infertility, easy miscarriage	Infertility
Premature delivery, stillbirth	
Production of breast milk when not nursing, elevated prolactin	
Decreased sex hormone binding globulin – means more available estrogen, estrogen dominance	Increased sex hormone binding globulin – means less available estrogen
Severe menopausal symptoms	Increased menopausal symptoms
Can be increased susceptibility to breast cancer and other cancers	Increased susceptibility to fibrocystic breast disease, breast cancer, and other cancers

Hypothyroidism

THYROID IMBALANCE SYMPTOMS	
HYPOTHYROID STATE	**HYPERTHYROID STATE**
CARDIOVASCULAR SYSTEM	
Slow pulse (< 60 beats/minute)	Fast pulse (> 100 beats/minute), heart palpitations
Low blood pressure	High blood pressure (systolic), shortness of breath
Sleep apnea	Swollen, red, bulging eyes
High cholesterol, high LDL and triglycerides, low HDL, macrocytic anemia	Reduced platelets causing easy bleeding
High homocysteine and lipoprotein (a)	Enlarged heart, angina, increased risk of heart disease, increased risk of mitral valve prolapse
	Palpable goiter (swelling) of thyroid gland in throat, atrial fibrillation (fluttering beat), arrhythmia
HAIR, SKIN, AND NAILS	
Hair is dry, brittle, falling out, loss of lateral one-third of eyebrow	Hair loss, thinning, and greasiness
Dry scaly skin, tendency to eczema, psoriasis, no perspiration	Increased perspiration, vitiligo (white patches)
Yellowing of the skin, especially on the palms	Raised thickened skin over shins
Thin, brittle nails with transverse grooves	Soft nails, easily torn, clubbing of fingertips
NERVOUS SYSTEM, MENTAL-EMOTIONAL SYMPTOMS	
Fatigue and muscle weakness, anemia	Overactivity, insomnia, eyes sensitive to light
Depression, memory loss, poor concentration	Confusion, disorganized thinking, depression
Slow thinking, emotional instability, agoraphobia, anxiety, irritability, apathy, dementia	Nervousness, anxiety, panic attacks, irritability, mood swings, paranoia, aggression, psychosis
Slow reflexes, particularly Achilles tendon reflex	Shakiness, tremor (especially in hands)
GASTROINTESTINAL TRACT	
Constipation, frequent headaches	Frequent bowel movements, diarrhea, increased thirst
Low stomach acid, mineral deficiencies — poor zinc absorption	Increased need for vitamins and minerals; zinc and calcium deficiency

GRADES OF HYPOTHYROIDISM

Hypothyroidism can be grouped into four classes, from severe to subtle or subclinical:

- **Grade I** is signified by low T3 and T4
- **Grade II** has normal T3 and T4 but elevated TSH (above 5.5; lower than 1.9 is ideal)
- **Grade III** has normal T3, T4 and TSH but an aggravated TSH response to TRH challenge
- **Grade IV** has elevated antimicrosomal antibodies and antithyroglobulin antibodies

Underarm Test

- The simplest way to test thyroid function is to take your underarm temperature in the morning before getting out of bed. A normal temperature is 97.8 to 98.2°F or 36.6 to 36.8°C with fluctuations that occur with your menstrual cycle.
- If your temperature is consistently lower than this, you may have an underactive thyroid (hypothyroid). If your temperature is often higher than 98.2°F, your thyroid gland may be overactive (hyperthyroid).
- Low progesterone, low cortisol, low iron, depression, post-traumatic stress disorder, fasting, eating disorders, poor circulation, and kidney failure may also contribute to a lowered body temperature.
- Several of these imbalances may be present simultaneously, so clinical judgment and further testing may be needed to differentiate the cause.
- Use the fertility chart from the Birth Control chapter of this section to record your temperature.

Blood Tests

- Blood tests for thyroid function include TSH, free T3, free T4, reverse T3, thyroid antimicrosomal antibodies (TPO Abs), antithyroglobulin antibodies (Tg Abs), and a thyrotropin-releasing hormone (TRH) challenge test.
- Commonly TSH is the only blood test ordered by many medical doctors – the range that is considered normal is 0.38 to 5.5 IU/mL, although many practitioners consider anything above 1.9 to be potentially hypothyroid.
- The TRH challenge test is the most sensitive thyroid test, and ideally all of them should be performed on women with low basal body temperature who present with symptoms of hypothyroidism.

DID YOU KNOW ...

Women are up to 10 times more prone to thyroid disorders than men, perhaps because higher estrogen levels suppress thyroid function. About 48% of American women over 60 have subclinical hypothyroidism. Hypothyroidism is chronically under-diagnosed, and blood tests may not reveal a problem.

WILSONS TEMPERATURE SYNDROME

Wilsons temperature syndrome is a thyroid disorder that occurs when there is a low temperature and an excess of reverse T3 (RT3) due to the liver's inefficiency in making the conversion of T4 to T3. The enzyme required to make this conversion is dependent upon the minerals selenium and zinc, vitamin B-12, and the amino acid cysteine. The heavy metals mercury, cadmium, and lead will block this conversion in the liver. Wilsons temperature syndrome can be suspected when standard blood tests for the thyroid are normal, and when the ratio of T3 to reverse T3 is less than 10:1.

DID YOU KNOW ...

To treat hypothyroidism, you should avoid or minimize raw goitrogenic foods. Raw brassicas – cabbage, broccoli, Brussels sprouts, cauliflower, kale, turnips, broccoli, kohlrabi, and rutabaga -- can interfere with the thyroid gland's ability to use iodine when dietary iodine is deficient. These foods are fine, however, when cooked. Other goitrogens include mustard seeds, cassava root, peanuts, pine nuts, millet, peaches, pears, spinach, and soy. Cooking usually inactivates goitrogens, and their effect will be minimized if you have seaweed regularly in your diet. Soy foods may prevent thyroid cancer.

Causes of Hypothyroidism

- Estrogen dominance, hormone replacement therapy or the birth control pill
- Progesterone deficiency
- High or low cortisol and low DHEA – excess cortisol causes diminished conversion of T4 to T3; low cortisol and adrenal fatigue may also precede hypothyroidism
- Increased stress or stressful event
- Times of hormonal transition, such as pregnancy, childbirth, and menopause
- Sluggish liver
- Iodine deficiency, which may cause a goiter, or thyroid swelling
- Tyrosine and dietary protein deficiency
- Iron deficiency anemia – when confirmed by blood tests of serum ferritin, % transferrin saturation, and hemoglobin levels
- Other nutritional deficiencies – low levels of zinc, selenium, copper, magnesium, manganese, or vitamins A, B-2, B-3, B-6, B-12, C, and E can cause or contribute to hypothyroidism
- Toxic metals — lead, cadmium, and mercury interfere with the liver's conversion of T4 to T3
- Fluoride in drinking water, bottled juices, soft drinks, and toothpaste may decrease thyroid function
- High mercury levels are often due to mercury amalgam dental fillings or consumption of fish, particularly tuna
- Injury to the neck with misalignment of cervical vertebrae
- Food sensitivities – gluten grains (wheat, rye, oats, barley, spelt, kamut), animal protein, dairy
- Candida overgrowth and bowel toxicity
- Cigarette smoke contains cadmium and thiocyanate, which increases autoimmune thyroid disease and decreases T3
- Radiation exposure from X-rays, radiation therapy, nuclear fallout, and proximity to nuclear power plants
- Goitrogenic foods and inadequate iodine

ENVIRONMENTAL AND PHARMACEUTICAL CAUSES OF THYROID IMBALANCE

Chemicals and pharmaceutical drugs can block thyroid function in several ways:

- Inhibit the ability of the thyroid gland to trap iodine. Thiocyanate, tamoxifen, and perchlorate in synthetic fertilizers and rocket fuel do this.
- Block the binding of iodine and the coupling of iodothyronines to form thyroid hormones. Sulfonamides, thiourea, methimazole, and aminotriazole do this.
- Inhibit thyroid hormone secretion. Lithium and an excess of iodine do this.
- Increase the metabolism of thyroid hormones so that they are used up faster where they are needed in the body. Many drugs do this — phenobarbitol, benzodiazepines, calcium channel blockers, and steroids, as do PCBs and organochlorine pesticides, such as chlordane, lindane, DDT, and TCDD.
- Mimic thyroid hormone and activate an autoimmune thyroid condition. Women with autoimmuine thyroid disease and high antithyroglobulin antibodies may have significantly higher levels of PCBs in their systems.
- Disrupt thyroid function in a mother and fetus, causing permanent neurological damage in the developing baby that may manifest as learning disabilities, attention problems, and hyperactivity throughout childhood and adult life. Low levels of PCBs and dioxins can do this.

- People with blood type A are more prone to hypothyroidism
- Kidney yang and/or spleen yang deficiency; or blood deficiency
- Unexpressed emotions and blocked creativity

Prevention and Treatment

Improve Nutrition

In addition to following the Women's Health Diet Plan (Section 2), these dietary and supplement strategies have proven to be effective for hypothyroidism:

Diet
- Eat sea vegetables, such as kelp, dulse, nori, hiziki, and wakame, as a source of iodine.
- Use warming foods, such as cinnamon, ginger, cayenne, and fennel.
- Eat three Brazil nuts daily to obtain selenium and a handful of pumpkin seeds daily for zinc and magnesium.
- Avoid animal protein, fish, and dairy, which are high in PCBs.
- Consume small frequent meals, eating every 3 hours, with vegetarian protein sources.
- Try to avoid wheat and gluten grains. They may be implicated in autoimmune thyroid disease.

DID YOU KNOW ...

Environmental chemicals and pharmaceuticals suppress thyroid function. Antidiabetic and sulfa drugs, birth control pills, hormone replacement therapy, some cough medicines, and aspirin do this, as well as food additives and tralomethrin, a pesticide used inside airplanes.

DID YOU KNOW ...

Our daily minimal requirement for iodine is 50 mcg or about 1 gram of seaweed, while a therapeutic dosage is between 300 and 400 mcg. However, excessive iodine can suppress thyroid function or trigger hyperthyroidism, so dosing needs to be approached with care.

Hypothyroidism

Tyrosine for Hypothyroidism

- Tyrosine is a building block for thyroid hormones. It is often low in vegetarians who avoid dairy. Aim to include in your diet at least 1500 mg daily of tyrosine for thyroid health from food sources or supplement with tyrosine. Sunflower seeds, soy, and aduki beans are excellent sources.

SOURCES OF L-TYROSINE		
FOOD	**QUANTITY**	**TYROSINE (MG)**
Cooked oatmeal	¾ cup	161
Wheat bran	½ cup	101
Low fat cottage cheese	1 cup	1655
Fish	3 oz.	500
Figs	10 dried	247
Soy flour	½ cup	555
Soy nuts	½ cup	1287
Almond butter	1 tbsp	85
Almonds	12	100
Cashews	1 oz	139
Filberts	1 oz	129
Sunflower seeds	1 oz	189
Meat	3.5 oz	600–1000
Adzuki beans	1 cup boiled	890
Soy beans	1 cup	1084
Other beans	1 cup	400
Nori	3.5 oz	254
Dried spirulina	3.5 oz	2584
Miso	½ cup	500
Tofu, firm	½ cup	665

NUTRIENT THERAPY FOR HYPOTHYROIDISM		
NUTRIENT	**ACTION**	**DAILY DOSE**
Kelp	Iodine content is necessary to make thyroid hormones	1,000 mg
Vitamin B-12 (sublingual) combined with folic acid and vitamin B-6	Increase hydrochloric acid Decrease homocysteine and prevent heart disease	B-12: 1,000 mcg Folic acid: 400 mcg Vitamin B-6: 100 mg
NAC, coenzyme Q10, and alpha lipoic acid	Improve the function of the mitochondria Protect from environmental contaminants	NAC: 1,500 mg Coenzyme Q10: 100 mg Alpha lipoic acid: 300 mg
Uncontaminated fish oil	Needed for healthy skin and hormone balance Protects against heart disease	3,000 mg
Vitamin A	Necessary for healthy skin and adrenal function	50,000 IU for 2-3 months until thyroid function improves
Vitamin E mixed tocopherols	Antioxidant	400 IU
Vitamin C	Protect from PCB and heavy metal toxicity	2,000 mg

Nutrient Supplements

- Use a multivitamin and mineral formula containing zinc (50 mg), selenium (200 mcg), chromium (200 mcg), manganese (30 mg), magnesium (400 mg), and vitamin B complex (50 mg) — all needed for proper thyroid function.
- Test serum ferritin and % transferrin saturation to determine if iron stores are low. If iron is low, supplement with iron daily, 30 mg, for 3 to 6 months; Floravit; or equal parts yellow dock (Rumex crispus), tang kuei (Angelica sinensis), and nettle (Urtica dioica).

Restore Balance

- Homeopathic remedies for hypothyroidism: Alumina, Baryta carb, Bromium, Calcarea carbonica, Calcarea iodatum, Ferrum metallicum, Graphites, Lycopodium, Natrum muriaticum, Silicea, Sepia, Spongia. Work with a homeopath to evaluate your symptoms and choose an appropriate remedy.
- Use 3 pellets once daily of thyroidinum 4CH to activate and 200K to regulate the thyroid.
- Exercise 40 to 60 minutes daily, preferably in the morning, to stimulate thyroid function and increase your tissue sensitivity

DID YOU KNOW...

Ashwagandha increases levels of T4, while myrrh enhances the conversion of T4 to T3. Recommended dosage of ashwagandha (standardized to contain 1.5 % withanolides) is 150 mg, while the dosage of myrrh (standardized to contain 2.5% guggulsterones) is 100 mg. Other natural tonics for the thyroid include bee pollen, spirulina or chlorella algae, wheatgrass, oats, watercress, kelp, bladderwrack, saw palmetto berries, damiana leaf, and globe artichoke. Use ashwaganda (150 mg) and guggul (100 mg), daily.

Hypothyroidism

to thyroid hormone. Practice yoga postures for the thyroid regularly, such as shoulder stands and plow poses.

- Assess progesterone levels with saliva testing between days 20 and 23 of your menstrual cycle. Increase progesterone levels with vitamin E, B-6, zinc, selenium, chaste tree, and progesterone cream if appropriate.
- Determine whether there is estrogen dominance by checking saliva levels of estradiol, estrone, and estriol. If the estrogen quotient is less than 0.8, there is too much estradiol and estrone, with too little estriol. Correct this imbalance. See the Hormone Balance chapter in the Living with Nature's Rhythms section for guidelines.
- Assess adrenal function and correct. See the Hormone Balance chapter in the Living with Nature's Rhythms section for guidelines.

TCM FOR HYPOTHYROIDISM

Work with a traditional Chinese medicine practitioner to address these imbalances with acupuncture and Chinese herbal formulas.

Causes

Kidney yang deficiency
Kidney and spleen yang deficiency
Blood deficiency

Treatments

Essential Yang Formula
Ginseng & Astragalus
Ginseng Nourishing Formula

- Use natural alternatives to the birth control pill and hormone replacement therapy.
- Use thyroid glandular extract (with the hormone removed) to stimulate thyroid function.
- Stimulate the thyroid gland by using alternating hot and cold packs over it – 3 minutes hot followed by 1 minute cold. Repeat this sequence 2-3 times once daily.
- Correct any misalignment of the cervical spine with massage, chiropractic, craniosacral therapy, physiotherapy, shiatsu, or acupuncture.

GEMMOTHERAPY FOR HYPOTHYROIDISM

- For an underactive or overactive thyroid, specifically to draw out cadmium, lead, and mercury: Cornus sanguinaria (dogwood tree bud) as drainage, 25-50 drops, once daily, for 2-3 months.
- To stimulate an underactive thyroid: Prunus amygdalus (almond tree root bark), 50 drops, once daily.

HOMEOPATHIC REMEDIES FOR HYPOTHYROIDISM

- Month 1: To begin liver drainage: use Unda 1, Unda 20, and Unda 258, 5 drops of each, 3x daily, for 3 weeks of the first month.
- Month 2: To continue liver drainage, improve breakdown of estrogen, and eliminate cellular toxins:use Unda 74, Unda 243, and Unda 48, 5 drops of each, 3x daily, for 3 weeks of the second month.
- Month 3: To normalize the thyroid: use Unda 16, Unda 273 and Unda 1000, 5 drops of each, 3x daily, for 3 weeks or more in the third month.

Detoxify and Rejuvenate

- Remove silver mercury amalgam dental fillings, replacing them with methacrylate or porcelain
- If you smoke, stop. See the Seasonal Cleansing and Rejuvenation Program section for guidelines.
- Detoxify the bowel for toxic metals and begin a 100-hour sauna detoxification program to eliminate environmental chemicals that may be interfering with thyroid function (PCBs, dioxin, pesticides). See the Seasonal Cleansing and Rejuvenation Program section for guidelines.
- Detoxify the liver using milk thistle, dandelion, bupleurum, and globe artichoke tinctures, along with NAC, curcumin, alpha lipoic acid, zinc, selenium, vitamin B complex, and magnesium so the liver is better able to manage estrogen and convert T4 into T3.
- Use the oligotherapy manganese-copper (Mn-Cu) twice weekly to stimulate the thyroid, along with the oligotherapy selenium once daily to improve conversion of T4 to T3.

Integrate Body, Mind, and Spirit

- Write out all the feelings you have suppressed or felt unable to express. Start a creative project or join a choir or chanting group to open the throat chakra. Don't be afraid of what others may think – listen to your inner voice and follow through.

DID YOU KNOW ...

In yoga, the thyroid gland is associated with the throat chakra. Imbalances may reflect difficulties with speaking one's truth, creative expression, communication, listening, surrendering to one's destiny, or taking responsibility for one's actions. Ask yourself if there is something you need to communicate or express. What is it and to whom? Do you speak your truth or do you bury the truth or avoid it?

HERBAL FORMULA FOR HYPOTHYROIDISM

20%	Bladderwrack	(*Fucus vesiculosis*)
20%	Siberian ginseng	(*Eleutherococcus senticosis*)
20%	Ashwaganda	(*Withania somnifera*)
20%	Myrrh	(*Cohmiphora mukul*)
10%	Bupleurum	(*Bupleurum scorzoneraefolium*)
10%	Tang kuei	(*Angelica sinensis*)

- **Dose:** Mix the above tinctures together and take 30-50 drops, 3 times daily. Do not use in pregnancy.

DID YOU KNOW ...

One-third of women taking Synthroid still have hypothyroid symptoms, such as depression, weight gain, sluggishness, and feeling cold. Many women have trouble converting T4 to T3. For those women this drug will not be effective, though blood tests for thyroid function may normalize. Improvement may occur with the addition of selenium and myrrh (guggul), or the addition of synthetic T3. Some women are best on a combination of T4 plus T3 – your T4 and T3 blood levels should be in the mid to high normal range after supplementation.

- Work with an NMT practitioner to balance the glandular system and eliminate the informational patterns that are disrupting thyroid function.
- Practice yoga, meditation, relaxation, visualization, music, dance, Tai Chi, or other technique for at least 11 minutes, twice daily, to help you adapt to stress and balance glandular function.

Conventional Medicine

Drug Therapy

Do not take calcium carbonate or iron supplements at the same time as your thyroid hormone supplement – they will interfere with its absorption.

- **Armour:** Conventional and naturopathic doctors in the United States may prescribe Armour thyroid, which is dessicated thyroid gland from a pig, at an initial dose of 60 to 120 mg, daily. Because it contains both T4 and T3, some individuals respond to it better than to synthetic thyroid hormone.
- **Levothyroxine:** The most commonly prescribed conventional medical drug treatment for hypothyroidism is Levothyroxine (Synthroid, Levothyroid), which is a synthetic form of T4. While this may work for some women, it suppresses function of the thyroid gland, so it usually must be taken for life.

KUNDALINI YOGA EXERCISE FOR THYROID BALANCE

1. Stand up with your hands pressed together as though praying, with your thumbs resting against the sternum between your breasts and your elbows relaxed at your sides.

2. Inhale deeply and extend your arms up and back to 60 degrees from the horizontal, dropping your head back to whatever extent feels comfortable.

3. Exhale as you return to the original position with the head straight.

4. Continue for 1 to 3 minutes.

TOP 5 STRATEGIES

1. Correct adrenal function.
2. Detoxify the liver and bowel of heavy metals and chemicals with a sauna detox.
3. Use tyrosine, selenium, zinc, vitamin B-12, fish oil, kelp.
4. Use the Herbal Formula for Hypothyroidism.
5. Express your creativity and be true to yourself.

Osteoporosis

Osteoporosis results when the rate of bone loss (resorption) is greater than the rate of bone building. Two types of cells manage bone tissue: osteoblasts build it up and osteoclasts break it down. During childhood and adolescence, our bone building or mineralization exceeds bone breakdown, but after we reach our peak bone mass in our late 20s, bone formation drops. The rate of bone loss after age 30 is related to diet, mineral intake, exercise patterns, hormone status, exposure to toxic substances, and diseases or medicines that speed up bone loss. This is accelerated when estrogen levels fall after menopause, since one of estrogen's roles is to suppress the tearing down of bone by osteoclasts. To improve bone density, we want to slow down the activity of the osteoclasts and speed up the activity of the osteoblasts. An alkaline diet, mineral-rich foods, supplements, and weight-bearing exercise help us to do this.

Bone Composition

- Bone consists of a network of calcium and phosphorus crystals (called hydroxyapatite) surrounded by protein fibers (called collagen). The mineral structure gives bones their hardness, while the collagen fibers lend flexibility. Both are needed for bone stability.
- The mineral crystalline structure forms 67% of bone by weight, while the collagen fibers make up 33%.
- Nutrients needed to form hydroxyapatite are calcium, phosphorus, magnesium, and sodium.
- Nutrients needed to form collagen are protein, zinc, copper, beta carotene, and vitamin C.
- The only bone-building supplement that nourishes both the collagen and the crystalline structure is MCHC (microcrystalline hydroxyapatite complex) derived from bovine bone.

Signs

Osteoporosis is a silent disease — there are usually no symptoms until we fracture a bone. However, there are some signs that may indicate decreased bone density.

- Compression or stress fractures
- Gum disease or excessive tooth decay
- Premature graying of hair (50% gray by age 40)
- Arthritis
- Low back pain
- Leg cramps at night
- Poor nail growth
- Decreased height

DID YOU KNOW ...

Women typically lose 30% of their skeletal structure between 45 and 75 years of age. With osteoporosis, the bones become porous, brittle, and fracture easily as calcium and phosphate salts are lost from bone tissue. We need to build our bone density in our 30s and 40s to prevent osteoporosis in our 50s and 60s.

DID YOU KNOW ...

By age 70, 35% of women have fractured a bone due to osteoporosis, and 12% to 15% of these women will die after a hip fracture. Hip fractures occur when bones have become so weak they can no longer support our weight. Hip fractures are the second leading cause of death in people 47 to 74 years old.

CAUSES OF BONE LOSS	SOLUTIONS FOR BONE BUILDING
DIETARY FACTORS	
• High animal protein diets • Sulfur-containing amino acids in animal protein are metabolized to sulfuric acid (the same thing that's in acid rain), which causes calcium to be removed from bone to buffer excess acidity. Women who eat 5 or more servings of red meat a week are at increased risk of fractures.	• Replace animal protein with tofu, legumes, nuts, and seeds • Eat no more than 40 grams of protein a day • Increase fruits, vegetables and seaweeds to 8 servings a day to stay more alkaline • Use alkaline powder away from meals to normalize pH if it is acid ($\frac{1}{2}$ tsp twice daily in warm water)
• Animal fats found in meat and dairy increase prostaglandin E2, which causes increased bone breakdown	• Take fish oil (3000 mg) and flaxseed oil (2 tbsp) to increase prostaglandin E3 and decrease E2
• Excess acid-forming grains (buckwheat, rice, oatmeal, barley, wheat, corn)	• Use millet more frequently (an alkaline grain) and always have vegetables and seaweeds (nori and dulse) with grain • Decrease serving size of grain
• Excess salt causes increased calcium loss through the kidneys	• Use dulse powder, rich in minerals, to replace salt
• Soft drinks contain phosphates, which lead to decreased calcium absorption	• Drink filtered water, at least 2 liters daily. The neutral pH of water will help flush acids out through your kidneys. You will retain acids if you are dehydrated
• Alcohol decreases bone mass	• Drink filtered water
• Sugar depletes calcium	• Eat fruit, avoid sugar
• Caffeine in coffee, black tea, chocolate, and coke stimulates calcium loss in urine	• Drink vegetable juices and herbal teas (nettle, red clover, horsetail) • Avoid caffeine
• Nutrient and mineral deficiencies • Potassium deficiency stimulates calcium loss	• Take a multivitamin and mineral formula • Eat foods high in potassium — carrot juice, oranges, banana, potato, avocado, azuki beans, kiwi — and use alkaline powder

CAUSES OF BONE LOSS	SOLUTIONS FOR BONE BUILDING
ABSORPTION FACTORS	
• Hydrochloric acid deficiency — we need enough hydrochloric acid in the stomach to absorb calcium	• Have your health-care practitioner check your hydrochloric acid levels with the string test or Gastro-test
• Antacids — increase stomach pH, neutralizing or decreasing hydrochloric acid, so calcium and minerals are not absorbed	• Use herbal bitters like gentian, wormwood, dandelion, apple cider vinegar, or lemon juice to stimulate hydrochloric acid production before taking calcium. Calcium is more soluble and absorbable in an acid environment
• Lactose intolerance	• Avoid dairy if intolerant
• Imbalanced bowel flora. The lower the pH in the ileum and cecum, the better the absorption of calcium and magnesium. *Lactobacilli* and *Bifidobacterium* maintain an acidic pH in these areas	• Supplement with *Lactobacillus acidophilus* and *Bifidobacterium bifidus* • Increase growth of these organisms with a diet high in fruits, vegetables, and fiber
• Disturbance in bowel flora will mean that less calcium is absorbed	• Increase growth of these organisms with a diet high in fruits, vegetables, and fiber
• Insufficient growth media for bowel flora will cause fewer *Bifidobacterium*, less absorption of calcium and magnesium	• Use inulin (20 grams) daily to increase numbers of *Bifidobacterium*
HORMONAL FACTORS	
• Low estrogen (amenorrhea, anorexia, menopause)	• Address cause of amenorrhea • Use phytoestrogens, such as soy and red clover sprouts in diet • Use estrogenic herbs, such as nettle, tang kuei • Use ipriflavone, boron, dietary soy
• Calcitonin deficiency	• Assess thyroid function and improve if necessary
• Decreased testosterone and androgens	• Use saw palmetto, ginseng, and zinc if testosterone is low
• Use of Depo-Provera for birth control	• Choose alternative birth control, such as barrier methods plus symptom-thermo method

Osteoporosis

CAUSES OF BONE LOSS	SOLUTIONS FOR BONE BUILDING
VITAMIN D	
• Vitamin D deficiency decreases absorption of calcium and phosphorus in the small intestine	• Spend an hour outside every day • Take vitamin D (800–1000) IU daily
ACTIVITY FACTORS	
• Sedentary lifestyle or immobilization due to sickness or injury • Without mechanical stimulation from exercise, osteoclasts tear down unnecessary bone • Trabeculae of bone are arranged in a longitudinal structure, which is capable of generating an electro-magnetic field as the structures are compressed when we walk. The electromagnetic field provides information to the body that directs the activity of osteoblasts and osteoclasts. Bone is constantly being reformed as it adapts to the ways our bodies are being used.	• Weight-bearing exercise causes calcium phosphate crystals in bone to produce tiny electrical currents, known as the piezoelectric effect, which stimulates osteoblasts to deposit mineral salts in stressed areas of bone • Exercise increases the secretion of calcitonin, a thyroid hormone that inhibits osteoclasts • Your exercise program should consist of: 1. Weight-bearing activities (walking, jogging, stair-climbing) 40–60 minutes daily 2. Strength-training activities (weight-training, yoga) 3 times weekly 3. Back-strengthening exercises (pilates, yoga) 3 times weekly. Check with your doctor first.
LIFESTYLE FACTORS	
• Smoking speeds up breakdown of estrogen in the liver. Women who smoke have earlier menopause	• Stop smoking and start doing deep breathing exercises. These will decrease your stress and increase alkalinity.
• Crash diets with mineral depletion	• Follow the Women's Health Diet Plan
• Stress can cause excess production of cortisol by the adrenal gland (cortisol increases bone loss)	• Reduce stress, practice relaxation or meditation • Practice slow, long, deep breathing 11 minutes daily, best before bed, to eliminate more carbon dioxide (an acid)
KIDNEY FACTORS	
• According to Chinese medicine, the kidney governs the bones and the hair on the head. Early graying hair indicates a kidney weakness, and may predict osteoporosis • Kidneys send bicarbonate into the blood and extracellular fluids, and excrete hydrogen ions. When the kidneys can't make enough bicarbonate to buffer acids in the extracellular fluid, calcium is borrowed from the bones	• Use Ho Shou Wu or Schizandra to restore kidney essence • Use alkaline powder and Abies pectinata to help the kidneys

CAUSES OF BONE LOSS	SOLUTIONS FOR BONE BUILDING
PHARMACEUTICAL DRUGS	
• Depo-Provera injections, cortisone, prednisone, chemotherapy drugs for breast cancer, estrogen-blocking drugs (aromatase inhibitors), SSRI antidepressants, antiseizure medications, cholesterol-lowering drugs, methotrexate — all interfere with bone health	• Do not use Depo-Provera (especially not longer than 2 years) • Do not use cortisone or prednisone longer than 3 months • Support bone health during chemotherapy or you will use 8% of your bone mass in 1 year • Be cautious about using SSRIs in adolescence when bone mass is building • Support bone health in adults taking any of the indicated medications
HEAVY METALS	
• Cadmium and lead accumulate in bone and increase bone breakdown	• Detoxify heavy metals and use urine testing to know when they are eliminated
DISEASE FACTORS	
• Kidney disease, liver disease, hyperthyroidism, rheumatoid arthritis, hyperparathyroidism, acromegaly, diabetes, osteogenesis imperfecta, iron overload, ulcerative colitis, celiac disease, Crohn's disease and many others may cause osteoporosis	• Rule out disease factors or treat them appropriately

Tests to Monitor Bone Density

Your conventional and naturopathic doctors can monitor your calcium levels and bone density with the following tests:
- Sulkowitch test measures calcium levels in urine.
- Urine test for bone resorption that measures deoxypyridinoline, a fragment of Type 1 collagen breakdown. This shows you how much bone is currently being resorbed. It should be done annually after age 35 and used to monitor treatment.
- Bone mineral density scan using dual energy bone densitometry (DEXA). Obtain a baseline at age 50 and have another every 2 to 4 years thereafter. If you have been a smoker, have had amenorrhea, have had chemotherapy for breast cancer, have taken Depo-Provera, reached menopause before age 45, or have a history of fractures, start earlier.
- This test uses low dose X-rays to measure bone density in the spine and hips. It will tell you what your current density is, but should be combined with the urine test to determine whether your bone-building regimen is effective.

Prevention and Treatment

Improve Nutrition

In addition to following the Women's Health Diet Plan (Section 2) and the solutions given in the previous chart, obtain 1000 to 1500 mg of calcium a day from food sources or supplements. Though listed here, fish and dairy are not recommended because of their elevated content of PCBs and dioxin.

CALCIUM CONTENT OF COMMON FOODS

TYPE OF FOOD	MEASURE	CALCIUM
FISH		
Sardines + bones	3 oz	325 mg
Pink salmon + bones	3 oz	179 mg
Chum, coho salmon + bones	4 oz	300 mg
Sockeye salmon + bones	3 oz	300 mg
Chinook salmon + bones	7 oz	300 mg
BEANS		
Kidney beans, boiled	1 cup	50 mg
Broad beans, boiled	1 cup	62 mg
Mung beans, boiled	1 cup	55 mg
Lentils, boiled	1 cup	37 mg
Black turtle beans, boiled	1 cup	103 mg
Black-eyed peas, boiled	1 cup	130 mg
Soybeans, boiled	1 cup	175 mg
Tofu, raw, firm	1 cup	258 mg
Miso	½ cup	92 mg
Adzuki beans, boiled	1 cup	63 mg
Great northern beans, boiled	1 cup	121 mg
White beans, boiled	1 cup	161 mg
Pinto beans, boiled	1 cup	82 mg
Navy beans, boiled	1 cup	128 mg
Chickpeas, boiled	1 cup	80 mg
Hummus	1 cup	124 mg
VEGETABLES		
Broccoli, steamed	½ cup	89 mg
Turnip greens, chopped, raw	½ cup	53 mg
Turnip greens, chopped, boiled	½ cup	99 mg
Bok choy, raw, shredded	½ cup	37 mg
Bok choy, steamed	½ cup	79 mg
Rutabaga	1 cup	100 mg

CALCIUM CONTENT OF COMMON FOODS

TYPE OF FOOD	MEASURE	CALCIUM
VEGETABLES *(continued)*		
Lambs-quarters, steamed	½ cup	232 mg
Dandelion greens	1 cup	150 mg
Collards, boiled, chopped	1 cup	148 mg
Rhubarb	1 cup	266 mg
Radish, long greens	½ cup	60 mg
Radish root, dried	100 g	400 mg
Mustard greens, steamed	½ cup	52 mg
Parsley, chopped	½ cup	39 mg
Beet greens, steamed	½ cup	82 mg
Spinach, chopped, raw	½ cup	28 mg
Spinach, steamed	½ cup	122 mg
Watercress, chopped	½ cup	20 mg
Shepherd's purse	1 cup	400 mg
Collard greens	1 cup	220 mg
Kale leaves	1 cup	210 mg
Broccoli	1 cup	150 mg
SEAWEEDS		
Hijiki	1 cup	300 mg
Wakame	1 cup	300 mg
Kombu	100 g	800 mg
Arame	100 g	1170 mg
Agar-agar, dried	3.5 oz	625 mg
Irish moss, raw	3.5 oz	100 mg
Nori, raw	3.5 oz	70 mg
Kelp or kombu, raw	1 tbsp	150 mg
SEEDS AND NUTS		
Brazil nuts	100 g	169 mg
Sesame seeds	100 g	630 mg
Sunflower seeds	100 g	140 mg
Sweet almonds	100 g	282 mg
Almond butter	1 tbsp	43 mg
Hazelnuts	100 g	186 mg
GRAINS		
Millet	3.5 oz	20 mg
Cornmeal, enriched	1 cup	140 mg
Carob flour	1 cup	359 mg
Soybean flour, defatted	1 cup	241 mg

MUSCULOSKELETAL CONDITIONS

CALCIUM CONTENT OF COMMON FOODS		
TYPE OF FOOD	MEASURE	CALCIUM
GRAINS (continued)		
Amaranth, boiled	½ cup	138 mg
Dark rye flour	1 cup	69 mg
FRUITS		
Papaya, raw, medium sized	1½ cups	72 mg
Figs, dried	10 figs	269 mg
DAIRY PRODUCTS		
Milk, 2%	1 cup	297 mg
Evaporated skim milk	½ cup	344 mg
Plain yogurt (2–4%)	1 cup	396 mg
Swiss cheese	1 oz	272 mg
Cheddar cheese	1 oz	150 mg
Blue cheese	3½ oz	300 mg
Cottage cheese	1⅓ cups	300 mg
MISCELLANEOUS		
Blackstrap molasses	1 tbsp	150 mg
Soy milk (not calcium fortified)	1 cup	50 mg

(Most of these values are extrapolated from Jean A.T. Pennington's *Food Values of Portions Commonly Used*.)

DID YOU KNOW ...

Our bones are our mineral reserve. They store 99% of our calcium, 85% of our phosphorus, 60% of our magnesium, and 35% of our sodium. They are also the favored storage bin for toxic metals, such as cadmium and lead, which may take years to eliminate as bone is recycled.

Restore Balance

- Walk an hour a day. Do weight training, yoga, or pilates at least 3 times a week.
- Traditional Chinese medicine considers osteoporosis a sign of kidney essence, yin and/or yang deficiency, as the kidneys govern the bones. One formula that addresses this is Eucommia 18.
- Use the gemmotherapy Juniperus, 25-50 drops, 3 times daily, for 6 weeks, to cleanse the liver and kidney. Follow this with Abies pectinata.
- Check the pH of your urine and saliva. If either is lower than 6.8, eat more vegetables, decrease animal protein and grains, and use alkaline powder when necessary.
- Work with a practitioner who uses biological terrain assessment and darkfield microscopy to provide a window into your body's biochemistry, the function of your kidneys, the degree of acidity, and possibility of dehydration.

BONE HEALTH COMPOUNDS

Several companies compound supplements that contain many of the nutrients important for bone health.

Nutrient	Manufacturer
Bone-Up	Jarrow
Ultra Bone-Up	Jarrow
OrthoBone	AOR
Osteo-guard plus Ipriflavone	Douglas Laboratories
OSX	Genestra
Osteoprime	Metagenics
Omnivite	Omnivite Nutrition
Strong Bones	New Roots Herbal

Bone Health Formula

Our usual recommendation for women is Bone-Up (Jarrow) 6 daily + Strontium Support (AOR) 3 in the morning + BioSil (AOR) 10 drops twice daily + Abies pectinata + a good multivitamin and mineral formula + alkaline powder _ tsp twice daily away from meals, along with an alkaline vegetarian diet, 2 liters or quarts of water and an hour of walking each day.

HOMEOPATHIC REMEDIES FOR OSTEOPOROSIS

- To begin drainage of the liver and kidneys and to remove small stones and scar tissue from the kidneys: use Unda 1, Unda 20, and Unda 258, 5 drops of each, 3x daily, for 3 weeks.
- To help the kidneys remove acid waste and balance the thyroid and parathyroid glands: follow with Unda 2, Unda 240, and Unda 1000, 5 drops of each, 3x daily, for 3 weeks of the month. Continue for several months.
- To stimulate bone mineralization: use the tissue salts Calc fluor 6X, 3 pellets every other day and Calc phos 6X, 3 pellets on alternating days
- Single remedies: bufo, calcarea carbonica, calcarea fluorica, calcarea phosphorica, carcinosin, silicea, symphytum, syphilinum and tuberculinum. Work with a practitioner to find a remedy that best fits your symptoms.

DID YOU KNOW ...

One of the main causes of osteoporosis is overacidity. The pH of our blood needs to be maintained in a narrow range of 7.35 to 7.45. When it drops too low, the parathyroid glands secrete a hormone that stimulates the osteoclasts to get to work, and our bones break down, releasing calcium into our bloodstream. When blood calcium is high, calcium is redeposited in bone. Parathyroid hormone is secreted mostly at night, so we want to take our largest calcium dose with a little food before bed.

DID YOU KNOW ...

Taking strontium (600 mg) daily can increase the rate of new bone formation by 172%. A large 3-year study showed a 41% reduction in fracture risk and an 11.4% increase in vertebrae density when women took 680 mg of strontium daily.

NUTRIENT THERAPY FOR OSTEOPOROSIS

NUTRIENT/SOURCES	DAILY DOSE	ACTION
CALCIUM *Best sources:* ossein microcrystalline hydroxyapatite complex (MCHC), calcium citrate malate, calcium citrate (but this may cause increased absorption of aluminum — check hair or urine for heavy metals) *Worst sources:* calcium hydroxyapatite (synthetic, poorly absorbed calcium salt), calcium carbonate (low bioavailability and neutralizes stomach acid, causing poor absorption of other minerals) *Natural sources:* see chart of calcium content of common foods	1,000–1,500 mg with food in divided doses • Have your largest dose at the end of the day	• Calcium suppresses bone breakdown • MCHC is a crystalline nutrient complex derived from bovine bone, complete with calcium, phosphorus, oxygen, hydrogen, zinc, strontium, silicon, iron, amino acids, and mucopolysaccharides. It is easily absorbed. It is the best calcium source, identical to what is found in our bones, but may be unacceptable to vegetarians. • Calcium citrate is absorbed 10 times more easily by women with low stomach acid than calcium carbonate
MAGNESIUM *Absorption rates:* magnesium aspartate (41.7%) magnesium citrate (29.6%) magnesium oxide (22.8%) *Natural sources:* soy, buckwheat, rye, figs, black-eyed peas, Swiss chard, almonds, cashews, brown rice, kidney beans, filberts, lima beans, Brazil nuts, pecans, kelp, walnuts, banana	500–750 mg	• Regulates parathyroid hormone and is necessary for absorption of vitamin D • Magnesium intake should be ½ of calcium intake. Taking more magnesium than calcium can suppress calcium levels and increase bone loss by decreasing production of the thyroid hormone calcitonin
VITAMIN D-3 (CHOLECALCIFEROL) *Natural sources:* fish oil, mushrooms, egg yolk	1000 IU	• Improves calcium absorption in the intestine • Needed especially in winter months
MENATETRENONE (VITAMIN K2) *Natural sources:* turnip greens, broccoli, cabbage, green tea, lettuce, spinach, asparagus, oats. It is also made by bowel bacteria	80 mcg	• Helps to form the hydroxyapatite crystalline structure of bone • Reduces release of calcium from bone by up to 50% • Reduces fracture rates in postmenopausal women
BORON (CITRATE) *Natural sources:* tomato, pear, apple, soy, prunes, raisins, almonds, filberts	3 mg	• Reduces urinary excretion of calcium by 40% • Increases estradiol

NUTRIENT THERAPY FOR OSTEOPOROSIS

NUTRIENT/SOURCES	DAILY DOSE	ACTION
STRONTIUM (CITRATE) *Natural sources:* spices, whole grains, root and leafy vegetables and legumes	700 mg • Do not take at the same time as calcium	• Take 1 hour before breakfast or away from meals • The only nutrient that builds new bone • Improves retention of calcium, phosphorus and protein, preventing the breakdown of old bone • Makes teeth harder and more resistant to decay
VITAMIN A (OR BETA CAROTENE) *Natural sources:* dunaliella algae, carrot juice, liver, spirulina, chlorella, dandelion leaf, sweet potato, mango, spinach, pumpkin	20,000 IU	• Helps form collagen in bone matrix
ZINC (CITRATE) *Natural sources:* oysters, beef, wheat germ, turkey, Swiss chard, lima beans, potato, oats, pumpkin seeds, soy, ginger, wild rice	30 mg	• Helps form collagen in bone matrix
MANGANESE (GLYCINATE) *Natural sources:* peas, brown rice, barley, rye, buckwheat, pecans, Brazil nuts, almonds, spinach	10-20 mg	• Helps form collagen in bone matrix
COPPER (CITRATE) *Natural sources:* liver, rye, dried beans, Brazil nuts, cashews, peas, molasses, other nuts and seeds	1–3 mg	• Helps form collagen in bone matrix
SILICON Best absorbed as orthosilicic acid *Natural sources:* oats (368 mg/cup), beets, barley, soybeans, brown rice, wheat bran	25 mg	• Acts as a semiconductor in the piezoelectric chemistry of bone, translating electrical signals from exercise into biochemistry that makes new bone matrix
FOLIC ACID *Natural sources:* liver, brewer's yeast, black-eyed peas, lentils, lima beans, orange juice, kidney beans, romaine lettuce, leeks, leafy greens	400 mcg	• Helps form collagen in bone matrix

Osteoporosis

NUTRIENT THERAPY FOR OSTEOPOROSIS		
NUTRIENT/SOURCES	**DAILY DOSE**	**ACTION**
VITAMIN B-12 *Natural sources:* meat, fish, chlorella, spirulina, nori, wakame, kombu, super blue green algae	400 mcg	• Helps form collagen in bone matrix
VITAMIN C *Natural sources:* orange juice, peppers, guava, grapefruit juice, watermelon, cantelope, kiwi, Brussels sprouts, cauliflower, broccoli	2,000 mg	• Helps form collagen in bone matrix; reduces risk of bone fracture in smokers
IPRIFLAVONE *Alternatively:* organic soy	600 mg	• Do not use if you are on Coumadin or have a stomach ulcer • A synthetic isoflavone that inhibits bone breakdown (slows down osteoclasts), increases bone building, decreases pain • Some women have a decreased white blood cell count after taking ipriflavone. Have your doctor check your white blood cell and lymphocyte count before using ipriflavone and then every 6 months thereafter
INULIN Prebiotic derived from chicory root *Natural sources:* Jerusalem artichoke, asparagus, leeks, onion, garlic, bran, dandelion greens	20 grams	• Growth medium for *Bifidobacterium*, which lowers the pH of the small and large intestine, allowing increased solubility and absorption of calcium and magnesium • *Bifidobacterium* predigests our minerals for easy absorption
ALKALINE POWDER: sodium bicarbonate (20%) calcium carbonate (26%) potassium bicarbonate (40%) magnesium carbonate (14%)	½ tsp in warm water twice daily away from meals	• Neutralizes acidity of extracellular fluid caused by acid-forming food, causing less calcium to be pulled from bone

Detoxify and Rejuvenate

- Do a bowel cleanse once a year to promote healthy intestinal flora, which helps with mineral absorption and manufacture vitamin K.
- Use the tissue salt Silicea 6X, 3 pellets twice daily to improve absorption and utilization of minerals and to improve kidney drainage. Do not use this if there is cancer or a transplant, implant, pacemaker, or any therapeutic foreign object in the body.

Integrate Body, Mind, and Spirit

- Examine issues around feeling supported and develop a support network with family, friends, a spiritual group, or other group.
- Look at your fears, which can weaken the kidney, and do whatever is necessary to alleviate fear.

Conventional Medicine

Drug Therapy

- All of the pharmaceutical drugs that conventional medicine uses to treat osteoporosis are anti-resorptive agents – they slow down the activity of the osteoclasts.
- These drugs include bisphosphonates, such as Fosamax, hormone replacement therapy, selective estrogen receptor modulators, such as raloxifene, and calcitonin. They promote maintenance and increased mineralization of old bone tissue, which becomes more brittle.

TOP 5 STRATEGIES

1. Eat a vegetarian, alkaline diet – follow the Women's Health Diet Plan.
2. Monitor pH of urine and saliva and use alkaline powder as needed.
3. Use calcium-magnesium with many of the nutrients listed in the chart above, taken at a different time of day as strontium.
4. Do one hour a day of weight-bearing exercise.
5. Take inulin (20 grams), daily.

DID YOU KNOW ...

Cadmium and lead are stored in bone and both increase bone resorption (breakdown), promoting osteoporosis. Do a hair or urine test for heavy metals once a year and follow through with a metal detoxification program and kidney cleanse once a year. See the Seasonal Cleansing and Rejuvenation Program section for guidelines.

DID YOU KNOW ...

The gemmotherapy Abies pectinata (fir tree bud), 25 to 50 drops, 3 times daily, improves kidney function, drains lead from bone tissue, improves bone calcification, and reverses osteoporosis.

CASE STUDY: *BONE RESORPTION NORMALIZED*

Belinda came to see us 4 years ago when her periods stopped at age 45 and she was experiencing hot flashes. At that time, we did the urine test for bone resorption and found that it was normal (less than 38). We have tested it every year since, and it has been gradually going up (to as high as 94), which indicates significant bone breakdown. Each year, we have adjusted diet and supplements and had her retested 2 months later. We were able to normalize it – until we retested again the following year.

Belinda comes from a family of beef farmers, and, last summer, they were having a hard time selling Canadian beef, so there were many family get-togethers around the barbecue, grilling local beef. Her blood type was O, and she believed she needed to eat meat regularly to feel well. So she did. Belinda was exercising 4 hours a week, taking 1500 mg of a quality calcium formula daily, using alkaline powder, and eating loads of vegetables. However, she had to cut out all meat before her pH and her bone resorption test normalized.

Heart Disease and Stroke

Our diligent hearts continuously pump blood through the 100,000 kilometers (60,000 miles) of arteries and veins traversing our bodies — highways for the transport of oxygen and nutrients, the removal of carbon dioxide and waste, and the transfer of electromagnetic energy to each one of our cells. Each day the heart beats at least 100,000 times and pumps 2,500 to 5,000 gallons of blood through the blood vessels. Without a strong heart and clear highways, this distribution system falters. Our blood vessels can become lined with plaque (known as atherosclerosis or hardening of the arteries) resulting from damage to the endothelium or the lining of the blood vessel. When plaque formation occurs in the blood vessels of the heart, causing decreased blood flow to the heart muscle, it is known as coronary artery disease or ischemic heart disease. If blood flow is insufficient, pain (angina) or death of heart cells (heart attack) may occur. When plaque formation occurs in a blood vessel in the brain, decreased blood supply causes damage to local brain tissue, resulting in a stroke. When it occurs in the kidneys, there may be kidney failure, and if it occurs in the legs, there may be cramping pain with exertion.

DID YOU KNOW ...

Coronary artery disease is the single leading cause of death in women over 50. In Canada and the United States, almost 40% of women die of either heart attacks or strokes. Black women between the ages of 35 and 74 are twice as likely to die of heart disease as white women.

DID YOU KNOW ...

Up to 50% of women with hypertension may have elevated insulin levels. Hypertension is defined as blood pressure above 140/90 mm/Hg. High blood pressure is very common in women over 50 and is a risk factor for stroke, heart disease, and kidney disease. Hypertension is a silent killer – we may not be aware that our arteries are damaged until a heart attack occurs.

Symptoms of Heart Disease in Women

- Fatigue with exertion
- Weakness, dizziness
- Sleep disturbances
- Shortness of breath
- Waking at night with shortness of breath
- Need to sit or stand to be comfortable
- Indigestion
- Anxiety
- Aching, tightness, or pressure in the chest (but not pain), worse with activity

Causes of Heart Disease in Women

- Body shape, hormone balance, and distribution of body fat influence our susceptibility to heart disease and stroke.
- If we are overweight or park fat in our abdomen (apple shape), we are more at risk than slim women or women who store fat in their hips and thighs (pear shape).
- Abdominal obesity is linked to impaired insulin action, higher insulin secretion, and elevated blood glucose, increasing risk of diabetes, high blood pressure (hypertension), and coronary artery disease.
- After menopause, HDL (good cholesterol) levels in women decrease and LDL (bad cholesterol) levels increase, making us more susceptible to heart disease.

Causes of Plaque Formation

- Imbalanced blood pH, caused by overacidity from too much animal protein, sugar, and grain, aging, anger, stress, worry, poor breathing, lactic acid buildup, excessive exercise.
- Increased dehydration and/or poor kidney function, allowing a higher concentration of circulating toxins in blood.
- Liver congestion or toxicity, with resulting increase in toxins and free radicals.
- Free radical damage and injury to the endothelial cells lining the blood vessels caused by heavy metals, iron excess, chemicals, bad fats, cigarette smoke, ultraviolet rays, barbecued meats, fried foods, drugs, and inflammatory molecules.
- Mineral and antioxidant deficiency and inability to neutralize free radicals.
- Presence of pathogenic fungus, bacteria, and viruses (chlamydia, cytomegalovirus, *Mucor racemosa,* herpes II simplex, *Helicobacter pylori,* treponema, borrelia, mycoplasma, coxsackie virus, *Porphyromonas gingivalis* in the mouth) that either attack the blood vessel lining or create chronic inflammation, which increases blood viscosity and clot formation. Their growth is promoted by imbalanced pH, deficient oxygen, increased toxic metals and chemicals, low trace minerals and antioxidants, iron overload, lowered immunity, and certain emotions.

Tests for Heart Disease in Women

Physical tests and laboratory tests are useful in assessing heart disease risk. If you are over 45, ask your naturopathic or medical doctor to do these for you annually or as required.

Physical Testing

- Blood pressure should be checked annually at every age. If elevated, check monthly until it is brought under control.

DID YOU KNOW...

Women experience heart disease symptoms differently than men.

DID YOU KNOW ...

Plaque formation is the result of damage to the lining of the artery combined with high levels of LDL cholesterol and low levels of HDL (due to high insulin, stress and lack of exercise). More than half the people who die of heart disease and stroke do not have elevated cholesterol.

CARDIOVASCULAR CONDITIONS

BLOOD PRESSURE RATES

BLOOD PRESSURE	SYSTOLIC	DIASTOLIC
Normal	90-120 mm/Hg	less than 80 mm/Hg
Borderline	120-160 mm/Hg	90-94 mm/Hg
Mild Hypertension	140-160 mm/Hg	95-104 mm/Hg
Moderate Hypertension	140-180 mm/Hg	105-114 mm/Hg
Severe Hypertension	over 160 mm/Hg	over 115 mm/Hg

- Be consistent with your dental exams and cleanings twice yearly, at every age, to prevent periodontal disease, which is directly linked to heart disease.

Annual Physical Testing for Women over 45
- Check pulse in carotid, femoral, and abdominal arteries
- Check peripheral pulses
- Electrocardiogram (ECG) at age 50, then every 3 years
- Treadmill stress test

Laboratory Testing
- Hair analysis or toxic metals urine test
- Blood test for platelet aggregation
- Total cholesterol, HDL, LDL, cholesterol/HDL ratio, LDL/HDL ratio, triglycerides
- Lipoprotein-a
- C-reactive protein
- Homocysteine
- Ferritin
- Fibrinogen
- Coenzyme Q10
- Vitamin E
- Lipid peroxides
- Glutathione peroxidase
- Red blood cell magnesium
- Red blood cell fatty acids
- Fasting insulin
- Fasting blood sugar
- Oxidata test for free radical burden
- Darkfield microscopy
- Biological terrain assessment

Prevention and Treatment

Improve Nutrition
In addition to following the Women's Health Diet Plan (Section 2), make these changes to your diet and your supplement schedule:

Drink More Water
Drink 2 to 3 liters or quarts of water daily to:
- **Reduce cholesterol:** Cholesterol plugs up gaps in cell membranes so that our cell walls can hold water inside. Cholesterol may be elevated when we are not drinking enough water, when the blood is too acidic, or when there are increased intracellular toxins that need to be diluted.

DID YOU KNOW ...

When there is a water deficiency, the hormone vasopressin may constrict blood vessels to ensure adequate water supply to the nervous system and brain. The hypertensive ability of vasopressin is needed to ensure a steady filtration of water into cells.

DID YOU KNOW ...

Women who drink more than 4 cups of coffee a day (which is very acidic and dehydrating) almost double their risk of heart attack. Drink green tea or herbal tea instead.

Heart Health Balance Sheet

Examine the risk factors and protective factors below to determine your heart disease risk and become familiar with protective strategies to promote lifetime heart health.

RISK FACTORS	PROTECTIVE FACTORS
FAMILIAL	
Father had heart attack or stroke before age 50	No history of heart attack or stroke on father's side
Mother had heart attack or stroke before age 65	No history of heart attack or stroke on mother's side
GENERAL	
Aging increases risk of heart disease and stroke	Begin heart health protection in childhood
Waist to hip ratio is > 0.8 (your waist measurement divided by your hip measurement)	Maintain healthy weight, exercise an hour a day
Body mass index > 29 triples risk (your weight in kilograms divided by the square of your height in meters)	Maintain healthy weight, exercise an hour a day
High blood pressure	Lower blood pressure with diet, exercise, meditation, crataegus, coenzyme Q10, magnesium, potassium, vitamin E, increased water, pH balance
Chronic infection in the blood vessels with chlamydia, cytomegalovirus, *Helicobacter pylori,* treponema, borrelia, mycoplasma, coxsackie virus, *Mucor racemosa,* herpes simplex II	Supplement with *Lactobacillus acidophilus* and *Bifidobacterium bifidus* Normalize pH and lower iron levels Test for and eliminate organisms with oil of oregano, goldenseal, colloidal silver, garlic
Gum disease, root canals — the oral bacteria *Porphyromonas gingivalis* and *Prevotella intermedia* are found in arterial plaque	Brush and floss teeth, regular dental checkups, see periodontal specialist, use vitamin C and coenzyme Q10, oregano oil on gums, remove root canal teeth
Increased inflammation (increases heart disease risk threefold; doubles risk of stroke; may be caused by infectious organism)	Wobenzyme, Rubozyme, Nattokinase, protein digesting enzymes, bromelain, onion, turmeric, curcumin, ginger, boswellia, fish oil, flax oil, vitamin E
Presence of a diagonal crease on the earlobe	No earlobe crease

Heart Disease and Stroke

RISK FACTORS	PROTECTIVE FACTORS
LIFESTYLE	
Smoking (increases risk 3–5 times)	Stop smoking
Excessive alcohol (more than 2 drinks a day)	Avoid alcohol or have one glass of red wine daily
Lack of exercise	Moderate aerobic exercise — 40–60 minutes daily
Increased stress; mental stress	Take time each day to relax, meditate, laugh
Exertion in cold weather (e.g., snow shoveling)	Don't overexert yourself in cold weather
BIOCHEMICAL	
High serum total cholesterol (>200 mg/dL)	Limit animal protein and fat, dairy and sweets Use psyllium, oat bran, *Lactobacillus acidophilus*, garlic, fish and flax oil, guggul, olive oil, folic acid, vitamin B-12, B-6, magnesium Treat gum disease
High LDL (> 130 mg/dL)	Garlic, olive oil, niacin, red yeast rice, polycosanol
Low HDL (< 55 mg/dL) — very strong risk factor	Fish and flax oil, garlic
Elevated triglycerides (> 400 mg/dL)	*L. acidophilus,* L-carnitine, choline, inositol, vitamin B-6
Low blood levels of vitamin E	Vitamin E (400 IU)
Elevated homocysteine (increases heart disease death sixfold) May be linked to hypothyroid	Vitamin B-6 (100 mg), folic acid (2–5 mg), vitamin B-12 (800 mcg)
Elevated C-reactive protein (increases risk 8.5 times) — elevated with Chlamydia pneumonia	Use olive oil, fish oil, vegetarian diet, no dairy, garlic, ginkgo biloba, Nattokinase, Wobenzyme
Low red blood cell magnesium	Eat foods high in magnesium (400 mg) daily
Impaired tolerance to glucose — insulin resistance	Chromium picolinate, niacin, Gymnema sylvestre
High blood sugar, diabetes (increases risk 3–7 times)	Fish oil, alpha lipoic acid
Iron excess — 1 in 10 people have hemochromatosis, a genetic predisposition to iron overload	Test serum ferritin and % transferrin saturation Use malic acid, rutin, lactoferrin, EDTA, donate blood to decrease iron
Increased fibrinogen — increased blood clotting	Garlic, ginger, onions, turmeric, niacin, fish oil, flax oil, vitamin E, magnesium, proteolytic enzymes, bromelain, curcumin, soy, vitamin C Eliminate source of infection

RISK FACTORS	PROTECTIVE FACTORS
HORMONAL	
High insulin (normal insulin action is impaired)	Avoid sugar, sweets, baked goods, high-glycemic carbohydrates; use salads, fruit, legumes, tofu, pearl barley, wild rice, whole rye, bran, nuts and seeds
Underactive thyroid	Use kelp, zinc, selenium, magnesium, manganese, L-tyrosine, adrenal support, ashwagandha, and guggul to improve thyroid function
Hormone replacement therapy	Use black cohosh, astragalus and schizandra for hot flashes Prevent osteoporosis naturally
Current use of birth control pill	Use symptom-thermo method and condoms
Taking Tamoxifen	Use Wobenzyme, fish oil, curcumin to thin blood
Postmenopausal with lower estrogen and progesterone	Support adrenals and thyroid Use ground flaxseed, soy
ENVIRONMENTAL	
Heavy metals — especially cadmium, lead, mercury	Test and detox heavy metals annually Decrease presence in environment Remove dental fillings Avoid fish
Excess free radicals from barbecued meat, chemicals, X-rays, ultraviolet light	Use Oxidata test to check free radical burden Take antioxidants to neutralize — vitamin C, E, selenium, zinc, coenzyme Q10, alpha lipoic acid, beta carotene
Chlorinated water creates more atherosclerosis	Filter chlorine from your water Store in glass
DIETARY	
Over-consumption of sugar, sweets, and high glycemic carbohydrates, which elevate insulin	Avoid sugar, sweets, boxed cereals, corn, white rice, bread and high glycemic carbs Use pearl barley, oatmeal with oat bran, legumes, whole rye, wild rice
Excess fruit sugar	Avoid fruit juice Use low-glycemic fruit, such as organic cherries, apricots, apples, pears, plums, grapefruit, oranges

Heart Disease and Stroke

RISK FACTORS	PROTECTIVE FACTORS
DIETARY	
Excess consumption of animal fats	Vegetarian diet (legumes, tofu, nuts and seeds) with olive oil, flax and fish oil
Smoked meats, barbecued foods, fried foods, rancid oils, margarine	Vegetarian diet (legumes, tofu, nuts and seeds) with olive oil, flax and fish oil
Animal protein	Use legumes, soy, nuts and seeds as protein
Low antioxidants	8 servings of fruits and vegetables, green tea
Deficiency of omega-3 fatty acids	Flaxseed oil (2 tbsp), fish oil (3000 mg), or algae oil
Excess processed foods	Avoid processed and canned food — cook from scratch
> 4 cups of coffee a day (increases risk 1.7 times)	Use green tea or herbal tea, drink 2 liters water
Low fiber	45 grams soluble fiber: 3 tsp psyllium, ½ cup oat bran, 2 tbsp ground flaxseed, 1 cup legumes, fruits, vegetables, nuts, grains
Food allergy to dairy and egg (increases mortality threefold)	Use ELIZA IgG test for food allergies Avoid dairy, eggs and allergenic foods
Homogenized milk contains the enzyme xanthine oxidase, which damages epithelial cells	Avoid milk, use organic soy milk
PSYCHOLOGICAL	
Feelings of aggression and hostility increase acidity and elevate cholesterol	Change situation or express yourself to decrease anger, let it go, forgive, cultivate joy
Chronic worriers are more apt to have elevated cholesterol	Practice meditation to calm your mind
Type A personality	Take a break for 20 minutes every 2 ½ hours
Depression, alienation, disconnection, heartbreak	Connect to others, love and be loved, serve

- **Flush sodium:** Sodium retention is also an effort to maintain water inside our cells. The water may be pulled inside the cell to decrease acidity or dilute cellular toxins. Swelling in the ankles or fingers may be a sign of sodium retention. By increasing water intake, the kidneys produce more urine, which, in time, will cause a decrease in swelling as excess acid and intracellular toxins are flushed out.

- **Support renin-angiotensin:** The renin-angiotensin system, regulated by the pituitary gland and kidneys, is activated when the fluid volume of the body is lower. It is activated to retain water, and promotes the absorption of more salt. If water and salt levels are too low, the renin-angiotensin system will cause a tightening of the blood vessel walls, causing blood pressure to go up.

Avoid Sugar, Sweets, and High-Glycemic Carbohydrates

- Sweets and high-glycemic carbohydrates (corn, white rice, millet, potatoes, cooked carrots, boxed cereals, baked goods) are converted into glucose quickly after digestion. Once absorbed, glucose causes a rise in blood sugar. Your pancreas makes insulin to clear glucose from the blood. Elevated insulin causes your liver to secrete more cholesterol. Most of the body's cholesterol is made in the liver, and does not come from food.
- Green vegetables, brassicas, most raw vegetables, cherries, apples, pears, plums, grapefruit, oranges, pearl barley, whole rye, wild rice, bran, psyllium, and legumes have a low glycemic index. Some of these should be included in every meal to decrease the glycemic load and reduce the rise in insulin after eating. A large salad with legumes and tofu or nuts and seeds makes a great lunch, as does a bean and barley soup.

Eat Small Meals Frequently

- By having five small meals rather than three large ones, you will keep insulin levels lower and improve thyroid and adrenal function, decreasing heart disease risk.

Limit Animal Protein

- Animal proteins are converted to strong acids that increase acidity in the extracellular fluid and blood. Acidity and excess iron promote pathogenic bacteria, viruses, and fungi (*Helicobacter pylori,* chlamydia, cytomegalovirus, treponema, *Mucor racemosa*), which cause inflammation and damage to the arterial lining.
- Substitute tofu, legumes, nuts and seeds (except peanuts), and nut butters for your protein sources.

Know Your Fats

- Eliminate harmful fats, which include saturated fats from red meat, cheese, butter, milk, and, to a lesser degree, poultry.
- Harmful trans fats are formed when vegetable oils are hardened to make margarine and shortening used in processed and fast food – on labels this might read "partially hydrogenated

CARDIOVASCULAR CONDITIONS

DID YOU KNOW ...

The more sugar and high-glycemic carbohydrates you eat, the more insulin your pancreas secretes, and the more LDL cholesterol your liver produces. High insulin decreases the liver's production of beneficial HDL.

DID YOU KNOW ...

Heart attack survivors with antibodies to cow's milk and/or egg white have a threefold increased risk of dying within 6 months. Food allergies can elevate blood pressure. Avoid dairy, eggs, and known food allergies.

DID YOU KNOW ...

Olive oil eaten with food reduces levels of harmful LDL cholesterol. Olive oil decreases inflammation linked to arterial damage, prevents arterial linings from contracting, and increases absorption of vitamins A, E, and K.

DID YOU KNOW ...

For a heart healthy meal, cook equal parts of oatmeal and oatbran for breakfast, add 1 tsp psyllium, 2 tbsp freshly ground flaxseed, 1 tsp cinnamon, sliced apple, walnuts, and organic soy milk. Oatmeal is high in silicon and vanadium, which protect against cardiovascular disease.

DID YOU KNOW ...

Eating 5 to 8 servings of fruits and vegetables daily cuts heart disease risk by 30%.

DID YOU KNOW ...

Eating two cloves or 4 grams of fresh raw garlic or 800 mg of garlic powder daily will help kill chronic infectious organisms that create inflammation, which damages blood vessel walls. Garlic reduces total serum cholesterol and LDL cholesterol (bad cholesterol) levels by 9% to12%, increases (good) HDL, reduces blood pressure by 5% to 7%, increases capillary blood flow, and helps prevent blood clots.

vegetable oil." These fats promote inflammation, increase free radical activity, which damages blood vessels, and cause elevation of insulin, cholesterol, triglycerides, and lipoprotein-a. They promote resistance to the hormone insulin and increase risk of diabetes.

- Do eat beneficial fats from nuts (except peanuts), seeds, whole grains, green vegetables, algae, olive oil, flaxseed oil, and fish oil (but don't eat fish). Freshly cracked walnuts are particularly healthy for the heart, containing omega-3 oil.

Increase Fiber

- Increase dietary fiber (particularly soluble fiber) to 45 or more grams daily, using 1 cup legumes (10 grams), ½ cup oat bran (10 grams), 4 tbsp ground flaxseed (15 grams), 3 to 5 tsp psyllium (more than15 grams).
- Soluble fiber lowers insulin levels and binds to cholesterol in the gut, promoting its elimination.
- Weaker sources of soluble fiber are bananas, apples, oranges, cabbage, carrots, potatoes, sesame seeds, and grapes.

Eat More Fruits and Vegetables

- Eat cooked tomatoes or tomato sauce several times a week (avoid if you have joint pain) for its lycopene content.
- Eat organic purple grapes or drink occasional red wine or purple grape juice for their resveratrol content, which prevents oxidative damage from LDL.
- Consume foods high in potassium, which include carrot juice, grapefruit juice, banana, kiwi, mango, potato, yam, squash, avocado, and azuki beans.

Use Soy Products

- Increased dietary soy (organic) reduces heart disease risk – use organic tofu and soy milk regularly if tolerated. Eat sea vegetables with soy to protect thyroid function.

Add Cayenne

- Cayenne helps to reduce and break up blood clot formation, stimulates blood flow, and functions as an antioxidant.

Eat Anti-inflammatory Foods

- Use several cups of organic green tea, 2 tsp or more of turmeric, an onion a day, and fresh gingerroot to decrease inflammation and supply antioxidants. Make a stir-fry of onions, garlic, and ginger sauteed in olive oil; stir in turmeric; add cubes of firm tofu, and then broccoli, cauliflower, carrots, mung bean sprouts, and a few almonds or walnuts for a heart-healthy meal.

Supplement Schedule for Preventing or Reversing Cardiovascular Disease

Work with your health care practitioner is choosing the most appropriate support and dosages from the following supplement list.

NUTRIENT THERAPY FOR HEART DISEASE AND STROKE		
NUTRIENT	**ACTION**	**DAILY DOSE**
Probiotic containing *Lactobacillus acidophilus* (DDS-1 and NAS super strains) and *Bifidobacterium bifidus* (malyoth super strain)	Normalize bowel flora and to lower blood pressure and total cholesterol by 22%, triglycerides by 33%	Twice daily
Hawthorne berry tincture	Prevents or reverses heart disease, dilates the coronary arteries, strengthens heart muscle contractions, decreases cholesterol and triglycerides, regulates arrhythmia, and decreases angina	30-50 drops, twice daily
Alpha lipoic acid, chromium picolinate, and niacin (or inositol hexaniacinate)	Lower insulin, LDL, and blood pressure	200 mg alpha lipoic acid 200 mcg chromium picolinate 300–2,000 mg niacin (or inositol hexaniacinate)
Antioxidants: vitamin E mixed tocopherols, selenium, zinc, vitamin C, grape seed extract	Antioxidant support Vitamins C and E help to reverse atherosclerosis	400 IU vitamin E 200 mcg selenium 50 mg zinc 3000 mg vitamin C 200 mg grape seed extract
Copper	Improves cholesterol metabolism	2 mg
Chlorella	Lowers blood pressure while increasing beta carotene levels	6 tablets
Coenzyme Q10	Increases oxygen and energy production of heart muscle cells, improves periodontal disease, and decreases blood pressure	100–300 mg
Uncontaminated fish oil	Lowers insulin and cholesterol, reduces inflammation and plaque formation	3,000 mg
Folic acid along with vitamin B-12 and vitamin B-6	Decreases homocysteine and blood pressure	2000–5000 mcg folic acid 800 mcg vitamin B-12 100 mg vitamin B-6
Calcium (from a microcrystalline hydroxyapatite source)	Decreases acidity, lowers blood pressure and LDL cholesterol	1,000–1,500 mg

NUTRIENT THERAPY FOR HEART DISEASE AND STROKE

NUTRIENT	ACTION	DAILY DOSE
Magnesium	Regulates heart rhythm, decreases angina, and reduces risk of heart attack. High doses of intramuscular magnesium are best after a heart attack to prevent death	400-800 mg
Potassium	Decreases blood pressure, prevents stroke	300 mg
Aged garlic extract	Reduces blood pressure, cholesterol, platelet aggregation, and plaque formation	Two 500 mg capsules
Policosanol	Can lower cholesterol just as well as standard cholesterol-lowering drugs by decreasing cholesterol production in the liver	12 mg before bed
L-arginine	Dilates blood vessels and lowers blood pressure, improves endothelial function and tolerance to exercise	1,000 mg for prevention, 2,000–3,000 mg after a heart attack in divided doses
L-carnitine	Increases energy production in heart cells, lowers cholesterol and triglycerides, normalizes an irregular heartbeat, repairs damage to the heart after a heart attack	1,000 mg for prevention, 2,000–3,000 mg after a heart attack in divided doses
Taurine	Improves the force of heart contractions and lowers blood pressure	500–2,000 mg, 3 times daily on an empty stomach
Plant sterols	Decrease cholesterol	1,500 mg
Ginkgo biloba	Prevents strokes by decreasing the stickiness of the blood, improving circulation to the brain	40 mg, 3 times daily
Curcumin	Decreases inflammation	1,500 mg
Wobenzyme N or Rubozym or Nattokinase	Decreases inflammation and dissolve clots	3 times daily on an empty stomach 45 minutes before meals with water or juice

CARDIOVASCULAR SUPPLEMENT SCHEDULE

NUTRIENT	On rising	Before brkfst	With brkfst	Betwn meals	Before lunch	With lunch	Betwn meals	Before dinner	With dinner	Before bed
Garlic (mg)			500						500	
Clean fish oil (mg)			1,000			1,000			1,000	
Chromium picolinate (mcg)			200			200			200	
Niacin (mg)			100			100			100	
Folic acid (mg)			1			1			1	
Vitamin B-12 (mcg)			1,000							
Vitamin B complex with 100 mg B-6			1							
Psyllium (tsp)			1			1			1	
Flaxseed (tbsp)			2						2	
Probiotic (tsp) with *L. acidophilus* & *B. bifidus*			½						½	
ANTIOXIDANTS										
Vitamin C with bioflavonanoids (mg)			1,000			1,000			1,000	
Vitamin E mixed tocopherols (IU)			400							
R-alpha lipoic acid (mg)			100			100			100	
Coenzyme Q10 (mg)			100						100	
Grapeseed extract (mg)			100						100	
MINERALS										
Zinc (mg)						50				
Selenium (mcg)						200				
Copper (mg)						2				
Potassium (mg)						300				
Calcium (mg)						300			300	400

CARDIOVASCULAR SUPPLEMENT SCHEDULE

NUTRIENT	On rising	Before brkfst	With brkfst	Betwn meals	Before lunch	With lunch	Betwn meals	Before dinner	With dinner	Before bed
Magnesium (mg)						150			150	200
Vanadium (mcg)						60				
Alkaline powder		½ tsp								½ tsp
Kelp for iodine (mg)			450						450	
TO KILL INFECTIOUS AGENTS										
Oil of oregano (drops)		4						4		
Copper-silver-gold oligotherapy	3x a week									
TO REDUCE INFLAMMATION										
Curcumin (mg)			500			500			500	
Wobenzyme, Rubozym or Nattokinase (tablets)				1–5			1–5			1–5
Bromelain (mg)				300			300			
TO LOWER CHOLESTEROL (if more help is needed)										
Policosanol (mg)										12
Guggul (mg) if low thyroid		1,000			1,000			1,000		
Red yeast rice (mg)		1,200						1,200		
Plant sterols (mg)			100			100			100	
Ganoderma (mg)		55			55			55		
Unda 1, Unda 20, Unda 243, Unda 258 (drops)		5 each			5 each			5 each		
TO STRENGTHEN HEART										
Crataegus gemmotherapy (drops)		50			50			50		
L-arginine (mg)	1,000								1,000	
L-carnitine (mg)	1,000									
Taurine (mg)	1,000								1,000	

CARDIOVASCULAR SUPPLEMENT SCHEDULE										
NUTRIENT	On rising	Before brkfst	With brkfst	Betwn meals	Before lunch	With lunch	Betwn meals	Before dinner	With dinner	Before bed
TO PREVENT STROKE										
Ginkgo biloba (mg)		40			40			40		
Alnus glutinosa gemmo therapy (drops)		30			30			30		
TO ASSIST LIVER (Choose 1)										
Ichol		1			1			1		
LVDTX		1			1			1		
L-trepein		1			1			1		

Restore Balance

- Walk for an hour twice daily. Fat-burning enzymes are activated after an hour walk and remain active for 12 hours. The more we exercise our muscles, the more our capillaries will open and hold a higher volume of blood in their circulatory reserves, which will help to decrease blood pressure.
- Practice meditation, yoga, tai chi, or pranayam daily to activate the parasympathetic nervous system.
- Monitor the pH or your urine and saliva, keeping it between 6.8 and 7.2. Increase fruits and vegetables, decrease grain and animal protein if pH is acidic (lower). Use ½ tsp alkaline powder in warm water twice daily as needed to normalize pH.
- Decrease insulin and blood sugar; keep strict regulation of blood sugar if diabetic.
- Many people with heart disease and high cholesterol have an underactive thyroid gland and don't know it. See the Hypothyroidism chapter in this section to determine if you are one of these people.
- Intravenous chelation therapy can remove atherosclerotic plaque fairly quickly when administered weekly for several months. Consult with an MD or ND who can do this for you. It may be particularly beneficial for those with diagnosed heart disease to eliminate the need for heart bypass surgery.

Detoxify and Rejuvenate

- Filter chlorine out of your drinking water. Chlorinated water increases risk.
- Detoxify for heavy metals. Cadmium, lead, and mercury are linked with atherosclerosis and heart disease. Cleanse the liver and do a liver flush at least once a year for 10 days. Do an

DID YOU KNOW ...

You can reduce cholesterol by using red yeast rice (Monascus purpureus), which is rice that has been fermented by the addition of yeast. Animal and human studies have shown it to reduce cholesterol concentrations by 11% to 32% and triglycerides by 12% to 19%. It works similarly to the statin class of lipid-lowering drugs, but without adverse effects. The recommended dose is 1,200 mg, twice daily.

DID YOU KNOW ...

Guggul (*Commiphora mukul*) can reduce LDL cholesterol levels by 10% to 12% by increasing fat metabolism in the liver, and reduce triglyceride levels by 16%, while raising (good) HDL levels. The dose is 1000 mg, 3 times per day, standardized to contain 2.5% guggulsterones, or 500 mg, 3 times per day, standardized to contain 5% guggulsterones. Guggul is well tolerated, but can reduce the bioavailability of the blood pressure medications propranolol and diltiazem, and may cause diarrhea.

DID YOU KNOW ...

According to traditional Chinese medicine, hypertension is caused by either an imbalance between yin and yang of the kidneys and liver, or an overabundance of phlegm and dampness. Chest pain can be related to several imbalances – usually a deficiency in the spleen, heart or kidney with stagnation of blood, cold or phlegm. Work with a TCM practitioner using herbs and acupuncture to address any imbalances.

annual kidney cleanse. Do a 100-hour sauna detox program if not too stressful. See the Seasonal Cleansing and Rejuvenation section for guidelines.

- Cleanse the bowel with increased fiber (2 tbsp ground flax, 1-2 tbsp psyllium or rice bran) and use a high quality probiotic containing *Lactobacillus acidophilus* and *Bifidobacterium bifidus* daily to normalize bowel flora.
- Improve oral hygiene with regular flossing and dental care. Remove root canal teeth to clear infectious organisms from the mouth. Replace mercury amalgam fillings with methacrylate or porcelain.

HOMEOPATHIC REMEDIES FOR HEART DISEASE AND STROKE

- For high cholesterol: use Unda 1, Unda 20, Unda 243, and Unda 258, 5 drops of each, 3x daily, for 3 weeks on, 1 week off, for 3 or more months. Consider use of Cholesterinum plex, 30 drops before bed to decrease cholesterol.
- To improve thyroid function (when the thyroid gland is underactive, cholesterol and homocysteine may be high): alternate the above protocol monthly with Unda 16, Unda 273, and Unda 1000, 5 drops of each, 3x daily.
- To promote healing and improve circulation to the brain after a stroke: use Arnica 200K hourly for 3 days, then 3x daily for the next 11 days. After this period, use Arnica 30K, 2x daily, for 2 months.

Integrate Body, Mind, and Spirit

- Depression predisposes us to heart disease. If you have hypertension or heart disease, you may be pushing yourself too hard so that cortisol and norepinephrine are high, and the sympathetic nervous system is on overdrive, which causes blood vessel constriction. To engage the parasympathetic nervous system, get plenty of rest, take a 20-minute break every $2\frac{1}{2}$ hours, use calcium and magnesium daily, develop an exercise routine and a meditation practice, practice left nostril breathing once or twice daily, and consider using one or more of the following herbs as tincture or tea — passionflower, lavender, chamomile, linden, lemon balm, or valerian.
- Reach out to others — and be receptive to what others want to give to you. Give and accept love and kindness. Acknowledge the ways in which you are connected to everything else in the universe. Find something or someone to serve.
- Participate in a spiritual community of some sort where you feel a sense of belonging and joy.

GEMMOTHERAPY FOR HEART DISEASE AND STROKE

- To decrease cholesterol, stimulate the thyroid gland, decrease atherosclerosis and blood pressure: use *Prunus amygdalis* (almond tree root bark), 50 to 75 drops, once daily.

- For atherosclerosis (the buildup of plaque in the arteries): use *Oleo europa* (olive tree shoot), 50 drops once daily, for several years, and *Viscum album* (mistletoe shoot), 25 drops, 3x times daily. *Oleo europa* will help to decrease atherosclerosis, lower blood pressure, lower cholesterol, and improve circulation to the brain. *Viscum album* breaks up plaque and scar tissue.

- To increase circulation to the coronary arteries quickly during or after a heart attack: use *Crataegus* (hawthorne tree bud), 50 drops, 3x daily, for 3 or more years, and *Alnus incana* (mountain alder bud), 50 to 75 drops, 3x times daily, for 2 weeks after a heart attack. After this 2-week period, use *Alnus glutinosa* (European alder tree bud), 25-50 drops, 3x daily with *Crataegus* for several years to thin the blood, decrease angina, and rebuild the coronary arteries.

- To improve circulation to the brain after a stroke: use *Alnus glutinosa* and *Ulmus campestre*, 50 drops, 3 times daily, after a stroke to improve kidney drainage. Do not use *Alnus glutinosa* if you have cancer — it may increase circulation to a tumor.

- To increase circulation to the coronary arteries, improving angina: use *Syringa vulgaris*, 5-25 drops, 1-3x daily.

DID YOU KNOW...

Cadmium destroys the thin layer of cells that line blood vessels, while lead prevents cell repair. They both prevent breakdown of fibrin on the arterial walls, so plaque builds up.

DID YOU KNOW...

When there is gum disease and a periodontal pocket probe depth of over 3 mm throughout the mouth, the bacteria present in the mouth increase the risk of heart disease. Gum disease causes increased fibrinogen, which promotes blood clotting. The severity of gum disease is proportional to levels of total cholesterol, triglycerides and LDL. Oil of oregano, goldenseal, and myrrh on the gums to deter infectious organisms, thereby decreasing inflammation.

HERBAL FORMULA TO LOWER BLOOD PRESSURE AND PREVENT HEART DISEASE

- 40%   Hawthorne (*Crataegus oxycantha*)
- 20%   Reishi (*Ganoderma lucidum*)
- 15%   Ginkgo (*Ginkgo biloba*)
- 10%   Motherwort (*Leonurus cardiaca*)
- 10%   Gymnema (*Gymnema sylvestre*)
- 5%   Ginger (*Zinziber officinalis*)

- **Dose:** Mix the tinctures in the above ratios and take 50 drops, 3 times daily. The formula will strengthen the heart, improve circulation, lower insulin, and reduce blood pressure. Do not use while pregnant.

CARDIOVASCULAR CONDITIONS

DRUG THERAPY FOR CARDIOVASCULAR DISEASE		
DRUG	**NUTRIENT LOSSES**	**POTENTIAL HEALTH PROBLEMS**
Hydralazine-containing vasodilators: No-Hydral, Apo-Hydralazine	Vitamin B-6 Coenzyme Q10	Anemia, fatigue, weakness, weak immune system, increased heart disease risk, increased breast cancer risk
Loop diuretics: Edecrin, Apo-Furosemide	Zinc, sodium, calcium, magnesium, potassium, vitamins B-1, B-6, C	Osteoporosis, heart and blood pressure irregularities, tooth decay, asthma, cramps, PMS, muscle weakness, fatigue, edema, depression, irritability, memory loss, insomnia, dehydration, appetite loss, poor wound healing
Thiazide diuretics: Zaroxolyn, Esidrix	Magnesium, potassium, zinc, coenzyme Q10, sodium	Cardiovascular problems, asthma, osteoporosis, cramps, PMS, irregular heartbeat, muscle weakness, fatigue, edema, lowered immunity, poor wound healing, decreased sense of smell and taste, increased breast cancer risk
Potassium-sparing diuretics: Dyrenium, Alactone	Calcium, folic acid, zinc	Osteoporosis, heart and blood pressure irregularities, tooth decay, cervical dysplasia, anemia, lowered immunity, poor wound healing, decreased sense of smell and taste
Centrally acting antihypertensives: Apo-Clonidine, Dixarit	Coenzyme Q10	Cardiovascular problems, weak immune system, low energy, increased breast cancer risk
ACE inhibitors: Accuretic, Prinzide	Sodium, zinc	Lowered immunity, poor wound healing, decreased sense of smell and taste
Cardiac glycosides: Novo-Digotin	Vitamin B-1, calcium, magnesium, phosphorus	Depression, irritability, memory loss, muscle weakness, edema, osteoporosis, heart problems, tooth decay, asthma, low energy
Beta blockers: Acebutolol, Atenolol	Coenzyme Q10 melatonin	Heart problems, lowered immunity, low energy, insomnia, increased cancer risk (especially breast cancer), faster aging
Calcium channel blockers: Adalat, Procardia	Potassium	Irregular heartbeat, muscle weakness, fatigue, edema
HMG-CoA reductase inhibitors to lower cholesterol: Mevacor (Lovastatin), Lipitor (Atorvastatin)	Coenzyme Q10	Heart problems, fatigue, lowered immunity, increased breast cancer risk

Conventional Medicine

Conventional medicine recommends a wide variety of drugs to lower cholesterol and reduce blood pressure. Unfortunately, they do not address the cause of these conditions and may deplete vital nutrients, which can cause further health problems. If you are taking any of the medications listed here, consult with your medical doctor about supplementing the nutrients that are being lost, or about trying a natural medicine approach with appropriate monitoring.

DID YOU KNOW...

Smokers are three times as likely to develop heart disease as non-smokers and die 7 to 8 years earlier. Tobacco contains 4000 chemicals that are carried in the bloodstream and damage the lining of the arteries.

DID YOU KNOW ...

The energies of the heart chakra connect us to others in love, compassion, service, and altruism. We recognize others as part of ourselves. Women with heart disease may feel alienated and disconnected from the world when the energy of the heart chakra is disturbed, closed, or stuck.

TOP 5 STRATEGIES

1. Follow the Women's Health Diet Plan.
2. Exercise an hour a day.
3. Take garlic, fish oil, coenzyme Q10.
4. Use crataegus (hawthorne berry).
5. Floss your teeth and take care of early gum disease.

KUNDALINI YOGA EXERCISE TO STRENGTHEN AND PROTECT THE HEART

1. Sit on your left heel, with the heel between the buttocks. Your right knee is up against the chest, with the right foot flat on the floor.

2. Hold your arms in front of your chest, with the forearms parallel to the floor, your right palm resting on the back of the left hand. Keep both hands flat with the tips of the thumbs touching.

3. Keep your eyes one-fifth open, and look down while keeping your head and neck straight.

4. Inhale slowly in four equal sniffs. Exhale completely, keeping the same rhythm, in four equal parts.

5. Use the mantra ONG ONG ONG ONG mentally as you inhale and SOHUNG SOHUNG SOHUNG SOHUNG as you exhale. (ONG means universal creative energy and SOHUNG means I am that.) Contunie for 11 minutes.

The four-part breath stimulates the flow of kundalini energy and increases oxygen absorption by the lungs, purifying the blood. The exhale helps eliminate 25% more carbon dioxide and waste than usual. The pressure of the right knee against the liver helps to balance the liver and spleen. The position of the hands (known as a mudra) regulates the pancreas, adrenals, and kidneys. Sitting on the heel balances the ovaries.

Resources

Most of the supplements mentioned in the book can be purchased from health-food stores or naturopathic pharmacies. If you are unable to find something, the information here should help.

Supplement Suppliers

Advantage Health Matters
250 Shields Court, Unit 8, Markham, ON L3R 9W7
Tel: 1-800-304-1497 or (905) 946-1011 Fax: (905) 946-0381
www.advantagehealthmatters.com
Recommended Products: Pure Synergy, New Chapter vitamins, Wobenzyme

AOR
4101 19th St NE, Bay 8, Calgary, AB T2E 6X8
Tel: 1-800-387-0177 or (403) 250-9997 Fax: 877-219-9974 or (403) 250-9974
For U.S. orders, e-mail: order_usa@aor.ca
Recommended Products: BioSil (Jarrow), Qabsorb, R-alpha lipoic acid, NAC, Curcumin, T100 (thyroid), Opti-Guggul, Strontium Support

Avena Botanicals
Tel: (207) 594-0694. www.avenaherbs.com.
Recommended Products: Phytolacca and calendula herbal oils

BioGenesis Nutraceuticals
18303 Bothell-Everett Hwy, Suite 110, Mill Creek, WA 98012
Tel: 1-866-272-0500 or (425) 487-0788 Fax: (425) 485-3518 www.bio-genesis.com
Recommended Products: Metal Cleanse, Intestinal Repair powder and capsules

Bio Lonreco Inc.
667 Meloche Ave, Dorval, QC H9P 2T1
Tel: 1-800-361-6663 or (514) 631-6627 Fax: 1-800-966-0903 or (514) 631-0903
www.dr-reckeweg.ca
Recommended Products: Dr. Reckeweg formulas, Schuessler tissue salts – silicea, mag phos, calc phos, calc fluor, etc.

Bioquest Imports
Box 27104, 1395 Marine Dr, West Vancouver, BC V7T 2X8
Tel: 1-888-922-0285 (604) 922-0285 Fax: (604) 922-4649 email: bioquest@greenalive.com
Recommended Products: ParaSave

Douglas Laboratories
In Canada: 255 Queens Ave, Suite 1615, London, ON N6A 5R8
Tel: 1-866-856-9954 or (519) 439-8424 Fax: 1-888-220-9441 or (519) 432-0071
In U.S.A: 600 Boyce Rd, Pittsburgh, PA 15205
Tel: 1-888-368-4522 or (412) 494-0122 Fax: (412) 494-0155
Recommended Products: Ultra Preventive X, CoQMelt, Ultra Indinol Plus, LVDTX (liver detox formula)

Ecotrend Ecologics
105 West 3rd Ave, Vancouver, BC V5Y 1E6
Tel: 1-800-665-7065 or (604) 876-9846 Fax: (604) 876-9846
Recommended Products: Citricidal, Nordic Naturals fish oil, Metal Cleanse, Intestinal Repair powder and capsules, Pekana remedies: apo-Hepat spag. drops, Renelix spag. drops, Itires spag. drops, Toxex spag. drops, Dalektro N drops, Upelva, Klifem

Enzymatic Therapy Inc.
827 Challenger Dr, Green Bay, WI 54311
Fax: (920) 469-4444
Recommended Products: Remifemin

Gaia Herbs
108 Island Ford Rd, Brevard, NC 28712
Tel: 1-888-917-8269 or (828) 883-4242 Fax: (828) 883-5960
www.gaiaherbs.com
Recommended Products: Quality single herbal tinctures or herbal formulas

Healthy Breast Products
235 9th St E, Owen Sound, ON N4K 1N8.
Tel: (519) 372-9212 Fax: (519) 372-2755. www.healthybreastprogram.on.ca.
Recommended Products: Healthy Breast Formula, Liver Loving Formula, Immune Power Formula, Healthy Breast Oil

Heel
In Canada: 11025, LH Lafontaine, Montreal, QC H1J 2Z4
Tel: 1-888-879-4335 or (514) 353-4335 Fax: (514) 353-4336 www.heel.ca
In U.S.A.: PO Box 11280, Albuquerque, NM 87192-0280
Tel: 1-800-621-7644 or (505) 293-3843 Fax: (505) 275-1672 www.heelusa.com
Recommended Products: Lyphosol, Nux vomica-Hommacord, Berberis-Homaccord, Hepar compositum, Klimakt-Heel, Echinacea Compositum drops, Nymeel

Herb Pharm
PO Box 116, Williams, OR 97544
Tel: 1-800-348-4372 www.herb-pharm.com
Recommended Products: Quality single herbal tinctures or herbal formulas

Jarrow Formulas
In U.S.A.: 1824 S. Robertson Blvd, Los Angeles, CA 90035
Tel: 1-800-726-0886 or (310) 204-6936 Fax: 1-800-890-8955
www.jarrow.com.
In Canada, available from Ecomax: Tel: 1-800-668-4559 or (514) 344-7008
Fax: (514) 344-3757
Recommended Products: Bone Up (Jarrow), Jarro-Dophilus + FOS, NAG (N-acetyl-glucosamine)

Kroeger Herbs
805 Walnut St, Boulder, CO 80302
Tel: 1-800-516-0690 or (303) 443-0261 Fax: (303) 443-0108
www.kroegerherb.com
Recommended Products: Triema Liva Liquid, Triema Blud Liquid,Triema Loongae Liquid (lung),Triema Lymf Liquid, Amoeba – Meeba Liquid, Giardia – Guardi Aqua Liquid

Pascoe

10023 Yonge St, Richmond Hill, ON L4C 1T7
Tel: 1-866-535-0099 or (905) 737-9837 Fax: 1-866-414-0028 or (905) 737-0950
Recommended Products: Lymphdiaral drops or cream

Poya Naturals

In Canada: 21-B Regan Road, Brampton, ON L7A 1C5
Tel: 1-877-255-7692 or (905) 840-5459 Fax: (905) 846-1784. www.poyanaturals.com
In U.S.A.: 2129 Watercress Rd, San Ramon, CA 94583
Tel: 1-800-844-5605 Fax: 1-800-246-8207
Recommended Products: Excellent quality essential oils

Professional Health Products

4307- 49th St, Innisfail, AB T4G 1P3
Tel: 1-800-661-1366 www.professionalhealthproducts.com
Recommended Products: Oxidata test, Sulkowitch test, Koenigsburg test, vitamin C test, zinc sufficiency taste test

ProMedics Nutraceutical Ltd.

PO Box 155, 2498 West 41st Ave, Vancouver, BC V6M 2A7
Tel: 1- 877-268-5057 or (604) 261-5057 Fax: (604) 730-71
Recommended Products: Magnetic clay; in the U.S.A., magnetic clay is available from www.magneticclay.com

Purity Life/ Purity Professionals

6 Commerce Cres, Acton, ON L7J 2X3
Tel: 1-866-831-4035 Fax: 1-800-930-9512 www.purityprofessionals.com
Recommended Products: Kroeger herbal products

Sanum

In Canada: Biomed International, 102-3738 North Fraser Way, Burnaby, BC V5J 5G7
Tel: 1-800-665-8308 or (604) 415-0535 Fax: 1-866-881-2888. www.biomedicine.com
In U.S.A.: Pleomorphic Sanum, Tel: (602) 439-7977 www.PleoSANUM.com
Recommended Products: Alkala, Basen Pulver, Mucokehl (Pleomuc), Nigersan (Pleonig), Sankombi, Notokehl (Pleonot), Pefrakehl (Pleopef), Fortakehl (Pleofort), Exmykehl, Albicansan, Pleo San Cand D5, Quentakehl (Pleoquent), Sanuvis, Citrokehl, Polysan formulas (Spenglersans)

Seroyal International Inc

44 East Beaver Creek Rd, Richmond Hill, ON L4B 1G8. Tel: 1-800-263-5861
Fax: 1-800-722-9953. In the U.S.A., Tel: 1-888-737-6925 Fax: 1-877-737-6925
Recommended Products: Genestra, Seroyal, and Unda single homeopathic remedies; Unda numbers, Chelidonium Plex; Cimicifuga Plex; Sepia Plex; Paeonia Plex; Hamemelis Plex; Unda gemmotherapies: Ficus carica, Juniperus, Rosemarinus, Sequoia, Ribes nigrum, Betula pubescens, Pinus montana, Acer campestre, Platanus, Juglans regia, Ulmus campestre, Corylus avellana, Tilia tomentosa, Rubus idaeus, Cornus sanguinaria, Prunus amygdalus, Abies pectinata; Oligotherapies: copper-silver-gold, zinc-nickel-cobalt; zinc-copper TAD+, Herbal GI , Scorbatate (vitamin C) powder; Candigen cream; Allicyn

St. Francis Herb Farm
104 Maika Road, PO Box 29, Combermere, ON K0J 1L0
Tel: (613) 756-6279, Fax: (613) 756-0002. www.stfrancisherbfarm.com.
Recommended Products: Quality single herbal tinctures or herbal formulas

Thorne
In Canada: #308, 19292 – 60th Ave, Surrey, BC V3S 3M2
Tel: 1-800-663-6369 or (604) 530-3639 Fax: (604) 530-0228
www.thorne.com
In U.S.A.: 25820 Highway 2 West, PO Box 25, Dover, ID 83825
Tel: 1-800-228-1966 or (208) 265-2488 Fax: (208) 265-2488
Recommended Products: Meta-Balance, Ipriflavone, Fractionated Pectin Powder, L-glutamine,
HMC Hesperidin, zinc picolinate

Young Living Essential Oils
Thanksgiving Point Business Park, 3125 Executive Parkway, Lehi, UT 84043
Tel: 1-888-880-1549 Fax: 1-866-203-5666 email: custserv@youngliving.com
Recommended Products: ParaFree and other essential oil blends

Chinese Herbal Suppliers

Eastern Currents
#200A-3540 West 41st Ave, Vancouver, BC V6N 3E6
Tel: (604) 263-5042 Fax: (604) 263-8781
Supplies Golden Flower, KPC, Health Concerns, and Kan Herbals
Recommended Products: Golden Flower Chinese Herbal Formulas: Bupleurum & Tang Kuei,
Tang Kuei & Salvia Formula, Stasis-Transforming Formula, Cinnamon & Poria Formula, True
Yin Formula, Jing Qi Formula, Ginseng & Astragalus Formula, Women's Precious Formula,
Tang Kuei & Salvia, San Qi Formula, Rehmannia & Scrophularia, Bupleurum D Formula,
Ginseng & Longan Combination, Citrus& Pinellia, Cinnamon & Poria, Gentiana Drain Fire
Formula, Essential Yang Formula, Ginseng Nourishing Formula

Health Concerns
8001 Capwell Dr, Oakland, CA 94621
Tel: 1-800-233-9355 Fax: (510) 639-9140
www.healthconcerns.com
Recommended Products: Health Concerns Formulas: Woman's Balance,
Ease Plus, Three Immortals, Rehmannia 8, Vagistatin, Channel Flow, Unlocking Formula,
Phellostatin

Institute for Traditional Medicine
2017 SE Hawthorne Blvd., Portland, Oregon 97214
Tel: (503) 233-4907, Fax: (503) 233-1017
itm@itmonline.org, www.itmonline.org
Seven Forests Chinese herbal formulas can be ordered from ITM.
Recommended Products: Seven Forests Formulas: Tang-kuei 18, Cinnamon and Rehmannia,
Chih-ko and Curcuma, Blue Citrus Tablets, Eucommia 18

Kan Herbals
6001 Butler Lane, Scotts Valley, CA 95066
Tel: 1-800-543-5233 or (831) 438-9450 Fax: (831) 438-9457
www.kanherb.com
Recommended Products: Kan Herbals Formulas: Relaxed Wanderer, Calm Dragon Formula, Two Immortals, Temper Fire, Quell Fire

KPC Products Inc
16 Goddard, Irvine, CA 92618
Tel: 1-800-572-8188, (949) 727-4000 Fax: (949) 727-3577
www.kpc.com
Recommended Products: KPC Formulas: Ginseng & Ginger Combination, Xiao Yao Wan, Tang Kuei Four Combination, Cinnamon and Hoelen Formula, Gu Yin Jian, Wen Wei Yin, Yunnan Paiyao, Chih Pai Pa Wei Wan, Anemarrhena Phellodendron & Rehmannia Formula, Bupleurum & Dragon Bone Combination, Bupleurum & Peony Formula, Tangkuei Four Combination, Curculigo & Epimedium, Eucommia & Rehmannia Formula, Rehmannia Eight Formula, Li Zhong Tang

Clinical Laboratories

Saliva Hormone Testing Laboratories
Rocky Mountain Analytic
Unit A, 253147 Bearspaw Rd NW, Calgary, AB T3L 2P5
Tel: (403) 241-4513 Fax: (403) 241-4516 www.rmalab.com

Aeron Life Cycles Clinical Laboratory
1933 Davis St, Suite 310, San Leandro, CA 94577
Tel: (510) 729-0375 Fax: (510) 729-0383 www.aeron@aeron.com

Pharmasan
373 280th St, Osceola, WI 54020
Tel: 1-888-342-7272 or (715) 755-3995 Fax: (715) 294-3921 www.pharmasan.com
Tests saliva, urine, and blood for hormone and neurotransmitter levels; tests urine for bone resorption; administers Post-Menopause I test for estrogen quotient, progesterone, testosterone, and DHEA

ZRT Laboratory
12505 NW Cornell Rd, Portland, OR 97229
Tel: (503) 469-0741 Fax: (503) 469-1305 www.salivatest.com

Hair, Urine, Stool, Saliva and Blood Tests
Great Smokies Diagnostic Laboratory
63 Zillicoa St, Asheville NC 28801
Tel: 1-800-522-4762 Fax: (828) 252-9303
www.gsdl.com
Recommended Tests: Comprehensive Digestive Stool Analysis with Parasitology

Doctor's Data Inc.
3755 Illinois Ave, St. Charles IL 60174-2420
Tel: 1-800-323-2784   Fax: (630) 587-7860 www.doctorsdata.com
Recommended Tests: hair analysis for toxic metals; urine test for toxic metals; Red Blood Cell Elements; Hepatic Detox Profile; Comprehensive Stool Analysis with Parasitology; Secretory Immunoglobulin A in stool; Yeast Culture and Sensitivities; Intestinal Permeability Test; Vaginosis Profile; Toxic Metal Analysis of Drinking Water

Metametrix Clinical Laboratory
4855 Peachtree Industrial Blvd, Suite 201, Norcross GA 30092
Tel: 1-800-221-4640 or (770) 446-5483 Fax: (770) 441-2237 www.metametrix.com
Recommended Tests: urine test for bone resorption; ION Profile; Cardiovascular Health Profile; 2/16 hydroxyestrone ratio; Metabolic Syndrome Profile; Amino Acids in plasma or urine; Fatty Acids in Red Blood Cells; Detoxification Capacity Test; Nutrient and Toxic Elements in blood, hair or urine; Dysbiosis Panel

Testing for Toxic Chemicals in Blood, Urine, Breastmilk and Tissue
Accu-Chem Laboratories
990 N Bowser Rd, Suite 800, Richardson, TX 75081
Tel: 1-800-451-0116. www.accuchem.com
Recommended Tests: blood tests for PCBs, pesticides, and/or brominated fire retardants

National Medical Services
3701 Welsh Rd, Willow Grove, PA 19090
Tel: 1-800-522-6671

Pacific Toxicology Laboratories
6160 Variel Ave, Woodland Hills, CA 91367
Tel: 1-800-328-6942

Testing for Bacterial Toxins in the Mouth and Gums
Affinity Labeling Technologies, Inc.
235 Bolivar St, Lexington, KY 40508
Tel: (859) 388-9445 Fax: (859) 388-9645 www.altcorp.com

Test Kit for Helicobacter Pylori
Source Medical Corporation
175 Brittania Rd E, Unit #1, Mississauga, ON L4Z 4B9
Tel: 1-866-307-4026 or (905) 502-3378 Fax: 1-866-892-2890 or (905) 502-3332
www.sourcemedical.com

Water and Soil Testing
Ontario Environment Farm Plan Program
Ontario Federation of Agriculture
Tel: (416) 485-3333 www.ofa.on.ca/water/default.htm.

Philip Analytical Services
921 Leathorne S, London, ON N5Z 3M7
Tel: 1-800-268-7396 or (519) 686-7558 www.philipanalytical.com

PSC Analytical Services
Northeastern U.S.A. 1-800-345-4026
Central U.S.A. 1-888-574-4547
Central Canada 1-800-263-9040
Quebec (514) 493-4733
Eastern Canada 1-800-565-7227
Western U.S.A, Canada, and Alaska 1-800-440-4808

Food Sensitivity and Candida Testing
Immuno Laboratories
1620 West Oakland Park Blvd, Fort Lauderdale, FL 33311
Tel: 1-800-231-9197 or (954) 486-4500 Fax: (954) 739-6563
Recommended Tests: IgG testing for food allergies or inhalants; ELISA antibody titer testing for candida

Information on Pollutants in Your Area
Commission for Environmental Cooperation of North America
393 rue St-Jacques Ouest, bureau 200, Montreal, QC H2Y 1N9
Tel: 514-350-4300 Fax: 514 350-4314. www.cec.org
Their annual publication is called Taking Stock: North American Pollutant Releases and Transfers. In Canada and the U.S.A, you can find out which industries are contaminating your area by entering your postal code or zip code into the websites www.pollutionwatch.org (Canada) or www.scorecard.org (U.S.A.).

Electromagnetic Field Testing Meters
Alphalab Inc.
www.trifield.com
Sells the Trifield Meter

BioAg Consultants and Distributors Inc
1400 Greenway Hill Rd, PO Box 189, Wellesley, ON N0B 2T0
Tel: 1-800-363-5278 www.bio-ag.com
Sells the Stetzer Meter, which measures dirty power or high frequency fields above 10,000 Hz

Stetzer Electric
www.stetzerelectric.com
Sells the Stetzer Meter, which measures dirty power or high frequency fields above 10,000 Hz

Gastro Test to Assess Hydrochloric Acid Production
HDC Corporation
688 Gibraltar Court, Milpitas, CA 95035
Tel: 1-800-227-8162 or (408) 942-7340 www.hdccorp.com
Measures pH of the stomach with a string test.

Micro Essential Laboratory Inc.
4224 Avenue H, Brooklyn, New York 11210
Tel: 1-800-227-8162.
Sells pH paper

Sauna Manufacturers
Saunaray
Collingwood, ON
Tel: 1-877-992-1100. www.saunaray.com

Saunacore
71 Strada Dr, Suite 8, Woodbridge, ON L4L 5V8.
Tel: 1-800-361-9485. www.saunacore.com

Heavenly Heat (California)
Tel: 1-800-653-8881 or (845) 679-2490

Associations

Kundalini Yoga Teachers Directory
Worldwide: www.kundaliniyoga.com

Holistic/ Biological Dentists Directory
In Canada: www.talkinternational.com
In U.S.A.: www.holisticdental.org

Naturopathic Associations
Canadian Naturopathic Association
Tel: 1-800-551-4381 or (416) 496-8633 www.naturopathicassoc.ca

American Association of Naturopathic Physicians
Tel: (206) 298-0125 www.naturopathic.org

American Naturopathic Medical Association
Tel: (702) 897-7053 www.anma.com

Dark Sky Protection Associations
The Durham Region Astronomical Association
728 Anderson St N, PO Box 59007, Whitby, ON L1N 0A4
www.drastronomy.com

International Dark Sky Association Inc.
3225 N. First Ave, Tucson, Arizona 85719-2103
Tel: (520) 293-3198 www.darksky.org

Selected References

Note: A complete list of references is available from the authors. E-mail: sdk@log.on.ca.

Adams, Mikhael. Seroyal seminar on Biotherapeutics and Drainage. 2003, from audiotape series.

Batmanghelidj F. Your Body's Many Cries for Water. Vienna, VA: Global Health Solutions, 1997.

Bedard J. Lotus in the Fire: The Healing Power of Zen. Boston, MA: Shambhala, 1999.

Bensky D, Gamble A. Chinese Herbal Medicine Materia Medica. Seattle, WA: Eastland Press, 1986.

Bhajan Y. The Aquarian Teacher: KRI International Kundalini Yoga Teacher Training, Level One Yoga Manual. Espanola, NM: KRI International, 2003.

Bhajan Y. The Kundalini Yoga Manual. Claremont, CA: KRI Publications, 1976.

Bhajan Y. Sadhana Guidelines for Kundalini Yoga Daily Practice. Los Angeles, CA: Kundalini Research Institute, 1980.

Bhajan Y. Survival Kit: Meditations and Exercises for Stress and Pressure of the Times. Compiled by S.S. Vikram K. Khalsa and Dharm Darshan K. Khalsa. San Diego, CA: Kundalini Research Institute, 1980.

Brennan B. Hands of Light. New York, N.Y: Bantam, 1987.

Colborn T, Dumanoski D, Peterson Myers J. Our Stolen Future. New York, NY: Penguin, 1996.

Crinnion W. Mercury and lead burden: Common sources, symptoms and treatment outcomes. OAND Convention. Hamilton, ON. Oct. 2004

De Villiers M. Water. Toronto, ON: Stoddart Publishing, 2000.

Dunne L. Nutrition Almanac. 3rd edition. Toronto: McGraw-Hill, 1990.

Feuerstein G. The Yoga Tradition: Its History, Literature, Philosophy and Practice. Prescott, AZ: Hohm Press, 2001.

Feuerstein, G. Yoga: The Technology of Ecstasy. Los Angeles, CA: Jeremy P. Tarcher, Inc, 1989.

Gibson G. Effects of prebiotics on human gut health. from Gut Ecology. Ed. Hart A, Stagg A, Graffner H, Glise H, Falk P, Kamm M. Martin Dunitz. London, UK: Martin Dunitz, 2002.

Guyton A. Textbook of Medical Physiology. Toronto, ON: W.B. Saunders, 1981.

Haley D. Politics in Healing: The Suppression and Manipulation of American Medicine. Washington, DC: Potomac Valley Press, 2000.

Hart A, Stagg A, Graffner H, Glise H, Falk P, Kamm M, eds. Gut Ecology. London, UK: Martin Dunitz, 2002.

Ganong W. Review of Medical Physiology. New York, NY: McGraw-Hill, 2003.

Brand Miller J, Foster-Powell K, Colagiuri S. The G.I. Factor: The Glycaemic Index Solution. Sydney, Australia: Hodder Headline, 1996.

Hering C. Preface, In Hahnemann, S.C. The Chronic Diseases, Trans. By C.J. Hempel, New York: William Raddle, n.d.

Hahnemann S. Organon of Medicine. Trans. W. Boericke, Philadelphia, PA: Boericke & Tafel, 1920.

Harper A, Rodwell VW, Mayes PA. Review of Physiological Chemistry. 16th ed. Los Altos, CA: Lange Medical Publications, 1977.

Hudson T. Women's Encyclopedia of Natural Medicine. Los Angeles, CA: Keats Publishing, 1999.

Leakey R, Lewin R. The Sixth Extinction. Patterns of Life and the Future of Humankind. Toronto, ON: Random House, 1995.

Lessard-Pereira B. Biotherapeutic drainage and product workshop. Toronto, ON: Seroyal, 2003.

Maciocia G. The Practice of Chinese Medicine. Toronto, ON: Churchill Livingstone, 1994.

Marz R. Medical Nutrition from Marz. 2nd edition. Portland, OR: Omni-Press, 1999.

Matsen J. The Secrets to Great Health. Goodwin Books Ltd.. 1998.

Mattman L. Cell Wall Deficient Forms. North Vancouver, BC: CRC Press, 2001.

McTaggart L. The Field: The Quest for the Secret Force of the Universe. New York, NY: HarperCollins, 2002.

Mishra RS. The Textbook of Yoga Psychology. New York, NY: The Julian Press, 1971.

Nissim R. Natural Healing in Gynecology. London, UK: HarperCollins, 1996.

Northrup C. Women's Bodies, Women's Wisdom. New York, NY: Bantam Books, 1994.

O'Connor J, Bensky D. Acupuncture: A Comprehensive Text. Shanghai College of Traditional Medicine. Seattle, WA: Eastland Press, 1981.

Oschman J. Energy Medicine. The Scientific Basis. New York, NY: Churchill Livingstone, 2000.

Pitchford P. Healing with Whole Foods. Berkeley, CA: North Atlantic Books, 1993.

Plummer N. Intestinal immunity, Candida albicans and dysbiosis, cardiovascular disease. Seroyal seminar, Toronto, ON, 2003.

Price W. Nutrition and Physical Degeneration. New Canaan, CT: Keats Publishing, 1997.

Rau T. Biological Medicine: The Future of Natural Healing. Lustmuhle, Switzerland: Biological Medicine Network, 2003

Simon GL, Gorbach SL. Intestinal Flora in Health and Disease: Physiology of the Gastrointestinal Tract. New York, NY: Raven Press, 1981.

Smith R P. Netter's Obstetrics, Gynecology and Women's Health. Teterboro, NJ: Icon Learning Systems, MediMedia, Inc, 2002.

Solomon G. Pesticides and Human Health: A Resource for Health Care Professionals. Physicians for Social Responsibility and Californians for Pesticide Reform, 2000.

Stamets Pl. The Role of Mushrooms in Nature. From Growing Gourmet and Medicinal Mushrooms. 3rd ed. Berkeley, CA: Ten Speed Press, 2000.

Walther D S. Applied Kinesiology. Pueblo, CO: SDC Systems, 1988.

Werthmann K, Schneider P. Isopathic/Homeopathic Materia Medica. Hoya, Germany: Semmelweis-Verlag, 1999.

Werthmann K. Successful Treatments for Allergies and Chronic Disorders. Salzburg, Austria: Semmelweiss-Verlag, 1999.

Wu Y, Fischer W. Practical Therapeutics of Traditional Chinese Medicine. Brookline, MA: Paradigm Productions, 1997.

Acknowledgments

I would like to thank those individuals who helped make the writing of this book possible. Firstly, Susi Schmidt, who spent months researching for me; Elinor Renny who cheerfully helped me in my office; MaryAnn Thomas who cheered me on as she heard me progress through the chapters and who reviewed a chunk of the book; Susan Gibson and Allan Stone for their many articles, medical journals, thoughtfulness, and encouragement; Jennifer Haessler ND and Kathleeen Finlay ND for helping me out when I felt stuck or overwhelmed; my co-authors Dr. Mary Danylak and Dr. Carolyn Dean for their research and contributions; my patients who have taught me so much and adapted graciously to canceled appointments as I needed to take time off to write; to Hans Burgschmidt for brainstorming sessions; to Mary Kovacs, Jan Palko, and Ann Pepper for their helpful input; to Jochen Schmidt for reviewing the manuscript in its early phase. Thank you to Yogi Bhajan whose glorious teachings have made their way into this book. I especially want to thank my editor Bob Hilderley for his midwifery and pruning skills in bringing this book into its present form and for knowing when to leave me alone and when to give me a push, and for persevering. Finally, thank you to my dear husband, Har Prakash, who took care of our three children while I was writing — I couldn't have done it without him. Thank you to my children for putting up with my absence at dinner for so many months. I am grateful to my publisher, Bob Dees at Robert Rose Inc., for granting me this project, and for the exquisite design team at PageWave Graphics. And as always, thank you to the great spirit that sustains us all.

Sat Dharam Kaur, ND

Index

A

abortion, 305-307
acupuncture, 15, 39, 295
adrenal glands, 204, 206, 207
air pollution, 149-153
alcohol, 38, 39, 59-60
alkalinizing powder, 189
allergies, 223-224
Alzheimer's disease, 37, 38, 40
amenorrhea
    categories, 249
    causes, 249-250
    conventional medicine, 255
    detoxification and rejuvenation, 255
    herbal formula, 255
    homeopathic remedies, 254
    hormone replacement therapy, 255-256
    prevention and treatment, 251-255
    resumed menstrual cycle, 256
    TCM, 250
    tests, 249
anger, 388
animals, dissection of, 23
antibiotics, 38, 175-176
antioxidants, 37, 44
aromatherapy, 26
arterial cleansing, 224-225
arthritis, 37, 40
arts
    creative, 41
    martial, 41
asbestos, 152
aspirin, 23
auriculomedicine, 9
Ayurvedic medicine, 12-14

B

bacteria, 135
Bacteroides, 172
Bastyr, Dr. John, 32
Bastyr University, 32
beta carotene, 37
Bhajan, Yogi, 13
Bifidobacterium bifidus, 89, 171, 172, 177
Bifidobacterium breve, 177

Bifidobacterium lognum, 177
biorhythms, 37, 69
birth control, 300-307
    charting ovulation, 304
    natural, 303-330
    oral contraceptives, 38, 247, 262, 306-308
    pros and cons of methods, 300-303
    sympto-thermo method, 305
black cohosh, 11
bladder, 204, 208
blood sugar, 38, 229, 231
blood vessels, 221
body ecology
    bacteria, fungi, and yeast, 173-175
    flora, 171-173
    gut disease, 172
    parasites, 173
    supplementation, 172
body energy, balancing, 39
body mineral content, 121
bodywork, 29-31
bones, 205, 208-209. *See also* osteoporosis
botanical medicine, 25-26
bowel cleansing, 190-193
brassica family vegetables, 53
breast cancer, 399-415
    breast health balance sheet, 399-406
    categories, 399
    chemotherapy, 414
    conventional medicine, 414
    detoxification and rejuvenation, 412-413
    drug therapy, 414
    gemmotherapy, 413
    healing, 415
    herbal formulas, 413
    homeopathic remedies, 413
    nutrition, 407-412
    prevention and treatment, 407-413
    radiation, 414
    restoring balance, 409-410
    surgery, 414
    symptoms, 399
breast conditions, 392-415
breast-feeding, 337-342

More Great Books from Robert Rose

Bestsellers

- 175 Best Babycakes™ Cupcake Maker Recipes
  by Kathy Moore and Roxanne Wyss
- 175 Best Babycakes™ Cake Pop Maker Recipes
  by Kathy Moore and Roxanne Wyss
- Ball Complete Book of Home Preserving
  edited by Judi Kingry and Lauren Devine

- Bernardin Complete Book of Home Preserving
  edited by Judi Kingry and Lauren Devine
- Best of Bridge Slow Cooker Cookbook
  by Best of Bridge and Sally Vaughan-Johnston
- The Food Substitutions Bible, Second Edition
  by David Joachim
- Zwilling J.A. Henckels Complete Book of Knife Skills
  by Jeffrey Elliot and James P. DeWan

Appliance Bestsellers

- 150 Best Indian, Thai, Vietnamese & More Slow Cooker Recipes
  by Sunil Vijayakar
- The Juicing Bible, Second Edition
  by Pat Crocker
- The Smoothies Bible, Second Edition
  by Pat Crocker

- The Healthy Slow Cooker
  by Judith Finlayson
- 200 Best Panini Recipes
  by Tiffany Collins
- The 150 Best Slow Cooker Recipes, Second Edition
  by Judith Finlayson
- The Vegetarian Slow Cooker
  by Judith Finlayson
- 175 Essential Slow Cooker Classics
  by Judith Finlayson
- 300 Best Rice Cooker Recipes
  by Katie Chin
- 650 Best Food Processor Recipes
  by George Geary and Judith Finlayson
- The Mixer Bible, Third Edition
  by Meredith Deeds and Carla Snyder
- 125 Best Indoor Grill Recipes
  by Ilana Simon
- The Convection Oven Bible
  by Linda Stephen
- 300 Best Canadian Bread Machine Recipes
  by Donna Washburn and Heather Butt
- 300 Best Bread Machine Recipes
  by Donna Washburn and Heather Butt
- Championship BBQ Secrets for Real Smoked Food, Second Edition
  by Karen Putman and Judith Fertig

Baking Bestsellers

- 150 Best Ebelskiver Recipes
  by Camilla V. Saulsbury
- Piece of Cake!
  by Camilla V. Saulsbury
- 400 Sensational Cookies
  by Linda J. Amendt
- 175 Best Mini-Pie Recipes
  by Julie Anne Hession
- 150 Best Donut Recipes
  by George Geary
- 750 Best Muffin Recipes
  by Camilla V. Saulsbury
- 200 Fast & Easy Artisan Breads
  by Judith Fertig

Healthy Cooking Bestsellers

- Canada's Diabetes Meals for Good Health, Second Edition
  by Karen Graham
- Diabetes Meals for Good Health, Second Edition
  by Karen Graham
- Eat Raw, Eat Well
  by Douglas McNish
- RawEssence
  by David Côté and Mathieu Gallant
- Complete Gluten-Free Diet & Nutrition Guide
  by Alexandra Anca and Theresa Santandrea-Cull
- The Gluten-Free Baking Book
  by Donna Washburn and Heather Butt

- 250 Gluten-Free Favorites
  by Donna Washburn and Heather Butt
- 5 Easy Steps to Healthy Cooking
  by Camilla V. Saulsbury
- The Vegetarian Kitchen Table Cookbook
  by Igor Brotto and Olivier Guiriec
- 350 Best Vegan Recipes
  by Deb Roussou
- The Complete Gluten-Free Whole Grains Cookbook
  by Judith Finlayson
- The Vegan Cook's Bible
  by Pat Crocker

Health Bestsellers

- The PCOS Health & Nutrition Guide
  by Dr. Jillian Stansbury, ND with Dr. Sheila Mitchell, MD
- 55 Most Common Medicinal Herbs, Second Edition
  by Dr. Heather Boon, BScPhm, PhD, and Michael Smith, BPharm, MRPharmS, ND
- The Complete Natural Medicine Guide to Breast Cancer
  by Sat Dharam Kaur, ND
- The Complete Doctor's Stress Solution
  by Penny Kendall-Reed, MSc, ND, and Dr. Stephen Reed, MD, FRCSC

Also Available
from Robert Rose

The Complete
Natural Medicine
Guide to

BREAST
CANCER

A Practical Manual
for Understanding,
Prevention & Care

SAT DHARAM KAUR
Naturopathic Doctor

Preface by Dr. Carolyn Dean, ND, MD

ISBN: 978-0-7788-0080-4

For more great books, see previous pages

Robert
ROSE